THE DRAGON KINGS OF FIRE AND ICE

SPECIAL EDITION OMNIBUS

BOOKS 1-5

AMELIA SHAW

THE DRAGON KINGS OF FIRE AND ICE: BOOKS 1-5

First edition. January 23, 2024.

Contact: harleyromancepublishing@gmail.com
Website: www.harleyromancepublishing.com

Written by Amelia Shaw.

Chapter 11   218
Chapter 12   224
Chapter 13   231
Chapter 14   240
Chapter 15   253
Epilogue   258

REBUILDING HIS DRAGON KINGDOM

Chapter 1   267
Chapter 2   273
Chapter 3   281
Chapter 4   287
Chapter 5   298
Chapter 6   303
Chapter 7   310
Chapter 8   318
Chapter 9   326
Chapter 10   331
Chapter 11   338
Chapter 12   345
Chapter 13   352
Chapter 14   359
Epilogue   366

THE HEIR OF WINTER

Chapter 1   377
Chapter 2   386
Chapter 3   395
Chapter 4   402
Chapter 5   410
Chapter 6   420
Chapter 7   429
Chapter 8   436
Chapter 9   445
Chapter 10   453
Chapter 11   461
Chapter 12   468

CONTENTS

TAKEN BY THE DRAGON KING

Chapter 1	3
Chapter 2	9
Chapter 3	16
Chapter 4	23
Chapter 5	29
Chapter 6	36
Chapter 7	42
Chapter 8	53
Chapter 9	58
Chapter 10	64
Chapter 11	70
Chapter 12	76
Chapter 13	83
Chapter 14	91
Chapter 15	97
Chapter 16	104
Chapter 17	113
Chapter 18	119
Chapter 19	128
Chapter 20	136
Epilogue	141

A KING FOR THE SORCERESS

Chapter 1	149
Chapter 2	156
Chapter 3	163
Chapter 4	170
Chapter 5	176
Chapter 6	182
Chapter 7	188
Chapter 8	194
Chapter 9	202
Chapter 10	209

Chapter 13   473
Epilogue   477

THE DRAGON'S TRUE MATE

Chapter 1   485
Chapter 2   493
Chapter 3   503
Chapter 4   509
Chapter 5   518
Chapter 6   525
Chapter 7   530
Chapter 8   538
Chapter 9   543
Chapter 10   549
Chapter 11   557
Chapter 12   566
Chapter 13   573
Chapter 14   581
Chapter 15   589
Chapter 16   596
Epilogue   605

FIRE AND ICE
TAKEN BY THE
DRAGON
KING
USA TODAY BESTSELLING AUTHOR
AMELIA SHAW

TAKEN BY THE DRAGON KING

CHAPTER
ONE

Stavrok

I glared at the elder standing before me. How dare he suggest something so barbaric? Sure, I hadn't found my fated mate. Sure, I was one of the only bachelor kings in our realm. But kidnap a woman from the closest human town?

He had to be fucking kidding me!

I slid my sword back into its sheath, finished with my morning training session, and handed it off to a nearby servant.

Then I narrowed my eyes at the elder. "I am your *king,* Hillsen! Do not presume to tell me what I must and must not do!" How dare he lecture me as though I was shirking my duties?

I stormed away from the elder, though I didn't want to walk away. I wanted to stay and tell him exactly where he could go.

Anger was sparking fire through my veins, and testosterone was pumping after a heavy fighting session with my training partner. I would do the old man serious bodily harm if I stayed here.

My shifter was enraged by everything going on around me. He wanted his mate as well, but the elder was suggesting I grab any woman that took my fancy—like King Magnik.

Not a chance.

Even though he was wrong about the route to my future queen, Hillsen didn't deserve to be on the wrong end of my dragon. He was, after all, only interested in the betterment of the kingdom. As was I. That had always been my focus.

But, kingdom or no kingdom, I would never stoop to mating with some random woman. Nor would I entertain what the elder had suggested: kidnap a woman to be my wife and mate, as was tradition.

My father had done it before me, and his father before him. Just because they couldn't control their shifting animal, didn't mean I would be so weak and give in to my baser urges. When I met my mate, I would woo her. Sweep her off her feet. Charm her.

I jogged over to the staircase, stepping underneath the large oil painting of my parents that hung high on the castle wall. Their faces stared down at everyone who passed through the great hall. In death as in life, they kept a faithful watch over their kingdom.

Love squeezed my heart as I remembered how caring they had been. The perfect parents, in truth, always taking care of me even when they had a whole kingdom to run.

They'd had everything a person could ask for, but... I had been their only son. Their only child and heir.

They'd left me with the crown only a handful of winters ago. Their deaths had both been accidents. That night still haunted me with all its unanswered questions.

Why had they been in the woods when the hunters had come? And why couldn't my father, the biggest of us all and the greatest fighter I'd ever known, survive the fire that broke out after he carried my mother's lifeless body back to the castle?

The courtiers whispered that he had died of a broken heart.

My parents' faces smiled down at me, golden and glowing as the sun crept in through the windows. I looked away before the bad memories could steal inside my mind and tarnish the rosy hue of my perfect memories before that terrible night.

I kept walking until I reached my bedchamber. I strode through the door and slammed it shut, still reeling with anger from my run-in.

As king, it was my duty to hear the counsel of my closest advisors—but that didn't mean I had to like what they said.

Out of nowhere, loneliness filled my gut, like an icy-cold soup.

A creak came from the huge wooden bed at the center of the room.

"Hello, my king," Daphne said, her tone seductive.

Once upon a time, she would have induced me to fall into bed with her. Not tonight though.

I sighed. My loneliness could be assuaged for an hour... a day... but not for long enough. And not by this one.

"Daphne. What are you doing here?"

She was sprawled across my bed, dressed only in her underwear, though it barely contained her ample curves.

I liked women with more flesh. Large breasts, huge ass. Something to hold during love-making and curl up against on long wintery nights.

My mate would need to be big and lush, strong enough to carry my heirs.

But this woman was not the one for me.

She pushed up onto her hands and pouted. "It's been so long, my king. Don't you crave me as you once did?"

She reached out her hand, and I was tempted by her words. Tempted to lose myself in her body. To forget my aching loneliness and the long, winding quest for my mate for a few lust-fueled hours. So far, the search for her had proven fruitless.

"No. I'm sorry Daphne. I can't."

Her wide, hopeful eyes narrowed, and her eyebrows drew together. A part of me was relieved that the savage side of her would always emerge sooner rather than later, especially when crossed.

She could be so innocent and meek in bed. When she was getting her way, that was. Deny her wishes, and you would soon see the *real* face of Daphne Montany.

Experience had taught me well in that regard.

"How can you say that to me?" she said. "We've been lovers for all our adult life. You know you want me. No one can please you as I do."

I chuckled at the arrogance in her words. She had no idea what I truly craved in the bedroom. She was a servant in my household, but nothing more.

I wanted someone who would love me, submit to me, give only to me.

Not to every man in the kingdom who looked her way.

I didn't voice these thoughts, but I let a healthy dose of irritation bleed into my tone, hoping she would get the message.

"Daphne, leave me. I need to take a shower, and if you stay, I'm afraid you'll see the rough side of my temper today."

She opened her mouth, clearly gunning for a fight. I held up my hand, letting loose the growl that had been building in my throat from the moment I'd stepped into the room.

"Daphne. I am your king. I am commanding you to leave me or face the consequences."

With a growl of frustration, she sprang up from the bed and scurried out of the room.

She knew my temper.

They *all* did.

I'd always had a stormy disposition, but the last couple of years had sent me over the edge. The loss of my parents, my lack of a mate. Most days I found it a challenge to rein in my moods, and no amount of anything—food, wine, or women—could sate my appetites for long.

I walked into the bathroom and stripped off my sweat-soaked shirt. The scent of my heat rose around me, making me groan with the need to fulfill my destiny.

To locate my mate. To fuck us both into sweet, sweet oblivion.

Maybe then I could finally find some peace.

I'd been told by my father that true happiness in the arms of your mate existed. He was the greatest king our clan had ever known. The most powerful. The most loved.

But I'd never experienced such peace for myself. Unlike my father, my mate had not been born into the local town. I couldn't smell her, despite all the nights I spent prowling down every alleyway and corner. Wherever she was, it wasn't nearby.

I'd been told, time and time over, that I would know her by sight, by taste, by smell.

I sighed. Until I found her, I had to deal with the heated dreams, the frenzies of rage, and the arousal that no number of trysts with easy women could abate.

I flicked on the hot water and walked beneath the flow, groaning out in the simple pleasure of the feeling.

I cast my mind back to Hillsen and the conversation that had interrupted my training session and had gotten me so riled up.

Aside from his bullish demands that I take a wife, there were more immediate troubles that I had to attend.

Our world was surrounded by the human world. We were enclosed, like a bubble hidden away from the eyes of ordinary souls, in a secret realm. A paranormal portal bridged the gap between us and the humans. The barrier kept us safe, and hidden, deep in the mountains of Siberia.

Our clan was one of six dragon shifter kingdoms that populated our hidden pocket of the world.

We lived in peace—most of the time. Of late, there had been rumours of an uprising, by Magnik, the king of the most southern tribe.

He had always wanted the land surrounding my castle. It was rich in rare, precious ore. We were sitting on a potential fortune if we chose to mine it and sell it to the humans beyond the portal.

But that wasn't my deal.

I avoided trading with the humans as much as possible. I didn't trust them. I'd met one, once. They were selfish. Without loyalty or bravery. It was for the best that our two worlds were separated, and we were hidden from them.

Before their death, my parents had made me vow that I would never mine the land that we'd owned for generations. It would see thousands of people lose their homes and would tear apart my kingdom.

All for the sake of money.

"Majesty. The evening guests are assembled. It's time to dress for dinner," Maddie, the housekeeper who'd looked after me since I was a child, said, stepping into the bathroom and laying out a fresh towel and my formal suit.

I groaned, venting my annoyance. "You *know* I don't like wearing that. It's too stiff."

She gave me a hard stare. Unfortunately, it was one I knew well. It told me I would do as she asked, or else.

"I know, sire. But unless you have lost your crown since we last spoke, I won't have you turning up to dinner wearing clothes fit for a farmer."

With a huff, I turned off the shower and grabbed the towel.

Maddie had been like a second mother to me since... forever. These days, with my parents gone, she barely left my side.

We'd had this argument on countless occasions.

"Who's coming tonight?" I asked. "Remind me."

"The leaders of the other five kingdoms, Majesty."

"What?"

I froze, halfway through drying my back. Had Maddie just said that *all* of the monarchs were dining here tonight?

"Since when?"

More to the point, why haven't I heard of it until now?

"Some of the elders decided to get everyone together to look over our yearly plans. The wedded monarchs are bringing their families with them."

"What?"

Four of us six were married already. Damon was the only other bachelor king and, as far as anyone could tell, he rarely stepped outside his castle.

"To make it more of an informal affair, as I understand it. Rather than an official one of state."

A growl began to rumble through my chest. With difficulty, I tamped it down.

Don't shoot the messenger, Stavrok.

"You've got to be kidding me," I said. "What do they want now?"

Maddie shrugged. "How would I know? I'm simply the maid, Your Majesty."

"Maddie, please." I crossed my arms and stared down at her, trying to maintain authority. "You know more about this kingdom than anyone. If you know why they're here, then you better tell me."

Her smile was secretive as she backed out of the bathroom. "See you downstairs, sire."

CHAPTER
TWO

Stavrok

I grabbed the suit Maddie had laid out for me and considered throwing it after her retreating form. Instead, I took a few deep breaths and pulled it on.

Was this a set up? Why was everyone conspiring against me today? This meal had to be in aid of something, but I couldn't for the life of me figure out what.

I rubbed the silk tie Maddie had laid out between finger and thumb, wrinkling my nose with distaste.

A tie as well? Shit. What am I, human?

I threw the narrow strip of material in the direction of the trash and tugged on the crisp white shirt.

Even custom made and tailored to perfection, these clothes did not sit right on me. It was expected, and befitted my position, but I never felt comfortable dressing like this.

I slicked back my long hair so that it didn't fall over my face and let out a slow exhale. I couldn't put it off any longer; it was time to make my way downstairs.

There was only one other king I got along with. Vlakid. He and I had hunted together many times. I was there when he found the woman who would be his queen. She was so beautiful that it made me sick with envy every time I saw them together. Even if she'd been a servant before he'd seen her.

As for the rest of them, well, where the night would take us was anyone's guess.

The rumble of deep male voices came from the formal dining room, and I paused before entering, gathering my strength to face them all.

Another thing my mate would make easier for me: formal gatherings.

She would be the perfect hostess, I was sure.

I craved my fated mate for more than the chance to secure my lineage. With her, I would have comfort, companionship. I wouldn't have to be the bachelor king a moment longer.

The elders and my kingdom would finally be happy with me.

I pushed open the door and everyone turned toward me. The men were standing, drinks in their hands. The women were already seated at the table.

They were all dressed as I'd been instructed to. In their royal robes. Rich fabrics topped with furs. Purples, reds and blacks. And when they looked at me, there was a mixture of jealousy and friendship written across their faces.

The men I'd known my whole life. But that was the price of power and privilege, living and knowing there were more than a few vipers in the nest.

Magnik especially. That one was a true bastard.

"Welcome." I surveyed the group before me, hands clasped behind my back. I had to look regal, self-assured. In control. "I trust your journeys were comfortable. Please, take your seats."

Delicious smells wafted through the air. The food was ready to be served. As I greeted my guests with the customary hand shaking and kisses, my stomach growled.

It had been too long since I'd last eaten.

And my dragon was hungry.

Always hungry.

I indicated the table where the women sat waiting for us. "Please. Let us eat before discussions begin."

The men around me nodded, their eyes lighting up as the servants entered, bearing platters piled high with delicacies.

A dragon shifter's hunger was ravenous all the time, especially through winter, when our metabolisms burned the hottest.

I grabbed for the cuts of stag and bear meat in front of me, loading my plate with a small mountain of food. I poured gravy over the lot and tore open the fresh, warm bread right in front of me, inhaling the steam that came from within.

I filled the bread up with meat and dipped it into a bowl of gravy before devouring the handmade sandwich in a handful of bites. My carnivorous nature really got the better of me sometimes; the dragon demanded meat, and lots of it.

I had barely slaked my hunger by the time Barrick called out to me from the other end of the table.

"Stavrok! I heard your elders are pushing you to enter the human realm to find your mate." He grunted, showing his disgust. "Are you willing to taint the pure blood of your dragon so easily?"

Barrick was the oldest of us, closer to fifty than forty. He was thinner and smaller, with long black hair that reminded me of a crow.

I shot a glare at him and picked up my wine glass, downing the thick red liquor and preparing my answer carefully. Though I agreed with him, that the mixing of my blood with a human would weaken my offspring, I wasn't going to give him the satisfaction of knowing that.

It was vital to show strength when conversing with another king. I took the remark for the challenge it was, and I knew I had to parry the blow with one of my own.

"I'm not going to grab the first woman who climbs into my bed, Barrick." I let my gaze wander over to the woman by his side. A peasant. His wife. Pregnant for the third time. Or was it the fourth?

I raised an eyebrow and watched as Barrick's face coloured with heat.

"You neglect the continuation of your bloodline, Stavrok," he said. "Your heirs. Without a son, your kingdom is weak, vulnerable."

I laughed aloud. "Vulnerable? I am not weak, and neither is my kingdom. I will find my true mate, no matter how long I have to wait."

I looked around the room at the five kings and four of their queens. Together, we ruled the kingdoms of *Fire and Ice.*

It wasn't the official name of our hidden country, but it was a name I'd given to my snowy lands a long time ago, when I was a child, and it had stuck.

"That may be a mistake, my friend. You're not getting any younger," Vlakid said to my right.

I glared at him, but there was no real heat behind the look. Vlakid was too relaxed to be a king, too kind. He had never been anything other than a firm friend and ally.

"Just because you found your mate working as a laundress in your town, Vlakid..." I gave his beautiful wife a smile, then shifted my gaze back to my friend. "You think such fortune will fall to everyone around you. Some of us aren't so lucky."

I'd scoured the city, and the surrounding towns. All the married kings in the room had found their wives practically on their doorstep, in their own hometowns, or thereabouts.

Everyone except for Damon and myself.

Mine had either never been born, died early, or she was yet to reach maturity. All of those possibilities were devastating and frustrating in the extreme. The worst part was, I simply didn't know.

A servant stepped forward and re-filled my glass. I reached for my wine and glanced down the table to Damon, the stoic quiet king who was also queen-less. He met my gaze and inclined his head in a silent moment of respect.

Marienne, Magnik's queen on the other side of me, reached out and touched my hand. Her long fingers were elegant, just like the rest of her, but the touch was brief as if she feared I might lash out at her forwardness. "Would you allow me the honor of reading your palm, King Stavrok?"

I moved my hand further away from her, feeling her subtle magic reach out after me like a shimmer across a pool.

"Readings?" My gaze snapped to her husband. "Is that why your kingdom has grown so prosperous of late, Magnik?"

He merely shrugged. "My wife has many talents," he said, a lecherous smile lifting his lips, "and she advises us regarding the weather and our crops. As she should. It is her duty and it benefits our people."

I gave him a knowing stare before sliding my gaze to Marienne. I was certain she helped with more than that. Magnik had renovated his palace in the past year and his clothes and jewels had multiplied in number. Their kingdom was more powerful than ever.

Perhaps she was predicting shifts in the humans' economy? The stock exchange, maybe. The practices weren't technically forbidden, but it was frowned upon to make money on the humans in such a way. Especially when Magnik had married a sorceress. It was the very definition of cheating.

Marienne was looking more tired than I'd ever seen her, with dark circles beneath her eyes. Did Magnik treat her well? As I pondered their relationship, she said to me again. "Stavrok. I implore you to let me help you. I may be able to tell you where to look."

Her purple irises whirled like rockpools, betraying some kind of emotion that I couldn't read.

"Why would you want to help me, Mari?"

She gave me a gentle smile that seemed genuine. "Because you are a good and kind man. And your dragon is growing impatient. I can feel him stirring. You will not be able to control him much longer."

I opened my mouth to tell her she was wrong. Not about her character assessment, but about the strength of my will against my dragon's restlessness. I had been fighting him all my life. But the heat of my dragon was stronger in my blood now. I could feel it flowing and shifting, ever impatient under my skin.

It was just as she said, though I wouldn't admit it out loud to anyone, even on my deathbed.

I relented, gritting the words out before I could rethink them. "Fine. Tell me. Where is she?"

She bit her lip. "I don't know yet. My magic isn't as strong as I would like at present. But if you'd let me hold both of your hands for a moment, the connection might help. I can try to give you the answers you seek."

A chuckle rose in my throat.

The sorceress wants me to let her inside my mind, does she?
Not a chance.

"Thank you for your offer, but I'm afraid I'll have to decline."

She sank back in her seat, her shoulders slumping a little as if my answer dejected her.

I turned away from her and focused my attention on Vlakid, who threw me an easy smile and started telling me about his youngest child, a baby girl born over the last winter.

Even in this den of powerful sovereign rulers, I had friends. People I could count on to turn my mind onto happier things.

After that exchange with Queen Marienne, I forced the conversation to politics, to trade and councils. After all, that was the purpose of our gathering. But I couldn't ignore Marienne's intent gaze upon me throughout the remainder of the meal. I sensed she was measuring me, weighing her options.

I wasn't convinced that her offer of help came solely from the goodness of her heart.

Witches and mages in our kingdoms regularly foretold the future, but such services always came with a price. Although Marienne was a queen by marriage, with all the wealth of her husband's kingdom already at her beck and call, I was concerned the payment she would require for this information would be more than I would willingly give.

We finished dinner, and to my relief, the subject of my future wife didn't come up again. In fact, everyone seemed to be steering clear of the topic entirely.

Perhaps they were fearful my temper might get the better of me.

It was infuriating to be the object of such speculation, but I knew it wouldn't end until I found my mate.

Why didn't they pester the solemn, quiet Damon? With his golden hair and bright blue eyes, it was a mystery why he was unmarried. And why he never spoke.

We moved into the grand hallway. My guests glittered in their finery; the women's skirts swirled in the candlelight, and the children ran in and out of their parents' legs, shrieking with the excitement of staying up so late.

I wished they would all leave. A pressure was starting to build behind my eyes. I just wanted to be somewhere else, alone. Preferably in a dark room.

Queen Marienne strolled up to me, unspeaking. What did she want? Surely not to offer me guidance once again about my mate. Her foot caught on a crooked flagstone. As she fell, crying out, I grabbed her hands to steady her.

I realized my error moments too late.

Her hands clasped mine, holding tight, and electricity shot through my palms as her magic and my dragon wove together.

Her head snapped up and our gazes locked onto each other.

I saw what she saw; it raced from her mind to my heart and back again, flowing in an unstoppable current that pooled together, forming a clear image that was almost vivid enough to reach out and touch.

It hit me like a thunderbolt.

My mate was a human. Alive, and whole, and beautiful. And entirely unaware of my presence, over all these years. She was just waiting to be found. Across the magical void that kept her land separate from mine.

CHAPTER
THREE

Stavrok

A gasp filled my throat, making it feel as though a hand squeezed tight around my heart. The shock of the realization pounded through my brain, over and over.

My mate. That was my mate!

Or was it? What, exactly, had I seen? A picture Marienne had possibly forced into my mind on behalf of her husband? A cunning deception intended to destabilize a rival king?

Or was that image the truth?

I dragged Marienne to her feet, and she came up, trembling. Her

16

husband materialized beside her, pulling her from me so quickly she stumbled backward and almost fell once again.

The moment her connection with me was broken, my mind cleared and all the feelings about the woman who was to be my queen, my fated mate, were gone.

"Stop that, Marienne. You're embarrassing me." Magnik hissed at her, and Marienne instantly flinched as though expecting him to strike her.

I frowned at the exchange, not enjoying see anyone flinch away from a loved one. I'd heard rumors over the years that Marienne and Magnik's marriage was not a happy one. She had no children, and it was clear he had chosen her for her powers, not for love. Had those rumors been true? And worse, did he raise his hand to her on occasion?

"I need to help him." She whispered the words in Magnik's direction but he was already storming away in a rage.

I narrowed my eyes again. If this was a deception, they didn't seem to be on it together.

"Did you see her?" Queen Marienne asked me, her strange, ethereal eyes wide. She sounded part-enthralled, part-fearful.

I stared at her, my arms twitching with a strange sort of energy. I could feel my shifter inside my chest, stretching, his wings unfurling. Ready for flight.

Damn. This was *not* the time to lose control.

"Did you put that vision inside my head, Marienne?" I demanded. It was a struggle to keep my voice steady.

She shook her head vehemently, purple magic swirling intensely behind her eyes. "No! I *told* you that if you would spare me a moment, I could try and help you find your mate."

I shivered and clenched my muscles, drawing my shoulder blades together in a fruitless attempt to control my dragon.

"That woman was my mate? Are you sure?" I asked, urgency growing in my tone.

I wouldn't be able to speak soon and I needed to know if what I saw was real.

Echoes of the vision flickered through my mind: a blonde woman, with hair that flowed and shone in the sunlight, curling all the way down to the small of her back. Her eyes were a brilliant emerald green, like the stones we mined from the caves near our home.

She had a fire about her, a vivacious energy that was a rarity in a human.

"Yes, I'm sure. I don't control my magic, King Stavrok," Marienne said, spreading out her hands in a supplicating manner. "The vision was a gift."

I stiffened against the word. "A gift I did not ask for, Mari, and you should not ask for payment."

Her eyes met mine. Her gaze was as unreadable as ever, but I could detect a shadow of hurt and frustration in her expression.

"Stavrok, your friendship alone is payment enough. We are to rule our kingdoms alongside one another for the rest of our lives, are we not? Let us try to be friends."

She turned away, as if not expecting an answer, and glided back across the room to Magnik's side. When she reached him, her husband turned his back on her and filled his goblet with wine once again.

I could almost see the defeat in Marienne's posture and, for a moment, my heart went out to the woman. But I had no time to dwell on the state of another's marriage.

I could see my mate so clearly in my mind. My dragon wanted to hunt for her, shake free. Leave the castle this very night.

Did I dare?

"Marienne?" I called after her, quickly crossing the room and closing the gap. "Tell me, what more do you know? Where should I look for her?"

The queen whirled and faced me squarely. "You must let me complete your reading if you want to know everything, Stavrok."

Damn. I didn't have much of a choice. She had me pressed into a corner. I wanted to know who my mate was, and where I could find her.

"No payment required," she added wryly.

"Very well."

It was a dangerous gamble.

If she probed too hard in my mind and found out too much about my kingdom, it could tip the balance of our world too far in her husband's favor. The six clans relied on a mutual fear and respect of the other kingdoms, and we kept our secrets closely guarded.

If I wanted answers, I had no choice.

Extending both of my hands, I kept my expression steely. Before she could take hold, I drew back. "Marienne. My mind is my own. Do not rifle through my thoughts. Tell me only what I want to know."

"I give you my word, Stavrok." She granted me a short nod, and I allowed her to clasp my hands.

Her gaze snapped to mine. This time, I willingly surrendered to her power.

Our eyes clashed and a myriad of images flashed across my mind as I struggled to keep calm and not fight against the jolts of electricity coursing through my veins.

I saw an image of the woman flowing through my mind again. She was with a child—no, with many children—laughing with them, helping them paint with their fingers on a giant sheet of paper.

Human children...

Then the picture changed. It was the same woman, sitting with an older couple on their front porch, clutching steaming mugs of coffee and talking quietly.

The images came faster, forming and reforming in front of my eyes. Now she was asleep, spread out in the middle of a large four-poster bed, alone. Her long golden hair was pale in the moonlight, fanned out over the pillow, and her arms were curved upwards, elongating her torso.

Her eyelashes brushed her cheeks, hiding her bright eyes. I watched her chest rise and fall, my eyes tracing over her full breasts and her long, pale throat...

I broke away, gasping for breath, unable to handle the force of my wanting for another minute.

My heart ached for the woman who would fulfill me.

And damn it all... she's human!

"Did you get enough? Do you know how to find her?" I panted as I spoke, my heart thundering as though I'd run up a thousand steps to the highest turret in the castle.

Marienne nodded, staggering backward. Her lips were pale, and her frame seemed smaller somehow.

Drained of energy, I guessed.

Her husband turned to watch our exchange, a snarl on his face as his wife stumbled then caught herself against a chair. He didn't step forward to help her.

I did, feeling the need to extend my arm and offer her the support she so obviously needed. That wasn't my place. It should have been Magnik's.

"She's human?" I asked, gently this time. I needed to confirm I'd gotten that part right, at least.

"Yes, she belongs to the human realm. But…"

I tilted my head, confused by the caveat. "But what?"

Marienne frowned, fiddling with the rings that studded her slender fingers. "I sense some magic in her. It's possible that one of our ancestors ventured out and bred with a human in that area a long time ago. I can't be sure. What I do know is, she is yours, Stavrok. Your fated mate. And she isn't far away. She lives in the first town past the border. You'll know her on sight."

The last thing I wanted was to head out there. I didn't trust the human race. But what choice did I have? Fate knew best. If she was my mate, surely there would be good in her.

I swallowed down the bile that rose. "Are the old stories true? Will my dragon kidnap her when he sees her?"

A small smile rose on Queen Marienne's face. "What's wrong, Stavrok? Never met a woman who didn't dive into your bed the moment you set eyes on her? Apart from me, of course."

I gave her a wry smile. "No, I haven't, actually."

My pride balked at the idea of kidnapping *anyone*, let alone the woman who I would make my queen, the mother of my children.

As Marienne had pointed out, I'd never wanted for willing women in my bed. As the king, every courtier all the way down to the lowliest townsperson wanted my favor. I was generous with bestowing it. As a virile man, I could have one, two, even three in a night without tiring.

"My father once told me that a true fated mate would not fall for me on sight. She would need to be taken and brought here, and only then would our bond be sealed."

The whole concept irked me. Why the hell would I force a woman into my bed who didn't want to be there?

Marienne shrugged her slender shoulders. "I can't help you any further, Stavrok. Your dragon will know what to do when the time comes."

She turned to her husband and I saw her recoil. Why… I wasn't sure. "Come, my king. Let us return home. I fear I have overexerted myself."

"Then go sit down, before you fall down," Magnik snapped. "And you will wait for me. I am not ready to return home yet."

I saw it again; the strain in her body, the faint lines that had appeared at the corners of her eyes and around the edges of her mouth. How much did it cost the sorceress to call upon her magic in such a way?

She pulled out a chair and sat upon it, and I saw her fighting to keep her posture straight.

"Mari," I said, feeling pity when I looked at her weary form. "I thank you."

She threw me a small smile. "Go, Stavrok. Fly there now. I know you need to. Don't hold out against it any longer."

My gaze went to the window on my right. It was huge and ancient, and bolted heavily. Its diamond-patterned glass winked at me, as if in invitation.

I couldn't, not now. It was pitch dark outside, and heavy snow tumbled from the skies above. The idea was absurd, surely...

"Sire, please." Hillsen's voice interrupted my reverie. The elder who had advised my father on many important decisions now advised me, and it seemed he had gleaned the current direction of my thoughts. "The council and I are in complete agreement. Surely you must see our point. As the only unmarried king you must..."

I put up my hand, silencing Hillsen.

"I quite agree, Hillsen. I will not return without a queen."

I unbolted the large window and pushed it open. The castle was built high up on the mountainside.

Cold blustery air blew in and snow landed on my overheated skin. I was glad for the relief of it, but the flakes melted as soon as they touched my flesh. I was as hot as a furnace, but exposure to the elements wouldn't be enough. Only one thing could sate the fire within.

I'd made my decision. I stripped off my coat jacket and tossed it to the floor. My shirt and my pants followed.

"My king, this is not advisable. Where are you going?"

I looked at the elder and raised a brow. "I told you, Hillsen. I need to find my queen. I will return home before the sun sets tomorrow."

Now completely unclothed, I stepped up onto the ledge and called to my dragon.

He wasn't far away. He had been under the surface of my skin for hours now, through the whole evening. Circling inside of me, impatient. Ready and waiting for my shift.

I dove out the window. The cold air whipped around my body as I plummeted through the snowfall toward the jagged rocks below.

My dragon jumped forward and my body transformed into an animal designed to cut through the air like a blade through silk. A creature of flight, huge and majestic.

My skin rippled, and my scales emerged. My toes curled into claws. Wings sprouted from my shoulder blades, stretching wide and catching the undercurrent of air in a heartbeat.

And, with that, I was soaring, skimming along the ground before shooting up and over the castle in a wide arc.

Fire lit up my throat and there was a heavy ache in my heart. I needed to find my mate, my queen. The woman who was born to complete me.

The one who would rule my kingdom by my side and provide me with my heirs, secure my dynasty for generations to come.

Children. Baby dragons. Hopefully... if a human could breed with a man such as me.

There was only one way to tell. And that was to do what my father had always said I would do, and what I always hoped to avoid.

I must find my mate and bring her back home with me, taking her away from her world and everything she held dear.

CHAPTER
FOUR

Stavrok

My wings carried me toward the border that connected the human world to ours.

I closed my eyes as I hit the invisible barrier. A cold shudder passed over my scales as I emerged through the other side.

It was warmer in the human world. As I sank down and flew close to the ground, it occurred to me that these people were not used to seeing dragons flying around in their airspace.

The last thing I needed was to collide with a passing aeroplane.

My feet hit the ground, as I shifted back to my human self. The transition was smooth and steady despite my agitated state.

My skin burned against the night air, and I looked around, wondering where I would be able to find clothes at this hour.

The most inconvenient part of shifting was not being able to carry clothes with me. Not that I worried much when I travelled in our world. Everyone knew who I was, and my noble standing ensured that they would come running with robes to cover my nakedness.

It was slightly humiliating to stand out here with no one around.

I walked through the woods, trudging along until I came upon a ploughed field. At the edge of it stood a small farmhouse with a flagpole in the front yard. The flag fluttered in the wind, and even from this distance I could make out a large red dragon emblazoned on it.

Happiness lit up my heart.

I knew that sign. It appeared that a tiny piece of my world had crept into theirs.

These people would help me.

I strode across the field and thumped several times on the door, covering myself the best I could with my hands. I was thankful that it was dark, at least.

After a few minutes, a man emerged. He took one look at me and called back into the house.

"Joanie! We have a visitor."

He opened the door wider and grabbed for a large fur greatcoat that hung in the entrance hall. "Here, take this. You'd better come in."

I had to duck my head through the low doorway. I wrapped myself in the coat and glanced around. It was a comfortable home with humble furnishings. A fire roared in the hearth, and I gravitated toward it.

"Thank you," I said, turning back to him. "For your hospitality."

The man gave me a tight smile. His gaze roamed up and down my body as though he'd never seen a dragon shifter before. Which didn't make sense. They had the flag flying and had welcomed me inside.

We were slightly different to humans. Far taller on average, and broader with it. My tattoos indicated my royal blood—not that these two people would know it.

A woman came into the hallway, carrying a steaming mug. Her eyes widened when she saw me.

Then her gaze dropped. "You're a Dragon *King.*"

Her husband blinked, staring at me. Slowly, he began to back away.

I lifted up my head. "How did you know?"

I knotted the tie around the coat and took the cup of hot drink the woman handed to me.

"I recognise your chest tattoo." She motioned to it, giving a shaky laugh. "My mother taught me all of the Royal Heraldic symbols in case I ever met one of your kind."

I nodded before taking a sip of the bitter drink. I couldn't complain, though. It spread much needed warmth through my belly. I turned my head toward the fire, staring into the flames.

"Your mother knew of our ways?" I asked.

The woman took a seat in the armchair beside the fire, motioning me to sit on the loveseat opposite. I sank into it and barely fit. The seat was tiny, made for humans.

"Yes. She was born in Jerriak, but she settled here with my father many years ago. We are the gatekeepers, Majesty. I have been charged with the responsibility of helping anyone who crosses the border."

I hadn't known such people existed until now. I was grateful for them; my kind had a friendly face to turn to when they entered this realm.

I set my cup down on a nearby coffee table that looked hand made. I leaned forward. "On behalf of my people, I thank you, madam. I shall need some clothes, though I'm afraid I don't have any coin with me."

My impromptu visit seemed more ridiculous with each passing moment. I hadn't brought clothes or money, and I had no plan that extended beyond making it to the human world.

I'd simply followed my instincts and the words of a witch.

Not one of my smarter moves, truth be told.

"Oh, that's no problem, sire," she said.

"Stavrok."

She got to her feet with a smile. "King Stavrok. Please, come this way. We have lots of clothes in storage, although I have to admit, you're bigger than most of the men we've seen cross the border."

I inclined my head at the awkward compliment.

Aside from the clear difference between me and human men, I was taller and broader than most of my kinsmen. Being of royal blood, and a man with a desire to be the fittest warrior I could be, I was unusually large.

I stood up, grateful to be out of the clutches of the loveseat. "Thank you. Anything you have will be appreciated."

The woman led me into a spare bedroom with a single small bed, then pointed to a huge closet. "In here," she said.

She opened the doors to the closet and revealed the contents. It was filled with clothes for every sort of person who may visit them. Winter dresses with long sleeves. Jackets and long coats. Shirts and pants. I wondered how long she had been helping people cross the border. My kingdom owed her a great debt it appeared.

And even more so, it seemed that I was wrong in my assumption that all humans were selfish creatures. There was a woman in front of me who came from a line of people who looked after my kind. I had to hope that my mate would be of the same ilk.

I grabbed some thick pants, a long-sleeved shirt, and a sweater. Simple human fare. If the clothes survived the journey home, I suspected Maddie would be most displeased to see me in such attire.

Once I was dressed, we walked back into the living room to re-join the woman's husband.

I turned to them. "Can I ask, how often do you see my kind pass through from the border?"

I'd had no idea that humans even knew about us. Perhaps I was more out of touch with my kingdom than I'd realized.

"Not often." She shrugged. "Maybe once or twice a month."

"A month?" I struggled to keep my voice level.

That was so much more than I'd anticipated.

I needed to investigate this further. Were people so unhappy in the kingdom they would abandon it for this strange land? Or did they only visit for a short while, then return? Did they want for things that our world couldn't provide? Whatever it was, it couldn't stand. I cared for my people, and they cared for me in return.

But those were considerations for another day. I had a big enough task ahead of me this night.

"I'm looking for a woman," I said. "I need to get into the closest town as soon as possible."

"Of course. We'll help in any way we can," the woman said. "Do you know her name, or where she works?"

I shook my head. "I know nothing, except what she looks like, and that she may have children. Or else, she cares for them in some capacity. It wasn't clear... I'm afraid the manner of her discovery was... unusual." I paused. "It's essential that I find her."

The couple glanced at each other. The woman gestured that I should follow them back into the living area.

I went with them. The man stoked the fire in the grate, his back toward me. I sensed his tension; my kind made human men nervous. Something in their biology saw us as a threat.

The woman walked out of the room and returned with a plate of food, fit for a common man.

"Forgive me, sire. We don't have anything special..."

I smiled and took a cake that she offered. "This is perfect."

We sat and they turned to me.

The woman leaned forward. "Perhaps if you described the woman, we might be able to help."

"She has bright emerald green eyes, and long blonde hair. She is striking, and strong, and though I haven't met her, I believe she will have a temper that could shake the foundations of this house."

The woman's eyes went wide.

"We, uh, know of such a woman. She lives in the next town over. She's quite famous around these parts."

"For what?" I ask, fear sinking into my gut.

Please, don't say that she is the town whore. I couldn't bear it.

"Well, for one thing, her striking looks." The woman furrowed her brow, staring into the roaring fireplace. "And for the other, turning down every guy that asks her out. She's had plenty of offers, I can tell you that much."

My heart leapt, threatening to burst out of my chest. That sounded like the beauty I'd seen in Marienne's vision.

"I must go to her, immediately. Do you know where she lives?"

The couple shared a look.

"Yes," the woman replied. "A few blocks over from the day-care center she works at. But she will be asleep now, so it may be better if you stop here for the night. We can take you to her in the morning. It's no trouble."

The idea didn't sit right with me. I looked at the clock. Yes, it was almost midnight, far past the time that humans typically went to bed.

Now that I knew her location, I could practically feel her presence. She was so close. Even sitting here was proving difficult. My urges were like an ever-present itch under my skin, and I needed to take care of them before my dragon took control.

"Thank you for your concern." I lowered my eyes, trying not to fidget in my impatience. It was unbecoming for a king. "I'm afraid there is a possibility I may shift when I meet her. It is best I go now, while the cloak of darkness can cover me."

I stood up, unsure whether I should have explained so much to complete strangers. And humans, at that.

Still, they'd provided me with warm clothing, shelter, and food. My trust in them hadn't been misplaced so far.

They got to their feet. The man seemed hesitant, but the woman carried a look of determination on her face that reminded me of Maddie.

"We will help you, King Stavrok," she said, drawing herself up to her full, if diminutive, height. "I'd consider it an honor."

"I'll get the keys to the truck," her husband said, before heading through a low doorway at the back of the room.

"You're sure you know where she lives?" I asked the woman.

I *had* to be sure. I had left too much of this excursion to chance already, and I couldn't afford to linger long in the human world.

The woman pulled on a winter jacket. "Yes, we do. My mother told me stories about her lands when I was a child. Is she your mate, sire?"

Technically I wouldn't know until my dragon sensed her. But I had hope.

"I have been told that she is," I said, my voice soft. "But I cannot tell until I meet her in person. So, we both shall see soon enough."

We headed outside to a large truck. It was a huge, rusty thing, older than me by the look of it. Hopefully, it would transport me to where we needed to go.

If it couldn't, I would walk. A hundred miles, if I had to.

Nothing, in this world or the next, was stopping me from meeting the woman who could be the mate I'd dreamed about for so long.

CHAPTER
FIVE

Lucy

The dream was back, swirling around me in the darkness.

I had dreamt the same dream for as long as I could remember. Over the years, it came and went, sometimes plaguing me for months on end, then disappearing for a time before returning, more vivid than ever.

It was always the same. I dreamed of a world of Fire and Ice, a dark, howling storm where the elements tore through my hair and clothes. The wind would whip around my form while I shivered, fear and awe rooting me to the spot.

At the center of it all was a man, standing on the clifftop. Thunderclaps shook the sky above his strong frame, and lighting flashed across his harsh features. He belonged in this hazardous world. He wasn't afraid of anything.

He held my gaze, unmoved by the chaos around him. He never spoke, but I knew that he was calling to me.

And I knew that I would go to him.

A bolt of lightning split the sky in two, and I screamed as the world darkened and my vision was obscured by a pair of huge, leathery wings.

I shuddered, crying out as my subconscious clawed its way back to reality.

Panting hard against the fear racing along my veins, I managed to struggle onto my elbows and pull myself into an upright position in bed.

What had woken me?

Surely not the dreams. I'd accepted them as a matter of course long ago.

A loud and persistent knocking came from downstairs. Someone was hammering on my front door like they were going to break it open.

I froze.

The clock told me it was just past midnight.

I relaxed back into the pillows with a huff. Who on *earth* would be knocking on my door in the middle of the night? On a Tuesday, no less?

Talk about rude.

I closed my eyes and prayed they would go away. Whatever it was, I would deal with it in the morning. I had an early start and a bunch of rowdy kids to manage tomorrow.

"Lucy! Open the door! *Lucy!*"

The call was loud and insistent, but I didn't recognise the voice. I groaned as I pushed back my thick, warm duvet and fumbled in the dark for my dressing gown.

There better be a major emergency to be disturbing my sleep like this. The noise was sure to wake the neighbours, which was the last thing I needed.

I shoved my feet into my slippers, cursing under my breath, and padded downstairs.

A glance through the spy hole told me my visitors were an elderly couple I knew vaguely by sight. I was more confused than ever. Both by their presence and the fact that they apparently knew where I lived.

I pulled open the door, trying to quell the worry that seeped through my chest.

I drew my robe tight around me, shivering at the blast of cold night air. "Can I help you?"

They moved apart, revealing a third figure in the group, standing in the darkness behind them. He was huge in stature, dwarfing the man and woman on either side of him. He stepped forward; his eyes fixed on mine.

I knew him.

I *knew* him. In the marrow of my bones. I felt a shiver pass through my body, and my breath caught in my throat.

"Who are you?" My voice came out as a shaky whisper.

He was the man who had haunted my dreams all these years. The recognition shocked me to the core. This figment of my imagination appearing on my doorstep in the dead of night... It was like falling under a spell.

Those eyes. Those silver-gray eyes. Glowing, lighting me up from within.

Calling to me.

The man moved as if to step into my house, and I held up a hand in warning.

"Don't come any further. You are not welcome in my house."

Despite my words, my body was overtaken by a sensation I'd never experienced before. I ached, throbbed, lusted for this giant of a man. My body curved toward his without my permission as I stared up at him.

He towered above me. His shoulders spanned the width of my doorway. He was the biggest man I'd ever met in my life. His thigh muscles bulged through the thick pants encasing them in a way that made my mouth dry.

Despite the anger in my gut that roared like a fire in the dead of winter, honey melted in my core. A sure sign of a pure lust. I'd been turned on before, but not like this.

This was... different.

This was *terrifying*.

"Stop. Seriously!" I put up my hands to try and halt him as he moved into my house.

The look in his eyes was strange. It was almost like he hadn't registered my defiance at all.

I backed up and pressed my hands into his chest, glaring at him with all my might.

My hidden desires, my carnal needs, spiralled up inside of me and my hands clung tight to his sweater. I stared at his mouth and knew, deep within my soul, that this man was meant to be mine.

No!

It was impossible. This was a stranger. I should be quaking with fear right now, not flushed and heated with desire. I especially shouldn't be raking my hands over his chest because I couldn't decide whether to push him back or pull him closer.

"You're coming with me," he said.

He bent down and lifted me up like I weighed nothing at all. The world tilted. I shrieked with rage, hammering my fists against his rock-hard ass as he marched outside into the cold with me over his shoulder.

"Put. Me. Down!"

As soon as I spoke, my feet hit the earth and I swayed, feeling the ground move under me. I staggered a little before regaining my footing.

The man in front of me was shaking. With rage? With desire?

"Get back. He's going to shift, and you need to get out of the way."

The woman who'd knocked on my door hooked a hand around my elbow and yanked me back. My breath caught in my throat as I watched, stricken.

Before me, the man began to glow.

An unreal shimmer of light encased his body. Suddenly, he changed.

He grew even bigger, his clothes ripping and shredding as a beast emerged from the man who'd once stood in his place.

"It's a... It's a..." I couldn't say it.

My heart burst into song and started pounding against my chest. Every part of me should be terrified of the creature looming over me, but I couldn't run. Couldn't hide. I could only stare at the magnificence before me.

"It's a dragon," the woman behind me whispered.

I dragged my gaze away to look at the couple surrounding me.

They stared at the mythical creature, awe shining in their eyes, like they were witnessing a miracle.

How were they not frightened?

Adrenaline zinged through my veins at a million miles an hour.

I twisted in the woman's grasp, managing to break away from her and stumble back a couple of paces.

"We have to get out of here!" I yelled.

"Don't run!" she said as I edged back toward my house. "Don't go back inside, Lucy. He'll destroy your house to get to you if he has to!"

At that, I froze.

I'd worked day and night for years to afford the deposit for this house. I wasn't letting some man... dragon... *thing*... destroy it right in front of my eyes.

"What does it want?" I yelled at her.

The sound of the dragon's ragged breathing was as noisy as a storm blowing through the trees around my house.

The woman turned toward me, and a strange smile tilted up her features.

"He wants you, Lucy. You'll have to go with him."

I didn't even hesitate in my answer. "No fucking way."

Dragon-clawed hands lifted me, holding me firm against the cold scales of his belly and chest. The grip of the dragon was strong, and the more I struggled, the tighter the hold became.

"Help!" I screamed, thrashing against my restraints.

It was absolutely no use. The clawed arms held me effortlessly, securing me as if I weighed no more than a sack of grain.

For a creature this size, I probably did.

My confusion and rage began to ebb away, and fear rippled through my body.

A cold sweat beaded at the back on my neck, and I shivered. The erratic pulse of my heart thundered in my chest, making my head spin.

This has to be a dream! Surely? There was no other rational explanation.

As soon as I'd had the thought, my breathing settled as I began to calm down.

Of course. Now it made sense. Trust *me* to dream up something this ludicrous.

I plummeted toward the earth as the great beast crouched down. I shrieked, pushing at its toes that held me firm. Then the dragon launched up, into the air with one powerful push of its wings.

My stomach lurched and I cried out. I heard a hysterical peal of laughter as the snow and cold wind blasted my face. It took me a second to realise the sound had come from me.

I had to wake up. This was totally insane.

"Wake up. Wake up. Wake up," I muttered to myself.

Beneath us, the ground flew past my eyes at a dizzying pace, spiralling and shrinking, familiar landmarks growing smaller and smaller as we climbed through the air.

Once we reached an altitude that made me dizzy, the dragon stopped flapping his wings and began to soar through the air.

Then suddenly, we struck against something. It was an invisible force-field of some sort, a barrier I couldn't see, but I felt the shift in the air as we passed through it.

I whipped my head around, trying to get a good look at it, but all I could make out was swirling darkness behind us.

I gasped and trembled, gazing down at the landscape below.

I was in a different world now. Below us stood craggy, snow-topped mountains. I glanced ahead and there in the distance stood an ancient castle, nestled amongst more mountains.

We flew over a dense, dark forest and off in the distance there were dark, soaring shapes in the black sky. *Oh my God.* They were riding the currents of air, spiraling through the heavens before swooping down into deep ravines. In the far distance, there were echoes of an unearthly roar.

More dragons.

I whimpered. "Wake up, Lucy. You have *got* to wake up."

This couldn't be real.

Maybe if I refused to accept what I was seeing, the images would dissolve, and my conscious mind would take over?

I squeezed my eyes shut, burying my face in the sleeve of my dressing gown and pictured my bedroom. I was tucked up in bed. Warm, snuggled under the covers.

Yes, that's it.

I had overheated under my duvet, and this nightmare was set to wake me up.

Oh, come on! Just push back the covers and wake up, stand up. Go to the toilet, wander to the bathroom, just move!

Anything to break this damn dream.

I was used to having vivid dreams about this mystery man. They were such a constant in my life that I hardly thought about them anymore. But this was getting ridiculous.

I had my eyes squeezed tightly shut. I dug my nails into the back of the opposite hand and prayed to every deity I could think of.

Nothing happened.

It didn't soften the grasp of the tight claws that circled my chest. It didn't lessen the bite of cold against my face and my hands. Thank goodness I'd remembered to put my dressing gown on before venturing to the door. And bed socks!

Lucy

The dragon pulled me tighter into his chest as the beating of its wings began to slow, morphing into a glide. I was glad for the gentler movement; the harsh motions were beginning to make me feel sick.

I chanced to open one eye a slit. Just to see what was going on.

We were circling atop the huge castle, over the tallest tower. Below us, people gathered, their heads upturned. From this vantage point they looked the size of ants.

If I could have slapped myself in the face, I would have done so.

The dragon's wing movements slowed almost to a standstill as he lowered us down onto the flagstones of the tower. It was like he'd transported us back in time a thousand years.

I managed to get a better look now and the people looked... human. The men wore formal suits, and the women wore high-necked dresses with fur around the collar. They looked like any wealthy group of people, though prepared for the cold climate.

The dragon set me down, more gently than I was expecting. My socked feet hit the flagstones, and I stumbled, disoriented, as he released his grip on me. He landed just behind me, the shadow of his wings falling across my body before they came to rest.

A man rushed forward with a warm blanket, catching me before I fell, and wrapped me up. He was dressed like a butler from some television drama, right down to the high collar and gloves.

My stress ebbed away slightly. I was impressed with the level of detail and accuracy my subconscious had managed to conjure up for this dream.

"Here you go, miss," he said. "Quickly, come inside. You'll catch your death out here."

I didn't argue as the warmth of the blanket engulfed me, and several hands tugged me forward.

I glanced over my shoulder as I went, just in time to see the dragon transform back into the gorgeous caveman who'd kidnapped me.

He stood in silhouette, and my face flushed as I realized he was naked. *Whoa.*

I looked away and tried to focus on getting myself safely inside, but the image of his perfect body was burned into my mind.

I'd never seen a man of that size. His muscles were huge, and his cock was bigger than any I'd seen. How was he real?

I giggled to myself.

He wasn't! I'd dreamed him up, obviously! To be my perfect man. All dark and mysterious, stealing me away to a foreign land. Taking me away from my boring life to a place where he would love me forever and keep me always by his side.

What a joke!

Should I just go with it and see where my imagination took me, or should I try to wake up again?

Not that it had worked the first time. I shook my head; I could think about that once we were in the castle.

The butler opened the door and we stepped inside. The warm air was a welcome change, and I shivered in anticipation of soon being toasty warm.

"Are you all right, miss?" he asked.

"Oh yes, I'm fine." I giggled, hearing the tone of my own voice and distantly admitting I sounded hysterical. "A man who turned into a dragon just kidnapped me from my home. How are you this evening?"

The man cocked his head in such an elegant way that I burst out laughing.

"I'm Lucy, by the way." I stuck out my hand.

I'd been raised to be polite, after all.

The man stared at it, like he wasn't sure what he was supposed to do, before putting his palm against mine.

"I'm James, miss. King Stavrok's head of house."

"Head of house?" I asked with a slight scowl. "You mean, like a manager?"

Sounded just like a butler to me.

James nodded once, then the rest of his words came flowing into my mind.

"Hang on a second, did you just say... king?"

"He did," a man boomed from behind me.

I whirled around to face off with my fantasy kidnapper.

I really hoped this wasn't one of those dreams where I got tied against some wall and ravaged. I had those on occasion, and they embarrassed me for weeks.

"What is going on here? You need to explain, because to me... this is simply..." I searched for the word, my mind exploding in a shower of light as it battled to string a sentence together while he was still so close to me. "This is unacceptable!"

The man laughed. The deep, rich sound rippled over my skin like a lover's caress.

He stalked toward me, his face set with single-minded determination.

"What are you..." I retreated, backing up and away from him until my back pressed flat against a cold stone wall.

He kept coming at me, not slowing his pace in the least.

Part of me was terrified, but as I watched each muscle flex and his intent became clear, my body melted. I knew that look in men; he was going to kiss me.

I moaned when he finally pressed his body against me and cupped my face.

"You're mine," he said with a growl.

His mouth descended, pressing against mine so firmly I gasped. I didn't even get to offer a blistering reply.

If I could have managed one.

He took my lips like they belonged to him. Like they were his territory, ripe for conquering.

My perfect lover.

My brain shut down as years of sexual deprivation soaked up every inch of this man's body against mine.

My hands slid up to his face and my fingers moved through his hair like I needed to touch him just to survive. He rumbled with approval and drew me even closer, his chest pressing against my breasts.

His mouth was magic. As my eyes slid shut, his arms encircled my waist like a vice, and he pressed his thickening cock up against me. A hot jolt of lust shot through me, pooling in my stomach.

I moaned again, shameless, parting my lips and thrusting my tongue into his mouth.

Then he pulled back. Pain sliced through my chest at the loss of him, and I held back a whimper.

"What's wrong?" I whispered.

Would even my fantasy lover reject me? As so many had done before in the real world.

His eyes roamed my face and body with lascivious intent. With an inhuman growl, he grabbed my hand.

"This way," he murmured. His voice was so low I felt it vibrate through my chest.

He led the way along the wide hallway, withdrawing from the crowd of astonished onlookers. I knew I should feel self-conscious after my little display, but I couldn't bring myself to care. This was *my* dream, after all.

Let them look.

I had to run to keep up with his long strides, and I found myself giggling as we hastened along the corridor.

This was an incredible dream! The level of detail was amazing. The stonework, the carved ceiling, the tapestries—even the paintings on the walls. They had a strange otherworldly beauty, like everything here. Their brushwork glowed in the dim, flickering candlelight as we rushed past.

The man, King Stavrok—what kind of a name was that?—pushed open a door, then turned and swung me up into his arms without hesitation.

"Oh, no! I'm too heavy," I squealed, then wanted to slap myself.

This was my fantasy man! As if he couldn't carry my size sixteen butt.

"You're light as a feather." His low tone rippled through my chest as he strode across the floor.

He threw me down onto the massive, four poster bed.

I laughed as I lay back and sprawled over the silk pillows. I was going to be so annoyed when I woke up in my cold bed alone after this. I may as well make the most of it while the dream lasted.

I threw 'playing hard to get' out the window and began pulling off my dressing gown, eager to get to the good part before the dream ended.

It always pissed me off when I woke up just before the sexy stuff started.

After my dressing gown came my pajamas. I tried to be as seductive as possible, not an easy feat when sprawled out across a huge bed, with a king staring down on me in wonderment.

I giggled again.

"What's funny?" He growled.

"You're a king," I said with the wave of one hand. "Of *course,* you're a king. What else would you be?"

He didn't seem to understand the joke, but he started to undress. Which was what I wanted.

He pushed off the robe he'd put around him, and he was standing before me in all his naked glory.

"Fuck, you're perfect," I sighed as I unbuttoned my pajama top and pushed it away.

The room was warm, with a fire burning and sparking in the grate not far away. I was already flushed as it was, my cheeks burning with anticipation and my stomach tingling.

"As are you," he said.

That sealed the deal for me; this had to be a dream. What real guy would say something like that?

"Ha! Sure, all of this is *so* perfect." I lay back and gestured to my huge thighs, soft tummy, and massive boobs.

He crawled on to the bed, his powerful frame looming over me. He grabbed for my hand and put it against his rock-hard erection.

"Yes."

I gasped as his flesh filled my hand.

"You're exactly the woman for me. You're exquisite."

He slid down and lay on his belly, pushing open my thighs and staring down at my pussy. I covered my face with my hands, feeling the heat rising from my neck, and not in a good way.

Why can't I be cool, even in my own dream?

Oh, fuck it. None of this was real. When would a guy like this ever want a woman like me? What the hell did I have to lose if I threw everything into this night? After all. It was just a dream.

Lucy

I moved my hands away from my scorching hot cheeks and opened my legs wider, displaying myself to him. He growled with approval and leaned in, licking me with slow, purposeful intent. I whimpered at the sensation, pushing myself up onto my trembling elbows so I could get a better view of him.

Then he licked me again, flicking his heated gaze up to meet mine. The sight was too much, and I collapsed onto the bed, arching my back helplessly, wanting him to come even closer.

He slid his hands firmly beneath my ass cheeks and lifted me up, bringing his food to him.

"Oh, oh God," I said with a moan.

He licked my clit from side to side, then suckled on the tender flesh until I screamed. He did this for an eternity, teasing me, then he brought his mouth to my core and drank from me like he couldn't get enough of my taste on his tongue.

"Oh, please. You've gotta stop." I grabbed for his hair, his shoulders. I was incoherent. I would do anything he asked, anything to make him stop, to come up and cover his body with mine.

My belly coiled tight with want, and my core ached for him. I needed to feel him inside me.

He kissed my inner thighs, his mouth lingering and worshipful, before moving to my belly and giving it equal attention. I slid a hand into his hair, and he crawled further up, sucking on each nipple until I bucked and gasped before he finally arrived back at my mouth.

"I'm going to make you mine," he said.

I nodded. What else could I do?

"Yes. Yes. Please, take me. I need you."

My voice was pitched up and desperate. I'd never begged before in my life.

How undignified.

But that was what dreams were for. Exploring the darkest, most wanton impulses I had. The ones that would never see the light of day.

He lifted my hips and positioned himself so the head of his cock rested against the entrance to my body, and every logical thought flew out of the window.

"Please." I fumbled for something to grab onto, hands curling around his massive biceps. I pulled him closer, offering my mouth for him to kiss me.

And kiss me he did.

He pressed down into my body, his firm chest sliding against my sensitized nipples, and he pushed his tongue into my mouth the moment he thrust his hips forward, impaling me in one smooth stroke.

I broke our kiss to cry out. It had been a long time, and the pressure bordered on painful as my long un-touched tissues stretched to accommodate him.

"You're so tight." He groaned and lay his forehead against mine, not moving.

I wanted to thank him for waiting for me to acclimatize, but I couldn't speak. I couldn't do anything but shudder underneath him, pinned down by his heft and bulk.

My sex throbbed in need. I wrapped my legs around his waist, which took him even deeper inside my body. We groaned in unison, and I looked up into his perfect face, loving the set of his jaw, the flint-like flecks in his ice-blue eyes.

"You're so big," I finally managed to say.

His expression was calm, though a drip of sweat ran down his face, suggesting that he was not as unruffled as he seemed.

I reached up to his face and pulled him down for a kiss, focusing on the mesh of our tongues, the way our mouths caught against each other. The scrape of his stubble against my cheek only heightened my arousal.

He retreated, then thrust home, snapping his hips into mine in a motion that sent the headboard crashing into the wall behind us.

I cried out again, my shout echoing off the stone walls of the bedchamber. The pleasure was too great. He slid a hand up to roll my nipple between his large fingers, and I was done for.

He began to thrust faster and harder and I shuddered as I felt a small climax sweep through my body. He moaned and bit into my shoulder as my pussy rippled around his cock.

I relaxed a little, the release of tension giving my body a moment of reprieve.

Then he began to ride me faster, hitting spots deep inside my body that I'd never known existed. I sank my teeth into the fleshy part of his shoulder and screamed with every thrust of his perfect cock. This was a dream. Who could hear me? I could be as loud as I wanted.

I shoved him, rolling us over, and he allowed me to manoeuvre our bodies until I was above him. If this was a dream, I could be anything I wanted—including a woman who was confident and exciting in bed, impulsive and daring.

Everything I was not in real life.

He landed on his back and pulled me with him, his broad hands settling on my hips, pushing me down onto his cock.

I panted, staring down at his chiseled face and the wild look in his eyes. Slowly, I began to ride him. Up and down on his thick, long cock, rolling my hips and meeting each of his upward thrusts with a downward move of my own.

I threw back my head and closed my eyes, focusing on the feelings of his roughened hands cupping my breasts, catching against my sensitive nipples. His cock thrust up inside me, until I wanted to cry out in ecstasy.

It was happening again. My belly was tightening, the pleasure cresting, sending me over the edge.

I gasped, every sensation in my body building to an incredible crescendo.

And that was when he flipped us over again.

I was on my back, Stavrok pounding into me over and over again. The sounds of our moans and cries echoed through the room until my head was filled with them. It drove me wild knowing such a stoic man was as affected by me as I was by him.

My orgasm began to peak, and I trembled beneath him helplessly as he kept up the force of his thrusts.

"This time, with me." He thrust inside me one more time, and his orgasm pulsed inside me.

It triggered my own release and stars flashed behind my closed eyelids as he filled me with his cum. We shuddered and shook together, grabbing onto one another like a life raft in a storm.

Eventually, he withdrew, and the energy in the room calmed and settled.

I winced at the pain as he pulled out of me, but I couldn't complain as an incredible lethargy stole over my body.

"Oh, my God," I groaned. "This is the best dream ever."

I rolled onto my side and wasn't surprised when he spooned me, his huge body making me feel small. Safe. Loved.

The perfect end to the perfect dream. And tomorrow I would wake up in my safe little world where dragons didn't exist.

Thank goodness.

Lucy

I ROLLED onto my back and tried to swim up to the surface of consciousness. It wasn't easy. My mind kept dragging me back down and into the deep sleep I'd been enjoying.

I'd had the craziest, most intense dream of my life last night. Part of me wanted to replay it before I woke up properly. I smirked to myself, eyes still closed.

I had to get up for work.

What time was it? Had I slept through my alarm? It wasn't a weekend, was it?

I reached out and blindly groped around for my phone on the bedside table. The surface my fingers hit was smooth, cold, and unfamiliar and there was no phone to be felt on it.

With a huff, I managed to force my eyes open. I stared up at the ceiling above me. My eyes widened and my stomach sank as my gaze focused, the last vestiges of sleep evaporating.

Was that... a *dragon* carved into my ceiling?

It was.

Holy shit!

I sat bolt upright and whipped my head around, looking left and right.

This isn't my room!

This was the room from the crazy dream I'd had last night.

I looked to the other side of the massive bed and gazed at the indent in the pillow where someone had slept beside me.

My hand flew to my mouth. It couldn't be. No. It wasn't possible. No matter how hard I blinked, the picture didn't change. My eyes weren't deceiving me.

I was in a castle room.

With a wolf skin rug laid over the flagstones and a small fire still simmering in the grate. The bed I was in was huge, with an intricately carved headboard.

Was that an *actual suit of armor* in the corner?

"What the fuck is going on?"

The blankets fell into my lap and my naked breasts tingled in the air. I looked down at myself. My *nude* self. Where the hell had my pajamas gone?

I leaned over the mattress and saw them on the floor, next to the bed —where I'd thrown them last night in my dream.

"Oh...no..."

I brought my arms together, reached my right hand over to my left, and pinched the skin. Hard.

Pain blistered my arm.

"Ow."

I rubbed at the offending limb and bit my lip, moaning. If I wasn't dreaming, then last night was real. And that man I'd had sex with was real. More than that. He was a...

Dragon.

It sounded crazy even in my head, but I could hardly deny the evidence of my own surroundings.

I threw back the covers and jumped out of bed, reaching for my pajamas and pulling them on as fast as I could. My belly was tight and sore. My thighs were still slick with last night's sexual escapades.

Oh, my God.

"How is this possible?"

I pulled at the tie on my dressing gown, tightening it around me. I rushed over to the wall and glanced out the narrow window. It was still snowing. Despite the warmth of the room, I shivered, remembering the wild journey last night.

How the hell am I going to get home?

One of the massive doors opened and I jumped, my heart pounding against my rib cage.

It wasn't the man from last night.

The king, I reminded myself.

A young, rather beautiful woman stepped into the room. Jealousy welled up in me at the sight of her slight figure. Her beautiful face.

"Oh, I'm so sorry, miss. Did I wake you?" she asked as she came forward.

She made a weird move, as though bowing to me in some way. I ignored her. I didn't know what that was all about; I wasn't a queen.

"You didn't. Can you tell me who I should speak to about going home, please?"

I pitched my voice to sound as authoritative as possible, pleased when it didn't tremble.

"Home, miss?" she asked, her eyes big and wide.

"Yes, home." I shook my head, gesturing vaguely at the window, though I didn't know which direction *home* was. "I'm late for work. I have bills to pay. People will be looking for me."

She frowned as if I were speaking a foreign language. I realized how alone I was, in this strange… town? Country?

"If you wouldn't mind… where *am* I right now, exactly?" I twisted my mouth, chagrined. "I had kind of a weird night."

She smiled shyly, but there was something in her eyes that told me she knew exactly what kind of night I'd had. I forced myself to maintain her gaze, praying I wasn't flushed.

"You are in the Kingdom of Bravdok, miss."

"Right…" There was no such place, as far I knew. Then again, I reminded myself, there were no such thing as *dragons* as of yesterday. "And how do I get back to Livia?"

"Livia?"

"Yes, it's a town about an hour outside of Munich." I swallowed. "My home."

"Are you talking about… the human city, miss?"

Now this was just getting *weird*.

"Uh…yes?"

The girl began to back away as though I was scaring *her*, and not the other way around.

What the hell had I fallen into here?

"I think you should speak to the king. He's training downstairs in the armory."

The king? My fantasy lover? The man I'd dreamt about my whole life?

Oh, God. I didn't want to face him after last night. But what choice did I have?

He was obviously the one in charge around here. He was the *king,* after all.

I seemed to have fallen into some crazy medieval wormhole by mistake.

My subconscious told me to pay attention. Though the woman's clothing was ordinary at first glance, there were strange patterns on her sleeves that weren't like anything I'd seen before.

The way she'd said the word *human*, like she wasn't one…

She looked human enough, but her eyes were a shade of amber that gleamed just a little too brightly for my liking.

I pushed down my fear and straightened my spine, brushing back the hair that had fallen over my face. I wished I could do something about my unkempt appearance.

Whatever. It was time to put on my big girl panties and deal with whatever fate had dealt me here.

"Take me to him, please."

The woman scurried, mouselike, toward the door. Wearing only my dressing gown, I followed her out of the massive suite and into the hallway that looked vaguely familiar.

My gaze skittered over the furnishings, from the magnificent paintings, to the thick rugs that scattered the floor.

This place looked like a fourteenth-century medieval castle. In daylight, I could fully appreciate how gorgeous everything was. Shafts of sunlight pierced the stonework and illuminated the intricate carvings. Dragons were everywhere; in the paintings, roaring from the carvings in the ceiling, even embroidered into the tapestries that covered the high stone walls.

What the hell was I doing in a place like this?

The maid, or servant—whoever my silent companion was—opened a door and indicated the stairs leading down into what I had to assume was a dungeon of sorts.

My belly twisted. First, I'd been kidnapped from my home, and now I was being imprisoned? It just added insult to injury.

"The king is down the stairs, just along the passage," she said. "It comes out to a courtyard. You can't miss it."

I stared, first at the dimly lit stairwell and then back at her. "You expect me to walk down those stairs by myself?"

She nodded. "The king doesn't like to be disturbed when he's training with his fencing master, miss. But, for his mate, I'm sure he will not mind the interruption."

"His *what?*"

Had she just said, 'mate'?

She bobbed another one of those weird curtsies at me and walked away.

I was left standing in an opulent hallway, by myself, staring at the stairwell that may or may not take me to the man who could clear up all this confusion.

At this point, anything could happen.

I waited, hoping that someone would arrive to help me decide whether to venture down, or try and find my own way out of here.

But no one came.

I leaned into the hallway, keeping an eye out for anyone who might push me, and heard the distant sounds of metal clinking against metal.

Had the servant said something about armor?

"Oh, come on." I blew out a breath and shoved my hands into my dressing gown pockets. "You can do this!"

I grabbed hold of the cold stone wall and took a deep breath.

The steps were narrow and crooked, and I took them one at a time, slowly and carefully, focusing on my breathing.

As the ground flattened out, my legs got more and more jelly-like, and I was ready to run and flee at a moment's notice.

No dungeon waited for me at the other end of the narrow corridor. Just a bright, massive courtyard that could have held a tournament, once upon a time.

Inside this courtyard, two bare-chested men fought with broadswords. They grunted with every blow.

I steeled myself against the feelings I knew I would experience when I saw him again. The bastard had kidnapped me. Surely, I'd be furious when I saw him.

But as I stared at him, the only feeling making my belly tighten and my heart pound... was lust. Unfulfilled, deep aching for the man.

God, he was magnificent.

The muscles of his chest and back shone with sweat and bunched with every swing of his sword. The sunlight caught every movement, and his blade cut through the air like an extension of his body. He made every strike look effortless.

When he saw me, he stopped the fight with a simple flick of his hand.

The man next to him let his sword fall and it clattered against the flag-stones. His chest heaved with the stress of the fight. He wasn't as big as the king, nor as old, but he was more exhausted from the fight than Stavrok.

My kidnapper turned to address me. "Good morning, my future queen. Did you sleep well?"

The other man bowed to us, falling back to a respectful distance, before practically running away in his haste to get out of there.

Maybe it was the look on my face that caused that? I wasn't sure, but I was glad that he was gone. This first conversation was going to be awkward enough as it was. I'd slept with this man... and I didn't even know him.

I took a couple of careful, measured steps toward Stavrok, tilting my head.

"What did you just call me?" I said, enunciating every word.

I could feel the lust draining away. In its place, there was an icy amount of fury.

Mate? Queen? Had I fallen into the twilight zone?

Stavrok grabbed a towel from the ground and rubbed down his body, tousling his hair as he went. It had the effect of making him even more gorgeously rumpled.

Dammit, concentrate!

"Answer me!"

"Are you always like this first thing in the morning?" He leveled a crooked grin at me, and I flushed, irritated.

I stamped my foot. "No. I am not. When I wake up at home, in my own bed, I'm pretty goddamn happy, actually. But when I wake up in a stranger's bed, in a bloody *castle*... Yeah, I guess I get a little grumpy!"

Ugh! Why do I sound like a petulant child, all of a sudden?

I took some steadying breaths and tried to suppress my anger as he chuckled to himself.

"Can you please just answer the question, King?"

"Please." His gaze was open and friendly in the face of my hostility. "Call me Stavrok."

Tingles coursed over my bare forearms at the sound of his deep voice, and I rubbed my hands over the traitorous skin, fruitlessly attempting to erase the effect he had on me.

"Okay... Stavrok. Can you please explain to me what I'm doing here?"

"What's your name, dear one?"

Heat blushed up my cheeks. He didn't even know my *name*, but he'd made me cum several times the night before.

I'd never had a one-night stand before. Shit, I hadn't even meant to have this one!

"I'm Lucy."

"Ah. Beautiful."

He pulled on a shirt that had been lying next to the towel, hiding his perfect physique from view—which was great for me. My concentration could only improve without the visual distraction.

"I must bathe, and then we shall talk," he said.

He moved to walk past me, and I grabbed for his arm.

"No. Please. Tell me what's going on here. I want to go home."

He turned and slipped his hands around my waist, squeezing me gently against him. "That is not possible, my dear one. We mated last night, and you will stay here and be my queen. The fates have already decided."

Despite the calm and happy feelings his touch brought me, his words shattered me.

I broke away from him.

"*What?* No! You can't do that! You kidnapped me last night, and now I want to go home!"

Said every kidnap victim, ever.

He smiled softly. "I'm sorry, but that's not possible, especially as you may be carrying the heirs to my kingdom."

"Heir*s?*" I squealed.

How many did he expect me to conceive after only one night?

"Yes. Dragons shifters are known to have up to four babes at a time, but as you are human, it may be different with us."

"Dragon shifters... Four babies... Oh, my God, I have to sit down."

My mind was whirling, the blackness beginning to cloud my mind.

I was going to faint for the first time in my life.

And then I did, and the whole world, such as it was, went black.

Stavrok

I rushed forward and caught my mate before she hit the ground.

"Humans..." I muttered, shaking my head as I swept her limp form up into my arms.

I didn't know if this swooning phase was normal for Lucy, or an early sign of her pregnancy. Either way, I needed to call my physician to attend to her.

I took the stairs two at a time, cradling her in my arms, and shouted for assistance. My voice carried down the corridor, and a couple of maid-servants came running at once.

"Lucy has fainted." I hefted her up, my stance protective. I forced myself not to scowl. "I'm going to take her back to my bedroom. Can you get the physician here as soon as possible?"

"Yes, sire."

They bobbed a curtsey in unison and scurried off.

I strolled to my bedroom slowly, loving the feel of my mate in my arms.

Last night had not been what I'd expected. I'd thought I would go to my mate and talk to her, perhaps even get to know her.

Instead, my shifter had recognised its mate and the dragon had ripped through me so fast, I had no control over him.

Then he'd taken her.

Kidnapped her.

It was something I had sworn I would never do to any woman. But I had. Just as my father had done before me, and my grandfather before him. This woman was my undoing, the thorn in my side. She'd broken through my defences, my carefully built control.

I entered our bedroom and laid her down on the bed.

Lucy had been incredible last night. Her passion and intensity had perfectly matched my own. She was utterly gorgeous, an ideal fit in every way.

I'd been pleasantly surprised that my mate would be my match in the bedroom. She'd taken my body as though she had a right to it. Which, of course, she did.

Now she was acting like she didn't even know who I was, or what had gone on last night.

Was that normal for humans?

The door opened, and the royal physician walked in, bowing when he saw me lingering at the foot of the bed.

"Hello, Arnold," I said. "I'm sorry to disturb you so early in the day. My mate fainted, and I am unsure if that is normal for her kind."

"Your mate, sire?" The physician's eyebrows shot upwards. "I didn't know that you'd found your intended queen."

I indicated the woman on the bed and didn't answer him past that. I couldn't blame him for his shock. I was still struggling with the idea myself.

Only yesterday, I'd been completely alone. A bachelor king, burning with frustration at the lack of change and transition with my life. No queen. No heirs. Nothing to give me the happiness that I saw in those who governed my neighboring kingdoms.

Overnight, everything had changed. My dragon had found its mate. I'd found my queen. And she may be pregnant already.

The physician checked her over gently before eventually turning to me. "It seems as though she has simply fainted, sire. When she wakes up, we can do some tests if you wish it."

"Thank you. I shall call you if we deem that necessary."

He bowed again and moved away from the bed as Lucy began to stir.

I couldn't help myself from reaching out. I walked around the side of the bed and touched her forehead, checking for a fever as her eyelids fluttered open.

There was a recognition of sorts, and for a split second her eyes softened. Then a blazing anger raced across her green irises, twisting up her face with a rage that came over her like a sudden storm.

"You!" she cried as she sat up, then grimaced before slumping back against the headboard.

"Don't move so fast, my love," I said. "You fainted. You must rest."

She swallowed strangely. I picked up the jug from the bedside table and poured her a glass of water. Thank goodness for servants.

"Here," I said, offering her the glass. "Sip this slowly and try to stay calm. No one is going to hurt you here, I promise."

She took the glass, though she eyed it as though I may have put poison in it.

After a moment's hesitation, she took a sip, then pressed a trembling hand to the side of her face and glared at me. She still looked pale, though color was slowly returning to her cheeks.

"Are you well? Should I call the physician back?"

It began to dawn on me then how little I knew about humans in general. Was their physiology exactly as ours was? Should I be worried about our offspring's health?

"No. I'll be fine, I think." Sighing, she set down the glass on the bedside table again, then pulled her knees up to her chest and wrapped her arms around them.

I sat down on the edge of the bed and tightened my fingers into the blankets around me. I ached to touch her, to roll her beneath me. To sink into her body once again and taste the essence of her lips.

But she was as frosty as the snow-topped cliff faces beyond the window.

"Stavrok... what am I doing here?"

Such a simple question; such a complicated answer. I stood up and moved around, pacing like a caged lion.

May as well tell her the truth.

"You're here because a sorceress told me you were my destiny, and that I ought to seek you out."

Lucy's eyes opened wide, then she nodded slowly. "Okay... assuming I believe you, what, pray tell, were you planning on doing with me once you found me? Because I hope the whole kidnapping thing was an oversight on your part."

She fiddled with the edge of the bedspread, glaring at the snowscape outside.

I frowned. Where was the confident, sensual woman from the night before?

"Lucy, I don't understand why you are so shocked about everything this morning. As I recall it, last night you had no objections to sharing my bed."

Redness blossomed over her cheeks as she glared at me. "Last night, I thought you were a *dream!* How could I have known, honestly, that you weren't? You turned into a dragon, for fuck's sake!"

She whipped her hair over her shoulder, and I got the strong impression that she still wasn't fully convinced any of this was real.

My eyebrows rose at her language. It wasn't exactly fitting for a queen, but who was I to judge at this point of our relationship?

She wasn't wrong, was she? I *had* taken her.

I shifted, uncomfortable now. "I suppose, for a human, dragons are uncommon creatures. But here, everyone can do it."

"Everyone? Even the children?" Lucy asked, her mouth dropping open.

"No, not the children." It was strange to have to relay such common knowledge to someone. Like I was describing the color of the sky to someone who was blind. "We begin shifting when we hit maturity. Around thirteen, fourteen, depending on the person."

"Okay, but you still haven't answered the question of why you grabbed me, or why everyone keeps bowing to me, or why on *earth* you said that thing before about me conceiving your babies. How many babies are we talking about? And why would you even assume I'd be *pregnant* after one night?"

The questions were coming hot and fast, and a laugh bubbled up and out of me before I could suppress it.

"Which would you like me to answer first?"

She crossed her arms over her chest.

"Stavrok."

A wave of something I'd never experienced passed over my back, before creeping up and over my face. A cold, yet totally invigorating sensation that made my dragon shiver all over.

I approached the bed and reached for Lucy, intent on sharing the sensation with her.

She jumped away from me so fast I barely saw her until she was over by the fireplace.

"No! We are *not* getting into bed together again until I know what's going on!"

I couldn't help but grin. She certainly wasn't ruling it out, which of course I didn't expect her to.

Even *this* angry, it was reassuring to know that she wasn't making any declarations that she knew she couldn't keep.

I smiled at her. "Let's make a deal. You'll let me escort you to breakfast, my dear one, and I'll tell you all you wish to know about how you came to be here."

She seemed to need a lot of information so she could process everything herself, an unusual characteristic in a female of my kind.

They were much more submissive, which was probably why I found them no challenge.

Lucy, on the other hand, would keep life interesting.

"I guess I could eat," she grumbled, but I could tell she was calming down.

It suddenly occurred to me that she was wearing the bedclothes she'd arrived here in and didn't have anything else.

As delicious as it would be to eat breakfast with her naked, I got the sense that suggestion wouldn't be welcome right now. She looked ready to get up and go home, back to the human world, and I couldn't let her leave.

Not now. Not ever.

CHAPTER
NINE

Stavrok

I pulled on the servants' bell that dangled from the roof by my bed and within moments, James stepped through the door.

"Yes, sire?"

"We're ready for breakfast." I turned toward Lucy. "Would you prefer to eat here or in the dining room?"

"The dining room," she answered quickly. Too quickly.

I quirked an eyebrow at her, then turned to James.

"Could you bring some things for Lucy to wear today? And we require the royal seamstresses to take her measurements. She'll need a full wardrobe."

"I won't be staying that long," Lucy interjected.

I ignored her comment and waited for James to leave before turning back to her. "I need a shower. Would you like to join me?"

She shook her head and I smiled.

The blush to her full cheeks said otherwise, but I was happy to allow her the illusion of control and space while she became comfortable with me again.

That didn't mean I couldn't tease her a little.

I stripped off my sweat-soaked shirt and threw it to the floor. Next, I unbuttoned the fly and pushed them past my hips, letting them gather around my ankles. I glanced at the bed but Lucy was turned away, focused intently on the scenery out the window.

I grinned to myself.

I worked hard every day to keep my body strong, fit, and ready for a war that could come at any moment. But I wasn't oblivious to the fact that womenfolk enjoyed my bulk and musculature.

I wanted my mate to desire me in the same way. I certainly wanted her.

I turned and sauntered toward the shower, feeling the heat of her gaze on my back. I glanced over my shoulder and caught her looking just as she whirled away.

I flipped on the shower head and stood beneath the warm water, letting the heat sink into my tired muscles.

I'd found my mate! She was here. The idea was finally resonating with me on a deeper level. All those years of emptiness would be behind me. The only thing that remained was for Lucy to accept my world, and all the changes that her new life would bring.

I'd never thought my queen would be human, or that she wouldn't know our ways. The concept of shifting was completely foreign to her, coming as she did from a world without magic.

The memory of grabbing her the night before now felt surreal, strangely out of body. Usually, I remained lucid when the dragon emerged, but this had been different. My shifter had taken over completely in a way that it never had before, and I'd been dragged along for the ride.

Perhaps that was what had happened to my ancestors also?

I'd always thought the way my father and grandfather had grabbed their brides had been primitive and barbaric, but the drive from our shifter to claim our fated mate was far stronger than I had anticipated.

Never mind that now. I've found her, at last!

Well, it had been Queen Marienne who had found her for me. She had sensed her through the magical boundary and handed me the key to a puzzle I'd been trying to solve my whole life. At the thought, a cold feeling washed over my skin. There was something about King Magnik that I didn't wholly trust, and I wasn't sure what role Marienne played in that scenario. There seemed to be no love lost between the king and his queen, but could that be a ruse, to lull me into complacence?

I couldn't guarantee that Marienne hadn't taken something from inside my head after she put Lucy into it. Nor could I understand why she'd want to help me in such a way and not demand payment.

The uncertainty weighed on me. I knew that, if it came to a choice between the payment or the woman, I was keeping Lucy no matter what. I could already feel our connection strengthening with each passing moment. My need was growing, to keep her safe, healthy, and satisfied.

Our bond would only grow with time and age. My own parents were besotted with each other until the day they died.

People were talking in the other room and I switched off the shower, interested to see what my servants had brought Lucy and what they were saying.

I toweled dry my body and grabbed a pair of comfortable pants from a nearby shelf.

The high voices of the women overlapped one other, chattering and gossiping away nineteen to the dozen. Lucy laughed at something one of them said, and my lips twitched up into a smile.

She was my mate, which meant fate had chosen her to be my queen, to rule my people. I wanted her to belong here, to feel this was her home.

I walked out of the bathroom to see Lucy standing in a simple shift dress, her luscious breasts pressed high and together, creating a cleavage that called to me to press my face against.

"Sire, how may dresses were you wanting for your new mate?" The seamstress asked me.

Lucy's gaze flicked straight to me. "What is this *mate* business? I don't understand it at all."

She was holding her arms out and turning this way and that as the seamstress asked, her earlier protests at odds with her actions.

"Get something on and we'll talk over breakfast," I assured her, before turning to the woman on the floor with pins stuck in her mouth. "As many as she will require. I trust she will let you know once she's had a chance to settle in."

I flicked my hand and the woman got up and curtsied deeply. "Yes, Your Highness."

She grabbed her materials and left the room.

Lucy drew up the dress and stockings they'd left for her in the meantime, draped over the back of a chair. The dress was finely woven, with rich purple hue. Befitting for a queen.

"I'm not really a dressy girl." She held up the dress, turning this way and that in front of my tall mirror that stood against the wall opposite the bed head. "I'm more of a jeans and t-shirt sort of woman."

"Why is that?" I asked her as I pulled on a shirt and my shoes.

"It's just easier to hide... all of this," she said, gesturing to her shapely, perfect body.

I laughed. "Why should you hide anything? Your body is strong, dear one. Healthy, beautiful. You should carry yourself with pride."

Lucy looked down at the ground and I reached over and touched her chin, tipping her head up and staring down into her eyes.

"In my eyes, you are perfection itself." I leaned closer, dropping my voice to a whisper. "Believe me, if I had my way, I'd strip both of us to nothing at all and devour you all over again this instant."

A smile trembled on her lips. "Do you like bigger women? Is that it? Because I can tell you, where I come from, men like you don't want women like me."

"Women like you?"

Confusion filled me. What did she mean?

"Yeah. Frumpy, chubby, big girls."

I let my hands run down her body, pausing at her tiny waist and then gripping her ass. She yelped in surprise but didn't fight me.

"Lucy, I don't 'like' big girls—I like you. *All* of you. I'm not sure how stupid human men are, but anyone who made you feel less than you are, is an imbecile. You're perfect in every way, and I desire you more than any other woman I've ever met. Can't you feel how much I want you?"

I pressed her pelvis closer to mine, where I was sure she could feel the hardening of my cock in my pants.

She bit her lip in an innocent, vulnerable way and then whispered, "Thank you."

It was too much for me—I had to kiss her.

I dropped my head and she lifted hers up to meet mine. Our lips met and a mutual moan was pulled from both our mouths.

Oh, God.

I wrapped my arms around her and pulled her closer, sliding my tongue into her mouth and tasting her. She gripped my face with her hands and held me to her, and I let the kiss go on and on.

My cock throbbed and my lust swirled in my heated blood, but I knew that the next time I took my mate to bed, it needed to be something she was desperate for.

I'd never taken a woman against her will, and I never would.

Finally, I pulled back and stared down at her beautiful face. Her cheeks were rosy, her green eyes dazed. Her lips were blood red from my kisses.

"Shall we go to breakfast?" I asked her and I could see her disappointment and rushed to reassure her. "I'd love to take you back to bed, so if you'd rather stay and make love first..."

She stepped away. "No, you're right. Breakfast. Talking. I'm sorry, but your kisses are just..."

"Intoxicating?" I finished for her.

She frowned. "Is that how everyone else feels about them, too?"

I laughed. "Who's everyone else? The women of my past were not interested in my kisses. I was referring to your taste for me. If my kisses have half the effect on you that your kisses have on me, I'm surprised we're still standing here dressed."

She giggled and tightened the belt around her waist. "Well, we have to be a little bit smart about this."

I took her hand and pulled her to the door and into the corridor, leading the way to the dining hall. Though I didn't say it, I was looking forward to eating in company for once. It was depressing, eating alone in a room designed to seat twenty.

I shook the thought away and turned to her. "Do you always do what is right, what is logical?"

That was a great attribute for a queen, though I hoped when it came to the bedroom, she would be more adventurous than that.

"Yes, I try to. But... I do have a bit of a temper, and I can sometimes be..."

"Less than perfect? Yes, I know that feeling well."

She smiled at me with an understanding that we hadn't shared yet and there was a moment that I recognized, of our souls linking and connecting.

It stole my breath away.

My God, what would I do if she left me now?

I shook away the feelings of dread and loneliness that such a thought gave me.

"Here we go." I pushed open the door and led her inside to the massive dining table. The chef and maidservants stood by the table, welcoming us with smiles.

As I had ordered, it was laden with everything anyone could possibly want for breakfast. Fresh breads piled high, a selection of jams and butter to accompany them, hot eggs and sausages on silver trays, and fruit and berries of all kinds. Jugs of sweet wine complemented the spread.

I nodded, satisfied.

I wanted Lucy to know that I could provide for her. She would want for nothing while she was here.

I looked over at my chef who still hovered nearby. "You've outdone yourself."

She smiled, then tapped the side of her nose. "I heard it was an important day, sire."

I walked to the head of the table and held out a chair for my mate.

"Thank you, Cherie." I smiled, waving her off. "That will be all for now."

I had a big job ahead of me. I had to convince my mate to stay with me. Even though I considered myself a civilized man, I didn't want to see what would happen if she tried to leave me.

My dragon wouldn't like that.

CHAPTER
TEN

Stavrok

My chef smiled as she left, accompanied by the maidservants, and I focused back on Lucy.

"Let's sit."

We took our places at the huge dining table and I glanced over at my mate.

"Wow, this looks amazing." Lucy smiled as big and excited as a child with new toys.

She obviously liked to eat and enjoyed food as I did, but something told me not to mention it.

I gestured toward the table. "Please, dig in. Take as much as you want."

I reached for the hot bread rolls and smothered them with butter, before grabbing the meat.

Lucy took a few berries and eyed the bread on my plate with envy.

"Please, eat." I pushed two rolls onto her plate and she practically shoved them straight off again.

"It's good food, I promise." I shot her a crooked smile. "Not poisoned."

She gave me a reluctant smile, before she sighed, fiddling with her fork. "It's not that... I can't. It's the carbs..."

She trailed off, looking longingly at the plates piled with steaming morsels.

I laughed. There were no such stupid rules in my kingdom. "Lucy, you're in a kingdom that must seem magical to you, a world full of dragons and castles. You've accepted these, yes? Why deny yourself the pleasure of good food?"

Her face twisted strangely before it cleared. She nodded, like she finally saw my logic.

"God, you're right. To hell with my diet!" She wrinkled her nose in a manner I found adorable. "They never work anyway."

She tore into the bread, slid a sausage into a roll, and bit into it in a way that had me groaning with need.

"You okay?" she asked, and I took a long drink of the sweet wine they'd poured for us.

"Yes."

She gestured with her hands that I should go on, but I didn't know where to start. I didn't know how to convey how much I wanted her. The best I could do, for now, was deflect.

"You have questions. What is it you want to know?"

She swallowed and glared at me, but this time there was a note of playfulness in her expression that made my chest spark with hope.

"Tell me why I'm here, for one thing," she said.

I leveled my gaze at her, considering. "It may be easier if I go back a bit and explain a few things. Is that all right?"

She nodded, sipping at the water in front of her. "Sure, tell me everything."

Where to begin?

"I may as well tell you about my history. My parents were married for thirty years before they both died a few winters ago."

Her face was stricken, pale and pained. "Oh, I'm so sorry."

"They died together," I said shortly. One day, I would tell her the full truth. But the story was a long one, and I didn't want it to cast a pall over our happiness. "It was what they would have wanted."

A soft smile filtered across Lucy's face. "Yeah, I think I can understand that. I've dreamt about that sort of love, but never experienced it."

And neither have I... until now.

"Well, you see, most dragon shifters have a mate that the fates choose for them. When we find them, we know them by their smell. There's an instant attraction. They are our perfect match in every way..." I dropped my gaze. "My parents had that. In fact, my father kidnapped my mother right out of her village and never took her home again."

Lucy laughed. "God, that must run in your family."

I grinned at her. "It does. My grandfather was the same. When our dragons see their fated mate, there is no holding him back. It is—it was, last night—uncontrollable."

"Hang on a second. Are you telling me that you think I'm your... fated mate, or whatever it's called?" She stared at me like I was insane.

"I don't just think it," I said, my voice solemn. "I know it. The feelings I'm experiencing, the way I shifted with no control last night, my dragon recognized its mate. I've been waiting for you for... a long time."

I didn't want to say something corny like 'forever' or 'my whole life' but now that I had her, I knew what it felt like to have that hole in my heart filled.

I wasn't letting her go.

"But that's impossible! I'm not like you!" she spluttered. "I'm human, in case you haven't noticed."

"Yes, I know. I don't know what sort of offspring you will have, but Fate has chosen you for me, and Fate is never wrong." I smiled. "I have every faith in you, Lucy."

I didn't want to tell her that Marienne believed she had a dragon shifter ancestor somewhere down the line. That may be too much for the woman to take in right now, on top of everything else.

Her face creased up, and I longed to pull her close and soothe her.

"But, but, but—no! Stavrok, come *on*. You can't be serious about this.

Fated mates... soul mates... it's not real. I don't know *what* you felt last night, or why we..." Her cheeks flushed. "But it isn't because some mythical thing like fate made us do it!"

I just grinned at her. She hadn't fled the room screaming yet. There was hope for this strong little human.

"What did you feel last night, Lucy? Tell me."

Her confident gaze dropped away from me.

I leaned forward. "Because for me, it wasn't a choice. I *had* to have you. You were the most beautiful woman I'd ever seen in my life, and I felt like I would die if I didn't kiss you."

Her eyes came up and met mine, and the fragility in her eyes broke my heart.

I reached out and took her hand, cradling it between my palms.

"I know you must be feeling lost and extremely overwhelmed at this point in time," I said, "but I need you stay with me, at least until we know if you're pregnant or not."

She stared down at her plate. Her eyes were filled with tears, but when she spoke her voice was strong. "Why? You must know that I can't simply vanish off the face of the planet. I have a job. I have friends! They'll all come looking for me soon enough."

I admired her courage. Even lost and disoriented as she was, she held her ground.

"We have access to the internet in some parts of the castle. Perhaps you could email them and tell them you've jumped on a plane for an unexpected holiday? Two weeks, that's all I'm asking for, Lucy. Can't you see that this is an opportunity to fulfill all of your wildest dreams?"

No woman had ever reacted like this to finding their soulmate—let alone finding out that their soulmate was a *king*. She would want for nothing for the rest of her life, and yet she was acting like I had given her a prison sentence.

"But my job. What if they fire me?"

I waved my hand around the room. "Then I will fill your bank account with whatever money you need. That is of no consequence to me. You are my first priority, now."

"Oh... I..."

I could tell she had nothing to say, and the topic of money seemed to embarrass her, which was interesting.

"If you need money..." I began.

Her gaze snapped to mine, and her tone was flinty. "I don't need money, thank you. I've paid off most of my house, completely by myself."

I tilted my head and gave her a broad smile. I had no idea what that meant. I was born into a royal family and would never have to pay for any piece of real estate for as long as I lived.

"You'll stay, then?" I pressed.

"You said..." Her voice was small, careful. "If I'm not pregnant, I can go home?"

No!

As much as my dragon resisted the idea of her leaving, she also hadn't asked what would happen if she *was* pregnant, and therefore I didn't need to tell her I would be using every opportunity to ensure it.

"Well..." I said, trying to balance the truth with a comfortable white lie.

Luckily, I didn't need to think of one, because she kept talking.

"The odds that I'm pregnant are low." She tilted her head, counting the days off on her fingers. "I'm quite late in my cycle, and at my age... we only slept together once. It's not likely, is all."

I grinned at her. She clearly had no idea how strong the bond between us was. If there was any chance at all of her becoming pregnant, then she already would be.

"How old are you, Lucy?"

"Thirty-three. And you?"

"Forty-two."

She gaped at me. "You don't look anywhere near that."

I shrugged. "Our shifter genes keep us young. So, my beautiful mate, the woman who will be my queen if you decide to stay in this land of Fire and Ice, do we have a deal?"

I stuck out my hand and she looked at my fingers like they might bite her.

"You know that saying things like that to me, a perfect stranger, makes you sound totally insane, right?" she asked.

"I wouldn't say we're strangers, Lucy. Not after last night... would you?"

She shook her head slowly. "I guess not..."

I kept my hand out, wanting her reassurance that she wouldn't run away the first chance she got. Not that an unaccompanied human would get far in this climate, but she was far too precious to lose to our brutal weather.

"Two weeks, you say?" She pursed her full lips. "And I get to use your computer?"

I nodded. She could do whatever she wanted, if it was within the castle walls.

"Absolutely," I said. "I want you to meet everyone in the castle. Then I'll take you out and show you our town."

She put her hand into mine, and a current of awareness passed over my skin, making a growl rise in the back of my throat.

"All right then. You have a deal," she said.

CHAPTER
ELEVEN

Lucy

The excitement fluttering through my belly was unlike anything I'd ever felt.

It was like waiting for an exam, a first date, and the beginning of a roller coaster all at once.

Stavrok spent the morning showing me his favorite parts of the castle. It was truly beautiful, like stepping into a fairy tale. He showed me his parents' portrait in the entrance hall, and the family tapestry hanging beside it. He drew me close and whispered that my name would be embroidered there before long, the glittering golden threads entwined with his, and I fervently hoped he couldn't hear my pulse fluttering at the thought.

We headed out, hand in hand, into the brisk morning air. I was glad for the thick scarf and muff a maid had brought me, because the weather was far chillier than I was used to.

Stavrok walked me down the narrow, cobblestoned path into the little town that lay below the castle. He took pleasure in introducing me to passers-by as we went, and it charmed me that he seemed to know so many of his subjects on sight and had a vested interest in their activities.

The town itself was a strange combination of modernity and old-world charm. The technology seemed to be similar to ours, but there were open-air markets that could've been pulled straight from another age, and I spotted apothecaries selling herbs and crystals that I'd never seen before.

The people were red-cheeked and happy, the streets were clean and inviting, and the castle loomed over everything with a majestic beauty.

As we wandered back toward the castle, I gestured to the people around me.

"You said that you were self-sustainable. How do you manage that in such cold weather?"

The chill in the air had me pulling the cloak around me even tighter.

I didn't know how it was possible, to go from my home, where we were enjoying a mild spring, to this place, where there was snow on the ground and the tip of my nose was frozen.

"We eat seasonally," Stavrok said. "Being dragon shifters, our diet does contain a high meat component. We only grow hardy animals that survive our winters."

"What are your winters like if *this* is spring?"

Stavrok laughed. "It gets colder, certainly. All homes in town have fire-places and a great heating system."

"And if someone can't afford to pay their bills?"

"Their bills?" He quirked his eyebrow at me as though he didn't know what I meant.

"Yes, for electricity, water. How does everyone pay for that?"

He grinned. "The royal family pays for the entire town, in all ways. As long as the townspeople are doing their jobs, all the essential amenities are taken care of."

I gaped at him, shivering as he opened one of the castle's great oak doors. I ducked inside, the heat enveloping me like a hug.

"So, there's no money?"

"Of course, there's money. We use a similar currency to the Euro, but when it comes to the basics of life—things like water, sewerage, heating, even food if the family is struggling due to illness—the castle takes care of it."

I stared at him, shocked to the core that there was such a place. "I wish our government did the same thing. There are so many homeless, struggling people…"

I shook my head, trying not to think about the depressing parts of the human world.

So many starving…

"Would you like some lunch?" he asked.

I looked around. Surely there were things he needed to attend to?

"I'm all right for the moment, although a shower and then access to a computer would be great," I said. "I really need to write to my work to let them know what's going on."

Or a version of it, anyway.

I'd meant to find the computer straight after breakfast, but Stavrok had wrapped me up in a cloak and encouraged me to come out with him and meet his people.

And how could I say no to a tour of his beautiful lands?

I smiled up at Stavrok. "Thank you so much for the tour. I loved it. Especially the shop full of all those silks. The clothes were spectacular."

Some of the fashions were far too feminine for me, or more feminine than I'd ever allowed myself to be. My job demanded simple and comfortable clothes. All that lace, silk, and ruffles, those intricate buttons—they weren't designed to end up covered in poster paint.

Modern women in my town were either high-powered career women or stay at home moms. I didn't really fit comfortably into either group.

"The dressmaker will return this evening," he said. "You can order anything you like from that shop. They'll have it made up for you to your specifications."

"But…" I wavered. "I won't be staying that long, surely?"

Besides, how would I pay for any of it? I didn't have any money on me.

Stavrok reached out for my hands and pulled me closer. His burning gaze made my knees weaken, and I moaned softly.

"Shall I join you in the shower?"

Images swirled in my head, of steam, and heat, and cold tiles at my back.

I'd always had a fantasy of having hot shower sex up against a wall, but no man had ever come close to fulfilling it for me.

How could they when I weighed more than most of my ex-boyfriends?

With Stavrok, I could see him easily overcoming my weight and clumsiness.

But the last thing I wanted to do was make him think that I had decided to stay, or that we were developing a relationship I wasn't certain about yet.

"I'd rather stay clean after my shower, thank you very much."

Stavrok kissed me, his lips tasting like snow, and sin.

I pushed away from him, the heat of his chest soaking into my palms as I tried to put some much-needed space between us.

"And I'm pretty sure, King Stavrok, that you have more important things to do than show me around and have showers in the middle of the day."

Stavrok grinned. "I do have a kingdom to run, it's true, but I'd prefer to have a shower with you, more than anything else."

When we were a respectable distance from each other, I could finally breathe more easily. "Please, let me do what I need to do, then I'll be more comfortable."

"More comfortable?" he asked, tilting his head.

"Yes, I have obligations that I need to fulfill. My work, my parents..."

I could hardly believe that I'd just left my whole world behind.

Then again, the day-care center probably assumed I was in bed sick, and my parents only called weekly.

That wasn't what rattled me, though. What disturbed me most was how little I'd thought about it all morning. I'd allowed myself to get swept up in Stavrok's icy world, seduced by more than the man himself.

This place called out to me like a siren song. Even though it had only been one night, it was the other world that was starting to feel like the dream.

Stavrok took my hand and held it as walked through the castle. "Well, after you finish all of that, I will meet you for dinner. I think you may like my proposal."

I wasn't sure I liked the sound of that. "What sort of proposal?"

The wolflike grin that sparked Stavrok's teeth made me jump.

"Wait and see. Until then, you need a guide. I'll have one sent to your room."

"What do you mean, a guide? Like your chief of staff?"

Stavrok backed away from me. He must have finally realized that he did indeed have things to do. "Not exactly. James runs everyone and everything, so he'll be somewhere making sure the house isn't burning down without me at the helm. But I'll send someone you'll like, I promise."

He waved, and strode off, the sounds of his leather heels tapping along the hallway until he disappeared into a room.

I sighed and let the happiness that I'd been holding at bay filter into my mind and fill me up.

What am I doing? This is utterly crazy.

I should be working out a way home, plotting my escape, but instead I was luxuriating in all this enjoyment.

Worst of all, memories of the heated moments from last night kept cropping up in my mind at the most inopportune times.

I wandered back to our room–*Stavrok's* room—and soon found myself alone in the large, hot shower.

The bathroom was fitted out with every modern convenience. The towel racks were heated, as were the flagstones underfoot. The walk-in shower had a giant overhead waterfall built into the wall, and there was a huge bathtub, sunken into the floor, with jets embedded in the sides.

And yet this was a castle.

If I didn't feel so awake, I could probably convince myself that I was still dreaming, because not much was making sense at this point.

It took a while before I could properly feel my toes again, but when I did, I was glad of it. It was cold here, much colder than I was used to. These dragon shifters were obviously immune to it, but I was not.

Maybe they ran hotter than I did? I swallowed, thinking of Stavrok's chest pressed up against mine. Even through my clothes, he was a total furnace. I would have to take precautions next time I went outside.

Thicker socks, more layers. Maybe I could find some earmuffs. I giggled at the thought.

Tilting back my head, I let the warmth of the water flow over me.

What am I doing?

Rearranging my life around Stavrok? I'd only known the guy for one night, and all his promises seemed way too good to be true.

Fairy tales like this didn't happen to women like me. I should get out of here before I got too attached. I didn't want to get myself hurt.

But what was I really rushing back to?

A job that paid me just above minimum wage to help raise other peoples' children, because I didn't have any of my own?

"Hello! Lucy! Can I come in?"

The sound of a young, chirpy female voice echoed through the room.

Did she want to come *into* the bathroom? I wasn't sure how comfortable I was with that.

"Just give me a second," I called. "I'll be out in a moment."

I switched off the water and grabbed a fluffy towel from a nearby rack. I rubbed the towel over every part of me. The room was so warm I was comfortable, but the knowledge of a stranger in the adjacent room made me want to get dressed as soon as possible.

Since my clothes were in the other room, I ventured out into the bedchamber wearing only the bath towel.

A young woman, who reminded me of our day-care center receptionist, greeted me with a beaming smile.

Her curly brown hair tumbled over her slight shoulders, and her eyes were the brightest blue I'd ever seen on a person.

Then again, those striking eyes seem to be common around these parts.

"Hello," I said, holding the towel tight against my huge breasts, which as usual threatened to spill out over the top.

"Hey! I'm Cass, His Majesty's cousin," the woman said. "And you must be the famous Lucy. It's so great to meet you!"

Cousin... All right. I could deal with that.

TWELVE

Lucy.

I lifted my chin and answered, "Yes, I am."

Cass clapped her hands together like an excited child. "This is going to be brilliant! When Stavrok told me you'd arrived, I couldn't believe it. People have been waiting for my cousin to marry for like... ages. Years! And now he's finally got his mate!"

I groaned and rolled my eyes. "Why does everyone keep jumping forward, planning out my whole life for me? I met Stavrok last night—last *night!* I'm not about to just marry him tomorrow because he thinks I'm some mythical mate... thing..."

The girl's face balked, her smile turning upside down as she went pale. "Oh...."

I clenched my teeth and forced some deep breaths.

"Look, Cass. You seem lovely, and I would really enjoy a rundown of how things work around here if you can spare the time, but I'm human. And I'm not used to being told what I must and mustn't do, so if you don't mind..."

She giggled. "You sound just like Stavrok."

That stopped me in my tracks. "In what way?"

"He's always said he wouldn't marry just because it was expected, and that he wouldn't succumb to the fated mates curse like his father did. But look at you! He snatched you out of a human town, didn't he?"

"Um..." I bit my lip. "Yes."

"I knew it!" She began pulling clothes from a huge oak wardrobe on the other side of the room. "The servants have left some things in here for you. Here. Try some stuff on. I wanna see!"

Cass wasn't looking in my direction, but I was still self-conscious. I didn't have much of a choice about changing in front of her, and as a fully grown woman, I knew I should get over myself. She was a girl. I was a girl.

Before I chickened out, I dropped the towel to the ground and grabbed for the thick stockings and the long-sleeved shift that had been laid out on the bed for me.

Layers, that was what I needed. Layers.

Over the shift, I slid on a soft, fine-knit sweater, following it with a low-necked garment that seemed to be a cross between a sweater and a dress. I smoothed it down against my body, finally feeling like I would be warm enough to face the rest of the day.

I didn't want to venture outside again, though. I'd always imagined huge castles of this kind to be drafty and uncomfortable, but with the crackling fire in the grate, I felt cosy as hell.

"That's better." I shuddered, remembering the icy air outside. "Goodness, it's cold here."

Cass turned around with her big smile. "You'll get used to it soon enough."

I gave her a smile in return, although my stomach twinged with unease.

That was my worry. I was already *far* too used to this place. I kept letting my guard down without realizing, sliding into the role Stavrok seemed so eager for me to play.

Cass was looking at me expectantly, and I shook my head to clear it.

Did she say something?

"Wow, you're miles away," she said, her eyes merry. "I said, you look the part! You should ask Stavrok about jewelry. I know he has some of his mother's old pieces squirreled away. You'll be the belle of the ball when the other royals come to dine here."

"What do you mean?" I asked, but Cass was too busy rummaging through the contents of the wardrobe.

As king, it was clear Stavrok had duties to his kingdom and people. I wondered what my duties would be, if I stayed here.

Hostess? Peacemaker? Diplomat?

I swallowed. I wasn't qualified for this— I couldn't even keep the peace through Christmas dinner with my extended family, let alone organize a feast for such important guests!

"You okay? You look like you've seen a ghost." Cass put her hand on my arm, frowning, and I jumped at the contact.

"Yeah," I managed to say, giving her a shaky smile. "Just processing."

She smirked at me before looping her arm through my elbow and tugging me toward the door. I yelped, having no choice but to follow her; for such a tiny thing, she had alarming strength.

Must be a dragon trait...

"You can *process* on the way. Come on! There's so much to see before dinner." Her curls bounced as she whipped her head round, flashing me a grin. "Stavrok wanted you to get the whole tour, and I'm the resident expert."

Cass continued chattering happily as we proceeded down the corridor, and I half-listened, catching glimpses through half-opened doors as we passed. There were a group of women working on a huge tapestry in one room who inclined their heads at the sight of us, and shouts echoed from another room, along with the sound of metal clashing together.

When we got closer, I realized the men were combat training, the way Stavrok had been when I'd confronted him and demanded answers.

It felt like such a long time ago. I was startled to realize that it was only this morning.

"The kitchens are in the basement, and the greenhouses are through there." Cass flung a hand, indicating a high archway at the end of the walkway we stood on. "We grow our own produce. Any surplus is donated to the townsfolk."

I craned my neck over the ledge of the huge glass window, gazing down into the valley that lay below the castle. The town looked tiny from here, the little houses and shops like toys.

"It's so..." I struggled to think of the right word. "Old fashioned?"

Cass giggled. "I guess it must seem that way to you, but we have our technological advances, same as your world. Have you ever been to Chicago? I spent a summer there once—"

I cut her off, remembering my request from earlier. "Speaking of technology, did Stavrok mention anything about a computer to you? I need to send some emails and check in on a couple of things."

Understatement of the century.

With any luck, I hadn't been gone long enough to raise any alarm bells.

Cass gave a heavy sigh. "I'm afraid the Wi-Fi kind of sucks here, but the east tower has a couple of hotspots. We have a small office space next to the library. You can use my laptop if you like."

"Perfect." I grinned.

"Can I show you the greenhouses first?" Cass drew her eyebrows together, eyes wide.

She looked so hopeful that I found myself softening.

"Fine," I said.

The greenhouses were beautiful, built into the center of the castle's intricate roof system and therefore sheltered from the strong winds of the rocky cliff faces on either side. The roof was paneled with multicolored glass, which dappled the floor with prismatic patterns.

After letting Cass show me the grapevines which produced the sweet wine I'd had at breakfast, the fragrant hothouse flowers, and the sunken pool where huge koi fish swam in and out of waterlilies, I finally turned to her with a sigh.

"It's gorgeous, but I *really* need..."

Cass threw her arm around my shoulders and steered me to the door. "I know, I know. I'll take you to your precious computer."

Her scrunched-up face made me chuckle; she reminded me of the face my toddlers made when I took away their crayons.

"Thank you for the tour, Cass," I said. It *was* useful to have a mental map of this place, after all. "Whoever built this place was really onto something."

I glanced back at the beautiful, bright hothouse flowers as we exited the greenhouse, breathing in their dizzying scent one last time. The place was like a little bubble of happiness, a pocket of summer hidden away in this icy, wintery landscape.

"I take it your ancestors put all this together?" I turned to her as we wandered back down the covered walkway, heading for the entrance hall.

She nodded.

"Back there, though?" She pointed toward the greenhouses. "Stavrok built all that."

My heart skipped a beat or two. "Really?"

She grinned, looking as if she could read my train of thought. "It's been a personal project of his for years. He spends time in there still when he can spare it. Self-sufficiency is very important to him."

I struggled to square my image of Stavrok—stoic, strong, the pinnacle of masculinity—with the leafy oasis at the heart of the castle. Still, I knew that first impressions didn't count for everything.

Maybe there was more to him than met the eye.

Cass was watching me carefully. "I know our ways must seem strange to you, Lucy. The human world is a far cry from ours."

We passed through another corridor, one with doors that opened into a large hallway where people sat along long tables, chattering as they worked.

When I looked askance at Cass, she smiled softly. "Everyone in this place plays a part, Lucy. Our kingdom is run, not by dominance and fear like some of the other kingdoms, but by understanding. Stavrok protects everyone, gives them the chance to hone their skills." She pointed to an old woman who spun thread on a giant spindle, while a young girl watched her closely. "They provide for us and themselves, and the kingdom prospers. In return, he will defend us to his dying breath."

I gazed at the scene, lost in thought.

This was what Stavrok was offering me.

A world where I could flourish, and nurture those around me.

Where I could be safe. Where our children would grow up, happy and loved.

I swallowed. "You say that like… it's different here."

She took my arm again, and we continued walking. "I guess it is. Stavrok can be fearsome, but there are parts of this world where true darkness lingers."

Cass bit her lip. It was strange to watch her mood change. The happy, cheery young woman from before disappeared in front of me, like a shadow passing over the sun.

"What do you mean, darkness?" I asked.

I thought about what she had said before. *Dominance and fear.*

Clearly, those other kingdoms Cass mentioned didn't run on the same playbook that Stavrok and his people did here.

"King Magnik rules the kingdom nearest to ours." Cass frowned out of a window as we passed it, like the man himself might suddenly appear. "He's a tyrant. He only cares about wealth and power, and his people suffer for it."

I was silent. My heart hammered as I thought about having to come face to face with such a man in the future. If I stayed with Stavrok, surely I'd need to see him at some point.

After all, what did I have to protect myself if I needed to? No magical powers, no mysterious shapeshifting ability. I was just an ordinary human.

Cass must have seen my face, because she nudged her shoulder into mine. "Hey, don't worry about that now. C'mon, we're almost there!"

I wanted to get her to tell me more about the kingdoms, about how things were done around here, but I forced myself to focus.

One thing at a time.

She led me into a gigantic library, full of floor-to-ceiling bookcases. We wove through the shelves, and I gaped up at the ornate gilded books that lined every wall. A spiral staircase in the corner led up to a small balcony, and through another door we came upon a smaller anteroom, complete with a desk, office supplies, and—

Bingo!

I made a beeline for the computer that sat on a small desk in the corner of the room, and Cass giggled.

"It should be all set up for you," she said. "Give me a shout if you have any problems, yeah? I'll be right outside."

I threw her a smile, grateful for the chance to be alone with my thoughts for the time being.

I opened my email and began to scan my inbox.

My depressingly empty inbox.

I had one unanswered email from the day-care center, asking me if I was sick. It wasn't like me to just not show up for work, and I detected a note of worry in the message underneath the polite annoyance.

I thought hard about what Stavrok had said. I knew the impromptu vacation excuse wouldn't cut it, but...

I began to type, my fingers flying across the keyboard. The more I typed, the more I thought about my life back home.

What I would be returning to, once I got out of here.

The small house, where I lived alone. My day job, where I cared for other people's children. The occasional drink I treated myself to, down at my small town's only bar. Spending the night getting hit on by guys who were only after one thing.

Rinse, and repeat.

Laying out the facts, it made for a pretty bleak existence.

Not that it was all bad. I liked my job well enough. I got on with my colleagues. I saw my parents every week or so.

It was all perfectly... fine.

I looked at the message I'd written, a simple, short email explaining that I had been taken ill suddenly. It didn't sound that convincing, but I hit send anyway.

I thought again about Stavrok. About the way he talked, offering to lay the world at my feet if that was what it took to get me to stay.

I had to admit it; there was something charming about his unwavering belief in me. His certainty that the fates had brought us together, and he wanted to build a life with me.

Granted, if a guy back home had told me he would father my children after only one night together, I would have turned tail and run.

But this wasn't my home.

The rules were different here.

Every time I thought I was beginning to understand them, something new came along and turned everything on its head.

I had to keep my wits about me. But it seemed like the longer I stayed here, the deeper down the rabbit hole I fell.

THIRTEEN

Stavrok

I looked over the perfectly set table. The candles were in place, and all the silverware was laid out precisely.

Normally, I didn't care about such things, but now...

Now I had someone to impress.

The double doors at the other end of the dining room opened a crack, and I straightened my spine, hands behind my back. I had elected to wear a simple navy shirt and slacks for tonight's meal: a nice halfway point between my training gear and the formalwear my advisors forced me into for diplomatic visits.

The door slid open, and Lucy slipped into the room. My heart lightened upon seeing her. She wore a simple low-necked dress, and her long hair flowed loose around her shoulders.

It was thrilling to see her embrace the fashions of the land so readily. She already looked like she belonged here. She looked like a queen.

My queen.

Her lips quirked upwards when she caught my eye, and she hurried over to meet me.

"Your Majesty," she said, giving me a small curtsey and giggling in a way that made me smile.

"My queen," I replied, giving her a bow in turn.

She scrunched up her face and waved away my remark, but she accepted the chair I pulled out for her without fuss. The woman was a conundrum. A delightful puzzle that I couldn't wait to spend the rest of my life figuring out.

Our food was brought in, and we began to eat in a comfortable silence. I surveyed her over the top of my wineglass, smiling at the way she flushed when she caught my eyes on her.

"This color suits you." I stroked a hand along her ruby red sleeve. "You should order more styles in this palette. You make a pleasing picture."

"Is that so?" she said, raising an eyebrow at me, but I could tell she wasn't angry at my remark.

On the contrary, she looked strangely shy. As if she wasn't used to men complimenting her in this way. I couldn't fathom the motivations of human men. To me, she was a feast for the eyes.

"I trust your day was pleasing?" I said, taking a bite of tender lamb shank and eyeing her.

She nodded. "Your cousin's fun."

"Cass." I smiled warmly. "I'm glad you like her. She's like a little sister to me—talkative, and always underfoot, but she means well. I hope she showed you all this place has to offer."

"She did." Lucy met my gaze, her tone careful. "I got the works."

"Good." I clinked my glass against hers. I wasn't hiding the fact that I wanted her to stay with me, after all. "Did you find the computer you requested?"

"I did, thank you." She cast her eyes downward, fiddling with her dessert fork. "I've tied up all the loose ends. So, I'm all yours—"

I grinned at her, and she snorted.

"For now." She pointed her fork at me, before taking another bite of lamb and groaning. "God, the food here is amazing."

"Care to join me for dessert?" I said, lowering my voice a shade.

She held my gaze. Her beauty was highlighted this evening, bathed by the candlelight's warm glow. She bit her plump lip, and it grew redder and fuller.

"Of course."

In due course, the strawberries were brought out, but I found myself watching her more than anything else. She dipped them in melted chocolate and brought them to her mouth, her eyelashes fluttering with pleasure at the taste.

Despite the servants standing by watching us, lust began to weave through my blood stream.

A drizzle of chocolate coated her little finger, and I couldn't help but take her hand and pull her finger toward my lips. I trailed my tongue over her flesh, and in answer she took a sharp intake of breath.

My heated gaze met hers.

Her pupils were large, and her flushed chest was rising and falling a little more rapidly than before. I let her hand fall to the table and leaned in closer, sliding my hand up the outside of her thigh.

She shoved away from the table, her chair scraping back as she stood up abruptly. Half a strawberry tumbled from her fingers, but she ignored it.

"I'm tired," she said, biting her words out. "It's been a long day."

I frowned. She clearly desired me just as much as I wanted her.

Something was holding her back.

"I'll take you to my bedchamber," I said, keeping my voice low.

I didn't understand how the mood of the evening had turned so quickly. I wanted to take her again. My dragon demanded its mate, roaring with frustration.

It would only be satisfied when Lucy and I were both sated and exhausted, but apparently my advances were unwelcome tonight.

"I want my own, uh, chamber." Lucy crossed her arms, staring me down. "You said I could have anything I wanted, right? I want this."

I gaped at her.

No woman had ever spoken to me in such a manner before.

It only made me want her more. She wasn't afraid of me at all, this small human woman.

I knew, in that moment, that I would level cities in order to keep her safe.

I also knew that we should be apart right now.

She wanted some space, and my baser urges were howling for me to throw her against the table and ravage her.

It was only a matter of time before one of these eventualities would prevail.

"Very well," I said, keeping my voice impassive. I gestured to a nearby servant, who sprang to attention. "See to it that my mate has everything she needs for the night."

Lucy turned to go, but before she could pull away completely, I took her hand in mine.

"Sleep well, dear one," I murmured, pressing my lips to the back of her hand.

Just before she withdrew it and walked out of the dining hall, I swore I felt her fingertips brush, light as a feather, against my cheek.

An hour later I found myself alone in my bedchamber, staring up at the ceiling.

I had spent my whole life in this bed, alone or in the company of an endless number of heartless women.

It had never bothered me. I always slept a deep, untroubled sleep, or spent my nights in the arms of a conquest.

Now the frustration itched under my skin. I ached for release, but I had nowhere to turn.

The one thing that would sate my burning desire was in the castle, tantalizingly close, but just out of reach. I buried my face in my pillow and groaned aloud, praying for sleep to come and put an end to my suffering.

Sleep did not come.

Instead, there was a knock at the door.

Hope flared in my chest, and I sat up, knocking my bedclothes aside.

She'd come back to me.

"Enter," I called, trying to keep the need out of my voice but hearing it anyway.

A figure entered the room, and my heart sank into my stomach.

"Majesty." The woman in the doorway gave a deep curtsey. "I came to make sure you were all right."

It was the maidservant Daisy, was it? No, Daphne.

"I'm fine," I said, dropping back onto my bed with a sigh. "I take it Lucy is settled?"

"She is, sire." Daphne edged the door shut behind her.

I cracked an eye open to watch her as she approached my bed.

"I was just wondering whether you required any other services before I departed for the night." Her hands came up to loosen the lacings at the front of her dress. "I could please you, if you wish it."

I eyed her, a wave of exhaustion crashing over me.

She was pretty. Her long black hair was fastened in a braid, and her brown eyes were fringed with long lashes.

In bygone days, I wouldn't have thought twice before pulling her into bed with me.

I'd had many beautiful women, including this one before me, but they were pale shadows to me now.

I looked at Daphne, and all I felt was emptiness. A longing for the touch of someone else. I knew in that moment that I would never have another woman again.

"Please." I passed a hand over my face, waving her away. "Leave me."

There was a small noise, like an inhale. Of shock, maybe. Perhaps the girl hadn't been expecting me to reject her so easily.

Tough. Things were different.

I'd found my mate now. I knew what true pleasure looked like, a real, deep intimacy that was already blooming into love.

I didn't hear her leave.

Sleep pulled me under like a tidal wave, and I succumbed to it with open arms. Tomorrow I would win back my queen. I wanted nothing more to do with any other woman, ever again.

Lucy

I woke up to what I thought was the sound of birdsong outside my window. I lay in the pale morning light with my eyes closed, coming to my senses.

As I regained consciousness, I realized the sound wasn't birds; it was the high, piercing sound of the icy winds that wrapped around the castle walls. I wasn't in my bed at home. The room I slept in was huge and high-ceilinged, and the silk sheets pooled around me where I lay in the center of a vast four-poster bed.

Memories of the night before flooded me, and I groaned, squeezing my eyes shut tight and sinking down underneath the covers.

I couldn't pretend any more. This wasn't a dream. This was my life.

I pushed the bedclothes back and shifted to the edge of the mattress, wincing when my bare feet touched the cold flagstones.

There were no clocks in the room, but judging by the dim light and the silence that surrounded me, it was still early.

I padded over to the empty fireplace and smiled as my feet sank into the lush rug that stretched in front of it. I traced the edge of the dragon woven into the center of the rug and sighed.

My night had been spent tossing and turning. The bed had been too big, too cold.

The memory of Stavrok's body curled up against mine, his heat, the safety I felt in his arms—it was too much. My body hummed with the knowledge that he was somewhere within the walls of the castle.

I craved him by my side, even after one day.

Walking away from him last night had been the hardest thing I'd ever done. I'd wanted nothing more than to melt into his touch, to open myself to him again. From the fire in his eyes, I could tell he felt the same way.

But I'd resolved to be cautious.

My judgement was already out the window. I didn't need another crazy, intense night to scramble my brain further.

When Stavrok was around, it was impossible to think rationally about anything. I refused to be a captive here; if I was going to stay, it would be *my* decision.

The stone walls that surrounded me were suddenly suffocating.

I turned and reached for the layers I had discarded last night on the chair beside my bed, dressing myself quickly. At this hour, a chill permeated the air, and I was glad for the soft fur against my skin. Toeing on my shoes, I headed out the door before I could overanalyze my actions.

With no particular direction in mind, I found myself wandering down the castle hallways.

My head ached as I thought about everything I'd learned yesterday.

About the town, its people. About the things Cass told me: Stavrok's vision for his kingdom.

For all the years of his rule, he'd been by himself. It humbled me, knowing how much he'd built, all on his own.

It was easier than it should've been to imagine myself by his side.

There were things I could help with. I'd spent my entire adult life working with children, hadn't I? There had to be plenty of projects to run, lessons to teach. I could do so much... I was sure of it.

In my mind's eye, I could see us, five or ten years from now, surrounded by our friends. Our servants. Keeping them safe from those who would threaten us.

The image expanded. I saw us surrounded by children.

Our children, running down the staircase in the great hall, playing together, swinging between our joined hands as we walked through these hallways.

My heart swelled.

Stavrok wanted me to be his queen. If I stayed, I would have a man who wanted me, just as I was.

Who didn't think I was too fat to be beautiful.

In his eyes, I was perfect.

I'd never have that at home, in my little town with narrow-minded men.

I was so caught up that I barely noticed the figure watching me at the foot of the stairs, and I almost walked into her.

"Oof!" I reached out a hand, steadying myself.

"Oh, I'm sorry, miss."

My eyes focused, and I exhaled heavily, shaking my head at the maid who stood in my path.

"No worries! My fault." I smiled.

The maid smiled back, but there was something guarded in her eyes.

Right. I was still a stranger in these lands. It would naturally take a while for its people to warm up to me.

Still, what was the harm in testing the waters?

"What's your name?" I asked, feeling a bit foolish.

I was probably distracting this girl from her chores for the sake of a little light conversation.

"Daphne, miss." The girl's eyes flicked up and down, and she bobbed a curtsey. A strange smile played at the corners of her mouth.

I already regretted starting the conversation, but I pressed on. "Have you been working here long, Daphne?"

She straightened her shoulders and flicked her hair back. She was pretty, like all the women were here, with her long hair and dark eyes. "The castle isn't my workplace. It's my home."

"Of course."

I'd put my foot in it, somehow, but in what way I didn't know.

Daphne took a neat step forward, looking me directly in the eye. "I'm not some naïve newcomer, miss. I'm devoted to my life here, just as I am devoted to the king."

I nodded, lowering my gaze. "I understand. I didn't mean—"

"I took care of the king's appetites last night," Daphne whispered.

My stomach swooped sickeningly.

She went on. "I consider it an honor to leave him well satisfied. I suggest if you can't keep up with our king's needs, human, you should fly off back to where you came from and leave him to those who can."

I stepped back. My hands clenched into fists. I wanted to slap the smug look off her face, but I managed to control myself, taking short, sharp breaths as I struggled to regain my composure.

Daphne's face settled into a placid smile. "Will that be all, miss?"

I was trembling with anger, but I knew when I was beaten.

The people here would never accept me. I wasn't one of them, and I never would be.

The women would hate me for being an outsider, for being the one to lay claim to their king after all these years.

The unfairness of it screamed out at me.

It wasn't my choice. Stavrok had found *me*, chosen *me*, brought *me* here to rule by his side.

But you claimed him too, a small voice said in the back of my mind. *He's yours now, fate or no fate. Everyone can see it.*

Apparently, fate had a twisted sense of humor.

I'd screwed up any chance I'd had of making things work between us. I'd driven him into the arms of another woman.

I gave her a short nod, and she turned tail, leaving me standing at the foot of the staircase with a swirling mind and a heart that was, despite all my best efforts, broken.

FOURTEEN

Lucy

I only wanted one thing: to hide.

The trouble was, I still didn't know the castle and all its hiding places well enough. Every time I ended up in some corner or other, a guard or servant wandered into the vicinity and looked at me like I was crazy.

Eventually I settled for prowling through the great hall before making my way to the dining room.

My blood was up, and there was nothing I could do to stop the rage that pooled in my stomach when I thought about my so-called "fated mate".

I prickled with frustration, pacing up and down in front of the roaring fireplace. The staff shot me nervous looks, but I ignored them. There was only one person I wanted to see.

When the man himself finally appeared, I had worked myself up into an anger that threatened to crack the very floor beneath my feet.

Stavrok was about to find out that this human woman had enough of a temper to take on a dragon.

He closed the door behind him and stepped into the room. I drew in a sharp intake of breath. He was pale and there were dark shadows under his eyes.

Maybe he'd slept as badly as I had.

Or maybe he's been up all night fucking other women.

When I met his gaze, his demeanor changed. He straightened up, and his face softened, a spark of hope shining in his eyes.

I met his eyes and kept my expression stony.

He'd brought me here, into his life, his world. And he wasn't going to take me for a fool.

"Good morning, dear one." He ventured closer, coming to a standstill about two feet away from me. "Did you have a restful night?"

I folded my arms. A hot pulse of irritation flooded through me at the way his eyes dropped to my chest. Folding my arms had pushed up my generous cleavage. I huffed and uncrossed them.

Men!

"Not really," I said shortly.

"I'm sorry to hear it." He moved closer, reaching out to touch my shoulder. "I missed you in my bed last night."

I pushed his hand off me and stepped back, narrowing my eyes. He actually sounded *regretful,* like he meant it. The audacity of his behavior threw me off my game a little, but I recovered myself.

"Did you?" I smoldered up at him, and he frowned, like I'd unbalanced him. *Good.* "Did you miss me, my *king?*"

"More than you can know," he replied, before tilting his head. "Lucy, is everything... all right? You seem agitated."

"There's no point in keeping up the charade, Stavrok," I snapped. "I know everything."

He scrunched up his face, which only sought to enrage me further.

He must think I'm a complete idiot!

"I ran into Daphne this morning." I let the words out in a rush of breath, relieved to finally release what I'd been holding back. "She told me what happened last night."

His gaze darkened, and I felt vindication sing through my veins.

Finally, we're going to have this out.

"The maidservant?"

"I can't believe I was actually starting to believe all the *bullshit* you fed me," I said. "All that crap about fate bringing us together—and *then*, the minute my back is turned, you go off and fuck the first willing woman you come across!"

Stavrok's mouth dropped open.

Dragon or no dragon, I was more than a match for this giant of a man.

"Lucy," he said, his shoulders squared off and taut with tension. "I have no idea what you're talking about."

"Is that how it is here?" I asked. A part of me thrilled at the heat building up between us. I wanted more of it. I wanted to stoke the flames until the inferno couldn't be contained any more. "You fuck other women whenever you please? What exactly am I here for, Stavrok? To give you heirs while you take your pleasures elsewhere?"

I pressed a hand to my stomach, feeling a wave of *something* pass through me.

I continued on, undeterred.

"You must think I'm an idiot." I gave a hollow laugh. "Well, I might not be anything special—I might not be a *magical shapeshifter*—but I know when I'm being played."

"You think I took Daphne to bed last night?" Stavrok's voice had dropped so low, I could feel it in my chest, even from this distance. "Lucy, I slept *alone*. She offered herself to me, yes, but I—"

"There it is!" I cut him off. "Finally."

I took a perverse kind of pleasure in getting the truth out of him like this, bit by bit. It was like touching a wound that hadn't healed yet. I couldn't stop the pain, but I liked being the one in control of it.

"Nothing happened!" Stavrok said, his voice booming off the walls. "Whatever she told you, it's a falsehood! I want no woman but you, Lucy."

I scoffed, but tears pricked my eyes. I dashed them away. On some level, I knew this rejection was going to happen. Maybe it was better it happened sooner rather than later.

A man like this—strong, handsome, virile—what did he want with a woman like me?

He could have anyone he wanted. He was the kind of man that beautiful women threw themselves at on a daily basis.

I swallowed around the lump in my throat. "I don't believe you!"

"What would you have me do to prove it to you?" he asked. "Have I not already offered you everything I have? Have I not laid it out at your feet, from the moment we first met?"

I shoved down the small piece of doubt that threatened to crack through my defences and took a step toward him.

"If it's not this one, it'll be another! Sooner or later, you'll see—"

"See what?"

"How much you're missing!" I said, running my hands through my hair so that it tumbled loosely around my shoulders. "The women here—I can't give you the things that they can! I'm not a shifter, I'm not beautiful. I'm not enough for you! You should never have taken me, Stavrok, because now I'll always know what it's supposed to feel like!"

I rushed forward and pushed at his chest with my fists. I gasped as he caught my wrists in his large hands and tugged me forwards until I curved into his body.

"I'll always know how it's meant to be between two people, and I'll *never* feel like this again! You've *ruined* me!"

He snarled, his eyes flashing. In the depths of his gaze, I caught a glimmer of the dragon that slumbered inside of the king.

Stavrok's hands tightened around my wrists, and his thunderous expression morphed into something deeper, raw and urgent. Lust raced through my veins as he pressed up against me, backing me into the wall and holding me there with ease.

"If you don't believe me," his said, his voice shooting through me, low and dangerous, "I'll have to show you."

I groaned and sank back. Anger and adrenaline pulsed through me, but it was impossible to keep up the fight when he had me pinned against the wall. I was surrounded by him. His skin pulsed with heat, and his fingers shifted and flexed against my wrists.

He must have felt my heartbeat fluttering just beneath the surface of my skin, because his eyes flicked upwards, assessing my ragged breaths, the way my chest rose and fell, the flush that spread out from my décolletage.

"Yes." The word tripped out of me, unbidden, and his eyes narrowed.

He dropped my wrists and his hands fell below my waist, pulling up my skirts with an urgency that I hadn't seen from him before. He hitched my legs up until he had me braced against the wall. My eyes rolled back, and I groaned, trying to pull him even closer.

The thin layers of fabric that separated us were torturous. I longed to feel his hot skin against mine, feel every inch of him pressed up against my body, but I had to settle for what I could reach. My hands dragged over his perfect torso, and his forehead pushed up against mine as he tore away the last of my underclothes, leaving nothing between us.

If I wasn't half-crazy with desire I would've chuckled.

So many layers, so little time.

I felt his fingers, blunt and insistent, against my entrance, and I shivered. He grunted, satisfied to find me slick and ready. I ached, the sense of emptiness overwhelming me.

I need him inside me.

I hooked my ankles against his hips and pulled, no longer caring about self-restraint or decorum, or the fact that we were in a public place where anyone might walk in on us.

All I cared about was this. I needed him to fuck me until neither of us could see straight.

His mouth found my neck, and he bit down as he sank into me. I wriggled, trapped between the wall and his hot, insistent body.

It was overwhelming, dizzying. Perfect.

He began to thrust, and I sobbed, fisting my hand into his hair and drumming my heels against his back in a silent plea for him to move faster, deeper.

He obliged, pounding into me relentlessly, and before long I felt myself start to tighten around his cock. My orgasm slammed into me, wave after wave of bliss rippling through my body, and I whimpered as his onslaught only increased in pace.

My whimpers tightened my throat. I murmured to him, high and breathy.

"Stavrok... please... I need you..."

He snarled, dropping his head to my shoulder as he continued to thrust.

"Mine," he breathed. "You're *mine.*"

"I'm yours," I said, and I opened my mouth, readily accepting his bruising kiss.

His thrusts began to grow less precise; something baser, more primal, took over. His grip on my hips grew firmer, and he began pulling down my hips as he hitched himself up to meet me, as if I were nothing more to him than an instrument for his pleasure. I moaned at the thought, at the way his breathing shifted, at the feeling of his thighs tensing up.

He spilled into me, and the feeling of his seed pulsing deep inside sent me over the edge again.

Little by little, our breathing returned to normal. The sound of it echoed loudly through the silent dining hall.

Slowly, inch by inch, he released me, and I trembled as I slid down from the wall, my hands reaching to adjust my skirt.

My legs felt like jelly, and my head spun. I stumbled, and his broad hand caught my elbow.

I looked up at him, and he looked down at me.

I couldn't know for sure, but I was willing to bet that our expressions were mirror images of one another.

There was only one feeling that raced through my mind, over and over, building until it could be encapsulated in a single expression.

Oh. Fuck.

It wasn't that I was falling for him.

I've already fallen.

FIFTEEN

Stavrok

Golden sunlight streamed in through the window. I stretched, eyes still half-closed, and reached out a hand. A smile grew on my face when my fingers brushed up against the form, warm and solid, curled up beside me.

Lucy.

I had worried the previous day had been an illusion. A fever dream, of sorts, conjured up by my fractured brain to mask the pain of my mate rejecting me.

It appeared not.

The real thing lay beside me, golden hair splayed out over the pillow.

One hand curled upwards beside her slumbering face, and I couldn't resist brushing those soft fingers, watching her hand twitch and her eyelashes flutter.

She looked like a princess, straight out of the stories my mother used to read to me as a child.

Her gorgeous green eyes opened, and her lovely features softened when she saw me. Sleepily, she raised a hand up to push a lock of hair off my brow. At the gentleness of her touch, I bowed my head, pressing a kiss into her outstretched palm.

"What a gentleman." She giggled. "Good morning."

"It is indeed," I murmured, pressing myself up against her side and combing my fingers through her hair, enjoying the soft texture.

She snuggled closer. I was gratified by the contact and pleased at the assurance of the motion. She had no problem dragging my free arm tight around her waist, and I growled in satisfaction as I traced a hand over the curve of her waist.

"What are your plans today?" Lucy whispered, pressing a kiss into my neck.

I stroked her arm absently, thinking. "Matters of state, a few meetings this afternoon. Nothing urgent."

She hummed approval and nuzzled into my neck. I wondered if the scratchiness of my stubble bothered her, but I didn't voice the thought. I was enjoying her kisses too much.

"Besides," I murmured, running a hand up her spine, "my advisors will understand. I've found my fated mate, after all these years. It's a cause for celebration."

There was a long silence.

I frowned. Lucy's back had grown tense at my words, and her body withdrew from mine under the bedcovers.

"Fated mates." She didn't turn her head, and her voice was quiet, but I was hanging on to every word. "You really believe in that stuff, don't you?"

My frown deepened. I pulled my arms back, and she flipped onto her back, staring up at me with a blank expression.

"Of course," I said, puzzled. "You feel it, don't you? The pull toward me, our connection? Don't talk of it as if..."

"As if what?"

"As if it's some"—I cast out a hand, struggling for the words—"fairy tale. I assure you, what's passed between us is real. It is a bond that cannot be broken. Neither time nor distance will weaken its power."

She pressed her lips together. The thin line of them grew white, and my anger bubbled to the surface.

"You *know* this." I growled. "I know you can feel it too, Lucy."

"Don't tell me what I feel," she snapped, and my stomach dropped. She pushed the bedsheets back, climbed out of bed, and grabbed a robe from my coat rack. "I *feel* like this is a load of shit, if you must know."

"What do you mean?"

I clambered to my feet, mirroring her movements. She had already circled the bed and walked out of reach. I resisted the urge to pace after her, sensing that it would only escalate things.

Escalate what? *We were having a pleasant conversation five minutes ago.*

The mood had changed so fast I had whiplash.

She rounded on me. Even though I stood a head taller than her, I backed up a couple of steps at the force of her glare.

"I mean, you promised me *time*," she said. "You promised me I could go home if I wanted to!"

"And I'll honor that promise!"

My heart hammered in my chest, and the blood rushed through my eardrums. *She wants to leave me.*

I couldn't believe it. I'd never heard of such a thing happening before. When a dragon shifter found their fated mate, that was it. They were bonded for life.

I swallowed.

Maybe it was because she was human. I should have known that crucial difference between us would come back to haunt me.

She stared at me, her face pale and her eyes flashing. Belatedly, I realized I had been yelling.

At length, she drew herself up to her full height and looked me square in the face, shoulders back. She was regal. She may not have been born into it, but she was certainly a queen in my eyes.

"I'm going for a shower," she said, her voice trembling with repressed emotion. "Alone."

Before I had a chance to respond, she turned and strode into the bathroom, slamming the door shut behind her. A few moments later, the water turned on.

I resisted the urge to release my dragon then and there. Love and rage warred within my chest. I wanted to scorch a forest to the ground, level fields and raze valleys in my fury.

Instead, I turned on my heel and walked out of the bedchamber.

It was time for a sparring session.

Whoever I was training with today, I didn't envy them one bit.

LUCY

By the time I climbed out of the shower, my skin was flushed and pruney, and my ire had cooled considerably. As I towelled off my hair, I cast a nervous glance at the door that led to the bedchamber.

The shower had washed away my prickling frustration, but I wasn't ready to face Stavrok yet.

When I pushed open the door, I revealed an empty room. The bed was neatly made, but there was no sign of the king anywhere.

My heart sank, caught somewhere between relief and sadness.

Ugh. I need to walk and clear my head. This place is driving me crazy.

I slipped on a simple velvet dress and, after a moment of hesitation, a fur mantle that I found hanging in the vast wardrobe.

It was fancier than anything I owned back home, but it was soft and warm.

I smoothed the fur around my shoulders, turning to assess myself in the mirror.

A knock at my door.

"Lucy? Are you awake yet?"

I smiled to myself. "Yep! Come in, Cass."

The door creaked open, and Cass slipped inside. She bounded over to me and bobbed up behind my shoulder. She grinned at me in the mirror, and I managed to smile back.

"The royal furs," she said. "It suits you!"

I let out a groan of dismay, and her brow furrowed. The gesture reminded me of Stavrok, and my mood sank even further.

"Oh, no!" She bit her lip, eyes wide. "What's wrong?"

I took her arm, shaking my head, lost for words. *Where to even begin.*

"I'm going for a walk." I led her to the doorway, out into the corridor. "And you're coming with me."

"Okay…" Cass's voice trailed after me as I strode down the corridor, not bothering to slow my pace for her. She trotted after me, panting. "Do I get to ask what this is about, or…?"

I shook my head, hurtling down the wide staircase and rounding the corner.

I was kind of impressed with myself. I knew the layout of this place like I'd lived here for years.

Like it's already home to me.

I forced the traitorous thought out of my mind and forced open the double doors, making for the outdoor walkway Cass had shown me a couple of days ago.

Air. That was what I needed. Fresh air, to clear away the storms swirling in my head.

"Lucy!" Cass burst through the doorway in a flurry of chestnut curls, laying a hand on my arm. "Tell me what's going on already!"

At her touch, I deflated, pulling back until we were walking side by side. I took a deep breath of the cool air, and exhaled, long and slow.

I started feeling better just for being outside.

"This is all happening so…" I flailed. "It's a *lot*, okay, and I'm… A week ago, I was living a totally normal life in my totally normal town, and suddenly, overnight, I'm the *soulmate* of a *king*—"

"Slow down…" Cass interjected, but I couldn't stop.

I always got like this when I was angry or upset. Once the words started, they kept on coming, faster and faster.

"He wants me to live in his castle and be his queen, and rule by his side, and have his babies, and—oh, my God." I ran my fingers through my hair, rounding on her. "My kids are going to be dragons, Cass. *Dragons.*"

"Well," Cass said weakly. "They won't be dragons all the time. It's more like… like a part of our souls."

I shot her an incredulous look and kept walking. The wide stone archways we passed through looked out over a snowy vista. A light flurry was falling, coating the castle roofs and turrets with white.

"We're shifters, Lucy." Cass's voice was gentle, reassuring. "And they won't just be his children. They'll be yours, too."

"That's exactly the problem!" I sighed. "You, Stavrok, everyone is talking as if I've already agreed to spend my life here, just because the fates have decided it."

Cass tilted her head to the side as though she was puzzled, so I sighed and tried to explain.

"In my world, there's no such thing as fate, or destiny." I looked out over the beautiful world I'd found myself in. I heard Stavrok's voice echo through my mind. *A world of Fire and Ice.* "I make my own choices, Cass. Nobody else. Not fate. Not even a dragon king."

We were silent for a few more paces. The wind howled around us, and I shivered, drawing my collar up around my neck.

"I hear you," Cass said eventually. "I just..."

She looked up at me, eyes piercing through mine. I felt exposed.

"I can't understand why you would ever want to leave this place," she said. "Or leave Stavrok."

I bit my lip. "I guess it must be kind of hard to wrap your head around, huh?"

Cass laughed. "Yes. If I found my fated mate..." She exhaled, fixing her eyes on the horizon, lost in thought. "I wouldn't ever want to be apart from them, let alone in another world entirely."

I didn't reply. I tried to imagine crossing the border and returning to the human world, starting my life again like none of this had ever happened.

Deep in my stomach, the thought didn't sit right with me.

I didn't want Cass to know that.

I sighed heavily. "Cass, I... I can't be a prisoner here. Whatever I feel for Stavrok, I'm my own person."

Cass opened her mouth to say something, but before she could, there was a tap on my shoulder.

Her eyes slid past mine, widening, and I whirled around to face two tall figures dressed in the livery of the castle guards.

I didn't recognise them.

That fact wouldn't have been unusual in itself—I hadn't been here that long, after all—but from Cass's expression I could tell she didn't know them either.

I straightened my shoulders, trying for an aura of confidence that I didn't feel.

"Yes?"

The one on the left spoke. His voice was low and gravelly. "Ma'am, you have to come with us."

Cass nudged me aside, stepping between me and the newcomers. "Why? Anything you can say to her, you can say to me."

A glow of warmth shot through me, but it vanished when the men's expressions darkened. Their eyes were glowing in a faintly familiar way.

"We were told to make this quiet," the one on the right said. He was shorter than his friend, and his voice had a mean undercurrent. "But we're authorized to use force if necessary."

I shivered, but Cass was getting angrier by the moment. Her brows were furrowed, her fists were clenched, and her face had gone an unhealthy shade of red.

"Authorized by *who?*"

Quick as a flash, the taller of the pair lashed out, swift and merciless. The uppercut sent Cass flying into the stone edge of the walkway. She hit it with a sharp *crack*, and fell to the floor, where she lay, unmoving.

"Cass!" I screamed.

I shot forward, stumbling toward her. She looked so still. I needed to check if she was breathing. She couldn't *possibly* be—

Firm hands grabbed me, and I struggled as I was pulled back, away from her. No matter how much I thrashed, the grip on my arms was as solid and immovable as iron.

"No! Let me go!" I twisted around, desperately casting around for anyone who might be nearby. "*Stavrok!*"

The last thing I saw were a pair of glittering, malevolent eyes, before a cloth was pressed against my nose and mouth.

And then everything went black.

SIXTEEN

Lucy

When I woke up, a single feeling slammed into me with inescapable force.

Cold.

I moaned and shuddered, curling into my side and wrapping my arms around myself in a futile attempt to warm up.

I'd been cold since I arrived in the land of Fire and Ice. But for the first time, the real arctic temperatures of this world were hitting me. I'd seen the fire first-hand, and now I was getting the ice.

I inched my eyes open, squinting as my eyes adjusted to the dim light.

I was in a cavernous, windowless room. Damp trickled down the stone walls, and a torch flickered in a hollow crevice, casting long shadows over the uneven floor.

I pushed myself up onto my hands, trying to keep my rising panic in check. I was lying on a thin wooden bench pushed up against the wall. There were iron brackets bolted into the stonework just above my head.

Wow, I really don't want to know what those are for.

I curled my legs up beside me on the bench, my eyes flickering back and forth, taking stock of my surroundings from the limited vantage point.

Dark, damp room. Stone walls.

Were those *chains* coiled up in the far corner?

I didn't care to get up and check.

I dropped my head, pressing my cheek against my knees.

It looked like I'd finally made it to the dungeons after all.

A cold, creeping misery swept through my chest, and I groaned.

Had I crossed Stavrok one too many times?

We'd fought badly this morning. Granted, it was just a continuation of the argument from the day before, but still.

He was the king. He must be unused to dealing with the sharp end of a temper like mine.

But to go so far as throwing me in the dungeons over it?

That just didn't square with the picture I had of him. He could be fierce, sure, but he treated me with a deference and respect I was unused to in a man.

Every scrap of evidence I had to go on told me that he was strong and just. A fair, kind leader of his people. I hadn't seen anything to point to the contrary.

A shiver rolled down my spine.

I pressed a hand to my stomach, and a jolt of rage sparked through me. I leapt to my feet, mentally and physically shaking myself out of my stupor.

Come on, Lucy! Get it together.

I began to pace, examining every inch of my prison as I went. A quick assessment told me I was still wearing the clothes I had put on this morning, before going out for my walk with—

Cass.

Whoever had kidnapped me, they had taken out Cass first.

Which suggested that Stavrok wasn't behind this whole thing. He wouldn't hurt Cass. She was family.

I frowned, pivoting on my heel. My hand crept over my stomach again, cradling it.

You may already be pregnant, he'd said.

If Stavrok thought the human world was too dangerous for any potential children I might be carrying, surely throwing me in a dungeon wasn't on the cards, either.

My gaze fell on the heavy oak door, set into the wall on the far side of the room.

I approached it slowly, cautiously, leaned in, and pressed my ear against the wood.

At first, I heard nothing but water dripping and the sound of my own breaths. My breath misted in the air in front of me, reminding me ironically of a dragon puffing smoke.

Damn, it really *was* cold.

Then, I heard voices.

They were faint at first, but they grew louder and louder, like their owners were travelling down the corridor toward me.

"...better be worth it, that's all I'm saying. If Magnik is wrong about her, it could bring our kingdom into open war."

More footsteps. Then, a second voice.

"Our king isn't wrong. She's Stavrok's mate. I know Stavrok—he'll do whatever it takes to get her back."

"Those lands have belonged to his family for generations. Do you really think he'll give them all up over one woman?" The speaker gave a snort. "A *human*, at that?"

"Maybe one day you'll find your fated mate, Tristan."

There was a grunt of protest, like someone just got elbowed in the ribs.

"Till then, you should keep your trap shut about it."

"Oh, yeah? Maybe Elsie's tired of you. I could swing by your house later, find out if you can have more than one soulmate... Ouch!"

The voices were moving off now, growing fainter. I waited, my body tense, but they passed right by my door without stopping.

My mind raced. The name Magnik was so familiar to me. Where had I heard it before? Wherever I was, it wasn't Stavrok's kingdom.

My stomach filled with ice. I was in enemy territory. And I was being used as a bargaining chip. All over some *land*.

I burned hot with rage and embarrassment. They hadn't even bothered to tie me up; to them, I was just a powerless human, a pawn to move around as they played their political games.

I watched my lonely flame flickering, casting strange shadows against the ancient stonework. Something curled in my stomach, something that made me stagger over to the bench and sit heavily. I sank my head into my hands.

It was a new sensation, something I hadn't felt since arriving here.

Dread.

~

STAVROK

I spent the morning working out my frustration in the courtyard.

The familiar, heavy clash of metal against metal, the adrenaline pounding through my veins, the satisfaction of besting our strongest fighters—all of it soothed me, and by mid-morning I found that my temper had cooled.

I waved off my sparring partner, standing alone in the center of the courtyard and staring up at the sky.

It was a cold, bright day, and I inhaled deep lungfuls of the fresh mountain air before stooping to pick up a water jug and gulping gratefully.

The fight had cleared my head, like it always did.

As I wiped down with a spare towel, my thoughts turned to the events of the morning.

Already I regretted the way things had gone with Lucy. I should've calmed her, the way only a soulmate could.

It seemed that I couldn't help myself with her. When we fought, all the adrenaline I had as a warrior sprang to the fore, mixed in with a hot, tantalising undercurrent of lust.

Lust which she met in equal force, every single time.

Our bond was a powder keg, and I kept lighting the fuse.

My limbs shifted, restless. My sparring practice had taken the edge off my frustration, but already the need for her was beginning to creep back in.

My mind was made up.

I pivoted on my heel, heading for the stairwell. I would track her down, and we could work through our heated feelings together—preferably up against a wall somewhere, or in our bathroom tub.

A shudder of anticipation ran through me, and a smile ghosted across my face.

Before I reached the stairs, a shout echoed from across the yard.

"Majesty!"

I scowled, not wanting to abandon my new mission.

"Yes, what is it?" I turned around.

James strode up to me. He was breathing heavily, like he had been running.

"Quickly," I said. "I have urgent business to attend to."

"Not as urgent as this." James brandished a letter, holding it out to me.

I wanted to brush him off, but there was an unfamiliar worry in his face that gave me pause. My eyes narrowed. I took the letter and opened it.

STAVROK —

I WANT to see which you value more: that goldmine of minerals you refuse to part with, or your precious soulmate.

Here is my offer. If you give up your lands to me, I will ensure your new queen is returned to you, alive and unharmed.

If not... I'm afraid that I can't be certain of her safety.

THINK IT OVER.

MAGNIK

· · ·

I READ THE WORDS CAREFULLY.

Then I read them again.

My brain refused to believe it. My queen, my love, my soulmate... held for ransom over some petty political argument.

I had never trusted Magnik, but even for him, this was beyond the pale.

The depth of the betrayal shook me to my core. Rage unlike anything I'd ever known, screaming inside my mind. My anger was so potent, I was surprised it didn't crack the stones beneath my feet. I let out a roar and shredded the letter, leaving the pieces to flutter to the ground.

James's face was pale and set, his mouth pressed into a thin line.

"What is this?" My voice boomed over the entire courtyard. "Where is she? Where is Lucy?"

People had begun to trickle into the courtyard, presumably to find out where all the noise was coming from.

"Sire, please," James said, "you must calm yourself." My vision was distorting, my muscles clenching. My dragon was waking up. I growled, and James backed up a couple of steps, wide-eyed.

With difficulty, I shoved my dragon shifter back down again. It could do me no good right now. I needed to be able to talk.

"I'm very far from calm. Tell me everything."

"Majesty," someone called out, pushing through the small gathering of people.

They grumbled and moved aside for her, and a small pathway formed through the sea of bodies.

My eyes narrowed as I caught sight of the strange procession of people.

The voice belonged to Maddie. She was leading a group of court officials through the crowd.

Their long robes clustered protectively around a slight figure, who was walking with the aid of two guards. I caught a flash of curly hair, and a fresh jolt of panic spiked through my chest.

"Cass?"

I rushed forward, jostling a guard out of the way as I took her by the elbow. My little cousin was ashen pale, and to my horror, there was a dark smear of blood at her temple.

In spite of her obvious wooziness, she shot me a weak smile. "Hey, Stavrok."

"What happened?"

Her large eyes fixed on mine. Her usual bouncy energy was gone, replaced by a stark seriousness.

"Lucy and I were taking a walk around the outer walkway, on the eastern side of the castle. Two men in guard uniforms approached us and asked her to come with them. I didn't recognize them. I got between them and Lucy. When I questioned them, they...they tossed me aside. The fall must have knocked me out, because I don't remember anything after that." She gave a hearty sniff, and her eyes filled with tears. "A guard—a *real* guard—found me. But Lucy was *gone*."

I nodded, putting the pieces together as she spoke. My heart clenched as I recognised the anguish in her face. It was my own pain, reflected back at me.

"Stavrok..." she said. Her slim hand found my arm. It was trembling. "I failed you. I couldn't keep her safe. I'm *so* sorry."

Her head dropped.

"No," I said. "This is not your fault, Cass. You couldn't have known."

"Will we get her back?" Cass wiped a tear from her face, listing to the side. She was still weak, clearly unable to stand unaided.

"We will," I replied. "I promise."

She gave me another weak smile and brought a hand up to her forehead, frowning when she saw blood. "Huh."

I turned to the guard on the other side of her.

"Take her to the infirmary and see to it that she gets immediate medical attention."

The guard snapped his heels and swept up Cass. She didn't protest, and her head lolled against his shoulder as he carried her off.

Assured that my cousin was being seen to, I turned back to the matter at hand.

Cass's state had distracted me from my initial spike of rage. Now my brain was cool and logical, drawing up plans, strategizing. I was in battle mode.

If Magnik wanted a war, he would get one.

～

I ASSEMBLED my chief advisors in the old map room in the center of the castle. The room had, at one time, been the scene of many war councils and state meetings, but there hadn't been a war waged in these lands since my grandfather's time. Consequently, it now lay quiet, the blinds drawn over the windows, slightly dingy from the years of abandonment.

With the help of Maddie and the others, I shook off the dust sheets and unfurled the maps that covered the walls, until the room was a flurry of activity.

Once everything was set up, I stood at the head of the table, looking out over the map of the country, laid out in miniature. I tried to imagine myself in my other form, flying low over the tiny hilltops and villages.

I glanced up, assessing all the expectant faces that sat around the table, waiting for me to speak. Maddie lingered in the corner of the room, her hands placed neatly behind her back. I nodded at her; grateful she had stayed.

In many ways, she was my only true ally in this room.

My hand dipped down, and I traced the carved, ridged hilltops that represented my ancestral lands. "Magnik has offered me a deal. If I give up these lands, he will guarantee Lucy's safe return."

The council absorbed my words. Looks of despair and anger passed over the heavily lined faces of the older men. They were my father's age, or older; old enough to know the stakes of Magnik's offer, and the value of the land beneath our feet.

They knew the magnitude of what lay ahead of us.

Slowly, but surely, I raised my head. I felt the weight of kingship settle across my shoulders, as heavy as it was on the day of my coronation.

"I'm not giving up *anything* to Magnik," I said, low and certain. "Not land, nor territory. And certainly not my queen."

"What are you going to do, sire?"

The question didn't come from any of the elders at the table.

It came from Maddie.

She gazed at me with hope and pride, like she could see something shining out of me that nobody else could.

"The only thing I can do. I'm going to launch an attack on Magnik's lands."

There was a rustle of movement around the table as the elders put their heads together and murmured to each other in low voices.

"Your Majesty, it has been over a century since any of the kingdoms have gone to war," Hillsen stated. "It would be... *could* be... catastrophic. For his people, and ours."

I bowed my head in acknowledgement, although frustration beat against the inside of my chest like a drum.

I was done with waiting around. I just wanted to get Lucy back, as soon as possible.

Even if I had to tear down every wall of Magnik's castle with my bare hands.

"Believe me, I am aware of the horrors that war will bring." I barely managed to keep the growl out of my voice. "But Magnik has left me with no choice. He struck first. He broke into my castle, hurt Cass, and stole away the woman I love."

The other council members looked grim, but I could see I was winning them over.

"My soulmate. You all know as well as I do, how long I've waited for her. I wish it hadn't come to this, but I won't rest until she's back where she belongs."

I knew in my heart I was right. There was no other choice.

I raised my chin, addressing the room. "Magnik must pay for what he has done."

CHAPTER
SEVENTEEN

Lucy

I don't know how, but I slept.

It was impossible to tell day from night in this place, and I didn't bother trying. I dozed on the thin wooden bench, imagining myself back in Stavrok's bed, surrounded by soft sheets and silk pillows.

Safe.

I jolted awake to the sound of heavy iron bars sliding free. The huge door swung open on its hinges for the first time since I'd arrived.

My chest tightened, and fear trickled down my spine.

A small, slight figure walked into the room. A woman, carrying a tray of food and a jug of water.

It would be impossible to mistake her for a servant. It wasn't just that her gown was a rich, deep blue color, and her hair elaborately decorated with crystal hairpins. There was something regal about her bearing. This woman was nobility.

She set down the tray on the bench beside me. I flinched, wondering if she might hurt me, and she quickly stepped back, her eyes wide and her expression sympathetic.

In fact, she looked about as nervous as I felt.

I gathered my wits, forcing myself to sit straight.

"Where am I?" I asked. "Where's Magnik? This *is* his dungeon, I presume."

Her eyes met mine and I was immediately drawn into her gaze. The irises were a startling shade of violet, and there almost seemed to be swirling mists in their depths, like there were hidden secrets in this woman that cried out to be explored.

I blinked a few times, dispelling the sense of mystery.

She smiled in a tentative manner, as if unsure of my response. "You're in Magnik's castle. Our castle," the woman said. Her voice was hesitant, apologetic.

Our castle?

"Who are you, his henchman?" I snapped. "No offense, but you're not exactly threatening."

That statement was only half-true. The woman was tiny—definitely a lot smaller than me—but those eyes hinted at an untold amount of power.

"I'm Marienne." Her voice was soft. She didn't seem perturbed by my sharp tone. "I'm King Magnik's wife."

Huh.

For some reason, I hadn't expected that. Magnik was a monster, and this woman—Marienne—did not fit with my idea of a monster's wife.

"Has he sent you here to get information?" I guessed. "Because I don't know *anything*. A few days ago, I didn't even know there were such things as dragons! And even if I did, I wouldn't tell you. You're wasting your time."

I crossed my arms, turning to face the wall.

"Magnik doesn't know I'm here." Marienne's voice was almost a whisper, and I detected a hint of fear in her tone.

I blinked. Despite myself, I inclined my head toward her, curious. "Seriously? Won't the guards tell him you stopped by?"

A wry smile ghosted across her face. "They didn't exactly notice me come in."

She held out her arm, and I watched as the air rippled around her fingers. Her outstretched limb grew fainter, fading until it became indistinguishable from the stone wall behind her.

"Whoa," I breathed, turning back properly to face her. "You're like a chameleon."

She laughed. The sound was light; it sparkled like silver bells. I thought how lovely it would be to hear such a sound on a regular basis, but instinct told me she didn't laugh often. "Let's just say I'm the master of hide and seek," she said.

No shit.

"Are you a witch?"

"The correct term is a sorceress." She fiddled with the ends of her hair. "Some of us are born with unusual abilities. My powers were the reason Magnik took me for his bride."

She looked downcast, and I didn't blame her. I couldn't imagine being married to someone like Magnik.

I felt a flash of pity for Marienne. Clearly, King Magnik was not the man of her dreams.

Still, what do I know?

"Aren't you his..." I fumbled. "Soulmate, or what-have-you?"

She flushed. "No. Not every monarch accepts his soulmate." Her voice dropped again into a whisper, even though we were completely alone. "Magnik bought me from my family because he craves power above all else. Total dominion, over his people and all the other kingdoms. To him, I am an instrument—I can give him these things, if I choose to."

"Do you want to?"

As soon as the question left my lips, I knew the answer. This was not an evil queen standing in front of me. Marienne was a victim, just as much as I currently was, sitting imprisoned in this dungeon.

She sighed, a deep, fractured sound that tore out of the very depths of her body.

"No." Crystalline tears welled up in those otherworldly eyes, making them almost luminescent. She blinked them back as if determined not to lose control of her emotions. "When I was a child, I hoped to be... more. I dreamed of marrying a man who loved me for *me*, not for my magic. I have never wanted to hurt anyone. The things Magnik wants, the things he has planned... they are wrong. I never wanted any of this. My parents sold me to him and forced me to be his queen."

She wiped her cheeks and shook her head fiercely.

My mind drifted back to my argument with Stavrok.

It could have only been a few hours ago, but it felt like a distant memory. I frowned. "I think I know how you feel. Kind of. I'm not really here by choice, either. This is all brand new to me. Stavrok just found me and carried me off." I snorted. "He's not exactly an expert on the human world. God only knows how he found me."

Marienne didn't reply. Instead, she bit her bottom lip.

I tilted my head. "What?"

"I showed him the way to you." She glanced away from me. "He... he was hurting, Lucy. He has been alone for years, waiting for his soulmate. I offered to help him look, and my vision led him straight to you."

Shock ran through me. Destiny, fate... these weren't things I'd held much faith in before. Maybe I'd been wrong to judge them so harshly.

"Are you telling me that it's true?" I croaked. "I *am* Stavrok's soulmate?"

She gave me a puzzled frown. "Yes, of course. I'm surprised you even have to ask. The fates have crafted you for each other. You're a perfect match."

I thought about fate. I pictured a golden thread, weaving through my life, connecting me to everyone I met. Stavrok, Cass... and now Marienne, seeing me in her vision, and us meeting again like this.

Marienne reached out a hand toward me, then dropped it again. Sadness filled her expression. "If my actions have caused you any pain, I am truly sorry, Lucy."

"It's not your fault," I said quickly, automatically, before I realized it was true. "You were trying to help."

"I was." She held out a hand again, palm upwards. "May I?"

When I nodded, I felt something pass over me, like a shadow.

"Is that your magic, Marienne?"

"It is. Don't be afraid."

I smiled at her. "I'm not." Her magic was feather-light and soft to the touch. It felt... comforting, more than anything.

Still, I hesitated before finally placing my palm in hers. Her eyes slid closed, and she was silent for a long moment.

I felt her going through my mind, turning over the chapters of my life like they were pages in a book. There were glimpses of my childhood, the house I grew up in, the children I had cared for.

There were one or two doors that I didn't want her to open. I turned her away, sharp, before she could peek into *those*.

Nope. Stay out!

She huffed a laugh, startled, and dropped my hand. When she opened her eyes and met my gaze, she grinned.

"You have a little natural magical ability yourself, Lucy. You protected your secrets from me without even thinking about it."

I had magic? If I thought about *that* for too long, my head would explode. "What did you find out? Anything interesting?"

Her eyebrows drew together. "Oh yes." She moved forward, as if to provide a hug, then clearly thought better of it. Instead, she gently patted my arm. "Lucy, you're pregnant."

I went cold. "What?"

She didn't say anything else. She didn't have to. As much as I wanted to protest, I knew, somewhere deep in my core, that she was right.

I had known for a while. I just hadn't been able to accept it. It was way too soon for any symptoms, and Stavrok and I had only slept together twice...

I groaned. *Stavrok.*

This was what he'd wanted, all along.

To my surprise, I felt a pang of *something* when I thought about him.

I miss him.

This was all wrong. We should have found out this information together. I would have broken the news quietly, in bed, or over the breakfast table. It would have been our little secret, a private joy we could have shared before we told the rest of the kingdom.

But he was God-only-knew where, and I was here.

Oh, shit.

"You realize that, once Magnik discovers your pregnancy, your value to him will only increase," Marienne said. She looked as panicked as I felt.

"An unwed soulmate is one thing, but the mother of Stavrok's heir? That's quite another."

I grabbed at her hand, still resting on my arm, and clasped it tightly.

"Please, I'm begging you. I know I'm asking for a lot here. And I know you have no reason to do me any favors, but from one woman to another." I took a deep, shaky gulp of air. "Please don't tell him."

"Of course, I won't." Her gaze was solemn. "I won't speak of it, Lucy. I promise."

I let out a breath I didn't even know I'd beenholding, and released her hand. "Thank you, Marienne."

"Call me Mari, please." She glanced at the door, as if she was worried her husband might burst in at any moment. "I'll do my best to protect you. But, aside from my magic, I have no real power here."

I thought about Stavrok. His strength, his fury. The way he looked at me, like he would do anything to keep me safe.

I thought about the child or children that I carried inside me. His children.

"I appreciate your kindness, Mari." I hoped her magic, along with my soulmate bond with Stavrok, would be enough to protect me and the baby. "Stavrok will be here soon to rescue me, and then all will be well once again."

I had to believe that, because the alternative was not an option.

CHAPTER

EIGHTEEN

Stavrok

In my dragon form, I glided through the air, zeroing in on my destination. There was no time to waste. Messages delivered to the other kingdoms had ensured that they would stay far away from this fight.

They had agreed, some more warily than others, but it wasn't their feud. My own guards were on standby and would head this way the moment I sent the signal. But I hoped I wouldn't have to.

This was personal. Between Magnik and me.

The peace that had protected us all for so long now hung in the balance, fragile as a gossamer thread. It was my duty to settle this. The lives of my people, of our whole world, hung in the balance.

Magnik's castle sat lower than mine. It was nestled into the black mountainside like a forbidden secret. It was small, as far as dragon castles went.

The front of the structure hid an elaborate sprawl of tunnels and caves that wound deep within the mountain, making it almost impossible to attack through traditional means.

The castle itself was just a façade, a deception. Just like Magnik himself.

I let the air currents carry me closer, barely moving my wings. I hoped the cloud cover would serve to conceal my approach, but I knew that every eye in that castle would be trained toward the sky.

Magnik would be waiting for me.

Well, I was coming for him.

My hackles were up. Why bother hiding anymore?

I let out a roar of displeasure that echoed around the rocky hilltops. A tongue of scalding flame shot from my mouth and illuminated the heavens like a lightning bolt.

If they didn't know I was here before, they certainly did now.

I wasn't some common thief, creeping into enemy territory under the cover of darkness. I was King Stavrok of Bravdok, son of Tyton and Eris.

I was coming to take back what had been stolen from me. Fire would rain down from the sky on whoever got in my way.

I swept into a low dive. My wings stretched wide, cutting through the air with ease. I cast a dark shadow over the ground as I flew.

I sent a silent prayer out into the swirling storm, hoping against hope that Lucy might somehow hear me.

Wherever you are, love, I'm coming for you.

I let out another billowing fireball, sweeping in a wide arc as I neared the castle's main watchtower.

Tiny figures stood on the parapets, aiming large crossbows into the sky.

Directly at me.

I roared, and my wings arched backwards.

I was close enough to watch as their eyes widened with fear.

They loosed their arrows, striking against my chest, snagging against my wings.

In human form, they would have killed me a hundred times over.

As a dragon? The arrows were as harmless as flies.

I shook myself, dislodging the arrows from my leathery wings. The thick scales that protected my chest smoothed back into place, and I continued my advance, unperturbed.

It would take far more than ordinary crossbow bolts to slow me down.

I was more than a dragon shifter. The blood that ran through my veins was the blood of a king. I was stronger than most others of my kind, and much harder to kill.

One of the archers dropped his weapon, fleeing from his post. The other cowered in the corner as I lit up the stone wall.

I barely spared him a glance. He wasn't my concern, after all.

I couldn't enter the castle in my dragon form. I was too large, too cumbersome. So, I landed on the wall and with difficulty, quieted the seething fire of rage in the pit of my stomach. I felt myself shrink down, my limbs reforming themselves, my vision changing.

Once in human form, I grabbed the abandoned crossbow and pointed it at the terrified archer.

"Where is she?" I snapped.

The archer pointed one trembling finger toward a low doorway set into the wall of the tower.

"That way, sire."

I ignored the numbness that settled through my bare limbs with the cold air and shouldered my crossbow. I half-turned in the direction he indicated before a thought occurred to me.

I was storming into the heart of enemy territory. It might be better if I weren't naked into the bargain.

"Let's make a trade," I said. "Your life for your trousers."

The archer didn't need to be told twice.

After I dressed, I strode through the castle doors, into the unknown.

MAGNIK'S CASTLE was chillier than the one I called home.

The walls were bare and dark. The only light came from the torches that burned at intervals in ornate iron cages.

I shivered.

Moving quietly, keeping my head low and my senses on high alert, I couldn't help but feel uneasy.

It had all been too simple. The lack of defenses, the empty hallway.

It was as if Magnik wanted me here.

Like I was playing right into his hands.

I shook off the prickle on the back of my neck and kept moving. I had no choice, after all.

I have to find Lucy.

Through my carelessness, I had broken the one promise I had sworn to her I would uphold. I had allowed her to fall into danger.

A cluster of voices emanated from the end of the corridor.

Finally.

As stealthily as possible, I slid the crossbow into position.

I would have preferred the familiar weight of a sword in my hands, but I was nothing if not adaptable.

It struck me again how impulsive I was being. My plan of attack was hasty, instinctive, fuelled by nothing more than the drive to rescue my mate.

Which, of course, was exactly what Magnik had anticipated.

My fingers tightened around the crossbow as I rounded the corner.

I took the guards by surprise. The nearest one didn't have time to draw his sword before I kicked him squarely in the chest and sent him flying into the opposite wall.

I whirled around, bringing the barrel of the crossbow up hard against the sword that swung down on me. I grunted with the force of the blow and twisted, lodging the sword in place and sending its owner staggering backwards without his weapon.

The third had taken advantage of my distraction; I hissed as the edge of a blade slashed into my arm.

I slid sideways. His sword cut through air and he staggered, off balance.

I pulled the sword free from the crossbow and turned it in my palm, testing the heft. Adrenaline coursed through me.

I may be far from home, in mortal danger, but I was in my element here.

And now I was properly armed.

The clang of metal against metal echoed off the stone walls as I faced down the two guards.

Their companion lay motionless on the ground, stunned by the force of my blow.

Even though the fight was two against one, I sensed my opponents growing tired. Their movements were clumsy, and I pressed my advantage, driving them further and further down the corridor.

Was this the first real fight they'd ever been in?

I wheeled around and slammed the hilt of my sword against the head of one of the men. He went down easily.

The last of the men fought with more determination than his friends, his face twisted into an ugly sneer.

A new thought occurred to me.

These men could have been the ones to infiltrate my castle. The ones who hurt Cass, the ones who snatched Lucy away…

I let out an inhuman snarl and pushed forward.

He staggered back, and I twisted my blade upwards, sending his weapon flying to the ground with a clatter.

I pressed the edge of my sword up against his neck, a savage thrill running through me at the way his eyes widened.

"Enough of this," I said. "Where is she?"

"The throne room."

I pushed the blade higher and watched his face grow paler.

"Ah! Please, it is no trick, Your Majesty. The king has your mate close by him, at the heart of the palace."

I narrowed my eyes. My mind raced; through vague memories of state dinners I had attended as a child, I knew that the throne room had to be somewhere nearby.

I moved as if to sheath my sword, and he scuttled away from me. I swung a glancing blow into the side of his head, and he slumped over, unconscious.

As I prowled through the castle, I stuck close to the shadows, pressing myself into alcoves and crevices as I neared my destination.

The voices ahead were growing louder. The corridor widened out, intricate marble stonework beneath my bare feet.

Magnik's family line was as ancient as my own. It pained me that he had thrown his noble heritage into the dirt by what he had done.

Outside the wide double doors leading to the throne room, I halted. Beyond the doors was only silence.

I pressed my hand against the handle. I could hear nothing but low murmuring from the other side of the doors. I had the element of surprise, but that would only last for a few seconds. I had to make that time count.

So far, the guards had been easy enough to handle.

Too easy...

I couldn't shake the sense that the battle hadn't yet started.

Whatever faced me on the other side of these doors, was when the real fight would begin.

If he's harmed her in any way, I'll kill him where he stands.

With a huff, I shouldered through the entranceway, and entered the cavernous throne room.

It was just as vast as I remembered. The walls stretched so high that the ceiling was barely visible. Black polished marble cast dark reflections underfoot, and the sparse décor was ornate, cold, and uncomfortable.

A raised platform held two thrones that were framed by carved columns.

Queen Marienne sat on one of the thrones, but she no longer looked like herself. One of her eyes was swollen shut, and that whole side of her face was black and purple with bruising. Instead of sitting straight and regal, she hunched over to one side. She barely seemed strong enough to hold herself upright at all.

Had Magnik beaten her? Was this new or something she'd endured from him many times? Pity filled me for the queen, but I had no time to dwell on that.

My gaze swept across the other throne, which was empty, and landed on Magnik. He stood in the center of the platform in front of another figure, his bulk hiding the person from my view. I could see the person had been tied to one of the dark columns rising up from the platform.

As Magnik bent close to his prisoner, I spotted a familiar head of blonde hair, and my pulse began to race. The bastard had Lucy in restraints.

He will pay dearly for this.

His back straightened, and slowly he turned. He must have sensed my presence.

"Stavrok." Magnik's voice echoed through the empty space with a note of satisfaction, and my skin prickled. "We were wondering when you would show up. I was beginning to worry you weren't coming."

Behind him, Lucy's eyes widened at the sight of me.

White cloth had been tied over her mouth, and my icy rage mounted.

There was nothing Magnik could do to contain her temper, though. It was plain to see, even from this distance. Lucy's eyes were bright and wild, and her cheeks were flushed with fury. She didn't wear the whole damsel-in-distress thing well. Perhaps they had expected a human to remain silent and compliant.

I could have told them otherwise. She twisted and turned against restraints that would never budge, but she didn't give up.

Pride sparked in my chest.

She wasn't one to go down without a fight, apparently. She may have been a human, surrounded by shapeshifters more powerful than she would ever be, but the courage in her eyes made my heart skip.

We were more alike than she knew.

"These are the actions of a coward, not a king," I snarled, turning my attention to Magnik. "Lucy has no part in this. Let her go."

Magnik spread his hands wide, moving away from her and descending the steps of the platform with unhurried ease.

"I gave you my terms, Stavrok. It's a fair trade. I get my lands, you get your mate back, safe and sound. Everyone's happy."

I fought the rage that simmered inside me, threatening to spill out and consume them all.

Up on the platform, a small movement caught my eye. Marienne?

She had slumped further in her seat, as if about to topple to the floor. But her gaze was fixed on me. I almost heard her voice in my head. *Hold onto your rage. Use it. But don't lose control.*

I blinked, and turned back to Magnik as he spoke.

"I have been waiting for this a long time, Stavrok. You've grown too comfortable, content to squander your riches. They lie buried in the earth, crumbling away."

I gave a growl. "My duty is to protect my own."

My gaze darted to Lucy. She had grown still in her confines; clearly, she was hanging on every word.

"Meanwhile," I said, "you hide away in your inner sanctum and let your men fight on your behalf! You're not fit to hold this kingdom."

"I tried to reason with you." Magnik strode close, his face twisting into an ugly scowl. "Year after year, I offered you trade agreements, business deals. You wouldn't take anything I offered you! So, now I have taken something of *yours.*"

He swept out a hand, indicating Lucy.

I said nothing. Anger rooted me to the spot. I focused on drawing long, measured breaths, in and out. *Don't lose control.*

But if he touches her...

I would tear down every wall in this godforsaken place and burn the lot. The hot fire of rage flooded through me, startling in its intensity. It burned brighter, building and building, until I could barely see the man standing in front of me.

"You've left me no choice, Stavrok." Magnik inclined his head, regarding me with narrowed eyes.

When I opened my mouth, it was the dragon within me who framed the words on my lips.

"Neither have you. King Magnik, I challenge you in combat. No armies to protect you. No more of your men will fall at my hand." I straightened and swung my sword in a circle through the air, the metal blade flashing in the flickering torchlight. "Just you against me."

Magnik's expression flickered as he absorbed my words.

I held firm. My gaze was sure and steady, but already I could feel adrenaline thrumming through my veins.

I spared a thought for my parents. I knew in the depths of my heart that it was *their* legacy I was protecting. For the first time since I took the throne, I saw the path ahead of me with perfect clarity.

And Lucy...

I had put her in grave peril.

She had been right, all along. I had been too blind and selfish to see it before. This wasn't her world, and she would never be safe here. It had been madness to ask her to stay.

I couldn't dwell on my pending heartbreak. I had to focus on the task at hand.

For the first time in a hundred years, a dragon king in this land of Fire and Ice had drawn his sword against another.

Magnik stepped forward. His eyes were steely, and when he spoke his voice was cold.

"Very well. I accept your challenge."

CHAPTER
NINETEEN

Lucy

I continued to struggle against the bonds that held me tight against the marble column, listing every curse I knew until they became a soothing, rhythmic chant in the back of my mind.

Fighting the bindings was pointless, but I couldn't just wait here and do nothing while Stavrok threw himself into this fight.

This wasn't some courtyard sparring match. There was an odd glitter in Magnik's eye, and something about the way he tilted his head as he and Stavrok circled each other made my blood run cold.

Nobody had to tell me; I knew the truth.

He won't stop fighting. Not until Stavrok is dead.

A flash of terror passed through me when I pictured Stavrok's lifeless body lying on the marble floor.

I feared for my own life too, held at the mercy of such a tyrant. But that fear was soon eclipsed by the realization that had been haunting me ever since I'd found out I held Stavrok's heirs inside me.

If I were to live, I would surely be kept as a prisoner here. And, sooner or later, I would begin to show...

Magnik will never allow Stavrok's bloodline to survive.

I narrowed my eyes and focused on drawing deep, cleansing breaths. From my position, I had a clear view of both kings as they circled each other, swords drawn.

This is insane. This is totally insane...

I chanced a glance at Marienne, whose throne lay a few feet to my left. I could only see the outline of her profile, but she was hunched over and from the looks of her, badly hurt.

What had that bastard done to her? Had he caught her visiting me in the dungeon? Delivering food, and a hint of kindness?

I wished I could somehow communicate with her. I was certain that she didn't support her husband's plan to kill Stavrok.

More than that, I knew, deep down, that she was just as afraid of him as I was.

At the sound of metal crashing against metal, my gaze snapped back to the duel at the center of the throne room.

The two men had moved closer to the platform, allowing me to get a good look at Stavrok. His chest glistened with effort as he drove Magnik back into the far corner, sword swinging through the air. There was a fresh cut on his arm, and he was grunting with exertion.

His words from earlier came back to me.

No more of your men will fall at my hand.

It seemed that Magnik had taken the coward's route, hiding in the shadows while his guardsmen took on Stavrok.

He's exhausted already.

Despite his injuries, Stavrok was clearly the better fighter. He stayed on the attack, forcing Magnik to parry a volley of savage blows in quick succession.

Frustrated, I bit down on the cloth that gagged me and craned my neck back, trying to work the material free against the column.

I was powerless to help, but if I was going to die, I didn't want to be without my voice.

I wouldn't give Magnik the satisfaction of killing me in silence.

I huffed with the effort of my task, and my heart thrummed in my chest when someone gave a loud shout of pain and fury.

The harsh panting of the two kings filled the hall.

Magnik toppled to his knees like a puppet whose strings had been cut. His sword clattered to the floor beside him; he clutched his right arm against his body, holding it while dark crimson seeped through his sleeve.

Stavrok staggered backwards. He kicked the sword away from Magnik and wiped a hand over his mouth.

Over Magnik's kneeling form, he caught my gaze.

Up until this moment, the dragon warrior was all I had seen. He was the one who had come to rescue me. Aggressive, domineering, driven by fury and power, the beast lit him up from within with unearthly force.

But for a single heart-wrenching moment, all I could see was the man beneath. Stavrok.

He held the sword high, poised to strike in cold blood. One blow, that was all it would take. His eyes were wide, filled with adrenaline and something else I couldn't decipher.

Those icy blue eyes, that only a few days ago had been so mysterious.

They pierced through me, and I froze to the spot. Stavrok seemed unsure, watching my face like he was transfixed.

Magnik reached for something strapped to his calf, and I caught the flash of a silver dagger as he slid it into his hand.

With a sharp jerk of my head, the cloth tied around my mouth loosened, and I managed to shimmy it down to my neck.

Magnik, still on his knees, lunged forward like a snake.

I screamed, "Look out!"

Stavrok whirled backwards. The dagger sliced through thin air, half a second too late.

Magnik hissed with anger.

"A cheap trick," Stavrok spat. "I should have known you would resort to low tactics, Magnik. You won't fool me again."

Magnik scrambled to his feet. He sliced upwards with the dagger, twisting the hilt of Stavrok's blade with his own.

"You gave me the chance to strike. You had the chance to kill me, but you didn't." His face twisted, and a taunting smile slid across his face. "You're weak. *Soft.* Just like your parents. What exactly happened to them, again?"

Stavrok gave a snarl and his attack intensified, the speed of his thrusts increasing. Magnik stumbled a little against the brute force of his onslaught. Both men were struggling to gain the upper hand. The air felt thick and heavy; it crackled with tension. I wanted to scream out again, do something to help, but I didn't want to distract Stavrok.

"How dare you?" Stavrok roared. His eyes were molten. I could feel his rage even from this distance; it burned like a brazier. "You're not worthy to hold this kingdom. You are no king!"

"Stand aside, Stavrok." Magnik's face split into a leering grin. His skin was pale and clammy from the fight, and his hair fell lankly across his face. I shuddered as his eyes darted to me momentarily. "I'll let you live. You can go free, walk out the door and find a new life, far from here. I'm sure there are other maidens who would have you. *Worthy* ones. Dragon-born, proud and strong."

His grin shifted until he was baring his teeth.

"I'll keep the human. She will bring me some amusement." His eyes crept over me again, taking in my body, lingering in a way that made my skin crawl. "For a night or two, at least."

Stavrok swung at Magnik's weapon, grunting with the effort. Repeatedly, he beat down on the arrogant king. There was a heat in the room, a fire in his eyes. His dragon was close to the surface. I could feel it.

Magnik's silver dagger was dislodged from his hand and went flying through the air, landing with a *clink* against the marble floor. I stared, amazed, as it came to rest just below my feet.

Then, with a final, earth-shaking growl, Stavrok raised his sword and drove it through Magnik's heart.

~

Stavrok

The moment Magnik's body hit the floor, Marienne stumbled off her throne. She didn't look grief-stricken, but *amazed*, like she couldn't quite believe what had just happened.

I raised my sword again, turning to face her, but the gesture was half-hearted.

The truth was, I had no idea what she was capable of or if she was truly friend or foe.

For all I knew, she was about to kill me right now, with nothing more than a magical incantation or a flicker of her fingers.

Slowly, her hands came up. She held them out in front of her in a gesture of peace, her one good eye fixed on me, her face drawn.

"Stavrok... please. This wasn't my doing." Her good eye swirled with color, blue mingling with deep purple and almost matching the bruises on her face. "You have to believe me. I never wanted any part of this. My husband—"

"Was an evil man." I found my voice at last.

Magnik's body lay between us where he'd fallen. Around him, scorch marks were burned into the marble, forming a crater.

The death of a dragon king was a rare event indeed. The marks proved what I already knew: his fire had gone out for good.

"He was. Truly, an evil man. One who has kept me as a slave and a prisoner for years." Marienne inclined her head. "Thank you for freeing me. At last. Your mate, she—"

"Would quite like to be untied now, thank you very much," Lucy called out.

My gaze snapped to Lucy, who was struggling against her restraints. I hurried over to her and broke the ties one by one.

She stretched, rotating her shoulders and groaning. "God, of course you can break them with your *bare hands*, Stavrok."

She rolled her eyes, and my heart swelled.

"Lucy," I said simply.

I reached out. I wanted to pull her close to me, kiss her deeply. We had been separated for what felt like an eternity. Her mere presence was intoxicating. I closed my eyes, steadying myself against the pulse of want that surged through me.

I'd never believed people when they'd said my father died of a broken heart the day my mother died. It didn't seem possible that a man as strong as he, could die so easily, so quickly.

But today, for the first time, I realized that I would not want to live without Lucy. And if such a love grew through the years, then I finally understood how my father could give up on life once his mate died.

I settled for running my hands over her arms, and then cupping her face. "Are you hurt? Did he—"

"Hey, hey!" Her hands found mine, and she wound our fingers together. "Stavrok, I'm fine. I'm absolutely fine. You, on the other hand, are *hurt.*"

I spared a glance down at the deep gash that cut into my shoulder. "Never mind that now."

She shook her head at me.

"I thought you worked in a day-care center, not a hospital." I sighed, allowing her to take my arm and wrap the cloth gag around the wound, securing it over my shoulder.

She frowned at the makeshift bandage, smoothing it several times before stepping back, satisfied. "I can play nurse with the best of them."

My eyes searched her face for a heated moment.

"I bet you can."

Somewhere behind us, Marienne coughed.

Right. There's unfinished business to attend to, here.

I placed a hand on Lucy's shoulder and turned to regard the sorceress.

She wrapped her arms around her middle and glanced at Magnik, whose remains lay at her feet.

"What happens now?" Her eyes dipped, and her voice filled with regret. "I can't tell you how sorry I am for all this."

I struggled with my warring impulses. On the one hand, this woman was a sorceress and possibly dangerous. Whether or not it was on purpose, she had started the chain of events that led to Lucy's capture and imprisonment.

On the other hand... I closed my eyes.

If it hadn't been for her, I never would have known Lucy existed.

"Stavrok..." Lucy laid a hand on my arm, and I turned into her body like a sapling toward the sun. "She helped me. She protected me from Magnik, as much as she could. And look what he did to her in return. I believe her."

I nodded. I couldn't understand what Marienne had gone through living with Magnik for the last ten years, but if she'd helped Lucy in her hour of need, then the sorceress had earned my mercy.

"Very well." I surveyed Marienne, the once beautiful queen, who appeared right now to be broken. "There remains the small matter of choosing a new king. You have no heirs, my lady."

There was no way of putting it delicately. Magnik's bloodline stopped with him.

Some might call that a mercy.

"No," Marienne said. "Magic has given me many things, but no child."

As though to prove her point, she lifted her hands and magic began to swirl around her face and torso.

She straightened up, and her face began to heal right in front of our eyes. The bruising disappeared first, then her eye opened, and finally she was her usual self again.

"If you could do that by yourself, why didn't you do it before?" Lucy demanded, reaching out to touch Marienne's freshly healed face.

A tremble of a smile lifted Marienne's lips. "He told me after the beating that if I took away any of my own pain and suffering, he would do the same to you, Lucy. Or worse." She shuddered. "He was very cruel."

Fresh anger rolled through me at her words. "He was no king." I growled, wishing I could kill the bastard again.

"Marienne, you know that only one of royal blood may anoint a dragon king," I said, primarily for Lucy's benefit. I could tell that she was listening closely to every word. "I will be in touch. We must find a new king for these lands. One worthy of the name, this time."

Marienne's eyes flickered. She bit her lip, her brows drawing together.

"What is it?" I asked.

"There was a boy. An illegitimate half-brother. Magnik told me of him, and a few years ago I secretly sought him out. He lives in the village." Her voice grew soft, dropping to a whisper, even though Lucy and I were the only people in the room. "His mother was sent away by Magnik's father when she was pregnant. I don't know much beyond that."

I processed the information and gave a final nod to her. She returned the nod, watching me with careful eyes.

Lucy murmured a farewell as we swept out of the throne room. Their eyes met with a friendliness that made me wonder what had passed between them while Lucy had been a prisoner here.

"Let's get out of here," I said, sliding my arm around her waist and squeezing. I craved her warmth, her proximity. "Time to return home."

"I don't know where the front entrance is." Lucy looked from left to right as we found ourselves at the end of a corridor. "I didn't exactly get the grand tour, I'm afraid."

I hoped that one day we would return to this castle as honored guests. I wanted to show Lucy that my world wasn't all darkness and bloodlust. There was laughter to be found here too, and friendship.

If all goes to plan, we shall be back.

"We're not leaving by the front door," I said, drawing away from her to pull open the door that led out onto a narrow rooftop.

"We're not?" Lucy wrapped her arms around herself, shivering from the rush of cold air. She had to shout to be heard over the howling wind. "Then how are... *oh.*"

I strode a few paces away from her and shook out my limbs. Deep within my chest, the dragon unfurled its wings. It was ready to go, fired from the fight and the joy of reuniting with Lucy.

My claws emerged. My scales rippled, smooth and dark, and my wings beat the air, making the snowdrifts swirl. Lucy tipped back her head and laughed, and in my mind's eye I saw the night we met.

The first time she had seen my dragon.

We had been strangers to each other, then. She had been nothing but terrified.

Now, there was a warmth in her face. Genuine affection in her eyes.

I didn't allow myself to believe it could be anything more than that.

If you really love her, you will let her go.

Without prompting, she clambered onto my back, throwing her arms around my neck, apparently having forgotten all about the cold.

Together, we took off into the snow-filled sky.

TWENTY

Lucy

After our exhilarating ride home, Stavrok swept me into the entrance hall, cradled in his arms, and demanded a warm cloak, which was duly provided. The heavy garment lay across my shoulders as I sat on a large chair in the hallway.

Stavrok paced up and down the marble floors. It was unsettling to watch, to say the least.

His eyes flashed, and he kept glancing back at me, over and over, like he was certain I would disappear right in front of him.

I wanted him to stop pacing the hallway. It was making me nervous. The longer the silence stretched out, the less I certain I became.

There was so much I wanted to say, but for the first time, I wasn't sure where we stood.

He had been all fire and rage from the moment he'd stepped into the throne room, but his behavior toward me had been different, even once he'd defeated Magnik.

I couldn't shake the feeling that he was holding me at arm's length, somehow.

He's just killed a rival king, and you're wondering why he hasn't taken you to bed already? Jeez, Lucy.

My face heated, and I went back to flicking stray snowflakes from my hair.

As much as the pacing annoyed me, I felt sure that it was the only thing keeping him from shifting into his dragon form and wreaking havoc.

"You could have been hurt, Lucy," he burst out, dragging his hands over his face.

I gaped, at a loss. I had never seen him like this. The stoicism that I'd come to expect from him had vanished. He looked terrified.

"You could have been killed," he said, "and it would have been my fault."

I reached out and put a hand on his arm. The motion stilled him. I pitched my voice so that it came out soft and soothing.

"I'm fine, Stavrok." I cupped his cheek and turned his face, looking deep into those mesmerizing eyes. "Look at me. You saved me."

After the darkness of Magnik's realm, this castle felt somehow lighter and airier than before. The light shafted through the windows, shading Stavrok's face with gold. I felt warmed just by being near him.

Stavrok shook his head even as he drew me closer. He slid one hand up my back, burying it in my hair.

"I'd rather be apart from you, if it would keep you safe," he murmured, dropping a kiss onto my forehead. "The human world carries far less dangers. It would better for you to return there, and be safe, than to stay here and risk your life in such a way again."

I gasped at his rejection. He wanted me to go home? No!

"You want me to leave?" I whispered, struggling to say the words through the pain of my heart breaking in my chest.

There was nothing for me back there. My future lay right here.

"Of course not." His voice rumbled through my chest, and I leaned into his solid frame with a sigh. "It would be the greatest pain imaginable to let you out of my sight. But I know now how much you mean to me. How precious you are. I can't risk you like that again, Lucy."

My heart skipped.

"Oh," was all I managed to say.

He's willing to let me go back.

I should be happy.

Why aren't I?

A couple of days ago, the prospect of freedom would have filled me with joy. Now, all I felt was a sharp ache at the thought of leaving this place.

"I'm so sorry for all the distress that I've caused you, my love." He stroked my cheek, cupping my chin with his broad hand. "More than I can say."

I clasped his hand with both of mine and brought it up to my mouth, pressing a kiss to his palm. His eyes widened, but he didn't pull away.

"I'm not." My voice was bold and steady. Suddenly, I knew exactly what I wanted to say. "Once upon a time, I would've chosen the safer option. But I had a lot of time to think when I was locked up in that dungeon."

I took a deep, shuddering breath. "Being here has made me realize what love is, Stavrok. What loyalty is. I don't want to stay because some magic vision says so. I want to stay because we belong together. My life is here, now. I belong by your side, as your queen."

"You... *want* to stay?"

"I do."

He eyed me for several heart-stopping moments, before his face broke into the sunniest grin I had ever seen. I grinned back, buoyed up by his joy.

"In the castle? In this land?"

"Yes!"

Before I knew what was happening, he had me in a tight bearhug. My feet lifted off the floor, and I giggled, pressing my face into his chest.

"It's probably for the best that I stay here, anyway," I added when he set me down. My grin softened into a loving smile, and I pressed a hand to my belly.

His gaze turned quizzical.

"I don't think human doctors know that much about shapeshifter babies," I said.

He looked at me, stunned, before he let out a sharp, delighted burst of laughter. "You're…"

"I am." I grabbed one of his hands, putting it on my stomach.

There was nothing to feel, not yet, but the warmth of his hand felt good against my skin. I imagined the sensations that would follow in the coming months; the tiny, growing life I held inside of me.

When he finally spoke, his voice was soft and wondering. "You are incredible."

"I know," I replied cheekily. "You're not so bad yourself."

"I suppose I have no choice but to keep you by my side now." He swept me in, kissing me hard until we both pulled back, breathless.

"How terrible for me," I said, running my hands over his arms and giggling. "However shall I cope?"

Stavrok's gaze turned serious. "Come with me."

Not like I had a choice, but I held tight to his neck as he swept me up into his arms and charged down the hall and into his bedroom.

He placed me on the bed and went straight for the dresser near the door. He opened a drawer, took something out, then turned to me with a bashful smile.

He came straight back and reached out for my hand.

"Lucy." He knelt gracefully in front of me.

My heart started hammering. If I hadn't already been flushed from his kiss, I was certain I would be glowing red.

"I have to ask. Officially, that is. Will you stay here, with me? Will you be my queen, now and always?"

"What about Daphne?" I whispered. He'd said she lied, but the pain of that moment still sat badly within me.

He growled. "How would you like her punished for lying to you so maliciously?"

I swallowed hard. I didn't want her punished… I wanted her, gone. "Um. Can we move her? I don't really want her in the castle anymore."

He nodded. "Done. She will be reassigned to a job at the other end of the village. You will never see her in our home, again."

I took a breath and let it out slowly. That was better.

I smiled this time. "Then... my answer is," I put my hands on either side of his face, drawing him up until his lips met mine. "I will. Of course."

His eyes glowed adoringly before they heated, darkened. He straightened fully before hitching me up like I weighed nothing at all.

I squealed.

Damn, I'm never going to get used to that.

I laughed freely as I wrapped my legs around his waist, uncaring of the fact that the door to the hallway was still open.

I had missed him. I *wanted* him.

I whispered a formless, breathy plea into his ear, and he pressed his hot mouth into my neck, growling when I gave a full body shudder. I could feel his hardness pressing into my core. Soon, there would be nothing between us. I wanted to feel all of him against me. Every inch of his powerful form.

My king, I thought, before he lay me down on the bed.

All mine.

EPILOGUE

Stavrok

"We're going to be late," I called through the open door of our bedchamber. "I can make excuses if you would rather stay, my love."

Lucy bobbed up into the doorway, face flushed with exertion. My impatience melted away at the sight of my beautiful wife, and I swept into the room behind her, wrapping my arms around her shoulders.

"Help me with my dress?" She looked over her shoulder, and I obliged, buttoning each of the tiny buttons from her waist to her neckline. Some maid or other would surely have to struggle with *those* later.

I peered over her shoulder at the finely carved trio of cribs that clustered around the wide, arched window, positioned to catch the best of the sunlight.

Or rather, I peered at what lay inside them.

Our babies nestled in their soft blankets. The girls, Jessa and Vanya, were fast asleep.

My son, Anselm, blinked up at me. His sleepy eyes were fringed with soft, downy lashes. They were wide, and the same guileless shade of blue as his mother's.

I leaned down to press a kiss onto the fluffy head of hair before drawing away reluctantly, smiling when he gave a gurgle.

Our brood was strong and healthy. Human and dragon blood flowed through their veins, and they were no weaker for it.

They had the fair coloring of their mother, but already they had a glimmer in their eyes, that tell-tale spark of light.

A light that told me, one day, they would be powerful shapeshifters.

I chanced a glance back at them before I drew my arm around my wife's waist and escorted her out of the room.

"They're in good hands," Lucy murmured, leaning up to press a palm against my cheek. I grimaced at the fact she could read me so easily, and she laughed. "Maddie will be with them the whole time!"

"I know, I know," I said, tugging at the formal collar of my jacket a little as we descended the wide central staircase. "I'm not worried."

She leveled me with a smirk. I could read the disbelief in her eyes.

"I'm picturing your dragon curled up around them like nest eggs," she joked. "Or a pile of golden treasure."

She had told me about some of the legends of our kind, fanciful stories that humans had been passing down to each other for generations. They amused me on the cold winter nights, when Lucy and I would sit beside a roaring fire and talk into the small hours.

"They *are* my treasures," I replied, simple and honest. "As are you, my Lucy."

She took my hand and squeezed it, before reaching up to straighten my crooked collar.

"I can't have you going to my first coronation looking so unkempt," she said, though her eyes were dancing. "Where's Cass, anyway? I thought she would be waiting for us."

As if summoned by the sound of her name, Cass skidded into view, buttoning her jacket up as she went. "I'm ready!"

"I wondered if you were joining us, cousin," Lucy said.

"What, and pass up the chance to witness the coronation of the bastard son? The mysterious King Bravadik? I wouldn't miss this for the world," Cass shot back with a grin.

She sounded a bit out of breath. I gave her a onceover, telegraphing my disapproval. "First my wife, now my cousin? Am I the only one who wants to be on time for this thing?"

Lucy and Cass shared a smirk.

Cass elbowed me in the ribs, none too gently. "*Definitely*, cousin."

"What do you think he's like, anyway?" Lucy leaned close, her fair head beside Cass's dark one. "I've heard rumors he didn't even know his true parentage. It must be a shock to the system, becoming a king when you're not expecting it. Maybe I should have a chat with him. I became a queen by surprise, after all."

"I've heard so many things, they can't possibly all be true," Cass replied.

"Maybe he'll be handsome." Lucy's eyes twinkled playfully. "How would you like a crown of your own, Cass?"

Cass scoffed and rolled her eyes, although a slight flush settled on her cheeks.

"I guess we'll have to wait and see." She clapped her hands together. "Now, let's get a move on. You're going to make us late, Stavrok!"

Ignoring my splutter of indignation, she slid her arm through Lucy's. They strode out of the front doors together into the bright sunshine, leaving me to trail in their wake.

A wide grin had lodged itself firmly onto my face, quite against my will. I couldn't shake it off all the way down the long, winding drive to the castle gates, where the carriages were waiting for us.

∾

2
FIRE AND ICE
A KING
FOR THE
SORCERESS
USA TODAY BESTSELLING AUTHOR
AMELIA SHAW

A KING FOR THE SORCERESS

CHAPTER
ONE

Erik

I knelt with my head bowed, every word the elder spoke placing the weight of the world on my shoulders.

"Bravadik Arman. Son of Sigmus, King of the Black Mountains. I anoint you and bestow upon you the kingdom and clan of your father. In your hands, I place responsibility, duty, and power. May this crown grow into a symbol of your strength. May you rise to be the leader your blood rite destines you to become."

I suppressed the shudder that passed through me. I'd dreaded this moment since the day my mother told me the name of my true sire. He had been the last person in the kingdom I expected. *The king.*

"Arise, King Bravadik," the elder said, startling me out of my reflections. I took a long deep breath before pushing to my feet and turning to face the room full of courtiers and honored guests, people who had traveled for the coronation ceremony of the new king. *Me.*

Cheers and applause rang through the room. The guests were on their feet, shouting for me. Praising me. They were all people I'd never seen before. People I didn't know.

My mother was gone. She had died the past winter, having been ill for many years.

Pain squeezed my chest at the thought of her, as though someone had reached inside my ribs and grasped hold of my heart. If I tried, I could picture her standing in the crowd, looking up at me, her eyes shining with devotion and love. She would have been so proud to see me take the throne.

Despite the fact I never wanted it.

I still didn't. Not the throne, nor the castle. And especially not the kingdom.

Hordes of well-wishers surged forward to congratulate me and, despite my misgivings, I held my head high as I made my way down the stairs, clasping hands with the first man to step forward.

"King Bravadik, it is an honor," the man said, smiling broadly. He had a kind, open face, and I couldn't help but smile back.

I made my way through the crowd, greeting people here and there as they waved to me. Disappointment surged through me when I realized that my half-brother's queen wasn't here.

Queen Marienne.

Five years ago, I laid eyes on her for the first time.

The first, and the last.

The crowds before me parted, and a man emerged. With one look, I straightened my spine and lifted my chin to look him in the eye. All of my dragon shifter kinsmen were tall and broad, but there was no mistaking this man for a mere courtier.

"Your Highness," I said, bowing my head, at least until the man's laugh rolled through his chest, coming out deep and loud.

"You're a king now. You bow to no-one."

I raised my head. It would take time to get used to the fact that I was now a leader.

He reached out, offering me his hand. I recognized the strength in his grip for the test that it was, and squeezed back, hard.

"Thank you for coming to the coronation," I said.

He grinned at me and pulled the woman next to him closer. Her breasts were so big and round they were practically toppling over the edge of her bodice.

"I'm Stavrok, King of Bravdok." His grin widened. "And this is my wife, Queen Lucy."

"Lucy?" I said, repeating the strange name.

She smiled, and her whole face lit up. "I'm not from around here."

My gaze slid back to Stavrok and I raised an eyebrow in question.

"I stole her." Stavrok grinned mischievously. "Out of the local village."

"The local... human village?" I was shocked by how casual they sounded.

"Yes," he said, puffing out his chest. "She'd never seen a dragon before me."

Lucy rolled her eyes, her expression fond. "It's very nice to meet you, Bravadik."

I scowled at the sound of my formal name. "My friends call me Erik."

Stavrok lifted his chin. A smirk tugged at his lips. "You have some of your father in you."

I took a step closer. "You knew him?"

Stavrok nodded. "Very well. Come to our castle for dinner one evening and we will discuss it at length. I've got plenty of old stories, if you wish to hear them?"

"I would appreciate that," I said, my voice rough with emotion. "Thank you."

"Come tomorrow night," Lucy said. "Bring Marienne with you. It has been too long since we've seen Mari. How is she?"

I made some low sound, deep in the back of my throat, and for some reason my dragon surged within my chest.

The mood shifted. Stavrok grabbed his wife and shoved her behind him, all the while rumbling out a growl that made my hackles rise and every muscle in my body clench to keep from shifting then and there.

What the hell?

My dragon was ferocious, sure. But my control was better than *this.*

"Get yourself together, or you're gonna force me to shift," Stavrok hissed through gritted teeth.

I caught a glimpse of his dragon in the way his nostrils flared, and the fire that burned in the depths of his gaze, and fought my own dragon's need to rise.

I clenched my fists until the knuckles whitened, trying to regain control.

Stavrok summoned a nearby male servant, who snapped to attention.

"A large glass of whiskey for King Bravadik. Now."

The servant dashed away. I forced myself to keep breathing in deep, even inhales and exhales.

Stavrok continued to hold Lucy back. The gorgeous little human fought against his arms, resolutely trying to peek around his barrel-like chest to get a look at me.

When the servant reappeared with the glass and a bottle, I ignored the glass and drank straight from the bottle, downing gulps. The whiskey burned my throat, all the way to my gut.

I swigged some more, and when that too reached my empty stomach, the need to shift finally began to subside.

My vision cleared and my shifter relaxed, yawning, and curling up to sleep inside me.

Stupid thing. We're trying to make a good impression, and you almost started a fight with our neighboring kingdom.

My self-anger must have shown on my face, because the servant took a couple of steps back like I was going to take a swing at him any moment.

"Thank you," I said belatedly.

The servant continued to stare at me with startled, wide eyes, not looking reassured in the slightest.

"Please, just..." I clutched the now half-empty bottle and waved him off. "You should leave."

I looked over at Stavrok, who allowed his little wife back around his huge body so that she could stare up at me with barely disguised curiosity.

"Did I say something wrong?" Lucy asked, then bit her lip in the sweetest way. "I'm still not sure about all the customs... Forgive me if I offended you."

I was too embarrassed to even *look* at her. "You did nothing wrong," I said stiffly, staring over her shoulder. Then I met Stavrok's gaze and inclined my head. "Thank you. That drink helped a lot."

Stavrok reached out and squeezed my shoulder. "We need to have that dinner sooner rather than later. Come tomorrow night, with or without Mari. No arguments."

"But..." Lucy began.

Stavrok gripped her hand and shook his head. "Marienne is the childless widow of the old king. She will not have a role in this kingdom unless the new king wishes it." His eyes found mine, narrowing. "If I were in his shoes, I would build a house somewhere at the edge of town and put her in it."

Stavrok's gaze intensified. I nodded and hummed as though agreeing.

Part of me could see his point. Marienne was part of the old court, the old ways. Her presence might divide loyalties.

Yes, sending her away would be the logical thing to do.

But the idea didn't sit right with me for a number of reasons, none of which, unfortunately, I could share in my present company.

"Where *is* Mari, by the way?" Lucy asked as she glanced around, scanning the crowd as if the woman might appear at any moment. "You haven't shipped her off already, have you?"

Mari. I liked the sound of the shortened name. Stavrok and Lucy obviously held an affection for my half-brother's widow, despite the fact that Stavrok had just urged me to ship her off.

I shook my head and lifted the bottle of whiskey, taking another sip to calm the way my frame was going rigid again.

"No." I looked down into the bottle, swirling around the liquid inside to avoid her gaze. "I wouldn't do such a thing."

"In that case..." Lucy's glare burned into the side of my head. I could feel it. "Where *is* she?"

I looked over toward Stavrok for support. "I would have assumed a human woman would be more malleable..."

Stavrok's bark of laughter was so loud, most of the people in the throne room turned to stare at us.

Lucy whacked him, and he calmed down a little, though nothing could pull the grin from his lips.

"No. Lucy is all fire." He looked down at her with pride. "Especially since giving birth to our triplets. She is the perfect mother dragon for my heirs."

"Triplets?" *Wow.*

My regard for the little human went up. Beauty, brains, and breeding. Stavrok had hit the perfect trifecta.

"Babies, Stavrok. We've talked about this. They are not simply... heirs." Lucy rolled her eyes.

"Our son *will* inherit the kingdom one day, my love."

I glanced between them with amusement. So, there seemed to be *some* cultural adjustments necessary when it came to human-dragon relationships.

Lucy huffed and puffed, apparently not having an argument for that one. Then, she turned that icy stare back on me. "You didn't answer my question. Where's Marienne?"

I released a deep sigh.

"I don't know," I admitted. "When I arrived, the staff said she was in mourning and would not be attending my coronation. So..." I turned away from them a little, pretending intense interest in a nearby marble column. "I've left her alone. But I have to assume she's still in the castle somewhere. Hiding from me, it would seem."

I neglected to mention that I was hiding from *her,* as well. Nothing would have stopped me from chasing her down if I'd truly wanted to know where she was.

"Maybe she's in the dungeons," Lucy said under her breath, casting a sidelong look at her husband.

Did she just say *dungeons?* "Why would my half-brother's queen be in the dungeons?"

Stavrok shook his head. "That's a long story, my friend. We'll have to tell it to you some other time."

He glanced over his shoulder, at the line of people waiting for me. I suppressed another sigh.

"We will see you tomorrow night, Erik," Stavrok said. "Eight o'clock. Bring your appetite."

I shook the king's hand again. This time, his grip seemed friendlier.

"Thank you again for your help." I lifted the bottle to indicate the alcohol, giving him a sheepish smile. My head was slightly buzzing, and my stomach burned with liquor. But my control was back intact. "I apologize if my behavior scared you, or your lovely wife."

Stavrok chortled, a growly laugh that set my dragon on edge. "Erik, the only reason I didn't take your damn head off was because you obviously don't have much experience controlling your emotions. That has to change, and I'll be happy to help."

I gave the king a small smile, trying to remain calm. Rumor was that Stavrok had killed my half-brother in hand-to-hand combat. He was a tough warrior. Not one to cross, that was for sure.

"No hard feelings, then?" I asked.

As the king, I needed allies. And, despite his ferocity and loud, bombastic manner, I sensed that Stavrok had a good heart underneath.

Stavrok grinned. "As long as you stop staring at my wife's breasts... we're all good."

"Oh... of course," *Had* I been looking there?

My mind was still on Marienne—or Mari, as they had called her—and whether I should insist she come out of hiding.

Inadvertent staring at Stavrok's wife was likely just the first of many royal fuck-ups.

How many more would I have before my time was done?

TWO

Marienne

I watched my husband, King Magnik of the Black Mountains, die at the hand of another dragon king in mortal combat. It was by far the most traumatic day of my life.

It was also the most liberating.

From the moment my magic began to show itself, my destiny had been set in stone. I'd been all of sixteen at the time; I didn't know how to control my powers, and I couldn't hide them.

The power that stirred within me made me a worthy prize. I was to be a royal bride. My parents had fought to make the king wait until I was eighteen to claim me.

For ten long years, I'd been the queen of a clan ruled by a tyrant.

In the town below us, the distant chime of bells rang out. They were still celebrating, ringing in their new king.

The day of Magnik's half-brother's coronation had been a long time coming. Hope was in the air, and the entire kingdom felt it. The servants carried the rumors all the way to my tower. This king would be different. Not capricious and power-hungry like the last, and the one before that.

A shiver coursed through my body at the mere thought of Bravadik.

"Erik…" I whispered the more familiar name into the silence.

Only the wind answered me. The silken curtains fluttered, billowing outwards. I collapsed onto the nearby couch, reveling in the soft velvet cushions that surrounded me. This place was my oasis; it sheltered me from the pain of the world outside.

But I couldn't stay in here forever. Sooner or later, these walls would come crashing down and reality would intrude.

I had to be ready. I had to *think*.

With a small sigh, I rose from the couch and paced around my room. It was a cozy space, full of books and plush decorations. Colorful rugs covered the floor, and a large lantern hung from the ceiling, casting the furniture with a warm glow.

Magnik himself had told me of Bravadik, many years ago. His father's bastard son, and the only true challenger for the throne. He was low-born, the child of some village woman and known in his home town as Erik. He had been raised down in the valley, far away from court, and that was likely the only reason Magnik had not had him killed.

I'd seen Bravadik only once, on a royal tour, five years into my marriage. The moment stood out sharply in my memory. Even now, the thought of that day filled me with a cacophony of feelings. Happiness, love, and terror.

From the moment I lay eyes on Bravadik, I knew.

He was my fated mate.

It had been more than five years since that day. The day my heart broke in my chest when I knew we would never have the chance to be together.

The original joy I had felt when I saw Erik had been crushed mere seconds later. I could never know him. Nor love him.

I'd been forced to marry a man who had claimed me for my magical power. Magnik was a distant, cold husband. He neither desired nor loved me. I was a tool to him, just another weapon in his arsenal.

The fates had cursed our union. My barren womb and untouched heart were a true testament to the emptiness of our marriage.

I turned my head toward the banging on the door, and called to whoever was on the other side. "I gave instructions that I don't wish to be disturbed."

"Queen Marienne."

My stomach dropped at the sound of the voice. I had never heard it before, and yet... I *knew* it.

Somewhere deep inside, the familiarity called to me. In my dreams, like an echo carried on the wind.

I raced to the door and bolted it with trembling hands. Then I pressed my forehead against the solid wood and took deep, steadying breaths.

"I know you're in there." The voice was low and smooth. Cautious, but not unfriendly. I took a deep breath and exhaled slowly. "What do you want?"

I forced the words out even as my defensive magic began to swirl around me. Purple infusions of light glimmered around the dim chamber, and I struggled to retain control.

"It's King Bravadik." Even muffled through the thick wood I could hear the discomfort when he announced himself. The title didn't exactly roll off his tongue.

A reluctant smile tugged at my lips.

What had become of the young man I'd seen in town, all those years ago? What sort of man was he now? How strong? How beautiful? I ached to know, but I had no right. I was the former king's barren widow, and as such, of little use to Bravadik, other than as a reminder of a past he might not want to remember.

"Sire." I swallowed. "How can I be of service?"

"Well," he said, "you could open the door, for a start."

I closed my eyes. *Goddess, if he only knew how much I wanted to.*

"I... I can't." I cast around for an excuse. "I'm undressed, and I am... unwell, Your Majesty."

"I see." An awkward pause ensued. "I have come to ask if you'd join me for dinner at Stavrok and Lucy's castle tonight? They attended my coronation and invited us both."

I couldn't help smiling again at his use of the king and queen's real names. It made sense that Erik wouldn't follow political protocol, given his upbringing. He would be a breath of fresh air in noble circles, and I wished, more than anything, to be there to see him flourish.

But it would break my heart all over again, to be so close to my intended mate and yet be unable to touch him.

I turned and pressed my back against the door. A deep ache was building inside my belly for the man who stood on the other side.

"If you are unwell, however..." His voice fell silent.

"You must go to dinner," I forced myself to say. "Stavrok is everything a king should be. Strong and kind, a true father to his people. And Lucy is a beautiful soul. She's a worthy queen, and a perfect match for him. You could not wish for better mentors, Erik."

There was a heavy silence. Then I realized my mistake.

My eyes squeezed shut. *Damn.*

"Erik? How do you know my name?"

"I..." I swallowed hard and wrapped my arms across my chest. "I saw you once," I said. "Years ago. Magnik pointed you out in the crowd." I cleared my throat at the silence from the other side of the door. "I confess, I kept tabs on you through the years. I hoped one day you would find the way to your rightful position, here at court."

He didn't answer for a long moment. "You're the one who told them where to find me."

I blinked rapidly as tears formed in my eyes. I wanted to hold him so much, kiss away the frown that was surely pulling at his perfect skin. But I had no right.

"I must lie down now, sire. Please, go to dinner. Give them my apologies." My eyes fluttered closed. "Send my blessings to Lucy and the new babies. They will be breathtaking, I know it."

This time I lost the battle, and hot tears slid down my cheeks. To have a baby of my own... it was a long-held dream. A fruitless one, of course, but that didn't stop the need from rising up on occasion.

"I will, Queen Marienne." There was a drawn-out pause from the other side of the door. I pictured him there, waiting. Lingering. "Thank you."

I turned back, and touched my palm to the wood. "I am no longer the queen, Your Majesty. You can call me Marienne. My husband is dead, and you will soon find your own bride who will be queen and rule alongside you."

I heard a soft, light scraping sound against the door, as though he too had pressed his hand against the wood.

"You'll always be a queen, Marienne," he said, and I moved my hand to my mouth to contain the sob that threatened to escape.

Eventually, I sensed him moving away from the door. "Goodnight."

I held my breath as his footsteps retreated down the stone hallway. Once nothing but silence remained, I collapsed onto my bed and began to cry.

My destined lover, my fated mate. He had walked away from me. And my heart broke all over again because I knew it was for the best.

Erik

"What's the fastest way to Stavrok's castle?" I asked Thomas, the head of the house.

I still hadn't quite worked it all out, but he seemed like someone I could trust.

"The fastest, sire?" A smile lit up his face, "Technically, that would be flight."

I grinned. I liked that idea; it would certainly make a statement. Though the lack of clothing on arrival might be a problem.

Thomas smiled even wider, as if he knew where my thoughts had gone. He obviously had a wicked sense of humor and I liked that about him. "Perhaps, since this is your first visit, sire, you could take the carriage?"

I frowned, disappointed. "Flying would be more fun."

Thomas snapped his fingers and several maids arrived holding clothes in their outstretched arms.

"I thought you might say that, so perhaps you would take the carriage today, and take along a few changes of clothes so that next time you wish to visit, you will have something to change into when you arrive."

I slapped him on the back. "You're a genius."

He checked his wristwatch. "And you will soon be late, sire. The carriage has been prepared. It is waiting for you at the castle gates. So please, my king, enjoy your evening and we will see you later tonight. Or tomorrow, if you so choose."

I flicked up my eyebrows. "Tomorrow?"

"Yes. King Stavrok may invite you to stay. If he does, please take the opportunity to view his kingdom in the daylight. There are many changes he has implemented that, if I'm allowed to be frank..."

"Always," I told him.

"That perhaps Your Highness would look at implementing here. In our clan. For our people." Thomas tilted his head, looking at me thoughtfully. "There is a lot of good you can do, sire."

I nodded. I was under no illusions about being able to rule the kingdom without support from others. This role was new to me, and I welcomed his guidance. "I will certainly take that advice. Thank you, Thomas."

He smiled and indicated the stairs behind me. "You must go. The maids will follow you and pack your clothes for you."

I glanced over at the little blonde woman who was eyeing me as though she would like to do more than lay out my clothes for me. Perhaps she would accompany me for the drive?

"How long is this carriage ride, Thomas?"

Thomas frowned, catching my drift. His eyes flickered over to the maidservant and he dismissed her with a wave of his hand. "Not long enough, sire."

I heaved a sigh and headed toward the stairs. "All right. See you when I see you."

I walked out to the carriage and climbed in, alone, and we set off.

My gut ached, my balls throbbed, and my veins pumped with a fire that was only associated with the need to shift, or fuck.

I needed a woman. It hadn't mattered that a door stood between us; even *speaking* to Marienne had left me hard and wanting. I needed some relief from the pain.

I wasn't sure what it was about that woman. The sound of her voice, so sweet, made my head spin. Even hearing her name spoken, as Lucy had done at the coronation, seemed to set me off.

But she was my half-brother's widow, and a sorceress to boot. She was off-limits.

Yet she stirred my dragon like no other, and I wasn't sure why.

If I ever got my hands on her, I was afraid I may never let her go.

Not that she would want me, I reminded myself, as I always did whenever my thoughts wandered to Marienne. She'd been wed to my older brother, the king. Surely, compared to him, I was a low-rate, pathetic bastard?

Queen Marienne would never look on me with anything but pity.

THREE

Erik

Arriving at Stavrok's kingdom was like driving through another dimension. The streets were clean, the houses were all brightly lit and smoke billowed from the chimneys.

His people were obviously wealthy, and it made my stomach churn to think of how my mother and I had lived for so long. The struggle of our friends and neighbors. The taxes on the people. *My* people, now.

When the carriage rolled to a stop outside the actual castle, I got out and stared up at the incredible monument in front of me.

Wow.

The idea that I was invited as a guest to such a place, still felt like a dream.

"This way, sire." A servant took my clothes and walked ahead, up the stairs before me.

I followed him, looking around and absorbing the atmosphere of the place. And once we stepped inside and the warm air hit my face, I sighed.

This was heaven.

There were expensive tapestries on the walls, lush carpets beneath my feet and from the sound of the general chatter and laughter in the castle, happy people around me.

The servant turned toward me. "I believe the main throne room is ahead, sire. I will take these clothes to King Stavrok's staff."

The servant headed off and I stared ahead at the well-lit doorway.

"Erik? Is that you?" Stavrok called from the end of the hallway.

I inhaled deeply and squared my shoulders. Time to be a king. I strode forward, entering the room and realizing it was a large sitting room. A huge fireplace was stoked with wood and welcoming flame, and in front, a set of large leather chairs seemed to beckon. Stavrok stood by with a bottle of alcohol.

I grinned at the huge man and walked forward to greet him. I clasped Stavrok's hand, giving it a firm shake, and smiled in greeting at his wife who stood nearby. "Thank you so much for having me."

"We're excited to have you here!" Lucy said. She had a baby on each broad hip and she juggled them with seeming ease. "But where's Marienne?"

I reached out a hand to the baby boy who grabbed my finger and smiled a toothless, gummy grin at me.

"She was unwell," I said shortly. "She sent her apologies, and told me to come along and learn all I could from you two."

Stavrok chuckled. "Well, she knows best. Come, follow me."

Lucy hoisted the babies on her hips. "I need to put these two back in their cribs. I'll meet you both in the dining room."

She headed off toward the broad staircase at the center of the hall.

I watched her large, swinging hips as she left, then realized I was staring and pulled my gaze back to the king before me. "I apologize. Your family is…"

Everything I could ever want. I couldn't express the thought without sounding odd, but it hung in the air between us.

Stavrok acknowledged my unspoken compliment with a broad, knowing smile. He led me into a huge dining room and poured us both a whiskey. The amber liquid sloshed in the glasses as he picked them up.

"I agree," he said. "I'm a lucky man."

We clinked glasses.

"To a successful alliance between our two great houses," he said.

I nodded. "Hear, hear!"

I took a sip and enjoyed the burn that rolled down my throat. "So, from what I gather, you and my half-brother were not on friendly terms?"

Stavrok let out a booming laugh. "Because I killed him, you mean?"

So, it's true.

I absorbed the information, careful not to let the shock show on my face.

Stavrok had been nothing but friendly to me, but I couldn't let myself forget that this man was powerful as hell. This man had killed the previous ruler of my kingdom.

I simply nodded. Stavrok's smile softened, and he led me over to the dining table. It was huge, and elaborately laid out with crystal glasses, white linen, and sparkling silverware. Seeming to pick up on my uncertainty, he indicated the chair to the left of him. I sat and nodded in gratitude.

He took his place at the head of the table, confident and stately. A true king.

There was a place setting to my left. A wave of sadness passed over me that Marienne would not be here to sit in what I saw as her rightful spot.

"Magnik wanted more than he had," Stavrok said. I put aside my bleak thoughts about Marienne and refocused. "Always. He craved power, wealth, and domination over the other dragon kingdoms. When he saw a way to force me to hand over my lands, and the mining rights that come with them, he took it."

"What did he do?" I asked.

"He kidnapped Lucy."

My mouth dropped open.

"Excuse me?" I placed my drink on the pristine white tablecloth so that I didn't spill it everywhere. "He... what?"

"He kidnapped me, held me in the dungeon, and threatened to kill me if Stavrok didn't agree to his ransom conditions," Lucy said, as she walked back into the room. Her tone was surprisingly breezy, given the horror of her tale. I wondered if all humans were this nonchalant, or if this one was unusual in that regard.

She sat down on the right side of her husband and laid a hand over his.

"Are our babes sleeping?" he asked her, in a gentle tone that I was surprised to hear from such a strong man.

She nodded, smiling. "Like little angels."

Then she turned her gaze back on me just as I lifted my drink to my lips.

"So... Erik. I assume you have a temper?" She smirked at Stavrok. "It seems to be a feature in the bloodline of dragon kings."

I choked on the whiskey, which shot up my nose and out of my mouth, making a general mess of everything around me.

Servants hurried over from every corner to clean up the spill, handing me napkin after napkin.

"I am sorry," I said, annoyed at myself and embarrassed more than anything.

Could I make it any more obvious that I wasn't raised to be anything other than a street urchin?

Stavrok grinned. "My wife has a wicked tongue. I should be the one apologizing to you."

Lucy glared at him. "I was just asking a question."

Question... question... What had she asked again?

Oh, that was right.

I bowed my head for a moment, gathering my thoughts.

"Well, yes," I answered eventually. "I struggled with my temper a lot when I was younger. Especially through my growth years when I was first shifting. I set the town alight one too many times." I winced. "The people named me Rage.... But my mother called me Erik."

"And you prefer it over your longer name?" Lucy asked.

I inhaled sharply, not sure if I should admit to such a thing. But I didn't wish to answer to Bravadik for the rest of my life, so I spoke honestly. "Yes."

Bravadik, my royal name, still threw me off-balance every time I heard it. My father had told my mother what to call me when I was born, and it had always stuck in my craw that she had allowed him to have such a say over my life as to actually name me.

I never even met the man. He hadn't sent me so much as a letter.

My hosts didn't ask why I preferred the name Erik, however, and the conversation soon turned toward the running of the kingdom. Stravrok was aware that I didn't know the first thing about statecraft, but he didn't seem to hold it against me.

"My father considered the happiness of the people to be the most important part of running a kingdom," Stavrok said. "If the townsfolk are warm, and well fed, then the whole land will prosper. That advice hasn't failed me yet."

I cast my mind back to the hardships I had faced, growing up in a humble village, far away from any finery. The long, dark winters. The famine. The cold nights where my mother had no kindling to keep us warm.

"Everything you told me about King Magnik..." I stared down at my plate. I knew I had to choose my words carefully; kings did not barrel through conversations like these. I had to be smart. "And everything I experienced in the past as one of his subjects... he is not a ruler I wish to emulate."

Lucy snorted.

"But I don't know the kingdom. Not as I should. Not as a *king* would. I..." I wavered. "There has to be a better way of doing things. I vowed to do right by my people when they placed the crown on my head. I want to honor that vow."

Stavrok studied me, as if sizing me up. I looked back, not breaking eye contact. The huge, open fireplace behind us flickered, casting golden light over the table and filling me with a sense of peace I hadn't felt in years.

Lucy opened her mouth as if she was going to say something. But before she could, however, the fireplace roared, flaring with light and heat. Flames shot upward and sparked out of the grate. The room filled with the sound of cutlery clattering against plates as Stavrok, Lucy, and I looked around with astonishment.

"What—" Stavrok began.

At the other end of the room, the double doors opened with a boom. A female figure stood in the doorway, flanked by two servants.

"Your Majesty, Dowager Queen Marienne of the Black Mountains."

I froze in my seat.

Stavrok and Lucy stood up from the table.

"Marienne!" Lucy swept toward the visitor, pleasure visible on her face. "Erik said you were ill! I'm so glad you made it."

Stavrok murmured something to me, but I couldn't understand his words. My head was buzzing. Panic and adrenaline flooded through me, and my heart thundered in my chest.

Marienne stood in the doorway for what felt like an eternity. I watched, transfixed, as she began to move toward us. Everything else in the room grew dimmer as she approached, as though she was giving off her own source of light. Her long dress shimmered and rippled, hugging her gorgeous frame, and her dark hair flowed loosely across her shoulders.

I had never seen anyone more beautiful.

Her eyes captivated me the most. They were a deep indigo, so dark they could have been black. When they caught the light, they glowed with magic and mystery.

My heart clenched at the sight of those eyes.

Something inside me snapped. The barrier that held back my dragon broke, and it thundered to life. My dragon roared, more powerful than ever before, and in that moment, I knew I'd lost all vestiges of control.

I didn't have time to shout a warning. My vision blurred, and the roaring inside my mind grew louder and louder as I slid off my chair, dropped to my knees and succumbed to the inevitable.

The dragon would not be silenced. It had seen Marienne, and in that split second, I was no longer the one calling the shots.

It had been years since I had shifted like this. Wild, spontaneous, and one hundred percent animal instinct. I couldn't do anything but cling on for the ride; already my claws were lengthening, my ribcage expanding. My blurred vision sharpened as the dragon took over, and I let out a roar as my wings unfurled from my back. I beat them through the air, causing the fireplace to flicker and cutlery and glassware to fall to the floor with a clatter and crash.

I twisted around, trying to get my bearings. My human mind screamed out, but it was locked deep within the scaly hide of the dragon.

The dragon was on a mission. It had zeroed in on Marienne. She stood, pale and unmoving, staring up at me with those beautiful eyes.

She was everything I wanted. Everything I needed.

Stavrok inched into my peripheral vision. He had circled around me in a wide arc, careful not to place himself between me and Marienne. Lucy was nowhere to be seen.

He shouted something. With a heroic amount of effort, I wrenched my gaze off the woman in front of me and onto Stavrok.

My claws dragged along the floor as I moved toward him, and I growled, but he didn't back down. He was still yelling.

What was he yelling?

"The windows! Get them open *now!*"

I knew—the part of me that was still a man, anyway—that I didn't want to hurt anyone. But the dragon in me would rip this place apart if anyone tried to stop me from taking Marienne.

The woman herself, in contrast to the chaos around her, stayed remarkably composed. She gazed up at me, like she was waiting for something. I extended my wings out to their full capacity and the rush of air swept her hair back from her face. It fluttered and resettled around her shoulders, and I caught the hint of a smile at the corners of her mouth.

Why was she not afraid of my dragon?

The wind picked up, cold and strong, and my head snapped up. The dragon was more alert than me, and I scanned the room, noting that the row of wide, floor-to-ceiling windows had been thrown open. The curtains billowed out like the sails of a ship, and the star-lit sky glittered beyond.

While I focused on Marienne, Stavrok had shifted, too. His dragon form loomed in the shadows, just as powerful and imposing as the man himself.

A tiny figure pressed up close against his dark, scaly side. *Lucy.*

Stavrok roared. A tongue of flame shot out through his open jaw.

I roared back, then stepped closer to Marienne. I crouched low, inviting her to climb onto my back. She came willingly, sliding over my shoulder and settling between my wings. I shuddered in delight as her tiny hands scrambled for purchase against my scales.

I spared a final glance at Stavrok. Our eyes met, and an understanding passed between us.

Then, I leapt to the closest open window, and launched with Marienne up and into the night.

CHAPTER
FOUR

Marienne

The harsh winter winds rushed around me, tearing at my hair and gown. If I were fully human, I would have been half-frozen by now.

But I wasn't just a woman. My magic shimmered and pulsed through the air, sending trails of heat through my core. Erik's huge shoulders shifted beneath me, and I moaned at the wonderful sensation of touching him. Could he feel my warmth spreading through his back as he flew? My legs clenched tight around him, and his wings beat the air with renewed force.

Power simmered in my veins. In that moment, I could have moved mountains if I had to. I needed Erik, and I was hopeful that nothing would stand in our way tonight.

I was so caught up in my musings I barely registered when his feet hit the stony parapet of the high North Tower. I let out a breathless laugh when his wings brushed against my back, preventing me from falling off during the abrupt landing.

Such a gentleman.

He released me, and I slid off his back, moving away so he had space to shift back to human when he was ready.

He staggered back from me. The air was already shimmering, and before my eyes the dragon dissolved away, leaving the man, naked and panting, in its place.

This moment—here and now—felt like our first true meeting.

There wasn't anything between us any longer. No husband, no ceremony, no court protocol to follow. We were completely alone.

Erik was tall and lean, with shaggy hair that fell to his sharp jawline. His stature was powerful; anyone could see at a glance that he was a true dragon king.

He was trembling. His eyes were shadowed, and his face turned away. He wouldn't look at me.

Was he afraid?

Had he felt my magic as we were flying back to the castle? A shock-wave of pain seared through my chest at the possibility of his rejection. Did he think I would hurt him?

I reached out a hand toward him, and he flinched.

"Don't," he said, his voice low and gravelly. The words shot right to my core, and warmth spread through my belly, even as a sob caught in my throat.

He didn't want my touch.

Slowly, I retracted my hand. We stood on the castle rooftop, at a stalemate. Neither of us moved. I was pretty sure neither of us breathed.

Then, his gaze slid to meet mine, just for a second, before darting away.

Oh.

He wasn't trembling out of fear. He was holding himself *back*.

I could see it now, the tightness in his strong frame. The way the muscles bunched together in his forearms as he squeezed his hands into white-knuckled fists.

It had been five long years since anyone had touched me.

The day I'd seen Erik, everything changed. From the moment I realized he was my fated mate, I knew I could never give myself to the king again. Magnik declared me barren when I said, 'no more', and he lost interest in me completely in a sexual way.

I hadn't been able to give Magnik heirs, but I could give him the power he sought. He valued the latter far more than anything else. He agreed to the physical separation happily enough. Our marriage bed had been cold ever since.

With Magnik, there had been no intimacy and, for years, I had convinced myself I didn't need such things in my life.

But I was wrong. So wrong. And standing here in front of Erik, the longing for him drowned me, flooding my senses until I couldn't think about anything else.

I *needed* him.

Slowly, so as not to startle him, I crept forward. My steps were feather-light against the flagstones—I could move soundlessly when I wanted to—and I kept my stance loose and relaxed.

I wasn't afraid.

He wouldn't hurt me.

We were so close now that I could feel the body heat coming off him in waves. It warmed the air around us and intensified my own desire. Gently, I reached out and cupped his forearm, encouraging it toward my body. His trembling increased. I placed his large, hot hand against my skin, over the neck of my low-cut gown.

My chest heaved beneath his touch, and ripples of warmth spread through me, undercutting the coldness of the night. The ripples became waves, lapping into every corner of my mind and body. Like a prism, the world exploded with light and color.

The images came to me in flashes. A silk canopy. A cheering crowd, flower petals thrown into a blue sky. Vows, an altar. Laughter, wine glasses sparkling in the sunlight. My hands trailing over his bare chest. His arms encircling me, protecting me. A kingdom—*our* kingdom—bright and thriving. Life renewing, fruit trees blossoming. Our children, running alongside us as we walked together, unhurried. Free, happy, fulfilled.

The visions vanished as quickly as they had come, slipping away into the darkness. All that remained was Erik.

His eyes flashed, and his hand flexed against me. I wanted to close the remaining distance between us, but I waited, mouth parted. If his hand slid down an inch, he would feel how hard my nipples had become.

His mouth crashed against mine without warning. I groaned at the feel of him as his other hand encircled my waist, drawing me up into him until I was on tiptoes and pressed against his hardness.

He pushed his tongue against mine and my legs trembled. No-one had ever held me like this—with such blatant raw need.

He kissed me with single-minded intensity, hands roaming all over my body until I gave up trying to kiss him back and simply clung onto his huge arms.

He gathered up my skirts, his hands spanned over my thighs, desperate, rough, and unrelenting.

I arched against him, impatient. I wanted him. So badly it *hurt*.

He pulled me up into his arms, fluid and decisive. I pressed my face into his shoulder, trailing my mouth over the hot skin of his neck, the angle of his jaw.

He was carrying me somewhere.

Inside?

I didn't care. I felt the wave of warmth settle across my skin, felt the motion of his long strides, but I couldn't bring myself to look up, or even open my eyes. If there was anyone around to see us, I preferred not to know.

We passed through a door, then another. The world spun around as he shifted me in his arms before dropping me onto a soft, warm, surface.

Is this a bed? How thoughtful of him.

I didn't have time to think beyond that, as he crawled up over me and lowered the entire length of his body down onto mine.

If he had been holding back before, he wasn't now. I groaned, pinned between him and the mattress. His hot breath huffed in my ear, and when he shifted on me, the hard length of his cock pressed against my stomach.

I rolled my hips up to meet his. He withdrew a little and loomed over me on all fours. He truly was beautiful, especially like this, his eyes slightly unfocused and swimming with lust.

"Erik..." I whispered.

"You want this? As much as I do?"

"Yes..."

He closed his hand around the neckline of my gown; the sheer, gauzy material crumpled in his fist. I moaned as he tugged sharply and tore the fabric in half, exposing my aroused breasts and belly to the air. His groan was deep and lustful, before his hot, damp mouth closed over one of my nipples, and I bit my lip to hold in the cry of pleasure that threatened to release.

He growled against my skin and palmed my other breast. I slid the remains of my gown off my shoulders to give him better access, writhing beneath him until the teasing became too much for both of us.

He reared back, ripping and tugging until the rest of my clothing was gone from the bed, then his mouth returned to my breasts where he laved first one, then the other, of my sensitized flesh with an expertise I reveled in.

"I need more," I whispered, and dragged his mouth up to meet mine. As he kissed me, deeply, I felt his essence tangle with mine and permeate the air around us. I pulled him down on me, encouraging the contact. My pussy was soaked, and I only grew more desperate when I finally felt every inch of his firm, naked body against mine.

We rocked together, rejoicing in the feeling. I groaned when his hand twisted into my hair and pulled my head back, exposing my neck under his mouth. He laved kisses over my throat, his tongue darting out to taste my skin. I moved again and my center dragged up over the length of his cock. We both shivered at the sensation, and his hands slid lower, bracketing my hips.

He panted hard. Every inhalation and exhalation shot through his body, like he'd been running for miles. I wasn't in a much better state myself.

Slowly, agonizingly slowly, he lifted me up by the hips and put me into position.

Then he sank into me, inch by inch. We both cried out at the connection. I was so tight, and his thickness felt so unbelievably good I had to take a moment to steady myself. My pussy rippled slowly around him, and I whimpered as I wrapped my legs around his waist, embracing the feeling of fullness.

I could have stayed that way forever. His ragged breaths were hot against my cheek. I bit at the corner of his mouth, and he grunted, thrusting up into me.

And again. And again. He fucked me hard and fast and... perfectly. The intensity of my pleasure shocked me. Sweetness rose like a cresting wave, and when his rough hand worked its way between us, fingers circling around my clit, I couldn't hold back a scream as a violent orgasm crashed over me.

I shuddered against him, working my hips up and down, urging him deeper with every thrust. Our mouths found each other, tasting, elevating the intensity of the experience.

His cock drove into me relentlessly, and he buried his face into my neck as he came. When I felt him pulse inside me, I gave myself over to the sensation completely. I panted his name over and over as I came again. I couldn't do anything but cling to him mindlessly as we kissed and shuddered in a mutual, mind-blowing climax.

He was still buried inside me, and nothing else mattered but the two of us, in this bed. Darkness filled the night, but here in his arms, I was completely safe.

The last thing I registered was Erik pressing a soft kiss against my temple, and then sleep pulled me under.

Erik

I don't know how long I lay there in the darkness, holding Marienne in my arms.

Even though I was exhausted, every muscle in my body wrung out and sated, my mind buzzed. In sleep, Marienne burrowed into my chest, and my heart melted. I brushed her long, dark hair off her bare shoulder and smiled to myself as I tucked her closer against me.

I couldn't make sense of what had just happened.

My shifter was a powerful one; my royal bloodline made sure of that. I had always been stronger than the other men in my village, and my dragon could fly great distances without tiring.

Sure, I had a reputation for losing my temper. But uncontrollable shifting, and then claiming my half-brother's wife? That was on a different level. In truth, the lack of control scared me.

There seemed to be one common denominator. One factor that set my dragon off like no other.

And I was currently sharing a bed with her.

If I hadn't just experienced the most mind-blowing sex of my life, I might have been more concerned. As it was, I couldn't bring myself to worry too much. The evening had taken an unexpected turn, but not an unwelcome one.

I should probably send Stavrok and Lucy a thank you gift basket.

I almost laughed aloud at the thought, but managed to keep in the sound, fearful I would wake my lover. I ran a hand over Marienne's soft hair and drifted into sleep.

~

Marienne

My eyes, still blurry with sleep, took a couple of seconds to adjust when I opened them.

Unless I was mistaken, I was in King Erik's bedchamber.

Huh.

The room was large and beautiful, and through an archway I spied a small sitting area with a vista through the window that overlooked the snowy mountains. The silk canopy over the bed exactly matched the one I had seen in my vision.

These rooms at the top of the North Tower had stood empty for years. Magnik and I had never slept here. He preferred to sleep nearer the heart of the castle, where the bank vaults lay filled with gold coins and other treasures.

My old rooms in the East Tower had been at the other end of the castle from Magnik. As far away from him as possible.

Erik didn't know about any of that.

To him, these rooms likely meant nothing. They were simply the king's rooms, prepared for him as befitted the man who currently sat upon the throne. The servants had removed dust sheets, polished the candelabra, and swept back the curtains to reveal the rolling hills of the valley below us. Glowing coals slumbered in the grate, and the bearskin rug spread out before the fire looked soft and inviting.

On a whim, I slipped out from between the sheets and padded over to sink my bare feet into the rug. I had always thought of this castle as gloomy and oppressive, but with Erik by my side, I was starting to appreciate its beauty.

A grumble came from the bed. Erik had flung out an arm into the empty space. His face was buried in the pillow, but I could already picture his furrowed, displeased brow. He was no good at hiding his emotions, even in sleep.

With a smile, I crept back to bed. He enveloped me with his long limbs, and I sighed with contentment and relaxed against him, readily submitting to the cuddling.

The king's bed in the royal suite. I never thought I'd actually end up here.

It was ironic, given I had been Magnik's wife, but somehow, I felt more like a queen right now, than ever before.

I fell asleep again wrapped in Erik's arms, with a smile lifting my lips.

When I woke, warm, golden sunlight poured into the bedchamber.

I was no longer within the tangle of his limbs. I lay curled up on my own side of the bed. I could feel the indentation of his weight behind me, but we must have separated at some point.

I suppressed my disappointment and rolled over to face him.

He was already awake. His gaze slid away from mine, his expression guilty, like I'd caught him out on something.

Had he been watching me sleep? My lips quirked into a smile.

After a minute, he grinned back. There was a hint of hesitation, but his expression was warm and genuine all the same.

"Marienne..." His eyes roved over my face, dipping lower before snapping up again. I suppressed a giggle. He had seen much more than my bare shoulders after all. "Last night... I must apologize."

I tilted my head, confused. I wanted nothing more than to curl into him once more, run my hands over his chest and press my mouth against his. But I resisted.

"I wasn't aware there was anything to apologize for," I said, keeping my tone gentle.

Unless...

The room was still toasty warm, but a shiver ran up my spine. "Did you not wish to have me, sire?"

"No!"

My mouth dropped open, and I met his gaze with wide eyes. *He didn't want me?* "I...err..." I didn't know what to say, but he shook his head.

"I mean... *yes.* I did, Marienne. I..." He swallowed. "I *do.*"

Relief and pleasure thrummed through me. "Then, sire—"

"Please," he interrupted. "Don't call me that."

"You're my king," I said carefully. "I will do as you wish, of course."

Somehow, he looked even more miserable. My heart sank. I wanted him, and he *clearly* wanted me.

So why did the space between us in this bed feel as though a chasm lay between us?

"Marienne... I just meant, call me Erik. Please." He reached out to lay a hand over mine. The touch was sweet and simple. A mile away from everything that had occurred last night.

I stared down at the bedsheets. His fingers over mine were light, as though he was afraid I might throw him off any second. He had big hands, and my smooth, pale fingers fluttered under his roughened palm.

Then the visions came.

It happened without warning. Usually, I got a couple of seconds to prepare before a premonition took over, but this one hit me like a sledge-hammer, pulling me under, drowning me in its intensity.

I gasped before reality ripped away from me and I was flung out into the darkness.

The world reformed; solidified. I found myself outside, on my knees, looking up at the castle. The sky overhead was black, but the castle was brighter than I had ever seen. Every turret, every window, *everything* burned. Hot tongues of flame shot into the sky, lighting up the night, and thick clouds of acrid smoke filled the air. I choked, coughing. I couldn't speak. My throat was raw from screaming. All I knew was heat and destruction.

The castle melted away. I was in a busy street. A town marketplace. I recognized it with a jolt; this was the village where I first saw Erik.

That day had been bright. The sky was blue, the trees laden with apple blossom, and the crowds cheered for their new young queen. *Me.*

This time, however, the sky thundered overhead. People ran, screaming, past me. I skittered backwards but they didn't notice. I was a ghost, powerless to help them, or to stop it. Death hung in the air.

It was then that I realized the flashes in the sky weren't lightning, but dragon fire.

The image changed again. I was back in the castle, on the rooftop. I knelt, cradling a man in my arms.

Erik gazed up at me. Despite the blood and dirt that covered his face, he looked peaceful. Serene, even.

A smattering of raindrops fell against his cheek. It took me a second to realize that they weren't raindrops. They were tears. Mine.

He reached up and touched my cheek. The motion clearly hurt him, and with horror I saw the wound in his chest. Beyond healing, even with magic.

"Erik..." I whispered, stricken.

He just smiled. His face was close to mine, and I bent so I could catch his soft words.

"Our baby," he breathed. "Get as far away from here as you can."

My breath hitched on a sob, and the vision melted away. I tumbled through darkness for what felt like forever, until I registered arms around me. Strong, solid and real.

"Marienne!" Erik—whole, uninjured, and frowning deeply—cradled my face, wiping away the tears that tracked down my cheeks with his thumbs. "Marienne. What is it? What's wrong?"

I gasped, trying to get a hold of myself. I ran my hands up and down his arms, feeling his warm skin beneath my palms to reassure myself he was there. That he was alive.

All the distance between us was gone. We were tangled together again in the bedsheets like one body; one being.

I pressed my forehead against his, allowing myself a couple of heart-beats to recover from the vision. I breathed Erik in, feeling him against me, warm and solid. He was safe. Unharmed. He held me against him. It felt so good.

I couldn't afford to become distracted. Something bad was coming this way and I needed time to gather my thoughts and work out what the visions had meant.

Reluctantly, I slid off the bed in search of some clothes. The ones I'd worn last night weren't in a state to be worn again. There wasn't anything in the walk-in wardrobe except large robes, so I slid one around my shoulders and tied the strap around the middle. It was awkward, but better than leaving this room naked.

When I reappeared in the main room, Erik lay exactly where I had left him in the middle of the bed. He looked like a lost puppy.

I walked toward the door.

"Wait."

I froze, one hand on the doorhandle. When I turned, his gaze was steady. I looked away, cheeks burning with the knowledge that he had just witnessed me in such a state.

"Tell me." Even from his position on the bed, he still commanded my attention. "Are you okay, Marienne?"

I managed to nod. In the face of everything I'd just seen, his concern warmed me straight to the core.

"Yes." I bit my lip. I wanted to explain myself, but I needed to make sense of it all first. "See you later?"

I stepped out of the room before he could reply.

CHAPTER
SIX

Erik

I'd been called into a meeting with the elders, and I was so out of my depth I could barely breathe.

Important matters were being discussed. Matters of state, matters that I had to attend to now, as the king.

I couldn't concentrate on any of it for a single, *stupid* reason.

I felt underdressed in my own damned Council meeting.

I eyed the thick gold chain that hung around the neck of Elder Kilgrave. It glinted as he turned, winking at me as if to say, *look at all this finery. Where's yours, boy?*

That chain could have fed my mother and me for a year. Longer, probably. The elder caught my eye, raising his brow, and I flushed, glaring down at the table.

It wasn't that I wanted a similar decoration for myself. I couldn't imagine anything worse than parading around in such a wasteful thing, in fact.

But maybe that was because I was too roughshod, too unsophisticated. A mere boy, playing at being a king.

"Sire?"

My head snapped up at the address. The other advisor, Elder Slater, pressed his lips into a thin, disapproving line as he stared at me.

He wasn't much friendlier than his counterpart. Every time I had to ask for clarification on a point of business, he gave an impatient *tut*, like I hadn't been paying attention or was too stupid to understand matters of grave importance.

I wanted to call an end to the whole meeting, and fly out to find a grassy field where I could spend the time roaming around and exploring the countryside like I used to do. Maybe I could take Marienne with me. The image of her laid out naked in a field somewhere filled my mind, and I grinned to myself.

Maybe we could go for round two...

I coughed loudly, forcing myself back into the present. "Sorry, what was the question?"

"We need to decide how to allocate our spending for the next quarter, sire. The old king raised taxes on the townsfolk last year, and now we have..." The elder paused, a smirk sliding over his face. "We have something of a surplus, it seems."

"That's excellent news." I spread out my hands. "I've been doing some thinking on that subject myself."

"Is that so?" Elder Slater interjected. He added, "Your Majesty," when I turned toward him and speared him with a look.

Somehow, the way he said it made the phrase sound like a question, rather than the statement of fact it was.

"Yes." I straightened up. I refused to be cowed by either of these men. I was now their king, whether they—or I—liked it or not. I knew my own instincts well enough, and they'd rarely let me down before. What I was about to say, felt right. "I want to issue a decree," I announced. "Our people shall have free heating, and water, and electricity. All of the costs will be covered by the Crown."

"But sire—"

I held up a hand, interrupting Elder Slater. "You won't change my mind. I've spoken to Stavrok about this," I continued, ignoring the matching glowers I received from both of the elders. "I don't see why the system that works so well for his kingdom can't also work for ours."

Elder Kilgrave clutched a hand over his heavy chain, like I was about to rip it off his neck at any moment and hand it over to the poor. "Your Majesty. Those funds are needed for castle upkeep." He pursed his mouth. "Not the trivial plight of the common folk."

I refrained from pointing out that, until very recently, *I* had been one of the common folk of whom he spoke with such disdain.

A single, pointed glance around the high-ceilinged chamber told me the whole story. The grand fireplace. The gilt mirrors. The sparkling gilded ceiling. This was where the money was spent. On excessive luxuries that were not necessary, nor had any function.

Perhaps I should consider taking that necklace of his and using it to feed the hungry.

"I can't see any urgent repairs that need doing." I tilted my head and narrowed my eyes, daring them to disagree. "Please, feel free to point out anything I might have missed."

"What Elder Kilgrave *means*, sire," Elder Slater began, rolling up the documents spread out over the table in front of us, "is that the royal funds are a serious matter. Frivolous spending such as this... it would not be a good start to your reign. Please trust that we are trying to *help* you."

The way he said it left no room for debate. He spoke as though I were an ignorant child who needed to be taught a lesson, instead of a full-grown man. Their leader.

I clenched my jaw, tight. The room, so cozy and elegant only moments before, felt stuffy and restrictive. The walls pressed in on me and a wave of crushing claustrophobia sent me reeling.

It wasn't in my nature to back away from a fight. But I couldn't let my temper rise. Now that I was king, I needed to wield far more control over my emotions than I ever had before.

This was a battle I didn't know how to win. This wasn't some bar fight; this was politics. I didn't have the right weapons, and the rulebook was a total mystery to me.

I was forced to retreat. My heart pounding, I yanked open the door and left the council chamber before they could patronize me further. And before my rage could fully ignite.

I was totally out of my depth. I may have forestalled my temper for today, but what about tomorrow? Or the next day? Or next week?

What did I know about statecraft? Or leadership? I was playing pretend, a dragon king in name only.

It was merely a matter of time before everyone in the whole kingdom would come to realize it.

~

MARIENNE

I spent the better part of the morning walking around my suite in the East Tower out of sheer force of habit.

I knew every nook and cranny, every pile of books, every cushion and candle. This was my domain, my sanctuary. Nobody was allowed inside without my express permission.

When Magnik had been alive, I wasn't queen of much. But this space, right here in the tower... this was my tiny little kingdom. My small tower room where I worked my magic, far away from the prying eyes of the court.

Now, I knew what I needed to do.

I steeled my nerves and set about pulling various herbs off the shelves and rifling through my library until I found the small, leather-bound volume I sought, right at the top of one of my bookshelves.

In silver letters, the title read: *Psychic Projection.*

I carried the book over to my desk, laid it carefully next to the small bowl I used for spell work, and leafed through the pages.

Projection was not a field of magic in which I had much experience. There were other sorcerers in the realm who specialized in the art of traveling to far-off places in their mind's eye, all while remaining physically safe inside their own territory.

Magnik had tried to force me to learn the art on more than one occasion, so I could spy on neighboring kingdoms for him, but I had never mastered it.

Now that he was dead, I could admit the truth to myself: I'd never really *wanted* to master it. Not for him.

I'd always wanted to *help* people with my magic, not spy on them.

However, this was different.

This time, it felt like I had no choice.

I *had* to know. I needed to find the source of the horrifying images that flashed to the forefront of my mind every time I closed my eyes.

The visions had splintered my happiness into tiny shards. I couldn't wait any longer. There was too much at stake to sit passively and wait for my kingdom to fall into ruin.

I murmured an incantation and a small ball of blue flame hovered over the palm of my hand. Slowly, I lowered it into the bowl and set fire to the bundle of herbs.

A thick, blue smoke rose from the bowl. I forced myself to lean in closer, breathing in the bitter fumes and trying not to cough.

This was the tricky part.

I had to clear my mind totally and *focus*. It was normally a challenge to shut my brain down and induce the visions, but this time, they were all I could think about.

My vision began to swirl. The world dissolved, melting away into blackness.

I concentrated on what I had seen before. The castle burning. People screaming. I flinched but forced myself to look deeper, beyond the pain and suffering.

I need to find the source...

In a flash, the world turned white.

I gasped in shock as phantom snow drifted against my face, settling on my cheeks and eyelashes. Cold air raked my skin, and I whirled, trying to get my bearings in the frozen iceland.

A castle loomed through the blizzard, with towering turrets and a heavy iron drawbridge, built to withstand a thousand winters.

Shock sent me reeling as I perceived the truth.

Damon.

The loner king. The Dragon of Winter.

He had many names. In truth, I knew more of those than I had memories of seeing him in person. He rarely ventured south. He preferred to stay in his icy domain, and usually stayed out of the politics and petty rivalries of the other kingdoms.

His people occasionally traveled south to trade. They were a distinctive sight, wearing thick, heavy furs draped across their shoulders, adding bulk and wildness to their broad, solid frames. Their rough-hewn weapons always looked as if they had seen their fair share of use.

Even Damon's shifters were unique. The northern dragons were pale shades of gray and white. They blended perfectly with their landscape, flying unseen through ice storms and nesting on snowy mountaintops. The fire they breathed was different: not orange, but a luminous, icy blue.

As I stared up at those spiky, foreboding towers, a chill of dread settled in the pit of my stomach.

In that moment, I knew I didn't need to look any further. The threat would come from the north.

CHAPTER
SEVEN

Erik

I managed to release my anger about my doomed meeting with the elders by pacing up and down the corridor outside the council room, practically wearing a hole in the stones underfoot.

After that, I wandered aimlessly through the castle hallways. Soon enough, I ended up totally disorientated.

It began to dawn on me all over again—I didn't know this place. I hadn't yet had a chance to become familiar with the layout. I had no bolt holes, no secret corners, nowhere I could go to lick my wounds.

This was my domain—my literal castle—and I was lost.

All the servants I passed along the way inclined their heads with deference, but from the sideways looks on their faces it was clear they saw me for what I was. A total stranger.

Worthy of respect, sure. I was their king, now. But they didn't know me, and I didn't know them. Perhaps they hated me? How could I live up to the legacy of my half-brother, even if he had been disliked for actions such as kidnapping Stavrok's mate? At least he'd been a true-born king. I was, at best, an interloper.

Eventually I found my way back to a section of the castle I recognized.

In the end, I returned to my office in the council chambers, out of a lack of a better idea on where to go.

The space was empty. The elders presumably gave up the meeting as a lost cause. It was just as well. A headache was building behind my eyes, and I wanted nothing more than a stiff drink and a fuck—in whichever order they came to me.

That was where Marienne found me half an hour later, with my head resting on my arms as I sat at my desk, surrounded by dozens of law codes, balance sheets, and tax bills.

I must have been a pathetic sight.

There was a tentative touch on my shoulder and I knew instantly it was her. I tried not to sink into her touch, though her hand was as light as a feather, and strangely comforting.

When I lifted my head, there was nothing of the fiery temptress who had shared my bed last night. In the mid-morning light, she was wan and frail, flitting around the side of the desk like a butterfly and settling into the unoccupied chair.

She truly is like no woman I've ever met.

And yet, there was something off about her today. She wasn't meeting my eyes.

Something had happened earlier, while we were in bed. Something that had shaken her to the core.

She had rushed off without explaining and instinct had told me not to stop her, but I sensed I was about to find out what had occurred.

"To what do I owe the pleasure?" I kept my voice light, trying not to show any hint of the anxiety that stirred within me.

"I..." She lay her hands, palm-side down, on the desk top and finally met my gaze. "I owe you an apology," she said.

My chin snapped up. Something churned in the pit of my stomach.

Does she regret what happened between us?

I raised an eyebrow. "For what?"

"For rushing off like that... after..." She bit her lip, looking embarrassed. I forced myself not to stare at the way she caught her full lower lip between her teeth.

"Oh." It was my turn to feel uncomfortable. "There's no need to apologize, Marienne. You were under no obligation to stay."

She seemed disappointed to hear that. My confusion grew by the second.

"Wait, is that why you're here?" I asked. "Simply to apologize?"

She sighed. "No. Not entirely."

I could sense that she was stalling, but I couldn't guess why. I raised my eyebrows, waiting.

"You know that I have magic." The words rushed out of her so fast I almost didn't catch them.

"Of course."

She flushed, tucking a long strand of hair behind her ear. "So, I'm a sorceress. That's why Magnik chose me to become his queen. Because he wanted access to my magic. For himself."

At the mention of the previous king, my stomach sank. "Why do you ask?"

"Sometimes I..." She swallowed. "Sometimes I have visions. And when we were together this morning..." Her eyes darted away again. "I saw something, Erik. A vision. That's why I... That's what happened. I had a vision, and I ran."

I exhaled, relief washing over me. She hadn't run because she regretted our coupling. I thought back to the moment she'd left. In truth, she'd looked scared and vulnerable. Like she was a thousand miles away, not safe with me, in our bed.

"Does it hurt?" I asked.

Marienne seemed thrown by the question. "What?"

"When you have your visions."

A strange look crossed her face. "No-one's ever asked me that before. I suppose I'm used to them. I've always had visions, ever since I can remember."

"That doesn't answer my question." My voice was gentle, but I couldn't hide my curiosity.

"It's not a physical pain," she said. "But it's like the world around me disappears. Sometimes I can't trust that what I'm seeing is really... real."

On impulse, I reached out across the desk and clasped her hand.

"There," I said simply. "That's real."

Her face softened, and her thumb stroked across the back of my hand. "It is indeed." She contemplated our joined hands for a moment, then raised her beautiful eyes to mine. "But Erik, I must tell you what I saw." Her expression was grave. She grew even paler than when she'd first entered the room. "I came to warn you."

I frowned. "Of what?"

"Something's coming. A darkness." She broke off, her eyes wide and distressed. "King Damon is planning to attack. I saw the castle burn. Our people, dead in the streets. I—I watched you die in my arms, Erik."

A tear fell down her cheek, glinting silver in the sunlight.

I stared at the open book in front of me without really seeing it. *She saw me die?*

My gaze drifted to our joined hands.

"In your vision. We were... together?"

Warmth bloomed in my chest when I said the words out loud. They felt right. Marienne and me. *Together.*

Her gaze slid away from me. Gently, she disentangled her fingers from mine and withdrew, leaving me oddly bereft.

"Yes." Those lovely eyes refused to meet mine.

My surprise hung in the air between us.

"Surely you've already noticed?" she said. "You must feel it."

My heart hammered in my chest. She sounded resigned; regretful.

"Noticed *what*?" I tried to hold back the harsh tone, but I was getting frustrated. "Feel what?"

"Our connection." Finally, she looked up.

"Of course, I have."

My heart rate increased when I stared as if hypnotized into her eyes. They swirled and shimmered like depthless pools. "The bond between us. The moment we laid eyes on one another, everything changed." She bit her lip, and I suppressed a sigh of longing. "Your dragon knows me, doesn't it? Why do you think it stirs every time you see me? Every time you hear my name. We were meant for each other, Erik. We are soul mates."

Soul mates? Fated to be together?

It was like a final puzzle piece falling into place.

That was why she had hidden from me when I first came to the castle. All these years, she must have known. And I hadn't had a clue.

Something had drawn us toward each other, binding us together. Like a thread running through our lives, winding us closer and closer. Right from the moment we'd seen each other, all those years ago.

My mind was blank with shock. *Soul mates. Fated mates.*

"You knew about this?" I whispered. "The whole time? Why didn't you say anything earlier?"

She looked utterly miserable. My chest tightened as realization struck. *She doesn't want this. Us.*

Why would she? Marienne was powerful, beautiful and strong in her own right. Anyone who laid eyes on her could see that she was in a different league to me.

Apparently, the fates had shackled her to me, a low-born lout who was only here by sheer dumb luck.

"It's complicated," she said. "Last night…"

My skin prickled as I remembered the way I had held her in my arms. The passion, the lust, the inescapable desire. It was all due to the fated mate bond?

My chair scraped back from the desk as I stood. My movements were abrupt and jerky; it took a second for me to realize I was shaking with anger.

"You don't have to explain yourself to me," I said, turning away. "I understand now." She didn't want me, but had no choice except to follow fate's design.

The magic had forced her into it. Was that the problem?

I didn't want to see the disgust in her expression. Or, worse, the pity.

"It wasn't my choice, Erik." Her voice was closer now, and when I turned my head, she stood right in front of me. "Neither of us have a choice in this. I'm sorry."

Her eyes flashed with repressed emotion.

I ached to pull her against me with every fiber of my being, but I resisted. I couldn't bear to face her inevitable rejection.

Our bond was inescapable, inevitable. I was still reeling from the truth, but I couldn't deny it: we *were* bonded. Worst of all, some part of me had already known, ever since that first day, when we were worlds apart. When she hung on the arm of King Magnik, her husband, radiant in the sunlight, waving out at the cheering crowds.

I closed my eyes.

"It seems that the fates have a sick sense of humor," I said. "Shackling you to your husband's low-born half-brother. You wanted the king, and you got the bastard."

As soon as I uttered the words, I regretted them. I knew I was being unfair; Marienne had already told me Magnik had chosen *her*, not the other way around. How could anyone say no to a king?

But pain made me harsh. The barbs that had twisted themselves into my heart tightened as her eyes filled with tears.

"Since you arrived in the castle, I wondered about you. Who you were, what kind of man you have become, since that day I saw you in the street." Her strong tone belied the tears that spilled over, tracking down her flushed cheeks. "I think I finally have my answer."

"I guess you do," I snarled. "I am truly sorry to disappoint you, Your Majesty."

I made sure to imbue the title with the same disdain I had received from the elders this morning. Her eyes widened, and then narrowed.

"So am I," she said. "Your *Majesty*."

We breathed in tandem, inches apart. I fought back the desire that pumped through my veins, the warmth I could feel radiating between us.

It didn't matter what our bodies wanted for us. I would never be good enough for her, and we both knew it.

At least we were on the same page. My status in life might have changed, but one thing was certain: last night had been a huge mistake.

She had just made that abundantly clear.

I wasn't worthy of touching her. And I never would be.

EIGHT

Marienne

I stared up at Erik.

His tall, lean body was stiff with tension, and his arms were crossed over his chest. His whole frame, which had been such a comforting haven to me only a few short hours ago, was now as impenetrable as a brick wall.

Hopelessness threatened to crush me. I scrubbed the tears off my cheeks and whirled around, determined to put some distance between the two of us.

I took a few deep breaths to stop the panic from rising up and choking me.

If my fated mate truly didn't want me...

Without Erik, my life would be pure loneliness.

My magic simmered in my veins, an ever-present reminder of the reason why I would always be an outcast. It was the one thing that truly set me apart from others. I'd spent my life gifted and cursed in equal measure.

I knew all the stories. Terrible things happened to sorcerers who were rejected by their mates because their magic could never be accepted. When I was a child, the villagers had whispered tales of madness and destruction wrought by those wielding magic when they had been abandoned by the ones who should have loved them.

I heard of sorceresses who flung themselves off high towers out of despair, or leveled entire towns with their magic. At best, if Erik fully rejected me, I could end up powerless. At worst, I could die.

Still, he had every reason to be upset.

I was hardly a desirable choice. Men had always lusted after my magic, but they feared it, too.

Whatever kindness Erik had shown me, it was clear he was no exception. He didn't see me as a woman, a true partner. He just saw a powerful sorceress who could pose a threat to his reign.

To add insult to injury, I had been Magnik's queen for years without ever conceiving a child. The castle physicians had all concluded I was barren.

Tears pricked my eyes. It was almost too much to bear.

But I couldn't let his rejection overwhelm me. I had to focus. Erik, and his kingdom, needed help.

I steadied myself and turned around. Erik was watching me with an unreadable expression. I forced my features to remain neutral in the face of his indifference. Internally, my heart was close to breaking.

"King Damon." I circled the table, drawing closer to Erik. "There's no time to waste."

It didn't matter how he felt about me right now. I could tell he was still angry, but we had to put aside our differences. We were still allies, first and foremost.

I might not be the queen any longer, but this kingdom is mine as well as his.

He gave a short nod. "How much time do we have?"

I shrugged. "I'm afraid the visions aren't precise. But..." I bit my lip, thinking hard. "It was snowing pretty heavily, which means it will still be winter when they attack."

"Very soon, then." He furrowed his brow as he leaned over the desk, sweeping papers and books aside. "The northern territories are three days' journey from here, correct?"

I adjusted to the swift change of tone in our conversation. He was addressing me in short, clipped phrases, like I was a member of his council.

Very well. I could keep this meeting professional. Maybe he would even let me stay in the castle, in my suite. *Could I learn to live like that, knowing my fated mate was so close by?*

Sooner or later, he would take a wife. And on that day, my heart would *truly* break.

I inclined my head. "By carriage ride, yes." I looked away, shame-faced. "It would be much faster to fly, but... I have no shifting ability, sire."

"Really?" he asked, his eyebrows lifting high on his forehead.

"It's the price of my magic." I shrugged. "You can't miss something you never had."

He opened his mouth, then closed it again.

"I could carry you," he said. "As long as we keep you warm enough."

I shook my head again. "Damon's mountains are dangerously cold. I'm not sure I would survive a long flight in that weather." *Even with my magic to keep me warm.* "Plus, it may be smarter to move with stealth. We would not be inconspicuous if we arrived by flight. Your dragon would be too obvious."

Erik nodded slowly, as though thinking over my words.

"I will lead an expedition to the northern territories." He stood upright, his jaw set and his eyes firm. "We'll gather what intel we can, and then go from there."

A flush of warmth rose in my chest as I looked at him. This man was a natural-born leader. He would make a wonderful king.

"Okay." I lifted my chin, meeting his gaze with more confidence than I felt. "When do we leave?"

Confusion filled his expression. "What?"

I tilted my head. "Sooner rather than later, I should think. Today, or tomorrow?"

"Marienne..." He shook his head at me. A frown fell over his face. "You can't really want to come with me, surely? It's too dangerous."

I bristled. "Excuse me?"

He swept a hand over his face, his features wrinkling as if with stress.

"It's the far north, Marienne! We don't know what we're up against yet, what kind of danger could be waiting for us. I'm not putting you—I mean..." He shook his head. "Thank you for your help, but I can take it from here."

Ugh!

"Erik." I fought to keep my voice steady. "I'm a *sorceress*. I can take care of myself perfectly well, I assure you."

"I don't doubt it," he replied, sounding frustrated. "Are you always this stubborn?"

I stared at him, saying nothing. A confusing mixture of pleasure and irritation flooded through me when I locked eyes with him. I stayed cool; patient. He clenched his jaw, his gaze heated.

I held on until he gave a huff of defeat and threw up his hands, glaring at the opposite wall.

"Fine," he muttered.

"Fine," I echoed, pleased. It looked like I had won that round.

So what if he didn't want me for a wife? I could be useful to him in other ways.

I ignored the stab of pain at the thought that I would serve this king just as I had my late husband—as a tool to further the betterment of the kingdom. Nothing more.

Erik stalked out of the room. I watched him leave in my peripheral vision. Presumably, he was off to find somewhere to brood until it was time to leave. I sighed internally and sank down into the nearest chair. My victory lasted all of ten seconds, before it occurred to me precisely *what* I'd signed up for: a carriage journey across a frozen tundra. Alone, for days on end, with the man I craved with every fiber of my being.

This should be interesting.

～

Erik

Stavrok—

I have reason to believe that my clan is in grave danger. Marienne had a vision: our castle burning, our people dead in the streets. She believes that King Damon is planning an attack. Whatever we discover, I'm sure you can appreciate the urgency of the situation. I'm determined to get to the heart of it; otherwise, I'm afraid my reign might be over before it has even started.

Marienne and I are travelling north to assess the situation. We want to scout Damon's kingdom before taking any action. I have instructed Magnik's army—my army—to remain on standby until our return.

This isn't your fight. But if you meant what you said the last time we met—about our alliance—I thought it best that you know what's coming.

I pray we meet again under better circumstances.

Erik

CONSCIOUS OF OUR TIME CONSTRAINTS, I'd written the letter while sitting in the carriage, so the handwriting wasn't great, but I think I got the message across.

I scanned the letter several times until I was satisfied that I'd said everything I wanted. With a grunt, I pulled the signet ring off my finger and pressed it into the inkpad that lay beside the paper. My signature was marked with my family seal, the royal crest emblazoned on the thick parchment.

The ring was a heavy, silver thing. It had been Magnik's, and my father's before him. And his father's. And on and on.

In moments of boredom or distraction I often found myself twisting it back and forth, uncomfortable with its presence on my finger. After stamping the letter, I wiped the ink off the ring and slipped it back on, making a fist while I waited for the bright ink to dry.

Then I folded the letter into quarters and rapped on the closed carriage door. The door opened, and my butler Thomas hovered outside. "Sire?"

I placed the letter into his hand. "See that this gets to Stavrok," I said, and he gave a short nod.

The cold blast of air into the carriage made a shiver run down my spine, and I yanked the door closed again.

The wind was picking up in earnest, and I wanted to get as far as possible before nightfall. I rapped on the roof of the carriage, and the driver shouted a reply. The horses whinnied as the wheels began to turn, and soon we were well on our way, trundling through the castle grounds at speed.

We had a procession behind us. A sleigh with our possessions and two additional carriages for my men. A small contingent of my army.

I chanced a glance at the seat opposite me.

Marienne sat with her hands folded in her lap. She was staring out at the changing scenery as it passed: dark mountains, trees, the small twinkling lights of the town below us. We weren't going that way, however; we were taking the road that wound up the rockface. The track was narrow and uneven, seldom used by travelers. It wasn't well-maintained, and the carriage wheels jolted over every pothole and lump of gravel.

Perhaps the kingdom should have paid to repair this road, rather than furnish gold chains around the elders' necks.

Marienne didn't seem uncomfortable to be sharing a carriage in dead silence. Her face appeared smooth and peaceful.

I left her alone with her thoughts. I couldn't think what to say.

An apology might be a good start.

A guilty prickle traveled up the back of my neck. It wasn't *her* fault she was saddled with me, after all.

The carriage was silent save for the whistling wind and the occasional distant rockfall. Unable to help myself, I continued to steal glances at her. Something in my chest tightened when my eyes tracked over her long, black hair. It was glossy, and looked almost blue in the shadows, like raven's wings. I remembered how soft it was to touch. A lock fell over her face, framing her jewel-bright eyes.

"Can I help you?"

Her voice startled me, and my cheeks heated with the realization I'd been caught out. I was too dazed to think up a good excuse. "I was just… hoping you packed for the weather."

I gestured lamely to the white skin showing above her low-necked blouse. She arched a delicate eyebrow, and I huffed, looking away.

What was I doing? We were going to be stuck like this for days.

Still, I was struck with a desire to fill the silence. If we couldn't be civil, we could at least use this time to talk tactics.

"We should be smart about this." I ran a hand over my jaw and noted absently that her eyes tracked the movement. "There's no point going in half-cocked. Just in case your visions…"

"They're not wrong," she snapped. "I know what I saw."

"I'm not *saying* they're wrong," I said, before brushing a hand through my hair. "We *are* mounting this expedition up north based on your visions, after all."

Her lips pressed together, before she finally nodded. "All right. I'll give you that."

"Look," I said. "There's too much at stake here—"

"You think I don't know what's at stake? If we don't act now, it will be too late!"

"Unless we get the full picture, we won't even know who our enemy is!" I growled, narrowing my eyes.

Opposite me, Marienne mirrored my posture. We both leaned in close, getting right into each other's space. The air between us simmered with heat.

Outside, the wind picked up. It was howling now, and large white flakes thudded against the glass of the carriage windows, building a thick white layer over the ledge. Snarling, I yanked the velvet curtain across the window to keep in some of the heat. Marienne's flimsy sleeves didn't look like they would provide much protection.

We lapsed back into prickly silence.

The carriage thundered on for a few more miles. The sky outside was dark with snowfall, and I found myself worrying about the remainder of the journey.

I'd never traveled so far north before. I'd heard tales, of course, but I had no idea what to expect.

Ravenous wolves. Frostbite, culminating in a slow, icy death.

Death at the end of a thick iron broadsword.

I wasn't afraid for myself as much as the woman sitting opposite me. Though we were now merely allies—and even *that* label seemed to be hanging by a thread—the thought that I was unknowingly leading her into danger was too much to bear.

For all I knew, we were playing right into Damon's hands.

The carriage wheels ground to a halt, wrenching me from my thoughts. I made eye contact with Marienne when she looked up at the delay. Our gazes darted away from each other, but it was clear her puzzlement equaled mine.

Why have we stopped?

The plan was to travel until we lost the daylight, then make camp. Unless...

I knocked a couple of times on the roof of the carriage, then slid over and opened the door a crack. The blizzard outside raged and a few stray snowflakes snuck through the gap. I craned my neck, squinting up at the driver. He dismounted and hurried toward the horses.

I called out to him. "What's going on?"

"The carriage won't make it any further in this, sire." He indicated the snow that was piling up against the wheels. "I'm afraid you and the queen will have to travel to your camp another way."

My alarm increased with every word he spoke. "What do you mean, another way?"

"The wheels won't make it through the pass in these conditions. You'll have to make the rest of the journey by sleigh."

Through the swirling whiteness that half-blinded me, I looked in the direction he was pointing. The snow was getting deeper by the minute.

Behind us, the small retinue of men that had followed us in a second and third carriage, began unfastening the ropes of the sleigh that carried our meager belongings behind the procession. The horses were led around and harnessed to the sleigh, and I glared out at the howling wilderness before ducking my head back into the carriage.

My eyes widened. From somewhere, Marienne had produced a thick cloak with a high fur collar, complete with a muff. She drew the garments around her small frame and gave me a short nod.

"Are you sure you want to do this?" I murmured. "You could still turn back."

She shook her head. Her eyes betrayed no hint of nervousness, but her face was paler than usual. Without thinking, I reached out and took the small hand that extended from her thick cloak. She clutched at me tightly, betraying her concern as clearly as her pale cheeks.

Without another word, I led us out into the storm.

Marienne

The snow outside fell continuously. I pressed myself up against Erik's side, using his body to shield myself from the worst of the wind as we hurried toward the sleigh.

The conveyance was much smaller than our carriage, but the men had lit the lanterns that hung inside the compartment, giving it a coziness that I gravitated toward.

Golden light spilled out over the snowdrift when Erik opened the door of the sleigh carriage. His hands found my waist, boosting me up, and I clambered inside, glad to be out of the elements.

Erik lingered outside. I listened to him exchange a few words with the men in a low, urgent voice, and then he slipped in behind me and fastened the door.

The crimson cushions inside were comfortable enough, but I came to the awkward realization we would have to share the bench. It was about the size of a loveseat, and Erik's large frame crowded up against mine no matter how we positioned ourselves.

He grunted, and his large hands curled around the horses' reins. He gave them a sharp tug and we were on the move once more.

"The men will rejoin us once the snow starts easing up," Erik muttered. He stared ahead, his jaw tight and his eyes like flint.

We traveled in silence. Dark, craggy rocks loomed on either side as we approached the pass, and I shivered, grateful for my thick furs.

He huffed, eyes flicking over my form. "Are you cold?"

I shook my head. The little nook had already warmed up due to our shared body heat.

Erik didn't say anything. His eyes were fixed on the road ahead, but I thought I felt him press a little closer.

"You keep asking me that," I whispered, eventually. I couldn't help myself. Despite his obvious lack of interest in me, he still showed the decency to ask if I was all right. "No one ever asked me things like that before you came along."

He shifted in his seat. "It's common courtesy."

"Well, I've lived a very uncommon life." My voice was soft, quiet, but I got the sense that he was hanging on every word. As if he *cared*.

"Yeah?"

"I'm not used to people asking *about* me," I said. "Usually, they want something *from* me. Magnik..."

His name hung in the air between us. I gave a deep sigh, relaxing into the cushions and the warmth of Erik's body.

"I was useful to him." I bit my lip. "But he never trusted me. Not completely. Even when I was a girl, the townsfolk always knew that I... I was... different."

Erik was silent. My heart thudded in my chest. Had I read the situation wrong? Then he reached out, and I found myself lifted and rearranged, so my back pressed against his torso, firm even through all the layers separating us. He tucked his huge arms around me, taking the reins up in his free hand.

"Well, then." He gave my shoulders a gentle squeeze. "I guess we have that in common, Your Majesty."

The tension that had built up between us started to thaw.

Your Majesty.

That title again, which he had said so scornfully the day before... now, it fell from his lips like a pet name.

Something shifted. Despite the storm, and the great, shadowy unknown that loomed from the other side of the mountain range, I felt a kernel of warmth spark inside my chest.

Lulled by the rhythmic sway of the sleigh ride, the thump of Erik's heart beneath my ear, and the whistle of the wind outside, I drifted off into sleep.

I woke to Erik's murmuring voice. My face was pressed against something firm and warm, and I curved in closer, sighing happily.

Once I realized what I was doing in my half-conscious state, I froze.

Blinking rapidly, I withdrew, brushing my tangled hair off my cheeks. The sleigh had stopped moving and Erik turned to me. A smile lingered at the corners of his mouth.

"Ah, Sleeping Beauty is back with us."

I scowled and rubbed at my eyes, straightening up. "How long was I out?"

"About thirty minutes." He paused, his eyes lingering over my face. "We've made it to camp."

Camp, I deduced, as I peered out of the window, was a small log cabin built into the mountainside. The snow had thankfully stopped for the time being, but it was over a foot deep in some places.

Erik held out his arms. "I'll carry you, if you wish. It'll save you from getting those dainty little shoes of yours damp."

I shook my head, cheeks heating up. "I'm sure I'll manage."

With a boyish grin, he flung open the door and pulled me out of the sleigh, his large hands curving around my waist. Before I could protest, he threw me over one shoulder and began wading through the snow toward the cabin.

"Erik!" I closed my fingers around the hair at the nape of his neck, and gave it a sharp tug to express my displeasure.

He let out a yelp before bursting into laughter.

Despite the depth of the snow, Erik got the door to the cabin open, and we tumbled through the doorway in a flurry of snow and tangled limbs. I righted myself and gave him a shove, and he held his hands up, still smiling at me with that crooked, unrepentant smile of his.

"See, your feet are still dry!" He pointed down, and I huffed, unable to deny that he was right. "I'll see to the horses and get them under shelter, and then let's get this place warmed up, shall we?"

While he strode off, I took stock of our surroundings.

The cabin was a simple, one room dwelling, with an adjoining bathroom, and a lean-to at the side where Erik would presumably lead the horses.

A heavy iron stove crouched in the corner, and snowshoes hung in the rafters over the one tiny bed.

Hanging in the corner was a rough-hewn, wooden cradle. I kept away from it, focusing my attention on the narrow bed and the rocking chair with the patchwork quilt thrown over it.

When Erik returned with kindling, he quickly started a fire for the stove while I set one in the hearth. In no time, the room began to warm up.

"Erik?"

"Hmm?"

I turned from the fireplace to see him poking at the stove, which now flickered and glowed. He handed me a piece of bread and I took it.

"Whoever chose this place didn't think very hard about our sleeping arrangements," I said wryly.

His eyes followed my gaze to the tiny bed. It was barely big enough for one person, let alone someone of Erik's size.

He chewed on his piece of bread for a beat or two, before swallowing. "I'll take the chair."

"Oh." Something inside my chest curled. "No. It's... You can't..."

There was that crooked grin again. The one that made my heart turn over in my chest.

"Marienne." He reached out and put a hand on my shoulder. "It's not a discussion."

We stared at each other.

Eventually, I sighed. "Very well."

We ate in companionable silence, positioned close to the stove. Erik even made me a hot coffee, which warmed me as we sat there. The crackling logs filled the cabin with a smoky smell, and I relaxed into it.

How was it that here, in the middle of nowhere with a man I barely knew, I felt safer than I had in... forever?

I laughed when Erik gathered up the quilt and draped it around his shoulders, posing in a mock-heroic stance, his arms crossed over his broad chest.

"Your Highness." I bowed low, accepting his outstretched hand.

He pressed a kiss to the back of my knuckles. For a moment, I forgot we were play-acting, and my breath caught as his mouth touched my skin.

He dropped my hand, and the laughter died from his eyes as he slumped back into the chair. I perched on the end of the bed, studying him. In the low light, all traces of the stoic warrior I had traveled with vanished. He looked like the young man he was, his hair rumpled, his shoulders set with unease.

"What you said earlier..." He looked up at me, and my gaze dropped. "About growing up... It was like that for me, too. I was always the strongest. The first boy my age to shift. My village didn't know who I truly was, but they could tell I was different."

"It wasn't right," I whispered. "Your father should have raised you in the castle. You were his son, his *blood*. It was your birthright."

He ran a hand through his hair and shrugged. "If that were the case, Magnik wouldn't have allowed me to live."

As much as I hated hearing that, I knew he was likely right.

His eyes met mine, his gaze lit by and reflecting the heat of the flames. "All I'm saying is, I know how it feels, Mari. To be misunderstood. To have people look at you like..."

He waved a hand. *He called me Mari.* I liked the sound of the nickname Lucy had given me, on Erik's lips. I smiled at him, and finished the sentence he'd started.

"Like you're a powder keg waiting to explode?"

He looked at me sharply. "Exactly." His serious expression melted away.

"I guess it's about finding the balance, right?" I wrapped my hands around the warm mug, breathing in the steam.

"How do you mean?"

"Well..." I paused, listening to the fire crackle. "I'm a sorceress, but I'm also a woman."

His eyes flickered over my face. I saw what he was imagining clear enough, and a heat rose in my cheeks.

"I don't mean like *that*. I just mean..." I bit my lip. "My power doesn't mean I'm some kind of heartless *force*. It's part of me, but I'm not driven by it. I want things just like any other woman. Love, companionship..."

Children. I trailed off once I realized what I was about to admit.

Erik gazed at me, his expression unreadable. I shook my head, letting the hair fall over my face to hide my blush.

"The way I see it, your shifter is the same as my magic." I inhaled deeply, breathing in the intoxicating combination of woodsmoke and the heady scent of Erik next to me. "It's part of you, so close that you couldn't imagine life without it. But... you're more than just the dragon, Erik. And I'm so much more than my magic."

He huffed, dropping his head down. My eyes traced over the broad span of his shoulders. In the firelight, the muscles in his back were particularly defined; they showed through his thin undershirt in a manner I found distracting.

"Never thought that you and I could have so much in common." He lifted his head and stared at me. My breath hitched at the look in his eyes.

I wanted him so badly. It would be easy, *too* easy, to lean in and kiss him.

But I had to respect his wishes. The bond between us was undeniable, but I could ignore it. I had to. I couldn't tempt him into losing control again, no matter how hungrily he was gazing at me.

"I guess there's a lot we don't know about each other," I said eventually, glancing up at him through my eyelashes.

"I guess so."

We laughed a little, our eyes lingering over each other, soft and warm. Heat coiled in my stomach.

It was a far cry from where we had started out that morning. Being away from the castle changed everything. All the tension and insecurity had fallen away, dropped somewhere along the road that lay behind us.

In some ways, I wanted it to go on like this forever.

Nevertheless, I couldn't suppress a yawn when it came. I pressed the back of my hand against my open mouth, but Erik wasn't fooled. His voice softened, low and quiet against the roar of the wind outside.

"You should get some rest."

I got up and lit the lantern, then carried it to the bedside. "You're sure you don't want to take the bed?"

He shrugged the quilt over his shoulders and nodded. "I'm used to roughing it, Majesty. Besides, I wouldn't fit in that thing in a million years."

I shook my head at him, but I couldn't argue with his logic. The bed was pretty small.

I slipped out of my shoes and pulled my long stockings down, folding them neatly and hanging them over the foot of the bed. Erik turned his face away, staring at the flames: ridiculous behavior, given the fact that he'd seen everything already.

I slid between the sheets, too tired to bother with nightclothes. I curled up on my side, my mind drifting already.

I studied his large frame in silhouette against the glow from the stove. It made for a comforting picture. The image of Erik grew more and more hazy as my eyelids fought to stay open. I was exhausted, but I didn't care.

Now that he was in my life, I wanted to look at him for as long as possible.

It was stupid, and irrational, but I couldn't shake the feeling that, if I closed my eyes and fell asleep, he might disappear forever.

CHAPTER
TEN

Erik

I woke to a sore back and a crick in my neck.

Groaning, I pulled myself up out of the rocking chair that had been my bed for the night and grimaced as I folded the quilt.

I'd had worse nights.

Marienne was stretched out on the little cot, fast asleep. Her dark hair feathered out over the pillow, framing her peaceful face.

I had a crazy impulse to lean down and place a kiss on her sleeping mouth, like a prince in a fairytale. After a minute, I snorted to myself and shook away the thought, moving to the window.

Last night had been strange, to say the least. I was glad we were on

209

friendly terms again, even if my heart wouldn't stop racing every time she came near.

Now I knew about the bond between us, I could rationalize it to myself. It must be the dragon that slumbered under my skin that hungered for her, not *me*. Every urge I had, every impulse to wrap my hands around her hips and pull her against me... it was all down to him. My dragon.

I glanced at her sleeping form.

I had to admit, though, our relationship was more complicated now. It wasn't lust crowding everything else out of my mind.

I actually *liked* her.

Gods, I had to focus. Like it or not, we had more pressing matters to deal with than my idiotic feelings.

Outside, the world was a bright, sparkling white. Mercifully, it hadn't snowed much more in the night, which would ease our journey considerably.

Sleepy murmurs sounded from across the room, and I looked over my shoulder to find Marienne staring at me shyly.

"Good morning." Her mouth curled upwards, sweet, pink, and tempting as sin.

I mumbled something in reply as I fumbled for my jacket and boots and shoved them on. She watched me as I trudged out the door, but I didn't look back.

Everything in me wanted to sweep her up into my arms and ravish her completely.

I had to get out of there before I did something I wasn't certain she wanted.

The horses whinnied in greeting as I checked them over, tending to them in preparation for the day ahead. If we made good progress, we should reach our destination by nightfall.

I stroked my hand down a horse's flank, gentling it. Truth be told, I was more at home out here than I was in the castle. *This* was the life in which I had been raised. It might be simple, but it was what I knew.

I glanced back toward the mountain pass. Behind us lay my castle. More council meetings, more jargon I couldn't get my head around. More petty power struggles and diplomatic entanglements.

I looked the other way, down the road we were traveling. I had no idea what lay around the corner, but it couldn't be good.

Marienne appeared at my side. She had changed into a thick fur coat and hat, and her hair hung in a long braid over her shoulder.

Her eyes traveled to my hands, as I went over the horses' tack again.

"You're good at that." She nodded in the direction of the horse, fiddling with the end of her braid.

I smiled. "It's what I know."

"Animals have always been nervous around me." Despite her words, she drew closer, like she couldn't help herself. "It's because of my magic, I think. They can sense it."

The horse huffed when Marienne came up alongside me. I hushed it until it calmed down and held out my hand.

Her eyes flicked up at me, long lashes shadowing her cheeks. I wiggled my fingers, and with a sigh she slid her palm against mine.

Gently, I turned her hand around and shadowed it with mine. We approached the horse together.

"If you're scared," I said, my voice ruffling the soft strands of hair around her ear, "they can tell. But if you're nice and calm... there, see?"

Her hand stroked along the horse's mane. The horse shuffled its feet a little but remained calm, allowing her to pet it without complaint. Marienne breathed out in amazement and my heart swelled in my chest.

Eventually, she drew away and gazed up at me. Her eyes were even more striking in contrast with the snow, but it was her expression that made her truly radiant. She looked so happy, all of a sudden.

"Thank you." She reached out and squeezed my hand, and I squeezed back before I could think better of it.

"We should make a move," I muttered, pulling away from her and heading back to the cabin to grab our supplies.

She bobbed along by my side.

"Not before I get some food into you." She nudged me out of the way at the door, batting her eyelashes at me over her shoulder. "Sire."

"Has anyone ever told you," I called after her, "for a royal subject, you're quite cheeky?"

"I think you'd be the first, Your Highness!"

I laughed, shaking my head. "I find that hard to believe."

~

THE BUOYANT MOOD drained away once we were on the road again.

Once the snowstorm cleared, we made good progress, but the further we journeyed, the closer we were to enemy territory.

Around mid-morning, we made it through the mountains. They loomed up behind us, stretching into the pale sky. For the first time, I sensed how truly vulnerable we were, just two people, heading into the vast unknown.

The procession would catch up with us once they found a way through the snow. But they were probably half a day behind us.

Marienne's hand found mine in the space between us, and our fingers tangled together.

Just yesterday, I had been terrified for her safety. I couldn't help but be glad she was here now. Whatever we found at Winter Castle, we would face it together.

Small farmsteads appeared on the horizon. The landscape was flat and sparse, and the settlements were bleak places without trees, or crops, or even signs of fire or life.

I shuddered to think of the life of pure survival the people in this place must live. Dragon shifters were a tall, proud people, and they needed a lot of food to survive.

How does this clan manage?

The snow drifted around us as we trundled through the frozen wasteland. We were nearing our checkpoint, where we would meet with the members of the expedition we had been forced to abandon in yesterday's snowstorm.

There was a rocky ridge up ahead. The back of my neck prickled as I drew the sleigh to a standstill.

Beside me, Marienne tensed. We exchanged glances and emerged from the sleigh together, sticking close to each other as we inched forward through the snow.

I didn't bother telling her to stay put. I would be wasting my breath.

I glanced up, something glinting in the sunlight on the ridge catching my eye. It was the shiny edge of an axe. The blood froze in my veins. These weren't our men. This was an ambush.

A raven wheeled in the sky overhead. Its sharp cry pierced through my chest. My heart thumped, and my head filled with white noise. Marienne whispered something to me in an urgent voice, but I didn't catch it. I had failed before the game had even started. I'd led us both into a trap, and we were about to pay the price.

"Put up your hands!" A male voice from behind me sounded, low and guttural. "Both of you!"

Slowly, I raised my hands. One glance via my peripheral vision told me that there were more soldiers behind us, bristling with weapons.

We were surrounded by the toughest men I'd ever seen. They were all huge, wearing long coats of fur suitable for their weather and they carried large weapons. Axes and swords aplenty.

Beside me, Marienne's eyes glowed with magic. I knew she was waiting for my signal. One look from me, and she would start throwing fireballs. Some buried instinct told me to wait.

They haven't attacked us. There's a reason for that; there has to be.

Instead, the men simply stood, tensed for action. But still, they didn't approach.

"I am King Bravadik of the Black Mountains. I've come here with Dowager Queen Marienne," I said, with all the confidence I didn't feel. "I wish to speak with King Damon."

If they so much as looked sideways at Marienne, I would transform into my dragon and fight our way out of here. But at the moment, my instincts were telling me to go along with the guards and find out exactly what was going on in this strange kingdom to the north.

Only time would tell if I'd been right to follow those instincts, or not.

MARIENNE

For the rest of the journey to Damon's castle, we traveled under armed guard.

Or, as I tried to think of it, a royal escort.

I held my head high, pretending for all the world that we'd been expecting this. If my years as Magnik's queen had taught me one thing, it was never to show fear in front of your enemy.

My response didn't seem to matter either way. Our captors barely glanced at me. They surrounded us on all sides, stone-faced, their focus purely on Erik. They were covered in thick furs, and their massive, hulking frames made it difficult for me to see the castle up ahead as we approached it.

By my side, Erik's profile was firm, unmoving, but his jaw was clenched tight. I could tell that it was taking every ounce of his concentration not to shift and fly us both out of there.

My magic simmered through my veins, sensing the threat that dragged us further and further into dangerous territory. But I knew better than to strike out at our captors. If I lost control, it would spell disaster for us all. War would break out between our clans, and all my visions—all the fire, bloodshed, and death—would come true. And it would be all my fault.

A huge black shape loomed out of the snowdrifts, dominating the skyline. Tall towers spiked upward, and the heavy iron gates of the drawbridge clanked open as we approached. Ravens perched along the high stone walls. They watched our progress with beady, inquisitive eyes.

I shivered. I could feel it in my bones; the birds were a bad omen.

As we trundled over the drawbridge, I caught flickers of movement from the parapets. How many people were hidden beyond these high walls? An army?

More to the point, the guards were totally silent. Almost sullen. Not what I expected from men who had captured such a powerful enemy.

As we climbed the uneven steps up to the entrance, Erik offered me his arm. I took it, half-amused that he was finally remembering court etiquette at a time like this, half-grateful I wouldn't slip and lose my footing on the icy stone.

We entered a huge, dark hallway. I shook the snow from my hair, glad to be out of the elements. My eyes struggled to adjust to the gloom; the man who seemed to lead the others held up a lantern, and in the soft light I could make out vague, dark shapes.

There were long, jagged cracks in the wooden beams that held up the ceiling. Cobwebs trailed from heavy candelabras above our heads, and all along the wall, pale squares suggested that paintings and tapestries had been torn down.

Huh.

All in all, it wasn't that different from our castle, or Stavrok's, but...

This one looked abandoned. Lifeless.

I frowned as we were led deeper inside the castle, through a high archway into a smaller antechamber. The lack of any sign of life didn't make sense. All the fireplaces were dark and empty, and a chilling wind howled through them, giving the place a desolate air.

I shuddered. I was no warmer now that we were inside. I puffed out a few breaths, noting the white clouds that formed.

"Something's wrong," I murmured to Erik. He tilted his head down so I could whisper directly into his ear. "Why is it so dark?"

We reached a set of ornately carved doors. Wolves and dragons intertwined in the dark grain, and I leaned in, impressed by the beauty of the artwork. But even here, once I got closer, I noted the scratches and cuts that marred the surface of the wood.

Dragon claws?

Erik pressed me further into his side and I tried to muffle the automatic sigh of relief at the feel of his strong body against mine.

Even now, when we were literally about to brave the lair of the beast, it felt so right to be with Erik.

Without a word or a backward glance at us, the guard strode forward and knocked on the door.

"Your Majesty. You have guests. King Bravadik of the Black Mountains, and Dowager Queen Marienne."

My chest tingled at the sound of our names. Spoken together like that, they sounded... good.

I hung my head, feeling foolish for having such a thought at a time like this.

"Enter."

The voice behind the door was low, but it pierced through the wooden door clear as crystal. The fear that I had managed to quell rose again, stronger than ever.

We were nudged forward by the guards, and the doors opened on either side of us, revealing a small room. Thankfully, this one had a small fire burning in the grate.

If we're about to be murdered, at least it'll be somewhere marginally warm.

Erik and I inched forward. The doors shut behind us with a final rush of cold air. We were both on high alert for any sign of sudden movement.

But none came. The room was just... a perfectly ordinary room. Half-office, half-sitting room, with a large oil painting over the fireplace and messy stacks of paperwork scattered over every available surface.

A lived-in room, unlike the rest of the castle.

We glanced at each other. Erik looked as puzzled as I did.

"Hello?" I called out, cautiously.

Something stirred at the large desk, behind stacks of papers. As one, we whirled to face it. Erik closed his hand over my arm, firm and protective.

Damon sat in a chair by the desk. I'd met him at several king's council dinners, but never truly spoken to him. He was tall and broad, like Erik, and his eyes were like ice. He wasn't old, and yet his hair was threaded with silver.

King Damon stared at us, and we stared back, too much in shock at his ravaged appearance to speak.

This was the man who had haunted my nightmares for days. And yet...

He didn't look like someone planning an attack. Dark shadows circled his eyes, and his huge frame was bowed inwards, like he had the weight of the world on his shoulders. He looked exhausted, almost ill.

What was going on here?

"Marienne." His voice was gravelly, like he didn't use it all that much these days. "It's nice to see you again."

I chose my words carefully. Even if it didn't seem like we were in immediate danger, we couldn't relax. I had lived through my entire marriage to Magnik on the edge of a tightrope. The threat of the dungeons always lurked in the back of my mind. I knew how to play the game.

Inclining my head, I emerged slightly from Erik's side so I could address Damon properly. "Your Majesty. It's been too long."

"And you decided to pay me a visit, it seems." Damon's eyes flicked to Erik. "With your new king. You're Magnik's half-brother?"

"That's right." Erik spoke evenly, but the forearm I was still gripping was tense. "They crowned me a week ago."

"Congratulations." Damon bowed his head. When he looked up, his pale eyes regarded us with an unreadable expression. "I'm sorry I couldn't make it to the ceremony."

"I won't hold it against you," Erik said, indicating the mess spread over the desk. "It looks like you have your hands full here."

His voice was conversational, diplomatic. I was impressed. This was a strange and unsettling place, and the odds were not stacked in our favor, but Erik was leading the conversation like we were chatting with friends over dinner.

The ghost of a smile crept over Damon's face. He looked down at the chaos, and then back up to us, arching a brow.

"You're not much like him, are you?"

Erik took half a step forward. "Who?"

"Your brother. Magnik." Damon glanced at me, then returned his gaze to Erik. "You don't seem very much like your father, either."

"I wouldn't know," Erik said. "I never met either of them, beyond having them pointed out to me by my mother."

King Damon circled around the desk, moving toward us with his hands behind his back. He walked slowly, casually, like we'd been invited here. Like we hadn't been marched to this room under guard.

I couldn't let myself forget that fact, no matter how friendly his manner. I squeezed Erik's arm, and he flicked a glance my way. His mouth was tight, and he gave me a tiny nod.

ELEVEN

Erik.

"I wish I could say I'd never met my father…" Damon trailed off with a sigh. I followed the line of his gaze, up to the painting that hung over the fireplace.

A fearsome-looking man stared back. He had Damon's pale, ice-blue eyes, but that was where the resemblance ended. His face was longer, and his jawline narrower. His expression was pinched, and his mouth had been painted with a cruel, foreboding twist.

The northern kings were known to be reclusive. They kept to themselves all year round. Nobody thought anything of it.

When Damon inherited the throne, none of the other clans had been present.

Were Erik and I the first outsiders to visit his court?

Erik strode forward, moving to stand beside Damon in front of the fireplace. Subtly, I crept away so I could study the documents that lay on the desk.

At a glance, they looked normal enough. Balance sheets. Payment notices.

"Did you not get along with your father?" Erik asked.

There was a long pause as Damon seemed to ponder his answer.

"My father ruled this clan like the tyrant he was." He spoke into the fireplace, gazing at the flames like they might reveal their secrets to him. "He drove my mother into an early grave. He cut off our clan from all outside influences. In his eyes, every other kingdom was a threat to his power."

Damon's words made me shiver. Memories of all the long years I'd spent at Magnik's side, helpless to stop his cruel nature, stirred up inside me. I may have been his wife, but to all intents and purposes I had been a prisoner in a gilded cage in my tower, subject like all of us in the kingdom to the whims of a power-hungry king...

Had Magnik been a tyrant, like Damon's father? Not quite, perhaps, but certainly close enough.

"Toward the end, his gambling got worse and worse." Damon practically spat out the words. "We lost so much. The castle fell to ruin, as you've probably already noticed, but even that wasn't enough for him. He raised taxes and drained the wealth from our land, all to feed his addiction."

He whirled around and strode over to the window, looking out at the barren, wintery landscape. "But all the money in the north couldn't settle the debts he racked up. Our whole clan is starving. Debtors took our entire crop yield, and it wasn't enough. They want blood and will be back for our heads by the end of the month. We are done for. The whole clan. There is nothing left."

My mind spiraled with the shock of his words. I stared blankly at the whirling snowflakes outside, a new realization dawning.

The visions hadn't been wrong, but they hadn't shown the full picture.

A burning castle. People dead in the street.

All this time, I had thought that it was *our* castle under siege. Our people in mortal danger.

I had been given fragments of a puzzle and put the pieces together as best I could. But I'd been wrong. And I had led Erik here, right into the heart of the danger.

Damon turned, standing framed in the window. From this angle he looked like a young, grim reflection of his father's painting.

"When my guards spotted you in the distance, I thought the other kingdoms had heard of our misfortune. We feared you had sent spies to check our defenses for weaknesses before sending in your army." He spread out his hands,. "Imagine my surprise when I was told it was the king and queen themselves, in the flesh."

"Why are you telling us this?" Erik asked, uncertainty in his tone.

Damon shrugged, his eyes hollow and blank. "Why not? I don't know why you've come, but it doesn't matter much to me, either way. Our clan is finished." His mouth twisted as he looked up at his father's portrait. "My father never thought much of my chances after I took the throne. It seems he was right. I'll forever be known as the king who destroyed the royal line of Ice Dragons."

"But..." I burst out.

The two men turned to look at me, and my cheeks heated.

"With respect, Your Majesty," I said, "we are only here because we thought you were planning to wage war on *us.*"

Damon's brow furrowed. "Why would you... ah." His face cleared as comprehension dawned. "The sorceress of the Black Mountains. The rumors of your skill at sorcery were not exaggerated, then."

"They weren't," Erik said. He spared a glance at me, then moved to stand beside me so he could also study the documents on the desk.

I stepped away from him, drawing Damon's attention, and drew my arms around my waist, suddenly self-conscious.

"I don't know about that. The visions, they're not always under my control. A few days ago, I saw... you." I glanced around at the desolate room, then out at the snowstorm. "I saw horrors I can't even explain. I thought..."

The memory of Erik in my arms, the life leaving his body, filled me with a wave of grief that almost choked me.

"Forgive me, Your Majesty," I said. "I thought you were responsible.

We traveled here because we had to know for sure. We had to at least try to avert war, if we could."

"It was brave of you to come all this way." Damon's eyes softened as he stared between us. "So far from everything you know. The southern clans don't usually bother themselves with us. It's a rare thing, to venture this far north beyond the mountains."

All these years, the northern kingdom had been the stuff of legend. Spoken about in whispers, in dark tales full of ice monsters with sharp claws and sharper teeth.

I now saw the loner king in a different light. Up close, he was just another young man thrust under the burden of leadership, trying to follow in the footsteps of a tyrant.

Damon and Erik had more in common than any of us had realized.

"Well." Damon clapped his hands together, interrupting my train of thought. "Now that you know the truth, I expect you'll want to begin the journey home."

I frowned and glanced at Erik, who was looking determined and resolute.

"Home?" I repeated.

Damon looked uncertain. "It's a long way, if I'm not mistaken. You'll want to set off before dark so that you may put as much distance between yourselves and my kingdom as possible."

"Damon." Erik cleared his throat. "With respect, I think I speak for both of us when I say that we'd like to stay here a little longer."

I nodded, moving back to stand beside Erik. Outside, the wind picked up again, howling so loudly it almost drowned out my words.

"We won't abandon you to your fate," I said. "Your people don't deserve to suffer for the sins of the past, and neither do you."

Damon's eyes widened as Erik approached him, moving with authority and grace. If I didn't know better, I would have thought he'd spent his whole life doing this. He didn't seem to know it, but Erik had stepped into the role of king quickly and already presented as a natural-born ruler.

Erik placed a hand over his heart and inclined his head. "I pledge allegiance to the northern dragon clan. I will send for my army at once. You won't fight this battle against your debtors alone."

Damon's mouth flattened into a hard line and his jaw tightened as he considered the proposal. Then, he reached out and grabbed Erik by the forearm. Erik grabbed Damon's arm, and they shook on it in the way of dragon kings, sealing the pact between our kingdoms.

A smile played at the corners of my mouth as I regarded them. This trip had taken an unexpected turn, but the terror that had plagued me for days melted away with the look on Erik's face.

He was capable. Confident. Righteous.

And sexy as hell.

I bit my lip, my thoughts veering off in a direction wholly inappropriate to the situation. Damon and Erik conversed in low voices, and I struggled to keep my thoughts on track when I heard my name.

"Hmm?" I blinked, coming back to the world to find the two men regarding me with amusement.

"We've been traveling for days." Erik turned to Damon. "My—Marienne—is a little tired."

I glared at him, and he threw me a smirk the moment Damon turned away. "I'm listening."

"I was saying that we should go to Stavrok, too. There's strength in numbers." Erik paced over the worn carpet. "I'm certain he will help your cause, Damon."

King Damon looked awe-struck. His mouth was open, his eyes wide. And he was barely blinking. Then he started to shake his head, as though Erik's plan was flawed.

"Stavrok is a good man," I added gently. "He spared my life, once. He will do what's right. I know it."

Damon sighed, and ran a frazzled hand through his hair.

"In that case, your journey will be longer by some distance." Damon glanced out of the window. "And the weather will only get worse, I'm afraid."

"Oh." Erik sauntered toward me, and I couldn't help but grin back. "We won't be traveling back the way we came. Right, Mari?"

We'd taken the carriage to hide from Damon, assuming he was the one responsible for the devastation I saw in my vision. We didn't need to hide Erik's dragon any longer.

My heart raced as I absorbed his use of the nickname Lucy had given me, and the confident way he held himself. Something smoldered behind his eyes, blazing through his body. I felt the pull toward him, always there just under the surface, intensify even further.

My grin widened and I nodded. I wouldn't miss this experience for anything.

Erik's dragon was waking up, and I was about to ride him.

CHAPTER
TWELVE

Erik

It was a whole new experience, flying through a storm like this.

The snow pelted against my wings as we flew hard against the force of the wind. Marienne gripped tight onto my back, and the warmth of her magic spread through my scales and tingled across my chest.

I threw back my head and roared, sending a jet stream of fire into the cold air, and I heard snatches of her delighted laughter before the gale whipped the sound away.

Despite the blizzard, we covered the barren ground in a matter of hours and approached the mountains. I was strong even for a dragon

224

shifter, and my broad wingspan cast long shadows as we moved over the earth below.

I dove low over the mountain range, banking in the air and swooping down into the valley. We passed over our castle, which looked like a child's toy nestled among the black hulking rocks.

Before long, Stavrok's castle emerged from the mists. As we passed through the snowstorm, shafts of sunlight pierced the clouds above us as I flew down toward our destination.

Mari leapt down off my back as I landed, her steps sure and confident as if we had been flying together for years.

As I shifted back to human, I couldn't keep the grin off my face. The woman I had by my side... she was truly extraordinary. She had journeyed with me to the edge of our world and braved the long flight home with no hesitation whatsoever.

She smiled back at me when she caught me looking. Her gaze lingered, trailing lower, and I realized with a jolt *why* her smile became a smirk.

I didn't have time to do anything about my naked and obviously hardening cock, however, because a group of guards were already approaching us. One was carrying an armful of fabric, which I took gratefully.

Once I was robed, we followed them inside, down a maze of hallways and corridors until we found ourselves in a small courtyard.

"Sire," the guard called out to the king as we approached. "You have visitors."

Stavrok turned, grinning broadly at us. I felt less underdressed when I realized he was shirtless, sweaty and disheveled. We'd interrupted his sparring practice.

"Erik!" he boomed, throwing out his arms and striding toward us. "And Marienne, too! I assume you're here about the letter?"

He reached out and swept Marienne into a tight hug, his broad arms around her slim waist. She looked taken-aback but accepted the hug with a peal of soft laughter.

A sharp wave of irrational anger flooded through me. I itched to pry his hands off her, drag her away from him...

It didn't make any sense. Stavrok was a friend, and I knew he wasn't a threat. He'd never hurt Marienne. So why was I glaring a hole in the side of his head?

Before I could think on it further, Stavrok pulled back and barked with laughter at the look on my face.

"Don't worry, Erik." He clapped a broad hand on my shoulder. "You can tell your dragon to stand down. I'm happily married."

I shuffled on my feet, awkward in his presence. Up until now, I had been certain of myself and my instincts, but... standing here, I was thrown. The whole journey to the north already felt like a lifetime ago.

Mari's small, soft hand slipped into mine and squeezed. I looked down; she smiled up at me softly.

I smiled back. Just having her by my side was enough to cool the protective instincts that threatened to swallow me whole.

I turned to Stavrok, my gaze sobering. "Marienne and I have just returned from the north. I decided to come straight here and meet with you in person."

Stavrok's face was grave; it wasn't an expression I associated with such a jovial man.

"I read your letter. You were right to reach out to me. Whatever Marienne's visions mean, they likely concern all of us." He picked up a heavy-looking broadsword that he'd been training with and slung it over his shoulder. "Come on, this isn't a conversation to be had in the yard. Let's find my wife."

With a glance at Marienne, I inclined my head, and we followed Stavrok through the courtyard to the open doors. Before we could go much further, however, Lucy found *us*.

"Mari!" She barreled forward, her blonde waves bouncing behind her. The two women hugged tightly. "Oh my gosh, it's so good to see you!"

"It's been too long." Marienne pulled back, her face shining with affection. "I'm sorry our visit was cut so short last time."

She pointedly did not look at me, but my face heated anyway. I pretended intense interest in the blank stone wall in front of me while Lucy giggled.

"I understand. Come, this way."

She looped her arm through Stavrok's, and the two led us through the castle corridors, Marienne and I following awkwardly behind.

The memory of my shift prickled hot and uncomfortable around the collar of my robe. Marienne seemed to be remembering it, too. Small spots of color appeared on her cheeks, and she wouldn't meet my gaze.

Lucy opened a door, and we entered a cozy round room with large, floor-length windows. She settled in an armchair and indicated we do the same opposite.

"I've called for some food," she said. "You must be hungry."

As soon as she said the words, my stomach growled. I smiled at her, relaxing onto a long, low sofa. "Indeed. My dragon flew a long way, and I am ravenous."

Mari cleared her throat and I glanced at her, to find her cheeks fully ablaze with pink. Suddenly, remembering the way her legs had gripped my scales and her hands clung to my dragon form as I flew, I was ravenous for something else altogether.

After an awkward moment, broken only by a bark of laughter from Stavrok, I forced my desire for Mari back down and tried to concentrate on the matter at hand.

"So," Stavrok began. "What happened on your northern expedition? Tell us everything."

Between the two of us, Marienne and I managed to relay everything that had happened on our travels, minus a few details here and there. I hoped that *getting captured* wouldn't make it into the history books when they talked of my reign.

Stavrok and Lucy listened attentively.

At some point the food arrived, and we took bites of delicious bread and cheese and drank steaming cups of hot chocolate while we talked. Their eyes grew wider and wider when they heard the truth about Damon, and when Marienne described the state of his kingdom, Lucy laid a hand on Stavrok's arm.

"We have to help them," she said.

"We will, my love." His brow furrowed as he stared off into the middle distance for a moment. "We must."

Lucy shifted, turning to Marienne. "Come and meet our little ones. You haven't had the chance yet, have you?"

She stood up, brushing her skirt down, and Marienne took the opportunity to get away, after a glance in my direction.

I recognized the gesture for what it was. A chance for me and Stavrok to talk, one-on-one. Ruler to ruler.

Smart little human, that Lucy.

Not much seemed to get past her. She may not have been born in this realm, but she fit into it perfectly.

If she can do it, maybe there's hope for me after all.

"So...." Stavrok leaned forward. "It seems that the loner king is nothing like he's rumored to be."

"I suppose it's easy for a king to be misunderstood," I replied, and Stavrok nodded. "My instincts told me he wasn't a threat. I think he's telling the truth."

"I met his father once." Stavrok squinted, like he was trying to recall a vague memory. "At a tournament, a long time ago. He was a brutish man. He hated the other clans and wanted nothing to do with them. Everyone assumed that all northerners followed his example. It seems we were wrong."

"Not all sons turn out like their fathers," I pointed out.

Stavrok chuckled. He lifted his mug, and I clinked it against mine, grinning.

"You've certainly shown that," he said. "I'll fight by your side, Erik. We're allies, and I'm a man of my word."

I bowed my head out of respect, but he shook the gesture off, putting his hands on my shoulders and looking me dead in the eye.

"You are a king, Erik," he said firmly. "It is your birthright, your blood-line. You bow to *no one*. Remember that."

As he spoke, sunlight pierced through the windows behind us and filled the room with a golden glow. Somehow, his words gave me a sense of purpose, of peace. I hadn't felt such a thing on the day of my coronation, but I felt it now.

I *was* the King of the Black Mountains. I accepted that role, now. And I would defend what was mine until my final, dying breath.

Marienne

I knew a ruse when I saw one, but I couldn't be annoyed at Lucy for separating me from Erik for the time being.

It was clear how much Erik respected Stavrok. Besides, it was good for us to be apart. I needed to get my head straight. Especially if we were going to fight this war that was coming, together.

"So," Lucy said, and grinned, leading me up the grand staircase. "Tell me everything."

"About what?" I asked.

"Marienne!" She huffed, slipping her arm through mine as we strode along the hallway. It was sunnier up here, and I tilted my head, grateful to feel the warmth on my face. "Come on. You and Erik!"

I bit my lip to stop the smile that threatened to appear. Lucy was as lively as ever. Her brief stint in Magnik's castle dungeons didn't seem to have dampened her spirit one bit.

"I don't know what you're talking about." I widened my eyes and batted my eyelashes, before breaking into giggles at the look on her face. "Okay, okay!"

"Is he your fated mate?" Lucy asked. "I know you, Marienne. Did you have a vision about him? How long have you known?"

"Whoa!" I held up my hands to stop the deluge of questions. "I've known about him for years. Ever since I saw him one day in the street, as Magnik and I passed through his town in a procession. As soon as I laid eyes on him, I knew."

Lucy's face fell. "Really? That long, and you couldn't..."

I hunched my shoulders as she trailed off. Her expression was full of pity. I didn't want her pity. And yet, I understood it. the thought of the long and lonely years I'd spent as Magnik's queen, knowing my fated mate was out there and I couldn't be with him, still left me hollow inside.

Luckily, I didn't have to change the subject. We had come to a standstill beside a high, arched door. Lucy pushed it open and I gasped as we entered a brightly lit room. Three cradles clustered around a window. Gauzy golden hangings swayed gently in the wind, and tiny mobiles hung from the ceiling.

I drew closer, and my heart softened when I saw that each mobile had tiny dragons hanging from it.

Reaching out one finger, I nudged the dragon in the middle, watching it spin around and catch the light. The baby in the cradle cooed, waving tiny, chubby fists at me.

"They're so precious." I smiled.

Lucy came up alongside me and brushed a hand through the baby's fluffy hair. "This little one is always causing me trouble, aren't you, Anselm? His sisters are good as gold—mostly."

Baby Anselm blinked up at me, and I reached out a hand, swirling a shimmering stream of magic through the air above his head. He gurgled with laughter, reaching up to try and grab the twinkling light before it dissolved.

As the light faded away, so did my smile. My hand fell away, and I traced the edge of the crib, lost in thought.

THIRTEEN

Marienne

"For someone who's finally able to be with their fated mate," Lucy said slowly, "you don't seem very happy."

"It isn't that simple." I turned away from the cribs, sighing. "None of it is."

"What do you mean?" Lucy put a hand on my arm. "I've seen the way he looks at you, Mari."

"It's not—it's not like that between us." I ran my hands over my face, hating the way my voice caught in my throat. "It shouldn't be! I'm hardly the perfect match, Lucy."

Lucy snorted. "Well, now you're just talking nonsense. Fated mates are, by definition, perfect for one another."

I held up my hand and counted off the reasons. "I was married for ten years to his half-brother. I'm not a dragon shifter. I don't think I'll ever be able to give him children—I was told years ago that I'm barren, Lucy. And sooner or later, he'll realize he wants someone without all this... this baggage! And of course, he will want an heir, one day."

I raised my hands and let out a sob as purplish mist swirled around me.

Lucy's face softened and she strode forward, sweeping me into a tight hug.

She drew back, wiping the tears from my cheeks. "But you're forgetting the most important thing."

I sniffed. "What's that?"

"He wants *you,* you idiot! It's obvious how crazy you are about each other."

As much as I wanted to believe her, I didn't dare. I cast my eyes downward as I mumbled, "The night he shifted, we slept together."

Lucy's face lit up. "And?"

I groaned, covering my face. "It was wonderful! Of *course,* it was." I shook my head, smiling weakly. "He's... he's everything I hoped he would be."

The grin slid from my face as I thought of the night we'd shared. "After all this time, I just can't trust that any of it is real," I said.

Lucy looked like she was about to say something else, but we were interrupted by a short knock at the door.

Before we could respond, the door opened a crack, and a young woman with a tumble of chestnut brown curls peered through the gap. "C'mon, Luce! Stavrok's looking for you guys! Dinner's ready."

The newcomer tossed a grin my way.

I smiled back at her, a bit startled at the casual intrusion.

"I don't think we've met. You're the... sorceress, right?" the girl said.

Lucy rolled her eyes good-naturedly. "Marienne, this is Cass. Cass, Marienne."

One of the babies began to cry, so Lucy rushed to soothe her.

Cass bounded up to me, and she shook my hand within an inch of its life. "I've heard so much about you! I'm Stavrok's cousin. I guess you could say that makes me royalty, but mostly I'm just here for the free food."

I chuckled. "Well, I could eat."

"Stavrok says you guys have been all the way up north." Cass's eyes glowed with enthusiasm, and I couldn't help but follow her as she led me out of the room. "What's it like? Tell me everything."

I turned to Lucy, who now had a red-faced infant in her arms. "You two go along," she said. "I'll stay here for a while."

"See you later." I smiled at my friend as she sat down in a nearby rocking chair and offered her breast to her babe.

"I read that the north men all have pointed teeth—is that true?" Cass asked as she led me from the room.

"Um... I don't think so. Not that I saw, anyway." I shrugged. "But we weren't there for that long."

"Is the loner king really as fearsome as they say?"

"What *do* they say?" I asked, curious.

Cass shrugged. "That he never comes out of his castle in daylight. That he keeps feral wolves for pets. That his dragon is untamable, and many have died fighting it."

That didn't square with my impression of King Damon, but I didn't want to disappoint Cass, so I just made a noncommittal noise. She didn't seem to mind, and I let her talk nineteen to the dozen while we approached the dining room.

Lucy's words were running through my head on a loop. No matter how hard I tried, I couldn't stay present; they flooded my mind, leaving no room for anything else.

I've seen the way he looks at you, Mari. It's obvious how crazy you are about each other.

I wanted so desperately to believe her. But I couldn't let my own feelings cloud my judgment: I was the first to know that simply wanting something didn't necessarily make it true.

Erik sat beside me at dinner. I barely registered what I put in my mouth, much less tasted it. I was totally entranced by his mere presence. Everything about him caught my eye: his hair, the way he smiled, the heat radiating from him as the night wore on. Once, we brushed hands while reaching for the wine decanter, and the spark that shot through me was so potent I almost gasped out loud.

The others talked easily enough, but they seemed to chalk up my silence to exhaustion and left me alone for the most part.

That suited me just fine.

At some point, underneath the table, Erik's thigh brushed up against mine and stayed there for the rest of the meal. He continued to laugh and joke with Stavrok, looking for all the world like he was none the wiser about what he was doing to me.

The singular point of contact was maddening. I ached for him, deep inside my core.

"It seems like Mari's ready to call it a night." Stavrok winked at me over the top of his wineglass. "A toast! Without her, we wouldn't be any the wiser about King Damon."

Everyone raised their glasses toward me, and I flushed and looked down.

"I've had the servants prepare your rooms," Lucy said. "Please, make yourself at home!"

Hang on... rooms?

It occurred to me that I wouldn't be sharing a bed with Erik tonight.

Why was that so surprising? We'd agreed it wasn't like that between us.

So why does it feel like ice has lodged itself in my chest?

Lucy caught my gaze. If I didn't know any better, I would say there was a glint of amusement in her eyes.

She knew exactly what I was thinking.

I stood up so suddenly my knees knocked against the underside of the table. All the glasses clinked, and everyone looked up at me with surprise.

"Excuse me," I mumbled. "Stavrok's right. We have work to do tomorrow. I should get some rest."

I pushed back my chair and began to make my way across the dining hall. A clatter behind me echoed off the marble floor. I paused and looked back over my shoulder.

Erik was standing, staring after me. He was still at the table, but the look on his face was pure fire.

I exhaled softly and turned away, beginning the lonely journey up the steps of the great hall toward my lodgings. Frustration followed me all the way into the lovely bedroom waiting for me, like an ever-present itch beneath the surface of my skin.

I fell face-first onto the soft mattress with a groan. The release I craved was far beyond my reach.

As a matter of fact, he was likely still sitting downstairs, seeming totally in control of his body and his emotions, while I lay here growing ever more desperate.

After a few minutes of silent despairing, I got up and slipped into a sheer nightgown someone had left out for me, then padded around the room in the half darkness.

The excitement of the past couple of days thrummed through me. Sleep felt a million miles away. My mind turned over possibility after possibility for what the future could bring.

One image still haunted me: Erik lying in my arms, the life draining out of him before my eyes.

It couldn't be true. Surely, with knowledge, the future *could* change.

With a huff, I turned and crept over to the bed, sliding between the cool, soft sheets. The castle was quiet around me, dark and still. I didn't know what time it was, but it had to be close to midnight.

I lay in the silence, breathing. In, out. In, out.

This was no use. I'd never get any sleep tonight with all this uncertainty.

I flung a hand above my head to trace the carvings on the headboard. Even in the dark, I could guess their shape by touch alone. Flame, smoke, fury.

Dragon fire.

I sat up and pulled back the sheets. The fabric of my nightgown rustled against my calves as I dropped both feet to the floor and strode over to the door with renewed determination.

Erik didn't want me in a permanent way. Of that, I was pretty sure.

But I had to be certain. The look on his face at dinner tugged at something in my chest. I had no choice but to follow my instincts.

I reached out and grasped the heavy bolt on the door, sliding it free. The old oak shifted under my hands, and I pulled it open before I could talk myself out of going to find him.

My breath caught in my throat and I almost jumped back in fright.

Standing just beyond the door, with one hand outstretched, as if about to knock, was Erik.

I blinked at him. From the way his eyes flickered across my face, I knew a flush had spread across my cheeks.

"What are—" I began.

"I was just—"

We both stopped, hovering on the threshold, waiting for the other to finish their sentence. Without realizing what my body was doing, I swayed closer. His hot breath ghosted over the side of my neck, and I trembled.

My hands moved without my permission, grasping the front of his shirt. Beneath my fingers I could feel the hot, firm planes of his chest, rising and falling rapidly as if he had been running.

With a growl, he pushed forward, walking me back into the room and tilting up my head. His mouth pressed against mine, and I opened for him with a moan of relief and desire.

I expected him to push me down onto the bed then, and have his way with me. I would have gone gladly.

But he didn't. His hand cradled the back of my neck, the other trailing down and sliding around my waist. He held me up against him, panting. His forehead pressed against mine. The intimacy was almost overwhelming; there was nowhere to look but straight into those burning eyes.

"I can't stand it, Mari." His voice, low and gravelly, made my stomach curl with heat. "I can't stay away from you."

I shook my head, hoping he understood; I was beyond words, beyond anything but the need that had me trembling, lips parted, aching for him to put his mouth on every part of me he could reach.

He cupped my face in his huge hands, holding me as if I was something precious to him. He kissed me again, soft and lingering, before angling us gently until I sat at the edge of the bed and he stood in between my open legs.

His hands inched up under the thin fabric of my nightgown. Even the slide of his fingers against the softness of my inner thighs had me squirming. In the dim light, I caught a flash of his crooked grin.

He leaned over me. His mouth found my cheek, the side of my neck, sliding hotly over my collarbone. He didn't seem to be in any hurry. The last time we did this, it had been relentless, inevitable; just pure, instinctual lust.

He was taking his time now. Mapping out my body, learning what made me gasp, what made me writhe and arch up against him. Slow and reverent.

No one had ever touched me like this.

No one had ever *seen* me the way Erik did.

He left a blazing trail up my inner thigh, closer and closer to where I really wanted him. Blindly, I reached out and slid a hand into his hair, anchoring him. He huffed as if in amusement, and my skin tingled at the sensation of his breath on me.

I groaned at the sight of his dark head buried between my thighs, and just barely managed to keep from crying out when he licked me, kissing around and over my clit while I bucked and rode up into his mouth like it was the only thing keeping me tethered to earth.

My other hand grabbed the head board, and his large palms slid under my thighs, pulling me impossibly closer. I lay there, trapped between his hot, damp mouth and the mattress beneath us. I could feel my climax approaching rapidly, and I squirmed, nudging at his broad back with my ankles to get his attention.

I didn't want it like this. I wanted to see him again, connect with him fully.

He glanced up. I shuddered at the wild look on his face, his mussed hair and wide pupils. I shifted beneath him, shuffling until I could wrap my hands around his huge forearms and guide him until he crawled up over me.

I leaned up and pressed a soft kiss against his mouth, heedless of where he had just been, and pushed his pants down his hips. I needed to feel his flesh against me.

He groaned as our kiss turned deeper, and our tongues slid together. My thighs trapped his pelvis against mine, and it wasn't long before his hips began sliding mindlessly downward.

Closer; closer. He got the message clear enough and reached down, taking his cock in hand and lining himself up. We both gasped when the head brushed against my entrance, and he slid inside slowly. I arched toward him, savoring the stretch and fullness of his organ inside my body.

I wrapped my hands around his shoulders, and pulled him down, pressing the length of his body against mine. He held himself rigid, clearly worried about crushing me under his weight, before relaxing into me. We rocked together, mouths brushing gracelessly against each other, lost to the world, and anything except the feel of each other.

His thrusts began to deepen. He growled against my neck, and I whimpered at the graze of his teeth against the skin there, tightening around him as my orgasm exploded through me. I gripped his jaw and dropped soft kisses onto his lips until he stiffened and roared. His cock pulsed with his own release deep inside me.

We both trembled as he withdrew and flopped down beside me on the bed.

I was utterly sated, wrung through with exhaustion and pleasure, but I smiled up at the canopy above us.

"What is it?" Erik murmured.

I turned my head to find he was studying me with a smile of his own.

I huffed a laugh, and his smile softened into a gentle grin. "It's just... I've been dreaming of you for so long."

Even in the darkness, I could see his eyebrows draw together. "Really?"

I reached out and pushed a loose strand of hair away from his gorgeous face. "Five years, in fact. Since the day I first saw you."

"So, you *did* see me that day," he murmured, turning fully onto his side and trailing a lazy hand through my hair, tangling it with his fingers. "You looked so beautiful, Mari, dressed in all your finery. I remember..."

"What?" I tilted back my head, allowing him to skim a hand over my collarbone.

He seemed caught up for a moment, lost in thought. "I'd never seen a woman so beautiful. And I knew that I'd never have you. We were so far apart... I thought the gods had cursed me. Set you in my path to punish me. I never stopped thinking of you, Marienne."

I inhaled sharply, catching his hand in mine and tangling our fingers together. "I'm sorry for all those years. All that pain." I sighed. "I wish it could've been different, Erik."

"The villagers whispered that you were a powerful sorceress," Erik mumbled, kissing my forehead, just below my tangled hair. "When I first saw you, I ran straight for the nearest field. I lost control completely... I shifted. I knew I had to get the hell away from the village, but I burned up an entire farmstead by accident. My mother was furious."

"Were *you* okay?" I stroked a hand down his bicep.

"Yes." He chuckled softly. "We had to pay for the damage for years, and no-one was hurt, but I thought you had *done* something to me. Some magic curse, or spell. I couldn't understand why my body reacted that way from just one look."

I wriggled closer, and he wrapped his long limbs around me. I sighed with satisfaction and rested my head on his chest.

"Well, I can assure you," I said with a smile, listening to the thud of his heart. "I'm just as much under your spell as you are under mine."

He pressed his face against my temple, and I felt his answering smile against my skin.

"I think I can live with that."

CHAPTER
FOURTEEN

Erik

After dozing, halfway between sleep and wakefulness for what felt like ages, I finally managed to open my eyes. I sighed deeply, contented. Marienne lay next to me, sound asleep, a warm comforting weight curled into my side.

Having her in my arms was perfect.

Just knowing that she felt the same way, after the doubt and turmoil of the last few days, was all I could ever have wished for.

As much as I wanted to stay here forever, we had to face what was coming for us. I couldn't stand aside and let Damon's kingdom fall because of his father's sins.

Stavrok felt the same way.

I glanced down to find Marienne awake. Her eyes were paler than usual in the morning light. The sun made their purple depths shimmer and sparkle, like the surface of a lake. Her expression was soft, but unsmiling.

It seemed I could now read her thoughts like a book. She was worried about me.

"I'll be fine." I stroked the side of her face. "The future can change, right? What you saw in that vision, it isn't set in stone."

She relaxed into my touch, but her eyes were still intent on mine.

"I'm going back there with you." She bowed her head, pressing a kiss onto my chest. It felt like a vow. "To the north."

Ice filled my veins. "It's not safe, Marienne."

Even as I spoke, I knew the words wouldn't change anything. It was just like last time. She had already made up her mind.

"I can help." Her voice was small, but firm. "I *want* to help."

I pulled her close against my chest. "I know," I murmured, cradling her against me. "I..."

The words that I wanted to say were on the tip of my tongue, but I couldn't let them out. It was too soon, too much. But I couldn't help how I felt.

I was falling in love with her.

So, I cut myself off, pushing the words back down and burying my face in her soft, sweet-smelling hair. Taking a few more stolen moments, before the world came crashing in again and destroyed our fragile, borrowed peace.

BY THE TIME we got downstairs, Stavrok and Lucy were waiting for us in the Great Hall.

"The troops are already on their way," Stavrok informed me, glancing at his wife. "Lucy's staying here with Cass and the babies. We should leave soon."

I nodded. Stavrok was wearing simple clothes, but his armor was piled up behind him. He followed my gaze and put a hand on my shoulder.

"This isn't your fight," he said. "Nor is it mine."

I had never fought in any kind of war before.

The memory of what I'd told Marienne last night resurfaced. My dragon, tearing through the countryside. Burning everything in its path, simply because I had spied a woman from afar. My shifter was strong, built for speed and stamina. I could do this.

"I know." I squared my jaw. "But we can't abandon the north, Stavrok. We can't abandon King Damon."

Stavrok's mouth twitched, and he shot me an approving smile. "Spoken like a true king." He turned his attention to Marienne, who had been watching our exchange with interest. "What about you, sorceress? Will you be joining us?"

Marienne inclined her head and her glance at me was warm. "My place is by my king's side, Your Majesty."

"Funny." Stavrok paused. "You used to say that when Magnik was alive. But now you actually sound like you *mean* it."

Marienne looked up sharply. Something passed between them, and I turned away. Stavrok clapped me on the shoulder, hard enough that I almost stumbled, then boomed with laughter.

"Better keep your wits about you, Erik." He winked at me. "There's steel behind those silk skirts, mark my words."

Marienne's eyes flashed, and she murmured something to Lucy. They both giggled.

"What is it?" I asked. Her voice had been too low, even for my astute shifter hearing.

Lucy turned to me, smirking. "She said, *he* should know. His wife is much the same, after all."

Stavrok scooped Lucy up by the waist with one massive arm, peppering her face with kisses while she squealed and tried half-heartedly to bat him away.

Something about their display of easy domesticity made me ache. Marienne met my eye, and in a flash, I could see that she was thinking the same thing.

The urge to lift her up and crush her against my chest in an embrace rose. I tried hard to tamp it down. I needed to concentrate on saving my energy for the coming flight.

The sun had already risen high in the sky by the time we set off. My shifter uncoiled itself lazily, sated after last night's activities but ready to fly nonetheless.

When I stretched out my wings, feeling Marienne's now-familiar weight settle onto my back, I almost relaxed. It felt like we'd done this a thousand times, her flying with me this way.

Stavrok flew by my side, dipping lower to skim through the cloud layer as we approached the Black Mountains. As I'd observed before, his dragon was bulkier than mine, with darker scales and piercing blue eyes as he turned his head back toward me. I made up for his bulk in wingspan, though, and I'd outpaced him by the time we flew over the mountain range into the northern territories.

We glided along, finding warmer air currents whenever we could, and I scanned the ground as we looked for signs of invasion. There was nothing amiss. Same sparse trees, same isolated little farmsteads, same snowdrifts.

Marienne's legs clamped tight against my back as she jerked. I turned my head, and my heart plummeted.

The small town outside the gates of Damon's castle was engulfed in flames.

Up ahead, dragons circled above the spires and turrets, locked in battle in the snowy sky. The enemy had already arrived. The castle itself appeared to be unharmed so far; its high stone walls and heavy drawbridge must have prevented the raiders from entering on foot.

Though by the ferocity of that attack, King Damon wouldn't be able to hold off the marauders forever.

I snapped out of my shock and refocused.

There wasn't time for distractions. I had to stick to the plan.

Soaring high above the castle, I circled, spotting a walkway where I could land safely. The moment my feet touched the battlements, Marienne slipped down off my scaly back.

She turned to look at me. Her eyes were full of unspoken promises. There were a thousand things I wanted to say, but I couldn't shift back and speak to her. There wasn't time.

Go, she mouthed at me.

I didn't need telling twice. With one final look in which I poured everything I was feeling but couldn't say, I pushed off from the wall and soared into the air, ready to join the fray.

~

Marienne

That look. Even in his dragon form, I almost melted at the heat and promise in Erik's eyes. But there was no time to dwell on it.

I sprinted down the narrow, twisting hallway as fast as my legs could carry me, glancing out of every window I passed to see if the raiders had breached the walls.

So far, Damon's people seemed to be holding strong—for now.

I followed the corridors until I heard people—dozens and dozens of frightened voices—and then I followed those sounds, dashing past suits of armor and old tapestries until I reached a dimly lit, musty hall.

A group of people huddled in a corner close to the small fire. All of them looked up when I rushed in. As far as I could tell, the group mostly consisted of women and children. Every face held an identical expression of complete terror.

"Have you come to help us?" A sharp voice rang through the crowd.

I craned my neck until I identified the source: a young woman with the same pale, ice-blue eyes as King Damon.

I nodded. "I'm Marienne."

The woman visibly relaxed. She moved through the crowd, which parted easily to let her past. "Erik's queen? Damon said you'd come."

Erik's queen? I didn't correct her. Didn't want to. It sounded wonderful, even if it wasn't true.

"I'm Lenora, Damon's sister," the woman added.

"Nice to meet you." I glanced around, taking stock of the huddled mass of refugees. "Is this everyone from the town?"

Lenora looked grim. "Yes. All the women and children, at least. We managed to get as many people out as possible before... *they* came." A shadow fell over her face. "But there are more people coming from further afield. Farmers and such. They don't have anywhere else to go, but..."

She bit her lip, looking anguished. "I don't know how they'll make it through the battle and the raging fires outside, and get safely into the castle."

"Leave it to me."

I spread my fingers, letting a shimmer of my magic swirl out into the open air. Several people gasped; children hid behind their mothers and peeked at me, half-frightened, half-awed.

This was what I knew. The curse I was born with. The terrible gift that I could never escape. I would turn it around, and use it to help these people who were staring at me with little hope in their eyes.

Without another word, I whirled around and stalked to the huge window overlooking the outer walls of the castle. I murmured incantations and spread my arms wide. The magic flowed out, glimmering, sinking into the stonework, trickling down every nook and cranny.

Protective enchantments.

I had plenty of practice with them. Under Magnik's orders, I'd covered every inch of our castle with binding spells. It wouldn't keep out raiders forever, but it should at least slow them down.

A roar outside trembled the glass in the window opposite, and a jet of flame rushed past. Several people screamed.

I turned around, finding Lenora in the crowd, and beckoned her over. "Keep everyone in here. Make sure they stay away from the walls, okay?"

"What?" Her eyes widened. "You're leaving?"

"You said there were people beyond the gates." I kept my voice soft and even, and placed a hand on her shoulder. "I'll help them if I can. You'll be safest in here. Bar the doors until you get my signal."

Lenora looked lost, but she nodded. There was a glint in her gaze, a semblance of steel behind the terror.

Good.

"Signal?" she asked. "What signal?"

I gave her a smile and, instead of answering, held out my palm and let the magic shimmer and dance across it.

"You really are a witch." Her eyes were round with amazement.

"I prefer sorceress." I shrugged. "And I'm going to use my magic to help as many of your people as I can." I didn't wait to hear her response. I hadn't come all this way to sit around in hiding. I had a job to do.

~

Erik

I flew higher and higher, touching the misty underside of clouds as I banked and turned. Below me, the castle shrunk in size. I circled it, assessing the high walls for signs of weakness.

The battle raged below. Outside the burning town, our armies clashed with a ravenous mass of raiders.

There were fewer of them in number, but they made up for it in ferocity and skill. The air was thick with the clash of swords and the cries of the wounded. I skimmed lower, spread my wings, and soared down to take a closer look.

The enemy hordes were like something out of a nightmare. Vicious and bloodthirsty, they hacked through our armies with battleaxes wielded with deadly precision. In amongst them were huge, deadly wolves. They fought alongside the raiders like attack dogs, tearing into anyone they could get their jaws on.

I spotted Stavrok in the thick of the battle, wielding a broadsword. I couldn't fight like him. It was safer for me to stay in dragon form and help those of Damon's men in the sky.

Stavrok was in his element, though, if the fire in his eyes was anything to go by.

I pushed higher, rolling in the air, and flew to the top of the castle where two dragons scorched the skies with their fury.

As I watched, a paler one, which I assumed was King Damon, released an icy blue stream of fire, hitting his opponent square on the wing. The opponent roared with fury.

My stomach dropped as the other dragon barreled forward, catching Damon's wing in its claws and dragging him down toward the earth.

Damon struggled, but it was no use. He was plummeting to the ground at a speed impossible to survive if they impacted.

I didn't think twice. I shot through the air and crashed into the side of the enemy hard enough to force him to release Damon, and sent the raider hurtling down against the castle wall.

Damon twisted in midair and recovered himself, shooting upwards to join me. Together, we turned to face our adversary.

We didn't need words; one silent glance was all it took. We brought down the dragon together, like we had been fighting side by side for years. Brothers on the battlefield, bound by blood and fire.

Below us, the tide of the battle was turning. Our army was beginning to overwhelm the raiders, forcing them back through the burning streets of the town and out into the flat, barren wilderness.

I spied one small group of Damon's soldiers near the center of the fighting. They were cornered, but like trapped animals they were even more ferocious, baring their teeth at anyone who dared to come close. They were guarding the drawbridge.

My heart plummeted when I saw the reason why.

A huddled group of stragglers stood in the middle of the fray. Women and children. They were trying to head to the castle, but a pack of wolves prevented them from getting past.

I roared with fury and spread my wings wide, swooping down, all set to burn the raiders to the ground. But as I flew closer, I realized I couldn't risk the fire spreading or hitting innocent people with the force of my wrath.

A small figure appeared on the drawbridge. Slender and fragile against the massive stone walls behind her, she was surrounded by a glowing purple mist.

My heart froze. *Marienne? Oh, gods, she would be harmed if she stayed there.*

She reached the edge of the drawbridge, moving with slow, delicate purpose. The raiders froze, slack-jawed. Like moths drawn to her flame, they stepped closer and closer. The purple clouds wavered and trembled and the raiders began to twitch, shaking off her enchantment.

There were too many of them for Marienne to handle on her own. She began to back away as their large wolves advanced, slavering at the sight of their prey.

It was too much. I couldn't bear the thought of anything happening to Mari.

My roar split open the sky above us. The ground trembled, and everyone looked up.

Marienne was in danger, and I would level entire cities before I let any harm come to my mate.

The burst of my fire swept through the raiders and wolves, clearing a pathway edged with molten, glowing flames. The group of stragglers rushed toward Marienne, and she quickly ushered them over the bridge. Her magic cocooned them, protecting them from my fire. Her spell melded and fused together, sparking in strange and beautiful patterns. Working together in this strange yet wonderful way, we soon got everyone safely inside the castle.

The battlefield faded into the background. All I could see was Marienne, picking her way through the rubble and ruin, casting spell after spell to protect the castle and all those who sheltered inside.

I landed on the battlements. My dragon itched to get back into the fray, to burn, to *destroy*.

I wanted to kill every vile raider who had dared to threaten my mate.

With difficulty, I pulled back, calmed myself and focused my energy inwards, already feeling the air start to shimmer and morph around me.

I knew it was a risk, to walk through the heat of battle as Erik instead of in the safe body of my shifter. But I had to get down to the ground level. I needed to find Stavrok and Damon...

Ignoring my nakedness, I grabbed a sword from a fallen soldier and paced along the top of the battlements, eyeing the chaos that continued to rage outside the castle walls.

Below me, Stavrok staggered out of the fray. He sported a nasty-looking wound on his shoulder, but other than that appeared unharmed. I raised a hand to get his attention, and his eyes brightened. He climbed up the side of the wall like it was nothing, and I reached down and helped him the final few steps to safety.

Together, we stood watching the battle from our elevated vantage point. Stavrok was panting hard.

"Some fight, huh?" He turned to look at me, grinning.

I nodded. I had just opened my mouth to ask him what to do next when he bellowed out a warning, lunging toward something just behind my left shoulder.

I didn't have time to react.

I felt rather than saw the axe blade that cut deep into my side. The pain was immediate, and excruciating. I twisted to face my attacker as he pulled his axe free.

His eyes... the hate-filled green. Those were the eyes of the dragon I'd taken down in defending Damon. I should have been more careful with his human half. I should have finished him off.

My attacker met the end of Stavrok's sword, but it was too late for me. The damage was already done. Marienne's scream pierced through the air. And then I collapsed to the ground.

~

MARIENNE

My legs threatened to fold out from under me. By some miracle, I managed to stagger closer to Erik, holding onto the wall for support as I went.

"No, *no. Erik!*"

I had been so close. I'd rounded the corner just a half-second too late.

Stavrok bellowed out a battle cry, tearing after the group of raiders who had managed to get past the castle walls. The lifeless body of Erik's attacker lay beside him.

I ignored the corpse, dropping to my knees, and tugged at Erik until his head was cradled in my lap.

This was my vision and it had come true. Nothing I had done today had changed the course of fate. And now I had to watch the man I loved die right before my eyes.

"Mari." Erik blinked up at me. His face was pale as ash, and he was clutching his side. He started to say something else, but broke away, coughing.

"Shh." I stroked back his hair, swallowing the tears that threatened to fall. "Shh. Erik, we did it. *You* did it. You were amazing."

He just stared up at me. There was a wonder in his eyes, like I was the most beautiful thing he had ever seen.

I pressed a hand against the crimson spot over his torso.

"No," I whispered, mostly to myself. "Not now. You don't get to leave me, Erik, you hear me? I have waited *too damn long* for you."

I squeezed my eyes shut, burning with grief and fury. Something was building inside me. My powers were coalescing, gathering, stronger than ever before. Fate may have brought us together, and I wouldn't let it tear us apart.

You don't get to take him from me! He's far too precious.

I threw back my head and let the power surge within me. Normally, I would dampen it down, keep it inside, afraid of what my magic would do if I let it free. But not this time. This time, I let go of my death grip and released my magic into the ether.

Wave upon wave of power pulsed out of me, pouring into the air. There were no incantations or rituals. No herbs or potions. No control.

Just sheer, raw instinct, lighting up the atmosphere around us. The sky rolled with dark, thunderous clouds, and white lightning struck overhead. For an instant, I thought the entire castle would come crashing down.

I was beyond caring.

This was *Erik*, and he was dying in my arms.

I focused on him with every ounce of my willpower.

Don't die. I love you. Please, Erik. Please. Do. Not. Die.

The wind lashed at my face, and the magic kept on coming.

Then, just as suddenly as it had started, the surge was over. I slumped back onto the cold flagstones, completely and utterly spent.

*E*RIK

Dying wasn't as painful as I'd once imagined it to be.

The world had taken on a dreamlike, hazy quality. Silver, and purple. My vision dimmed at the edges, then brightened and warmed. Marienne appeared, hovering over me like an angel.

I must be dreaming.

I didn't care. I wanted to reach up and touch her. She was so beautiful, so perfect. But I didn't have the strength to move.

I couldn't believe that, for a brief, shining moment in time, she had been mine.

Her lovely eyes were full of tears that threatened to spill down her cheeks.

No, that's not right...

She didn't have to worry about me now. I had given my life to save Damon's kingdom, but I knew I'd made the right choice. I couldn't have done anything else.

Mari's beauty pierced my soul. I could barely stand to look directly at her; she was like the sun, haloed by light, almost glowing with radiance. Except, there was no *almost* about it. She was *literally* glowing.

I wanted to raise my hand again, but I still couldn't move. She was so bright; *too* bright. The light engulfed her completely, and a searing, blinding pain shot through the wound in my side. I grit my teeth to stop from screaming out.

The light spread, unfurling in all directions, darkening the sky above us and making the very earth tremble beneath me. At the center of it all, Marienne's small frame swayed like a reed, right at the heart of the chaos she had somehow unleashed.

She looked strikingly vulnerable. It was too much. She was going to hurt herself, but I was powerless to help her.

At long last, the light faded, and it was over.

I gasped like a landed fish, taking in lungful after lungful of air and marveling at the lack of pain when I inhaled and exhaled.

Marienne slouched beside me. Her dark hair pooled to her waist, obscuring her face. Gently, I tucked a few strands behind her ear. Alarm bells rang in my head. Her skin was pale. Too pale. Her eyes were no longer the luminous, swirling mass of indigo blue-purple I had come to know so well. They were dull and magic-less. She looked up and met my gaze, smiling softly. I found her hand and squeezed it, trying not to show my shock at how cold she was to the touch.

"You're alive," she whispered. There was wonder in her tone.

I sat up, staring down at my side. My wound appeared to be healed. Her magic had put me back together. But what had it done to *her*?

"Can you walk?" I asked. I could hear the worry in my own voice, but she didn't seem to register it.

She nodded. "I... I think so."

Slowly, I helped her climb to her feet. She stood there, listing slightly to one side, and I darted in to slide a firm hand around her waist before she could keel over.

"Marienne." I pulled her close, pressing my fingers to her wrist to check her pulse. It was faint and irregular, but the sound of it reassured me. "What did you do?"

She reached up and touched my face. I turned my head and pressed a kiss into her palm, watching her eyelashes flutter at my touch.

"You saved me," she whispered. "I had to save you, too."

She made it sound so simple.

I wanted to yell, to tell her she'd been reckless. The truth was, it frightened me to see her like this. I didn't know what the power drain meant, if she would recover her energy. What if she'd weakened herself too much? What if...

I couldn't think it. I focused instead on what I *could* do: find the others.

The sounds of battle had grown fainter in the time we'd spent up here. It sounded like our forces had taken control of the situation.

Good.

I'd done all I could. Now it was time to take care of my own. I needed to take Marienne home.

Erik

Eerie silence hung in the air around us.

The burnt-out shell of the town was utterly still. The blackened ruins of hollowed-out buildings were all that remained, some standing, most of them lying in piles of still-smoldering ash.

Thin, wispy trails of smoke were all that remained.

Most of the raiders were dead. The ones that survived had fled back toward the mountains.

Hopefully the raiders had gotten the message.

The northern clan is protected. The people will not pay for the old king's mistakes.

Damon surveyed the destruction with empty eyes. I could tell that he was thinking of the long road ahead. He would have to rebuild his kingdom from the ground up, repairing and restoring what had been lost.

Stavrok, Marienne, and I stood opposite him.

Out of the three of us, thanks to Marienne, I was the only one who had emerged unscathed from the fight.

Stavrok was gritting his teeth and clutching a nasty shoulder wound. It wasn't life-threatening, thank God.

More worryingly, Marienne clung to my side like I was the only thing keeping her standing. Which I likely was. I had to pay my respects to Damon, but I needed to take her away from this place. Soon.

"I can't express how grateful I am to you," Damon said. "All of you. I vow one day to repay your kindness."

"Let this be a new chapter in our realm's history." Stavrok spoke slowly, letting every word hang in the air. "An alliance to last for generations to come."

We shook hands, and I gripped Damon's arm when it came to my turn.

"Any manpower, supplies, building materials you need..." I trailed off, surveying the frozen landscape around us. "You shall have them."

Damon's eyes flickered with gratitude, and he nodded. His attention turned to Marienne.

"You must get her home, Erik," he said softly. "As much as I appreciate your help, don't hang around on my account."

I squeezed Marienne's hand, and she gave a faint squeeze in response. "I know."

"I would offer you the use of my castle, but I'm afraid it's not fit for purpose right now." Damon glanced up at the huge mass of stone behind us. "My people need me."

"Can you fly?" I asked Stavrok, and he gave me a nod.

"It's a flesh wound. I've had worse." He shot me a sharp grin, and then wandered away. He glanced at us behind his shoulder just before he turned the corner of a nearby, smoke-blackened wall. "May we all meet again soon."

He shifted into his dragon form and flew away.

My mind was already on the logistics of getting Marienne home safely. She couldn't ride on my back. She wasn't strong enough.

"I'll carry you," I murmured into her hair. "We're going home, Marienne."

The journey seemed to last a lifetime. I carried Marienne in my talons, imagining the flutter of her heartbeat. She felt impossibly small and fragile. I flew as fast as I dared, but every flap of my wings felt like hours too long. I exhaled in relief when the mountains appeared on the horizon.

The sky was clearer than it had been in days. The snow had stopped falling, and a beautiful sunset streaked across the sky.

I thought about the raiders in the mountains, and the wilderness we had just left behind. Would we ever return?

My chest twinged with relief when we passed over the mountains. On the other side, the valleys rolled out in shades of green and blue, warm and inviting.

Familiar. We were home.

I drifted to the top of the nearest tower, setting Marienne down as gently as possible. The servants ran out to greet us. Thomas took the lead, carrying a robe for me.

Good man.

I shifted quickly and threw on the robe before hurrying over to Marienne. She was on her feet, at least.

I took her slender shoulders and gazed down at her. She smiled, her eyes tracking over my face as if she were trying to commit it to memory.

Then the last of her energy seemed to leave her. She let out a deep sigh, and her body sagged against mine.

"Marienne?" I held her against me, as tightly as I dared. I slid my hands into her hair and turned her face up to mine. "Mari, please..."

Her eyes were closed. She was so cold.

I fell to my knees, pulling her down with me. I could feel the servants hovering around me, but I paid them no mind. Nobody dared to come near us.

My shout echoed through the mountains, and into the valleys below. "Marienne!"

~

MARIENNE

The first thing I registered was warmth, and softness.

I stirred. In my half-conscious state, confusion filled me. I didn't remember falling asleep. It was all a blur. The last thing I remembered was...

Oh.

My eyes snapped open.

A gauzy canopy filled my vision. I blinked up at it, trying to put the pieces together in my mind.

I'm in the master suite bed again? How did I get here?

I shifted. Warm fingers curled around my hand, outstretched across the covers. I turned my head on the pillow and smiled.

A chair had been pulled up at the side of the bed. Erik sat, slumped over with his face against the mattress. His hair had fallen over his face. He was dozing. Both of his huge hands cradled mine.

Moving slowly, I extracted my hand. My fingers reached out and carded through his hair, brushing it back. He stirred.

He sat up, blinking a few times. His eyes were shadowed. He looked like he hadn't slept for a long while.

"Hey," I whispered, and his face broke into that crooked grin I'd come to love so much.

"You're awake." Relief flooded his face as he looked over me.

"How long was I out?"

"Too damn long." He huffed a laugh, shaking his head in disbelief. "Couple of days."

"Days?" I grimaced and then relaxed back into the pillows. My head still tingled; I sensed that getting up wasn't the best idea right now. "Did I miss anything good?"

He laughed again, before glaring at me. "Other than me almost losing it because I thought you were *dead?* Not much."

"What?" I reached out and took his hand, forcing him to look at me.

"These past two days..." He broke off, clenching his jaw. "It made me picture what it would be like to lose you."

I wanted to say something, to interject. I didn't.

"I don't want to rule, Marienne," Erik said, lowering his gaze, "unless you're by my side."

"Oh," I breathed.

He drew up my hand and pressed a kiss there as he continued.

"I love you. All of you. I never want you to change, Marienne, and I never want you to leave. Stay with me." He slid to his knees, keeping a gentle grip on my hand as I peered over the bedside, amazed. "*Marry* me."

I froze, astounded. After everything we'd been through together, everything he'd seen, Erik still wanted me. *He wants to marry me!*

He didn't care about my past, or the strength of my magic.

This man—this wonderful, ridiculous man—wanted me. For *me*.

"I—" I stopped, joy spilling over in my chest. "Yes. I'll marry you."

His whole expression lit up, and he launched himself onto the bed, careful not to jostle me. His eyes shone with happiness when I cupped his face in my hands.

"You will?" He grinned at me. "Say it again."

"Yes," I repeated, laughing. "Of *course*, I'll marry you!"

I squealed when he dived in and kissed me, over and over in spite of my protests.

After all, I didn't put up *too* much of a fight.

EPILOGUE

Marienne

"I have been married *before*, you know," I said to Lucy as she clucked over me like a mother hen.

Behind me, in the mirror of my dressing table, Lucy's eyes rolled in exasperation. We were sitting in my new bedroom. Erik's room.

"I know, but not to someone you actually—"

"Love?" I smirked.

"Exactly." Lucy held up two heavily jeweled tiaras and I turned to face her.

I wrinkled my nose at them, and she let out a sigh.

"These are traditional! I got them out of the Treasury. They are meant for a queen. And you *are* a queen." She brushed a loose strand of hair over my shoulder, and I couldn't help but smile at her. "You're going to be the Queen of the Black Mountains, Marienne! For *real* this time."

I eyed the tiaras, trying to keep an open mind.

Nope, I was right the first time. They're still hideous.

My gaze drifted past Lucy, to the elaborate floral arrangement on the table behind her. Sprigs of white flowers clustered together, interspersed with pale lilac and gold.

"Screw tradition," I said, standing up and arranging my dress behind me. "Let's do something different."

Lucy raised an eyebrow, and then caught on to my train of thought.

She smiled broadly. "Ah. Yes, I think that will work."

My hand curled protectively over my belly, and I smiled.

It had turned out that conceiving with my fated mate was simpler than I ever thought possible. Whether Magnik was infertile, and blamed it on me instead, or he didn't know... none of it mattered now.

I'd thought I was the problem, and that my magic refused to allow me to grow a child. But instead, I had just needed the right man. *My* man. My fated mate.

I wasn't showing yet, but that wouldn't last for long. Nobody knew except Erik and I that we were expecting. We planned to announce it at the wedding reception.

Things between me and my soon-to-be husband hadn't gone the way everyone expected they would.

They'd turned out even better.

~

Erik

I gazed out over the crowd of onlookers, trying not to let the nerves show on my face.

The hall was as busy as it had been on my coronation day. I thought back to that moment, standing here in a sea of strangers with no idea of what lay ahead.

The memory made me smile, now. Such a short time, and yet so much had changed.

The wedding preparations had been simple. Neither of us wanted a huge show.

We had other things on our mind.

Ruling my own kingdom took priority, but I spent time in the north when I could afford to spare it, traveling up with Stavrok and checking in on Damon to see how the rebuilding efforts were going.

His father's debtors had been scared off for good by our alliance. Pride and happiness filled me when I thought of how much we'd achieved in such a short period of time.

Speaking of which...

I grinned to myself, thinking of the news that Marienne and I had to share later tonight.

"Something on your mind, my friend?" Stavrok's voice startled me out of my thoughts. I glared at him, and he promptly burst out laughing. "Stop scowling! You have plenty to smile about. You're marrying your fated mate, Erik. Not many people get to say that."

My scowl instantly cleared. I could hardly believe it myself.

It had taken me a long time to trust that I was worthy of someone like Marienne. But we fit together, flaws and all.

"It could have ended very differently," I reminded Stavrok, as well as myself.

His face darkened.

"Indeed." He pointed at me, looking stern. "You—you need some sparring practice, my friend."

"Hey, I know!" I held up my hands and burst out laughing. "You won't hear any complaints from me on that front!"

If I had to go a few rounds in the castle courtyard with a training master to ready myself for battle one day, I would. But I couldn't think about that today.

My gaze wandered down the aisle and flickered through the rows of guests, all decked out in their finery. All the kingdoms were here. Cass was sitting in a nearby row and I smiled at her. She grinned back, before catching sight of Stavrok and sticking her tongue out at him.

"Hey Stavrok, have you considered taking Cass up to the northern kingdom?"

Stavrok drew his eyebrows together. "No, why?"

I grinned at him, having heard from Marienne that she'd had a premonition the day she'd shaken Cass's hand. The young girl had been interested in knowing more about the castle to the north, and Marienne believed Cass would do well up there.

"Damon's still looking for his fated mate, and Marienne suggested to me that you might want to take Cass along on your next visit up there."

Stavrok's eyes widened a little. "But, she's only nineteen."

I shrugged. "Then wait a year or two. I'm sure Damon's not going anywhere."

Stavrok nodded once, though his jaw was tight with sudden tension and indecision. I'd wanted to impart that knowledge to him for months, and it was a burden I was grateful to now shift onto his shoulders.

The winter king had sent his congratulations, but he'd declined our invitation to attend. I understood; he had his hands full for the foreseeable future. If the loner king ever did decide to venture south, at least he knew he had friends waiting for him.

On the other side of the aisle, my new councilors sat whispering amongst themselves. They included representation from all over the kingdom: both the town, and the outlying countryside. One of them, my butler Thomas, caught my eye and nodded his head respectfully.

There was not a single gold chain to be seen among them. I smiled to myself.

I hope the old elders are keeping themselves warm with their gold, now that they are no longer welcome in my castle.

Stavrok leaned in again, and I turned toward him.

"Word has it that you're quite the natural statesman," he said. "If the rumors from my wife are to be believed."

"That's all Marienne." I shrugged. "I can't claim any credit. I couldn't have done it without her."

"I'm sure she'd say the same about you."

I shot Stavrok a grateful smile. I had chosen the right guy to be my best man today.

The hall began to fill with the sounds of soft, ethereal music, and the double doors swung open. My heart clenched with nerves and anticipation.

It was finally time.

Mari stood there, haloed by sunlight. I couldn't keep the smile off my face. Her dress floated and swirled around her, and her perfect face was framed by dozens and dozens of flowers.

She had a whole crown of them. They tumbled through her long hair, their tendrils trailing through her veil, the latter held up by a smiling Lucy. As she walked along the aisle, the whole room seemed to come alive in her wake.

I almost forgot to breathe. She looked like a goddess.

The tension in my shoulders drained away, and my heart warmed. Meeting Marienne's gaze, all I felt was peace, and certainty about the future.

This was just the beginning.

~

3
FIRE AND ICE
REBUILDING HIS
DRAGON
KINGDOM
USA TODAY BESTSELLING AUTHOR
AMELIA SHAW

REBUILDING HIS DRAGON KINGDOM

CHAPTER
ONE

Cass

I couldn't believe this was now my life.

Stavrok and Lucy were out tonight, again, negotiating a new trade agreement near the border between our kingdom and the human world. They were always off doing important things. Things that would improve the lives of our people.

And I was left here, holding the babies. *Literally.*

I loved my nephew and his sisters more than anything in the world, but on days like this I longed to be somewhere else. *Anywhere* else.

The urge to explore new horizons was becoming almost over-whelming.

I clenched my jaw and tightened my hands into fists as I strode along the corridor, a walk I could do with my eyes shut. I knew every inch of this palace back to front. The castle had been my home since I was a little girl. When my parents died, my cousin Stavrok had taken me in and raised me like his own.

He'd been young then, barely a year on the throne, and yet he hadn't turned me away when I needed him. He'd always treated me like the little sister he never had, far more than simply a cousin. He was part big brother, part father to me.

I was lucky to have Stavrok in my life, but lately the walls and ceilings of the castle had begun to press in on me from all sides. I felt like a prisoner in my own home. No matter how far I explored, or which paths I took, I always ended up exactly where I started.

That was probably because I wasn't allowed outside the castle walls—had never been, really. At first, I'd been deemed too young to leave, but then Stavrok's rule had become even tighter since that fateful day three years ago when Lucy had been kidnapped and I'd been hurt in the process. Stavrok had really locked things down after that.

I understood why he kept us close. He wanted to keep those he loved safe. But I was turning twenty-one tomorrow, for crying out loud! I was a woman now. My own person, with my own destiny.

I wanted more. I wanted *adventure.* I needed to know what was out there, beyond our green fields and sleepy village.

Most of all, in the heart of my secret desires, I craved one thing. To go north. To visit the Kingdom of Winter.

Since Stavrok had visited the north and helped Erik save the North Kingdom, I'd wanted to go myself. See the town that no-one else had seen. Meet the people no-one had known about, until now.

I spent most days now, tucked away in the castle library trying to find out more about the town everyone had thought was just a myth. I read about ice storms and ravenous wolves, harsh winters that lasted for years on end. And huge, powerful dragons that breathed ice instead of fire.

I wanted to see everything I read about in the books... for myself.

I walked across the room to a large window and glared out. The view was beautiful, as always, but it was as familiar as the nose on my face. The snow-peaked mountains, the rolling hills... It seemed very tame, in comparison to the harsh wilds I'd been reading about.

An urge struck me: to fling open the windows and release my dragon. I wanted to stretch my wings and soar. My dragon stirred inside me, and the call for adventure sang through my veins.

I inhaled sharply, trying to push away the desire. Then I turned away from the view.

Stavrok forbade me from leaving the castle without an armed guard. As a princess of his realm, I could be a valuable hostage; journeying alone was risky. If somebody recognized me, I would make a worthy bride for any upstart warlord or ambitious noble who dared to challenge the king.

I hated being stuck here, no more than a pawn in the games played by dragon kings and their lords.

I wanted to carve out my own destiny. And yet, as Stavrok's cousin, I wasn't sure how I was ever going to do that.

THAT EVENING, Stavrok and Lucy returned to the castle.

I smiled with relief when they walked into the dining room, still shaking the last of the snow from their hair. The table was already laid with silver candlesticks and the maids had decorated the white cloth with sweet floral arrangements. Platters of meat and warm, soft bread were waiting for them.

I stood up from the chair where I rested by the fire and rushed toward them. Lucy greeted me with a hug. She was still cold from being outside, and I shivered in my light evening clothes, pressing my hands to her pink cheeks.

"You're so cold," I said, trying to warm her. As a human, Lucy wasn't as adaptable to our climate as dragon shifters.

"How were my little ones?" Lucy clasped my hands, still shivering as she held my warm palms to her cheeks a moment longer.

I laughed. "They were good as gold...Well, the girls were!"

Stavrok let out a booming laugh as he took his seat at the head of the table. "My son has a strong will, even now. He will make a fine dragon king one day."

Lucy chuckled and moved from the fireplace to take a seat beside her husband. I did the same, and Lucy reached out to brush her hand over mine as we all sat down to dinner. "Thanks for watching them, Cass. I know I can always count on you. You're an angel."

I forced out a laugh. "Any time, Lucy."

What else did I have to do?

I fiddled with my fork. "You know I'll always be here."

Always and forever. Until I die of old age, in my library tower, surrounded by my books. Dreaming of adventures, I never undertook.

There were worse fates, and yet I couldn't help but want *more.*

Some note of frustration must have come through in my voice, because when I looked up, Stavrok had set down the turkey leg he'd been gnawing on and was watching me with a contemplative expression.

I tilted my head. "What's up, cuz?"

A grin slid over his face, and his eyes twinkled. "Cass. Dear Cass."

Uh oh. What have I done now?

"It's your twenty-first birthday tomorrow," Stavrok continued, and my stomach, which had lurched at his initial words, relaxed.

A matching grin sparked over Lucy's face, and the two of them turned to me. My heart started to race.

"You're not the child I met anymore, all those years ago." He reached out and took my hand. "You've grown into a smart, strong and beautiful woman. I'm proud of you."

My eyes widened in alarm. "Don't go getting all emotional on me, Stavrok!"

Still, I couldn't help but be a *tiny* bit pleased. If Stavrok finally saw me as an adult, then that could mean...

"I think what my husband is *trying* to say," Lucy interjected, "is that you deserve a treat. A birthday present that will let you... spread your wings, so to speak."

Spread my wings? Like, *actually* spread my wings? Excitement burst through me, but I tried to hold it in. What if I had misinterpreted what Lucy meant? What if...

"I'm taking you with me to the north," Stavrok said.

I gasped, both hands lifting to cover my mouth.

Stavrok grinned, obviously relishing the look of total shock on my face. "To meet the Dragon of Winter himself."

My hands dropped down and my mouth gaped open. The two of them sat there looking pleased as they watched me process the news.

"*Oh. My. God!*" I squealed, launching myself out of my chair and forward to throw my arms around my cousin's neck.

As Stavrok spluttered, struggling to free himself from the embrace, Lucy sat back and laughed.

Stavrok patted me a few too many times, and I dragged myself back to my seat, barely able to sit still. Finally, I was getting out of this kingdom! And not just going anywhere. He was going to take me to the one place I wanted to see most!

"I take it this means you're on board with your present?" Lucy said, wiping tears of mirth from her eyes.

"Of *course,* I am! I can't believe it!" I leant back in my seat. A thousand questions sprang to mind; I didn't know where to begin. "You're being serious, right? You wouldn't trick me with something like this?"

I glanced between my cousin and his wife, both of whom just laughed and shook their heads.

I clapped, too excited to eat anymore. "When do we leave? What do I pack—is it really as cold as they say? Will there be wolves? Will—"

"Whoa!" Stavrok reached out and put a cautionary hand on my shoulder, but his eyes expressed fondness. "How about we finish this meal first? Then we can talk about the rest."

"Of course. Thank you, guys! This is seriously..." I couldn't settle on the right word. Eventually, I just went with, "Amazing."

Stavrok and Lucy turned back to their meals. The conversation shifted to their three kids, so I drifted off.

I ate mechanically, without tasting another bite. I wanted to race off to the library at once and bury myself in the old books I had loved since I was little—the tales of the northern explorers, battling against icy storms and fearsome beasts.

I wanted to reacquaint myself with all the stories so I could prepare for actually going there in person.

I'd never met Damon, the King of Winter, despite the few times he'd come to the castle for royal errands. Stavrok had always kept him, and many of the other kings, away from me for some reason I hadn't yet worked out. I'd only heard stories about Damon, and they were enough to pique my interest to a mountainous level.

The servants passed rumors and I'd gotten snatches of tales traded from person to person, third-or-fourth hand, from Stavrok's expeditions and hunting parties.

Everyone knew that the north was a wild place, inhabited by unruly people. Things were different there... survival was harsher. People fought tooth and nail for everything they had.

Their king, according to the rumors, was the wildest one of all. He was said to be a ferocious fighter with piercing eyes and a cold, stoic demeanor. A lifetime spent in the frozen wilderness had rendered him more dragon than man.

An image formed in my mind: a dark, shadowy figure at the center of a snowstorm.

I shivered, and not just from the imagined cold.

"When do we leave?" I managed, at last.

Stavrok looked up from his plate of food. "Tomorrow."

We would leave tomorrow? On my actual birthday? I breathed deeply, trying to contain the excited squeal that wanted to rise. Best birthday present ever!

My fate was in the north, that much I knew.

The why? That was still a mystery.

CHAPTER
TWO

Cass

When I woke the next day—the day we were set to travel—sunlight was already filtering through the curtains and warming my face. I lay there, reveling in the joy and excitement that flooded through me.

It had been so long since I'd traveled, and I didn't even care that Stavrok would be babysitting me the whole time. It was a clear, bright day. I was itching to set out on our journey.

I bounced out of bed, flinging the windows wide open, and inhaled the cool springtime air.

"Someone's ready for their big day," a dry, amused voice said from behind me. "Little Cass, twenty-one years old! You're making me feel my age, child."

I turned around and grinned at Maddie. She was our head housekeeper; except she was so much more than that. She was part nanny, part adoptive mother. She'd raised me as much as Stavrok had. Probably more.

She stood in the doorway, hands on her hips. She shook her head at me before moving over to sort out the bedsheets.

I crossed the room and hugged her from behind, making her huff with disapproval at my lack of 'appropriateness'.

"You don't look a day over twenty, Maddie!"

"Flattery will get you nowhere, young lady." Maddie smacked my hands until I backed off, but her eyes were dancing. I was her favorite, and we both knew it. "Now, a little birdie told me about your trip... I take it we've got some packing to do."

I groaned. Packing and choosing clothes was the last thing I wanted to focus on right now. But Maddie merely tutted at me, opened my huge closet, and ran her hand along the rows of fabrics.

She began pulling everything out and placing each item on the bed, shaking her head as she went.

It soon became clear that I wasn't exactly prepared for a trip to the far north.

My clothes aren't, anyway.

I was used to the warmth of the castle: if I ventured outside, it was never further than the edge of town. My wardrobe was made up mostly of silk gowns and soft slippers. I found a couple of sweaters tucked at the back, but that was all I had that would save me from freezing to death.

I headed down to the Great Hall, only to find Stavrok already there, pacing up and down. Which was odd. He was obviously in a strange mood because, instead of wishing me a happy birthday, he gave me an unreadable look, like he was agitated about something.

Ugh, forget about him. This is the day everything changes!

"Come this way," Stavrok said, and I let him drag me into the next room.

Lucy and the babies were waiting for me there in the sunroom, along with a luscious birthday breakfast. I shoved aside whatever Stavrok's problem was because I would figure it out later.

Lucy gave me a broad smile.

"I had a surprise for you," she said as she jiggled the toddler on her hip, "but I'm afraid Anselm ate half of it already."

On the low table, a stack of pancakes lay in the centre of a plate, surrounded by strawberries. I squinted at the writing on the top; it was clearly meant to read HAPPY BIRTHDAY CASS, but the top layer had chunks missing. It now read HAP BIR AY CA.

I eyed Anselm with suspicion; he blinked back at me, his eyes wide and innocent.

"I love it!" I smiled, then stuck out my tongue at him while Lucy was distracted by the other two.

He giggled and blew a raspberry back at me.

"Happy birthday, Cass!" Lucy set Anselm down on the floor, then leaned forward to give me a big hug.

Anselm toddled over to where his sisters were stacking wooden bricks. Now that they were all walking, it was impossible to keep them in one place.

"Are you excited?" Lucy asked.

"Finally, a chance to get out of here," I said, trying to sound like I meant it as a joke, but her eyes softened in understanding.

"You deserve it."

I pulled her aside for a moment. "Did something happen this morning?"

She looked puzzled. "Nothing out of the ordinary, why?"

I shook off the uncomfortable feeling about Stavrok's mood, pasting a smile back onto my face. "I'm sure it's nothing."

Ugh, forget about Stavrok!

This was my birthday, and I was going to enjoy every second of it.

"Anything I can help you with?" Lucy asked. "Do you need to borrow a beanie, or muff, or anything?"

"I do, actually! I have nothing suitable for traveling to the north. I'm too used to being here in the cozy warmth of the castle."

Lucy giggled. "And I'm used to being cold all the time! My clothes might be a little big for you, but I'm sure we can get the seamstresses to take a few pieces in."

Lucy and I were the same height, but she was much curvier than I was. Especially since giving birth to the triplets.

"Sounds perfect! Thank you so much, Lucy."

Lucy winked at me. "Leave it to me. I'll go have a chat with the head seamstress now."

Lucy headed off and I sat on the floor to play with the babies. Only yesterday I was lamenting never being able to leave. And now... I was going to miss them while I was gone.

After breakfast, I went back to my room where three seamstresses came by with a dozen pieces from Lucy for me to try on. They were all heavy and warm, and I was sweating by the time they were done.

"We'll have these ready by the time you leave, Princess," one of the women said, before she hurried from the room.

"Thank you!" I called out to them, relieved beyond measure that Lucy cared enough to make sure I was comfortable and warm, and still able to go on my dream visit.

By the time we were ready to leave, Stavrok seemed to have gotten over whatever was bothering him earlier. He met me in the Great Hall with the easy smile that usually dominated his face these days, ever since he'd found Lucy.

"I've sent word to Damon. We will fly to an outpost half a day's journey from the castle, then take the rest of the journey on foot."

Huh?

"Why not fly the whole way?" I tilted my head, my confusion only growing when his laughter boomed through the hall.

Several servants turned their heads. His laugh always attracted attention.

"It would be quicker, right?" I asked him.

"I thought you would prefer to be properly dressed for our arrival, Cassie."

Oh. Right.

Shifters didn't return to human form fully clothed.

I pictured arriving in a strange land, in a strange throne room, naked in front of the fearsome, mysterious King of Winter...

Heat spread across my cheeks.

Stavrok's smile turned fond. "I thought I would spare my favorite cousin the embarrassment of appearing nude on your first meeting with Damon."

Favorite... and *only* cousin!

Irritation prickled over my skin as I realized that he was still trying to *protect* me. I didn't want to be sheltered any more. I wasn't the helpless, vulnerable little girl that everyone around here thought I was.

I was twenty-one, and officially an adult!

Still, I couldn't deny the fact I was kind of relieved he'd thought of such a thing. I certainly hadn't.

I didn't want Stavrok to know that, so I just glared and punched him on the arm. It rebounded off his solid frame and he ruffled my hair.

"I've already sent your trunks ahead. The seamstresses worked for hours to alter the pieces for you. My men will be waiting for us at a check-point just beyond the mountains," he said. "I hope you're ready to stretch your wings."

I grinned. My dragon itched to unleash. "Absolutely."

We walked through the main hall and stepped onto the balcony. Stavrok stripped off most of his clothes, leaving only his underwear for modesty.

I almost laughed. He only did that for me. Everyone else in the castle had seen him naked a hundred times. In fact, over the years I had seen him naked too as he left and returned from his many flights, but I allowed him his moment of modesty right now.

I followed his lead and stripped to my thin chemise and underwear, lamenting that I was wearing some of my favorite knickers. They'd be shredded soon. I really should have planned that better.

I grabbed my cousin's hand, stepped up onto the balustrade next to him, and took a deep breath as I stared down at the town beneath us. Excitement whipped through my stomach in the same way the wind was messing with my hair. Crazy. Invigorating.

"You ready?" Stavrok said.

I nodded. *I've been ready for this for years.*

He jumped, shifting mid-air and swooping low over the town.

I let out a little excited squeal and, letting my shifter take hold of me, threw my human self into the wind. My dragon roared with excitement, rushing forward to take over.

Taking to the skies again was like a dream.

It had been so long since I'd flown further than the edge of town, and I glided over cloud banks and dipped low over the hilltops, spiraling through the air with the adrenaline of the shift and the freedom singing through my veins.

Stavrok indulged my excitement, but eventually he steered me back on course. I followed him toward the mountains, and together we flew over the smoke-wreathed town in the foothills of the Black Castle.

Erik and Marienne were somewhere below us, tending to their own kingdom. Part of me wanted to swoop down and say hello, but I was eager to push on.

This was the furthest I'd ever flown from Stavrok's castle. The furthest I'd ever journeyed. *Ever.*

I drank in the colors of the sky, enjoyed the wind rushing past my wings, and reveled in the sharp icy chill of the air as we pushed onwards.

Eventually, we started to spiral lower to land. I followed Stavrok until we touched down beside a small cabin in a sparse cluster of trees. A group of men rushed out to meet us carrying thick robes.

As I shifted, I found myself trembling the instant the cold touched my bare skin. As a dragon, the cold didn't touch me. As a human, it was very different. I'd never felt such cold temperatures before. I wrapped my arms around my bare breasts, my nipples pebbling into hard points from the frost.

And we're not even in the far north yet...

The man who passed me my robe averted his gaze out of respect, though I was sure the men had seen more than they should. I pulled on the robe, hugging the fabric tight around my body and trying not to show my embarrassment. It was hard to hide that, though, with my cheeks flushing with heat.

No man had ever seen my naked body, other than in this moment. And now that the day had finally come, a cold mountainside and a bunch of Stavrok's guards wasn't exactly the scenario I'd had in mind.

Luckily, we were ushered into the cabin before the moment could get too awkward.

Stavrok let out his trademark booming laugh. "Don't worry, Cass." He clapped a heavy hand on my shoulder as he ducked through the doorway. "If any of my men fancy themselves a peek, I'll put their eyes out myself!"

I looked away in horror, only half-sure he was joking. Stavrok could get like that—particularly with Lucy.

I chalked it up to his protective nature, but it was more than that with me. I was a royal dragon shifter, and the men around me sensed the power that came with that title. No one would dare lay a finger on me, but I'd caught their eyes on me more and more often over the past few years as my body had changed into one of a breeding-aged woman.

Still chilled to the bone, I scuttled closer to the roaring fire, focusing on warming my face to cover how flustered I was.

"I'm starving," Stavrok said, settling down beside me on the ground and stretching out his legs.

As if on cue, a plate of hot soup and bread was presented to each of us by one of Stavrok's servants. My stomach lurched and I put my hand to my belly. Damn, I was hungry too. Flying so far had really engaged my appetite. I ate with gusto, tearing into the bread and dipping it into the soup.

"See," Stavrok said, with a note of pride. "You're a little wild thing already!"

I made a face at him but didn't slow down on eating.

When the meal was over, we sat in comfortable silence and stared into the fire's glowing embers.

"I have another surprise for you," Stavrok said. "Lucy and I took a trip to the seamstress last week... She had a hand in the design. Consider it an extra birthday present."

He signaled to the man behind him, and the servant came forward carrying something over his arm. When he held it out for me, I gasped.

"Stavrok!"

He smiled as I held up the garment in the firelight. It was a long black coat lined with thick gray fur around the collar. The lining was soft and velvety, and when I slipped it on it fit me like a glove. I ran my hands over the delicate patterns stitched into the material, a warmth tingling in my chest.

Something brand new and made just for me. It was such a thoughtful, useful gift.

"It's beautiful." I couldn't help rubbing my cheek over the soft collar. "And so warm!"

"Where we're going, dear one," Stavrok said in a soft voice, "you'll need it."

I was silent, pretending to examine the coat as I mulled over my words. "Stavrok?"

"Yes?"

"What's he like? King Damon?" I bit my lip, regretting my pointed question.

I would never admit it in a thousand years, but a wave of nervous energy flooded through me every time I thought about the King of Winter. I was no stranger to meeting noble families, and powerful men. But this felt... different. And I wasn't quite sure why.

It was my first time visiting his kingdom, and I wanted to know what to expect.

What if I make a fool of myself?

Stavrok gave me a strange look. "He inherited a broken kingdom, Cass. A king needs to be extremely strong to overcome such a tragedy."

"But what's he *like?*" I pressed. "Tall? Short? Funny? Boring? I need details, Stavrok."

Stavrok huffed, like I was being unreasonable.

"He's..." He trailed off, staring into the fireplace. "Tall. Are you satisfied, little one?"

Satisfied with "tall"? Hardly!

"Don't call me little one!" I rolled my eyes. "And *don't* avoid the question."

"He's a king like any other," Stavrok said eventually. "We only met once, and we were fighting a battle together. There wasn't much time for small talk, Cass."

I released a long, drawn-out sigh.

There was something he wasn't telling me, but Stavrok wasn't someone I could persuade information out of if he wasn't ready to share it. He'd tell me in his own time.

CHAPTER
THREE

Cass

Our carriages were waiting for us when we passed the treeline, with all the belongings we would need for the trip. Given that I hadn't been given any information about how long the trip would be, I'd packed practically everything I owned, plus everything Lucy had altered for me before we left.

I grimaced with sympathy at the thought of the servants lugging all that heavy baggage over the mountains.

The men bowed low to Stavrok and me as we stepped up into the carriage.

Once inside, I realized we were on a true royal mission, one royal family visiting another. And I was part of that. My heart started to hammer. The anticipation gnawed at me. This was it: the trip I had been waiting for. The journey of a lifetime.

When I looked up, Stavrok was watching me again, a frown on his face.

Annoyance flashed through me.

"What?" I huffed, crossing my arms. "Are you ever going to tell me what's going on? You've been sulking about something since the morning of my birthday."

He looked down, then stared out of the window at the landscape as we trundled on. I began to wonder if we'd spend the rest of the journey in silence.

"I received word from Queen Marienne," he said at last.

I brightened up at that. Marienne came to visit Lucy and I whenever she could. She was a natural with the kids, using her magic to make pretty floating lights for them. They loved her as much as we did.

But she had her own kingdom to run, and a new husband, to boot. It had been weeks since I'd heard from her.

"What's wrong?" My heart clenched. "Wait, is she okay?"

"Yes, yes." He waved a hand. "She and Erik are fine... better than fine. She had some news for me, is all."

He paused. The silence weighed heavily between us.

"About you," he added.

I stilled. Marienne's visions were well-known throughout the realm, but this was the first time *my* name had ever been thrown into the mix.

I didn't know what to think.

"What news?" I twisted my hands in my lap. *Was it bad?* "Did she see something?"

She must have, or Stavrok would never have brought it up.

His mouth pressed together in a thin line. Whatever he was about to tell me, I could see that it troubled him. My stomach tightened beneath my new coat. How bad could the news be?

"She had a vision," he said. "A vision of you. With King Damon. She believes that the two of you are... connected."

He glanced out the window. I could tell he really didn't want to be having this conversation.

I shook my head, totally lost. I couldn't see what the big deal was. We were going to the north to see King Damon, weren't we?

If Marienne saw the future, her vision made sense.

But Stavrok looked *angry*.

"Is *that* what you've been so worked up about?" I snorted. "Some vision of me meeting the king? Hell, I could've predicted that—and I don't have the sight! We're heading there right now, remember?"

Stavrok twisted around to look at me, his eyes hard. "Cass. You don't understand... Marienne's visions, they don't happen every day. She wouldn't have foreseen this if it wasn't important. She believes that the two of you are fated for one another."

Shock flooded through me.

That can't be true.

"I wanted to cancel this trip," I heard Stavrok say.

I wasn't fully listening anymore, just staring into space, processing the words, hearing them echo in my mind.

Fated for one another.

"But I knew how disappointed you would be. Cass, I'm not saying Marienne is right—"

"Has she ever been wrong?" I asked, my tone sharper than I intended.

Stavrok's face could have been carved from granite. His huge features, usually so warm, were deadly serious. He was more than my cousin. For the first time, I saw him for the man he truly was: a powerful Dragon King.

"All I'm saying is that you need to be prepared."

Prepared for what?

I wanted to call the carriage to a halt. I needed to ask a million questions.

Truth be told, I was terrified. I knew about fated mates—I'd seen it play out right in front of me on the day Stavrok brought Lucy home to the castle.

But it was rare for a dragon shifter to find their perfect match. Like... crazy rare.

I'd never once imagined it might happen to me.

To complicate matters further, I was a virgin. On the occasions I imagined the man I would marry, the idea was hazy and indistinct, but I'd always pictured something sweet, something romantic. Rose petals and soft music. *Definitely* not the crazed, lust-fueled pursuit that came to mind when I pictured a mate's heat.

Something must have shown on my face, because Stavrok leaned forward. I looked up to meet his gaze.

"Cass, listen to me. I won't let anything happen to you. I swear." He straightened up, his bulk spanning almost the width of the carriage. "I'm here as your guardian. I'll protect you—like I always have."

Outside, the scenery was changing. The trees were gone; the landscape consisted of miles of frozen ground, as far as the eye could see. Inside the carriage we remained warm, but I shivered all the same.

"How much further?" I mumbled.

I forced the whole conversation out of my mind. I had come here to explore, to see the world, and I was going to do that no matter what.

Stavrok pointed at a distant tower poking over the horizon out of the carriage window. "We're almost there."

As the carriage wheels turned and the horses picked up the pace, I barely heard the small talk from Stavrok. I couldn't hear anything beyond the rushing in my ears, and my own thudding heart. It completely drowned out everything else.

Why did it feel like I was about to meet my destiny head-on?

It was mid-afternoon by the time we arrived at the castle gates. The sky was pale gray, and snow blustered in through the door when Stavrok opened it. A blast of icy air hit me, and I turned up the collar of my coat as I stepped outside.

My eyes widened as I took in the huge castle with its ancient drawbridge. A wide moat surrounded the fortress; laid out around it was what looked like a giant building site.

"King Damon's enemies razed the whole town to the ground," Stavrok said as we walked along a winding, makeshift path. Everywhere I looked, townsfolk were hard at work, bricklaying, sawing, and heaving huge blocks of stone over the frozen ground. "They've been slow to rebuild. The conditions up here can be brutal."

I craned my neck to watch the drawbridge as it lowered to let us over the moat. Everywhere I looked there were remnants of the battle, deep gouges in the stonework and burn marks over the battlements that could have only been caused by dragon fire.

"It's so..." I trailed off, lost for words at the huge, imposing structure.

Harsh was the word that finally came to mind.

All the castles I had seen were square and smooth, made of sandstone. This castle was all dizzying turrets and spiky towers, edged with snowdrifts.

"So tall," I said eventually, trying to remain polite, and letting out a nervous laugh at my lame description.

Stavrok grinned, leading me up to the huge front doors. The guardsmen stepped aside, bowing low, to let us pass.

Back home, the palace guards were friendly and open with me. I knew all their names; after all, most of them had watched me grow up.

These guards were different. They were fearsome in their thick over-coats, and the broadswords hanging by their sides looked like they had seen their fair share of use.

The hallway was as grand and stately as I expected from the imposing exterior, and even Stavrok looked impressed. He glanced up at a huge window as we passed underneath an elaborate stone archway, whistling.

"The last time I was here, this room was nothing but rubble," he said, catching my eye. "I hardly even recognize the place."

As Stavrok continued to admire the repair work, I trailed after him, my eyes wide. I tried to keep up, but in truth I was barely paying attention to the running commentary.

Now that we were in the castle, it was impossible to forget about Marienne's vision. The man I was about to meet could very well be my intended mate. The one person who was designed for me, and me for him.

Part of me wanted to run screaming from the place. The other part was so excited I could barely walk straight. I'd wanted a life, and an adventure, outside the safety of Stavrok's castle, and I'd gotten it. In spades.

We were led deeper and deeper into the castle, down the cavernous hallways. Our guide, another stone-faced guard, made me nervous. I stuck close to Stavrok's side, my mind racing.

My palms itched with anticipation and my dragon shifter stirred closer to the surface than usual. I tried to imagine this king, a total stranger, somewhere in the castle. Could he feel my presence?

Was this nervous anticipation just normal-level excitement at getting out and having an adventure, or was it more? What if what Marienne had foretold was true?

I swallowed as Stavrok indicated I should move forward, and together we walked into a small antechamber. Two more guards waited on either side of a set of huge doors. They stared at us impassively as we approached and knocked once on the double doors.

My heart stalled in my chest. It was too late to turn back now.

Damon

"Sire." The voice of my chief advisor echoing across the Great Hall startled me out of my thoughts. "They're here."

I straightened and stood up from my throne, stepping down from the dais and striding forward into the center of the large space. It was customary to greet a fellow king on equal ground. I could not meet my guests from up high on my throne.

The formal clothes I wore were stiff and uncomfortable. I much preferred my everyday attire, but my advisors had cautioned against it for this meeting. I found all the court rules and regulations stifling, especially when my mind and my focus was on the repair work I'd been carrying out with my men only this morning.

Still. Stravrok had shown me great generosity during the battle by coming to our aid. Not to mention what he'd done for us since we started repairing. It was only fitting that I return that favor by allowing him and his cousin to visit and see the renovations.

Plus, it gave me a chance to show another kingdom that we were slowly regaining our former strength. Hopefully, the word would spread. My ancient house—the family of ice dragons that had ruled the north for generations—had survived the raiders.

The castle wasn't the only thing my father had driven to ruin. I needed to rebuild alliances and treaties. The best way to do that was to make peace with my fellow rulers.

The corners of my mouth lifted into a polite, welcoming smile as the double doors opened.

"His Majesty, King Stavrok of the Bravdok Clan, and his cousin, the Princess Cassandra."

Stavrok strode into the room with all the brazen confidence I remembered. The years since the battle hadn't changed him that much; only a few more threads of silver in his hair indicated that time had passed.

I greeted him with a nod, and he grinned back, charging over with his hand outstretched, ready to pull me into a friendly bear hug.

He only managed to get halfway across to me, however, before I caught sight of the other newcomer standing behind him.

My dragon instantly woke from its slumber, uncoiling inside my chest. I growled, trying to push him down.

Something I'd never felt before pulsed through my veins, dark and hot, filling me with a single-minded purpose: a *desire* like I'd never known before.

What the hell is this?

Whatever it was, I had no power to stop it. The force rolled through me like a tidal wave.

My vision began to change. Everything in the room faded out of focus. And nothing else mattered. Not Stavrok, nor my kingdom. Not my castle repairs. Not the fact that I was a king.

Only *she* remained.

Her chestnut brown hair hung in loose curls, dusted with snowflakes from her journey. Her eyes were wide and fringed with dark lashes. Unlike most of the shifters I had met, who all had icy, pale blue eyes, hers were a deep, warm brown.

I need her.

The realization hit me like an anvil. I didn't have time to consider what it meant. I strode forward, my gaze zeroed in on my prize.

Stavrok stepped in front of her, blocking my path. He knocked away my hands that were already outstretched for her. I released a deep snarl, prepared to shift fully if I needed to fight the other man. My neighboring king. The obstacle in the path of my need.

Stavrok was on the brink of shifting as well. I caught sight of his dragon when his angry gaze flashed to meet mine. Hot rage curled within me and I lowered my stance. Stavrok would not keep her from me.

She wasn't any woman. This one was *mine*.

On some level, where my brain still operated rationally, I knew the difference. I'd had women before. I was a Dragon King, and I had to satisfy my appetite for pleasure alongside everything else.

The stresses of recent years meant I'd tamped down my desires. In the face of all I had to rebuild, a fumble with a maid or some woman in town felt like a waste of time. I had responsibilities; more important things to deal with than my sex drive.

Not that plenty of women hadn't put themselves in my path. I was their king. More often than not, I'd rebuffed them.

And this was why. *She* was why.

All thought of polite pleasantries and formal introductions were long gone. We circled each other, Stavrok managing to keep himself between me and the girl as I snarled with impatience.

We weren't two kings anymore, meeting for an official royal visit. This was deeper. Primal.

We were dragon shifters and the need to fight this invader, this intruder in my kingdom, coursed through me as strong as the ocean.

For whatever reason, the mere sight of this girl inflamed my dragon like no other.

Only one thing remained: the feral, frenzied, uncontrollable urge to take her and carry her out of here.

Stavrok shouted something, but I was too far gone to hear it. I could only watch, burning with fury, as he grabbed the girl by the arm and practically dragged her out of the room.

The moment the heavy doors thudded closed behind them, I was there, pounding against the wood. My shifter writhed in frustration; it was all I could do not to release my anger, shift, and burn down my own door to get to her.

"Stavrok!" I bellowed, fists balled against the immovable oak door. "Open the door, right now. Before I burn the damn thing down!"

"So, it is true," the voice came back, muffled, from the other side of the door. "Marienne was right."

I was losing patience. As every minute passed, shifting looked like a more and more appealing plan.

"*What* is true?"

"You're my cousin's true match. Her fated mate," Stavrok yelled through the door.

I forced myself to take deep, ragged breaths, fighting to regain control. It was easier now that the girl—Princess Cassandra—wasn't in the same room, but knowing exactly where she was, just out of reach... the feeling of it, the knowledge... It was pure torture. I groaned and again smashed my fist against the wood.

"The two of you are destined for each other," Stavrok added.

I pressed my forehead against the door, growling. "Then what are you waiting for? Let me through!"

"You're not in control, Damon!"

I bared my teeth at him, even though he couldn't see it. Frustration pounded through me.

"She's young..." Stavrok hissed. "And still a virgin!"

"*Stavrok!*" Another voice cut in. A sweet, light voice, admonishing him for revealing a truth that had my dragon slowly retreating.

A *virgin?* Then I would be her first. Her *only*.

"Open the door, cousin," she said, and the sound washed over me like silk. She sounded... perfect. Right down to that thrum of desire I heard in her tone. Oh, yes. She had felt the lick of need too, it seemed.

But I needed to get myself under control, so I could meet her properly. I straightened, crowding as close as possible up against the door and hoping she would speak again.

"Get yourself together," Stavrok said, as if he knew exactly how hard I was struggling. Perhaps he did. His wife Lucy was Stavrok's mate. Perhaps it had been like this for him?

"I'm warning you, Damon. If you can't control your dragon, I will leave, and I'll take Cass with me. You'll never see her again."

He sounded dangerous; deadly. If I were fully in my right mind, I might have been afraid. Stavrok was a fearsome warrior. I had no doubt that if anything happened to his beloved cousin, he would have my head for it. Literally.

I focused on breathing, clearing the fog that had spread through my senses.

"Okay." I took a few steps back from the door. "I'm ready." Slowly, the doors opened.

Stavrok stood with his arms crossed, half in front of Cassandra. She sidled out from around his body shield.

Had my behavior terrified her? One glance told me otherwise, from the lust burning in her gaze, to the way a light flush spread over her cheeks.

I forced down a shiver and turned my attention back to Stavrok.

"My apologies," I said through gritted teeth. "Your cousin caught me by surprise."

Stavrok's face was stony, and I could tell he was holding back for Cass's sake. He nodded, straightening up, his posture remaining protective.

My dragon simmered with rage at the show of strength. I knew better than to challenge him, though, because when it came to the safety of his cousin, Stavrok was indeed doing the right thing. Even if my dragon couldn't see it yet.

You could have cut the tension in the room with a blade. One wrong move, and the peace I'd built—this fragile alliance I wanted to strengthen between my kingdom and Stavrok's—could be reduced to ashes.

We stood in silence, my head buzzing.

"Well," Stavrok said loudly, clapping his hands together. "Do we get the grand tour?"

"Of course," I replied, grateful for the suggestion. It would give us all something to concentrate on, other than my need to shift and fly away with my mate. "Follow me."

I LED them through the castle, focusing my mind on anything but the woman walking with Stavrok. I pointed out all the changes I'd made and moved as if in a trance. The voices around me were muffled, like I was underwater.

After a while, Stavrok stepped out in front and led the way, talking loudly and asking question after question. He seemed keen to put as much space between me and his cousin as possible.

Cass herself was an enigma.

I could barely keep my eyes off her. She flitted through the hallways, her gaze wide and excited at every detail, every new discovery. Occasionally she stole a glance at me, and I looked away the moment our eyes met, glaring down at the floor.

I didn't trust my dragon not to grab her if he had half the chance.

Her long dark hair tumbled around her shoulders in loose curls, and her eyes were warm and bright. Everything about her was a breath of fresh air in this cold, gloomy place. She reminded me of a butterfly, the way she darted from window to window.

And yet, somehow, I knew that she was as aware of me as I was, of her. Even though she seemed more able to throw it off and act normally, I sensed the desire simmering beneath the surface of her beautiful exterior.

My dragon ached for her. More than anything, I wanted to grab her and haul her away somewhere, *anywhere* we could be alone. Then I could unleash all my passion and drive her into ecstasy.

But a small part of me—the tiny shred of reason buried in the back of my mind—told me that Stavrok was right about not rushing this connection I felt for Cass.

I couldn't risk offending Stavrok. And I couldn't risk her safety. Especially if she was as innocent and virginal as Stavrok said.

Outside, the snowflakes tumbled thicker and faster as we reached the rear of the castle, where the high walls overlooked the small gardens below.

Cass tapped on the windows. "What's that down there?"

"The hedge maze," I said.

Her eyes lit up at the prospect of an adventure.

"My ancestors planted it centuries ago," I added, wanting to prolong the conversation with her but still having trouble with my dragon staying under control.

Stavrok's eyes narrowed. "Cass, you're not going out there in this weather. There's going to be a blizzard before long."

Cass tilted her chin up at him defiantly. "It's my birthday, isn't it? We didn't come all this way so I could end up stuck inside another castle... No offence," she added, glancing at me.

Heat gathered in my chest as her eyelashes swept across her cheeks.

"None taken," I murmured, pretending intense interest in the weather beyond the window as Stavrok and Cass debated beside me.

Eventually, Cass won the argument and, as I turned to look at them, Stavrok scowled at me.

I wasn't going to be the ally he hoped for. In this state, I could hardly deny her request. My dragon wanted to give Cass everything.

I'll protect her.

As we headed down to the small gatehouse at the foot of the castle, emerging into the frosty air on the long, winding path that took us toward the gardens, Cass appeared suddenly, bobbing up beside my elbow.

I shuddered with longing as she brushed against my arm. The pink that rose in her cheeks had nothing to do with the cold air and suggested she felt the same way as me.

"What's in the middle?" she asked.

I turned to stare at her, my eyes trailing downward. She was a petite little thing, only coming up to my shoulder. I didn't trust myself to speak, so I waited for her to clarify.

"Of the maze," she added, and then bit her lip.

I groaned internally, imagining what it would be like to sink my teeth into her soft flesh, right where her teeth currently nibbled.

"Don't mazes usually have a prize in the middle?"

Her gaze lingered on mine. I couldn't help but wonder what kind of *prize* she was imagining.

There were plenty of places for two people to get lost inside a maze.

Perhaps that's what she's counting on?

I shrugged, not trusting my voice. She would see soon enough what was at the center of the maze.

Stavrok was glowering by the time we reached the entrance. The tall hedges on either side were already covered in a fine bank of snow. A glance up to the sky didn't tell me much. The weather could turn, or it could hold.

Behind Stavrok, Cass was admiring a frost-tipped rose. The color matched her glowing cheeks. She was utterly bewitching.

I would give her anything she wanted.

The knowledge terrified me. I glowered, hoping that my fascination didn't show on my face.

"Are you sure you want to do this?" Stavrok grumbled, flicking snow off the edge of his coat.

Cass grinned up at him. He sighed, mumbling something about birthdays and annoying cousins, but followed her into the maze without a backward glance.

I trailed after them. My dragon was still simmering inside me, barely contained; the urge to grab her thudded continuously in the back of my mind. If anything, it was growing stronger with each twist and turn of the maze. Cass led us deeper and deeper. Stavrok swore when he stumbled over an exposed tree root, grumbling to himself.

The hedges closed around us.

Cass practically ran around each bend in the hedgerows. It turned into a game of chase. My heart raced as I tracked her through the maze. My dragon was single-minded and greedy; it wanted her.

She skipped ahead, throwing a cheeky smile back at me. I caught the edge of a skirt, a loose curl, before she slipped out of sight around the corner.

I glanced behind me. Stavrok was nowhere to be seen.

I was alone.

There was nothing for it but to go on. The sky above was white with snowflakes, which were falling thicker and faster than ever.

"Cass?" I shouted. "Stavrok?"

I listened intently but there was no answer, only the wind rustling through the leaves around me.

I knew the maze better than most. When I was a child, I often played in it, or hid away where the servants couldn't find me when my father was on one of his temper-fueled rampages. But as I got closer to the middle, my worry grew. I could make it out of here, but Cass and Stavrok...

Get to Cass, my dragon growled. *Find her. Protect her. Take her.*

I rounded the corner and got my bearings, realizing I was close to the center. My heart rate picked up when I heard a voice behind me, high and sweet.

"King Damon?"

I turned. Cass stood in the middle of the path. She had her arms wrapped around her body, tucked into herself, and she was trembling as gust after gust of cold air buffeted the hedgerows around us and sent her hair tumbling and flying within a cascade of snowflakes.

"This way," I said, not trusting myself to get too near her.

I strode down the path, leading the way. Her footsteps trotted as she caught up with me.

"We need to get out of here!" Her voice trembled.

The snowstorm was building, and it wouldn't be long before we were trapped in it.

"Shouldn't we turn around?"

She was right. We needed to get under cover, and fast.

There wasn't time to get back to the entrance and make our way back to the castle. I swallowed thickly as I realized that we only had one option.

"You wanted to know what was at the center of the maze?" I strode onwards. The path narrowed, and I knew what waited for us around the next corner. "Didn't you?"

"Well, yes, but..."

I turned and stared at her. "Trust me."

Our eyes met. Heat sparked through my veins. Her breathing grew ragged. The fur on her collar rose and fell with each exhale.

She nodded.

Together, we turned the final corner.

We had reached the center of the maze. Without Stavrok.

In the middle of the clearing stood the entrance to the stone grotto that led to the caves.

I ushered Cass toward the entrance. The snow was falling so thickly that I could barely make out the stony entrance. As Cass hurried into the grotto, I ducked back outside to take a final look around for Stavrok.

He was nowhere to be seen.

Cursing the weather, I ran back into the cave after her.

"Cass!" My voice echoed off the rocky walls. I climbed down the steps cut into the rock.

The sound of soft footsteps shuffled up ahead. My heart pounded with adrenaline. We were alone.

I should never have agreed to show them the maze. I knew the weather would get worse.

They aren't from around here. They don't know how harsh our winters are. They're used to rolling hills and mild snowdrifts.

I admonished myself but it was too late to change anything now. I could only blame my misjudgment on my foggy head and the overpowering lust that I couldn't shake. It was more potent than anything I'd felt before, and my body wouldn't let me forget that the source of my misery was a scant few feet away from me.

"Damon?" Cass called again, nearer this time.

I stepped into the cavern. Dim light flickered from a torch set into the stone wall, casting a golden glow over the stone. Cass had her back to me, staring into the pool that dominated the room, watching the steam rise from it and spiral upwards.

"It's a hot spring," I said, coming over to stand beside her. From this close I could feel the warmth from her body. "People swim here sometimes. It's said that the water has healing properties."

She glanced up at me. "Can I...?"

Once I realized what she was asking, I stiffened.

We would be stuck here for some time, until the storm lifted. She was cold and wanted to go in to warm up, and with her staring at me like that I couldn't think of a good reason why not.

The second I nodded, she began to unbutton her coat, sliding the fabric down and off her shoulders.

A growl rose unbidden to my lips. I turned my back on her and strode over to the other side of the cave, facing the mouth of the tunnel.

"Where are you going?"

Her voice was light, teasing. She was taunting me.

"Nowhere," I forced out as I stared down at a wooden chest by the entrance to the cave. It held clean clothes and towels, if I remembered correctly, but I couldn't make myself reach down to open the lid. My body was wound far too tightly.

A soft rustle reached my ears, the sound of fabric dropping to the floor. I clenched my hands into fists when the gentle sounds of lapping water reached me. Then I heard her body slide beneath the surface.

I swallowed, squeezing my eyes closed.

"It's so warm!" Her tone was startled, as though she couldn't believe that up here in the freezing mountains, beneath the arid earth, were warm springs.

But I heard the sweet undercurrent of pleasure in her words and began to imagine how she'd look floating in the water.

I forced myself to relax and draw deep, even breaths.

The mere thought of her naked body sliding beneath the water was maddening. I could hear the gentle splash as she moved around, but I didn't dare look.

"Aren't you joining me, my king?" Her tone was teasing, and her words even more so.

That was the last straw.

I rounded on her. "What game are you playing at?"

She was in the middle of the pool, submerged up to her bare shoulders. Curly tendrils of her dark hair lay on the water's surface. She looked like a nymph.

Or a siren. Come to lead me to my doom.

"What do you mean?"

She sounded shocked. Her eyes, however, raked up and down my body. I had only deigned to remove my outer coat, and I stood before her in my shirt and slacks. Strangely, I felt like I was the naked one.

"You want me to swim with you? Alone, in this cave? With..." I gritted my teeth, waving a hand to indicate her bare form. "Your cousin—"

"My cousin," Cass interrupted, her eyes flashing with impatience, "is not here."

Damon

Cass stilled, and then looked up at me again. There was a new fire in her eyes, burning even brighter than before.

I hadn't realized that she must have been kneeling until slowly, she stood up in the pool and revealed herself to me. Droplets of water rolled down the contours of her naked body, hugging her curvaceous frame. My eyes raked over every inch of her small high breasts, her hips, her pale thighs and the alluring valley between them.

She was still, silent. It was a challenge.

She had thrown down the gauntlet, baring herself to me.

My dragon ignited inside me, recognizing its mate once again. I let out an inhuman growl and crashed into the water, still clothed. Cass squealed with surprise as I wrapped my arms around her waist and hoisted her body flush against mine.

We both groaned at the feel of finally being able to touch each other. Her legs tightened around my waist. I backed her through the water until I reached the place where I knew the rock leveled out, creating a natural shelf in the side of the cave. I pressed her against the shelf, and she arched her back, revealing her long, pale throat to me.

It was an act of submission in the boldest possible way.

She wants this. Wants me to claim her.

My dragon was in control now. My teeth scraped against the sensitive flesh, and she whimpered, her hands running along my forearms as she bucked and writhed against me. I gripped her hips, holding her in place, while she pulled my shirt out of my trousers, tracing over the planes of my chest with exploring fingers.

I drew back, breathing harshly. Her lips were red and full where she'd bitten into them, and her eyes were hazy, pupils blown out with desire. I was willing to bet I didn't look much saner.

My fingers slid up her thighs and she squirmed with delight. Knowing I was the first man to touch her in such a way was intoxicating.

My dragon pushed for more, *more*, and I gave into the demands fully.

I grunted when her hand closed around the nape of my neck, tugging my hair with impatience. Her eyes flashed, and I knew her own dragon guided her every movement, from the way her hips bucked up into mine to her other hand clinging against my back, pushing up my shirt, greedy for more contact.

When my hands slid between her thighs and my fingers pushed inside her slick pussy, we both gasped. Her hot, open mouth pressed against my shoulder, and I groaned at the feel of her sharp teeth against my skin, and how tight she was around me.

She clung to me, wet hair sticking to my shoulders as we moved together. My thumb circled her clit and she tensed, tightening even further.

When she reached for my trousers as if to release my cock, I growled, grabbing both of her hands in one of mine and pinning them above her head, to the cave wall behind her. My own pleasure could wait.

She acquiesced to the restriction, staring up at me with wide, lust-filled eyes.

I teased her, withdrawing my fingers from her body so that I could run my free hand over her breasts, cupping them as I bruised her throat with kisses before returning to her pussy. Even submerged in warm water, I could feel how hot she was inside, and it drove me wild.

When she squeezed tight around my fingers, a long moan sounding in my ear, I couldn't hold back my dragon any longer.

When I pulled my fingers out again, she whimpered at the loss of contact. Her hands fumbled for me, and together we pushed down my trousers so that there was nothing standing between us.

I lined up my cock with her still-squirming body and thrust into her as slowly as I could considering the lust riding me hard, and her virginal status. She cried out in shock and I instantly halted.

"No," she whispered. "Don't stop. I want more."

I complied, thrusting again and seating myself fully, and this time her cry was pure pleasure. She wrapped her arms and legs around me tight, holding me close.

Around us the surface of the water trembled, and the torch flames fluttered. The force of our shifters joining together filled the cave with an energy I'd never seen before, a light that drove the shadows away and illuminated the pool and the whole cavern. I could feel the power flowing through my body, and from the look on Cass's face, I could tell that she did, too.

I thrust into her over and over again, feeling her squeeze tighter and tighter around my cock with every forward motion of my hips. Nothing had ever felt so right, so perfect. Every cry, every moan, every gasp from her lips was like a symphony to my ears.

Then her small frame began to stiffen against me, and her sharp cry filled the cave as her orgasm overtook her. She rode it out against me, and after a couple of harsh thrusts I followed her over the edge.

For several endless moments I stood there in the water, braced against her, feeling nothing but sheer ecstasy and joy.

We were both panting and the water around us suddenly felt cold against my overheated skin. I pulled out of her, stroking a shaking hand down her side before I could stop myself. I pulled up my trousers and tucked my cock away before staggering out of the water.

Guilt hammered me, choking the life out of the afterglow that flowed through me. I was sated, satisfied, and utterly screwed.

This beautiful, innocent girl... I'd taken her. Without a second thought about her innocence. My dragon had overruled my better judgment and I'd done the one thing I swore I would not do until my kingdom was repaired: I had claimed my mate.

My kingdom still lay in ruins around me. I spent all my days, and many of my nights, rebuilding the castle and the land surrounding it, shoring up our defences in preparation for winter. My world was one of ice and fire. The land was harsh and hostile, and only harsh things grew here.

My people were tough. They had to be, in order to weather anything that the north threw at them. Cass was slender, beautiful, and delicate. She was a hothouse flower, a rare creature in a such a cold climate.

Such beauty surely couldn't survive the ice world in which I lived?

I swallowed as she climbed out of the water behind me. Droplets cascaded down her body, making her look even more ethereal and delicate.

After everything was said and done, I was no better than my father. The man had terrorized this country for so long. He'd been selfish and weak. He'd taken without a second thought.

And now I'd done exactly the same to Cass.

"Damon?"

I half-turned my head. Mercifully, she'd slipped on her dress. It clung to her damp body, and I looked away before my baser instincts could wreck further havoc.

"The snow should have eased off by now," I said. "We need to return to the castle before nightfall, or your cousin might..."

I trailed off and we stared guiltily at each other. What would Stavrok do? That was the burning question. "Okay." She sounded so despondent that I turned to look at her properly. A stab of remorse ran through me when I realized she was shivering.

I strode over to the wooden chest near the entrance to the cave, rifling through it until I found a large, fluffy towel.

"Here." I returned to her, draping the towel around the exposed skin of her shoulders and wrapping it firmly around her. "Use this as an extra layer."

She gave me a wan smile, and I picked up her coat, helping her into it.

"What about you?" Her eyes flicked over my soaking form, and I remembered abruptly that I had been almost fully clothed when I rushed into the water.

At the sight of her naked body, all of my common sense had gone out the window. I couldn't help the sheepish smile that crept over my face.

I played it cool, shrugging. "I'm from the north. We're cold-blooded up here."

Her eyes glimmered, and the corners of her mouth twitched. "Is that so? Well, you could've fooled me."

She glanced at the hot pool behind her, as if to remind me wordlessly of our heated encounter.

Like I needed reminding. My face remained stoic, but my heart was still beating a mile a minute in my chest. I regretted the loss of control, regardless of the current sated feeling in my body. Whatever the dragon inside me wanted, my actions had been reckless.

Who am I kidding? If my dragon had its way, we'd already be going for round two.

"Come on," I said, changing the subject. "Your cousin is probably worried sick."

Without waiting for a response, I picked up my own coat from where it lay in a crumpled heap on the floor and haphazardly pulled it on. Then, I strode toward the mouth of the cave.

I needed to put some space between me and Cass. That was all I needed. Time to think, to clear my head.

The cold air hit me and my wet clothes hard as we exited the cave, but the snow had thankfully eased off.

The sooner we were out of this maze and back under the watchful gaze of Stavrok, the better. At least, for Cass.

CHAPTER

SIX

Cass

The journey back through the maze to the castle, despite my best attempts at conversation, was mostly silent.

Damon didn't hesitate in choosing the path out of the maze. He probably had the route memorized. With his longer legs, I had to almost jog to keep pace with him, but I didn't mind that. It helped take my mind off the cold.

Occasionally I felt his eyes on me, but he always dropped his gaze before I could get a read on him. There was worry in his expression though, and his broad shoulders were stiff with tension.

It didn't make sense. Back in the cave, he'd been passionate and intense. Everything I'd ever dreamed a lover could be.

Things had been simple between us there, when it was just the two of us. I wanted him, and he wanted me.

Now he was evasive.

I tried to make the best of the heavy silence and use the time to organize my thoughts. Everything had happened so fast. The last few hours were a jumbled-up blur of sensations. It was hard not to let the excitement of the day overwhelm me. I felt like a totally different person to the girl who had woken up that morning.

From the second I'd laid eyes on Damon, my dragon had responded, hungry for his touch. We'd gone from room to room, down every hallway and explored every inch of his castle. Nothing slaked the burning fire in my belly.

I was all I could do not to launch myself at him and demand he drag me away somewhere to ravish me. Which was so out of character I couldn't understand what had overtaken me.

I'd thought the fresh air might help matters, exploring the maze, but I had no such luck. I had been aching for him to take me: my only thought by then had been to lure him deeper, somewhere away from prying eyes. Somewhere away from my chaperone, Stavrok.

I thought we'd both gotten what we wanted. But Damon's attitude now suggested otherwise.

I guess I was wrong.

The second we were back inside the castle, he muttered something about needing a change of clothes and hurried off into another room. The door slammed shut behind him with a resounding *thud*.

I lingered in the hallway. My hair was still dripping from melted snow and water from the heated spring pool. The soft sounds of water dripping against the tiles on the floor was the only noise in the empty space.

The ecstasy I had experienced in the cave felt like a far-off dream. I'd stepped back into the cold, harsh light of day, and my happiness gave way to doubt.

What does this mean? What will happen if he doesn't want me?

Ice filled the pit of my stomach.

I wasn't sure how I long I stood there, turning every detail of our encounter over in my mind. Now that the initial frenzy of lust had been satisfied, I could look at things more objectively.

Did I do something wrong?

I thought back to the way Damon held me against him, his firm hands on my hips, his hot mouth on my neck. The way he thrust into me, claiming me...

I bit my lip, the heat rising in my cheeks once again as lust twisted in my belly, making me ache for more.

He *had* wanted me, that much had been clear.

So why can he barely look at me now?

"Cass?"

I turned, relief flooding me at the familiar voice. I'd never been so happy to see my cousin.

"Stavrok!" I rushed over to him. "We lost you back there. Are you all right?"

Stavrok's eyes flickered on the word *we* but he otherwise ignored my phrasing.

He grunted, looking unhappy. "The way back to the castle was easy enough from the air," he said. "I shifted as soon as the weather turned. I looked for you, Cass, but I couldn't see you. I thought you must have returned to the castle, but..."

He tilted his head. I could see the cogs turning in his mind, and I fiddled with my fingers, twisting them around each other, uncomfortable under his intense scrutiny.

"Damon found me." My eyes flicked over to a nearby tapestry.

Stavrok's gaze burned a hole in the side of my face, but I ignored him.

"There were these underground caves, and..."

I trailed off. My cheeks grew hot. I reached up and pressed a hand against one, trying to hide my face behind my still-wet hair.

"I see," Stavrok said.

After his earlier attitude, I expected him to explode with anger. In the back of my mind, I feared he would tear apart the castle, kill Damon, and carry me home with him.

But he didn't sound enraged. Instead, he seemed... resigned.

I looked up. "You're not mad at me?"

His gaze softened as he looked down at me. "Cass, I could never be mad at you."

"We just..." I scrambled for a way to explain. A thousand excuses for my behavior fell into my head: the weather, the cave, the water. The way Damon looked at me, how good his hands had felt...

Stavrok *definitely* wouldn't appreciate hearing all the details.

But I had to make him *understand.*

"It just happened," I whispered. "It's like Marienne said. Like *you* said. I think it was always going to happen."

Stavrok huffed, but he nodded. His hands rested on my shoulders, and we stood together in the quiet.

"When I look at you, I still see that tiny girl who showed up at the castle gates one night with nowhere else to go." In a familiar, comforting gesture, Stavrok tugged gently on a lock of my hair. "You've always been more than a cousin to me, Cass. You're like my baby sister. It's hard for me to admit that you've grown up."

"I know. But I have."

He gave a heavy sigh and stepped backwards. "It seems that I owe Marienne once again."

We smiled at each other.

Then Stavrok's face turned serious. "Cass, it's probably best if I head home. I only came to introduce you to Damon, and to protect you from his dragon if it was needed. But you've proven you can handle him well enough on your own, and well... I need to return. I have my own kingdom to run."

A shiver of loss ran through me.

All this time, Stavrok had been a necessary endurance. My chaperone, an annoying brother figure standing in the way of my destiny.

The thought of him leaving, left me cold. He was the one constant in this stark and forbidding place, my only reminder of home.

He gave me a regretful smile. "You don't need me here, Cass."

"I *know*, but..."

I bit my lip to stop from continuing. I sounded petulant.

The truth was, I was afraid, alone in a frozen fortress with a mate who was a stranger to me.

"That's only if you want to stay?" Stavrok lifted an eyebrow. "Or have I read you wrong? You can come home with me also, if you'd like?"

The idea of leaving now filled me with an even greater dread. King Damon was my destiny, my fate. I was sure of it. I couldn't leave him now.

I looked straight at my cousin and smiled as confidently as I could. "I want to stay."

Stavrok nodded. "I knew you would. I'm so proud of the woman you've become, Cass. I know you'll do *me* proud as my royal representative here, and if you have any issues with the Winter King, you know you can always come home."

I grinned at him. "In this weather?"

He shrugged. "You're a royal, Cass. Shift and fly home. We'll be there waiting with open arms, no matter what."

Tears filled my eyes as I embraced my cousin, my protector, my king. "Thank you, Stavrok."

He was right.

I was a grown woman now.

If I wanted a life of my own, I'd have to take the opportunity on offer, and make it my own.

~

STAVROK HAD TAKEN his leave and night had fallen in the castle. Damon did not reappear.

Luckily, I was considered a valued royal guest, so I was not left to wander aimlessly or lament being alone. The servants showed me up the winding staircase to a cozy suite of rooms. I huddled gratefully beside a roaring fire in the grate, watching snow drift past the windows. The fur throws strewn all over the bed were thick and soft to the touch, and I tugged one over my shoulders while I sat and stared into the flames.

It was quite obvious. Damon was avoiding me.

I rang the bell that had been left for me, and called for a maidservant. It was a matter of minutes before the door opened, and a woman entered. She was a slip of a thing, scarcely older than I was, and she eyed me with poorly disguised anxiety.

"Can I help you, Your Highness?"

"King Damon." I stood, letting the fur blanket slide back onto my chair. "Where is he?"

The maid looked even more nervous at my question. I softened my expression, hearing Stavrok's words echo around my head.

You're a stranger to them, remember? They're not used to outsiders. You'll have to win over their trust, little by little.

"I... I'm not sure, ma'am."

We stared at each other.

We both knew she was lying.

In all likelihood, he slept in another part of the castle altogether. He had tucked me away in one of the guest bedrooms, probably as far from his chambers as he could.

Out of sight, out of mind.

"Very well," I said eventually, defeated. For now.

The maid bobbed a curtsy before she turned to leave. A thought struck me, and I put up a hand.

"Wait."

She turned back, her eyebrows drawing together. "Can I help you with anything else, Your Highness?"

I bit my lip. *Win over their trust.* "I only wanted to ask... your name."

"My name?" She sounded surprised. "It's Isla, ma'am."

"Isla." I repeated the unfamiliar name, giving her a genuine smile. "Thank you for your help, Isla."

Her brows rose and she almost smiled back, before her nerves kicked in again. With one final, curious glance at me, the maid was gone.

I thought longingly of my maids at home. Of Maddie, who scolded me constantly over reading too much, leaving my clothes in a mess and failing to follow the formal etiquette of the royal houses—among other things—and she didn't suffer fools lightly.

I re-wrapped myself in the blanket and burrowed down into its warmth, staring into the flames. I would give anything to see Maddie again, even if I would most likely receive a lecture on disappearing into hedge mazes with strange men...

Hell, I even miss the babies.

Coming here had turned my world upside down. Nothing was what I expected. I'd flown farther than I ever had before, lost my virginity, and found the man that Marienne claimed was my fated mate.

A fated mate who can barely look at me since our encounter in that cave. And I have no idea why.

I gave myself a mental shake.

Damn it. I was the Princess Cassandra of the Kingdom of Bravdok, cousin to King Stavrok. I was a dragon shifter, and a powerful one at that.

Nothing was going to dampen my spirits.

Not even Damon and his strange mood.

I *wanted* to be here. No matter how nervous I was, how alone I felt now that Stavrok was gone...

Maybe winning over Damon was impossible. I could be fighting a losing battle, wanting love from a man who had none to give?

Something told me not to give up hope. I'd wanted adventure, hadn't I? Well, now I was right in the middle of one.

I stared at the carved dragons and wolves over the fireplace. In the flickering orange glow of firelight, they almost seemed alive, twisting and fighting with each other along the wooden panel. The broad reindeer antlers hanging over the mantelpiece cast long shadows against the back wall.

Maybe I could *belong here.*

The question was, how could I get Damon to see that?

CHAPTER
SEVEN

Cass

I woke the next day bright and early, my mind made up.

I sat bolt upright, smiling broadly to myself like a mad woman. I had a plan.

Damon could be as stoic and silent as he wanted.

I wasn't going to let it get to me. I would enjoy myself, just as I'd intended to before all this business of soul mates, and the irresistible desire that came with it, got in the way.

He can like it or lump it. I don't care.

I flung off the covers and toed on the fur-lined slippers that lay waiting for me by the fireplace. A glance out of the window told me that the snowfall was lighter today. *Yes*! I would get a chance to see the countryside I'd been aching to explore for years. My stomach tightened with anticipation as I thought about the day that lay ahead.

A sharp knock at the door startled me.

"Come in!" I called out as I bounced over to the huge wardrobe. All my clothes were hung up neatly inside, waiting for me.

"Your Highness." The door creaked open, and I smiled over my shoulder in the general direction of Isla's voice. "I came to ask if you'd like me to bring you some breakfast."

I waved her off.

"I'll eat with Damon," I said happily, then did a double-take as her eyes widened. "What's wrong?"

"The king... usually doesn't like to be disturbed, ma'am. He takes his meals in his study."

I wrinkled my nose. "Well, let's surprise him."

Isla looked frightened by this prospect, but I grinned at her.

"You know, Isla, I'm a visiting royal, and I think I deserve at least a little of the king's company, don't you think?"

"I... err... yes, I believe you do, ma'am." Isla gave me a tentative smile back, and I counted that as a small win. Cass one, Damon yet to score.

I grabbed her elbow and steered her toward the open wardrobe. "Can you help me pick out some suitable clothing?"

"Um." Isla glanced at the rows of garments, then back at me, seemingly at a total loss. "I suppose... yes?"

I grinned with triumph. Did that count as win number two? Rifling through my dresses, I pulled out a simple blouse with a lacy, open neck. "This is one of my favorites. What do you think? Pair it with a long skirt?"

"I think you'll freeze before you take a step outside," Isla muttered, before slapping a hand over her mouth. "I intended no disrespect, Your Highness. I only meant..."

I snorted and pushed the offending garment back into place.

"Don't apologize! I *really* need your advice." I ducked my head. "I'm not exactly... used to traveling. In fact, it's kind of a first-time thing for me."

"I've never been south," Isla admitted. Her voice was quiet, but full of curiosity. She rubbed her fingers against the soft lining of a skirt. "All your clothes are so pretty. I've never seen fabrics like these before."

I stared at the clothes and shrugged. "Pretty, but useless for this weather up here in the north."

The only exception was Lucy's clothing that had been altered for me, but I didn't see many of those hanging up. Perhaps they were still being transferred here?

Isla frowned with concentration as she scanned through the rack holding my dresses. Eventually she made a noise of victory, pulling out a soft pair of trousers and a sweater.

She handed me the items before stepping back and looking me up and down, assessing.

"Wait here," she said, before turning tail and leaving me holding the garments—and feeling more confused than ever.

I held them up in front of the mirror and smiled. It was hardly my usual style, but maybe I could get used to it. The whole point of the trip was to try new things. I kind of liked the idea of trousers. It offered more freedom than a long and often cumbersome skirt.

"Winter chic," I whispered to myself. My reflection smiled back at me in the long mirror. In spite of Damon's disappearance, this trip was turning out to be rather fun.

Isla returned with a dust-covered box tucked under one arm.

"I found these stored away in the old queen's quarters," she said, handing over the box.

I took it, puzzled. The old queen? Was that... Damon's mother?

"They look about your size. You'll need them if you want to stand a chance on frozen ground."

She stared pointedly at the soft shoes I'd worn yesterday. They hadn't survived the hedge maze; they lay abandoned, still drying out in front of the fireplace. The silk was crumpled and stained with mud.

A flush heated my cheeks at the memory of yesterday.

To distract myself, I brushed away the dust on the box and opened the lid, pulling the soft tissue paper away to reveal a sturdy pair of boots nestled within.

I pulled them out one by one, then plopped down on the armchair and tugged them on over my nightclothes. I felt kind of ridiculous, but wouldn't risk insulting my newfound friend by waiting until later to try them on. Isla had to help with the laces, but pretty soon I had them figured out.

The boots were calf-length, soft and supple. They fit me perfectly and they were so comfortable.

I turned this way and that in front of the mirror, unable to remember the last time I'd worn clothes built for practicality as well as beauty.

It felt surprisingly good.

"They suit you, Your Highness," Isla remarked. "Will you need any help with the rest?"

I shook my head. "I can manage from here, thank you, Isla."

As she left the room, I grinned. So far, so good. I dressed and threw my hair back into a simple braid, before hurrying out of the room.

Retracing my steps from the day before turned out to be something of a challenge. After encountering several dead-ends and having an embarrassing run-in with a couple of confused guards, I found myself lingering in the doorway of a huge, darkened chamber.

The dining hall. I peered inside, frowning around at the gloomy space. All the curtains were pulled shut, and the tapestries hanging from the walls were faded and worn.

Guess he doesn't throw many parties in here...

I shut the door softly and crept back along the corridor. Unwilling to ask for help, I ended up following my instinct, until I came to a standstill outside a room where light spilled out from underneath the closed doors.

Bingo.

I hesitated, and then knocked.

"Come in." Damon's voice traveled through the door. His tone was muffled, but he sounded weary, like he hadn't had much sleep.

Now or never. I turned the handle and slipped over the threshold before I could talk myself out of it.

Damon was sitting behind a huge, old desk. There was only candlelight filling the room with a soft light, and very little else in the room. There were none of the riches I'd come to expect from a kingdom's inner rooms, but apparently this king was like none other. I was beginning to understand that, even though I'd only been here a day or so.

He looked up at the sound of the door closing behind me. His eyes widened before the blank, stoic mask resettled on his face.

"Cassandra." He stood, straight-backed and formal.

Okay, so this is how it's gonna go.

"How can I help you?" His tone was stiff and formal.

"The servants said you don't usually have breakfast." I bit my lip, noting the way his eyes tracked the motion of my teeth. "So, I thought I'd come ask if you'd join me?"

He blinked, as if shocked. There were shadows under his eyes, and thin lines of tension at the corners of his mouth. I ached to know what weighed on him so heavily.

He seemed at a loss for words. "That's very thoughtful of you."

"Thank you." I shot him a smile, edging closer. "I am a visiting royal, remember?"

For a moment, it seemed as if I'd won a smile from him. But then his lips resettled into their non-committal expression.

I settled for sitting at the edge of his desk, toying at the loose papers strewn over the surface.

"What are you working on?" I asked.

"Farming ledgers... it's all boring. Paperwork, mostly," he said, shuffling the papers away out of sight. "I'm heading out to the tenant farms today. I need to see how much grain the kingdom will yield before next winter."

As he spoke, his hands rested on the desk in front of him. They were rough, expressive hands, large and calloused with use. The hands of someone who built things, crafted things. Who worked hard alongside his men. Not a spoilt rich king.

Those same hands had only yesterday pressed relentlessly into my soft flesh, touched me everywhere, greedy and possessive. I swallowed at the memory, looking away.

"I'd like to come with you, if that's all right?" I said. "I'd like to see more of your kingdom, and meet the people."

Damon ran a hand through his hair, staring at me with a strange look in his eyes. "Are you sure that's what you want?"

I nodded. "Yes, very much so. But with respect, Your Majesty. You need to eat something first."

"Is that so?" he murmured.

The look in his eyes told me he had something else in mind. Another kind of hunger altogether.

Our eyes met. After what felt like an eternity, my cheeks heated, and I ducked my head.

To hide my glowing face, I turned and hurried over to the door, peeking out of it. The footman who waited on the other side looked at me with curiosity.

"His Majesty and I will take breakfast in here this morning," I said, trying to sound confident.

Hell, everyone needs to eat, right? Even the king of the ice dragons!

If the footman was surprised by the request, he didn't show it, merely nodding before turning away. I shut the door and ambled over to a nearby bookshelf.

I felt Damon's eyes burning into my back, tracking my every move. I didn't turn around, shifting my focus instead to all the unfamiliar titles. I ran my fingers along the decorated spines, my heart pounding in my chest.

Some of the books looked ancient. I burned with curiosity, forgetting myself for a second and sliding free a book with embellished silver wolves on the cover. I leafed through it.

"You like reading?"

The sound of his voice in the hushed room made me jump. Although he hadn't moved from his position on the other side of the desk, the low notes raised goosebumps on the back of my neck. The effect was the same as if he was pressed right up against me.

"I do, Your Majesty." I slanted a glance behind me, only to meet his intense gaze.

He stared at me like I was a puzzle he couldn't figure out.

"I didn't have much else to do, growing up."

I said nothing of the loneliness that had carved a deep furrow into my upbringing. My life had been full of music and companionship... but also captivity. Other children were allowed to explore the fields and forests of our kingdom. They roamed free, flying and fighting and playing together from sunrise until sunset.

They weren't afraid of roadside kidnappers. Raiders. Bandits who would gladly hold a young princess for ransom or sell her off to the highest bidder.

Although I didn't say any of this out loud, something in Damon's eyes told me he understood the isolation that came with growing up in a royal house.

I wondered what his own upbringing had been like.

Stavrok had told me his father was a tyrant. *Was that true?*

"Where did you get those?"

I followed the line of his gaze down toward my borrowed boots. "Oh. A maid found them for me. She said I'd need them if I wanted to go out into the fields today."

A shadow crossed over Damon's face. I glanced down at the boots again, feeling awkward. These were likely his mother's boots, I remembered. I tilted my head. The look in his eyes threw me off.

"I can take them off if you want, Sire?"

"No." He rounded the desk and came to a stop halfway across the room with his arms outstretched.

Before he could reach me, his arms fell to his sides. I ached for him to come nearer, but he didn't.

"No... I was just..." He frowned. His gaze darted away from mine, settling somewhere on the far wall. "Those boots belonged to my mother."

"I'm so sorry," I whispered. "I knew that, from what the maid said, but I didn't realize it might upset you. I should have asked."

Embarrassment sent me spiraling. What was he going to think of me, rifling through his family's possessions like that?

He held up a hand. "Please, I won't hear you apologize. You're welcome to them." He paused, staring down at the floor. "It's been a long time since I've seen them, that's all."

His tone was stiff, overly formal, but sincere.

I nodded, still not trusting myself to speak. I wanted to ask him questions—about his mother, his life growing up here—but now didn't seem to be the time. He still looked distracted. He glanced out the window and picked up a handful of papers, shuffling through them, but his eyes had glazed over.

"Cassandra." He was still frowning when he finally addressed me again. "Are you sure you want to go out into the fields today? Wouldn't you rather stay inside the castle, or walk around the rose garden?"

Inside? Trading one castle prison for another? No, thank you!

I opened my mouth, but before I could answer, there was a soft knock at the door. Damon strode over and opened it, and the sweet smell of breakfast drifted in.

I smiled, grateful for the distraction. I slid past him and took the tray from the maid, thanking her, before setting it down on the desk between us.

I picked up a piece of buttered toast and nibbled on it while I considered my answer.

I knew what Damon was trying to do: palm me off on the castle and its grounds, confine me to ladylike pursuits in the hope that I'd be content to wander around exploring every nook and cranny of this place.

Stay inside. Warm and safe.

The thought was tempting, but I knew he had another reason for wanting me out of the way.

He wants to put as much distance between us as possible.

The thought lanced through my heart. I was determined not to give into the pain of it. I wanted Damon to take me seriously. To prove to him that I *could* do this. Whatever *this* turned out to be.

Finally, I looked up at him, raising an eyebrow in challenge. "I would *not* rather stay inside the castle, Sire. So, when do we leave?"

EIGHT

Cass

The wind howled around us, battering the open carriage as it bumped and trundled along over the barren fields. I pressed my face lower into the collar of my coat, trying not to shiver.

Seemingly unbothered by the cold, Damon rode up ahead on horseback. He made an indistinct, lone figure against the horizon. Only the bare skeletal trees marked the landscape. It was a far cry from the lush orchards and grassy meadows I was used to.

When I confessed that I'd never ridden before, Damon had looked surprised, but he didn't pass comment on my lack of skill. I guessed it was just another weakness in his eyes, fitting in with his image of the pampered princess flitting around her tower in satin slippers. Which, in many ways, was actually the truth.

I squinted at the farmstead up ahead as we approached. It was a simple building, with cozy-looking gables overhanging the wraparound porch. The farmer and his wife waited for us outside, on the steps. Damon arrived first, and he dismounted, handing off the reins to his footman and striding up to the farmhouse.

I was struck by the way he carried himself. Every line of his body spoke of an easy confidence, commanding, yet open and friendly.

The couple bowed their heads to him, and the farmer struck up a conversation. From their tone of voice, it was clear that Damon knew them well.

All told, it was hard to imagine that this was the same man I'd shared breakfast with. The one who looked at me like a spooked animal and shied away every time I got too close for comfort.

One of Damon's men helped me down from the carriage. I nodded to him, and picked my way over the uneven ground. A deep permafrost made the earth hard and unyielding, and I would have slipped without my borrowed footwear.

The farmer's wife looked at me as I stepped up to join Damon, her eyes widening in astonishment. She sank into a low curtsy, and I smiled at her when she straightened up.

Damon's eyes darted to mine before glancing away again.

"Allow me to present the Princess Cassandra of the Bravdok Clan," he said, as if reading from a script. "She is currently... visiting our kingdom."

I inclined my head at the couple, silently noting Damon's phrasing. *Visiting.*

Well, if that's how you want to play it...

"It's an honor, Your Highness," the farmer said. Like most of the men in the north, his weather-beaten, heavily lined face spoke of a harsh life. "How long will you be staying with us?"

"As long as I'm welcome here." I smiled back at him. I felt Damon's eyes on me, but didn't look at him. "You see, I've wanted to visit these lands my whole life."

"Well, you're certainly welcome here on our farm." The farmer's wife gave me another warm smile. Her tone was pleasant, but her eyes were burning with curiosity. "And—forgive me for saying so, my king—we're so used to you coming out here alone. It's good to see you with company, for a change."

I heard the implication in her words, the way she lingered on *company*, and ducked my head, a blush coming on. I could feel the couple still eyeing me curiously.

Damon cleared his throat. "So. I was glad to receive your letters. I take it you've made progress cultivating the southern fields for livestock?"

"Oh, yes, Sire." The farmer rocked back and forth on his heels before waving his hand. "Please, follow me..."

As the two men strode off over the field, Damon glanced back at me, just once, like he was checking I was okay. I nodded at him. He turned away, apparently satisfied, resuming his conversation with the farmer.

The farmer's wife was watching me when I turned to look at her. There was a knowing twinkle in her eyes that only grew as her face lifted into a broad smile.

"Would you like some tea, Your Highness?"

I rubbed my hands together, attempting to chase away the chill, and nodded.

She led the way inside, taking me to a comfortable kitchen with a view of the fields out back. It was rustic, simple, and not unlike the cabin Stavrok and I had stopped at on our journey here. A fire burned merrily in the grate, and a small copper kettle hung above it.

I relaxed onto a window seat covered with a patchwork quilt. As the woman poured the tea, I traced my finger over the rich patterns, letting myself be comforted by the soft noises of her whistling and the crackle of the fire.

There was so little about this land that I understood. Bravdok seemed like a lifetime away.

I took the teacup from her, before frowning. "I didn't catch your name."

"It's Molly, ma'am." The woman settled in a sturdy armchair and eyed me like she was measuring me up for something. "So. You're to be our new queen?"

I blanched, almost spilling the tea all over myself. I set the cup down on the small table in front of me. "What?"

"Oh, don't worry." Molly gave me a conspiratorial smile. "I saw the way the two of you looked at each other. I know how it goes. When it's meant to be, it's meant to be."

I chewed over her words. She wasn't wrong: my dragon had recognized Damon's immediately. I remembered the way it uncoiled in my chest, reaching out to him from the moment we laid eyes on each other.

My eyebrows drew together. I picked up my teacup again and looked down into the brew, like the answers I sought were in there somewhere.

"What if it's not that simple?" I said.

Maybe it was wrong to spill all my troubles onto the first person to take any interest, but I needed to talk to someone. Hell, I needed *advice*.

Something about this woman told me I could trust her.

"What could be simpler?" Molly cocked her head to the side. Like her husband, she had lines around her eyes, but her gaze was softer, friendlier. Those were *laughter* lines, I could tell. "He cares for you. You care for him."

Well. When she put it like that, it *did* sound simple.

"He doesn't even know me," I whispered. Needing something to do with my hands, I ran my fingers along the floral rim of the cup.

"But he *will*."

Molly said it with such certainty, I half-wondered if she, like Marienne, had the gift of sight in her. I sensed it wasn't polite to ask.

I stared blindly out the window. Somewhere out there, Damon was pacing the fields, checking over his ancestral homelands, doing the job he had been born to do.

I pressed a hand to the cup, half-wishing I was out there with him.

I turned back to Molly. "You seem very certain about all this."

"I've lived a long life." She shrugged. "And he is my King."

"Then you must know him," I said, leaning forward again to face her. "Better than me, anyway. Tell me. *Why* is he so..."

Withdrawn? Moody? Unreasonable? Infuriating?

Her mouth quirked with amusement. I flushed, feeling that uncomfortable sensation again.

She can read me like a book.

"His Majesty had... a difficult upbringing," she said carefully.

"In what way?"

"You know of his father, of course."

I nodded. Stavrok had told me about the old king. How he'd drained his people of money and driven his kingdom into debt. Stavrok and Erik had joined forces with Damon to put an end to the scavengers and raiders who wanted to pillage the north and settle old scores. Those raiders hadn't cared how many lives were lost, as long as the debt was paid in blood.

The sins of Damon's father were legendary all over the realm.

But what sort of father had the old king been, to his son? Had Damon suffered, at his father's hands?

"His mother died shortly after Damon's sister was born." Molly frowned into the distance, lost in memories. "It drove the old king mad with grief. They say he was never the same afterwards."

I thought of the look on Damon's face that morning when he'd spoken of his mother.

"Damon's father took his pain out on the whole kingdom." Molly's face darkened. "Crops failed; cattle starved. All the while, he stood by and did nothing. Locked himself away in his castle, growing more paranoid by the day... and he locked away the young prince, too."

"Damon?"

"Aye. People barely saw him until his father died, and he became king. By then, the castle was a wreck. There's so much darkness in that place." The woman clicked her tongue. "Bad, bad memories. It's a wonder that King Damon has managed at all."

I stared into space, processing everything she'd said. I tried not to let the shock I felt show on my face.

Despite my overprotective upbringing, I couldn't deny that my life had been full of love. Music and laughter filled my memories when I thought of my childhood. I had a cousin who loved me, and a kingdom that welcomed me with open arms.

It sounded like Damon hadn't been so lucky.

"More tea?" she asked, holding the pot in her hand.

"No, but thank you."

Molly smiled at me kindly. "Try not to worry so much, my dear. You'll clear out the cobwebs of that old place, I just know it."

By the time Damon and the farmer arrived at the door, stamping the snow off their boots, I was warmed through. I wandered over to stand by the king. As we turned to leave, Molly dropped into a low curtsy, her eyes twinkling with pleasure.

"You're welcome to drop by whenever you want to, Your Highness," she said, looking directly at me.

I was hyperaware of Damon's presence at my side. His body had brought the cold in with it. He smelled of fresh air and snow. Snowflakes littered his hair and the collar of his dark coat. I jumped at the shock of coldness as his fingers brushed against mine.

Molly's smile grew.

"Thank you," I told her. "For everything."

~

I FELT Damon's eyes on me as we walked back to the horses and the carriage.

"What?" I quirked an eyebrow in his direction.

"Nothing," he replied, a little too hastily.

I raised both eyebrows, a smile playing at the corners of my mouth.

"You're good at that," he said quietly. He opened his mouth, like he wanted to say more, then closed it again.

Good at what?

I wanted to challenge him, ask him why he was so surprised I could hold a conversation with a farming woman. What kind of girl did he take me for?

But I didn't push him for anything more. I accepted the compliment for what it was.

We came to a standstill by the men, who were holding the carriage horses by the bridles, waiting for me to climb up into the carriage. Both of us were lingering. I wasn't sure about Damon, but I didn't want to be separated just yet. I can only assume he felt the same way.

"Come on." Damon closed his hand around the reins of his horse. He offered his other hand to me, and I took it, though I was confused. He tugged me closer, his large hand gentle around my own. "You ride with me."

Before I could say anything in reply, his hands wrapped around my waist. I gasped at their firmness, and the warmth I could feel even through the layers of outerwear. He boosted me into the air, and I swung my leg over the horse, clutching the mane and panting with shock.

"Oh, my—"

It was very high, up on this horse. And very... um... *close* to Damon's hard, strong body.

His hand clenched around the horse's bridle, and the animal trembled, huffing a little as he climbed up behind me.

Damon exhaled, the motion pressing his chest against my back. He leaned forward, and his breath tickled the side of my neck. I shivered and closed my eyes, knowing he couldn't see how I trembled with desire for him. He could likely feel it, though, against him.

He clutched the reins, an arm on either side of my waist. Then he spoke into my ear, his voice rumbling straight through me. "Comfortable?"

That's not exactly the word I would use.

I nodded to his question. I didn't trust myself to turn around and give him a response with words. That would bring our faces dangerously close to one another.

He shouted something to his men and clicked the reins.

And then we were off.

I swallowed the scream that rose as I clung to the saddle in front of me, the huge arms of Damon surrounding me on each side and his body behind.

I had to trust that he could hold me in place, because I sure as heck didn't know how to stay atop a horse without assistance.

We thundered over the countryside like the hounds of hell were on our tail. Initially, there was only terror in my heart, but as I relaxed, I began to enjoy the exhilaration of the cold against my face, and the horse beneath me. The blood sang through my veins. Riding with Damon was almost like flying, that same exhilaration, except this time, I wasn't in control. *He* was.

His body crowded close to me. It was impossible to ignore every flex of his thighs behind my ass. Every brush of his arms against my chest as he adjusted our course.

I could barely pay attention to the world around me, or what was going on outside of the feelings inside me. That need was building up again: the need to claim what was mine.

But I knew that wasn't what he wanted.

My mind and body screamed at each other, tortured by the mixed signals. I was powerless to do anything in my current position. I could only let Damon ride us to our destination.

He grunted behind me, and his hand pressed against my belly, pulling me more firmly against his chest. I wanted to arch back into him until I realized that he was merely adjusting my position, making sure I didn't fall.

By the time Damon slowed the horse to a trot, we were approaching a shallow slope that led down onto a rocky scree. Several wagons had pulled up at the side of the road around us, and there were people everywhere, hard at work digging and toiling in the earth.

"When the raiders came, they burned many homes to the ground," Damon said, speaking for the first time since we started this journey. "My people needed raw materials to rebuild. Stone, mostly."

A team of people manoeuvred a huge machine to the base of the slope. Damon slowed the horse to a standstill. He jumped off with ease and held out a hand for me.

I climbed down more gingerly, running a shaky hand over the horse's mane.

"Thank you," I whispered to the horse. "Sorry for being nervous of you before."

Just before he turned away, I caught the edge of a smile on Damon's face and my heart lifted as hope twisted within my chest.

CHAPTER
NINE

Damon

My heart was still pounding heavily beneath my shirt as I approached my men.

I regretted my foolish impulse to ride with Cass as soon as I felt her small frame settle in my arms. She'd been so distracting I'd struggled with the simple task of sterring the horse in the right direction. The scent of her hair, the softness of her thighs pressed up against mine... It was all far too tantalizing.

Pull yourself together.

The voice inside my head, cold and stoic, sounded remarkably like my father.

He was probably right. I couldn't afford distractions; not today. *Not any day.*

I let out a deep sigh and walked on.

Cass trotted up alongside me as we drew closer to the stone quarry. "Can I walk down there and get a better look?"

I shook my head, frowning at the very idea that she'd wander off exploring. "You need to keep close to me. For safety."

Several of the men put down their tools as we approached, giving her a furtive once-over as they did so. My hackles rose as a possessive instinct pulsed through me. I clenched my jaw and forced myself to keep walking.

I ached to take her far away from them. I wanted to shift and fly us both back to the castle, just to get her out of their sight. There, I would claim her all over again, leaving her gasping my name until she could barely remember her own.

I am their king. Nobody will hurt her. Nobody will touch her. She is safe.

The mantra did little to calm me down. My dragon was inflamed and the men seemed to notice, because they dropped their gazes, mumbling amongst themselves.

I drew level with them. "Is it ready?"

"Yes, Sire." Jace, my well-built foreman, spoke up. "We're waiting for your go-ahead."

I nodded. "Very well, then. Fire away."

Cass looked up at me curiously as we strode toward the edge of the rocky slope. I bent closer, letting my mouth almost brush against her ear.

The quarry is so noisy; she won't be able to hear me otherwise.

It was a flimsy excuse at best. Luckily, if she noticed the way I wasn't breathing normally, she didn't say anything.

"We drilled down into the side of the rock yesterday. Now we're packing it with explosives," I said. "It's the best way to break up the stone."

As I drew away, a shiver ran through her slender frame. It was no wonder. A chill wind was buffeting us, and the sky once again threatened snow.

"Are you cold?" I asked. Worry sharpened my tone. When I spoke again, I made sure my voice was softer. "Because I'll take you back to the castle, if you want. You only have to say the word."

Her eyes flashed up to mine. "No! I..."

Before she could continue, a loud whistle broke through the air.

I grabbed her by the arm and pulled her into my body for protection. "Cover your ears. Quickly."

She did so, just as a loud *boom* shook the ground beneath us. Rubble rained down everywhere. The men cheered, and I smiled proudly.

Where there had been a huge shelf of rock, there was now a slope, leading to a stone-filled crevice. My men descended into the new quarry, carrying their tools with them and setting to work.

"What now?" she asked, lowering her hands from where they'd been pressed against her ears.

I scrambled down the slope after them. She followed me, surprisingly nimble, ignoring the hand that I held out for her. My mouth quirked at her stubbornness.

"Now, we break up the larger pieces of rock for transport back to the town."

"We?" Cass tilted her head as I shrugged off my coat and rolled up my shirtsleeves.

"Of course." I smiled. "What sort of king doesn't get into the trenches and dig alongside his men? I'm their leader. I'm hardly going to stand on the side lines while they do all the work."

I watched her absorb my words.

"In that case," she said, jutting out her chin, "neither am I."

I could already see that there would be no arguing with her, and since I'd all but given her the lines to use against me, why would I bother fighting her? She at least wore pants, and my mother's boots provided protection for her feet.

"Very well, then. Let's get to work."

For the next few hours, we worked in the quarry, picking away at the fragments of rock that lay around us. I showed Cass how to look for the highest quality stone, and she soon began working alongside the men in the processing section, talking with them as if she'd been doing this for years.

The now-familiar bond between us *insisted* I keep a close eye on things. I didn't want her to think I was hovering, but I hated to leave her alone amongst all those men. In fact, I *couldn't* leave her alone, no matter how many times I tried to walk away. It didn't matter that I knew rationally she wasn't in danger.

My dragon didn't give a damn.

I mostly hung around in the background, trying and mostly failing to concentrate on the task at hand.

Jace sidled up to me. The two of us worked well together, and I trusted him implicitly.

He nodded toward the group. "She's in her element out there."

I couldn't help but agree. Watching Cass working with my people stoked a fire inside my chest. It was impossible to keep on task. I could have watched her all day, a small, bright butterfly flitting around all those hardened men like she was born to it.

"If you don't mind me saying so, Sire..." Jace paused for a long time. He was usually a man of few words, but even so, this pause was longer than usual. I tilted my head, curious to see how he'd finish. "It's good to see a smile on your face. Been a long time."

I wasn't even aware I *was* smiling.

"Oh. Thank you Jace," I managed, then turned back to look at the little princess I'd assumed would never fit in here.

But watching her out here, it began to dawn on me that I may have misjudged her. Clearly, she wasn't afraid to get her hands dirty... literally. I'd given her the option of staying at the castle, cozy and warm by the fireside, and instead she was out here working on the frozen tundra with me and my men.

She turned her head, and my breath caught at the sight she made. A curly strand of hair pulled loose from her braid, floated in the wind and brushed along her cheek, unnoticed by her. She had a smudge of dirt on the tip of her nose that took everything in me not to race over there and wipe it off with my thumb tip.

When she caught my eye, I realized I was staring, but she didn't seem to mind. She gave me a small smile and I couldn't help but smile back, even though I was faintly embarrassed at being caught staring. I inclined my head, giving her a stiff nod, and tried to get back to work.

At midday, when a weak sun shone above us in the pale gray sky, I called a halt to the work. Cass and I sat on a rocky outcrop, a little apart from the others, and passed pieces of a sourdough loaf between us in comfortable silence.

"I'm sure you're used to fancier fare," I mumbled, fingering a scrap of the coarse bread.

I was used to this, but Cass had grown up surrounded by beauty and luxury. Through her eyes, I saw the northern way of life in a new light.

We must look like barbarians to her.

To my surprise, she only shrugged. "I've always preferred bread and cheese to huge elaborate dinners." A dreamy expression crossed her face. "Although, I do miss strawberries."

I laughed. "Good luck finding those up here." I put out my hand, catching a few drifting snowflakes in the palm of my hand. It was snowing lightly again. "I can't recall the last time I ate a strawberry."

Her answering laughter was a soothing melody to my ears. I couldn't help but lean in closer to her. My hand came out, unbidden, and I brushed off the snow that had settled on her shoulder.

She swayed into my touch, seemingly unconscious of her body's movement.

"Come on," I found myself saying. "I have to show you something."

CHAPTER
TEN

Cass

This time, I was expecting the horse ride, which made it a little bit easier to handle.

But only a little. That was a skill that would clearly take a little time to master.

My legs were still trembling by the time Damon dismounted. He didn't offer me a hand. Instead, he simply caught me around the waist and lifted me down off the horse. I swayed into him when he set me on the ground and for a moment I forgot where we were.

He felt so good against me. Solid and warm. I wanted to lean into his strength and stay there forever.

He seemed to need a moment to gather himself too, because he didn't move away very quickly.

"So," I began, and as I spoke, I was surprised to hear the husky undertones in my voice. Was that what being in close proximity to Damon did to my vocal cords? "What did you want to show me?"

Instead of answering, he merely took my hand. There was a tantalizing mystery in his eyes, and I couldn't help but be drawn in by it. We weren't on the open plains anymore. High rocks loomed above us, and a pale, watery sun shone in the sky above.

"Come with me." He winked at me, apparently determined to remain mysterious.

I rolled my eyes but let him lead me down the narrow mountain track we were on. The air felt warmer here. We were probably sheltered from the harsh elements by the hills around us.

Odd patches of greenery grew in amongst the rocky terrain. It was the first true sign of nature I'd seen since arriving in the north. The sight warmed my heart.

"Damon." I squeezed his hand, drawing his attention. "Where *are* we?"

"You'll have to wait and see."

I trotted along beside him, trying to match his long strides. Curiosity burned within me, mingling with the ache that had taken up residence in the pit of my stomach.

I need him. So much. How does he not feel the same way?

I was almost frightened by the strength of my feelings, despite knowing that they were due to the mating bond. I wondered if I'd always feel this burning pull, this *desire* that colored every interaction with this man and made it impossible to stay away.

It was my dragon who felt it most. But that desire, that need, had grown bigger now. It was more than just pure, naked *want.*

I'd never felt this way before. When his eyes met mine, my stomach swooped like I'd missed a step on a staircase.

Maybe I should've asked Stavrok more questions...

I dismissed the thought. There was no way I was talking to Stavrok about any of this! He'd already seen and deduced more than enough as it was.

Damon stopped in the middle of the path. He bent his head, and I shivered as his mouth brushed the edge of my ear. Did he know the effect he had on me?

"Do you trust me?" he whispered.

The words took me back to our encounter in the maze. The first words we'd properly spoken to each other. A spark of heat had passed between us then, just as it did now.

"Yes," I breathed.

Sheer instinct spoke for me, but as soon as I said it, I realized it was true.

He'll protect me. He won't let any harm come to me.

My thoughts were exhilarating.

He stepped behind me, and his palms came up to cover my eyes. I could barely breathe as he guided me forward.

I felt like I was on the edge of a precipice, about to fall.

It was the best goddamn feeling in the world.

Soon enough, we came to a standstill. His hands fell away, and I opened my eyes.

I gasped at the sight that lay before me.

We stood in the middle of a lush, green valley. The rocks underfoot were carpeted in moss, and the hillside around us was scattered with flowers. I could hear running water nearby and I soon spotted a mountain spring trickling down from the rockface.

In the middle of such a barren, frozen land, it was like I'd fallen into a dream.

I turned to Damon. The astonishment must have shown on my face because he huffed out a pleased laugh.

The stiffness in his shoulders was gone, and the color had returned to his face.

"What is this place?" I whispered.

"A secret hideaway." His mouth flickered with amusement, but his eyes were soft. He put his hands in his pockets, surveying our surroundings. "I come here sometimes, to get away from..."

He trailed off, shrugging, but I caught his drift. To get away from the palace. From his father. From his responsibilities. His life.

The crown obviously weighed heavily on him. This place was his solace, a temporary respite from the stresses of day-to-day life.

"Who else knows about this place?"

"Nobody," Damon murmured. "It's my place. And now yours, Cass."

Oh... my...

The thought that he'd led me here, allowed me in to his private hideaway, overwhelmed me. To cover my rising blush, I turned away from him, drawn by the sound of the water. I sat down beside the small waterfall, feeling the heat of Damon's presence as he came up behind me. My skin tingled at his proximity, yearning for his touch.

"You can drink from this stream," he said, leaning over me and dipping his fingers into the clear water. I watched, oddly transfixed by the motion. "The water comes directly from the mountain. It's totally pure."

I scooped up a handful of water and held it to my lips. It tasted sweet and fresh, just as he said.

"How does this place..." I cast around, searching for the right words. "How does this exist?"

Damon sat back and ran a hand through his hair. He'd taken off his jacket, and my eyes were drawn to the flex of his forearms as he relaxed back onto his elbows.

"I've thought about that a lot." He frowned. "I think the rockface must form a kind of natural shelter from the ice and snow. It protects these plants and gives them a chance at life. Outside this area, they would just wither away and die, like everything else that tries to grow in the cold."

As he spoke, he plucked a stray daisy beside him and leaned over, threading it through the end of my braid.

It was a sad thought, that all this tranquil beauty would not exist, if not for the rockface protection. I ran a hand over the daisy, fiddling with it.

"So, it's only here because it's protected?"

"I guess so."

From the weather, and the rest of the world. If everyone knew about this place, it would surely be trashed within a few weeks.

I let my hand dangle in the edge of the stream. I watched the flow of water before something else occurred to me.

"But I've seen fields. People farm in your kingdom, don't they?"

Damon frowned. "Of course. But they farm the tough plants. Root vegetables. Things that can survive the frost, not delicate flowers like these. Our crops are hardly beautiful. They're just tough."

"Maybe they're beautiful *because* they're tough."

Damon didn't look convinced. "Maybe."

It seemed like a pointless argument. Anyway, we weren't really talking about the vegetation anymore. I huffed out a sigh.

Flopping onto my back, I tilted my head toward him. "You're quite stubborn, do you know that?"

He snorted. "*I'm* stubborn?"

His playful tone emboldened me.

"Yes." I reached out and wrapped my fingers around his forearm, tugging gently.

I hope I'm playing this right...

He came willingly, crawling up over me until his arms were either side of my head.

"I can't fight this, Cass." His eyes burned into mine. "No matter what I do, I can't."

"Then stop trying," I whispered.

He lowered his head and pressed his lips against mine.

I returned the kiss eagerly, wrapping a hand around the back of his neck to bring him even closer. He inhaled sharply, and I smiled against his mouth.

With a shock, I realized that it was the first time we'd kissed.

In the cave, it had been all fire and lust. We'd been strangers then, drawn together by our bodies' urges. This time it was different. Slower. Softer.

We were taking our time with each other. He trailed his lips beyond my mouth, kissing behind my ear, and I moaned with a sudden, unexpected burst of pleasure.

His hands skimmed over my body and peeled off the winter layers of clothing one by one. He moved like he was handling something precious, as if I might break with one wrong move.

Eventually I grew impatient and dragged him back on top of me, digging my heels into the small of his back to get him where I wanted him.

He growled, and the light of his dragon glowered in his eyes.

It was tempered this time though—the glow a burning ember rather than a roaring flame.

His fingers curved over my side and brushed against my inner thighs. He ducked his head and pressed delicious kisses into the hollow of my throat, against my collarbone, between my breasts, down onto my stomach.

My face heated once I realized his intention, but I didn't stop him from exploring my body further. I reached out a shaking hand to thread my fingers through his hair, and he looked up.

His eyes met mine, our gazes clashing together like steel against steel. Against our lush surroundings, Damon's eyes were even paler than normal, like shards of ice.

Whatever he read on my face, he seemed satisfied, because his head dropped again and I arched up at the sudden hot press of his mouth against my hip.

I bit my lip, but I couldn't stop the moan that escaped me as his mouth skated across my inner thigh.

He hadn't even reached his destination yet, and already my voice was wrecked.

When his tongue found my clit, I groaned. My legs clenched over his shoulders, and I trembled at the roughness of his stubble against the soft skin of my thighs. He circled the sweet spot for several delirious minutes until I was bucking up into him, fingers alternately grasping against the mossy bank and raking through his hair in turn.

I wailed as my orgasm crashed over me. He carried me through it, tasting me greedily, buried between my thighs until the sensation was too much and I was forced to drag him up.

We kissed deeply and my face burned at the thought of where his mouth had just been, but I couldn't dwell on it. I had another goal in mind.

My legs came up again, wrapping themselves around his waist, and I raked my hand up underneath his shirt.

He seemed to get the message. He disentangled from my legs, then sat back on his haunches, stripping quickly before settling back down over me. I was still hazy from my climax, and I blinked up at him, taking in the set of his jaw and the clench of his muscled arms on either side of me.

Something hard trailed down against my chest, and I blinked lazily. I caught a flash of metal glinting in the light as he tossed it over his shoulder, out of the way. It was a chain of some sort, with something on the end of it...

I was too distracted to think on it further. His hot weight was finally against me, and his hard length pressed against my inner thigh. I trembled.

"I need you," I murmured, reaching down between our bodies to take his cock in my hand.

He sucked in a sharp breath, and his head dropped onto my shoulder. He mumbled something unintelligible before looking up again. This time his eyes had lost their icy paleness. Instead, they were almost black with arousal.

"The things you do to me, Cass..."

We both groaned as he slid inside me.

The fire, the need I'd felt in the cave was still there; it always would be, I realized, whenever we were joined like this. Our dragons were greedy for each other, and the heat inside my chest only increased when I caught a glimpse of Damon's shifter in the burn of his gaze.

"So beautiful..." Damon stroked the hair back from my face. His blunt, broad fingers traced over my cheek, the bud of my lips.

He looked at me like I was a priceless jewel. Like he couldn't believe what we were doing.

I surged up and caught his mouth in a kiss. Our tongues brushed against each other as he rode into me, and before long I felt a second orgasm building. With every thrust of his hips, he pushed me closer to the edge.

This time though, he was right there with me. As I dug my fingernails into his arms, crying out as my orgasm pulsed through me, he growled, chasing my climax, thrusting into me faster, deeper, before spilling hotly inside of me.

He brushed the tangled hair from my forehead, and pressed a final kiss onto my damp, heated skin.

Sweet oblivion.

For the first time in a long time, I felt truly at peace. The mossy bank under me was pillow-soft, and the gentle flow of water lulled my senses.

Damon settled down beside me. He folded an arm over my chest, and his breathing slowed. I felt so safe, in his embrace.

I reached out blindly, pressing my hand to his chest to feel the comforting *thud* of his heartbeat.

My eyes fluttered closed, and I drifted off to sleep.

ELEVEN

Damon

"Cass," I whispered. "Cass, it's time to go."

She curled closer into me, mumbling something in her sleep I didn't catch. I smiled and kissed the top of her head, turning my face upwards to the darkening sky.

It was late afternoon now. The days were long here, but the nights were even longer: soon it would be dark, and we needed to return to the workers and the castle before it became impossible to navigate the path.

"Cass," I said again, more firmly this time.

Finally, her eyelashes fluttered, and her eyes fixed hazily on mine.

"Come on, sleepyhead."

We found our clothes, pulling them on. The temperature had dropped considerably since we'd arrived in the clearing, and I moved closer to her, turning up the collar of her coat to keep the chill away.

Her fingers paused on the buttons of her coat. She reached out, one finger running down the chain that lay partly exposed under the neck of my shirt.

"What's this?"

I glanced down at her wandering fingers, enjoying the sensation on my skin, before stepping away. I tucked the chain away and buttoned up my coat properly. The metal seemed to burn my skin through the fabric, like a beacon.

"Nothing important," I murmured. "Just a family heirloom."

She seemed to accept this, although the tilt of her eyebrows told me she'd get the truth out of me sooner or later. Her expression was still questioning.

"What changed your mind?"

I was caught off-guard by the sudden topic change. "About what?"

She lifted her chin, putting her hands on her hips. "About me."

I just stood there, wracking my brain over what to say. She didn't seem bothered by my pause. She waited, both eyebrows raised.

I'd been in a tailspin all day, determined to keep my distance yet unable to resist her sweet allure. But it was more than that.

She doesn't miss a trick, this one. That's for sure.

"You did well today," I said eventually. "My people don't take kindly to outsiders. Today, at the farmhouse, and at the quarry, you won them over with what seemed to be effortless ease. You're... not what I expected."

Cass shook her head, like I'd amused her in some way. "I'm used to talking to people who find my status intimidating. The guardsmen back home. The servants. I grew up in the palace so I know non-royals probably find me hard to relate to. But I try my best to make everyone see me as a person, and if not, a distraction, right?" She shrugged. "Something to lighten the mood."

I frowned. That wasn't the case at all.

"That's not true." I came over to stand in front of her. I reached out and took her hands in mine, forcing her to meet my eye. "You want to know what I think? I think they saw a queen. A queen who cares about others."

Cass looked up at me. Her eyes were shining, but her face was smooth and calm.

I drew up her hand and kissed it.

The gesture was overly formal, considering what we'd just done, but it felt right. I was giving her the respect that should have been afforded to her the first time we met. A princess's welcome.

Before our shifters got in the way.

They were gone, for now, sated by the pleasure in which we'd just drowned ourselves. My dragon slept lazily inside my chest, content to have his mate close by.

We stood there in the twilight. I leaned down to brush a loose strand of hair off her face. When I straightened up, she was still regarding me. Chin up, shoulders back.

Anyone in the realm, down to the lowliest kitchen boy, would have been able to see the royal blood flowing through her in that moment.

A sharp whistle from somewhere beyond the rocks caught my attention.

We had been gone too long. My men had sent out a search party to look for us.

"Come on," I said.

She tucked herself easily into my side, and together we picked our way through the valley, emerging on the other side of the rocks.

I strode over to untie my horse, but we didn't have time to get into the saddle. Lanterns bobbed through the dusk, casting long shadows over the rockface around them.

"Over here!" I waved, and the lanterns drew closer.

"Sire." Jace, who was leading the men, hurried forward, relief plain across his face. "We thought the raiders had come."

A flicker of regret passed through me as I caught a couple of worried looks from others in the group.

My people were fearful for good reason. The mountain-dwellers that had ransacked our kingdom two years earlier were still out there some-where. We had thinned their ranks, but that didn't mean they were gone for good.

They were biding their time, likely hungry for revenge.

"No, nothing like that," I said. "Cass and I just wanted to... explore."

Judging by the expression on Jace's face, I could tell that he knew exactly the kind of *exploring* I meant, but thankfully he didn't remark on it.

He took my horse's bridle and led it toward the search party. They were all waiting in a huddle, their bulky shadows looming over the gravel terrain.

After spending all afternoon with Cass, the contrast between her and my kinsmen was even more pronounced. She stood at least half a foot below the shortest of them, but she greeted them like old friends, dragging me along with her. They were careful not to get too close to her, obviously fearing my dragon.

We set off. The terrain was too unstable in parts to go on horseback, so we had to travel on foot. We climbed down the rocky slope in tandem. I barely thought about where I was putting my feet. I'd spent years walking over these rocks.

Cass picked her way over the ground more carefully than me. I pointed out the sturdiest stones for her and guided her around the deadly black ice that lay in wait of unsuspecting travelers.

Then Cass spotted Rob, the kind, elderly man she had been working with earlier that day, and she was off like a rocket.

Before I could stop her, she'd slithered halfway down the slope in front of us in order to catch up with him. I'd only taken my eyes off her for one second, just enough time for her to dart ahead of me, out of reach.

A sharp cry echoed through the valley.

Cass. My stomach plummeted sickeningly.

I broke into a run and shouldered aside a couple of concerned bystanders before dropping onto my knees beside Cass. She was curled up against a rock, cradling her ankle in her hands.

Gently, I pried off her fingers and ran my hands over the skin, pulling away when she grimaced with pain.

"It's just a sprain." She looked up at me. "Damon. Come on. I'll be *fine.*"

Her words were soothing, but I could tell she was in pain. For some reason, she seemed more concerned with *me* than the injury.

I turned her foot slightly to look at the side of her leg and she winced. There was a rip in her pants, and red stained the thick material.

"Is that..." I reached out and touched the wet patch, and stared down at my hands.

Cass's bright red blood coated my fingers. I swallowed hard, my dragon roaring inside my head.

"One of the rocks just cut me a bit," she said. "I'm a shifter. I'll be fine. You know that."

I couldn't concentrate on any of her words, or the calm energy she was trying to push toward me. All around me, the noise of the men murmuring amongst themselves buzzed through my head, growing louder and louder. Nobody got too close, but they set my teeth on edge, nonetheless.

"Leave us!" I barked.

I had never spoken in anger like that before. I startled them, but I didn't care.

My men obeyed, and we were alone. Only the wind whistling against the rocks around us broke the silence.

I stroked my hands over Cass's hair until we were both calmer. Eventually, Cass looked up at me.

"You shouldn't have done that." Her mouth turned down at the edges. "I'm okay, really."

"You're *not* okay. You're hurt."

A voice in the back of my mind pulsed like a drumbeat.

This is all my fault. I brought her out here, into danger... and now look what's come of it.

My rational side insisted I was taking it too far. The injury wasn't bad—she just wasn't used to the terrain—but I didn't listen to it.

In that moment, I wasn't King Damon.

There was only the dragon inside me, snarling and helpless, confronted with its injured mate—and ready to lash out at any threat, real or imagined, that got too close.

I helped her to sit up, but when I put my arms under her to carry her the rest of the way her body stiffened against mine.

"I can walk just fine on my own." She glared up at me. "You don't need to act like I'm going to break."

I sat back on my heels, stung by the force of her words. "Cass, you're being unreasonable."

"No." Her eyes flashed with anger. "I'm not. You think I haven't noticed how you treat me?"

I ducked my head, but I wasn't about to back down now.

"You can't walk on that ankle," I said, reasonably enough, I thought. "You'll only injure it further."

I gazed down at her slender legs, sprawled out against the rocks. She was so beautiful, so perfect.

So soft.

She couldn't survive in this place.

In that moment, my mind was made up. I would rather spend the rest of my life knowing that she was safe before I let anything happen to her... even if that meant I could never see her again.

Ignoring my warnings, Cass struggled to her feet. She leaned on her side, obviously favoring her uninjured ankle, but I didn't dare touch her.

She put her hands on her hips. "Why can't you accept that I *want* to be here, Damon? That I want to stay?"

I threw out my hands. "Why would you want to spend the rest of your life somewhere like *this*?"

"Because *you're* here!" Petite as she was, Cass had a way of making her presence felt, like no other woman I'd ever known.

I took a step back, struck by the force of her words.

"I know how I feel, Damon. And I know how *you* feel. The bond between us—"

"I don't care about the bond! All I care about is keeping you safe." I ran a hand over my face, suddenly exhausted. "And I can't do that by letting you shackle yourself to me."

"What are you trying to say?" Cass's face was inches from mine. Her eyes filled with tears.

"That you should never have come here!" My voice echoed over the empty landscape, reverberating off the barren gray rocks. "This place will destroy you. Just as it did my mother."

As soon as I said the words, I wanted to take them back. But it was too late.

"You're a coward," she whispered. Her eyes were still dewy with tears, but now they turned hard. "Rejecting me? You're ready to give up. On me. On *us*. Even after what we've shared. I thought you were better than that."

I felt the blood drain from my face.

It's not like that, I wanted to say.

I didn't know how to make her understand. I wasn't rejecting her.

"Cass, I—"

I reached out to her. She ducked out of reach, turning her back on me, and limped away.

My dragon grumbled inside my chest, but I ignored it.

This is all your fault, Damon.

The air shimmered around Cass's form, and my heart almost stopped.

"Cass! No!"

It was too late. Cass shifted in front of me, and I saw her dragon for the first time.

She was slender, and smaller than shifters tended to be this far north. As her wings extended, they shimmered pale violet. She turned to look at me one last time, and with a flash of her jewel-like eyes, she launched herself into the sky.

I could only stare in shock as she flew off into the distance. Each beat of her wings broke something inside my chest. She was flying away from me. Leaving me. Going home to where she'd be safe.

Despair filled me as she climbed higher and higher, edging further toward the forest that lay at the foothills of the mountains.

Then, out of nowhere, two dragons swooped out from the thick bank of cloud that wreathed the mountaintop.

"*No!*"

I didn't recognize those dragons. They weren't my people.

They divebombed Cass on either side, releasing twin jets of ice over her as she twisted and thrashed her wings in an attempt to get away from them.

My dragon roared up inside me and I began to shift, keeping my eyes on the sky above.

Hang on Cass. I'm coming.

It was no use. The ambush was short, and swift. I was only halfway shifted when Cass's now-frozen wings collapsed around her, and she dropped out of the sky like a stone.

TWELVE

Cass

T hit the earth with a thud that would have broken every bone in my body if I hadn't been in my dragon form.

Staring helplessly up at the thick canopy of leaves above me, I could only lie there, winded, as my shifter curled up inside my chest. Damn it. I couldn't sustain my dragon.

Soon enough I was human again, naked and shivering in the freezing cold of the north. I curled onto my side and crossed my arms over my chest, closing my eyes and trying to draw in breaths.

If I fall asleep, maybe I'll wake up and this will all have been a dream...

With a groan, I opened my eyes again.

I couldn't fall asleep, not now.

But moving *hurt*. It hurt a whole damn lot.

My attackers had damaged my wings, somehow. Frozen them, maybe? And the pain of the fall stung through my body, especially my arms and each side of my ribs. They ached, like I'd been repeatedly punched.

Before I could consider my next move, the undergrowth rustled, and sharp voices pierced through.

"— saw her fall down here somewhere. We can't return without the girl."

My heartbeat picked up as I realized they were talking about me.

I squealed as something hot and wet dragged along the side of my face. Terror filled me as I rolled over, only to come face to face with the jaws of a huge wolf.

"Here! She's over here!" a man called out.

Footsteps trampled over the ground toward me, and I was surrounded. Hands reached out for my naked body. I tried to bat them away, but they easily caught hold of my wrists. I was totally outnumbered. On all sides of me, tall men with long, shaggy furs loomed over me, holding leashes on the creatures that had haunted my nightmares since I was a little girl: giant wolves.

I began to shake and tremble. Blessedly, a fur was thrown over my shoulders, partially covering me from the cold and the gazes of the men.

I pulled the fur around me and my lip wobbled. What were they going to do to me?

"Scream all you want," the leader of the men told me with a broad grin. "Nobody will hear you out here."

That didn't stop me.

I screamed all the way through the forest and beyond.

～

Damon

One moment I was staring up at the sky, feet planted firmly on the ground, and the next I was soaring high over the clouds. I let out an earth-shattering roar of rage and despair as I climbed higher and higher, beating my wings against the howling wind.

Cass! I could feel my mate slipping away from me, somewhere far below, in the forest at the edge of the horizon.

In the distance, a pale shape rose above the trees. My heart skipped, and for a brief second, I thought she'd managed to fight off the attackers and was free.

When a second dragon flew up to join the first, my hope vanished. It was them. The monsters who had taken her. *Hurt* her.

She was gone.

Muscles straining, I pounded my wings through the air. The wind had turned. While Cass had sped through the air, I was forced to fight through a gathering storm.

My rage urged me onwards, the anger that pumped through my body so strong I could have broken through any barrier. The gates of hell could have opened beneath me, and I wouldn't have batted an eye.

Beneath the sheer fury of the dragon, my mind whirled with panic.

What if she's dead?

It was my fault, all my fault. I'd put her in harm's way. If she was dead... I couldn't live with myself. I couldn't live. Period.

The ground passing beneath me flooded with greenery, and I wheeled in mid-air, realizing I'd reached the edge of the forest.

I reared up, beating my wings against the sky and letting out a roar. An icy jet of blue fire shot out from my throat.

Come and get me, you bastards.

I caught a flicker of movement in the forest canopy, the edge of a wing sticking out of the trees below.

I dove toward the branches, like a hawk spotting a mouse. I caught the dragon in my talons and we tumbled down to the earth together, crashing through branches and bushes. The dragon fell from my clutches and staggered away, but I knew I had injured him.

Good. I wanted to kill the bastard, for endangering Cass in that way.

The forest was cool and dark. The density of the trees dimmed the light, and I stumbled backwards, struggling to get my bearings. I was still in dragon form, and didn't intend to shift back until my mate was by my side once again.

My anger and panic turned me clumsy and my claws raked the ground, trying to get a foot hold as I tried to locate the other dragon in the shadows. I blinked in the unfamiliar, greenish light, panting hard. This wasn't my terrain. I was used to the open tundra, frozen and unforgiving though it was. The trees above pressed down, trapping me in what felt like a cage.

A sharp pain lanced across my back as the enemy shifter dropped down on me from above.

I roared in fury and lashed out, blasting a patch of foliage nearby and reducing it to ice. My blast managed to catch the edge of the shifter's wing, stunning him long enough for me to roll over, shake him off, and send him flying.

The sharp talons at the edges of my wings gave me an advantage, as did my size. Whoever this shifter was, I stood at least two feet taller. Not to mention my wingspan, which dwarfed his own.

His scales, however, were a pale icy color. Just like mine. *Were we kin?*

I couldn't think about that. Not now. Cass was in danger; nothing mattered beyond that.

The fight was vicious and short. The red haze that swirled through my veins turned me merciless; cold blooded. I lashed out, sharp talons tearing through scales, and before long, my opponent lay dead at my feet.

I stood over him, panting.

The bushes trembled. A low, deadly growl sounded. I froze.

Another dragon. This one was bigger and, when he emerged, the undergrowth rustled on either side of him. Yellow eyes came forward, followed by huge paws, soundless and far more graceful than mine on the forest floor.

Beside the dragon stood a wolf. Huge and powerful, its hackles were up, lips pulled back to expose its long white teeth. The wolf's unblinking gaze fixed on me, waiting for me to make my move.

Another wolf appeared, then another. Before I knew it, the clearing was full of them. A circle of wolves.

And I was in the center.

This was an ambush.

The dragon's gaze flicked to the dead dragon at my feet. I lowered my head, muscles coiled with tension.

Logically, I knew there were too many of them to fight. My dragon didn't care. Inside, I was roaring, screaming for my mate. And if my dragon couldn't get to her, well, then I'd have to destroy those who stood in my way.

I lunged at the dragon, knocking him to the ground. We tousled in a vicious fight for our lives. There were sharp jabs against my hide as dozens of wolves piled on us. The air was thick with fur, and blood, and hide, and teeth. We twisted over each other and I snapped at every creature that came at me.

The dragon took advantage of my distraction, snapping at my tail, raking sharp talons over my wings until I scorched the ground in icy fury.

But any shifter, no matter how powerful, was no match for me.

I was a Dragon King.

And I had a mission. To rescue my mate.

I drew in a deep breath, threw back my head and *roared.*

The air filled with white ice flames. The blast knocked back every beast that climbed my flanks, carving a deep crevice through the trees and down into the very ground itself.

By the time I was done obliterating the area, the second dragon shifter and many of the wolves were dead.

Yet still more wolves kept coming. How many of the creatures were there? There was a long, low whistle through the trees. I staggered to my feet, bleeding, injured, and exhausted.

If I stayed, I could die.

More shifters would come. I could already hear them heading this way. This wasn't a battle I could win. Not today. And not on my own. I needed my people. I needed my army.

Frustration clawed its way up my throat, and I considered throwing caution to the wind and pushing through my fear, slaughtering everyone in my path until I found Cass.

But a small voice, a mere echo in the back of my mind—the part that was still human—said, *Damon, no. You're smarter than that. If you want to save Cass, then we need reinforcements.*

I hated that voice, but I couldn't argue with it.

If I wanted any chance to get Cass back safe, I had to be smart.

Cursing the name of every god I could think of, I launched up through the tree canopy and back into the sky.

～

Cass

I huddled on the ground in some godforsaken corner of a cell-type prison room, curled up beneath the furs they'd thrown into the room with me. At least I wasn't going to freeze to death.

Small comfort. I stifled a sob against the crook of my arm. I was scared out of my mind. At least none of them had tried to hurt me. Not yet, anyway.

I wish I'd never come here.

I wish I was home. Somewhere warm, where everyone knows me and no-one would ever try to hurt me like this...

I clenched my jaw, willing the faint dragon spark inside me—the shifter that was currently nothing but a shadow—to warm my chest.

Pull yourself together. You are Princess Cassandra of Clan Bravdok, and you are better than this. You wanted adventure, didn't you? Well, things don't get much more adventurous than this.

In all those books I'd read about the north, I tried to think what those explorers did, when they were in a life-or-death situation?

"Found their resources," I muttered out loud.

It wasn't much, but it was a direction at least, a momentary chance to make myself feel a little less powerless.

I lifted my head and took stock of my surroundings, though I couldn't see much. There wasn't any light inside my prison cell, but through the gaps in the walls, the flickering torchlight gave me enough light to make out the dim interior of a hut.

The walls were made of rough-hewn wood, and the floor was one step above dirt. Whoever my captors were, they weren't advanced.

Or maybe they just don't plan on keeping me here for long.

I pushed away the unhelpful thought and uncurled my legs, stretching out. They hadn't bothered to tie me up, which I took as another clue that they didn't expect me to be able to run away.

I could try to shift, attack them, or fight my way out of here. But these men were ice dragons and had taken me out of the sky once already today. I didn't want to die, and since they didn't seem to want to kill me—at least right now—I would bide my time and save my strength in case I needed to fight my way out in the end.

The door swung open and a shaft of orange light filtered through, startling me. I ducked as something was thrown at me, but when it landed on the floor with a soft *thud,* I realized what it was. A bundle of clothing.

"Get dressed," someone ordered, just out of view. Then the person slammed the door and I was alone again.

I crawled toward the dark pile, fingers closing around the cloth. It was soft to the touch, but spun out of simple fibers.

I didn't care. I would've worn a freshly stripped wolf pelt in that moment. My hands were stiff as I slipped on the tunic and pulled up the supple leggings.

My final garment, a loosely knitted shrug, was wholly unfamiliar to me, but I slipped it on. Mercifully, the shivering began to ease as I warmed up, and in turn my mind grew clearer.

I shuffled around the small cell, the blood pumping through my veins and reaching my arms and legs. Everything hurt from the cold, but thanks to my shifter blood, I was healthy and well. The small ankle injury I'd sustained before I left Damon and the few injuries from my fall had healed.

They haven't tied me up, and they've given me clothes... What kind of raiders are these?

A dark thought occurred to me. If I was being held for ransom, I'd be no use to them dead.

I paced faster around the edge of my small enclosure, checking for weak spots on every inch of the walls. My cage was well-built, and from the sounds on the other side of the door, I had guards.

Finally, I found a gap in the wood big enough to peer through. I caught glimpses of a few people sitting around the fireside, talking amongst themselves.

They weren't all men, either. My heart clenched as three women carried children across to sit beside the flames. They looked sleepy, but relaxed and content.

This was hardly the stuff of nightmares.

My spying was rudely interrupted by the sound of the deadbolt sliding back from the door, and light spilling through the gap.

I whirled, my fists clenched. I'd never physically fought anyone in my life before, but I wasn't going to cower in the corner like they wanted me to.

"What's going on?" I hissed. "Where the hell am I?"

The man merely stared at me, blank-faced.

"Your Highness," he said. "Come with me."

THIRTEEN

Damon

By the time I found my way back to the castle, the sky had faded into a purplish hue, and a canopy of stars glittered overhead. I had no time to stop and appreciate their beauty. The flight had calmed my mind and body, and as I landed, my mind was clear. My rescue plan had formed. All that remained was to set it in motion.

I looked around me as I shifted, vaguely aware that I'd landed in the middle of the drawbridge. I was sure the townsfolk didn't appreciate the sudden sight of their naked king, but I didn't care.

We had to move fast. A shiver ran up my spine. I had failed to protect Stavrok's beloved cousin.

He'll have my head on a spike.

If it came to that, I would deserve it. Hell, I'd *support* it.

The realization flooded over me then and there.

I loved Cass. I needed her by my side. And I was going to do whatever it took to bring her back to me.

Jace strode up to me, his expression clouded with worry. He held out a robe and I dragged it over my shoulders, falling into step beside him as we entered the castle.

"Gather the men," I instructed my commander, Eric, who snapped to attention at once. All around me, people whispered to each other, hushed and frantic. "There's no time to waste."

"Sire?" Jace put a broad hand on my shoulder. It was a familiar gesture, and one I appreciated. Right now, I needed people I could trust, not servants bowing before their king. "What happened?"

"Cass, she…" The words lodged in my throat and I swallowed hard, jaw tightening. The very mention of her name sent my shifter reeling. "They've taken her."

Keeping my voice low, I told him about the dragon shifters I'd fought in the woods, plus the hordes of wolves trained like attack dogs to take down anything in their path.

Jace's eyes darkened. "Raiders."

There it was. The word that had haunted our kingdom for years. The dark figures that still filled my people's nightmares, crowding their thoughts with smoke, death, and ruin.

"Yes." I bowed my head. Although we were speaking quietly, I glanced around, making sure no-one could overhear us. "In the woods, by the mountains. I'm not sure how many. But there were too many for me to fight off on my own."

"Thought we'd wiped most of them out." Jace frowned, running a hand over his thick beard. "I guess scavengers find a way to survive. You sure we have the strength to face them, Sire?"

I stared at the ground, gathering the strength to say what needed to be said.

In truth, I didn't know if we would survive this, but I wasn't going to stop until Cass was safe again.

Eventually I lifted my head and looked him right in the eye. "We leave at sunset."

Jace simply nodded. He trusted me. I wouldn't send my men into a fight they had no hope of winning.

As I watched him walk away, I knew what I had to do.

~

Cass

I had no option but to follow the guy who'd come into my hut.

We bypassed the fire pit, circling around it and heading toward the largest hut in the small encampment.

For whatever reason, they hadn't blindfolded me. Small faces peered at me as I passed, with people coming and going out of the thick forest around us. They were fetching firewood and mending things. The wolves were nowhere to be seen.

My guard came to a standstill at the doorway of the hut. He gestured silently in the direction of the door. I hesitated, terrified to discover what was on the other side.

The guard gave me a nudge. It wasn't a harsh one, but it told me I didn't have a choice in the matter.

Reluctantly, I walked through the door.

The hut was dim inside, although a small fire burned under a bubbling pot. Two men sat on low seats just behind it. They stood when I came in, and the tiny hairs on the back of my neck rose up.

"Where am I?" I asked, trying not to let fear bleed into my voice.

Then I remembered something. The guard had called me *Your Highness.* I definitely wasn't some random girl to them.

"You know who I am." I crept forward. They regarded me impassively, still mostly in shadow. "Why have you done this?"

"Princess Cassandra," the one on the left said. His voice was rough, as if not often put to use. It reminded me of woodsmoke, or the logs crackling over the fire pit. "Welcome to our camp."

He moved a fraction closer. As his face caught the light, I froze with shock.

His face was strikingly similar to the man who had just broken my heart. He had the same high cheekbones, the same piercing, ice-blue eyes.

His face was broader, however, and his hair longer and wilder. He had a fair amount of stubble, and a scar at the edge of his jaw. The scars on his bare arms told me he'd seen his share of combat.

"Who are you?" I whispered.

I wanted to remain afraid, but some part of me whispered that I wasn't in danger. My dragon settled, slumbering in my chest, unphased by the unfolding action.

"He's Dymitri," the man on the right said. He had a smoother voice, a deep, rich baritone, and when the flames fell across his face, he too bore a striking resemblance to Damon. "And I'm Lucian."

"This is your camp."

"Yes." Dymitri crouched before the fire, drawing out a cup and filling it with something that smelled delicious. "Please, eat. You must be hungry."

I was, but I took the cup from him without bringing it to my lips. I had no reason to trust these people. Not after what they had done.

I pressed my lips together, considering the two of them. "You shot me out of the sky and then dragged me here and flung me into a prison room."

Dymitri looked downcast. "We're deeply sorry. You have to understand... my brother and I wish you no harm, Princess."

I wrinkled my nose and corrected them. "Just Cassandra."

Dymitri nodded. Wordlessly, he swept out an arm, indicating a cushion by the fireside. I sank down onto it, curling my hands around my cup, letting the flames from the fire warm me.

"We seek an audience with the new king." Lucian returned to his seat. Despite the fact that he was the speaker, he seemed less forthcoming than his brother, content to stare into the flames. "We needed a bargaining tool."

"And I just happened to fall out of the sky," I said dryly, mouth twisting. "Quite literally."

"Please." Dymitri glared at Lucian, who merely raised an eyebrow. The former leaned forward, catching my gaze. "Our people are desperate. Survival out here is... perilous, to say the least."

Lucian snorted but didn't comment.

Pieces of the puzzle were falling into place in my mind.

"The raiders who burned and ransacked Damon's kingdom..." I stared into the flames, frowning as if the answers lay there. "That wasn't you, was it?"

"No." Dymitri pressed a hand against his forearm, thumb tracing over a white, raised scar. "We've run into them ourselves on many occasions. When they were defeated, that's when word got back to us that the old king was dead."

Lucian smiled, but it didn't reach his eyes. "We've spent our lives in exile, along with our entire village."

"Why?"

As our conversation progressed, the wild men of my imagination transformed, growing less and less fearsome the longer I looked at them. I began to see them as they truly were: two young men who were just as scared as I was.

"The old king didn't take kindly to reminders that he was less than a perfect husband; a perfect father." Dymitri exchanged a grim look with his brother. "We were living proof."

"You're his sons." As I said it, I knew it was true. I'd known it from the moment I saw them. "Damon's brothers."

"Half-brothers," Lucian corrected. "But yes."

"We want to talk with King Damon." Dymitri folded his hands together, looking at me intently. "But we knew we had to be careful. Nobody here knows him; knows what kind of man he is. If he's anything like his father..."

"He isn't," I interjected. "He... he cares about his people. He wants to rebuild his kingdom. That's his main priority."

I could hardly think of Damon without ice flooding into my heart, but I wouldn't lie about him. He may have rejected me as his mate, but I *could* say that much for him. He only wanted to recover what his father had lost. Nothing mattered more to him than that.

Not even me.

Something of my anguish must have shown on my face. If the brothers noticed, they didn't say anything, much to my relief.

"We have no interest in challenging his rule." Lucian turned to me. "We just want to live in peace."

They both stared at me for a lengthy moment. I narrowed my eyes at them, and then turned my attention to the delicious broth in my cup. I took a big sip, savoring the flavor.

Finally, I set down the cup and turned to face them fully.

"You two..." I stared between them. "Are *idiots*."

Their eyes widened in shock, but I wasn't done.

I've been blasted with dragon ice fire, dragged through the woods, and held hostage. I am going to say my piece, and they're gonna listen!

"You should have come and talked to him! Like rational people! Damon is *good*. He won't turn you away, or hurt you, or whatever it is you're so afraid of! He's a good man, and he needs good, strong men to help him rebuild the kingdom." I drew a shuddering breath. "And if you take me back with you, *I* can smooth over this huge misunderstanding, and we can all move on with our lives."

I crossed my arms over my chest and glowered at them.

Dymitri and Lucian gaped at me.

I raised one eyebrow, and then the other crept up to join it.

"Got it," Dymitri said eventually.

I exhaled.

"Good!" I kicked out my legs, stretching them before the fire. I was warmed through now, and relaxed. Finally. "By the way, Damon won't take kindly to the whole kidnapping thing, so you might want to let *me* do the talking to start with."

By the looks on their faces, it was clear they hadn't considered the ramifications of holding me hostage.

I gave them a cheery smile. "Can I have some more broth now?"

An hour later, we were ready to leave.

Lucian disappeared outside to tell the others that the camp was on the move.

Dymitri and I stayed by the fire, trading stories. He had never been south of the mountains, and he wanted to know everything about what it was like to grow up in green, peaceful valleys, where life wasn't a continuous struggle for survival.

In return, he told me more about the kingdom of the north.

"Damon's father was happy, once." He twirled the stick in his hand, which he had been using to poke at the fire, as he considered his words. "His mother... she wasn't born here, in the north. Did you know that?"

I shook my head. Curiosity burned in my chest.

"Damon's father saw her one day, when he was visiting the southern kingdoms to sign a trade deal. He carried her off."

Dymitri glanced at me, and I nodded. I knew how these things typically went, after all. Stavrok was a prime example, except Lucy had been in a human village when he'd carried her off.

"She was adored by the people... and by the king. But when she died, it was whispered that the ice and snow killed her. She wasn't made for the north. She didn't belong here." His head dropped. "Forgive me, Cassandra. I don't mean to suggest that you..."

"It's okay," I was quick to reassure him. "I know."

Well, that definitely explains a lot about Damon's fears for my safety.

"Come on," Dymitri said eventually, clambering to his feet and offering a hand. "We should be on the move shortly."

We emerged from the tent.

"That was fast!" I said, startled.

The camp site had been completely dismantled. All that remained of the fire pit was a smoldering pile of ash. A huddle of caravans, laden with belongings, waited for us at the edge of the tree line.

Dymitri gave a loose shrug. "We're used to packing up in a hurry, I guess."

A wolf prowled the edge of the forest, and fear trickled down my spine as a small girl rushed up to it and buried her hands deep in its thick pelt.

The wolf lowered its head and let the girl pet it. It was strange to see such a large, ferocious beast act so gentle.

Maybe I've misjudged this place. In more ways than one.

"Ready when you are, Cassandra," Lucian shouted. He held the reins of a sturdy-looking horse. "Your carriage awaits."

I smiled at him.

The sky above us went dark. Several people screamed as they stared up into the clouds.

I glanced upwards, and my eyes widened as I made out the shadow of wings, so vast they blocked out the sun.

A jet of silver fire burst across the sky, and my heart almost stopped.

"No!" I screamed, waving my hands frantically. For a heartbeat, I considered shifting, but by then it would be too late.

I could only watch as Damon circled the clearing above us, like a giant killing machine.

CHAPTER
FOURTEEN

Cass

Dymitri and Lucian rushed forward, and fresh panic gripped me as their dragons gleamed in their eyes. They were about to shift, and if they did, he'd kill them both.

"Stop! He wants me!" I ran toward them, and they stopped in their tracks. "He won't hurt you. He's just looking for me!"

I had no idea how true that was, but I had to believe Damon wouldn't attack an entire camp just to get to me.

The sky lit up again with icy flames.

Dymitri wheeled to face me. "Are you sure about that?"

I closed my eyes, reaching out with every ounce of mental strength I had in me. My soul searched for its mate, up into the cloud bank above our heads. A flash of coldness ran through me, a fury unlike anything I'd felt before.

Damon.

It was his rage I felt. His anger, his terror.

Damon... Damon, I'm here. I'm safe. Please...

I let out a gasp, and my eyes opened.

The huge dragon descended into the clearing, its clawed feet leaving deep gouge marks in the earth. He roared, and the deep, powerful sound shook the earth beneath our feet.

Damon's dragon was huge. Bigger than I could've imagined, with a wingspan that easily stretched across the whole camp.

His hide was pale, shimmering silver in the dim light. His eyes were the same icy blue as they were in his human form. The spikes that covered his head were sharp and deadly. As he lowered his head, they reminded me of a crown.

He was magnificent.

I stepped forward, separating myself from the group. I spared a glance behind me and kept my voice quiet but firm as I instructed a woman nearby. "Bring me a robe for the king."

She hurried off.

I turned and faced him. His eyes were already fixed on me. Even from this distance I could see his huge chest rise and fall with barely suppressed fury.

"I'm here," I said. "I'm unhurt, look."

The woman scuttled up behind me and I took the robe from her with a nod.

I sensed the tension in the clearing. At any moment, it could break.

It's all up to me.

All my life I'd been told what to do. By my courtiers, or my own family. None of that mattered any more. I wasn't about to hide from Damon and let him destroy these innocents in my name.

I moved closer, positioning myself between the dragon and the frightened villagers. I knew that Damon wouldn't harm them if there was a chance that he'd hurt me in the process.

As I got within range, he moved sharply, as if to grab me. I stepped back and glared at him, shaking my head. He huffed with annoyance and glowered at me but lowered his head.

I tilted up my chin at him, triumphant.

I'm not going to be carried back to the castle like a sack of potatoes.

I raised an eyebrow at him, and watched the fire in his gaze flicker, smoldering into embers. A hazy mist built up as he shifted, and when it cleared, Damon stood in the middle of the clearing.

Even unclothed, his human form was imposing. His gaze was fixed directly on me, but his sheer presence was enough to freeze everyone to the spot.

I stepped forward with the robe held between my two hands.

He looked at me, his burning gaze unreadable.

Then, he fell to his knees and bowed his head—to my shock, and likely the shock of everyone else in the clearing.

I knew what I had to do. Gently, I lay the robe over his shoulders. It was a coronation of sorts. The movement felt ceremonial, regal. When he rose to his feet, he drew the robe around to cover himself and took my hand.

"My king," I murmured.

He bent and kissed my fingers.

The gesture was formal, more for the benefit of those watching than anything else. Nevertheless, when his mouth brushed against my skin a tremor ran through my body.

He dropped my hand, and his gaze moved past me, onto the crowd at the edge of the trees.

"Who is in charge here?"

"We are." Dymitri's voice rang out across the clearing.

Lucian stood by his side, unspeaking and unsmiling. Tension was written into every muscle in their bodies.

Damon narrowed his eyes, but the expression mingled with surprise, which morphed into open astonishment.

He'd picked up on the likeness between the two men and himself.

Good. That will hopefully make this easier.

I gripped Damon's arm tight, and his gaze flicked down to meet mine.

"Come on." I smiled up at him. "Let's go meet your brothers."

"Brothers?" he whispered, seemingly to himself. We moved together, crossing the ground at a slow, careful pace. Damon looked like he was in a dream.

Finally, we drew level with them.

"Your Majesty," I said, looping my arm through his, so he didn't swing out at them. "Allow me to introduce Dymitri and Lucian."

Damon regarded the two men, who both inclined their heads at him in an identical fashion.

"Cass tells me we're brothers." Damon's voice was low, and still held an edge of danger. "I'll admit that I can see it. That's the only reason I haven't reduced this entire clearing to ash."

Lucian's lip curled, and Dymitri flashed him a glare of warning.

"King Damon," Dymitri said. "Our mother was the daughter of our village's blacksmith. The old king sent us into exile after the queen's death... along with half the village, as you can see."

As he spoke, Damon sidled closer to me, tucking me in against his side. Shielding me.

Internally, I sighed.

Is stubbornness a genetic trait amongst these ice dragons?

"Damon," I interjected, pulling away slightly. "They were never going to hurt me. They needed some way to get your attention, and I was just in the wrong place at the wrong time."

"My attention?" Damon's eyes flashed, although thankfully there was now no trace of the dragon behind his gaze. "Why?"

"We wish to come back, Your Majesty," Lucian said. Although his face was as somber as ever, his tone was sincere. "We were banished from the kingdom many years ago, but now that our father is dead, we hoped you might let us return."

"The old king threatened our lives," Dymitri added. "We had no idea what kind of man you were. We thought we needed... leverage."

"Then you got more than you bargained for," Damon said fiercely. "Cass is *not* a bargaining chip."

"Damon." I placed a soothing hand on his shoulder, and he relaxed beneath my touch. "They know. They only want to talk. That's all. Look at them. They want to be safe again. These people deserve protection. Your brothers deserve protection."

Damon stared down at me. Then, he took my face in his hands and pressed a gentle kiss to my forehead.

"Of course," he murmured. "Thank you, Cass."

Our argument earlier felt like a distant dream. I tried to recall my anger, how furious I'd been, but seeing him like this now, I could feel only love.

He had listened to me. Actually *listened*.

Relief flooded Dymitri and Lucian's faces, and all those behind them began to relax and chatter amongst themselves in low, excited voices. I couldn't help but feel a spark of pride.

Damon straightened up, looking over the entire gathering, although his gaze soon returned to his brothers.

"You are all welcome to return. The kingdom is your home, and its gates will always be open to you." He lowered his voice, addressing Dymitri and Lucian directly. "Come to live with us in the castle. For as long as you want. God knows we've got the space." The use of the word *we* lifted my heart, but I couldn't question it right now.

There was too much going on to worry about whether Damon meant what he said, or if I'd gotten the wrong end of the stick from him yet again.

~

*D*AMON

I waited until the last of the caravans trundled out of the clearing before turning to Cass.

We stood in the middle of the empty space, surrounded by bare patches of earth, where tents had been pitched only a short time ago.

Cass refused to meet my gaze.

"Cass, please." I reached out a hand, and then pulled it back, uncertain. "Allow me to explain myself."

She tucked her arms around her body, biting her lip. The dark fringe of her lashes hid her eyes from me. "What is there to explain?"

"When I first saw you, I..." Unable to help it, I rushed forward, but I didn't dare touch her yet. "You know how I felt. How we felt. It terrified me. I couldn't see anything beyond your youth, your inexperience. In my eyes, you were this delicate, beautiful woman who had stumbled into a harsh wilderness... I knew there was no way you could survive it. Just like my mother. And I had trapped you here. I hated myself for putting you in that position."

"Thanks," Cass said tonelessly. Her eyes were flat and dull, all traces of their usual spark snuffed out.

"I was wrong."

Cass looked up sharply. "What?"

I drew a deep, shuddering breath, and lay a hand on her shoulder. "I was wrong, Cass. And you were right. I was so wrapped up in the past, my father's mistakes, that I couldn't see what was right in front of me. When I watched you drop out of the sky—" I broke off, shaking my head against the terror of that memory. "I've never been so afraid in my life. And I realized, I can't keep focusing on the what-ifs anymore."

"What are you saying?" Cass whispered.

"I've been so caught up with wanting you gone..." I leaned forward, forcing her to meet my eye. "I wanted what I thought was best for you, for us. I wasn't seeing you for who you are. You're brave, smart..."

"Keep talking." The corners of her mouth curled upwards, and some of the light crept back into her eyes.

"You brought me to life, Cass." There it was. The truth I had been running from all this time. "I can't live without you. I know that now. I'd give up my kingdom, I'd give the whole world, just to keep you by my side."

"I'm stronger than you think," she said, as her hand came up and clutched mine, squeezing my fingers gently. Emboldened by the gesture, I reached up and brushed her hair off her face, running my fingers through her curls. "I still want to stay, Damon."

My heart swelled, and I pressed a kiss against her mouth. She returned it eagerly, and for a moment we stood there in the clearing, tangled up in each other.

"Then stay," I breathed, watching her cheeks flush. "Stay and be my queen."

"Is this a proposal?"

Despite everything that had passed between us, the nerves still crowded my stomach.

"It is." I bowed my head, before falling to my knees and taking her small hands in mine. "All that I have is yours. It's not all you're used to, I know."

I looked up at her. She was gazing down at me, her expression soft.

"Maybe," Cass whispered, "but it's all I need."

I reached into my shirt and drew out my thin silver chain, fingering the ring on the end. Cass's eyes widened, and she watched in rapt focus as I undid the chain and held the ring up to the light.

"This belonged to my mother." I turned the ring over in my fingers, memories crowding my mind. "My father gave it to her not long after they met."

It was small, silver-wrought, and delicate. Roses crept along the band, entwined with thorns.

"It's beautiful," Cass said.

I held it out to her.

"It's too small for me to wear," I said. "So, I kept it on a chain."

Close to my heart.

"Ever since she…" I swallowed, not being able to say the words. But from the look on her face, she caught my meaning. "I want you to have it, Cass. *She* would want you to have it."

Cass fiddled with the ring. Gently, I took it back from her and slid it onto her finger. It fit her perfectly.

"Roses and thorns." She chuckled to herself.

"Beauty and harshness." I straightened and stood up. As I drew my arms tightly around her waist, she leaned into my body. "In this land, you'll have to get used to both, I'm afraid."

"Well, then, I guess I'll need some warmer clothing," she said, and stood on her tiptoes, lifting her face.

I tilted my head down, and readily gave her the kiss she wordlessly asked for.

As I knew I always would.

EPILOGUE

Cass

A dish was set down in front of us by a servant and I gasped as the cover was removed with a flourish. Beside me, Damon's eyes danced with amusement.

"Strawberries!" I shouted, loud enough for several of the wedding guests' heads to swivel around. "You remembered!"

Undeterred by the eyes on me, I reached forward and shoved a strawberry into my mouth, groaning as the sweetness burst across my tongue.

Damon chuckled, watching me. He accepted the strawberry I pressed into his hand and raised an eyebrow as he bit into it, clearly surprised by the sweet taste.

"Good, right?" I grinned.

He nodded. He was humoring me to some degree, but I didn't care.

I snuggled in against his side, humming with contentment. I turned my face up to him. "I can't believe you remembered what I said about strawberries."

"Of course, my love." He trailed a finger over the back of my hand. I turned my palm up and let him lace our fingers together. "Anything for you."

The hall was packed with well-wishers and admirers. It was hard to believe that a few short months ago, this place was so dark and still. Now, the carved wooden paneling gleamed, and the high arched windows framed the snow drifting down outside.

Granted, it was a little different to the celebrations I was used to. The decorations around the hall mixed the north and south together, symbolizing our union; delicate sprigs of blossom and pink ribbons were dotted around the tables, and shiny glass icicles hung from the high ceiling, sparkling in the sunlight.

It shouldn't work, but it did. I smiled, catching sight of the banner hanging on the far wall. Wolves and dragons interwoven together, and the whole thing entwined with a border of roses.

Summer and winter.

I wasn't stupid. I knew that life would never be the same again. That there would be challenges thrown our way. But I didn't care. Besides, who *didn't* have challenges?

I'd chosen my destiny. Where others might see danger lurking around every corner of this land, I only saw adventure.

Not to mention the man I love.

Along the top table, we sat with our friends and fellow rulers. The smaller round tables filled the rest of the space in the Great Hall. I caught sight of Rob, who I'd learnt knew everything there was to know about the history of the kingdom. At another table sat Dymitri and Lucian. They had declined the offer to sit beside us, but seemed content enough to observe the proceedings, if slightly unnerved by the number of people at mine and Damon's wedding.

I let my eyes wander, smiling every time I spotted a familiar face. More and more of them *were* familiar, these days. The change in their king had won over most of the townsfolk, and every day it got easier to chat to them.

They weren't really as cold and hard as people said. You just needed to get to know them.

And I had all the time in the world for that.

"It's time," Damon murmured, and I straightened up in excitement, squeezing his hand as he got up from the table.

As his chair scraped backwards, I locked eyes with Marienne who sat a couple of seats away. She waggled her fingers at me playfully. Damon headed across the floor, weaving his way through the tables, and as I watched him go, Marienne chuckled.

"What?"

Marienne raised her glass of tonic water with one hand and cradled her round belly with the other.

"Nothing, nothing." A smug smile played around her mouth. "I'm pleased you've found your happiness here, Cass."

Erik leaned over and draped an arm over her shoulder. "My wife is the matchmaker of the various kingdoms." He smirked. "I think it's gone to her head."

He sounded a little annoyed, but the way he looked at her said otherwise. Pride shone in his eyes.

"Not at all." Marienne stuck out her tongue at him, and he laughed. "It's just nice to use my powers for something good, for a change."

Erik's eyes softened, and something unspoken passed between them. I turned my head away to give them their privacy, scanning the crowd for Damon.

My husband!

I still couldn't believe it. I was a married woman now, a queen.

A broad hand fell on my shoulder, and I looked up to be confronted with the full force of Stavrok's broad, beaming smile.

"Cass." He hauled me up out of my seat.

I wheezed as he pulled me into a bone-crushing hug.

"Oof!" I pulled away from him a little, laughing. "Stavrok!"

My cousin gazed down at me, misty-eyed. "I'm so proud of you, Cass."

"Looks like I figured things out on my own, huh?" I tilted my head, unable to resist teasing him a little. "No rescues necessary."

"Look at you." He glanced around at the bright hallway, and the snowy landscape outside. "You're the Queen of Winter."

I let out a chuckle. Lucy appeared at Stavrok's side, flushed and happy, her long fair hair braided up at the top of her head. It had been some months since I'd seen her, and I gasped at the bump under her dress.

"He's all smiles now, isn't he?" She looped an easy arm around Stavrok's waist. "Be glad you didn't have to see me wrestle him into his tux this morning."

"Lucy!" She let me pull her into a tight hug, giggling as I squealed and hopped up and down with excitement. "Oh, my God! Why didn't you tell me you were expecting?"

I drew back. I couldn't punch her in the shoulder, so I punched Stavrok instead, who glared and rubbed his arm.

"Jeez, Cass! You're lucky it's your wedding day."

Lucy looked unconcerned with her husband's plight. Her eyes danced with happiness. "I wanted it to be a surprise!"

"Hang on..." I glanced over at Marienne, who was deep in conversation with Erik, still cradling her own pregnant belly. "Did you do this on purpose?"

Lucy just shrugged, but a smirk appeared at the corner of her mouth. "What? They'll all grow up together! It'll be so cute."

Stavrok shot me a look that said, *don't even ask.*

Not that I wanted to. The less I knew about their sex life, the better, given some of the things I'd had the misfortune to hear back when I lived with them.

Luckily, Damon chose that moment to reappear out of the crowd, his two half-brothers in tow.

They were both dressed in suits in honor of the day. They obviously felt as uncomfortable as Stavrok did in their fine garments, judging by the way they kept tugging at their collars. They looked good, strong and regal. A far cry from the rough-hewn shifter men I'd met in the woods, all those weeks ago.

Although Damon and his newfound brothers had warmed to each other considerably since their first meeting, Dymitri looked apprehensive, his pale eyes narrow and his brow furrowed. Lucian looked downright suspicious as they reached the foot of the table.

"What is this?" Dymitri asked.

"You'll see," Damon said with a wink.

I grinned back at him. I'd been looking forward to this moment.

"Marienne, would you mind?" I turned back to Dymitri. "Marienne has a very special gift. She's agreed to use it on the two of you."

"My wedding present." Marienne stepped up from the table. "To Cass and Damon."

Dymitri still looked unsure. "That's very generous of you, Damon, but it's not necessary..."

Damon held up a hand. "After everything the two of you suffered at the hands of our father, I want to give you a gift. Something you'll treasure forever. It's the least I can do."

As he slid back into his seat, I turned to him and gave him a big smile. "What?"

"Nothing!" My smile grew bigger. "I'm just happy."

He let out a huff, but I could tell he was pleased. My head dropped into the crook of his neck and his arm came up around my shoulder, his fingers tracing lazy patterns against the back of my neck.

"Have I told you how gorgeous you look right now?" he murmured.

"Yes." I glanced up at him. "Many times, actually."

Whatever his reply was, I found myself distracted by a sudden purple haze of light that erupted over the floor before us, flowing out from Marienne's outstretched hands.

Several onlookers gasped, but the crowd wasn't fearful. Most of our guests knew Marienne, and watched, fascinated, as the shimmering smoke continued to spiral outwards. Lucy had told me all about Marienne's courage, how she'd risked her life fighting in the battle. It was clear that she was a heroine in the eyes of these people. I was glad her powers were a source of admiration to them, rather than fear.

With a deep, shuddering breath, she collapsed to her knees, utterly spent. In a flash, Erik was by her side, stroking a hand over her back. When she looked up, however, her eyes were wide with excitement.

"I know where they are!"

As she spoke, her eyes wandered over to... Lucy, of all people.

"Where?" I asked. Why was she looking at Lucy?

"Not here, that's for sure." Marienne got to her feet, still trembling a little. She was fast regaining her strength, stronger than she had been the last time we met. "They're beyond the portal. In the human realm."

"Who are?" Dymitri asked. "What are you talking about? What's going on?"

Lucian said nothing, but he looked equally impatient to know the answer.

Marienne blinked, like she'd forgotten about them altogether. She glanced at Damon. "You... didn't tell them?"

"Tell us *what?*" Dymitri demanded.

"Damon asked me to find them for you. Like I did for him and Cass. And Stavrok and Lucy. I used my magic to find the women you're fated to be with," Marienne said. Her shoulders rose and fell as she shrugged, and the sleeves of her elegant gown fluttered around her. Her eyes were wide. "They're in danger."

My stomach twisted. "What do you mean?"

Marienne swayed against Erik, who put an arm around her waist and drew her into his side. She pressed a hand to her temple, like the memory pained her.

"I saw... an old house. A farmhouse. A pickup truck. And..." She looked up, her long dark hair falling over her face. She'd gone pale. "A locked door. The women are together, but they're—they're trapped."

"Hold on a second," Lucian demanded. "Are you saying our soulmates are human?"

"Yes," Marienne snapped. "There's no time for the finer details. You have to hurry."

Dymitri was already tugging loose his tie, unbuttoning his shirt like he was getting ready to shift then and there. The entire hall was hushed, agog. Dymitri and Lucian's gazes flicked back and forth between Marienne and the others like they were watching a tennis match.

Lucian's hand shot out and he grabbed his brother's wrist. "Wait. Where exactly are these women?"

Marienne strode forward. Instead of replying, she simply pressed two fingers against Lucian's forehead. His eyes slid shut and when he opened them, his astonishment chased away the last remaining shreds of doubt and confusion.

"Thank you," he said, and she nodded, satisfied.

Marienne turned toward the table, where the rest of us were still looking on in shock.

"I've just given them directions. They know how to get there…" She paused, looking worried. "In theory, anyway."

Stavrok stood so fast that the silverware and glasses clattered over the table. "I'll go with them. They'll need a guide, someone who understands the human realm. And human women, come to that."

He glanced down at Lucy, who patted him on the arm.

"My husband isn't the type to back down from a fight," Lucy added darkly. "Promise me you'll come back in one piece?"

Stavrok bent to kiss the top of her head. "Always. You know I'd take you with me, but…" His gaze fell pointedly on her belly. "I won't be gone long, love."

He was already shrugging out of his jacket, the light of his dragon surging in his eyes. Damon sauntered up beside me. I took his hand in mine, and together we watched Stavrok stride out of the hall, Dymitri and Lucian hot on his heels.

"Well, that was exciting," I said.

Damon's mouth quirked. "Did you expect anything else?"

I laughed and shook my head. Soon it would be time to cut the cake, and after that there would be dancing, and the snow-covered grounds would be full of people, music, and laughter.

And after that? I fiddled with the silver ring around my finger, smiling. It had company now—my wedding band.

There were many more adventures to come and, with Damon at my side, I couldn't wait to get started.

4
FIRE AND ICE
THE HEIR OF WINTER
USA TODAY BESTSELLING AUTHOR
AMELIA SHAW

THE HEIR OF WINTER

CHAPTER
ONE

Dymitri

In the blink of an eye, everything had changed. One minute, I was sitting awkwardly in the royal hall of my ancestors, hardly able to believe our reversal of fortune. The next, my brother and I were told that our fated mates were *human* women.

That would have been enough of a surprise. My brother and I had always assumed that we didn't have fated mates. Only the luckiest of shifters enjoyed that privilege.

But the real shock came when Marienne told us that these women—these strangers—were in danger. She said we had to fly to the human realm immediately and save them, before they were lost forever.

My brother and I shifted into our dragons and launched off the palace balcony into the air. We followed King Stavrok, who had agreed to accompany us. We'd never been south of our kingdom, let alone to another world. But our mates needed us, so we didn't hesitate. Though the fear and trepidation that pulsed through my heart was very real indeed.

The cold air nipped at my face as we flew closer to the magical barrier that divided my world from the human realm, with no idea of what lay waiting on the other side.

We were dizzyingly high already, but we kept climbing. The air was thinner up here; there were no birds, nothing around us but thin strands of cloud. Beside me, my brother's wings beat hard, but he managed to keep pace as we followed Stavrok to the portal.

Lucian and I had always pushed each other, spurred each other on with every challenge. We'd always competed fiercely. It was what had enabled us to survive all these years of exile out in the wilderness.

But we weren't alone anymore. Our half-brother, King Damon, had agreed to take us in and allow our people to live within the safety of the kingdom's walls. But even more so, Damon had asked us to live in the castle with him. That had changed our lives in many ways. Especially now. Without his contacts we would never have met the sorceress who had given us a glimpse into our future. With our mates.

Stavrok let out a puff of fire when we reached the barrier as a signal to us. I slowed, flapping my wings hard and stared at the space before us. It was little more than a ripple in the air. The faint golden color would have been easy to miss if you weren't looking for it.

Lucian pulled up next to me, hovering in mid-air.

Stavrok went through first, disappearing into oblivion. I swallowed my fear and, after a glance at my brother, I followed, slipping through the portal after Stavrok.

I inhaled sharply when I emerged.

The change in the air was stark. In our world, a cold wind had been blasting over the frozen tundra of the north. But here it was warmer. Even the sky was different: a pale, peach color in the glow of the setting sun.

Stavrok circled down to earth below me, but I waited for my brother.

When Lucian flew through the portal and appeared at my shoulder, a sense of relief and happiness swept over me. I could tell from Lucian's expression that he felt the same. We'd made it through unharmed.

We fell into a simultaneous dive in perfect sync, wings spiraling outwards. It was a neat trick—impressive, according to those who had seen it in the past. We'd been doing it since we were kids. We didn't need a signal. In the air, our shifters could practically read each other's minds.

We landed in the middle of a cornfield, and I found myself panting for breath. We were ice dragons. We breathed ice, not fire. And we weren't as used to this warmth as Stavrok.

The king was waiting for us, hands on his now-human hips. He gestured toward a small farmhouse to show us where we would be going next.

I glanced at my brother, and together, we let go of our shifters and became human once more. Naked humans, like Stavrok after his shift. Would this be an issue, here in the human world?

As if he'd read my mind, Stavrok said, "These people are loyal to our kind. They will clothe us and provide some means of transport."

"All right." I nodded at the king. We had to trust him, but everything in me was tense and on guard. I was ready to shift back and launch into the air at a moment's notice.

This was not our world and nothing about this situation felt natural.

I followed Stavrok, together with Lucian, without voicing the questions that were shouting inside my head. Judging by his relaxed body language, Stavrok wasn't worried about the fact that we had all arrived naked in the middle of a field.

But, I couldn't help the nerves that ran through me. When I looked at Lucian, he seemed equally tense: jaw tightly clenched, hands held in fists at his side.

We stepped out of the field and walked toward the farmhouse.

Lucian and I hung back while Stavrok rapped on the door. I had no idea what to expect, but a small buxom woman who seemed glad to see us, was not on my list.

"Come in, come in. Out of the cold," she said, and ushered us into a small cloakroom. "Help yourself to anything that will fit you."

The woman looked at Stavrok with the kind of reverence I wasn't expecting from a human.

When we were left alone to dress, I grabbed Stavrok's arm. "Do they know about us? About you being one of our dragon kings?"

Her behavior didn't make sense with any other explanation.

"Yes. This family guards the entrance to the human world." He pulled on a pair of slacks designed to fit a man with his large frame.

These people were obviously accustomed to our size as I found clothes that fit me perfectly well, even though I'd heard that the men in this realm tended to be smaller in stature than our kind.

"I have been meaning to return here for some time," Stavrok went on. "They did me a great kindness when I came here to find Lucy."

I spared a glance at Lucian, who was buttoning his shirt with clumsy fingers. There was a frown on his face and I knew that look too well. He hadn't spoken since we arrived, which didn't surprise me. He was always the more stoic one of us. I was used to doing the talking.

When we stepped back into the main living area of the small house, the woman had returned with a man in tow. He had the look of a farmer. Although he was much shorter than us, he was stocky and strong-looking. His eyes darted between the three of us and in contrast to the wife, it seemed like he couldn't wait for us to leave.

"There's a car waiting for you out front." The woman smiled at us as she spoke, digging around in her pocket before pulling out a wad of cash and handing it to Stavrok. "This should be enough, Sire. Please call us if you need anything else."

Stavrok bent his head and kissed the woman's hand, making her giggle. "I thank you. I will return when we find what we're looking for."

The woman's gaze fell on my brother and me, and her eyes softened. I wasn't sure how much she knew, but I felt warmed by her kindness, nonetheless.

"Good luck," she said, waving as we left her small home and went on our way.

⌒

"Forgive me," Stavrok said as he jammed the gearstick into position with a crunch. "It's been many years since I've driven a car."

"Don't worry about it," I said between clenched teeth as we rumbled over a pothole. The bump lurched the car down and sideways. My fingers tightened around the edges of the seat. In the rear-view mirror, Lucian was looking distinctly green. "My brother and I aren't used to them either."

That was an understatement. We'd lived our whole lives in the wilds of the north; for the most part, such modes of transport were totally foreign. We were aware that vehicles like existed, but this was the first time I had actually seen one, let alone dared to ride inside one.

My heart hammered in my chest like I was being chased by a wolf.

Thankfully, the ride became smoother once we reached a main road that widened out into two carriageways. Stavrok's driving became less frantic, which gave me the chance to absorb our surroundings, rather than fearing for my life.

I stared in fascination at the strange markings on the surface of the road, and the giant metal signs that hung overhead.

"Which way?" Stavrok looked in the rear-vision mirror at Lucian when we reached the first intersection.

Marienne the sorceress had put the directions inside Lucian's mind back at the castle. Wordlessly, my brother pointed to the right.

This happened a few more times, and soon enough we were on the outskirts of a city. It was like nothing I'd ever seen before. There were bright, multicolored lights everywhere and pavements full of bustling people and glittering storefronts. As the lights faded outside the car, I didn't know which way to look.

Stavrok tapping his fingers impatiently against the steering wheel was a constant reminder of our mission. The traffic around us was thick, but we snaked through the crowded streets.

I'd never given much thought to who my mate could be. My life up until very recently had been one of survival. Harsh winters and brutal raids had left little time for pleasure, and women had been few and far between.

Some had come and gone over the years. People drifted through our small clan of outlaws, tagging along for a season before disappearing again. They'd warmed my bed, that was all. No woman had left her mark on my heart, and as far as I knew, I hadn't left mine on any, either.

I stared grimly out the window at the blur of lights. Night was falling, and fast.

I glanced at Lucian out of the corner of my eye. I was accustomed to reading his stoic expression, but right now I had no idea what he was thinking.

From what the sorceress Marienne had told us, there would be trouble when we reached our destination. We could hold our own in any battle when we knew the terrain, but this was unfamiliar territory on every level. I'd never fought against humans before.

But I knew in my bones, even though the shock of the revelation had yet to wear off, that I would do anything to protect my mate. Even though I hadn't met her yet.

My mate... I shook my head. As the bastard son of the northern king, thrown out of the kingdom a long time ago, the last thing I ever expected to find, was a human fated mate. I didn't feel worthy, or deserving of such a gift.

It was late evening by the time we left the city behind.

At Lucian's instructions, Stavrok turned down a dark, winding country lane. Then we were once again bumping over potholes and loose stones, the car rumbling as it crept forward.

Stavrok dipped the headlights as we approached so hopefully they wouldn't see us coming.

I couldn't see much outside thanks to the darkness of night. The vague shapes of trees loomed ahead.

I stared hard and through the gaps in the undergrowth, I made out a handful of small outbuildings. Once we cleared the trees, a small yard lay in front of a seemingly empty farmhouse.

"Are you sure this is the right place?" I muttered to Lucian. It looked like no-one had lived here in a long time.

Lucian nodded, his expression grim.

Stavrok shut off the engine and we climbed out of the vehicle.

The wind whistled around the seemingly abandoned dwelling as we approached. Our footsteps echoed loudly in the silence. As we grew closer, the sense of foreboding increased. Something didn't feel right about this place. It was so still and quiet, and yet...

All the windows were boarded up with planks of wood. Why would they need to do that if it was abandoned?

Then I saw it. A thin strip of light beneath the doorway. Stavrok caught the direction of my gaze and nodded before pressing a finger to his lips. I took my place on the other side of the doorway to Lucian.

In one blow, Stavrok shouldered open the door. Light spilled out, along with a gust of warmth and a clatter of surprise from the inhabitants inside.

Crates bound in packing tape were piled around the edges of the room. In the center lay a long table under a single, bare lightbulb, around which a small group of women sat, huddled together. Their eyes were wide with fear. They were all thin, and their hollowed cheeks spoke of weeks of untold suffering.

Clear plastic bags littered the table, along with powder and cutting tools.

Human drugs, then.

I couldn't focus on any of it. Like a fishhook in my gut, my attention was yanked elsewhere.

I almost fell to my knees with the force of the call coming from somewhere inside the house. My hand clamped around Stavrok's shoulder. In normal circumstances, I would never dare touch a king in such a way.

But these weren't normal circumstances.

"She's here," I said with a pained breath. "Somewhere else. Not in this room."

"Are you sure?" Stavrok asked.

I closed my eyes briefly, trying to block out the overwhelming force of the siren song that had led us here. It still threatened to bring me to my knees.

I forced myself to nod. "Yes."

My gaze roved the frightened faces. But there was no flicker of recognition among them. There was only terror staring back.

"She's not in here." I fought to keep the rising panic out of my voice. "But she's close. I can feel it."

I caught Lucian's eye. I don't know what I expected to find. A reflection of my own feelings, perhaps? If my mate was somewhere close by, then my brother's mate was likely with her. But there was no trace of a reaction on his face—only concern.

I dragged my gaze back to the room at large.

"Who's in charge here?" I called, addressing the women.

Silence greeted my words.

Beside me, Stavrok stepped forward. "We do not seek to harm you. We are here to help. Tell us—are there more of you? Are there others being held captive in this place?"

Slowly, one of the women looked up. Her pale face was fraught with anxiety, but she didn't look as spaced out as the others.

She met Stavrok's eye bravely. "There's a basement beneath the house."

She pointed to the corner of the room. My eyes followed her gesture, and a heated pulse shot through me as my eyes landed on a door.

By now, I could hear faint voices coming from another part of the building. They were low and rough—it sounded like a group of men.

A door slammed and the woman who had spoken jerked upright. "They're coming. You have to hurry!"

Stavrok strode toward the source of the male voices. I remained in the center of the room, paralyzed by the flow of hormones that raced through my body. Lucian seemed to sense my altered state, because he took charge, rushing to the front door and beckoning the women forward. They drifted uncertainly toward him, heading out into the darkness.

"There's a car parked in the yard out front. Keys are in the ignition," Lucian told the leader of the women.

I eyed her threadbare clothes and frail physique with worry, but she nodded fiercely at his words.

"Head for the main road."

With whispered thanks, the women slipped off into the night. The car's engine started up just as the door on the other side of the room slammed open.

Stavrok let out an almighty, inhuman roar, and immediately shifted into his dragon form.

A pulse of fury sparked through my chest when I laid eyes on the monsters who'd held these women prisoner. The rage on their faces lasted for only a second before terror replaced it. Bright, hot flames reflected in their eyes as Stavrok released a jet of fire that annihilated the nearest packing crate, reducing it to ashes.

The men turned tail and fled the scene, leaving Stavrok to obliterate the entire room.

"I'll check for stragglers," Lucian yelled over the roar of the flames. "You get to the basement."

As shifters, my brother and I were impervious to the fire that raged around us, but that wouldn't be the case for any humans left behind.

Stavrok came to a halt beside me and shifted back into his human form. His chest heaved with anger.

"Let us finish this." He growled, nodding with narrowed eyes at the door in the corner of the room.

Lucian appeared in the empty doorway, the back rooms still smoldering away behind him. "All clear."

Before any of us could do anything, a dirty, ragged arm appeared through another doorway, followed by the hulking form of a man. His face was twisted with fury as he pointed a gun at Stavrok.

The shot rang out. Stavrok recoiled from the impact. My blood ran cold as I started towards him. I braced the king against my side before he could sink to the floor.

No, no...

With a swift, merciless movement, Lucian raced forward and snapped the human's neck. He fell to the floor, lifeless, and Lucian turned to us with the same blank, calm expression I'd seen hundreds of times before.

"It's a mere flesh wound." Stavrok shrugged me off, staggering backwards. Sure enough, the bullet had pierced through his shoulder; dark blood ran from the hole in his bare skin. He didn't seem bothered, though, merely shocked that such a thing could happen. "I'll be fine. We must get to the basement."

I didn't need telling twice. Leaving Lucian and Stavrok behind, I hurried to the door in the corner of the room.

My mate was on the other side.

CHAPTER
TWO

Dymitri

The door was locked when I tried the knob. As if that would stop me. I took a step back, lifted my leg and kicked it in. The door was flimsy and once partly open, I twisted it off its hinges and tossed it aside. A dark stairwell lay beyond the door.

At the bottom of the darkness, a faint light buzzed on the side of the wall—a meager lightbulb illuminating the crooked stairs and peeling walls.

With the door out of the way, the call grew even stronger. It was almost deafening, buzzing through every cell in my body.

I descended the stairs two at a time, landing at the bottom with a grunt. As I straightened, my breath caught in my throat.

Two women were chained up against the far wall. One of them sat slumped over. The small movements of her chest were the only sign of life; she was deathly pale, and her hands lay limply by her sides.

The other one had gotten to her feet at my arrival. Despite her obvious weakness, along with the heavy shackles that bound her wrists and ankles, she stood half in front of the other woman as if to protect her, a determined glare on her face.

"Who are you?"

Her voice was low and rasping, perhaps from dehydration. Even so, the sound was music to my ears. Her words soothed the ache in my chest. I didn't know how long the pained feeling had been there, but it felt like forever.

I took a half-step forward. This was the one. This was my human mate.

Her hand shot outwards, the handcuff clinking around her thin wrist. "Don't come any closer!"

I froze on the spot. The need for her was inside me, building. It was burning hotter and hotter—and I didn't know what to do to ease it.

Stavrok and Lucian came down the stairs more slowly than me, and stopped just behind me. The spell was broken, though, their sudden presence forcing me into action.

The shift began inside me before I could stop it. I couldn't control what was happening even though I fought it. *Now is not the time.* But my dragon would not listen. My vision blurred and I stumbled to my knees, the familiar sensation taking over my body.

As I straightened, my head now hit the low ceiling. My mate gaped up at me. She was glued to the spot, still hovering over the other woman. I let out a snarl and lashed out with my claws, breaking open the chains that bound her in place. She backed away from me, but I advanced on her, grabbing her around the waist and hauling her toward me.

I could feel the tension in her human body as she tried to resist. I realized she was saying something—*pleading.*

"Take me, but please, please—don't hurt my sister! I'll do anything you want—I swear, just let her go!"

Lucian rushed forward and crouched down beside the unconscious girl. He pressed a hand against her forehead, brushing back her hair. He didn't seem affected by her at all, though his actions were possibly gentler than I would normally expect from him. Despite my haze of euphoria, my brain registered his response as strange.

But I couldn't focus on that. My only priority was the woman I held in my grasp.

When she saw Lucian reach for her sister, her thrashing intensified. *"Please!"*

"Get them back to the castle!" Stavrok roared from behind us.

Lucian jumped up and shifted, grabbing the other woman up in his claws. I arched my head back and blasted the ceiling above us with a cold jet of ice. The wooden beams broke apart, shattering in a spectacular fashion and raining debris down on us.

I bent my head and folded my wings over my mate, feeling bits of wood fall onto my wings as I waited for the collapse to finish.

When the area calmed, I looked up once more. The ceiling was gone, leaving the dark, clear night sky beyond open to our flight.

The woman sagged against me. I glanced down. Her eyes had closed. The shock of the roof caving in above us must have been too much for her to handle.

The need was stirring within me, fierce and uncontrollable. I had to get this woman to safety, to take her far away from this place. Back to my home, where I could protect her.

"Tell Lucy I will return to our castle." Stavrok's voice rumbled through the wreckage. He was pulling more rubble down from the hole in the ceiling, making sure the gap was large enough for us to fly through. "I have to take care of things here first."

As if suddenly remembering he was wounded, he pressed a hand against his shoulder. "Tell her our doctors will attend me. She'll worry otherwise."

Lucian launched himself into the sky. I watched his silhouette against the stars, the dark trees framing his steadily shrinking form as he rose.

With one final, parting glance at Stavrok, I followed Lucian into the sky.

~

THE JOURNEY back to the portal between worlds was brief compared to the long, winding car ride from the farmhouse.

Human roads seemed to be full of traffic and pointless diversions. The sky, in comparison, was a vast and mostly empty expanse that we were able to traverse quickly. Our only company was the strange metallic machines covered with blinking lights—the humans' airplanes. Because we were carrying human women, we had to fly far lower than those airplanes, instead of high above them where we would normally choose to travel.

At the altitudes Lucian, Stavrok and I normally flew, these women would not be able to breathe.

It made things slightly trickier on the way back to the portal. We had to fly extra-fast, to avoid detection from the humans below us and ensure that anyone seeing us would have to rub their eyes and look twice. By the time they did that, we'd have been long gone.

My wings beat through the sky until they ached. I pushed on, faster, inhaling deep lungfuls of the cold night air. My blood was burning, my fear for the woman I carried greater than anything I'd ever known.

I didn't know any humans. The only one I had met was Stavrok's wife, Queen Lucy, and I'd hardly said two words to her. I'd certainly never spoken with her properly.

I had no idea how strong they were, or how much trauma their bodies could withstand before they just gave up. What if I hurt the one thing I was destined to protect? What if I accidently *killed* her?

As the thought passed through my mind, I let out a roar into the night sky. The sound shot through the clouds way above us, the icy flames jetting from my mouth and lighting up the surrounding sky like a bolt of lightning.

I couldn't live with myself if anything happened to my mate.

It was a wild shock to me, how quickly everything had changed.

Ever since my brother and I had been welcomed into Damon's castle, our lives had been turned upside down. He had accepted us as his kin, his half-brothers—royalty in our own right. After all these years of scavenging and raids, warfare and the constant, desperate struggle for survival, it was strange to feel as if we had finally been allowed to come home.

But as tough as those exile years had been, at least I'd known my purpose in life. The last few weeks had been amazing… but I was adrift. I'd had no idea what I was supposed to do.

Now? Now I *knew*.

It had been just as the sorceress Marienne had said. My future was in my grasp. My path lay ahead of me. This woman clutched in my talons was the answer to everything.

Now, all that was left was to protect her. Cherish her. And claim her for myself.

~

WHEN WE FINALLY MADE IT to the shimmering air around the portal, I exhaled with relief. We were almost home.

How I longed to set foot on our home turf once again. The sky changed when we passed through the gateway between the worlds. The blackness around us was replaced by a pale dawn sky. It was disorientating, and I blinked to clear my vision as we swooped down into the lush, green valley that lay beyond the portal.

Lucian flew up beside me, dipping his wing in greeting. We must have made a strange sight, flying in tandem with our unusual cargo. Beneath us, Stavrok's palace lay glittering in the early morning sunlight, its multitude of windows shining up at us.

Hopefully the king wouldn't stay long in the human world. He needed medical attention, and his wife would not be happy when she found out he'd stayed behind.

We flew toward our own home, the weather shifting into our winter wonderland.

By the time we flew over the mountain range that divided Damon's kingdom from Stavrok's, even the colder, thinner air couldn't dampen my spirits. I clutched the still-unconscious woman close to my chest, hoping the warmth of my dragon body was enough to protect her from the harsh elements of the north.

Up ahead, my half-brother's castle loomed on the horizon. I steeled myself and prepared for the descent.

There were people already standing on the castle battlements, waiting for us, as we flew homeward.

I circled overhead, eyeing Lucy, Marienne, and Erik's upturned faces.

As Lucian and I landed on the rough flagstones, they rushed us from every direction.

"What happened?" Lucy asked, her forehead creased with worry. She kept looking up at the sky, until she must have figured out Stavrok wasn't with us.

She reached out to grab hold of the girl in my grasp and a faint ripple of anger swept through me, demanding that my mate stay close by my side, but I shoved it down. "Where's Stavrok?"

I let go of my dragon and shifted back, standing on two feet once more. Marienne rushed forward, handing Lucy a blanket for my mate, and a thick robe for me, which I took gratefully.

"He's heading back to your castle. He had some things to take care of first."

Lucy's gaze narrowed, before studying my faintly singed hair. Beside me, Lucian straightened. There was a purpling bruise on his cheekbone; he must have been hit by a piece of falling rubble when we'd been at the house.

"Dymitri," Lucy said, putting her hands on her hips. "What *happened?*"

I didn't have the energy to pretend. "Stavrok got shot."

The queen's hands flew up to cover her mouth, and I spoke quickly before she had a chance to interrupt. Or panic.

"He's fine. Injured, but alive. He said he'll get the palace doctors to attend to him, and he'll be waiting for you when you return."

"He better be," Lucy grumbled. "All right. I'll tell the servants to get the carriage ready."

On the ground a few feet away, Marienne wrapped my mate in a blanket. Lucian had the other human woman over his shoulder, and he and Erik were already striding toward the doors of a nearby tower.

I turned away from Lucy and hurried over to Marienne. I could barely take my eyes off my mate's pale, serene face. Her beautiful blonde hair spread out like a halo. My breath caught in my chest and I crouched down, unable to resist putting my hand against her neck to check her pulse.

Despite her unconscious state, it was still strong, thank goodness.

"Where are Damon and Cass?" I asked.

"They left for their honeymoon last night," Marienne murmured, watching me carefully. Despite her kindness toward us, I felt uneasy being alone with her. The sorceress's intense, violet eyes made me uncomfortable. It was like she could read my mind.

For all I know, she can.

"We need to get her inside. Warm her up properly." I grunted, hefting my mate's dead weight into my arms. Her fair hair spilled over my arms as I marched to the castle entrance.

Marienne fell into step beside me. Her apparent calmness was unsettling, considering my urgency. She held the door open for me and I swept through, letting her lead the way down the maze of passageways until finally we were at the door to an unfamiliar chamber.

"We had this wing of the castle prepared for the two women," Marienne said. "My vision showed me the state they would be in when they arrived. I knew they would need urgent care, and warmth."

Her brow furrowed as her eyes fell on the woman in my arms.

"Thank you," I said, sincerely grateful for everything she'd done.

Marienne nodded at me as I shouldered open the door, finding my brother already in the room. Erik and Lucy were nowhere to be seen.

The room was dark, softly lit by a few lamps set into the alcoves. Two beds had been placed side by side under a white canopy. On top of a cupboard opposite the beds, several medications were arranged in neat rows.

I ignored the anxiety that twanged in my chest at the sight of the make-shift hospital and made my way over to the empty bed. Gently, I deposited my mate onto it, and pulled the sheets up over her small body. Her skin was almost as pale as the bedsheets, and the deep shadows under her eyes were even more pronounced in the low light.

How can this delicate-looking woman be a dragon's mate?

I stared down at her unmoving face. I couldn't deny the possessive *want* that surged through my body every time I laid eyes on her.

Her proximity was satisfying on some bone-deep, primal level; I couldn't explain it, but I knew it was real. This was it. Somehow, impossibly, she was the one.

My hands skimmed over her shoulders as I tucked the sheets around her. She seemed tiny beneath my hands. Most of the women in this realm were sturdily built and as tough as the menfolk—especially in the north. They had to be to survive the harshness of life. But this woman was a slip of a thing. One wrong move, and she would melt away with the morning snow.

When I glanced up at Lucian, I saw that he was staring down at the other woman, frowning.

I held back a grin.

Typical Lucian. Even seeing his mate for the first time can't make the guy crack a smile.

I opened my mouth to say as much to my brother, but before I could, Marienne slipped silently into the room. I straightened up again, feeling like a kid caught with his hand in the cookie jar.

Marienne swept over to the beds and stood between the women. She reached out and put one hand on each of the women's temples, closing her eyes for a moment. When she opened them, she nodded to herself, before turning to us.

"These girls have been through hell," she said, her face grave. Her eyes sharpened, their purple hue darkening into midnight blue as she pointed a finger at me and then Lucian. "They aren't like us. You will have to win them over slowly. Even when they heal physically, their mental suffering has been great. I don't know how long it will take before—or *if*—they will trust again."

She stared down again at the girls, and the expression on her face shifted as she took in the face of the girl Lucian hovered over. She frowned, a small wrinkle appearing between her usually flawless brows.

My unease grew and a shiver ran over my skin. "What's wrong?"

Marienne's eyes snapped up to meet mine.

"I... Nothing." She bit her lip, glancing at the woman again. "I'm just confused, is all. I saw two sisters, but this one—she wasn't in my vision."

I stared down at the sleeping, peaceful face. The resemblance between the women was clear: long, fair hair, pale skin. The one Lucian had brought back looked a little younger than my mate; perhaps still in her late teens.

"What are you trying to say?" Lucian demanded.

"I'm sure it's nothing." Marienne's hasty tone didn't match the nervousness in her eyes. "My visions are... sometimes a little unreliable. Perhaps I misinterpreted something."

I found myself nodding. The feelings swirling inside me were so real, so intense... I knew who my mate was, and if the sorceress had seen two sisters in her vision, then there was no doubt this young woman must be the one for Lucian.

When they wake up, that's when everything will start to make sense.

At least, I hoped so.

~

Too soon, Erik and Marienne took to the battlements to begin their long journey home. I watched with a heavy heart as the sorceress climbed onto the back of her mate. Even though she unnerved me, it was tough that our only source of guidance was leaving.

I wanted Marienne to be here when the girls woke up, but I knew this was something my brother and I had to experience for ourselves. Erik lifted into the sky, but before his powerful wings carried them away, Marienne twisted around and shouted down to us.

"Don't forget what I said!" Her voice traveled through the whistling air as her flowing hair twisted in the wind. "Take your time with them. Please."

I nodded to let her know I'd heard, and then Erik's huge, leathery wings soared into the distance. Soon enough, they were nothing but a speck on the horizon.

I headed back inside the castle thrumming with nerves and anger. Who had done this to our mates? And what level of suffering had they endured, that Marienne was so nervous about their ability to heal?

Would we ever get the revenge my dragon already demanded for their suffering?

THREE

Dymitri

The court physician was an elderly man who peered at us through half-rimmed spectacles as we ushered him inside the chamber.

"I've never treated human women before," he said, before reaching out to pick up my mate's limp arm. As he took her pulse, a throb of possessive rage rushed through me. I shoved it down. The physician was only trying to help them.

"But the basic principles are the same as for our kind," he continued. "They are dehydrated and exhausted, chafed from being in restraints, but I can't find anything else physically wrong with them at the moment. Not without speaking to them and doing a more thorough exam. When they wake up, they will both need bed rest, and lots of fluids."

I nodded my thanks and the physician soon took his leave. Like most of the staff in the castle, he was uneasy around my brother and me, not speaking unless necessary and slow to meet my eye.

Many people here thought King Damon had been a fool to let the likes of *us* into the royal court. The courtiers saw us as thieves and scoundrels, trying to drag the land to ruin.

I could only hope that, over time, we would manage to change their minds. But it didn't really matter to me whether or not we achieved that. If we had to leave the castle and return to our rougher lives, I would do it. I had learned the hard way through life, that Lucian was the only person I could truly count on; we were used to living in a hostile world.

Though now, I had a mate I had to consider. I wasn't yet sure how that might change things, for my future.

I took a jug off the top of the dresser and filled the empty glass at her bedside with water. I hated being so powerless, but there was nothing to do except wait for my mate and her sister to wake up.

"Dymitri."

My brother's voice dragged me out of my thoughts. "Yeah?"

"Those feelings everyone describes getting when you first see your mate..." He didn't meet my eyes. "Do you feel them?"

I thought about the intense pull in the pit of my stomach. The desire that raged through me. My shifter burned with passion for this stranger who lay unconscious between us.

"I do." I swallowed, clenching my fists and then releasing them.

"What's it like?" he whispered.

I frowned, taking a closer look at Lucian. He was staring down at the other woman, focused intently on her face, like he was willing her to wake up. A ripple of confusion shot through me.

"What do you mean, what's it like?" I tilted my head, trying to get a read on him. "Don't you *feel* it?"

Lucian hesitated, then shook his head. "I... don't feel anything. She's pretty, I suppose... but there's no *attraction*. I rescued her because she was in trouble... but I would have done the same for anyone in that situation."

I thought back to what Marienne had said. Her confusion over her vision.

Maybe she's made a mistake...

No, surely it wasn't possible. It *couldn't* be. I wanted my brother to have *everything*. The fierce joy that burned through me dampened at the possibility that he didn't share in my passion for his mate.

"When she wakes up," I found myself saying, "Your shifter's bond will likely activate then. That must be the difference—my mate was awake when we found them."

"Maybe." Lucian didn't seem convinced, but I was.

Surely Fate wouldn't be so cruel as to deliver me my mate, and at the same time deny Lucian the mate he'd always craved?

Sarah

I woke up warm, beneath a deep, soft cloud. At least that was what it felt like as I slowly pulled myself out of the depths of sleep. I was almost drowning under the comfortable weight. I could sleep forever cocooned in its delicious warmth, and my body certainly wanted to.

But something at the back of my mind prodded me to *wake up*. There was something I was meant to do... something I'd forgotten.

I opened my eyes a fraction and my fingers closed around the cloudy substance which turned out to be a thick, plush blanket.

Wait. A *blanket*?

My eyes slowly adjusted to the dim light and I took in the room. It was lit with candles and had stone walls like a medieval castle.

This must be a dream...

My heart hammered inside my chest. Was I in a hospital?

It didn't feel like one. There were no nurses, no blinking lights. It didn't smell like a hospital ward, either; instead of antiseptic, the air was scented with woodsmoke. The scent was divine, permeating my nostrils and causing me to inhale deeply.

What is that beautiful scent? Who does it belong to?

We'd been saved! That was certain.

Thank God for that. Our nightmare might finally be over.

My eyes opened a little wider. In the corner of my field of vision, I made out a fireplace full of bright, flickering flames.

What the...?

My breathing picked up as panic set in. I wanted to speak, but when I opened my mouth, nothing came out.

Nadia! Nadia, where are you?

Through my half-closed eyelids, a dark shape appeared. A cool glass was pressed to my lips, and I swallowed rapidly.

The sensation of water passing through my parched lips was pure bliss and I collapsed back on the pillow with a sigh, my eyes closing even though I tried to keep them open.

Where am I? And who are you? I wanted to ask my water bringer, but the dark shape receded out of view. I was too weak to open my eyes again, or even lift a finger.

I slipped away into darkness once more.

THE NEXT TIME I WOKE, daylight cast brightly over my face.

This time my eyes flew open easily.

There was a thick canopy, woven with strange patterns, above my head. It stretched right over the bed and draped down on either side, then tied at the bases of the ornately carved pillars.

I squinted in confusion. *Why am I in a four-poster bed?*

I shifted experimentally, pressing down. My fingers met a soft, downy mattress. I rolled my head to one side, feeling the lush pile of pillows beneath me.

Is this some kind of hotel?

My heart squeezed with elation. Had we been rescued? I must have passed out because I couldn't remember how we got here. The memories leading up to this moment were a dark blur as well.

I had a faint memory of the delicious smell of woodsmoke, and the sound of our captors shouting in panic.

And then... I must have dreamed the next part. It was... impossible.

Nadia!

I sat bolt upright with a gasp, instantly taking in the room around me. There were stone walls, huge, arched windows, a roaring fireplace—and my sister's small frame, half-buried in blankets, asleep in the bed across from mine.

Oh, thank God!

I scrambled to push my sheets away and stumbled to my feet, my heart thumping wildly in my chest. I took a step forward, and the world tilted. My fingers grasped for the bedside table, but before they could make contact, something warm and solid collided with my back, and strong fingers wrapped around my hand.

"Whoa!" The deep voice came from behind me and it made the hair on the back of my neck stand on end. "Easy, little one."

I wanted to tell him I wasn't a horse, and despite my size I wasn't helpless, and he didn't need to treat me that way. But my knees were wobbling, practically knocking together like a new-born foal.

I tried to move forward, but the stranger held me back. "You must rest, woman. You're too weak to move about just yet."

I struggled against him. "My sister! She's—"

"She's fine, but weak. She's still recovering from her ordeal." The voice was firm, which was oddly reassuring. "As are you."

I stopped fighting him and allowed myself to be led back to my own bed. The world was spinning again.

Damn it. I hated being so weak.

As I settled back down onto the pillows, I got a good look at the owner of the deep voice. My heart leapt with a mixture of fear and fascination as I met his eyes for the first time.

I know those eyes...

"You," I blurted out. "You're the one who broke into the basement. You're the one who... who..." *He saved us.*

I fumbled, lost for words. Fragments of memory slipped through the fingers of my consciousness. I remembered clawed talons, and dark, scaly skin... the shadow of wings against a blackened sky...

And most vivid of all, fire. Blazing bright and hot, destroying everything in its path. Reducing the house that had been our prison into a pile of smoldering ash.

Large hands wrapped around my wrists, and I realized I was clutching the bedsheets in my fists.

"You're safe here," he said. "I promise."

I twisted away from his touch. "Where am I? What is this place?"

The room was like something out of a painting. My gaze landed on the plush rug in front of the fire, on the crossed swords and shield that hung above the fireplace. I wanted answers, but everywhere I looked only increased my confusion.

"Somewhere you can rest," the man said. "Trust me. You are safe."

I couldn't escape those piercing eyes. They were such a light blue they bordered on gray. The color reminded me of a frozen river. They were still and guarded at their surface level, but a storm of emotion raged beneath. I wasn't sure how I knew that, but in my heart, it was the truth.

The intensity of his gaze made my breath catch in my chest.

He appeared to mistake my flushed cheeks for something else, because he pressed the back of his hand against my forehead.

"Are you feverish?"

I shook my head. Some instinct made me draw the bedsheets up over my arms, cocooning myself from his touch. I craved his touch, which was the exact opposite of what I wanted or needed at this time. It made my evasion of him, even more necessary.

"Where am I?" I forced myself to meet his gaze. Even though my pulse was racing, I tried not to let the fear show on my face.

He didn't look like any of the men who had kept my sister and me captive. Truth be told, he didn't look like any man I'd ever met in my life.

His dark, shaggy hair curled around his ears, and the dark stubble on his face made me question just how long he'd been keeping watch over me. A scar cut through the stubble on one side of his face, running down to the edge of his jaw. His bare forearms were weathered, and more scars crisscrossed the tanned skin there, faint, pale lines that intersected, some old, some new. He looked like a warrior of old, but that was insane. Nothing in my experience had prepared me for someone like this guy.

He watched me calmly. "You are in my brother's castle."

My mouth dropped open. Did he just say... *castle*?

My fingers didn't budge from their death grip on the sheets. I couldn't help but feel like a cornered animal on high alert. A glance downwards confirmed that I was still wearing my clothes, at least, but it was cold comfort.

"Okay," I snapped, terror and annoyance warring within me. "How did I get to this... *castle*?"

"I brought you here."

Simple as that. My stomach twisted at his words.

"And you'll let me go once my sister wakes up?" I persisted. "We're not prisoners here, are we?"

As we had been back at the farm.

He shook his head. "No, of course you're not a prisoner. You're only here to recover from your injuries."

I relaxed a little, though I noticed he hadn't totally answered my question.

"My name is Dymitri," he said, when the silence stretched out between us. "I still don't know yours."

Despite everything, I almost smiled. He had brought my sister and me to this unknown castle, surrounded by who-knew-what, totally at his mercy. But he didn't know my name. And clearly, he wanted to.

"Sarah," I managed eventually. To my relief, my voice didn't tremble, and I managed to keep my head held high. "My name is Sarah."

I'd never thought my name was anything but plain. But from the way Dymitri's eyes suddenly darkened, and my belly did an answering flip-flop, my name suddenly seemed like the most erotic word in the world.

FOUR

Dymitri

I held my breath as I walked to the bedroom door to let myself out. I had to force my dragon down with every step I took.

When I reached the door, I turned the handle, then glanced back at her. "I will return shortly."

I waited on the threshold, eyeing her until she nodded. She was still looking at me warily, but she was no longer half-buried in the blankets, which I took to be a good sign.

The sight of her threadbare clothes reminded me that she needed something new to wear. Food, too. Who knew when she last ate?

I headed into the corridor, only to find Lucian hovering just outside the room.

"How are they?" he asked, barely giving me time to shut the door.

"The one I rescued—Sarah—she's woken up." I fought to keep my voice even. I wanted to shift, to fly far above the clouds. I could have burned the whole place down with my desire for her. But I had to keep myself in check for now. "The other one is still out cold."

I caught the attention of a passing servant and waved him over. "Some bread and hot soup, please. For two people. Quick as you can."

The man gave me a smile which looked more like a sneer, turned on his heel, and strode down the hallway. My hands clenched into fists. I knew very well what most of the servants saw when they looked at me: a bastard son of the old king.

Rejected. Unwanted. Desperate.

The reminder always stung, though King Damon made sure we never felt it in his presence. Cass and Damon treated us like family.

"I'll go to the kitchens," Lucian said. "Just to make sure the cooks know we need food up here."

I nodded as he followed the manservant out of sight. I listened to the echo of their footsteps until silence fell once more.

I was abruptly aware that I was alone... and Sarah was waiting for me on the other side of the door. My heart hammered in my chest as I pushed it open and peeked in.

Maybe she's gone back to sleep.

I swallowed hard at the sight of the empty bed. The bedcovers were rumpled, and Sarah was gone.

My blood ran cold. I stepped into the room, ready to bellow out for help, and woe betide anyone who didn't respond.

Then I saw a small figure, sitting beneath the window.

Sarah turned her head as I moved to stand beside her. She was curled up on the narrow window seat, feet tucked underneath her, staring with seeming calm out at the frozen landscape beyond.

"I thought you were gone." I tried to keep the note of accusation out of my voice.

I wouldn't have blamed her if she'd tried to escape; after everything she'd been through, it would have made sense.

"I just wanted to stretch my legs. And see it for myself." She turned back to the window, pointing at the snow that drifted past the glass. "I guess you were telling the truth about this being a castle."

I hesitated before dropping down onto the other end of the seat, shifting awkwardly to accommodate my large frame. She still seemed calm enough, but from the way her eyes kept darting toward me, I could tell she was on edge.

"I would never mislead you." I kept my reply soft and as non-threatening as possible. "This is an ancient fortress. It's been in my father's family for generations."

Her bright blue eyes widened as they met mine. Her lips hovered apart, like she was on the verge of questioning me further. I was transfixed by the soft bow-shape of her mouth.

God, she's perfect.

Then the door opened, and Sarah's mouth snapped shut. Her gaze dropped down to her lap, and I frowned as she shrunk into herself, shoulders hunching.

Lucian approached with a tray and set it down on a nearby table. I smiled when, despite her obvious anxiety, Sarah leaned forward. I inhaled the scent of the fragrant soup and hot bread that my brother had brought and my stomach tightened in hunger.

"Please, eat." I gestured toward the tray.

When her eyes narrowed, I shrugged, reaching for a hunk of bread and tearing off a piece.

"Suit yourself," I said, dipping the bread into one of the mugs of soup and then shoving the food into my mouth. I grinned at her.

Her mouth curled into a nervous smile. She reached out, took her mug from the table, then took a few careful sips of soup before hunger seemed to get the better of her and she grabbed for the bread and began eating in earnest. Before long, she had demolished half the tray.

By the time she was finished, her eyes were brighter, and her skin had lost that deathly pallor.

"You must have been hungry." Lucian raised an eyebrow at her.

Sarah's hands were still curled protectively around the mug, but she nodded. The movement made her fair hair shift around her shoulders and catch in a momentary ray of sunlight. I wanted to reach out, to run my fingers through the strands of her hair... I struggled to focus back in on the conversation.

"I haven't had a meal like that in…" She trailed off, fingers tapping against the mug. "I don't know how long."

"Those men," I growled, and her eyes snapped up to meet mine. "Who were they?"

Her cheeks paled so much I almost regretted my question. Lucian frowned at me, and I knew what he was thinking. She was too weak right now; any unnecessary stress might impede her recovery.

I needed to find out what those bastards did to her and her sister and punish them for it, but I wanted to see her get better first. That was the only thing standing in the way of me going back through the portal right now and killing every last one of them.

At first, I thought my anger had scared her into silence. But after a moment, she started to speak. Her voice was quiet and hesitant at first, but the more she spoke, the stronger she seemed to become.

"I was… well, I *am*… in my final year of college. My little sister Nadia had come up for the weekend, just for a visit." Sarah's eyes darted to her sister's still-motionless form. "She'd always been the one of us to stay at home. She went to a community college close by, so she could look after our parents. I was the one who wanted excitement, the adventure of the city… Anyway, on the last night of her stay, I wanted to go out. She didn't want to… but I insisted."

Sarah's voice wobbled and her eyes shone with unshed tears. I wanted to reach out and pull her close, but I resisted, giving her the space to continue in her own time.

"Anyway, we eventually went out. After hitting a few clubs, I wanted to try this new place, on the edge of town. She went along with it… but I knew she wanted to go home. The street was dark, and we'd been walking for…God knows how long. Anyway, at some point a man stepped out of the shadows. Before I could do anything, something hit me in the back of the head… and I woke up in the back of a van, with Nadia by my side."

"What did the men want with you?" Lucian asked.

My hands were clenched together in my lap and I breathed shallowly through my nose. Sarah wiped a stray tear from her cheek.

"They told us they'd kidnapped dozens of girls—girls like us—from all over the place. Some of them ended up working for their business." She sniffed.

My mind flashed back to the women gathered around the table in that dimly lit room, handling the drugs.

"But they said we were too valuable for that. A pretty face could fetch a high price. They'd have buyers lined up for both of us soon enough."

Sarah's voice trembled and she collapsed as she burst into tears. The stress of everything had apparently caught up with her. I put my arm around her shoulders, wanting to offer comfort. At first she stiffened up, then relaxed into my touch.

My heart ached with happiness to hold her, and my dragon was calm knowing his mate was here, and safe at last.

When she spoke again, her voice was barely above a whisper. "I don't know long they kept us in there. At first, we were held in one of the back rooms... and Nadia thought we could escape. She waited until she thought everyone was asleep, and tried to slip out." Sarah closed her eyes and shuddered. "When they brought her back, the man in charge got angry. He—he hit her, hard, and she fell. She didn't get back up. After that, they put us both down in the basement in those chains."

I pulled her closer, feeling her ragged breathing against my chest. "I'm sorry you had to go through all that. Rest assured, no harm will come to you here."

She pulled back from me and wiped her hands over her face. "I just want to go home."

I exchanged a glance with Lucian. Minutely, he shook his head at me.

He's right. I need to be careful what I say. don't want to shock her any more than I already have.

Instead of answering her directly, I decided to change the subject. "Now that you're awake, I'll see about getting you some clothes." I plucked at her threadbare sleeve. "You must be half frozen."

"Why are you doing all this, Dymitri?" Her eyes met mine, sharp and suspicious. "How did you know where to find us in the first place? Why are we here?"

Whatever I'd expected from this human woman, I could see that things weren't going to be as straightforward as her recognizing me as her mate and simply falling into my arms with joy.

I reluctantly pulled myself away from her and stood up. "Excuse us for a few moments. I'm going to see about some garments for you."

Once Lucian and I were out in the hallway, he rounded on me, arms crossed.

"You can only stall for so long," he said, as we fell into step. "Sooner or later, you're going to have to tell her the truth."

"I know."

She was beginning to trust me; I could see that. But how long could I keep her in the dark about our bond? About her new life in this land? Would she change her mind and want to stay? Or would she still want to go 'home'—to the human world?

Our connection was so new and still so fragile.

I stole a glance through a window as we passed, eyeing the stormy sky with trepidation.

How long before it all came crashing down?

SARAH

I don't know how long I sat at the window, watching the snow falling over the frozen landscape.

From what I could see from my high vantage point, the castle was expansive. Below us, stone gargoyles scowled from ornately carved cornices, and the spikes of various towers rose into the sky.

There were snow-covered hedges in the gardens below, and the occasional staff member hurried along the steps that snaked down toward a heavy iron drawbridge.

It was like a castle from a fairy tale, or a dream. I kept expecting to wake up in the cold basement. But the longer I sat there, the more I realized that this was real. We had been rescued, and now Nadia and I could begin the road to recovery.

I pressed my fingertips against the leaded glass window, watching my breath fog up the surface. I shivered, reminded of Dymitri's promise to find me something to wear. It was warm enough in this room, with the fire roaring in the grate, but some warmer clothing would be welcome.

Right on cue, a soft tap sounded on the door.

"Come in!" I called out.

I was expecting Dymitri, or his solemn-faced brother, but instead a petite woman entered the room. Her arms were piled high with fabric. I was up out of my seat in an instant.

"Don't trouble yourself, ma'am." She ushered me down again, before dumping the pile onto my bed and giving me a once-over, her hands on her hips. "By the looks of you, picking this lot up would finish you off, so to speak."

She paused, biting her lip. "Sorry to speak out of turn."

She didn't look that sorry, but I didn't care. I was just relieved to have some friendly conversation to interrupt my whirling thoughts.

I shook my head at her. "You're probably right. What have you got there, anyway?"

"New clothes for you, ma'am." Her sharp gaze flickered over me, lingering on my face and hands. I tucked them into my lap, suddenly self-conscious. When was the last time I'd had a bath? As if she'd read my thoughts, the woman said, "Perhaps I can show you the facilities first?"

"That would be great." I clambered up, relieved at the prospect. Earlier, I'd been half-starved, and too traumatized to think of such things. But now...

The maid opened the door at the far end of the room.

There was a bathroom in here? Amazing!

She held the door open so I rushed over and slipped across the threshold. My mouth dropped in wonder.

Instead of cold gray stone, the room was covered from floor to ceiling in a warm, honey-colored marble. In the center, a giant sunken bathtub dominated the space. I craned my neck to admire the cascade of multi-colored light filtering through the stained-glass skylight above our heads.

"Wow." I couldn't help but laugh a little with amazement.

How the hell had I ended up here? Maybe I'd died in that rotten base-ment, and this was my version of heaven? Food, warmth, incredible bath-room facilities... and a huge hulking man who generated strange feelings deep inside me, especially when he looked at me with more desire than I was used to.

"There are towels and robes in that cupboard." The maid pointed to a huge armoire in the corner. "Will that be all for now, ma'am?"

"I guess." I gave her an awkward shrug. "Uh, there's no need to call me ma'am. Please, I'm Sarah."

"Of course." The maid gave me a smile. "I'll be just outside."

Once I was alone, I turned my attention to the giant bathtub. The prospect of soaking in a mountain of bubbles had never been more tempting.

After a frustrating fight with the taps, I managed to fill the tub with hot water. The plumbing was unlike anything I'd ever seen. But then, I hadn't exactly visited a castle before.

A quick search in the cabinet across from the sink yielded a wide assortment of jars and bottles, full of all kinds of scented products. Some of them smelled familiar and reassuring—lavender, rose, violet—but some of them I couldn't place at all.

I sank into the hot, fragrant water with a moan. Whatever my reasons for being here, I might as well enjoy the opportunity to have a good wash.

I soaked until I began to get impatient to be really clean. So, I grabbed some of the soaps and washed every inch of my body, then finger-combed my hair and scrubbed it the best I could. My hair was matted and disgusting until now, and once I was done, my arms ached from exhaustion.

It was all so strange. This castle. The wild weather outside. My confusion over how exactly we had been rescued...

But the strangest thing of all, by far, was the man who'd been watching over me when I awoke.

Dymitri.

For some reason, my mind kept turning back to him. I couldn't get his face out of my mind, or the intensity in his ice-blue eyes whenever he stared at me. Which was basically all the time.

I shivered as a gust of cold air grazed over my bare, wet shoulders. I stood up quickly and wrapped myself in a soft towel from a nearby pile. My heart rate had picked up again, and my toes curled against the marble floor when I remembered Dymitri's fierce expression. The expression belied the gentle warmth of his hands as they wrapped around my wrists, holding me steady.

No harm will come to you here.

My mouth twisted into a soft smile. I didn't know why, but when he said it like that... I'd actually believed him.

But what of Nadia? Was she safe here, too? And what would happen to her when she finally awoke?

She was the most important thing to me, and I owed her so much. It was my fault we were in this whole mess, and I had to make sure I never forgot that fact.

CHAPTER
FIVE

Sarah

I opened the door and stepped back into the warm bedroom. "Sorry, I didn't catch your name."

The maid looked up as I re-entered the room, wrapped in a fluffy robe. I was loose-limbed and warmed through after my bath, and I smiled when I saw she had laid out some garments for me over the bed.

"It's Isla, ma'am—I mean, Sarah."

"Isla." I padded toward her, sparing a glance at the other bed. "My sister... did she wake at all while I was gone?"

My heart sank when Isla shook her head.

"No. I kept an eye on her, but she didn't stir. She seems peaceful enough," the maid added, clearly catching my look of dismay. "And the physician came earlier and checked you both over. He said you will both need food and drink and rest, but that, physically, you will be all right."

Physically? What about mentally? Oh Nadia. What have I done to you, dear sister?

I leaned over Nadia's bedside and put my hand to her forehead. Her face remained perfectly still. Only the soft rise and fall of her chest under the bedsheets reassured me that she was still alive.

With a deep sigh, I brushed the hair back off her face, and then turned to Isla.

I plastered a cheery smile on my face. "So, what do people wear to keep warm around here?"

The answer to that question, apparently, was way more complicated than I expected.

Isla handed me stockings, silk dresses, jackets made from soft wool, fur trimmed hats and coats, lace-up boots, and a multitude of other items until the room looked like a hurricane had swept through it. A lot of the stuff was familiar, but some wasn't.

There were boots made out of something tougher and thicker than leather, and a gauzy dress that reminded me of dragonfly wings, but somehow it was warm and seemed sturdy.

"Where did all this stuff come from?" I struck a pose in a floor-length fur coat that was much too big for me, making Isla laugh. "Did you raid a mall or something?"

A puzzled expression crossed Isla's face. "Some of it belongs to Queen Cassandra. The rest used to belong to the king's mother, rest her soul."

My skin prickled with discomfort. These clothes belonged to royalty. I'd never heard of a Queen Cassandra, but still...

"Are you sure it's okay for me to borrow them?" I laid the coat over the back of a nearby chair, smoothing it nervously.

"Of course." The confusion on Isla's face grew. "Why wouldn't it be?"

Before I could give her an answer, the door opened, and that put an end to our conversation.

Dymitri was back.

～

Dymitri

Now that Sarah was in the castle, it was torture to stay away from her.

Lucian and I had been sparring in the yard in an attempt to keep my passion in check. It worked well enough; that familiar burst of adrenaline that came from a good fight managed to distract me from the constant itch under my skin.

But once the sun began to dip lower in the sky, I didn't have the strength to avoid her any longer.

After I took a shower, my feet carried me back to the door of her room. I hesitated before entering.

Her scent hit me as soon as I crossed the threshold. I fought to keep my expression neutral, but the shifter inside me rumbled in satisfaction at the mere sight of her.

She met my eyes with a nervous expression. The maid had decked her out in clothing from our realm; she wore a simple fur trimmed dress with a neckline that skimmed just below her collarbones.

She looked exquisite. The very sight of her made me want to push her down onto the bed behind us and take her right there and then. Claim her as my own.

I managed to meet her eyes, hopefully without telegraphing my lascivious thoughts, and she gave me a small smile. I returned it, clenching my hands into fists so that I wouldn't do anything stupid.

"What do you think?" She gave a small twirl, holding her hands out expectantly.

"Better," I bit out, my dragon desperate to take over my human body. I shoved it back down. "C'mon, let me show you around."

Sarah's gaze strayed toward her sister's bed. "Maybe I should stay..."

"Don't worry," Isla said from the other side of the room. "I'll stay here with her, and take care of her if she wakes. We'll get her some food and a bath, like you had."

"Thank you, Isla." Sarah smiled at the woman, before following me toward the door.

Once we were out in the hallway, I glanced down at her, surprised by how quickly she seemed to have found her footing around here. That didn't seem to extend to me, however; every time we locked eyes, her cheeks reddened.

Not that I was doing much better. My shifter stirred restlessly; every time our hands brushed, or I caught a waft of her delicious scent, the dragon inside me leapt up, ready and eager.

At the end of the corridor, Lucian appeared. When he saw the two of us together, his eyes narrowed as if with suspicion. He could tell how close my dragon was to the surface.

"I am just going to give Sarah a tour of the castle." I raised my eyebrows at my brother, trying to project an innocent aura. "And the village."

"While I'm here, I might as well see it," Sarah added. "I've never been inside a castle before."

My chest twinged with unease. I didn't want to lie to my mate, but I didn't see much of an alternative. It was better this way; too much too soon might cause her to completely shut down on me.

Lucian caught my eye. I could feel his disapproval, but he said nothing.

After we had turned the corner, Sarah looked up to me with a questioning expression. "Your brother seems... quiet."

My mouth twisted into a smile. "Yeah, always has been."

"I don't think he likes me very much."

"Don't take it personally." I moved to touch her arm, before thinking better of it. "He's like that with everyone."

"You're not. You're different." Sarah's gaze burned into the side of my face.

I stared blankly at the tapestry in front of us, trying to quiet the shifter inside me.

Control yourself.

As I led her around the castle, the quiet, frightened woman I'd met disappeared; her eyes were brighter, and the way she held herself became more confident. With her long blonde hair and regal clothes, she looked every inch a dragon princess.

She paused in front of a giant portrait in the hall. It towered over us, looming from above.

The old king stared down at me with foreboding, judgmental eyes. Beside him, his queen sat with a serene expression, with baby Damon on her knee.

"Who is *that?*" Sarah whispered.

I took a long pause before answering her. "That's my father."

Her eyes widened. I could see the wheels turning in her head, trying to connect the dots.

"Does that mean…" She pointed at Damon. "Is that you?"

I let out a humorless laugh. "No, that's not me. That's the current king, Damon. C'mon, this way."

We wandered over to the doors that led into the main hall, Sarah eyeing me curiously the whole time. I pretended not to notice her regard.

I didn't want to talk about my father. Not now. Not ever, in truth.

Sarah lingered in front of the huge stained-glass window that dominated the front of the hall. The glimmering, colored panes told the story of the winter kings. How they had come to this land, hundreds of years ago, and built the castle where we now stood.

"See those mountains?" I pointed to the images in the bottom of the stained-glass window, and Sarah nodded. "Those lie to the south. Damon's ancestors journeyed over them so they could build this kingdom here in the north."

Sarah's upturned face was filled with wonder. The colors of the window shimmered over her skin and tangled in her long hair.

A spike of desire pierced through my soul.

I looked away, choking on the maelstrom of feelings that surfaced for the human before me.

"And those creatures?" Sarah indicated the top of the window, where several large dragons circled overhead. Their glassy wings shone in a multitude of colors: deep reds, vibrant greens, and pale blues that scattered light over the floor down by our feet. "I've never seen anything like *that* in a window this old."

I gazed up at the dragons, my heart sinking.

I can't keep lying to her forever.

But for now, I had to settle for a half-truth. "You could say that they're an important emblem in the royal family."

Sarah's eyebrows rose, and I could tell that she was on the precipice of another question.

"This way," I interjected, ushering her over to the door. "I want to show you the village."

～

SARAH

Something wasn't adding up.

With every hour that passed, I felt stronger. My mind got clearer, and the world around me became real again. How long had I spent in a dream-like stupor, just trying to make it from one day to the next, while my sister and I had been imprisoned?

But now, I had food in my belly and warm clothes on my back.

I could *think* again.

And every instinct was telling me to hold my cards close to my chest.

I glanced over at the man walking beside me. I couldn't understand why, but when he was around, I felt... better. Calmer, safer.

Even though I was in a strange place, surrounded by strange people. He had shown me great kindness, even if he occasionally seemed unsettled by me.

From the way he mentioned his father, I sensed that there was a lot more to the story.

I shivered as a blast of cold air hit my face. Dymitri grinned at me.

"Now you know why all our clothing has a fur lining." He laughed, holding the front door to the castle open for me.

I descended the uneven stone steps carefully. My shoes had a good grip to them, but a thin layer of ice beneath my feet made the going difficult. I almost took a tumble, but at the last second, he grabbed my elbow.

"You should watch where you're going." Dymitri's deep voice murmured in my ear. "I might not always be around to catch you, Sarah."

I am not *blushing. It's the cold air biting my cheeks, that's all.*

"Easy for you to say," I retorted. Dymitri moved with an enviable confidence and ease, taking my weight against his shoulder like it was nothing.

Which, given his size, it probably *was*.

Dymitri laughed, and my stomach flipped over at the sound. "I've navigated harsher terrain than this, believe me."

Once we crossed over the narrow wooden drawbridge and hit the cobblestones, I could breathe easier.

We were in a tiny village and, as we made our way down the narrow, crooked street, I took in all the sights and sounds. Overhead, the sky was a pale gray, and white flakes were still lightly spiraling onto our heads.

Where in heaven's name are we?

"Welcome to the village." Dymitri's voice rose above the hubbub. "This is where the castle gets its supplies. People from the outlying farms come to trade, to pay tithes, that kind of thing."

"Wow." I paused beside an old woman selling bundles of fragrant herbs, before glancing up at Dymitri. "Tithes? That sounds pretty old-fashioned."

Like... medieval.

"I suppose it would," Dymitri said with a shrug. His pale eyes scanned our surroundings, like he was half-expecting someone to attack us at any moment.

A dozen follow-up questions sprung to my lips, but before I could voice any of them, I got distracted by another seller: a cheerful, red-cheeked man selling sweet, candied apples in the next stall. They smelled mouth-wateringly delicious.

Dymitri followed my gaze. "Do you want one?"

"Oh..." I bit my lip. "No, it's okay."

"One toffee apple," Dymitri said firmly to the man. "Thank you."

"Right away, Sire." The apple seller skewered one of the apples for me and handed it over. When Dymitri dug around in his pockets for the cash, the man waved him off. "No charge. Your royal custom is payment enough, my prince."

"Nonsense." Dymitri pulled out a handful of coins and shoved them into the bewildered seller's hand. "I always pay my debts. I'm no *prince*."

"My deepest apologies..." The seller seemed uncertain which form of address to use and trailed off.

To spare him any more embarrassment, I gave him our thanks and dragged Dymitri further down the street.

Dymitri's eyebrows had drawn down, but I kept my hand on his arm hoping to distract him a little. When I took a bite of the apple, his eyes tracked the movement of my mouth. For some reason I liked that he did that, and I deliberately licked my lips, chasing the sugar at the edges of my mouth.

God, what is happening?

"So, let me get this straight." I took another bite of the apple, smiling at the explosion of sweetness over my tongue. *So good.* "Your father was the king, but you're *not* a prince?"

"It doesn't work like that." Dymitri hesitated, eyes searching my face. I waited. "I wasn't born here in the castle. My father was king... but my mother wasn't the queen."

Oh.

"I'm sorry." I stared down at the red glazing on my apple, my cheeks burning. "I didn't mean to pry."

"It's nothing." Dymitri's finger nudged against the side of my chin. Gently, he tilted my face upwards, then brushed a strand of my hair away from my lips. "That's better."

I stood there, transfixed by the look on his face. No man had ever looked at me the way Dymitri did... especially not one that I'd only just met.

Despite the fact that I barely knew him, I couldn't deny my racing heart. Nor could I explain the way my body leaned into his, like it wanted to close the space between us and hadn't consulted with my mind about its intentions.

Abruptly, Dymitri stepped away from me. His jaw was tight, a hard line against the dark fall of his hair.

"Let's continue." He forced the words out through gritted teeth, and turned his back on me entirely.

I had to run to catch up with him as we wound our way through the street.

I was certain the flush in my cheeks had spread to my neck. In fact, it felt like my whole body burned with heat beneath the thick winter layers of clothing.

When he finally slowed his pace, I took a deep breath and exhaled. "So..." I adopted a casual, bright tone that rang hollow. "Where to next?"

We stopped at half a dozen more stalls. Every time I thought we were done, something new caught my eye: a stall hung with huge, dried mushrooms, a cart laden with different smoked cheeses, a black velvet tablecloth covered in smoky quartz. It was all so beautiful. And different to anything I had ever known in my life.

The dank basement and those terrifying rough men felt like a lifetime ago.

So long ago, in fact, it now seemed like a distant nightmare, and I'd finally awoken. The relief was enough to send me staggering.

Eventually, we reached the edge of the village. I frowned at the narrow dirt track that led out toward what looked like miles of bare, frozen wilderness.

I couldn't understand how such a thriving community could exist in the middle of nowhere. How had they even gotten here?

A shout pierced the air, and my attention shifted to a small group of men on the other side of the road. Three of them held a wooden frame, and after a second, I worked out what it was—the bones of a house.

One of the men yelled something to the others. The words got whipped away in the wind before I could understand them, but they caught Dymitri's attention. We watched as the man struggled; one of the support beams at the corner of the structure had shifted out of place.

"That thing will come crashing down if they're not careful," Dymitri muttered, seemingly to himself.

A creaking groan came from the frame. It was bending in the wind, twisting even more out of shape, threatening to snap altogether under the strain. A volley of shouts followed the noise. A small crowd gathered around the men but no one seemed willing or able to step in and help. It would take inhuman strength to hold the beam in place.

Dymitri and I glanced at each other. Without a word, he darted forward, ushering people aside. When the village folk near to us got a good look at him, they stepped aside, murmuring to each other, their eyes wide. Dymitri hardly seemed to notice. I hurried after him. Once we reached the center of the crowd, he stepped forward and grasped the errant beam with both hands.

"On my count," Dymitri shouted at the men on either side of him. "Lift!"

Despite a sea of dumbfounded looks, they did what Dymitri told them to do. Dymitri, seemingly stronger than the rest of the men put together, eased the frame into place with no difficulty.

Once the structure was secure, a scattered round of applause started up amongst the onlookers. The other men offered their thanks to Dymitri, who waved them away. He didn't seem comfortable with all the attention. In fact, the longer we stood there, the more he started to glower.

I was beginning to wonder if his seemingly natural propensity toward anger was actually a mask to hide his awkwardness with others.

An elderly woman stopped us as we headed away from the crowd. The deep wrinkles around her eyes grew as she smiled up at Dymitri. Her eyes shone. "Blessings to you, Sire."

Dymitri shifted uncomfortably, and I fought back a smile. I was right. He was uncomfortable—especially, it seemed, when people showed kindness toward him. He must have had a difficult life indeed, if he didn't feel worthy of receiving niceties from others.

I could see that he wanted to correct her address, but he didn't want to come off as disrespectful. Eventually, he settled for a half-nod, lowering his gaze.

"Thank you. And to you," he mumbled.

Once we were out of earshot from the gathering, I put my hand on his arm. He seemed startled by the sudden contact, but he didn't push me away.

Our footsteps echoed loudly across the cobblestones.

"You know..." I bit my lip, feeling a little bit cheeky. "I've never met royalty before, but you aren't what I expected."

Dymitri tilted his head down to look at me.

"I told you." His pale blue eyes were intent. My skin prickled under his scrutiny, but I didn't drop my gaze. "My brother and I aren't royals."

"But you're not one of the villagers, either. What you did back there... it was a true kindness. It also showed exceptional strength. You did a good thing, Dymitri."

His expression twisted, and he glanced away from me, rubbing a hand across the back of his neck. "I saw a problem and stepped in to fix it. Anyone would have done the same in my position."

Unconsciously, my hand had found its way back onto his arm. I squeezed gently to make him look at me again. "That's not true."

I didn't know if it was the softness in my voice, or the way I was holding on to him, but something shifted in his expression. He moved closer to me, and for a dizzying second, I wondered if he might actually lean in and kiss me.

I should have been scared and jumped back. But I wasn't, and I didn't. Instead, I waited, my heart beating strangely fast.

In the end, he stopped just short. His tone was grave when he finally spoke, and something in his eyes made my heart rate speed up even more.

"Sarah. There's..." He cleared his throat. "I have to show you something."

Sarah

"Where are we going?"

I didn't know how many times I'd asked that question. It didn't matter—Dymitri gave me the same answer he had all the other times.

"You'll see."

It was maddening, and yet I had no choice but to follow him. If I turned around and left him now, I'd get lost for one thing. For another, I had to admit that he'd piqued my curiosity.

He led me all the way back to the castle, then through a network of hallways and corridors, until we reached new doors and went out into the gardens. I thought at first we were heading toward the massive hedge maze lying beyond the rose garden, but instead Dymitri drew me to a halt in the little courtyard at the bottom of the steps.

"Well?" I crossed my arms, waiting. "What is it?"

Dymitri looked... nervous. He took a few steps back from me, coming to halt about ten feet away.

"I need you to promise me something."

I shuffled from foot to foot, beginning to grow uneasy. "Okay."

Dymitri bowed his head. "Promise me you won't be afraid. I would never harm you. *Never*. Do you understand?"

I wanted to laugh out loud. After everything I'd just been through, he wanted me to trust he'd never hurt me? I wasn't sure I could promise that. I wasn't sure I would ever trust anyone fully again.

But something in his demeanor told me to take this seriously. After a moment I nodded, once, my fingers tightening protectively around my forearms.

"All right. I'll do my best." It was all I could offer.

He looked at me for a long moment. "Very well."

He crouched to the ground. My eyes narrowed, wondering what he was doing, then widened in disbelief as a thick mist filled the air around us. The cloud rose up, higher and higher, until it blocked out the sky.

I inhaled sharply as the impossible happened right before my eyes. The man before me disappeared. His limbs grew larger, his fingers turned into claws, and, most terrifying of all, a huge pair of wings, with curved spikes crowning each wingtip, rose up out of the swirling fog, like great, dark shadows.

The enormous monster before me threw back its head and let out a roar that shook the ground beneath my feet and rippled into the air.

"Holy shit."

He looks like... My blood froze with terror. *A dragon?*

I took a stumbling step backwards, then another, backing up until I was at the bottom of the stairs.

I couldn't think as the enormous creature advanced on me. In that moment, everything Dymitri had said vanished into the ether. I was nothing but prey for the monster that was stalking toward me.

My heart pounded like a war drum in my chest. The roar of my blood in my ears was so loud I couldn't hear anything else.

I wanted to run, to hide, but my feet were rooted to the ground. I could do nothing but watch as the mist began to clear, and the massive dragon stood before me, head lowered, staring at me expectantly.

Dymitri...?

My breath caught in my throat as my eyes climbed up over the creature's thick, scaly hide. The light glinted wickedly off its claws. In contrast with the pale landscape, the dragon was an inky black color, aside from its eyes...

Which were as piercing and intense as the man himself.

When I locked eyes with the dragon, something inside my chest eased. My fear began to drain away.

That gaze was so familiar. This creature—this *man*—wasn't going to hurt me. Deep down in my soul, I knew it.

I inched forward, reaching up into the air between us, my fingers outstretched.

There was nothing but silence around us, and the softness of the still falling snow. My own shallow, uneven breaths came out in little puffs of fog.

When my fingers made contact with the creature's chest, I inhaled with shock. I had expected ice-cold scales, but instead, my fingertips were met with a smoldering heat, like I'd touched glowing coals.

I jerked back, but then I realized the warmth wasn't burning me. It was *caressing my skin,* wrapping me up like a thick, soft blanket.

I put my hand to the dragon's scales and stroked down them, keeping my touch light and gentle.

The creature lowered its head, eyes sliding shut. It let out a deep rumble of satisfaction that resonated through my whole body.

This is impossible.

But I couldn't deny the evidence of my own eyes. I let out a breathless, slightly hysterical chuckle.

My roaming fingers encountered a deep gouge of old scar tissue. I frowned, moving to the side, peering closer to get a better look.

The dragon's thick shoulder was covered in a mass of scars, running all the way down from its neck. In a flash, I remembered the scar on Dymitri's jaw.

Who could have done this to such a beautiful, majestic creature?

I pressed my forehead against the scales, feeling the warmth emanating from within, comforting myself by listening to the slow, steady pulse of the dragon's heartbeat. A wave of sorrow for his suffering threatened to pull me under as tears rose in my eyes.

I sniffled, and let out a soft sob, squeezing my eyes shut. It was no use, though; a few salty tears leaked out and fell.

Under my hands, the scales fell away, and bare skin returned in its place.

"Shh." At the sound of Dymitri's deep, rumbling voice, my breathing slowly evened out, and I relaxed against him. When I opened my eyes, I realized that the warmth surrounding me was his embrace; strong arms, holding me steady on my feet. "It's all right. I told you, nothing will hurt you here."

"What happened to you?" I whispered.

"Many things."

I sniffed, wiping my face and drawing back enough to look him in the eye.

"In time, I'll tell you." He reached out and swept a strand of my hair back behind my ear. "I'll tell you everything, Sarah."

DYMITRI

I'd controlled myself long enough for Sarah to drag her hands over my body. In my shifter form, I was even more volatile in relation to the mating call, but somehow I'd managed not to react to her touch in the way I truly wanted to.

It was only when her tears wet my skin that I couldn't hold back. The dragon retreated, and I was left standing before her. Just a man, standing in front of the woman he was meant to love.

I pressed my body against hers until she got a hold of herself. It broke my heart to see her like this, to feel how vulnerable she truly was.

I pressed my lips to her forehead as she looked up at me in wonder. There were still tears in her eyes, but awe as well.

"How..." She bit her lip, shaking her head. "How is this even *possible?*"

"For my people, it's normal." I swept an arm out around us, indicating the castle and the vast lands beyond it.

Her eyes brightened further in recognition. "Wait... so those dragons in the window..."

I nodded. "Almost everyone in this realm is a shifter." I stared down at my feet. "I happen to come from one of the royal bloodlines, that's all."

If I'm telling her everything, I might as well get it over with.

"This is insane," Sarah murmured. She glanced toward the horizon, shaking her head.

"Sarah." I reached up to grip her shoulders before I could stop myself. "Search your memories. How do you think we rescued you from that farmhouse, back in your world?"

She frowned. "Hang on... what do you mean, *my* world?"

"Come inside," I said. "Let's get warm. I'll explain everything, I promise."

Her gaze drifted downwards, and her cheeks flushed as she seemed to realize for the first time that I was completely naked. I watched with amusement as her gaze fluttered around, not knowing where to look.

Of course. Humans have hang-ups about such things.

"When we shift, our clothing shreds," I murmured.

"Oh. Err... okay..." She still couldn't look at me, and I had to bite my cheek to stop from laughing.

Once we were back inside, I found a thick robe and slipped it on. I caught Sarah sneaking glances more than once at my bare chest still exposed, but this only served to further heighten my excitement. It was becoming clearer than ever that our interest in each other was mutual.

Remember to take it slow. A voice that sounded suspiciously like Lucian's protested in the back of my mind. *This is all new for her.*

Once we were situated in front of the huge, roaring fireplace in the Great Hall, it was difficult to think about anything else. Sarah stared into the flickering flames, her skin bathed in golden light. Her long hair flowed down her back, brushing against her bare neck as she leaned into the warmth.

"So?" She arched a brow toward me.

My mind turned blank. I struggled to remember what we were talking about. All I could think about was how beautiful she looked in the flickering firelight.

Oh. Right. Worlds.

"Outside," Sara said patiently. "What did you mean, *my* world?"

"This place," I said, gesturing to the stone walls, the gargoyles peering down from the rafters, the snow that swirled outside the huge windows, "is not part of the human realm. It exists beyond a portal."

A small crease of confusion appeared between Sarah's eyebrows. "Portals... dragons... those words tell me I'm dreaming. I must have been knocked on the head or something."

I smiled softly at her. "You're not dreaming. We found you and brought you here."

"Let's assume that what you're saying is true." She tucked her feet up under her. I mirrored her position, sitting cross-legged on the cushion opposite. "How did you know where to find me? It's not that I'm not grateful, but... why am I even here?"

This was it. The moment of truth.

I still wasn't sure she was ready, but her face was open and inviting, and the way she kept biting her full lower lip was driving me to distraction.

"Our kind... we're not like humans. In life, we're fated to end up with one partner. Some of us never find that one person, but when we're lucky enough... they stay with us forever."

Sarah tilted her head, puzzled. "Like... a soul mate?"

I didn't know how to describe something I barely understood myself, but I nodded.

"Yes. A soul mate. Two halves of the same whole, who are only complete when they find each other."

Reflecting the firelight, her eyes brightened as she mulled over my words. "What does this have to do with Nadia and me?"

"My brother and I... we have a friend. A sorceress. Her name is Marienne. It was her vision that led us to you."

Sarah's eyes widened. "A *sorceress?* Hang on, wait a second. Are you saying... do you think *I'm* this fated person?"

I nodded, my heart thundering. "Nadia is Lucian's fated mate. And you, Sarah, are mine."

The silence that followed my words lay between us. The unspoken tension that had been building since she woke up had finally reached a breaking point; from the look on her face, we were both feeling it.

"Is it really so hard to believe? Can you really tell me that since we met, you haven't felt anything?" I reached out to hold her wrist loosely in my hand. "I can feel your heart rate pick up when I touch your skin. I see the way your pupils widen when you look at me."

Sarah just stared at me, dumbfounded. "I..."

I slid my hand over hers, and her fingers automatically turned to slide over the bare skin at my wrist. "Even now, you can't deny yourself."

"This can't be happening," Sarah said in a small voice. "I barely know you."

But her hands had already moved of their own accord; one of them had come up to rest on my shoulder, and the other dipped down to my chest. The shifter inside me growled in satisfaction under her touch, and I smiled.

"You will," I whispered, just before I brought my mouth down to meet hers.

～

Sarah

Dymitri's kiss surprised me, but not for long. I couldn't stop myself from responding, tentatively at first by lifting my chin and returning his kiss, before eagerly grabbing hold of his hair to tug him closer.

I wasn't sure what had come over me. Perhaps I was still in shock from seeing him transform into a dragon and back. A *dragon*!

But I knew it was far deeper and more elemental than shock. I could not resist him, and I did not want to.

My enthusiasm only seemed to spur him on. His kiss began softly, with light, melting brushes against my lips. Then the connection shifted, deepening further and further. Eventually he groaned and tilted my head backwards, dragging his mouth down my neck and sucking hard at my pulse point.

My breath hitched in my throat as he grabbed my waist and tugged me closer.

I climbed on top of him and straddled his thick thighs, moaning as his big hands clamped around my hips and held me tight.

He plundered my mouth, and I wanted more. *Desperately.* I *needed* more. I slid my arms around his shoulders and then up to his neck, trying to give as good as I got.

I squeezed my arms tight, a slow, lazy warmth coiling in the pit of my stomach at the feel of his hard muscled form against my body. My reservations melted away, replaced by a haze of desire.

Dymitri arched up with a growl, rolling us over. I found myself pinned to the floor as he lavished open-mouthed kisses onto my neck and chest, dragging his teeth lower, over my racing heart.

I swallowed thickly. My arousal mingled with surprise. Then worry. This was all going so fast. He was on top of me, surrounding me, bending me to his will.

Our eyes met, and I fought back a gasp. His pupils were blown out, inky black with a thin sliver of ice blue around them. His mouth was red, and as he panted down at me, there was a flash of white teeth.

I squirmed, my hands grasping for purchase. He groaned and rolled his hips into mine. It felt good, but I couldn't push away my fear. He was so strong, and his passion threatened to drown me.

His hips bore down into me again. His hard length pressed down into my belly. It felt so good and so right, but my fear continued to grow. I shuddered, twisting, and he snarled at the sensation of me moving beneath him.

When his fingers slid up beneath my skirt, the fright consumed me. I urged us over, and he rolled onto his back, looking up at me. His chest heaved, robe-half open.

He was so damn sexy, but suddenly, I couldn't breathe.

What am I doing?

I scrambled off him and stumbled away. His hands shot out as if to draw me back, but I darted out of reach.

I have to get out of here.

He growled again, and for a split second, I thought his dragon was going to emerge. But when I caught a flash of his expression, I realized he was fighting to keep control of himself. To stay as Dymitri the man, and hold the dragon inside.

He stretched out his fingers toward me. "Sarah... Please..."

He sounded like a dying man, on the verge of his last breath. I ached to return to his arms, but my fear had taken hold and threatened to consume me.

"I'm sorry," I whispered in a broken tone, before I turned and ran.

Sarah

I tore down the dark hallways, taking random turns until I was totally lost. Behind me, Dymitri's faint voice called for me, but I ignored him and kept running until I was certain I was out of his reach.

I came to a trembling halt beside a huge tapestry and slid down the stone wall opposite, collapsing into a heap on the floor and heaving in deep, ragged breaths.

I glared at the swirling patterns in front of me. Embroidered dragons flew through a woven landscape, strong and majestic. I dropped my gaze to my lap and hugged my knees in close.

I want to go home.

But I couldn't leave. Not while my sister was still lying unconscious in another part of the castle. I had to stay and ensure her safety.

Plus, there was a huge part of me that ached to return to that warm fireside. To be held in Dymitri's arms again, to listen to him tell me that everything was going to be okay. That I was safe.

What is wrong with me?

I rested my head on my knees and squeezed my eyes shut.

At the faint sound of footsteps coming from the other end of the corridor, I stiffened, on high alert. I tried to remain as still as possible, praying that the shadows would conceal me.

I'm not ready to talk to him. Not yet.

But the voice that called out to me wasn't Dymitri. It was a female.

"Hello?" The pattering footsteps grew closer. "Is anyone there?"

I sniffed and drew my legs in closer. "Please leave me alone."

My voice was trembling and thready in the echoey space. Instead of retreating, the stranger came right up to me, dropping into a crouch in front of me.

"Are you okay?"

Although I'd buried my head in my arms, I could almost make out a mass of curly dark hair, and a sweet, heart-shaped face. The voice was kind and gentle. Despite my fear, I looked up, meeting the eyes of the young woman.

"I'm fine," I lied, wiping a hand over my face. "I just got lost, that's all."

Instead of offering me a hand up, the girl shuffled onto the floor beside me, resting her back against the wall.

"This place is kind of a maze, huh?" She smiled at me, her cheeks dimpling. "Not to mention the *literal* hedge maze outside. Have you explored it yet?"

After a small pause, I shook my head.

"You should—it's great." She released a small sigh and stretched out her legs over the floor. "I'm Cass, by the way. What's your name?"

"Sarah."

"Nice to meet you, Sarah." Cass's cheerful voice made me relax a little. "What brings you to our castle?"

Other than a mythical beast? Not much.

Oh, my God. Didn't someone mention the king's wife was named... Cassandra?

I took a closer look at her. The thick, fur-trimmed collar around her neck, the cuffs at the end of her sleeves... her outfit was almost identical to my own. She wasn't one of the servants who roamed the halls, which meant that...

"Your Majesty," I stammered. "I—I'm so sorry—"

"Hey, stop!" Cass put a hand on my arm before I could embarrass myself any further. "It's okay, Sarah. Don't worry! We just got back from our trip, that's all. You surprised me!"

"I didn't know where else to go," I said. "I just needed some space to clear my head."

"What happened?" Cass folded her arms under her chin, studying me carefully.

I let out a deep sigh. "Dymitri brought me here."

Her eyes widened as realization set in. "Oh, my... you're *her,* aren't you? The human woman that Marienne saw in her vision?"

Human woman? "I guess I am," I mumbled. "He told me that we're... fated to be together, or something. And then he... changed."

I didn't know how else to describe a guy turning into a huge dragon right in front of me, but Cass seemed to get the gist, nodding along. Hell, Dymitri told me that they were all like him. That probably meant she had the same power.

"So, what's the problem?" Cass prompted me softly. "Don't you like him?"

"It's not that." I struggled to get the words out; my thoughts still tangled together with my knee-jerk desire to *escape.* "He's amazing. Like no guy I've ever known, to be honest."

I let out a nervous chuckle, and Cass smiled encouragingly.

"But the way he *looks* at me... it's like there's something inside him, driving him to... take me. *Claim* me. It's so intense." I sighed. "I had to get out of there."

I looked up, fearful of her response.

But her expression was understanding. "You're a human, Sarah. This is all new for you."

"I don't want to hurt him." My voice trembled as the tears threatened. "I don't want to hurt anyone."

Especially someone who'd shown me nothing but kindness since I woke up.

"You haven't." Cass laid a hand on my arm. "Dymitri knows the score, Sarah. He'll understand. It's difficult for dragon shifters to resist the call to mate. He wouldn't have meant to scare you. I'm sure he was being as gentle as it was possible to be, in the circumstances."

I thought back to the ferocity with which he'd held me, the inhuman growl he'd let out as I'd run away. I shivered.

Cass seemed to sense my wariness. "Look—I don't claim to know much about the human world. I'd love to visit it one day, but... I know that things are different there. Dymitri would never harm you, Sarah. He'll let you take things at your own pace."

"How can you be sure?"

"Because I know him. And his brother," Cass replied. A soft smile played on her lips. "They captured me once—Dymitri and Lucian. I thought they were going to hurt me, but they gave me food, warmth, and shelter. They're loyal men, Sarah. Loyal to my husband, and to you and your sister."

"Your husband..." I remembered the painting of the royal family in the hall. "King Damon."

Cass nodded. "We just got back from our honeymoon. Things weren't easy with us, at first. I'm from the south, you see. We're from different worlds."

"I know the feeling." I shared a weak smile with her. But her kindness had calmed my anxiety somewhat. Slowly, I unfurled my legs and sat upright. "So, what's the deal with this bond? How does it work?"

"No one is sure." Cass shrugged. "Even the sorceress, Marienne. But all dragon shifters have a mate. Some just happen to be human. You probably have shifter ancestry in your bloodline, if you go back far enough."

I didn't know how to begin unpacking *that.* The thought that one of my grandparents, my great-grandparents, could be one of those creatures...

My alarm must have shown on my face because Cass chuckled. "Come on. Why don't we go down to the kitchens and get some hot chocolate? It's so draughty up here."

I clambered to my feet alongside her and shook my head. "Thanks for the offer, but I think I should go back and find Dymitri."

I had no idea what I wanted to say, but talking to Cass had cleared away some of my worries. I was going home anyway. My time here was limited only to the time it took for Nadia to wake up and become well enough to travel.

Maybe I could just take this one step at a time and see where the road led me—and the first step was to talk things through with my so-called "mate".

Cass smirked. "Okay. Go find him."

I turned to walk away, then chuckled. "I could use a hand getting back, if you don't mind?"

Cass laughed and slid her arm into mine. "Not at all."

DYMITRI

I stood with my eyes closed under the jet of scalding water, inhaling the steam that rose around me. I pushed my wet hair back from my face before letting my hands drop to my sides again.

My fists clenched as another wave of regret swept through me.

I've screwed everything up. I've driven her away, forever.

Lust still churned inside me, and my shifter thrashed ceaselessly, furious at being ignored. But it was muted due to the pain. I'd made my mate run away, and I couldn't forgive myself for that.

I let out a deep sigh. She would want to leave now; I was sure of it. And it was no one's fault but my own.

I was in the middle of working out how I would explain myself to Cass and Damon when the door to the room outside opened and closed softly, and light footsteps followed.

They paused outside the bathroom door. Whoever was out there was listening to the shower, hesitating.

I imagined one of the servants there on the threshold, one hand on the doorknob.

I opened my mouth to tell them to leave. Whatever royal business it was could wait; I needed to clear my head and make preparations to take Sarah home.

The thought pierced like a knife through my heart.

If she won't stay with me, the least I can do is make sure she gets back to her family safely.

Before I could say anything, the door opened, and the person stepped into the bathroom. I watched their progress as they crossed the room. The shower cubicle was large, but the glass was too fogged up to see clearly who it was. I caught a blur of movement as they came closer.

My heart rate picked up. I recognized that small frame, the blonde hair, and that scent. Her beautiful, enticing scent.

Sarah stepped out of her garments, one after the other, leaving them on the floor where they lay. By the time she reached the glass door behind me, I was hard and wanting.

The door opened.

Sarah stood naked before me. My gaze raked over every inch of her creamy skin, devouring the vision she presented. Her pert breasts, her rosebud nipples, the graceful curve of her hipbones... all of it set me on fire.

My cock was already skyward. I couldn't remember ever wanting—no, *needing*—anyone as much as I wanted Sarah in this moment. I didn't know where I wanted to put my mouth first, but I stopped myself from moving, staying rooted to the spot as she joined me under the hot spray of water.

She looked up at me with wide eyes. She stood a hair's breadth away, close enough that I could feel the heat from her skin. Small droplets ran down from her hair, racing over her chest and stomach.

Still, I waited. "Are you sure?" I managed, though my voice was a mere croak. The last thing I wanted to do was scare her away again.

"Yes. Touch me," she whispered.

Those three words were all it took. With a groan, I took her face in my hands and kissed her, bringing her up on tiptoe and pressing her against my body. She was so soft, so willing.

I didn't know what had changed between earlier and now, but it wasn't the moment to stop and ask. From the way she was nibbling my bottom lip it was clear that she wanted me now. And that was enough for me, and my shifter.

We stumbled over to the tiled wall, and my hands slid under her wet thighs. I urged her upwards, wordlessly encouraging her to wrap her legs around my waist. She gasped, clinging to me like a lifeline. Her lips brushed my neck, and I shuddered, driving forward with her until she was pressed up against the damp tiles, spread out for me.

I lifted her higher and set my lips to her breasts, suckling her nipple deep into my mouth. First one perfect rose tip, then the other.

Sarah writhed against the wall, clinging to my head and filling the shower stall with her gasps.

I held her with one arm and moved my other hand to tease her flesh. I flicked my thumb over her clit, again and again, until she was crying out against me. Then, and only then, did I slowly slide one finger up into her tight pussy.

I groaned as she wrapped around my finger, her walls slick and ready for me. I added a second finger to stretch her some more. She wriggled and groaned as I thrust inside of her, listening to her gasps as a guide to what she wanted.

When she tightened around my finger, and her gasps became too loud to hold back anymore, I withdrew my fingers and grabbed her thighs with both hands.

With her arms looped around my shoulders, it was easy for me to slide into her. She was slick even under the force of the shower, and I groaned as I sank into her depths. *Perfection.*

Her heels drummed into the small of my back, and I began to thrust into her tight pussy, listening to her cry out in pleasure and allowing the sounds to drive my own desire higher.

"Please," she whined, pressing her face into my shoulder. "Dymitri... *please.*"

I groaned at the sound of her pleading, and continued to drive into her over and over, unrelenting with the need to claim her as mine. She weighed practically nothing, and it was easy to slide a hand free to get between our bodies and circle her clit with my fingers.

She squirmed with the extra teasing and her channel walls clamped tight on my cock. We were both wound up from earlier, and it wasn't long before the desperation in her voice told me she was about to climax.

I dropped my head to her neck, growling into the damp skin, sensing her fluttering pulse under my tongue. When I nipped at the skin, she cried out and began to buck in my arms as I felt her cum around me.

My shifter growled in satisfaction, and I tumbled over the edge after her, filling her with my seed and bonding us together at last.

CHAPTER
EIGHT

Sarah

I woke up in a sea of soft sheets, a deep blue canopy above my head.

Blinking the sleep out of my eyes, I sat up, confused. This bed was massive, much bigger than the one in the room my sister still slept in...

My eyes landed on the man standing opposite the bed. He was staring out the window, lost in thought. My eyes lingered on the broad line of his shoulders, and my stomach curled with satisfaction as I remembered the night before.

My limbs dragged under the weight of the heavy blankets, soft and sated with the multiple orgasms Dymitri had given me last night. I stretched my arms above my head, taking a second to luxuriate.

"Good morning." Dymitri's deep voice provoked a smile across my face. "Did you sleep well?"

I nodded shyly, pulling back the sheets and hopping out of bed. I was still naked from last night's activities, but I found a robe lying over the back of a nearby chair and slipped it on before joining him at the window.

"I want you to join me today." Dymitri slid his arm around my waist, and I leaned into his warmth. "Damon and Cass are back from their honeymoon. They're waiting for us down in the Great Hall."

"I actually bumped into Cass yesterday," I admitted, my face heating. At Dymitri's questioning look, I shook my head. "Doesn't matter. Sure, that sounds great."

We headed downstairs together, pausing to check on Nadia. She was exactly the way I'd left her yesterday. The maid, Isla, was there watching over her.

"Any change?" I brushed my fingers over Nadia's forehead and squeezed her hand briefly.

"It's hard to tell," Isla said with a small frown. "Her heartbeat seems stronger today. But only time will tell when she wakes up."

"Thank you for looking after her," I murmured, a wave of guilt crashing over me. I hadn't been here watching her. Isla had. I'd been enjoying myself, making love to Dymitri while my sister lay here unconscious.

"Of course." Isla bobbed a curtsey to me as we left the room.

Dymitri pressed a kiss against the top of my head.

"She's in good hands," he murmured. His gaze slid back toward the room as we wandered further down the corridor. "Strange. I expected to find my brother in there."

I looked up at him, confused. "What do you mean?"

Dymitri shrugged. "If you were the one in that bed, I wouldn't have left your side. I'd be in there night and day until you woke."

A flood of warmth filled my chest.

"I guess he doesn't know her. She's just a stranger to him... and it's not like she's not well looked after."

A small crease appeared between Dymitri's brows. "I suppose."

I stood on tiptoe so I could kiss the frown off his face. "Come on. I'm hungry."

As soon as we stepped into the Great Hall, I gasped. A fire roared in the fireplace and a huge oak dining table was laden with all kinds of delicious-smelling food.

Dymitri laughed at the amazed look on my face. "It's something, isn't it?"

My eyes skimmed over the plates heaped with bread, the trays of sweet pastries, the huge silver coffee pot.

"I..."

It was like something out of a movie... or a long-forgotten dream. It was amazing.

At the head of a nearby table, Cass stood up and waved to me, her fork clattering onto her plate in obvious excitement.

"Sarah!"

King Damon himself stood up more slowly, subdued and regal in his movements. He nodded toward me and Dymitri. "Good to see you again, brother."

I glanced at Dymitri, not sure what to do.

Do I bow? Curtsey? Oh, God...

Before I could worry myself further, Dymitri strode forward and grasped Damon's hand, pulling him into a loose hug. When he stepped back, he was grinning. "How was the honeymoon?"

Damon's face relaxed into a smile. "A little warmer than I'm used to."

"We saw the coral reefs!" Cass interjected, sending a dimpled grin her husband's way. "It was *amazing*."

She turned to me, grabbing my arm and tugging me over to sit beside her. "I wish we could build a diving pool here, but it's way too cold. We might as well build an ice rink."

She picked up a piece of fruit, nibbling on it thoughtfully.

"We have the hot springs, love." Damon poured her a cup of something red from a nearby jug. The look they shared as he handed it to her was full of love.

"Hot springs?" I raised an eyebrow at Dymitri.

"The castle is built on top of a system of them," he said, passing me the plate of pastries. "I'll show you later. But right now, please eat."

I took a bite of pastry, closing my eyes in pleasure. It was heaven to eat proper food again, after all this time.

The door opened at the other end of the hall and Lucian appeared, looking as downcast as he had when I saw him previously. Dymitri hurried over to speak to his brother. They stood in front of the fireplace exchanging words in low, hushed voices.

Cass nudged my shoulder, and I tore my gaze away from the scene.

"Are they always like that—so private?" I asked the queen.

"Pretty much." Cass took a bite out of a roll and chewed thoughtfully. "They only had each other to depend on for years. And old habits die hard, I guess."

A deep frown appeared on Dymitri's face. Whatever Lucian was saying, it looked like Dymitri didn't want to hear it.

Seeing the two of them like that, silhouetted against the fireplace, it occurred to me once again just how different Dymitri was to me. He and his brother were so alike: tall and strong, with striking pale eyes. As the firelight flickered across the planes of their faces, they looked... formidable. *Inhuman.*

Which I guessed, was the actual truth.

Soon after their discussion ended, Lucian left the hall without even speaking to the rest of us. Dymitri returned to the table and his unsmiling face filled me with unease. His apprehensive expression was a far cry from the warmth and intimacy we'd shared this morning.

"Isn't Lucian joining us?" Cass leaned forward, sounding concerned.

Dymitri shook his head. "He's going for a walk. He needs some... space."

Damon and Cass exchanged worried glances. I couldn't help but feel out of the loop, but the sensation faded away when Dymitri put his hand on mine, drawing my attention.

"Come on." He pushed a strand of hair behind my ear and tilted my chin upwards with his fingertips. "Let's finish eating, then I'll show you around the gardens."

~

THE NEXT FEW days followed a strange, but increasingly familiar pattern.

I would wake up with the sunlight hitting my face every morning, cocooned by Dymitri's warmth and solid arms. After an hour or so of mind-blowing sexual pleasure, we usually wandered downstairs to eat breakfast with the others.

I always checked on Nadia on the way to the breakfast room, and while she seemed to have a better color and was breathing more easily now, she still had not woken. The physician assured me my sister was mending, and would wake when she was ready. He had added a tube to her arm, via which she was receiving valuable hydration, and she seemed to be cared for very well.

At breakfast, Dymitri and I would chat with Cass and Damon, and I would ask as many questions as I could. They were helping me to understand the way things operated within the castle and this kingdom, and I found everything about the wintry palace fascinating.

Through the three of them, I learned something of the history between the brothers and their father... but only fragments. Whenever I tried to question Dymitri further on the king, he would often clam up, or drag me toward some distraction or other.

The castle itself was huge and rambling, with hundreds of abandoned rooms. Dymitri often went out on scouting trips with Damon or his brother. Their dragons kept an eye out for enemies that might be crossing the vastness to attack us.

When they did that, I would check in on Nadia, and then Cass and I busied ourselves with exploring the castle.

According to Cass, a couple of years ago, the castle had been, in her words, "a total wreck". Things were changing now that Damon had taken the throne. But there was still a ton of renovation work to be done, not only here at the castle, but right throughout the kingdom. But before the rest of the healing could happen, all the junk from centuries past had to be organized.

That was where we came in.

One day, Cass and I were in a small tower room that felt like it hadn't seen daylight for years. She was standing on top of a small pile of broken furniture and old boxes, digging around like a determined hamster.

"Ah, ha!" She stood upright and grinned at me. "Victory!"

I peered at the object she'd unearthed. "A cradle? *That's* what we've been searching for this whole time?"

"I *knew* I'd seen it somewhere." Cass hopped down from the pile and began to tug on a box almost half her size, trying to shift it over. "It doesn't look like anyone's used it for years."

With a sigh, I moved forward to help her. "What do you need a cradle for?"

"You know," Cass said evasively. "Just in case."

I stared at her, puzzled. Then it dawned on me. She was newly married, and from what I knew about dragon mates, they were insatiable in the bedroom. My own experience with Dymitri had already taught me that.

"Are you pregnant? Not that you look it, of course..." My cheeks heated, and Cass burst out laughing.

"No! But it's never a bad idea to look to the future, right?"

"I guess." I still felt confused as to why she'd been so determined to find the cradle, but I figured it was best to go along with her.

Cass tugged the carved wooden cradle free from a tangle of old curtains, wiped away the dust on her hands, and turned to me.

"Sarah, are you happy?"

I looked up at her, startled. "Under the circumstances... surprisingly, yes." I bit my lip, fiddling with the cuff of my sleeve. "Other than my sister's condition, of course. I know she's healing, but I do wish she'd wake up."

Sometimes, I caught myself feeling terrified, right in the middle of a moment of pure bliss. It was a horrible feeling, but my worry for Nadia cast a shadow over the surreal happiness I'd found here. Until she woke up and I saw for myself that she really was going to be okay, I'd never be truly at peace.

Cass seemed satisfied with my answer. We climbed down from the tower to move on to other rooms, and I put the conversation out of my mind.

Until a couple of days later, when Dymitri and I were enjoying the hot springs, and he asked a similar question.

"Do you like it here?" His voice came out of the silence, echoing along the damp cave walls.

I was floating in the beautifully warm water with closed eyes when he spoke. I opened my eyes and lowered my feet to the floor of the pool, lazily regarding him. Condensation dripped all around us, and the steam rising from the surface of the water obscured his expression. I moved closer through the water and took one of his hands loosely in mine beneath the surface.

"Of course." I leaned backwards, floating on my back and staring up at the arched ceiling above us. "Everyone keeps asking me that. What's not to like?"

Dymitri was silent for a long moment. I reach out and brushed my fingers over his chest, tracing loose patterns across his firm shoulders. By now I knew every scar, every burn. Some of them I'd heard stories about, but the origin of other scars was still a mystery to me.

"The weather?" he said with a smile, trailing his fingertips along my collarbones. We were both naked, and the sensation made me shiver despite the lightness of his touch.

"I don't know." I slid through the water, and his hand dropped lower, cupping my breasts and thumbing my nipples with his broad, calloused fingers. I arched against him encouragingly. "It's growing on me."

His face broke into a grin, and he dipped his head to kiss me. I returned the kiss eagerly, groaning when he caught my bottom lip between his teeth.

When he pulled back, I whined, wanting more. But his eyes had turned serious. He held me at arm's length, just gazing deep into my eyes. My heart started to patter.

"What is it?"

Dymitri's hands slid up to cup my face, his touch achingly gentle. "Sarah... I want you to stay here."

My heart fluttered and a wash of confusion swept over me. "I'm already staying here. Until Nadia wakes up, right?"

I thought I'd been clear about that?

He huffed. "I mean, I want you to stay here with *me*, Sarah. Forever. You're my mate. I don't want us to be apart."

My shock must have shown on my face because he slid his fingers under my chin, forcing me to meet his eye. "You said it yourself—you're happy here. And for the first time in my life, I feel..." He closed his eyes and drew a deep breath before opening them again. "I feel at peace. There's nothing I want more than to share my life with you."

Was it my imagination, or did the water temperature suddenly drop several degrees? It felt as if the previous tranquility of the moment shattered; the steam around us pressed against my skin, and a jolt of claustrophobia made me reel back from his touch.

"Sarah." Dymitri's eyes darkened with confusion. "Surely you can't be surprised by this. You're my mate—it's natural I should want you here. I *need* you."

But I was already backing away, swimming over to the edge of the pool and climbing out of the water. I grabbed blindly for the nearest towel and began drying myself. My hands trembled.

"Come on." The tension in Dymitri's voice made me flinch. "At least let's talk about this!"

"I have to check on my sister," I informed him, pulling my overshirt down and drawing the laces on my boots. "She needs me."

"Sarah!" The water lapped over the edge of the pool as Dymitri swam across. "You're being unreasonable."

Anger burned in my chest. "*I'm* being unreasonable? You're the one who wants me to leave *everything* behind—my family, my home, my own *world*—to live in a place I don't even know! I'm not part of this world, Dymitri! I never will be!"

He opened his mouth as if to speak, those pale eyes gleaming like shards of ice. But instead of replying as I expected him to, with more placating tones to try and persuade me to stay, he gritted his teeth and growled at me. "Go, then!"

"Fine!"

I stormed over to the exit and blundered out of the cave, tears blurring my vision. I thought Dymitri might follow me, but he didn't, so I made my way back to the castle alone. By the time I arrived at the oak doors, a light fall of snow dusted the tops of my boots. I stamped them clean and hurried toward the main staircase.

He's crazy. I'm crazy! I got so caught up with him I forgot why I'm still here in the first place!

After all, didn't I have a family and a whole life waiting for me back home?

By the time I made it to Nadia's room, my anger had cooled down significantly. I was beginning to feel the first pangs of regret. Dymitri was a wonderful person and I knew that I'd never find anyone else who made me feel the way he did.

I need to talk to him.

That could wait, however. First, I needed to check on my sister because everything hinged on her and her health. Once she awoke, I knew that she'd be desperate to get home. To our family, our friends. Our lives.

And I'd have to go with her, because, just like I'd said to Dymitri, I didn't belong here in this world. Going home, to my own world, and my own life, was the right thing to do.

It was strange how that thought didn't feel *right* at all.

CHAPTER
NINE

Dymitri

I waited in the pool until I was certain Sarah had gone.

My head thundered with pain, and regret pushed through me with the strength and heat of dragon fire. I'd been so sure that she felt the same way I did, but the look on her face when I'd asked her to stay here told me otherwise.

How could I have gotten it so wrong?

With a deep sigh, I heaved up to sit on the stone ledge. I glared down at my darkened reflection in the water as another wave of guilt crashed over me.

Ever since Damon had asked Lucian and I to stay in the castle with him, I'd been waiting for the other shoe to drop. For final confirmation, once and for all, that everyone would realize I didn't belong here. That I wasn't *worth* saving from the life I'd once barely survived.

I hadn't expected trouble to come in the form of a small human woman. She'd turned my world upside down in a few short days, and my life would never be the same.

My father's face swam up to the surface in my memories, just as foreboding and distant as he looked in that royal portrait in the castle.

"You're no son of mine." His remembered words reverberated through my brain. *"You are nothing."*

And now, my mate had rejected me, too. I was nothing to anyone.

Even Lucian had grown distant recently. At first, I'd attributed it to his worry over his mate, but whatever it was seemed to run deeper than that. He had always been taciturn, but now his continued silence had started to weigh heavily on me. Whatever it was, he had cut me off, which left me powerless to help him.

I had no place in the castle. Not anymore.

I swirled the water, breaking my reflection into pieces. Perhaps it was time to give up this life for good. I could head back out into the wilds. I'd survived there my whole life, after all. The life of a nomad was a lonely one—little more than hunting, ice-fishing, and basic survival. But at least I wouldn't hurt anyone else.

Everyone I loved, I hurt.

I jerked upright, my chest tight with a sudden realization.

I *loved* Sarah. With everything I had. This wasn't just passion and desire. This was *love*.

She was my mate, and I'd ruined things with her when they'd barely even begun.

And now I sitting here wallowing in self-pity, thinking about giving up on that love.

No. I was stronger than that. Better. And she deserved more than that from me.

As terrifying as it was to face the thought of more rejection, I knew I couldn't give up on Sarah. On us. Not at the first obstacle thrown in our path.

I scrambled up, disregarding the slick, damp stone underfoot as I raced to get dressed.

If she was truly my mate, then I would never give up on her.

~

I BURST through the castle doors and almost barreled into Lucian, who steadied me with both hands.

"Dymitri! What's wrong?"

I gaped at him, unsure where to begin. I felt like I'd just solved the world's greatest puzzle... and he was looking at me like I'd lost my mind.

"Nothing," I said, shrugging him off. "I'm fine. Just looking for Sarah."

Lucian arched an eyebrow. "Funnily enough, she just sent me down here to find *you*. Is everything okay between you two?"

My stomach twisted.

"I don't know," I admitted. "Wait, she's trying to find me? Why?"

Lucian's face was so pale and still, it may as well have been carved from stone. "Nadia's waking up."

My heart jumped at what that might mean. Without another word, I followed him toward the huge staircase. For once, I didn't pause to glance at the royal portrait that hung above the stairwell landing. Still, I could feel our father's eyes burning into the back of my head with every step.

I jogged to catch up with Lucian's retreating back. "Your mate is finally waking up. That's a good thing, right?"

Lucian glanced at me with a blank expression. "Of course."

His tone didn't fill me with confidence. The distance between us yawned like a vast expanse.

He nudged my shoulder. "What's the matter with Sarah?"

Quickly, I told him about our argument. How she wanted to return to the human realm and considered her time here nothing but a brief, forced holiday.

I fought to keep the misery out of my voice, but from the look on my brother's face, I could tell he wasn't buying it.

"Give her time," he said.

"She's a human and we're not." I sighed. "I understand her reservations, kind of. But I don't know if I can just... let her go. Now that I've found her, I can't imagine ever going back to the way things were before."

Lucian frowned. "Maybe that's the problem. She needs to talk to someone in her position, someone who's been through this before. You should take her south, to meet Queen Lucy. A human woman who became a dragon queen." He nudged me again. "She's bound to give her some good advice, from a perspective that we simply don't have."

I mulled his suggestion over in my mind. It wasn't actually a bad idea. I had to fight against my natural instinct to solve the problem on my own, but this wasn't about my ego, after all. It was about what was best for Sarah.

I hadn't met a happier couple than Lucy and Stavrok. I'd heard of their family, too: three healthy babies for the royal bloodline.

I suppressed a wave of envy.

I'd never given much thought to having a family. Up until recently, my life had been an unpredictable gauntlet of chaos and danger, hardly a fit environment in which to bring up a child. I'd lived the life of a warrior. Things like tenderness and beauty were distant dreams; they belonged to other lives, not mine.

Until the day I met Sarah.

"Maybe," I said with a grunt, eventually.

To my relief, Lucian didn't press me further. We reached the door to Nadia's room, and he paused.

"Hey." I put my hand on his shoulder. "You've got this."

I waited until he gave me a nod before I pushed open the door.

Sarah

I sat at the edge of Nadia's bed, holding my breath. Beside me, Isla hovered, folding blankets and fluffing the pillows on my old bed. The silence stretched out as we both watched the face of the sleeping woman.

Nadia sighed and frowned a little in her sleep. She drew a small breath, and her eyes opened softly.

"There," Isla whispered. "And just like that, she's back with us."

I couldn't contain the smile that broke across my face. "Hey, sleeping beauty."

My sister waking up was the most beautiful thing I'd ever seen, even with dark shadows under her eyes and hair that hadn't been washed in weeks.

Tears gathered in my eyes.

"Sarah…" Nadia mumbled, then lifted her head a little. A puzzled frown scrunched her forehead. "What happened? Where am I?"

Her expression was so familiar my heart clenched in my chest. I flung my arms around her neck, pressing my damp face into her hair.

"It's a long story." I sobbed. "I'm so glad you're okay."

Gently, Nadia extracted herself from my hug and blinked. "How long was I out?"

"Okay, don't freak out." I took her hand gently in both of mine. "Just over a week."

Not counting the time we were trapped under that house.

Nadia's face turned ashen. I picked up a glass of water from the bedside table and helped her take a shaky sip.

"Sarah…" she said, once I put down the glass. "Where *are* we?"

I glanced up at Isla. She gave a small shrug, looking just as lost as I felt.

How the hell do I explain this situation? I can barely wrap my head around it myself.

Luckily for me, a distraction arrived when the door opened and Lucian and Dymitri slipped through into the room.

My eyes locked onto Dymitri. A hundred emotions raced through me when I met those familiar ice-blue eyes. Guilt, regret, and confusion were the strongest ones of all.

"Sarah?" Nadia said in a small voice. She swung her legs off the side of the mattress and sat up slowly, gripping my arm for support. "Who are they?"

Right. The drama between Dymitri and me could wait. There were far more pressing matters to hand.

Like the fact that Lucian's mate had woken up, and he was confronting her for the first time. Would it be instant, like it had been for Dymitri and me?

Dymitri took another step into the room, shutting the door behind them. Lucian remained where he was, rooted to the spot. His face looked like a thunderstorm was brewing within him.

Dymitri glanced over his shoulder. "Brother, she's awake. Aren't you going to talk to her?"

Lucian still didn't move. He stared intently at Nadia. With every second that passed, the chill in the air grew stronger and stronger until it threatened to drown everything out.

"Lucian," Dymitri urged his brother again, then he glanced at me.

I was unsettled by the worry in his expression. Something was wrong.

I moved closer to Nadia, half-shielding her with my body. "What's wrong with him?"

"I don't know." Dymitri moved toward his brother and put a hand on his arm.

Lucian shook him off. His fists clenched tight. Even from my position beside the bed, I could see his white, strained knuckles.

"Lucian," Dymitri said, "you need to control yourself."

Lucian's lips pulled back into an unmistakable snarl, one I had only seen on Dymitri when he was about to change form. *Oh no.* I shrank back, pressing Nadia against the bed.

My sister wriggled out from around me and stood up, her hands on her hips. "Can someone *please* tell me what's going on?"

That was the last straw for Lucian, it seemed. The air thickened with dark fog, and a deafening roar reverberated off the stone walls around us.

"Sarah!" Dymitri shouted. *"Run!"*

A huge shadow loomed out of the mist. Lucian was in dragon form, his wings outstretched toward the high ceiling. One talon caught the candelabra above us and sent it swinging, before it crashed to the floor with a mighty boom.

I jumped as a burst of icy fire shot into the air. Nadia screamed.

I was afraid, too, but beyond the fear, fury rose. *How dare he threaten my sister? She's supposed to be his mate!*

My heart pounded in my chest at the realization that Lucian had gone insane.

Bloody hell.

"Stay behind me!" I yelled at Nadia, as the dragon circled around the edge of the room.

Before it could reach us, Dymitri dived in front of Nadia's bed to shield us from the monster.

I wanted to reach for him, but forced my arms back, trying to protect my terrified sister. "It's going to be okay," I gasped to her, not knowing if I believed the words.

Dymitri shifted right in front of us. Nadia cried out again, digging her nails into my arms, but I couldn't look away from him. He was magnificent.

Dymitri spread out his wings and snarled at his brother. Lucian barely paused at the sound, continuing to advance towards Nadia and me.

Oncethe mist cleared, I could see his eyes, narrow pale slits above sharp teeth. His scales were paler than his brother's, more of a dark gray. Icy flames rose up and burst out of his mouth, burning cold and dangerous. If Dymitri didn't do something to stop him, there would be nothing left of Nadia and me.

I turned to my sister and wrapped my arms around her, pulling her close. "Close your eyes. Hold on to me."

With a rumbling roar, Dymitri launched himself at Lucian. From behind, me, I heard the sounds of them fighting.

My breath caught in my throat, fear pulsing through my blood. Not just for myself and my sister, but for Dymitri. He was fighting his only family, his brother. The man everyone had said was his best friend. His closest ally.

He was fighting his brother... to protect Nadia and me.

The room was huge and high-ceilinged, but even the castle's strong architecture was no match for dragon wrath. Wings caught against wall hangings, claws tore into curtains, and tables and chairs were upended as they fought savagely.

I screamed and jumped out of reach, pulling my sister with me as a chair clattered against my leg. I hurried her over to the wall, pressing her into the stones and covering her with my body as best as I could.

Lucian released a jet of icy flames that blasted a nearby wardrobe; Nadia screamed and I forced her out of its path just in time to feel the icy chill whizz over our heads.

Dymitri snarled in my direction, and for a second, our eyes met.

Get out! he seemed to be screaming at me. *Take your sister and run!*

But I couldn't move. I couldn't leave him, useless as I was in this situation. If I left him alone in this fight, he might not walk out of it alive.

Lucian seemed to be savage with rage, tearing into everything in his path. I could feel the pain and heartbreak radiating off him, and I knew Dymitri would only be able to hold him off for so long. That much pain... he was inconsolable that Nadia was not his mate.

Nadia's hand squeezed tight around my arm.

"Sarah!" she screamed into my ear. "We need to leave! Right now. Hurry!"

My feet were rooted to the floor. I was torn; my brain told me I needed to take my sister and go, but my heart said something else.

Nadia grabbed my arm and half-dragged me over to the door. She threw it open and yanked us both into the corridor, slamming the door shut behind us.

"I have to go back in there." The words spilled out of my mouth before I could stop them, and my sister's eyes widened.

"Go back?" she hissed. "Are you *crazy*?"

"It's Dymitri." I twisted in her grasp, trying to break free, but she held me firm. "I *have* to make sure. I need him to be okay!"

More crashing and howling issued from inside that room, and I had no idea what was happening.

Was Dymitri hurt? What could I do to help him?

Tears of frustration filled my eyes and spilled down my cheeks.

"Dymitri?" Nadia repeated. "You *know* one of those—those *things*?" Her eyebrows crept to the top of her forehead. "No. You're not going back in there. We're getting out of here, Sarah. We're lucky we weren't killed already!"

Her eyes flickered across my face. There was a desperation in her expression that was new.

My heart sank. This was my baby sister. It didn't matter what I wanted, what I *needed*; I had to make sure that she was safe.

And if I went back into that room, I couldn't guarantee that she would be.

Another screaming roar echoed from inside the bedchamber, and we both flinched back from the door.

"All right," I said, admitting defeat. A small part of my heart broke, as I added, "Let's go."

TEN

Sarah

Nadia tugged me further and further away from Dymitri, my heart aching in my chest with every step.

"Come on, come on! We've gotta go!" she cried, dragging me down the main staircase and toward the front door.

It was only when we reached the bottom of the grand staircase that Nadia stumbled to a halt.

She stared up at the huge windows and elaborate stonework. "Whoa. What is this place?"

Our footsteps echoed loudly as we crossed the marble floor. I glanced down and realized that my sister was barefoot, and only wearing the long nightgown that the maids had dressed her in.

Damn it. She's going to freeze to death in this place.

I pulled off my jacket and wrapped it around her shoulders.

"A castle," I whispered. "Far away from home. Trust me, I'll explain everything."

Nadia shivered and pulled my jacket tighter around her. "Explain? You don't need to explain anything! We need to find a car and get home!"

Nadia's voice reached a squealing pitch and I reached out to grab her hand. "Please, calm down. We need to talk about this."

"What's there to talk about?" Nadia glared on me. "I wake up around strangers, and one of them suddenly turns into a monster and tries to kill me. Sound familiar?"

I remembered with a jolt that Nadia had been unconscious since the farmhouse. She knew nothing about this place. All the trauma and fear we'd suffered together was fresh in her memory.

"It's not like that," I replied, my voice weak. "These are good people."

"I'm leaving." Nadia's voice rang out, clear and certain. "And you should come with me. Please, Sarah. Let's go *home*."

Tears welled up in my eyes as I stared at her. I didn't know what to do anymore. Seeing Lucian as an out-of-control beast had horrified me, but I also knew it couldn't have come out of nowhere. Some shifter instinct had made him snap... something about Nadia.

If Nadia *wasn't* his mate, then who was?

Dymitri had shifted when he'd seen me, but he hadn't wanted to kill me; quite the opposite in fact. He'd been in complete control, desperate to seduce me but not without my cooperation in that fact. So, what had happened to Lucian for this to occur?

I frowned. When Dymitri had described the sorceress's vision, he'd seemed so certain about both of us. When I'd asked Cass about it, she'd agreed that Marienne had never been wrong before.

But everything was starting to add up. Lucian's cold demeanor around me and the way he seemed to have withdrawn from Dymitri since I'd arrived, even though the two of them had always been close.

"We should wait," I said.

"For *what?*" Nadia shook her head. "Come on, no one's guarding the doors. We have to get out while we still can!"

I opened my mouth to protest further, but before I could say anything, the sound of glass shattering from an upstairs window made us both scream and dive for the floor. Another crash of broken glass, this time closer, set cold air rushing over our bodies.

Oh, no. What was that? Did one of them escape the castle? That wasn't good.

"Nadia! Oh, my God!" I clutched my sister's hand, and we raced each other to the front door.

I glanced at the scene unfolding at the top of the stairs. Lucian and Dymitri twisted and rolled over one another, locked in battle on the hallway floor. Dymitri was trying desperately to stop Lucian from continuing his rampage of destruction, though I didn't know if he could do it. Not alone.

Where was Damon? Surely, he could step in and help Dymitri. These were his brothers, after all.

While I debated whether to start searching for Damon, Cass or in fact, anyone who might be able to assist, Nadia pulled open the front doors. A blast of chilly air hit me.

I spun around. "Nadia. No!"

But it was too late. My sister was fleeing down the castle stairs and out into the snow. Freezing air swept in. Behind me, the huge window, where the colored dragons had once danced through a glassy sky, lay in pieces on the floor. Bits of glass crunched under my boots as I headed for the doors, breaking into a run.

I didn't have a choice now. I had to follow her. The last time I didn't go after her, she'd almost died. I couldn't have that happen again.

"Nadia, come back!"

I chased her over the drawbridge, and through the narrow, winding streets of town. She was running in a hurried zigzag, like a scared rabbit, not paying attention to where she was going in her terror.

She knocked into food carts and market stalls, barreled through astonished onlookers, and carried on without stopping. She ran all the way to the narrow track that led out of the village and across the flat, barren wilderness that stretched as far as the eye could see.

"Nadia." I almost reached her, and tried to grab a hold of her, but she shrugged me off, continuing forward with her jaw set and her eyes narrowed. Her cheeks were streaked with dried tears. "Please," I begged. "You'll freeze. It's going to be dark soon. We have to go back."

"I'm not going back there." Nadia sniffed. Her bare toes curled against the snow-covered track, and I winced. "I'm going home."

I jumped in front of her and pushed my hands out, trying to stop her. She had no idea where we were, or just how far from home we really were. "You don't even know where home is from here."

"We're bound to run into a car eventually," she said, wrapping her arms around her chest. The jacket I'd given her covered her hands, making her look even younger than she was. "Seriously, you've been here this whole time?"

"I have." I ducked my head as I fell into step beside her. "I've been waiting for you to get better, so we could go home."

I thought back to the argument Dymitri and I had earlier, and my cheeks burned. The cold wind sliced into my face, and I pulled up the collar of my sweater. Now that I said it out loud, it sounded like a weak excuse.

It's not like I've sat by her bedside this whole time, waiting for her to wake up.

I shoved away the traitorous thought.

We were silent as we continued our trek. The terrain underfoot was getting rockier, and the sky overhead darkened by the minute. I wanted to turn back, but I sensed that Nadia wouldn't have any of it.

She would have to be freezing. Her poor feet must be numb by now.

I shivered, the clothes I wore not suitable for the cold air without my jacket.

"What were those things?" Her small voice broke through the stillness.

Inhaling a shaky breath, I answered her honestly. "Dragons."

I saw her eye-roll coming from a million miles away. "Very funny."

"I'm not joking." I waited until she caught my eye, and her expression sobered. "They're men who turn into dragons, and they're from a royal bloodline. Dymitri never really explained it beyond that. I'm not sure they even know how it works."

Nadia was quiet and my heart thumped as I watched the cogs turn in her head, putting the pieces together. The ancient, lavish castle she'd woken up in. The huge wings, the claws. The wardrobe engulfed in icy flames.

When she finally spoke, however, her question surprised me.

"You said that name before, back in that room. Dymitri." She nudged into my shoulder. "Who is he?"

I bit my lip, taking my time before answering her question. "He was there when I woke up. He thinks we're meant to be together."

Nadia snorted. "Like fate, and all that crap?"

"Actually..." My mouth twisted into a chagrined smile. "It's exactly like that, yeah."

"That's some crazy Stockholm Syndrome you've got there." Nadia shoved her hands into the pockets of my jacket. "Seriously, you meet a guy, he tells you he loves you and you don't ask any other questions? The Sarah I know would *never* have acted like that."

"That's not..." My cheeks burned.

I didn't know how to make her understand. My feelings for Dymitri ran deep, but I could barely understand them myself, let alone talk about them out loud.

"It's not like that," I said eventually. "He's a good man. He was trying to protect us earlier, Nadia."

"I know what I saw back there," Nadia replied. "Two out-of-control monsters fighting. I don't care what you think he is—he's no different from the one who tried to kill us."

I sighed, with no idea what to say in response.

We continued on in silence. But with every step we took, the panic in my chest twisted tighter and tighter. The castle was nothing but a dark, murky expanse on the bare horizon behind us now.

I can't abandon her, and I can't convince her to come back to the castle with me. We're stuck.

What the hell am I going to do?

~

By the time I finally managed to persuade Nadia to stop, a howling wind had picked up in the shallow ravine in which we found ourselves.

The snow, which had started off light enough, brushing our shoulders like icing sugar, began to fall faster and thicker. Every direction was a haze of swirling whiteness; it didn't matter which way we turned, everything looked the same. We had no way of knowing which direction the castle lay.

At some point I'd forced Nadia to put on my boots, because her feet were cut and bleeding from walking so long without shoes. I cursed loudly as I struggled over the rocky terrain in my socks.

Now it was my feet almost numb with cold, and I began to worry about frostbite. Or worse.

My heart hammered with terror and disorientation.

We are in so much trouble.

When Nadia's hand slackened in mine, I tightened my grip in alarm. If I lost her out here, we might never find each other.

But she was signaling toward something. Blinking back the driving snow, I made out a shallow crevice in the rocks up ahead, large enough for two people to wriggle into.

It was the only chance of shelter that had presented itself. Staying outside in these conditions would get us nowhere; our only chance was to stay put somewhere sheltered, like this small crevice, and hope that the snow eased up enough that we could get our bearings.

Or maybe Dymitri will find us. I tucked the stray thought away. Given he was probably still in battle with his brother, that scenario was unlikely.

Nadia curled up around me once we were inside the tiny shelter. Her head dropped onto my shoulder, and within a couple of minutes she was asleep.

Was that a good thing? I had read somewhere about not going to sleep in the snow, but she had literally just woken up from a long illness. Perhaps I should leave her to sleep for a while?

I tugged my jacket around the both of us as best I could.

How did this happen? It seemed like minutes ago, I was in Dymitri's arms in the heat of the hot springs cave, safe, warm, and protected.

Loved.

Now, we were miles away from the castle, trapped in what was fast becoming a blizzard of epic proportions. At least in this tiny crevice, we were shielded from the worst of it.

Nadia snuggled closer to me, letting out a soft breath. I could feel her heartbeat against mine and cuddled her close. She wasn't a baby anymore. She was nineteen, but still, I could remember what it was like to hold her when she was really young.

She was still weak, and despite how incredibly stupid it had been to walk this far in the snow, tears gathered in my eyes for how grateful I was to have her alive, and with me. I'd been so close to losing her forever.

I pressed my face against the top of her head. Despite everything, I couldn't blame her for reacting the way she had in her fragile, traumatized state. I could imagine how it had looked to her. How it *sounded.* If I were in her shoes, I might have fled just as fast.

My thoughts drifted back to the castle.

What if Lucian has totally lost control? It might take Dymitri all night to calm him down. If he is able to, at all. What if Lucian hurt Dymitri? What if he... No. Don't think the worst.

My toes curled up in the thick socks. At least, I think they did. It was hard to tell, as my whole feet were numb from all the time we'd spent out here in the frozen weather.

I don't think we'll last all night out here.

I tried to distract myself by wondering what the sorceress had in mind for Lucian. If Nadia wasn't his mate, then who was? *Sisters.*

A thought glowed in the back of my mind. A fragment of conversation, something Dymitri had said.

You probably have shifter ancestry in your bloodline, if you go back far enough.

A realization began to form in my mind. Something that was so obvious, now that I looked at it, I wondered why I hadn't thought of it before.

If we ever made it through this night alive, and I found my way back to Dymitri, I would let him know. *I wonder...*

I DIDN'T KNOW how much time had passed.

All I knew was that it was pitch black. The wind howled over the rocks above us, and the occasional blast of snow made me squeeze my eyes shut tight against the cold.

The night seemed endless. The storm raged on around us, huge and unstoppable. Nadia and I were just two tiny specks in the face of such a vast and untamable beast.

I'm sorry, sister. I've failed you. I've failed both of us.

Weirdly, I didn't feel as cold as I had before. A lazy warmth was burrowing its way through my bones like a thick blanket. My eyelids were heavy; I wanted desperately to close them, to go to sleep for just a second...

My eyes snapped open. A single thought struck through my mind, clear and simple: *If you go to sleep, you'll die.*

I pulled my sister closer to share our body heat and forced myself to stay awake. My thoughts immediately went to Dymitri, and what had passed between us during this time.

I'd fallen in love with him, and that hadn't been in my plans. Not at all. A month ago I'd been a college student, wanting to party, and study, and have fun while I was young. But then we'd been taken, and every breath had been painful. At times I'd wanted it all to be over. Just so I could get away from the tragedy of what had become of us.

And then we'd been given a second chance at life. Or at least, *I* had been. And while I was with Dymitri, all my college plans had seemed stupid. Small in the bigger scheme of things.

I'd had a dragon prince rescue me and want to be with me forever. What more could there be in this world than to be with him? If I really was honest with myself, all I wanted to do was love Dymitri, and make him feel needed. He'd never had that, and he deserved it. I wanted to give him a baby, who would adore him as much as I did.

And if I got another chance, I'd tell him all of this. That I was his. And he was mine. And despite everything, family obligation, my plans, nothing else mattered now.

The more my thoughts wandered, the more I struggled to remember why that would be such a bad thing. My limbs were stiff, and my thoughts were sluggish, weighed down by the snow and cold.

I sent a silent prayer out to the world. There was nothing we could do now; our only hope of rescue came from the man whose love I had turned away mere hours ago.

My eyelids drooped as my vision became hazy. With every ounce of strength I had left in me, I repeated one thing in my mind, again and again. *Dymitri. Please... we're here. Come find us!*

ELEVEN

Dymitri

The wind howled down through the shattered window above us.

I stood over my brother, glaring down on him. We had shifted back to human, and our chests heaved with residual anger. Twin furies simmered in the air between us, and for a hot second, I thought he was going to get up and take another swing at me, this time in human form.

But he didn't. His head slumped down against his chest, face falling into shadow.

"She's not my mate, brother." Lucian's voice was broken with despair. "When I looked at her... I... I felt *nothing*."

I dropped my gaze, my chest twisting. It had always been the same way between us: Lucian's sorrow was my sorrow; his happiness was my happiness. This was all wrong. We should be celebrating the recovery of his mate right now...

Instead, both Sarah and Nadia were gone. Vanished.

By the time Lucian had calmed down enough to shift back, dusk was gathering, and long shadows crept toward us over the marble floor.

I cast my eye around at the destruction we'd wrought on our brother's castle. We were surrounded by a mass of broken shards.

"I know," I whispered. "I'm sorry."

"How could the sorceress have been wrong?" Lucian met my eyes. Now all the rage and destruction had passed, I saw him for what he was. What he'd always been. My little brother. Grieving for something that had never existed at all. "You and Sarah..."

"She's my mate," I said, my voice firm. "But she wants to leave. So, it looks like we'll both be alone after all."

My bitter voice echoed off the cold stone. Lucian rose to his feet, shaking his head.

"No." He tilted his chin up. "You hear me? No. We're going to get them back. *Both* of them."

"You don't have to help me do that."

"Yes, I do." Lucian wiped a hand over his face before surveying the chaos around us. "I owe you that much. They left because of me."

I didn't have an answer for that. He wasn't wrong, after all.

"I'm not going to endanger your happiness any more, just because I haven't found mine." Lucian's eyes were like shards of ice as they stared past me, out through the open doors where snow had begun to fall. "Let's find them, and bring them back alive."

Lucian and I took to the air.

Flying in tandem like this again, it was like things were back where they should be. With Lucian by my side, I soared up toward the cloud banks that scudded high above the uppermost towers, circling around so I could look at the ground spread out far below us.

Even with full winter gear, this terrain was dangerous for two human women. On foot, there was only one track that led from the village below the castle; they wouldn't have had any option but to follow it.

I turned into a graceful spiral and dived through the air, dropping close to the ground to see if I could pick up their trail. Lucian followed me, right at my shoulder as always.

Fighting him had gone against every instinct I had, but in some ways, I was glad for it. Now the air between us was clearer, and we were on the same page again.

Lucian shifted course slightly as the road narrowed. Shallow, rocky outcrops sprouted up below us, snaking toward a dip in the landscape.

I had a good mental map of the terrain; Damon had shown us the king's lands from the air and on foot, and we were used to tracking our enemies over both.

But this was different. This was Sarah—and she was in danger. I could *feel* it.

I followed Lucian as we flew. The sun had vanished below the horizon and both the wind and snow had picked up. The weather and the cold got worse, and worse, until the storm was raging around us.

Sarah! My mind screamed for her. *Where are you?*

All around us, thick snowflakes whirled in icy droves. The wind battered our wings and darkness threatened to drown everything out. We pushed on through it all, searching through the storm, to no avail.

Sarah!

We couldn't give up. If we couldn't find them in time, they would both die.

Up ahead, the swirling blackness gave way. I spotted a faint light. It was nothing more than a blur at first, and I thought I was seeing things. But it didn't go away. It just hovered there, like a bright beacon.

I started toward the light. I met Lucian's eyes in the darkness. His gaze was blank; he hadn't seen anything.

But he trusted me, so we headed in that direction.

The light was coming from a shallow cave. It was little more than a crevice in the rockface, scarcely big enough for one person, let alone two.

But when I ducked my head, my heart almost stopped inside my chest.

Nadia and Sarah lay curled up around one another. I landed and nudged Sarah's shoulder, but she was unconscious.

At least, that was what I told myself. After everything we'd gone through together, I couldn't contemplate the alternative.

I leaned in and clawed my way through the stone, knocking aside a boulder, and pulled the two bodies from the wreckage. They were like rag dolls in my grasp, limp and icy.

My heart thudded with fear as I clutched Sarah close to my chest.

Please, let her be alive. Oh, God... please. I can't lose her. Not like this. If she wants to go home, so be it. But not like this.

Lucian took Nadia from me. We both inhaled deeply, letting our chests fill with smoldering warmth before we clutched their limp forms against us. For now, it was the best we could do to keep them warm, until we could get them back to the castle.

I stared into the black sky while the blizzard continued to howl around us. I pulled Sarah close with my claws and extended my wings out.

As one, Lucian and I launched ourselves into the air and flew the women home, to our brother's castle.

~

SARAH

My dreams were muddled and hazy. I'd been dipping in and out of them for what seemed to be an eternity, hovering in the space between sleep and wakefulness.

In one dream, I was back home, and my parents were talking in the next room. In another, I was at college. At one point, I had a nightmare. I was back in the basement, Nadia slumped beside me. And this time, it was my fault. It was *all* my fault...

When I finally came back to reality, a hand was holding mine, warm and soft. I gripped the fingers like they were a lifeline.

"Sarah...."

Hearing Dymitri's whispered voice, I turned my head to peer at him through half-opened eyelids. His other hand came up to cradle my fingers.

"You're awake."

Déjà vu. We've been here before.

I squeezed his hand again, harder this time.

"Ouch," he said. He didn't look hurt, though. With my human strength, I probably hadn't affected him at all.

"Sorry." I scrunched my face at the sound of my own voice. It was so thin and raspy, like I'd been crawling through a desert. *The irony.* "Just checking you're real, that's all."

"I'm real." His eyes were soft, and full of relief. "For a little while there, I thought I might lose you."

Nadia! I sucked in a quick breath. "My sister?"

Dymitri nodded. "She's fine. Recovering, like you, but she'll be okay."

I sagged with relief, then, with his help, I struggled upright. He shoved a couple more pillows behind my head until I was only half-reclined. I felt kind of stupid, but I let him fuss over me. It felt nice to have someone who cared that much.

"I'm not going anywhere," I said. "I promise."

He looked up sharply, taking in the weight of my words. We stared at each other for a long moment. We were alone. There were no other priorities. No distractions. Just the two of us.

"Do you mean that?" He lowered his gaze. "Because if you don't..."

"I do," I told him honestly. "When we were in that storm, I thought we were going to die. I had a lot of time to think about life. About what I wanted."

I took his face in my hands, tilting his head toward me. "Dymitri, it's you. You're what I want. I couldn't stop thinking about you... what I'd be letting go if I just walked away and went back to my old life." I pushed my forehead against his, inhaling softly. That delicious scent, always there to entice me. "I'm not sure I *can* walk away."

I felt the familiar rumble of his voice through my body when he answered. "I meant what I said, Sarah. I'd never hold you against your will. When you ran... I thought of how you must see me. A vicious beast. A monster." His voice turned fierce. "I'm not like those men who kept you in that basement, Sarah. With me, you'll always have a choice."

"I know." I pressed a kiss to his forehead. "And if we're really doing this, I need you to accept me. All of me. The human world will always be part of that."

"I can live with that." His face broke into a smile. "And to think, until recently, I'd never been south of the mountains."

I thought of all the things I wanted to do with him. Take him to the city, to my college. Introduce him to the rest of my family. Maybe we could have a road trip. My heart soared with the possibilities.

"You're not the only one caught between two worlds, Sarah." In a gesture that was now familiar to me, Dymitri tucked a loose strand of hair behind my ear. "My father never accepted me. For the longest time, I thought King Damon was my enemy. Even now, I walk these hallways wondering if everyone sees me the way I see myself—the bastard son of a tyrant."

He glanced toward the window, as if it was difficult for him to meet my gaze. I shifted closer, taking his hand and pulling him properly onto the bed. He came willingly, joining me under the mass of blankets.

"But you taught me that I was enough," he said. His arms slid down to my waist. I was still warm with sleep, but I shivered under his touch, nevertheless. "Everything—the good and the bad. Thanks to you, I can finally see a future for myself here."

I surged forward, catching his mouth with mine. He kissed me back passionately, tangling his hands in my hair. Before I could deepen the kiss, however, he pulled back.

"Wait," he panted, ignoring my frustrated whine. "Does this mean... you'll stay forever? You'll mate with me?"

"Yes." I pressed kisses everywhere on him I could reach. I burned with want, eager for his touch. "*Yes.* I'm yours, Dymitri."

His eyes darkened, and he let out an inhuman growl.

"That's right." His voice dropped even lower than usual. "You're mine."

I'd heard that growl once before, by the fireside. Then, it had frightened me enough that I ran to the other side of the castle.

Now, I felt the folds between my legs becoming wet and slick with anticipation.

He leaned into me and tightened his grip on my waist, pulling me into his lap. I slid my knees onto either side of him, rocking into his already hard length. I groaned as his cock pressed up against me, shivers of pleasure racing through my body.

It was the work of a moment for him to slide off my nightgown. Feeling my naked body against his clothed one was amazing, but I wanted to taste his bare skin. Without pausing, I pulled open his shirt halfway and began pressing open-mouthed kisses to his flesh.

You don't understand, I thought wildly. *You're* mine, *just as much as I'm yours.*

Once he shoved off his clothes, we came together again, twisting and rolling as our bodies slid together in ecstasy. He pinned me underneath him, holding my arms up against the headboard. I whined with need and arched against him as one of his huge hands bracketed my wrists. The other drifted downwards, toying with my nipple.

I bucked up again, grinding my hips into his until we both groaned.

"I need you inside me. Dymitri, *please.*"

His eyes darkened even further, and his lips came down onto mine as he lined himself up. He slid into me in one smooth stroke. I moaned and pushed back against him as much as I could, and he met my hips with his own, rutting into me over and over.

This wasn't like before. Before, our joining had been delicate and soft... almost sweet.

Now, it was a true claiming. I was his mate, and he was making me his own. I submitted to it willingly, taking everything he had to give, my body opening up around his cock like it was made just for him. Perhaps it was.

He surrounded me completely, covering my body with his as he made love to me. His hands slid down to my hips and pulled them higher so he could get a deeper angle, and I whimpered as he found my g-spot, my fingers clawing uselessly at the bedsheets. I was going to come soon; I could feel it building up inside me, like the crest of a wave, forceful and inevitable.

"Mine." He sucked at my bare neck as he continued to thrust relentlessly.

"Yours," I gasped out.

He released a low groan and I felt his cock pulse as he filled me with his seed. My pussy tightened around him at the realization that we were unprotected—he could be making me pregnant, right here and right now.

I couldn't hold it back anymore. The thoughts of everything our future might hold sent me tumbling over the edge, and wave after wave of pleasure crashed through my body. Dymitri fucked me through it, still pumping me full, and I took it all gladly.

When we finally collapsed beside one another, my head swam with happiness. I pressed a hand to my belly, letting out a long sigh.

All I wanted to do now was drift off to sleep. Safe and warm and replete in the arms of my mate.

Sarah

I must have fallen asleep, because too soon I woke to the sound of Dymitri shutting the door and re-entering the room.

I sat up in bed and smiled at him. "Hey. Where'd you go?"

"I went to check on your sister, and she's awake. Which is great."

I threw back the blankets and jumped out of bed. "I want to see her. Can we go now?"

Dymitri nodded, his jaw tight. "I think we all need to."

I frowned, not quite understanding. "Who's we?"

"Lucian and I. He wants to apologize to her, and sort things out between them. The castle has been very tense since our fight."

I bit my lip, then nodded. "Okay. But I'll word Nadia up first. She's only nineteen and has always been a little afraid of big men like your brother."

I pulled on the fresh clothes laid out for me on the side table, shivering with the coolness in the air. We'd been so cold in that small crevice, it gave me chills just thinking about it now.

"I'll take you to Nadia, then go and get Lucian. There's a lot to discuss."

I didn't ask what he meant. My only concern was getting to Nadia as soon as possible and seeing her alive and well again.

I'd really thought we were going to die out in the wilderness. Frozen to death, never to be seen again.

When I opened the door to her bedroom, Nadia jumped up from the bed. "Sarah!"

She raced for me, and I swept her up in my arms, holding her tight.

"I am so sorry." She sobbed against me, her small frame shuddering. "We almost died. And it's all my fault."

I pulled back from her and grabbed her hands. "Nadia, listen to me. You were terrified and had no idea where you were. Then those two brothers turned into dragons. Trust me, I know why you ran. I would have done the same thing the day I met them, if it wasn't for the fact that you were still unconscious and I had to wait for you to wake up."

Nadia brushed the tears from her cheeks. "Well... you did have another reason to stay."

I smiled and straightened up. "Dymitri."

I glanced behind me. He hadn't arrived yet. I took her hand and tugged her to the windowsill so we could speak quietly together.

"He's the one I want to be with, Nadia. I'm sorry I didn't get a chance to properly explain it all to you. Before."

She smiled softly at me. "It's okay. I understand."

I gripped her hand and squeezed her fingers. "You probably can't understand, but please know, he makes me so happy. I am totally in love with him."

She laughed. "I know. I can see it all over your face."

The guys were coming, their footsteps echoing in the hallway. "Then please trust me when I say, these men are good people."

The door opened and Dymitri stuck his head in. "Do you two want to join us for a drink in the dining hall?"

I jumped to my feet. "That's a great idea. We'll be right there."

Dymitri shut the door again and I couldn't help but smile at how thoughtful he was being.

"What's that about?" Nadia asked, already grabbing her coat.

"Lucian wants to apologize for what happened."

"Oh."

I slid my hand into the crook of her elbow and gently directed her out of the bedroom, and into the hallway. "He feels terrible about it. So please... just let him apologize, hun."

"Okay."

I led my sister to the dining hall, though I could feel her reticence. As far as she was concerned, these two men were monsters. I just happened to be in love with one of them.

The fire was blazing in the grate, and Dymitri sat with his brother at the table, waiting for us.

"Hot chocolates?" he asked, gesturing to the table where hot drinks were waiting, along with platters of sweets.

"Thank you," I said, sitting down and grabbing for a drink. "I'm famished."

I took a long sip of my hot chocolate and sighed as the sweetness ran over my tongue.

Dymitri cleared his throat. Lucian stared at the table, looking worried and slightly sick.

"Go on, brother."

Lucian looked up, his face hard and his jaw tight. "I need to apologize to you both, for my abhorrent behavior. I am... ashamed to have scared you in the way that I did."

Nadia gulped. "Oh. Lucian, I..."

"No," he said fiercely, shaking his head. "You both could have died, and that would have been my fault. If I'd only retained control over my dragon, none of this would have happened."

I glanced over at Nadia, whose eyes were filling with tears.

"It's okay. Really," I said. "You weren't in your right mind."

Lucian shook his head. "No, I was not."

Nadia stared at him. "Isla told me you saved me from those men back at the farm. You brought me here. You saved my life."

Lucian looked at her, his eyes wide and fearful. "Yes. But then I—"

"Why did you freak out like that?" she asked suddenly. "Was it something I said? Or did?"

"No! It was…" Lucian sighed, running a hand through his long dark hair and pushing it off his face. "I was ashamed. And angry. I'd been told you were my fated mate, but I don't feel those things for you that Dymitri obviously feels for Sarah."

"And when I woke up, I confirmed it was true, didn't I?" Nadia asked gently. "That I wasn't your soul mate."

He nodded, his throat working as he swallowed his pain. "Yes, and I… we…"

Dymitri cleared his throat loudly. "My brother and I have grown up in the wilderness, together. Only recently have we been welcomed back into the castle, and our feelings of abandonment and pain have not gone away."

Nadia wiped at a tear that had fallen on her cheek. "I'm so sorry I hurt you."

I reached over and touched my sister's arm. "It's not your fault. Fated mates are created, born for each other. Neither Lucian, nor you, chose this. And it's no one's fault."

"Except Marienne's." Lucian growled.

I laughed. I couldn't help it. "Yes! Let's shoot the messenger."

Dymitri frowned at me in disapproval, and I waved my hand at him.

"It's just a human joke. Oh, forget about it." I turned to Nadia. "They were told by a fortune teller, of sorts, that we were their mates. By a sorceress called Marienne. She was right about me and Dymitri, but unfortunately, she was wrong about you two."

A smile quivered on Nadia's lips. "Well, one out of two isn't bad."

I glanced across at Dymitri. "I'm grateful for it."

Nadia stood up and reached for Lucian's arm. "Can you stand up? I need to hug you."

"What for?" he asked, though he got to his feet anyway.

"For saving my life." Nadia pressed herself into the huge dragon's chest.

His eyes went wide, and worried, then he softened, wrapping his arms around her.

A soft sigh filled the air and I smiled at my mate.

"I never had a little sister before," Lucian whispered.

I grinned as Nadia pulled back and stared up at Lucian. "And I never had a brother before."

They settled back into their seats and the atmosphere in the room buzzed with energy.

"Now that that's settled, Nadia, we have a question for you," Dymitri said, his deep voice booming in the room.

"We do?" I asked him.

He smiled at me, then focused on my sister. "Would you like to stay here, with us? In the winter palace? Damon and Cass have said you can both stay, for as long as you like."

My heart dropped in my chest, and I turned to my sister.

Nadia stared at me with a similar type of anguish.

"You're staying?" she whispered.

Tears welled in my eyes, burning the back of my throat. "I have to. I can't leave Dymitri."

Nadia nodded. "I knew that, but to hear it..." She wiped at the tears that dropped onto her cheeks. "I'm going to miss you so much."

"Stay," I whispered. "Please. There's no reason for you to leave."

Nadia glared at me. "No reason? Sarah, I have college, and my friends. Mom and Dad!"

I pressed my lips together, pain ricocheting through my chest. "I know."

She put out her hand to me. "I'll tell them all you met the guy of your dreams and can't possibly leave him."

I laughed, choking on the sound. "That's pretty close to the truth."

I got to my feet and pulled my little sister into my arms for a hug.

Dymitri said from behind me, "We'll organize a way to get you home, Nadia."

I closed my eyes. I didn't want to think about her leaving me, but it was my turn to focus on my future. And my future was here. With my dragon prince.

THIRTEEN

Dymitri

I finally understood what true bliss felt like: having my mate, holding her safe in my arms, her head resting softly on my shoulder as we drifted in the afterglow of our love-making.

The morning sunlight shone through our window. Faint noises echoed down distant hallways, and the clatter of plates downstairs told me that breakfast was almost ready.

I didn't care. I wanted to stay here forever, just like this.

But reality came knocking on the door sooner rather than later.

I groaned, throwing a pillow in the direction of the door, but the hammering increased.

"Dymitri!" Cass's muffled, irate voice came through the wood. "I know you're in there! Come on!"

Sarah frowned sleepily and looked up at me. "What's that all about?"

"It's time to take your sister back to the human world."

Sarah sat upright in bed. A faint look of dismay crossed her beautiful features. It had been three days since we'd had our talk in the dining hall, though I'm sure Sarah had deliberately put it out of her head, hoping this day would never come.

"You must have known this was coming." I kept my voice soft. I hated to hurt her in any way. "She doesn't want to stay here, my love. And we can't keep her if she doesn't wish it."

"No, I know." Sarah drew up her shoulders before letting out a long sigh. "I just... I'll miss her. That's all. She's my baby sister. I'll always worry about her."

I gathered Sarah up in my arms. "I understand. She's much better, though. She can travel now."

"Okay." Sarah sighed, and we begrudgingly tugged on some clothes and headed downstairs.

We were the last ones down to breakfast. A chorus of smiling faces greeted us, ranging from genuinely happy grins from Damon and Cass, to knowing smirks from our siblings, Lucian and Nadia.

We took our seats, and my stomach lurched with hunger. I was starving.

I didn't care what the others thought about our lazy hours in bed. Sarah was mine. I wanted the whole world to know it.

Nadia and Sarah sat at one end of the table, speaking in quiet voices, their heads close. Cass sat next to them, with Damon at the head of the table. Lucian was on the other side, sitting a little apart from the others.

Lucian's apology to Nadia, along with him saving her life, seemed to have changed her perspective on dragon shifters. Since yesterday, she'd let Cass drag her around on a tour of the castle, and even expressed an interest in some of the rare herbs and mushrooms that the village market had to offer.

So far, she'd flat-out refused to actually *ride* on the back of a dragon, however. Which might pose something of a problem when the time came to take her home.

I nudged my brother in the back of the head, and he scowled at me.

When Nadia had initially woken up and we realized she wasn't his mate, he'd torn the palace apart in his frustrations.

But now he seemed to have accepted the fact, and he'd brightened up considerably since realizing he wasn't broken. She just wasn't the one for him. He'd even suggested that he could be the one to take her home, but I turned him down.

I needed to make sure Sarah's sister got back safely. I wanted to be the one to tell her family she was okay.

"Is it time?" Nadia's voice broke through my thoughts. I realized she and Sarah were both standing up at the table, looking at me.

"It's time."

The morning air was crisp and bright, the perfect conditions for flying—not too windy, and a clear sky for navigation. Cass, Damon, and Lucian joined us in the cobblestoned courtyard as Sarah and Nadia hugged each other tightly.

"I love you," Sarah said, face muffled against her sister's shoulder. "We'll see each other again soon, okay? Tell Mum and Dad and Katerina that I love them."

Nadia sniffled and laughed as she pulled away, wiping her tears with her sleeve. "Katerina won't believe a word of this, will she?"

"Probably not." Sarah looked close to tears as well, but she was holding it together for now.

"Wait." Cass frowned. "Who the hell is Katerina?"

"Oh..." Nadia raised an eyebrow at Sarah before turning to the rest of us. "Right. Sorry. She's our older sister. We don't see her that often, but she'll come back home for this, I'm sure of it."

My heart flipped over in my chest.

Another sister?

The conversation moved on quickly, but I couldn't stop turning it over in my mind, and wondering...

~

Sarah

I watched Nadia and Dymitri soar high into the sky, Nadia's shrieks piercing my ears until they were out of earshot.

She hadn't wanted to get on the dragon's back, but the other option was being held in Dymitri's claws. To Nadia, riding on his back was the lesser of the two evils.

The silhouette of Dymitri's huge wings covered the sun. My heart ached. I knew I'd be returning home soon to see her again—Dymitri had promised that I would be able to traverse between the worlds on occasion—but tears still blurred my vision. I watched them until they were nothing but a pinprick on the horizon.

Cass and I returned to breakfast together. My appetite had vanished, and I sank back into my chair with a heavy heart.

"Do you want to walk through the maze after breakfast?" Cass's unusually soft tone broke me out of my thoughts. "Or we could get the cooks to make something sweet."

"I'm fine," I replied automatically. My shoulders hunched inwards, and I sighed. "I'm... I'm worried about her. I can't help feeling like..."

Cass tilted her head to one side. "Like what?"

"Like I'm being selfish." I let my head thud back against the heavy oak chair. "All this... It's wonderful. I want to be here, with Dymitri, but she's my sister. What if she needs me?"

"Nadia is a grown woman. She can make her own choices. And *you*," she said, prodding my shoulder, "deserve to be happy. Life is short. You need to grab happiness with both hands and live it. Fated mates don't come around every day, trust me."

At the head of the table, Damon grinned. He put his hand on Cass's and tangled their fingers together. The gesture was sweet, and surprising from the king who wasn't known for being outwardly affectionate to anyone other than his wife.

"She's right, you know," he told me, eyes twinkling.

I tipped my head back and laughed. "Thanks, guys."

The pep talk hadn't fixed everything, but the knot of guilt in my chest eased slightly.

Cass was right. There was no point in worrying about what could have been, or what I should have done better in the past. Life would carry on regardless, and Dymitri was part of my life. Now, and forever.

A soft beam of sunlight hit my face, and I basked in the warmth of it. Dymitri would be back soon. I wasn't a shifter, but the love in my heart in that moment could have rivalled that of any dragon.

And, if I can't hold onto anything else... I can hold onto that.

EPILOGUE

A Month later
Sarah

"You look amazing." Nadia grinned widely, her gaze running up and down my body. She held a bouquet of trailing holly, ivy, and winter roses in her hands—the only plants we could find in the garden to cobble together at this time of year. "A true dragon princess."

I rolled my eyes, fighting back a blush. "It's too much, isn't it?"

"Definitely not." Katerina reached over to rearrange the bouquet a little, pulling out some wilting flowers here and there. "This is your wedding, Sarah! You have to look the part."

I glanced down at myself, smoothing out the gauzy fabric of my skirt.

The dress was simple, but it was topped off by a long fur-lined cloak. I flushed happily and accepted the flowers from Nadia.

"Oh, I almost forgot." Nadia picked up a delicate circlet that Cass had given to me as an early wedding gift and fitted it over my hair. "*Now* you're ready."

"You know..." Katerina reached down to adjust the back of the coat as I stepped up to the doorway. "It's okay if you want to postpone. We can still call it off."

She made a muffled sound of pain, like Nadia had stepped on her foot.

"What? It's kind of soon to be marrying this guy, sis. I'm just saying."

"They're eloping!" Nadia retorted. "It's *romantic,* Kat."

"Shh!" I hissed, and they fell silent. Inwardly, I rolled my eyes.

Sisters.

The guards on either side of the doorway clicked their heels, and the doors opened. I smiled when I saw the tall candles decorated with ivy and roses. Cass had refused to be a bridesmaid with my sisters and decided instead to decorate the hall for our small ceremony.

It didn't bother her that there was no-one here to see it except us. In her mind, even a simple ceremony should be beautiful.

We hadn't wanted to wait, and with my friends being human, and Dymitri being, well, Dymitri, everyone who was important was here anyway.

Except my parents. My father was unwell, and unable to travel. I hadn't wanted to push him, especially with the truth of who I was marrying. A royal dragon shifter from another realm. It had been hard enough to convince Katerina to come, and she didn't even know the extent of everything. I'd taken her to the airport, given her a sleeping tablet for flying, and met Dymitri once Kat fell asleep.

He'd been the one to fly us home, and I still hadn't explained everything to my sister yet. That was a problem for another day.

Today was my wedding day.

"Let's go," I said, nodding at my beautiful sisters.

They both smiled at me, then walked through the doors. I followed them down the aisle.

Damon and Cass stood to one side, their faces glowing with happiness.

Lucian stood beside Dymitri, who waited for me at the end of the small aisle.

My heart lifted as my groom locked eyes with me. His face broke into a smile as I made my way toward him.

"You look incredible," he murmured when I reached him.

I ran my hand over the lapel of his jacket. It was the most dressed up I'd ever seen him. I wondered if Cass was the one who'd gotten him into that suit.

"You don't look so bad yourself," I whispered with a smile.

That was an understatement. His suit fit him perfectly, his broad shoulders tapering down to his waist. I was already thinking about peeling his clothes off him later. My teeth caught on my bottom lip with the thought.

Someone gasped behind me and I turned to see Katerina gaping at Lucian, her mouth open in surprise.

I followed her gaze and caught sight of Lucian's expression. He was standing just behind Dymitri's right shoulder, staring past me.

My heart jumped. He was staring at Katerina, the same way Dymitri stared at me.

Lucian's eyes darkened. His pupils were black in an eerie resemblance to his brother's, and I realized immediately what was happening.

Katerina is his mate.

My sisters and I had been in our own rooms, in another part of the castle, while we prepared for the wedding. Lucian hadn't had a chance to cross paths with her until now.

Marienne wasn't wrong. All this time, my sister *was* Lucian's mate.

But not Nadia.

Katerina.

"I'm sorry..." Lucian muttered into Dymitri's ear.

I was close enough to hear the pain in his words. His hands clenched into fists at his sides, and I realized that he was barely holding it together.

"I... I have to go."

Dymitri turned, and comprehension dawned on his face. "Brother..."

Before Dymitri could touch him, Lucian stumbled back, knocking over one of Cass's floral arrangements. It clattered to the ground but he kept running, almost barreling into Cass herself in his rush to get away.

It was horrible to see him run from his mate when his dragon wanted her so badly, but he strode out of the hall as fast as his legs would carry him.

Katerina gripped my elbow and whispered into my ear. "Who was that?"

I gave her a reassuring smile. "My brother-in-law. I'll explain later."

I had a wedding to get through first.

Dymitri's face was crestfallen as he watched his brother go. I put a hand on his arm, gently drawing his attention back to me.

"Do you want to go after him?" I whispered.

"Shall I proceed?" the minister asked in a low voice, leaning forwards.

Dymitri hesitated.

"It's okay." He caught my eye and took my hand, lacing our fingers together. "Once upon a time, it was just us, Lucian and I. But it looks like he's not going to be alone any longer. And neither am I."

He squeezed my fingers.

My chest filled with warmth as I looked into the eyes of the man I loved.

Dymitri was right. Our families went beyond blood now. I would always love my sisters, and Dymitri would always love Lucian... but we had our own life to build now. Together.

The trauma in our pasts had made it hard for us to trust each other, but we were beyond that now. I wasn't interested in the past any longer.

It was time to look to the future.

Hand in hand, we turned to the minister, ready to exchange our vows.

∾

5
FIRE AND ICE
THE DRAGON'S TRUE MATE
USA TODAY BESTSELLING AUTHOR
AMELIA SHAW

THE DRAGON'S TRUE MATE

CHAPTER ONE

Lucian

I staggered out of the hall, away from my brother's wedding and the woman he'd taken as his bride. His fated mate.

Sarah and Dymitri had been perfect together from the very start. From the moment they met, I'd been able to sense the intensity of the feelings Dymitri had for her.

Desperately, I'd hoped it would be the same for me and my mate. Marienne had said it would be, but that wasn't the case. I'd felt nothing except sympathy for Nadia when we found her injured and unconscious.

When she woke up, there had been none of the intense feelings I'd been promised. No passion. No quivering desire. No dragon rearing his possessive head.

The lack of those feelings had sent me into a rage unlike any other. I'd felt so hurt and betrayed. So disappointed. But I'd gotten through it and hoped to one day find my own mate. Perhaps a servant in the castle or one of the women in town.

But no... today I'd met my own fated mate. It was another human woman. Just like my brother. And my dragon was bursting to be free.

I erupted through the door of the grand ballroom, my gut tightening to the point of having to run bent over.

"Hold it together," I muttered to myself, not sure that I could.

Running for the entrance of the castle, I passed through the foyer that had only recently been patched up. Dymitri and I had done enormous damage to the once-grand colored glass windows when I'd flown into a rage over Nadia not being my mate. Not my finest hour. Nor my dragon's.

I burst through the front doors, feeling the cold blast of our icy winter breeze on my face.

Reveling in the sensation of the crisp chill, I deeply breathed in the air. *Calm down, calm down.*

My dragon was furious at me for running away, snarling and snapping inside my mind. He wanted to go back and find his mate, but I couldn't.

I was teetering on the verge of being out of control and if I returned to the wedding party, I'd destroy everything in sight. There was no hope of containing my dragon any longer.

He needed to be free.

My dragon rose up inside of me as I stripped off my suit jacket and threw it on the ground. Wings sprouted from my back, and my skin transformed into the leathery scales of my shifter form.

I closed my eyes and let my mind go as mist swirled up around me, and I became my dragon.

When I opened my eyes, the world around me looked different. But the feelings inside of me weren't.

My mate was here, and Marienne had been right after all. My fated mate was human, and a sister to Sarah. But it hadn't been her tiny, younger sister Nadia as we'd all thought. Instead, my mate was her older sister. The gorgeous, generously curvy Katerina, with dark, curly hair and a sexy smile that made my skin catch fire.

Not to mention her ass... *oh my God*. My cock ached just thinking about her curves.

I leaped into the air, beating my wings against the sky.

Everything that I'd been told about fated mates was true. My dragon was uncontrollable in his need, my human side having no chance of dominance. My heart was thudding against my chest with the power of a steaming locomotive. Lust poured through me, all for a stranger. A woman who would never understand my world or our customs.

I'd never been good enough for my father to accept, nor any woman I'd known in the past. Why would this gorgeous human want me now?

Memories of my anger and hurt from past traumas poured through me like molten lava, eating away at any hope I had for my future. None of this made any sense to me, and in my growing fury, I couldn't see a way around the problem except to gain altitude and fly away.

I soared higher and higher, until I couldn't move my wings any longer. Until I was afraid I might fall from the sky if I didn't stop ascending.

Soaring back down to a lower altitude, I continued until I was far away from my half-brother's kingdom. Until sunshine heated my wings in place of winter chill, and my skin ached from the rapid change in temperature.

There was another kingdom ahead of me, with a huge castle perched high above the surrounding lands and villages. I could only hope it was Stavrok and Lucy's castle. I'd never been to visit them in their home but had met the royal couple when they'd visited Damon and Cass.

I glanced back the way I'd come, weak now from hunger and fatigue. I'd never make it back. Not tonight. Not without a rest. I used the last of my strength to fly down and land on a high balcony attached to the castle and there I collapsed against a railing.

I let my dragon go and shifted back to human, my chest heaving with the strain and my legs trembling in their attempts to hold me up. An older male servant hurried out onto the balcony to greet me, his gaze narrowing as my human body replaced my dragon.

"Let me get you a robe, sir," he said with a polite incline of his head, then stepped inside once more.

I sighed with relief at the confirmation I was in the right place. That was definitely a royal servant, so this had to be Stavrok's palace. None of the servants in the winter palace treated a stranger so well.

The man returned with a warm robe that I slipped on gratefully. "Thank you."

Then he handed me a glass of water, which I downed immediately. The coolness flowed over my aching throat, soothing it, making me moan with gratitude.

"Can I help you, sir?" he inquired. "Are you here to see King Stavrok?"

I nodded, though it wasn't entirely true. I'd ended up here purely by accident. "Could you tell Stavrok and Lucy that I'm here? My name is Lucian. He'll know who I am."

The servant bowed and walked away. I managed to put down the glass of water and tie up the robe just as an older man dressed in fine clothes stepped out onto the balcony.

"Lucian, sir, please follow me."

"Thank you."

I followed the man, who was likely the steward, into the castle, marveling at the richness of the carpet underfoot and the beautiful paintings that lined the halls.

What a difference it made when the king in charge of his kingdom actually looked after his wealth. Unlike my father, who'd been a tyrant king and let his people and his castle fall to ruin.

He'd been the worst of men.

You're not him, and you're far away from his memories. Let it go.

I gazed about Stavrok's castle and briefly indulged myself in the fantasy of what life might have been like if I'd grown up as the bastard son of this king. Raised in this home, or within the castle's walls. Perhaps then I wouldn't be such a fucking mess.

The steward stopped in front of a large, wooden door. "King Stavrok is waiting for you in here, sir. He's aware of your arrival."

Wonderful. Hopefully he doesn't kick me straight back out again. It wasn't like he knew me well.

The man opened the door and held it open for me to head inside. I took a deep breath and moved forward. Part of me had expected an office or a sitting room, but instead I was staring down the length of a grand dining hall with an impressively long wooden table.

At the head of the table sat King Stavrok, food laid out before him and a glass of red wine in hand. When he saw me, he grinned and waved a hand toward the seat across from him. "Lucian, take a seat. What brings you here to my humble home? Isn't your brother getting married today? That's the rumor I heard, at least."

King Stavrok was a huge man, and even seated, cast an imposing figure.

"You heard correctly," I mumbled as I sat down in my robe, feeling more naked than before. "The ceremony took place earlier and I expect the reception is well underway as we speak, in fact."

"Please, help yourself." Stavrok gestured to the feast before him.

I poured myself a glass of wine and picked up a bread roll, my gut still churning with the accumulation of stress. I wasn't very hungry, but I wasn't going to turn down the king's generosity.

"So, Lucian, tell me why you aren't at the wedding." The king tilted his head to the side, no doubt curious as to why I would leave such a joyous occasion and travel so far away.

I wanted to tell him it was none of his business. That he could stick his nose elsewhere and leave me be.

But I'd shown up at his home unannounced, and owed him an explanation. He had a human mate from the other side of the veil, his wife, Lucy, so perhaps he'd offer me some advice.

Certainly, my brother, Dymitri, would have tried to help me. However, I had no intention of burdening him further. Not on his wedding day, of all days. Just seeing me flee the ceremony had probably left him worried enough.

I needed a sounding board. "My fated mate is at the ceremony."

Stavrok's brows rose. "I repeat then, why aren't you there?" He chuckled.

I saw nothing amusing about the situation but instead of answering immediately, I took a bite of my roll and a sip of the wine. Then another. I hadn't realized how much I needed sustenance.

I inhaled deeply to regain some control, then released my breath slowly. "I'd just come to terms with the fact that I wasn't going to have a fated mate. That the sorceress, Marienne, had been wrong about my future. After all, she'd been so sure it was Nadia. She's the—"

"The other woman we rescued from that human hell hole." King Stavrok shuddered. "I remember."

"I thought Marienne's vision had been wrong, and prepared myself for never finding my true mate. I'd made peace with that."

Stavrok grinned at me as though he knew what I was about to say. "Marienne hasn't been wrong about our fated mates. Not yet, anyway. She was the reason I found Lucy."

"Oh, I didn't know that." And I hadn't. So, Marienne had been a royal matchmaker from the beginning? Somehow, that made this story even more credible now.

"I didn't mean to interrupt," Stavrok said, pouring us both some more wine. "Go on."

I blew out a breath. "Well, it turns out Sarah has another sister and the moment I saw her... everything fell into place. I wanted her. I still want her. And the only thing I could do to keep myself from taking her on the spot—or destroying everything around me—was to flee." I paused, the shame of my lack of self-control washing over me. "I felt like a monster, getting lost in that lust."

The king's expression softened. "You're a better man than me. I kidnapped Lucy from her home. I had no control."

My jaw dropped. "You..." *He kidnapped her?*

He nodded. "Yes. Literally picked her up and flew her home."

I didn't know Stavrok well, but I knew men. And he was serious.

"Did she forgive you?" I couldn't imagine Katerina letting me pick her up and carry her to my bedroom.

Stavrok cackled out a laugh. "Of course. Eventually. But tell me more about your mate. Why don't you believe she'd forgive you for letting your dragon have his head? After all, it's the most natural instinct we have."

I reached for some fruit, picking apart the grapes and orange. "Katerina might not want me at all. I'm not exactly the easiest to love."

A fact that had gotten drilled into me at an early age. I'd spent so much of my young life being told I wasn't worthy. Why would that change now? What would she see that everyone else missed?

The answer was nothing. Once she got to know me, she'd come to the same conclusion. Having her and then losing her might kill me.

Stavrok sighed then motioned for a butler who had been patiently waiting nearby to come closer. "A bottle of whiskey, I think."

"Yes, my king." The butler bowed and left in a hurry.

"Here's what you're going to do," King Stavrok said. "You're going to calm down and get out of this spiral of doom you've placed yourself in. Then you'll remember this woman is your fated mate. She was created *specifically* for you. Her soul is the other half of yours. She is what will complete you, and she is going to love all sides of you. Even the ones that are difficult or not really that loveable."

"How do you—"

He gave me a sharp look that shut me up. "Because we all go through those thoughts, and we all have difficult pieces to love. No one is perfect, Lucian."

I pressed my lips together tightly, wanting to argue. Stavrok didn't know me, and he couldn't imagine what my life had been like.

But I kept my thoughts to myself. He was a king, and I was a bastard son. Even though he was allowing me to sit at his table and drink his wine, we weren't on the same level.

The butler returned with a bottle of golden whiskey. Stavrok poured me a glass and placed it right in front of me. "Once you've collected yourself and rested a little, go back to the wedding and be with your mate. Show her the depth of your feelings for her."

"She's human. What if she doesn't understand? They don't feel the pull the same way we do." Or so I'd heard.

Stavrok laughed. "I guarantee you, she will. It might not be the exact same sensation, as she doesn't have the dragon inside of her. Her heart will know, though. It will beat faster when you're around. Her gut will twist whenever you're near. Her body will have the pull of extreme desire, and her heart will war with her head until she gives in. Sound familiar?"

"Yes." So similar. Perhaps humans weren't as strange as I'd originally thought.

"She is going to love you." He sounded confident. "But it will take a lot longer if you keep running from her every time her presence makes you a bit uncomfortable."

A bit uncomfortable is an understatement.

The moment I'd laid eyes on her, my cock was at full attention and every part of me had been eager to explore every inch of her curvy figure. No other woman compared. I'd never been set ablaze in such a way before in my life. If I couldn't do something about that discomfort soon, I might explode.

"Next time, I'll be more prepared," I said, much calmer than I felt. I couldn't guarantee that, but I'd pretend for the moment. "If nothing else, it won't be such a big surprise."

"I need to go and speak to my wife. Shall I leave you with your thoughts?" Stavrok asked.

No. My thoughts frightened me. All the same, I said, "Yes." I picked up my glass of whiskey. I'd intruded on his hospitality long enough.

"I'm always happy to help," Stavrok said in a soft voice. "I'm glad you felt enough trust in me to come here."

I appreciated him saying that more than I could express. He was treating me as an equal when I was only King Damon's bastard brother.

"Thank you for your assistance." Despite the fear creeping through me, I knew what I had to do, and I had a plan of action to take.

Stavrok left me, and I took the time to finish my whiskey, letting the warmth soothe my inner dragon. My strength began to return, and a new determination stirred within me. A determination to face my fear, and seek out my fated mate.

Once I was able, I transformed into my dragon and flew back to Damon's castle. It was indeed, a long way, though I did not ascend so high this time and the air was better for breathing. When I arrived, I found a private place to change back into human form.

I'd obviously missed the ceremony, and felt terrible for that. But Dymitri would understand, I felt sure, as would Sarah. I'd seen it in my brother's eyes just before I fled the castle, and he would explain what had happened to Sarah. Everyone would understand, except for *her*. My one true mate.

By the end of the night, I would make it up to her. I did not want to be the mate who ran away.

I gathered all the courage I had and made my way to the hall where the reception was still underway. My heart was pounding like a battering ram, but after my long flights, I had enough control over my dragon to walk into the room without feeling like I was going to shift.

My gaze settled on my mate sitting across the room, and a piece of me I thought long dead sprang to life once more.

TWO

Katerina

Even though we were in a castle, my sister's wedding was small and simple, which was fitting for her. The fact that she was marrying a guy she'd just met wasn't very typical, but I tried not to judge her too harshly for that.

It was easy to understand her falling in love so quickly, especially considering her new husband was one of the men who'd rescued her and Nadia from hell.

I wouldn't be following that path any time soon, of course. Love at first sight just wasn't my style. But I was glad at least one of us was getting an epic, whirlwind romance worthy of a romance novel. As long as he loved her and took good care of her, he'd stay off my shit list. I'd give this Dymitri guy the benefit of the doubt, especially when I saw the way they looked at each other.

Dymitri. Even his name sounded like something from a fairytale. I tried to keep my jealousy at bay, not wanting to be bitter. That wasn't right. Instead, I focused on the joy I felt for my sister as she walked down the aisle. She glowed as she gazed into the eyes of her new husband.

As Sarah and Dymitri exchanged their vows, a strong yearning tugged at my heart. That part of me that didn't want to be alone anymore. I knew nothing came easy. As a chubby girl, I understood that I had to work a lot harder to stand out in a crowd full of size-zero wannabe supermodels.

Easy would be a nice change.

I gazed through the small crowd of mostly strangers and noted the original best man still missing from the group. I'd caught one glimpse of him earlier, and then he'd disappeared. Strange. And even stranger was how much I'd felt his absence. I tried to shake off the feeling and refocus my attention on Sarah. This was *her* day.

Tears were shed as the bride and groom were officially pronounced husband and wife. Up next was the reception where I fully intended on hiding behind a drink and pretending I belonged. Something about the party guests seemed unique. Not bad, just different, but I couldn't quite put my finger on what it was.

Everything about the wedding was different, in fact. Sarah was being married in a picturesque mountain village, over which the castle loomed like a medieval dream. I had so many questions, and yet I didn't want to ask, not wanting the magic of the day destroyed.

And then, speaking of magic, *he* walked back into the room. As soon as the best man stepped through the door, it was like a spell had been cast over my body. My legs quivered. Actually quivered! Something I only thought happened in fiction.

I clung to my glass of wine, suddenly fearful I wasn't going to be able to stand much longer. My knees got wobbly and there was a tingle between my legs I hadn't felt in too long to count. I swallowed hard, unable to drag my eyes away from him. My whole body flushed with heat, and I finally looked down to try and get some control back over my physical reaction to his presence.

Holy hell! All that from *looking* at one of the most majestic men to ever walk the earth.

The best man. Now I was sad I'd only caught a glance earlier. Clearly, I'd missed out on quite the specimen. Long, dark hair that gracefully fell to his shoulders. And he was so tall! Even from a distance, he towered over everyone and everything. A broad frame, too. Those arms... that chest... I'd kill to have them wrapped around me.

I'd kill to wrap parts of me around him too, for that matter. He was imposing enough I wouldn't feel like I was squishing a bug.

A gentle hand on my arm startled me out of my trance. My sister, the happy bride, smiled at me.

"Let's go say hi," Sarah said, nodding her head toward Tall, Dark and Dangerous.

More heat flushed through me, this time primarily in my cheeks. "What? To him? Why?"

"He's my husband's brother, and family should meet family, right?" She winked suddenly. "Besides, I think you two would hit it off."

Smashingly well, I hope.

I cleared my throat. "Good point."

Sarah slipped her arm in the crook of my elbow, and we walked across the room together. Each step toward him was like floating on a cloud. No way was my sister about to introduce me to the most gorgeous guy on the planet. No way!

Then, the next thing I knew, I was standing in front of him and gazing up into his deep, soulful, dark eyes. *Hot damn...*

"Lucian," Sarah said and gestured between us. "This is my other sister, Katerina."

He gazed down at me with such intensity, I lost my footing and stumbled just a tiny bit. Toward him, I should add—much to my embarrassment. Lucian caught me before I face planted into his rock-hard abs. I didn't know they were rock-hard for sure, but based on what I'd seen it was easy to assume. His whole body was probably chiseled from stone.

"Heels," I said, struggling to find an excuse for my clumsiness. "They're big. Long. Tall."

Oh God, I was mortified, because immediately my mind went to other things that were big, long, and tall. In my four-inch heels, I barely made it to his shoulder. He was just so fucking tall in comparison, and I was all for it. But I doubted a guy like that would be into a woman like *me*.

"You should be careful with those," he said, his voice a low rumble that caused my insides to churn with desire.

I laughed, awkward and too loud. "Just need more practice with this pair. I bought them for the wedding." The conversation was tanking fast. "Anyway, it was really nice to meet you..."

I turned back toward my sister and shot her a warning look that suggested she better not stop me from leaving.

"Kat!" Sarah insisted, clearly not caring or not catching what I was trying to communicate. I walked past her, and she turned her attention to Lucian. "We'll be right back."

I found an empty table to sit at. The music for the dancing had started, and the loud thumping of the bass was a nice distraction from my thoughts, but also made it impossible to think clearly.

No, if I were being honest, Lucian made it impossible to think. Simply having him in the same room turned my brain into a pile of glittery, hopeful mush. Story of my life... I see an attractive guy and let lust cloud my logic, which always resulted in heartbreak.

"What is wrong with you?" Sarah gasped out, standing over me with her hands on her hips. "Katerina... you bolted before you even got a chance to actually *talk*!"

"Clearly, the conversation wasn't too riveting," I snapped, pressing the palm of my hand to my forehead. "My shoes, of all things... I had to talk about those. He's going to think I'm some kind of shallow ditz!"

"No, he's not."

"No, who's not?" our other sister, Nadia, asked, joining us at the table. "What did I miss?"

I groaned. "My humiliation with Tall, Dark and Dangerous."

"Lucian?" Nadia asked, looking over at him.

We all did, and I noticed he was staring intently back... at me. He wore a deep frown that seemed almost concerned. For me? I gave him a small wave, and that brought a smile to his face. It was such a beautiful sight to behold that I had a difficult time looking away.

"Yes," I said at last. "Lucian. Sarah thought I should meet him since he's our new brother-in-law's brother, or whatever. Then I lost my footing and almost fell into him, and it spiraled from there."

"It did not," Sarah insisted. "It was not that bad!"

She didn't understand. At all. For someone like her, it'd be cute. For me... I shook my head. "I'll talk to him later when I'm not so..." I made a vague gesture around me, hoping that explained everything. No such luck.

Nadia reached out and grabbed my hand. "I'm with Sarah on this one. Go and say hello to him. Talk. Dance!"

"Oh, yes, dancing! That's a great idea." Sarah pulled on my arm to try to get me out of my seat. "Then you'll be a little more relaxed. Small talk is always hard to get past, so maybe just skip it. I don't think Lucian is into that anyway."

Why were they being so pushy?

I looked back toward him, and he gave me a small wave, his eyebrows raised in an inviting fashion.

"Is there something I don't know that you're not telling me?"

"No," they both said at once, making it even more suspicious.

After a brief moment of silence and one shared glance, Sarah spoke. "Dymitri seemed to think you and Lucian would hit it off well, and I agree. In fact, I heard he's nervous to talk to you."

"Seriously?" I didn't buy it. A guy like that wouldn't get nervous.

She nodded. "He's... not exactly a people person. Kind of rough around the edges. I know you haven't had a lot of luck with guys, but I wouldn't suggest you two talk if I thought it was a bad idea."

"I feel really good about it too," Nadia added. "Neither of us would lie to you or set you up for failure."

They'd conspired against me! I couldn't believe it.

That being said, Lucian was... wow. And I did trust them. They'd never let me down before. I just wish the set-up didn't have to seem so desperate. Guys never found that attractive. But if he truly wanted to talk to me, then maybe I'd judged him too quickly.

"All right, I'll ask him to dance," I said. For the moment, I had my nerve, and I wouldn't let my head talk me out of it.

Sarah grinned and Nadia clapped.

I took a few steps forward, and Lucian's eyes seemed to light up. He moved toward me, meeting me halfway in front of the buffet table where the night's feast was spread.

"You seem to have practiced walking," he teased.

I shook the joke off, my legs going weak again. I wouldn't stumble any more. I would show him how confident and sexy I could be. "What can I say? I'm a fast learner." I paused. "Would you like to—"

"I was just about to get something to eat," he said. "I took a long journey unexpectedly and it'd be nice to replenish that spent energy."

"Oh." So much for my sisters steering me in the right direction.

"And I'd like you to join me," he added. "Because after…"

"After?" I asked, gazing up into his eyes. Immediately, I was lost.

He smirked. "After, I'm sure I'll have plenty of energy."

Doubt tried to creep into my head. This guy was way too hot for me. But I shoved it aside. Trust. I knew I had to trust my instincts about him. I couldn't say how I was so certain of that fact, but it felt right. I'd never get anywhere if I always played it safe.

"Sounds perfect. I'm pretty hungry too, to be honest."

He walked me to the table, and we loaded up our plates. I followed my instinct there too, not going crazy, but not sticking to only the veggies from the salad tray either. The way my heart was continuing to race in his presence, he wasn't the only one who had to stock up on energy!

Soon, we sat down at a table together and tucked into our plates.

"You went on a journey," I said. "Everything okay? I saw you missed the ceremony."

His gaze never left me, instead wandering over my body more than once. "Everything is perfect. Now, I mean. It was a personal problem that needed attending to."

"Sounds like you found the resolution to your problem then," I said. "I'm glad. I noticed you were missing."

"You did?" He seemed surprised.

I nodded. "I only saw you for a second, but I put two and two together when you rushed out. Something was up."

"You're observant," he said. "And kindhearted."

I felt the heat return to my face. "When I want to be."

"May I always inspire you to keep being so," he murmured. He cleared his throat. "Are you enjoying your time in my half-brother's castle?"

"How could I not? It's a castle!"

I cleared my plate a lot faster than was probably lady-like, but Lucian seemed to be on pace right along with me. Almost like we both wanted to finish our food and get to whatever came next.

"Ready to dance?" I asked. "Feel replenished?"

"Very much so." He offered his hand to me, and the second our fingers touched, an electric shock ran through my body.

I heard a sharp intake of breath from him, and then his arm slid around my waist and he led me through a waltz as a slow song conveniently started playing. My hips and chest pressed against his. God... I had no resistance in me when it came to this man.

"Confession," I said softly, just barely loud enough for him to hear over the music. "These aren't actually new shoes. You just... have a way of making me forget how to function."

He leaned his mouth to my ear. "I'm relieved. I was worried I'd scared you off, or that you thought I was disgusting."

"No woman in her right mind would think you're disgusting." I giggled at the preposterous thought.

"You'd be surprised." He pressed his cheek against mine. "But I don't care what other women think. You're the only one whose opinion matters."

My heart began to beat even faster and my whole body grew hot. "You're still talking about me, right? I'm not being punked, am I?"

"I don't know what that means but yes, this is a two-person conversation. No one else is around. It's only us." He took in a heavy breath. "I'd love to kiss you. Would that put your mind at ease?"

"It certainly wouldn't hurt," I managed.

He wants to kiss me? Someone pinch me, because I have to be dreaming.

Then his lips were against mine, firm and sweet, in a kiss that started out chaste and pure but quickly morphed into more. I opened my mouth and teased his tongue with mine. It was only a small taste of what I wanted to give him. Passion pulsed through me, hot and insistent. I had to have him. Logic be damned.

"I have a room," he said, his voice rough with need.

I nodded, growing wet just thinking about being in private with him. "Lead the way."

He took me by the hand and led me from the grand ballroom. I glanced around to see if my sisters were still watching, wondering what they'd think if they caught me. Sarah was too busy with her new husband, and Nadia was nowhere nearby. I shook my head. They'd lose their minds once I told them. A one-night stand was the last thing anyone expected from *me*. I'd always been into feeling secure with a commitment before taking things to such a level of intimacy.

But Lucian felt different. I might never get a chance with such a god of a man again. Seriously, it wasn't every day someone so incredibly sexy wanted *me*. If I declined his invitation, I knew I'd regret it.

He led me up the stairs, stopping halfway up to push me against the wall and claim another kiss. I was more than happy to oblige him. His lips were warm, his arms were strong. Tingles flooded my body. We couldn't get to his bedroom fast enough as far as I was concerned.

We hit a landing and started running down the hallway. I picked up the hem of my dress so I wouldn't trip on it, and laughed at his enthusiasm. We stopped outside a room, he opened the door, then tugged me inside.

As soon as the door was closed, I pushed off his suit jacket. His hands moved to slide the straps of my dress down and in seconds, he had the zipper at the back moving as well.

This guy was an expert at undressing women, that was for sure.

I ripped open his button-down shirt, buttons popping off and rolling onto the floor. Underneath that fabric was a body made for a billboard. His abdomen was so defined, it could have been made of stone. It had to be. There was no way a human man could be so chiseled and rock-hard. And that wasn't the only thing rock-hard.

I could feel the power of his erection as he pressed against me. I was wet in anticipation and clawing at his pants to break him loose. When his cock was finally freed, the sight of his length made me shiver.

He was hard and long, the head red and engorged. Wanting *me*. Needing *me*.

I had to have him inside me.

Now.

I dragged Lucian over to the bed and crawled backwards over the mattress. He moved over me, nibbling up and down my torso. His kisses were everywhere, starting between my breasts, then he moved down my abdomen to my mound.

I gasped out as he pushed apart my legs, then his tongue teased me in the most sensitive of places and I moaned the loudest I've ever moaned in my life. Normally, I'd have been embarrassed if I made a sound like that, but God, it felt so fucking good, I didn't care who heard.

I twisted in the silken sheets, grabbing at his hair to anchor myself. He didn't stop, flicking over my throbbing clit with his lips and tongue until I was screaming for him.

"Get inside me, please," I begged. "Stop being a tease!"

His head came up and he said with a smirk, "If that's what my lady wishes."

"Yes!" *Of course, it fucking is!*

Lucian didn't wait. He crawled up between my legs, spread me even further apart with one of his thighs, and readied his cock at my entrance. Then he plunged hard, sinking his cock into my channel. I cried out at the welcome invasion. My back arched involuntarily, my body receiving his fierce invasion as if it had been waiting for him my whole life.

I dug my nails into his back, holding him tightly to me as he withdrew slightly, then filled me again. We were ravenous with one another, each giving as good as the other. Lucian began to move faster, harder, claiming me like his life depended on it. Every thrust sent a powerful wave of pleasure through my body, driving me toward climax at a level I'd never experienced before.

And even when I tipped right over the edge and screamed and shuddered as the release took me, he wasn't done.

He showered my face and body with kisses, withdrawing so that he could suck on my hard nipples and twirl them with his tongue. I moaned again, unsure of how much more I could stand.

When he grabbed my ass and entered me again, I sobbed with relief. Nothing had ever felt so good before. So right. He pushed me to orgasm yet again, only this time when I began to climax, he released a might roar and came deep inside me at the same time I lost control and arched up and into him, screaming.

My belly rippled as he shuddered within me, my body shivered beneath his, and it was minutes before I came back to earth from the most amazing climax of my life.

"Oh. My. God," I gasped out, breathing hard.

He let out a satisfied groan, then rolled onto his side, facing me.

"I... is it okay if I stay for a while?" I asked. "I know that's presumptuous but I don't think my legs will work right now."

There was no way I was jumping up and leaving if I didn't have to. My belly was still tight and aching, and the need to be close to this man had only amplified.

Lucian gazed over at me, smiling, only... were those tears in his eyes? No, I had to be imagining that. It must only be the afterglow of an epic fuck.

He kissed my forehead. "Stay as long as you'd like. I have no intention of letting you go."

I raised an eyebrow, but who was I to argue? He wrapped me in his arms, and, surrounded by his warmth, I drifted off to sleep.

CHAPTER
THREE

Lucian

I slept long and deep, possibly the most satisfying sleep I'd ever had in my life. Never before had I felt so content, so at peace. For the first time ever, all the missing pieces in my heart seemed to be there, whole and complete.

All of it felt like a dream, too surreal to be true. And I would have doubted the whole night had occurred until I rolled over and Katerina's luscious, warm body pressed into mine.

I didn't want to let her out of my sight for fear she might disappear. She could have snuck away in the middle of the night but chose to stay. That had to mean something.

Gazing down at her beautiful face and with her dark curls lying across my pillow, my inner dragon stirred. Once I'd returned to the wedding for the reception, I had somehow found the strength to stay in control of the beast lurking within. *Stay calm. Soon enough.*

I'd kept the dragon quiet so Katerina wouldn't see that side of me too soon. When Nadia had witnessed me transform, she'd run away and taken Sarah with her. We'd almost lost both of them that night. Humans weren't used to seeing any sort of magic, let alone mythical creatures. In her world, I was nothing more than a myth... and a monster.

Upon waking and seeing her still there in my bed, I relaxed, letting my guard down.

Katerina shifted in her sleep, her lush body moving closer to mine as if by instinct. The fresh touch of her skin against mine ignited a fire in my soul.

It's her. She's the one. The other half. I'm complete.

My stomach churned with the immediate change within my body. I tensed and recited calming words inside my head.

Stay in control. Stay calm. It's okay to be excited, but I have to be careful. I don't want to scare her away.

I squeezed my eyes shut, trying to focus on the war raging inside my mind as two sides of me fought for dominance.

We're bonded now. We're one now. My dragon's celebration grew as Katerina's eyes opened and her gaze landed on my naked chest.

"Morning," she said, and an adorable blush spread across her cheeks.

"Morning," I murmured back, pushing a lock of hair away from her eyes. "How did you sleep?"

"Wonderfully." She let out a blissful-sounding sigh. "I'll be honest. I don't do this kind of thing, like, ever."

I gazed down at her curiously, unsure how to interpret her statement. "Do what kind of thing, exactly?"

"Fall into bed with someone I just met." Her voice got awfully quiet. "Totally worth every second."

A grin spread across my face. "Definitely worth the leap of faith on my part, as well." If only she knew how much of a leap it was on my end. My dragon stirred at the memory of becoming one. How much that alone meant...

Calm down!

"I'm sorry, I didn't mean to stay all night," she said. "But I was so tired and so content."

I frowned. "Why would you leave?"

"Isn't that how these things work?" she asked.

These things... did she mean a one-night stand? "I wasn't intending for this to be the only time we—"

Her beautiful eyes grew wide, though I couldn't tell if it was excitement or surprise that colored her expression. "No?"

"No."

"That's a relief, because I was kind of hoping for seconds this morning. Or is that selfish and forward of me to presume?" She placed a hand on my upper thigh and, at the feel of her exploring fingertips, that's when I lost all control.

I groaned as my body started to respond to my shifter's elation. "E-excuse me, I..."

I rolled out of the bed and staggered toward the door. I had to leave the room before I shifted in front of her.

When she saw my dragon for the first time, I wanted it to be after I'd explained more about the world she was now going to be a part of. Throwing her straight into the thick of it without any pre-warning would be far too overwhelming.

My dragon had other plans, though.

"Lucian, are you okay?" She sat up in bed, holding the sheets up to cover her chest. "Maybe I should leave. We can talk later... or if this is your way of kicking me out so that my feelings aren't hurt..."

"No!" My voice came out in a growl. "I want you to stay. I want to talk. I want..." *A whole life with you.* That's what I wanted to say. But I couldn't get the damn words past my shifting throat. "Just...a few... minutes..."

I reached the door but before I could stagger through it, the change began to happen.

Fuuuck!

I fought it hard but lost. My body grew bigger, my eyesight shifted, and wings unfurled from my back.

In moments, I was in my dragon form. He demanded a celebration for finding our mate, and I'd fought him back for too long.

I beat my wings to stabilize myself before setting my clawed feet on the ground.

Oh, no. Please, Katerina, don't freak out.

My dragon form took up the space between the bed and the door. Luckily there was more than enough room, as all the rooms in the castle were designed with our transformation in mind.

I turned to look at my mate, horror curling around my mind. What was she going to say?

Katerina sat on the bed, frozen. Her jaw slowly dropped, and her eyes grew wide. "Oh... wow..."

If that was her whole reaction, then perhaps things wouldn't be so bad after all.

But it seemed she was in shock. And the initial effect wore off more rapidly than I thought it would. Suddenly, she let out a blood-curdling scream. I automatically roared in response, the pitch of her voice piercing my ears. Not my finest moment.

"Oh my God! Ohmygod, ohmygod, ohmygod!" She covered her ears, squeezed her eyes shut and threw the blankets over her head. "Don't eat me! I am not food! Ohmygod."

I needed to speak to her and there was only one way. I gathered all of my strength and forced my shifter back inside. Slowly, too slowly, I became a man once more.

"Katerina? No! I'm not going to—"

A small squeak escaped her lips as she sat bolt upright again and pulled the sheets down once more. Her face was bright red and flustered. "You talk? Are you a demon? You have to be some kind of unholy monster from Hell to talk! To change shape! You were just... a man and then a dragon... ohmygod..." She started to breathe, heavy and fast.

"Katerina, I'm still Lucian. I'm a—"

"No! Stop! I'm not going to fall for it! I've seen this movie! A million times! It never ends well." She whimpered. "Oh, God... please tell me this is all a dream. None of this is real. All a dream. All. A. Dream."

My heart felt as if it broke in half. Pain tore through my chest as the intensity of her fear amplified. Of course, she was frightened. Why wouldn't she be? To her, I was a predator searching for its next meal.

The question was, should I run?

Yes. In fact, the further I distanced myself from her, the better. She sounded on the verge of hyperventilation, and someone else in the castle must have heard the scream and my roar. They might even be on their way already.

I'd distressed her, my presence terrifying her. One of her sisters could provide her with the care and comfort she'd need, and I would be far away, unable to cause her more harm. Yes, that was definitely the best course of action. Then she wouldn't be able to watch me fall apart from her rejection. She didn't even try to listen...

I let my dragon loose, allowing him to fly up into my body once more, the panic within my heart settling as my beast took over. I flew out the nearest window, glass crashing to the ground as I took to the sky. I'd already caused plenty of damage to Damon's castle fighting with Dymitri. What was one more window?

The wind kissed my scales, and I barreled toward the forest—toward home. Not the castle that Damon insisted was now my home, but my true one. The one in exile. That's where I belonged, in the land of banishment where my asshole father had put me. Why did I think I could ever leave? Why did I think I could make a home in the castle and have a happily ever after?

I didn't deserve anything like that.

How could I have been so stupid?

I wanted to rip the world apart. To destroy the trees, the buildings, whatever got in my way. Wanted to but didn't. Enough of my humanity remained to remind my dragon that setting the world ablaze would do more damage than good. A mournful cry left my lungs as I soared into the clouds. There, I could wallow in my misery as much as I wanted.

She was supposed to understand. Her heart was supposed to respond to mine and give her the compassion and grace to accept the dragon inside me. It hadn't, probably because I wasn't worthy of her love. At least I'd had one night with her. I'd rewind and replay the night over and over again for the rest of my life.

The cool air calmed me some. I felt more human than dragon again. I almost turned back toward the castle, so I could transform once more and try to comfort her now that my rational and more logical side had returned. Perhaps we could talk. She might still listen...

Then I remembered the large, terrified eyes staring up at me, pleading with me not to eat her. The way she'd nearly gone into shock. Leaving her alone was still the best option. She didn't need my presence complicating things further. One of her sisters might have more success at getting her to understand, then maybe I could take over from there.

I just had to wait things out. Steer clear so I couldn't cause her any more pain or angst.

I found the small shack I'd called home through my formative years and landed in the small clearing near the front stoop. There, I changed back into a human and made my way inside.

"It'll be fine," I said to myself as I walked into the kitchen to splash some water onto my face. I groaned. "Who am I kidding? It's not going to be fine. She hates me. My fated mate hates me and thinks I'm a monster."

It had been all over her face. Not just fear, but loathing as well. She'd called me a *demon*! That was how she made sense of my shifting ability, jumping to the worst possible conclusion.

Maybe she was right. A monster's blood did course through my veins. My father had been a terrible creature. He'd banished Dymitri and me when we were children, leaving us for dead. He'd preyed on the people who relied on him for their survival. Everything he did was for his own selfish gain, no matter the cost or who got hurt along the way.

As much as I wanted to be a better man—as much as my brother told me I *could* be one—I wasn't a fool. I was doomed to repeat my father's mistakes.

There's a reason the phrase, "Like father, like son" exists. Perhaps Dymitri lucked out and most of his nature came from our mother. I clearly hadn't, though. I'd seen parts of my father in my soul in the past. The fact I couldn't control my dragon as easily as others could was another sign. I desperately wanted to *not* be like him. But I was his flesh and blood, and it showed.

If I didn't mate, then I couldn't have my own children, and that meant I wouldn't keep the cycle of his insanity going.

Katerina deserved someone who was able to love her to the fullest and provide the best future possible. I wasn't capable of either of those things. I wasn't worthy to even try. Failing her would kill me far faster than her rejection.

No, I would spend the rest of my days alone, living on the memory of our one beautiful night together. At least one of us might then have a chance at happiness.

Katerina

Oh my God! Oh... my... God.

Did I just see what I thought I saw? One moment, Lucian was his tall, handsome, sexy self, staggering around the room naked like he had a stomach ache. The next, his skin melted into scales and his long limbs became wings growing from his body.

He turned into some kind of dragon, right in front of my eyes! I said demon, but a dragon felt a lot more accurate somehow. How was that even possible? There was no way dragons could be real. They belonged in fairytales and movies, not real life!

I didn't wait for anyone to come to me. I threw on my dress and underwear from the night before and ran from the room with my shoes in hand. Not the leisurely post-sex morning walk I'd planned on taking, that was for sure.

I'd been hoping for a more subtle approach to leaving Lucian's room. One that didn't scream the "bridesmaid just fucked the best man!" cliche to the whole damn castle. Instead, I'd screamed my lungs out, and probably woke everyone up.

There was a definite lack of commotion in response, which to me seemed odd. A scream and an inhuman roar should have had everyone scrambling to help. At the very least, spark an investigative curiosity. I didn't run into a single soul until I was halfway down the grand stairway and met my youngest sister coming up toward me.

I must have looked half-crazy, because Nadia suddenly picked up her pace and ran to me. "Kat!" She flung her arms around me. "Are you okay? I thought I heard you scream but wasn't sure you needed help."

"Why would you think... *oh*!" She'd thought I was screaming as part of my lovemaking with Lucian. "Took you long enough," I said, breathing heavily.

Nadia squeezed me harder. "I was on the other side of the castle eating breakfast. It's kind of a huge place, if you hadn't noticed. Are you okay?"

"I'm not hurt," I said. Not physically anyway, I figured. Just my pride. Tears pooled in my eyes. "I'm not okay, though."

She urged me to sit down on the steps. "What happened?"

That was when Sarah arrived. She stood at the top of the stairs with her new husband beside her, took one look at me and her shoulders sank. "Oh, Kat..."

I gazed up at her and shook my head. "Go back to your honeymoon." I could see from her disheveled hair and swollen lips that I'd interrupted something.

"Dymitri will understand." She gave him a pointed look. He nodded and whispered something into her ear before disappearing back along the hallway. Sarah walked down the stairs and sat on my other side. Both of my sisters held me close and I felt comforted and slightly less disconnected in their presence. "Tell us everything."

"I took your advice and danced with Lucian," I said. That seemed the easiest place to start. Maybe if I put it all together from the beginning, it might make more sense to me as well. Everything about coming to the castle felt like a dream. "We hit it off, like you said we would."

"That's wonderful!" Sarah's eyes grew wide with excitement.

I bit my lip and shifted uncomfortably. "We hit it off *really* well, and I stayed the night in his room."

"Ooh-la-la!" Nadia teased.

I shot her a glare. "Our morning started great. We woke up and were kind of canoodling in bed. Then he started acting funny. Like he was sick. I thought maybe he was faking it so he could get rid of me. That he'd gotten what he wanted from me and everything else had just been a line."

I want you to stay. I want to talk. I want... What had been that third thing he wanted but never got to say? His eyes had been so sincere, his words so pure.

"It wasn't a line," Sarah said. "Kat, he—"

"I'm not finished," I said stiffly. "So, he's pacing madly around the room, trying to get me to understand he's honestly not well. Just as I'm about to believe him, he... he..." The memory of his transformation and the way he'd spoken to me in that rough growl sent a shiver down my spine. "You're not going to believe this, but he turned into a monster."

"A dragon," Nadia said.

"Right, it looked like a—" I frowned. "Wait a second, you *knew*?"

She pressed her lips together tightly, her eyes avoiding mine. "We met before the wedding, and he might have done the same thing in front of me, too." She hurriedly added, "Not after having sex with him. I never touched him, I promise! But he has a tendency to get overly emotional and then—"

"Changes into a dragon!" Sarah finished. "Lucian is passionate, and he's passionate about *you*, Kat."

I held up my hands. "You *both* knew?"

"Yes," they said together, both quiet after.

I took in a slow breath, trying to keep my rage at bay. "Why didn't you tell me all of this *before* I met him! Before we... we..." Had the most incredible sex of my life. Oh, goodness. I'd never been loved so thoroughly. "That one detail changes so much!"

"Would you have believed us?" Sarah asked. "I certainly didn't believe it until I saw it with my own eyes."

Nadia nodded slowly. "It's a lot to take in. I had the same reaction you did, Katerina. I ran away!"

"We both did, because it was almost too much to handle," Sarah continued. "But then I saw the softer side. The man behind the beast. Lucian is still in there. You have to look past the scales and the rough exterior and then you'll realize nothing about him has actually changed. That's what I did with Dymitri."

"*He's* one of those things too?" I gasped. Of course, he was. They were brothers, so why not? "How many of these dragons are there?"

"A few," Nadia said. "This town is their home. It's in another realm. Again, I know this is a lot to take in."

Another. Fucking. *Realm?* She had to be joking. "So, I'm not even on Earth anymore? I'm not in some fancy small European country? I'm in another... what? Dimension?"

Nadia winced. "Kind of. There's a magical veil we cross over to get here that separates the world we know from theirs. There are other shifters and witches and—"

"This is impossible." I shook my head and slowly got to my feet. "This is *insane.*"

"But it's true!" Sarah put a hand on my arm and urged me to sit with her again. "And you know it's true because your heart just... knows that it is! We wouldn't lie to you. We didn't lie about Lucian, either. He's special and thinks the world of you. You're..." She looked down and shook her head, as if she wanted to say more but wasn't sure if she should.

"I'm *what*, Sarah?" I pressed, using my firmest voice.

"You're his fated mate," she whispered. "That's part of why he's losing so much control whenever he's with you. The two of you are meant to be together as one."

That was the icing on the cake for me. "Fated mate? Like a *soulmate?*"

"Yes, exactly like that!" Sarah exclaimed. "He left the ceremony because he saw you for the first time and just the sight of you pulled at his inner dragon. If he hadn't left, he'd have made a huge scene in front of everyone! While the servants in the castle and his family understand, I think it would have been way more than you could have handled at that point in time."

"You think?" I didn't know how to process all this information. It sounded so surreal.

"The last time he had an emotional explosion like that, he nearly destroyed a whole wing of the castle," Nadia added. "That was when he was told I was his fated mate, then realized I wasn't."

I glared at her, all of a sudden feeling possessive of Lucian. "What do you mean he was told you were his?"

"A witch told him that one of my sisters belonged to him," Sarah said gently. "He didn't realize I had more than one, so when he met Nadia and the mating call didn't pull at him like it should have, he got upset." She gave my arm a squeeze. "And then he saw you and freaked out even more because he saw his true love did exist after all."

"True love? He barely knows me!" I certainly didn't know anything about him beyond the fact that he was tall, dreamy, amazing in bed, a little rough around the edges, and apparently, a dragon. We'd clicked right away, yes. Our chemistry was incredible. He'd certainly made love to me like he meant it.

I just struggled with the fact that he actually *did* mean it.

Guys who looked like Lucian didn't date chubby girls like me. We were fun for a little while, but not the kind of woman most guys wanted hanging on their arm in public, let alone be married to. Sure, our sparkling personalities were hard to match, but there were smart, funny, *skinny* women out there.

How could a woman who looked like me be the soulmate of a guy who might as well have been a god? I didn't believe it.

"This is ridiculous," I said, shaking my head. "You're both full of it."

"Kat!" Nadia huffed. "You're the one being ridiculous here. I get the dragon part is a stretch, but you've seen the shifting with your own eyes. You've experienced some of the magic when you crossed over the veil to get here. Haven't you noticed how different this place is from home?"

"Yes," I admitted. This place was vastly different from home. "But there is no way I'm the soulmate of Lucian! There's just no way. Whoever told him that was seriously wrong."

I stood and this time neither of my sisters stopped me. "Maybe she had it wrong and it really is you, Nadia."

"Trust me, it's not," Nadia said. "I feel absolutely nothing for him. It does go both ways. We might be human, but we also have hearts capable of discerning the truth. Don't you feel it? Deep inside of you?"

Yes. I felt it.

My heart ached for him in a whole new sort of way. I'd never felt anything like it, and that was saying quite a bit, since I had the tendency to fall for the wrong guy all the time. One look, one kind word, and hope ignited within me. Fluffy, cute hope.

Lucian did something else to me completely. I didn't merely hope for him. I *craved* him like a drug. I needed him to survive. We might have been in the beginning stages of getting to know one another, but I knew for certain the places we would be going together were amazing.

I didn't dare admit any of those thoughts to my sisters. Instead, I said nothing. They claimed to not lie to me, so I would give them that same courtesy.

"I'm going home," I somehow managed to get out. In truth, I wanted to break down into deep sobs. And then I wanted Lucian's arms wrapped around me.

God. Too many emotions had been stirred within me. Lucian was a dragon, for goodness' sake! In retrospect, he'd been a beautiful creature to behold, even in such a terrifying form. Magical and terrifying, but beautiful.

However, his lack of control scared me. So much raw passion inside of one man could easily lead to my heart snapping in two. Who was I kidding? It already had! I'd bounced from the high of a one-night stand, to the hope of starting a relationship with a guy who had fangs and claws and scales, to being told he was my *soulmate*.

My one true love.

That last one hurt the most. If they were wrong, I'd never bounce back from that level of hurt.

"Do you need help with your stuff?" Nadia asked.

"No. I want to be alone," I said, and began to walk away, then stopped at the top of the stairs. "How can I get back, anyway? You said I'm in another realm."

I couldn't believe I was actually saying that out loud, and meaning it!

Sarah let out a heavy sigh. "I'll talk to someone about giving you a ride home."

"Thanks." I paused. "Not just for that, but for not arguing with me about this decision. And for telling me everything. It's not your fault this is difficult. I won't shoot the messengers."

"Keep an open mind. That's the last thing I'll say about it." Sarah toyed with the gold ring now on her left hand. "I don't want you to shut yourself off from something amazing because you're scared. Or uncomfortable."

Uncomfortable was an understatement. I didn't want to get into all of that with her. For the time being, I'd do as she asked. Thinking about the possibilities stung, but I could leave the door open a crack. *I guess.* Only because I wanted more of that warmth from last night.

No. This is dangerous.

"Okay," I said. That was me not committing to, nor rejecting, her proposal.

I returned to the room that I'd been assigned upon my arrival—the one I'd barely spent any time in. The garment bag for my dress still lay across the bed, my duffel bag with all of my normal clothes next to it. I shut the door, changed into a pair of leggings and a t-shirt, returned my dress to its proper place, then walked back out of the room with all my stuff in tow.

"We can return that for you," Nadia offered.

I gratefully put my bag in her hands. "Thanks."

A man stepped forward. "I'm Damon, the owner of this castle, and Lucian's half-brother. I'm sorry to hear that you want to depart so soon, however, I'm happy to give you a lift back."

This was the king? He looked so normal. "Thank you. I appreciate that."

"Your sisters tell me you're aware of our secret," he continued. "You should know that the journey back is best made while on the back of a dragon. I wanted to give you a warning, so it didn't startle you too much. I understand this is all very new to you."

I looked him over. He had short, blond hair and gorgeous blue eyes. But he didn't look like a dragon either, just a normal, ordinary guy. Like Lucian had.

"Yes, this is definitely new," I said at last.

"You will need a warm jacket for traveling." He waved to a servant, who hurried forward with a long, fur-lined coat.

I slid it on even though I'd already layered up for the cold air outside.

"It gets very chilly when you're flying," Nadia added.

I glanced at her, ready to ask how she knew that, but the answer was clear. My sisters had been hiding things from me. Disappointment hit me, but with all the other emotions buffeting my system at the moment, my sisters' actions didn't affect me as badly as they would have in the past.

Damon waved for me to follow him outside and I did, my sisters close behind me. A solid lump started forming in my stomach. He walked a few feet away from the castle before transforming. The process was so smooth and elegant, quite different from the abrupt and chaotic way Lucian had done it in the bedroom. Damon stretched out his wings and neck, and while he was still imposing to behold, I didn't feel anywhere near as afraid.

Just a dragon, not a demon, my heart told me. *Lucian's the same way.*

I shook the thought away. How could a normal, human woman like me, be with a beautiful creature like that? Plus, where exactly was Lucian? For someone who claimed to be my soulmate, he sure had run away in a hurry. One would think he'd want to stay and help me make sense of it all.

The sooner I got home and tried to forget all of this, the better.

Nadia gave me a hug. "I'll come see you soon."

"Me, too," Sarah said.

"After your honeymoon," I insisted. "I'm okay, ladies. I just need to return to something familiar and then I'll be fine."

"I understand," Sarah said. "When Lucian comes back, we'll be sure to tell him."

"Sure thing." *If* he came back. I wasn't going to hold my breath, not with the way he'd been so quick to flee. We were *not* soulmates. We couldn't be. Dragons might be real, but I didn't want to be a part of their strange and unfamiliar world.

I gazed over at Damon and sucked in a deep breath, not wanting to climb on his back but desperate to return home. "I'll let you know once I'm settled in."

Damon lowered himself to the ground so I could get on his back.

For fuck's sake. I held back a half-hysterical need to laugh. My life was seriously upside down right now.

I took a step toward him and climbed up on his shiny, hard back like I would a horse, swinging my leg over then lying down flat.

Oh my God.

Once I was settled, he raised his body up and flapped his powerful wings.

I screamed, because I couldn't help it.

"Hold on!" Sarah called out.

She didn't have to tell me twice! I grabbed onto what bit of him I could and clung for dear life. As we rose in the air, I closed my eyes tightly. However high up we were going, I didn't need to see it, right? I just had to trust he would get me over—or was it through?—the magic veil in one piece.

We soared through the atmosphere, and there was a strange tingling against my skin. For a second, I opened my eyes and saw a shimmer in the sky—a shift in the very fabric of existence—but before I could focus on it properly, we had passed through. That must have been the veil. Immediately, I noticed a difference in the air.

It was normal again. Warmer, too.

Damon glided through the air for a few more miles before finding a place to land. Once I slid off his back, I stroked his scales in thanks, still weirded out by the dragon body, but not terrified anymore. A step in the right direction. My brother-in-law was a dragon. I didn't have to be part of their world, but I did need to accept it if I had any hope of maintaining a relationship with Sarah.

He shifted back to human for a moment, and I averted my eyes to avoid staring at his nakedness. If I was honest, he did nothing for me. Not like Lucian.

"From here, will you be able to make your way home?" he asked.

"Yes, thank you," I said. "It's not far."

"I'm going to take a moment to rest and make sure you get a ride back. Then I'll be on my way."

Such a gentleman. Lucian had been as well. Had I been too quick to judge him? Maybe. But he'd still left me and stayed away. That was the other thing—he hadn't come back. He'd barely tried, and that spoke volumes to me.

I used my phone to call for a ride, glad I had that and my purse on me. It didn't take long for a car to get there. By the time I got back to my house, I was absolutely exhausted.

Exhausted and heartbroken. I'd taken a leap of faith last night by letting Lucian charm me into his bed. Once again, it was a misplaced hope.

Our two worlds did not belong together.

Lucian

I stayed at the small house in the woods for two days. During that time, I did everything in my power to regain control over my emotions. I talked myself into returning to the castle to properly woo my mate, only to talk myself out of it again.

Since I was already there, I tried to sort through the lingering baggage from my father. Perhaps I should have turned around and returned within a few hours, but I felt like I owed it to Katerina to sort through the toxic emotions brewing inside me.

If I didn't, how could I ever love her the way she deserved to be loved?

I was proud of myself for coming back at all. Those dark places in my heart still tried to tell me I should stay away; that I wasn't worthy.

Katerina should have cooled off a while ago, and her sisters must have told her everything about our world by now. Once she knew we were fated mates, she'd welcome me back with open arms. Or that was my hope, anyway.

I landed within the castle grounds, slightly unnerved by how quiet it was. The wedding festivities were obviously well over. Most of the mess had been cleaned up. I walked into the palace, looking for evidence of my mate.

"Katerina?" I called out. My voice echoed through the halls. "Katerina, where are you?"

A soft clearing of the throat startled me. One of the servants was hiding by the doorframe. "She's... returned to the human realm."

"What?" My hands clenched into fists, and I stormed up the stairs. "That's not possible! How did she get back there? She isn't scheduled to leave for another week, at least."

Hadn't that been the original plan? Sarah's out-of-town family were to stay for a while.

"It's true, sir. We cleaned up her room today," the servant said from below.

I stalked to the room that had belonged to Katerina and found it empty and far too pristine. Sadness crushed the hope in my chest. "Why did you leave?" I spoke to the empty walls. "I don't understand."

The memory of her calling me a demon crept back into my head. Had she left, because she truly believed I was evil?

She was supposed to stay so we could talk. Why didn't anyone try to stop her? Everyone knew she was my fated mate, and they all understood how important that was. I'd never have stood back and watched Sarah walk away from Dymitri.

Is it because they know I'm not good enough for her? That I'm too broken to be a worthy husband?

Were they saving both of us the heartache of disappointment? Could they see how our relationship was destined to crash and burn?

I didn't even get to say a proper goodbye. Fuck! I'd screwed up royally. If only I'd managed to control myself, then none of this would have happened. We could have languished in our bliss for a while longer, and then I would have gently brought her into my world, the way I'd planned to, originally. But, no, I had to act like an animal. No wonder she'd left. If the situation was reversed, I wouldn't stay, either.

I sighed and walked toward my room. Anger and hurt still pulsed through me, and I needed to be alone to squash it down before I destroyed even more of the castle. Why did I have to be such an idiot?

Somehow, I had to work out how to become resigned to a life of solitude. I accepted Katerina's rejection with a heavy heart, and tried to think of ways to fill my time.

I could at least make things right for my brothers, by fixing all the damage I'd caused to the castle. They'd suffered considerably because of my lack of self-control. Then once I was done, I'd see to it that I never caused harm again.

My initial instincts had been right. I knew too little about love to be able to give it to another. Fated mate or not, if I couldn't behave the way a man should, I'd never succeed.

I didn't try to find Nadia or Sarah. I just changed into warmer clothes and began repairs on the damage I'd caused, starting with the stonework. Using my body in a physical way kept me distracted from my feelings, at least a little. Laying brick and mortar down gave me a different kind of satisfaction. With each slab I placed came a piece of healing to my soul. I might not forgive myself, but I could earn forgiveness from my brothers. They'd said it was all water under the bridge, but I didn't believe them. I could feel the burden I'd placed on them unnecessarily.

A week passed, then two, filled with long days of work. My progress on the castle repairs was steady and when I wasn't fixing what I'd broken, I dove headfirst into training.

I'd always kept myself physically active, but the need to exhaust myself so I couldn't think about *her* was great, indeed. If I could lay my head on the pillow at the end of the day and fall straight to sleep from pure exhaustion, that was a good day. Unfortunately, by that definition, most of my days were bad. No matter how hard I pushed myself, I always had a few thoughts left for Katerina. Memories of her smile, her body, her warmth. My inner dragon yearned for her. *I* yearned for her... the sweet taste of love I didn't deserve.

After too many nights without sleep, tortured by my memories, I began to push myself twice as hard.

My brothers checked in on me from time to time. They weren't wrong to do so, since I was battling depression like I never had before. I did a fairly good job of hiding it. Or so I thought.

"Still sulking?" Dymitri asked one morning.

I glanced up at him and narrowed my eyes. He was leaning against the doorframe and shook his head when I scowled. "Damon and I have a bet going on how long this pity party will continue. He seems to think you'll bounce back any day now. I, on the other hand, know you're stubborn enough to continue in this vein forever."

I snorted. "It's nice to know my misery is amusing to you both."

"It's far from amusing, actually," he said, and walked toward me. "I want to lose this wager, so prove me wrong, brother. Snap out of this funk and return to the human realm so you can win Katerina back."

"She left me!" I snapped. "And she had every reason to. I lost myself in my dragon. I frightened her, just like I did with Nadia. I fucked up, just like I always do. She deserves someone mature. When women say they want a man who would kill for them, they never mean it literally."

"True." Dymitri nodded, considering my words. "That being said, I don't think you give yourself enough credit."

I shrugged. My brother was biased. He was the only person in this world who truly loved me. "She still left."

"*You* rushed off and never came back. Maybe that had something to do with her leaving?"

I glared at him. "She was about to hyperventilate! She thought I was going to *eat* her! What was I supposed to do? Let her pass out?"

"You stay and you calm her down!" He pinched the bridge of his nose. "Running away is the perfect way to make a woman to feel unwanted."

"Right. I fucked up," I growled. "And that's why I'm staying away, because I don't know what I'm doing. I don't know how to love her and I'm going to keep hurting her. I'm just like Father."

"No!" He grabbed me by the shoulders and shook me hard. "You are not! You are kind and caring. Father would have laughed and tormented her. You left because you were worried for her and stayed away because you're afraid of hurting her more. Believe me, brother, I understand those feelings all too well. But every morning, I dedicate myself to proving I can be different. I think you want to do that, too. You came back. Maybe not when you should have, but you did. You returned."

I swallowed, looking away, unable to take the weight of his gaze any longer. "I didn't mean to wait so long. I couldn't return until I was at peace with myself. Then I got here and unraveled all over again."

"You didn't decimate the building this time," Dymitri pointed out with a smirk. "You're making progress."

I let out a sour laugh. "There's no way I can win her back. She was so frightened. I know it's a lot to take in, but..."

"Damon flew her back, you know."

Damon? My heart lurched at the thought of my mate on the king's back. It should have been me, carrying her in that way.

"She might have been afraid, but she accepted him in dragon form, and she will accept you too if you give her the chance." He exhaled heavily. "Lucian, there is so much happiness to be had by embracing the mate bond fully. Stop talking yourself out of the possibility. You do know that you deserve that, right? To be happy. We are not our father. We do not have to pay for his sins. Don't you miss her?"

"With every breath," I whispered.

"Why keep fighting, then?" He let out an angry huff. "Please, go to her! Talk to her! She'll understand so much more than you think."

"It's been too long."

"You're fated to be together. It doesn't matter how long it's been. Don't quit before you've even started." He closed his eyes and our foreheads touched. "It'll be okay."

Hopefully he was right. I closed my eyes as well and took in a slow breath. "Promise?"

"I swear it." He patted my shoulder and pulled away. "I'm sure her sisters will help too."

I'd struggled with facing them. Every so often I would see Sarah in the distance and when she looked at me, all I saw was pity. So embarrassing... Nadia avoided me equally as much as I avoided her. Given our history, the last thing I needed was to hear her opinion of my latest blunder.

Naturally, Dymitri led me to Nadia rather than his wife. Of course, he did. It was as if he knew how little I wanted to see her. I let out a groan.

"Stop that," he hissed, then turned to Nadia. "You'll be nice, won't you?"

She nodded. "I won't say anything bad. Promise." She stared up at me.

"I'm sure you already know how the conversation would go. Imagine your worst, and just pretend it was all actually said. How's that?"

My jaw tightened. "That isn't nice, Nadia."

I instantly regretted my words. Her eyes flashed, and even though she held her tongue, I understood right away just how much she was holding back.

"I'm sorry," I mumbled. "And yes, I have imagined our conversation and it was pretty rough."

Her mouth lifted in a little smile. "I bet it was."

"Can you help me get to Katerina?"

"Of course." She smiled properly then, tears pooling in her eyes. "I want you two to have all the happiness in the world."

I let out a sigh of relief. "Be honest, then, please. Do you think it's too late?"

"No. But we shouldn't make her wait any longer, right?" She winked, then frowned. "Wait, you're not going to wear *that,* are you?"

I looked down at my clothes to see what was wrong with them. I'd been wearing old, ripped jeans and a gray sweatshirt because they were easier to work in. The fact that they were currently covered in dust probably made them not the best choice of clothing, I had to admit.

"An outfit change isn't necessary," Dymitri said. "He'll be shifting anyway."

That was true. I'd end up naked on the other side of the veil if I wasn't organized.

"Fine," Nadia said. "I suppose you're right. She'll just be happy he's at her door."

Hope ignited within me. "Do you think so?"

"I know so. Come on."

She grabbed a large cloak from the front door hook, and we hurried out of the castle. I was so eager to get going I just about took off without Nadia, but then I remembered I couldn't find Katerina without her sister's help. I needed an address, and someone to make sure I didn't change my mind and turn around.

"Want me to carry your clothes?" she asked, rather sensibly.

"Yes. Thank you." I stripped off and folded the clothes, handing her the jeans and shirt before letting go of my humanity and shifting into my dragon.

The small seeds of doubt planted so deeply by my father had grown for a long time and they still threatened to rear up.

Dymitri is right, though. I am not my father, nor should I be punished for his sins. Just because Father never loved me, doesn't mean a thing. All it proves is how terrible a person he actually was.

Nadia climbed onto my back, and we flew into the sky. I took her across the veil and into the human realm, praying the whole way that she was right and that I hadn't left it too late to fix things with Katerina.

Katerina

"Miss Kat! Miss Kat!" One of my students ran over holding up her latest drawing of... a bear? *I think that's what it's supposed to be.* "I made this for you!"

"It's beautiful," I said, taking the drawing and setting it on my desk. "I especially love your use of purple and blue. Did you know those were my two favorite colors?"

The little girl nodded enthusiastically. "I hope you feel happier soon!"

"I'm very happy," I said, meaning it in that moment.

All my kindergarteners made life a million times better for me. I loved them so much. Even when they acted out and frustrated me to tears, I wouldn't have traded them for any other job. There was always *something* to smile about.

"Okay," the girl said and shrugged, almost like she didn't believe me.

Kids had a way of being able to read me better than most adults. They were also far more honest and braver than anyone gave them credit for. I'd never tell her just how much happier her noticing my sadness made me feel.

I looked at the clock. "All right, class, it's time to start cleaning up so we can get ready to go home!"

The kids all excitedly tidied up their tables. I couldn't help but share their excitement. So much so, that I opted to bring all my work back home with me to do there rather than stay at school for my usual extra two hours after class had been dismissed.

I loved my job but was exhausted at the moment. Ever since my adventure across the veil, I hadn't felt like myself. My body just wasn't as energetic as it used to be, and I'd wondered—several times—if maybe the magic messed me up somehow. Was that possible? I was an ordinary human, after all. I didn't belong over there. What if my molecules had scrambled when I crossed over? Was that why I felt like death warmed over every morning? Like I could never get enough sleep.

The exhaustion was more than physical. It was mental, too. My mind kept wandering back to the night of the wedding, the night I'd spent with Lucian. Not just the incredible sex we'd had, but all the subtler ways he'd expressed his desire for me. The intense gaze across the room, the hands catching me as I almost fell, the smile... oh, the smile. All those memories haunted me like a ghost with unfinished business.

Then I'd remember the huge dragon, and how scared I'd been when he first shifted. And the fact that he'd left me and hadn't so much as *tried* to contact me since then. It had been more than two weeks. If we were supposed to be together, then where was he?

The whole experience was an emotional rollercoaster and it was just too much to deal with.

I drove home early from the school, glad it was Friday and the weekend was around the corner. I'd have a couple of days to re-group and eat a pint of ice cream... or three. Maybe. That was how I normally comforted myself after a difficult week, yet even the thought of my beloved Chocolate Chip Cookie Dough left me feeling nauseous. How sad was that?

In short, I was a hot mess, and the stress was taking its toll. Even my period was late in protest. That only freaked me out a little. Okay, more than a little, but I was determined to not jump to conclusions until more time had passed. Periods could be late for all kinds of reasons, not just because I'd had unprotected sex with a dragon.

I shook the idea out of my head. Nope, not going to doom-spiral over a "what if".

And I hated that I'd let myself get so emotionally crazed over a one-night stand. I went into his room with the intention of just enjoying myself. One night of hot passion and then letting him go, because he'd *want* to be set free. With that expectation, I shouldn't have ended up getting hurt.

He just had to be a freaking dragon, didn't he?

Fated soulmate business aside, just the fact that he was a shifter blew my mind several times over. I'd grown up not believing in much beyond what I could observe.

If I could see it, taste it, touch it and so on, then I knew it was real and true. It would make sense. People shifting into dragons? *Actual* dragons? That was harder to pull into my sphere of logic. Magic was for fairytales, and fairytales weren't real.

Well, I'd had that belief blown right out of the water, that's for sure.

I'd seen it with my own eyes. I'd heard his roar. Felt the scales on Damon's back as he carried me back here to my own world. My five senses were backing up the truth—dragons *were* real.

I walked into my house and did the first thing I did every day when I got home from work—checked in on my sick father. Part of the reason I lived away from Nadia and Sarah was so that I could take care of him. As the oldest, that duty fell on my shoulders. Okay, it was also something I chose. My sisters did not need to help shoulder the burden. I handled it fine on my own.

How are you feeling today? I texted. He usually was awake at this time.

Feeling good! Which didn't mean much, but we celebrated all those small victories.

Love you! I'll be in to visit soon. I promised.

I set the phone down, knowing he probably wanted to talk more but I just couldn't do it. My head and heart weren't in the right space for a full conversation. If I started talking to him, he'd know something was wrong. That's why I texted instead of called. He couldn't hear the waver in my voice through a text message.

Looking forward to it. Love you too.

I stared at those words, feeling guilty. My dad meant the world to me. He'd helped hold me together more times than I could count. I almost changed my mind and called him so we could talk about all my life problems. Almost.

Telling him I'd had an intense night of sexual relations with the hottest man alive was probably going to be too much information. Telling him that man was also a dragon, might have him questioning my sanity. Pretending everything was okay would result in me spilling my guts. No, I had to wait. We'd catch up later.

I sighed, at a loss for what to do.

If Nadia and Sarah were home, then maybe I'd call them. Sarah was staying in the other realm, apparently. Nadia wasn't planning on coming back just yet, so I'd have to wait to talk to her, too. We hadn't always been super-close, but there was comfort in knowing they were around. Having them not be a phone call away left a strange void in my life.

They were a part of Lucian's world now. That magical place with the dragons. Sarah had married one, and Nadia sure seemed attached to castle life despite not having a dragon of her own. And just like that, my mind was back on Lucian and the night we'd spent together.

Lucian was *my* dragon. I had one to love and call my own.

Had, being the keyword there. Past tense. He might have felt drawn to me initially, but that clearly didn't last.

I rummaged through my refrigerator, knowing I should eat something but not really wanting to. Partly because of the exhaustion and nausea constantly lurking under the surface, and partly because maybe if I was a little more mindful of what I ate, then I could be more attractive. Because I'd be, well, *smaller*.

Stupid train of thought, I know. But I kept going back to one fact—I wasn't a size two. I wasn't even a size six. I was a size sixteen. Full-on curves and rolls. I'd always looked this way. Whatever cute, petite genetics my sisters had gotten from our parents completely bypassed me.

Most days, I accepted it. Embraced it, even. When I looked in the mirror, I saw beauty staring back at me. I'd had enough long-term boyfriends to know that I was loveable. But all those boyfriends had eventually moved onto a smaller version of me. Seeing them with their new girlfriends always brought on the doubt. Had I been lied to? And lied to myself? Was I really not worthy of being loved, after all?

And that's where my head went every time I thought of Lucian. We'd had an amazing time together. I let myself give in to his charms because I'd instantly felt safe *and* desirable. I didn't just feel beautiful when I looked into his eyes, I felt out-of-this-world gorgeous. Like he only had eyes for me, and no one could ever turn his head elsewhere. For once, someone saw my true worth.

It was that thought that made me miss him more than I should. Our instant, magnetic attraction to one another that continued to attempt to cloud my logic. I'd gone in with no expectations for more, and left thinking there would be far more than I ever imagined possible. Even post-dragon grand reveal and return to my human reality, I'd spent a few days hoping he'd knock on my front door.

Soulmate. I'm not sure how much of that I bought, anyway. It always felt like a line any time I'd heard it.

"You wouldn't understand. She's my soulmate. You aren't." That's how it usually went.

But why did I let myself get so caught up in him? Why was I still letting myself get lost in those dark eyes? Why couldn't I just let him go? Why did I feel like my heart was being ripped in half for a man I barely knew?

None of it made sense.

I groaned, settling down with the small serving of leftover pasta I'd discovered in the fridge. I didn't put anything on it. Bland sounded soothing to my upset stomach. Once again, just thinking of Lucian had my belly in knots.

I'd taken two bites when there was a knock on my door.

I scowled toward the sound. Who would be coming to my house?

I peeked through the peephole and my mouth dropped open. Was I seeing right? I swung the door open and stood there gaping. Nadia was standing on my front stoop.

With Lucian beside her.

CHAPTER
SEVEN

Lucian

Nadia motioned for me to knock on the door. "Go on. You can do it."

"I can," I whispered, my breath short with nervous tension. I raised my hand and knocked against the wooden surface, waiting, hoping, praying that Katerina didn't slam the door in my face the moment she saw me.

The door opened wide, and Katerina stood in front of us, her eyes widening as she gazed briefly at her sister then up at me. "You... you came?"

"Yes," I said, my heart beating hard and fast.

Damn, she's beautiful.

She stood there, staring at me almost as if she expected something more. After a moment, her gaze shifted back to her sister, and she frowned. "O... kay?"

Nadia nudged me.

"May I come in so we can talk?" I asked, my heart pounding even louder in my ears with every passing second. I could barely focus. The moment Katerina appeared, my body craved hers, and my heart sang in a way I'd never thought possible.

I'd never experienced such a reaction before.

"I don't know," Katerina said. "I'm not sure I have anything to say to you."

"Please," I stressed.

"You had your chance to talk to me before," she pointed out. "And you didn't take it."

"It's hard to get a word in when you're screaming your head off," I grumbled. Nadia gave me a sharp elbow in the side. "Ow."

She glared up at me, and didn't need to say more.

Control my temper. Message received.

I took a slow breath and released it in a measured way. "I would very much like to talk to you. May I please come in so I can do so?"

For a few seconds, Katerina didn't say anything. I wasn't sure if she'd heard me.

Eventually, she stepped aside. "Uh, yeah... I guess."

Not the elated reaction I'd been hoping to receive. I almost turned and left. Being an asshole for self-preservation reasons was better than sitting in her living room so she could reject me all over again. I'd promised myself I'd do right by her, though, and I was determined to stick with it.

Nadia pushed me through the door as if she could sense my urge to flee.

I staggered inside and sat down on a chair in her living room.

"Sure, make yourself comfortable," Katerina mumbled. "No problem."

I scowled. What was I doing wrong *now*?

Before I could say anything, Nadia spoke up. "Since you two are getting settled so nicely, I'm going to head out. Kat, call me later, okay?"

"Okay," Katerina said softly. I could tell she didn't want her sister to leave us alone.

Nadia hurried away and the front door closed with a resounding thud. A long silence passed between Katerina and me.

"How have you been?" I asked, wanting to fill the silence.

"Confused," she said. She stared down at me from where she stood. Why wouldn't she sit? Her arms were folded across her chest in a less than inviting stance. "It's a lot, you know. Having you turn into a… a…"

"Dragon?" I supplied.

She nodded. "Yeah, that. It would have been nice to receive a gentle introduction to the idea."

"I agree. That's what I had planned to give you. It's why I tried to leave before you could see me change." I gazed down at my hands and sighed. "For that, I apologize. I should have had better control. I was too excited. After so long wondering if I had—no, *hoping* I had—a fated mate, I discovered it was true. At long last, you were there. The one thing I'd dreamed of —the other half of my soul. My fated mate."

"See, that's the part I think is shit," she said. "There's no way *I'm* the girl you'd been dreaming about. I couldn't be."

Why did she always doubt me? "I'm not lying."

"Explain it to me better, please. All of it. Nothing about this makes any sense."

"Sit," I said. "Please. I think it'll be easier to listen."

She huffed and rolled her eyes but did what I said. "Fine."

Without her looming over me, I felt more confident. Where to begin, though? "You've seen that I can turn into a dragon. I think that part doesn't need to be talked about in any more detail."

"Well, maybe, but I do actually have questions about that, too," she said. "There's a lot about it I don't understand. How? Why? And where were we exactly, for that matter? How different is your home from here? Were you born like that? Was everybody in your… realm… able to change into a dragon, too?"

Her questions helped guide me with what to answer first. "The how and why are the same, I suppose. I'm a shifter. It's what we do. We can change into the creature of our bloodline. In my case, that's a dragon. There are others. Bears, wolves, just about any animal, to be honest. There are some humans and non-shifters who live among us, too. But those of us who can shift… yes, we are born that way. We live with both human instincts and those of our animal form. Dragons are by far the most regal and sentient of the bunch, in my opinion."

"I can see that," she said. "And the why you change is just... because that's what you do?"

"Yes. It's just what we do." I ran my hands over my jeans, my nerves slowly starting to fade. Her decreasing hostility gave me hope. "As for where... we were staying in my brother's castle on the other side of the veil. Over there, my kind are normal."

I gazed at her as I spoke. Our eyes met, and my heart fluttered in my chest. "Over in my realm, our territories are divided by kingdoms, much like the world you live in. Unlike your world, though, there are still kings to rule them. My brother, Damon, is one of those kings."

She blinked. "So, you're a prince?"

"No." I said. "We're half-brothers. Same father, different mothers. My mother, who I share with Dymitri, was not the queen. When my father passed on, Damon took over to rule the kingdom. However, I don't have any birthright to the throne. Damon is gracious and has said Dymitri and I are welcome on his lands. A stark change from my father's attitude toward us."

"Your dad didn't want you around?" She gasped. "Are you serious?"

"Yes." I shifted in my chair, not caring to dwell on this part of my story. It was the part that had kept me away from her, after all.

I cleared my throat before she could say more. "Anyway, I have slowly learned to accept my brother Damon's hospitality. Actually, I'm still learning, I think. We are dragons of the north. He seems to think all of us should work as a unit to unite the kingdom. My father wasn't the best of rulers, as I'm sure you can imagine."

Katerina nodded slowly. "My sisters mentioned something about soul mates?"

"Fated mates," I clarified. "We call them fated mates. Every shifter is born with one. You are the other half of my soul. When we are together, we feel whole because our souls are bonded as one at last."

"If that's the case, why did Nadia say you thought she was your fated mate?" Her gaze narrowed. "I know you said a witch told you, but that feels awfully convenient for an out. How do I know you're not just using that as an excuse?"

I wanted to know who had hurt her so badly to make her distrust me so deeply. "Marienne can see things others can't because of her magic. She is a sorceress and if you would like to meet her, we could organize a trip to her castle. But her magic isn't completely reliable. What she told me was that my fated mate was Sarah's sister. I didn't know about you, and I made the mistake of assuming it was Nadia. However, the moment I laid eyes on your younger sister, I knew she wasn't the one. Everyone else told me to give it time and the instinct would kick in once she awakened from her injuries. It never did. My gut was right. She wasn't the one. I didn't even try to pursue her."

I had to make that last part clear.

"So, you just... knew? The moment you saw her?" Katerina asked. "And when you saw me, you knew I *was* the one? How does that work?"

"The dragon inside of me recognized the other half of my soul instantly," I explained. "That's how I knew Nadia wasn't the one despite everyone's insistence. Initially, I thought Marienne's magic had been wrong. That there was no hope for me. Part of me thought..." I swallowed, unsure if I wanted to confess the truth. But to gain more of Katerina's trust, I had to show her all of me. "Part of me thought that perhaps I didn't have a fated mate at all. That I was impossible to love."

Katerina's frown deepened. "Why would your mind ever go there?"

"Remember, I'd been cast out by my father."

"So?"

"So, if he couldn't love me, how could I expect anyone else to do so?" It made sense in my head.

Katerina shook her head. "Right. Your dad who *chose* to not love you. That is different than *couldn't*. And I don't know a whole lot about the situation, but of the few things you've just said, I don't know why you'd let this one guy dictate your self-worth. He's clearly an asshole."

"Yes, yes he was." I chuckled. Rather than try to explain in another way, I let the topic drop for the time being. "Regardless of how logical my reasoning is or isn't, I'd come to terms with the idea of being alone. Then you entered the castle and all of that changed. I wanted to properly woo you. To bring you into my world and show you the possibilities of our future together. And then I messed it all up."

"Turning into a dragon first thing in the morning is definitely far from a gentle introduction," Katerina said.

A small smile lifted her lips as she spoke. My heart jumped. I was making ground.

"I left because I didn't want you to go into shock. While I was gone, I came up with all the reasons I should stay away." I held up a hand when she opened her mouth, probably to protest. "I know it's no excuse. Leaving, and especially not returning, was not the right course of action to take. In the moment, I wanted to protect you. Then, I decided you could do so much better than me."

She laughed. "Funny, I've been thinking the same thing myself. That you could do better than *me*."

That broke my heart to hear. "But you're perfection."

She gazed at me for a second, then cleared her throat. "What now?"

"I want another chance. I want to show you how true our connection is." I gazed down at my hands in my lap. "Please, Katerina, will you forgive me for running off?"

"I can't deny there is a connection," she said softly. "I felt it that night, and I feel it now. As much as I tell myself there's nothing going on, nothing between us, I know it's a lie. Fighting it is starting to get exhausting."

"Then we can return to my realm and—"

She shook her head. "No, I'm not going back there. It's cold and bleak and my life is here! I have a class of students who are counting on me, as well as my dad. If Sarah and Nadia stay over there, then who is going to look after him? He's really sick. I'm not sure if Sarah told you. Our relationship with him isn't stellar, but I could never abandon him."

I nodded, my heart sinking once more. Rejected again. "I understand. Then I will take my leave."

"You're going?" She gasped. "Just like that?"

"If you don't want me..."

"I said I'm not going back to your realm," she snapped. "But you can stay here... with me. If you want to."

My heart began to beat faster at the idea, excitement and fear pulsing through me. She wanted me to stay! However, staying in the human realm would be tricky. No other shifters. I'd be forced to live the life of a human man. Was I capable of *only* being human? What if I couldn't blend in?

But when I looked at Katerina, with her big, beautiful eyes and stunning face, I couldn't refuse. This was my chance to prove to her that I wanted her. All of her.

I nodded. "All right, I'll stay with you. Long enough for us to figure out something more long-term."

"Sure," she mumbled. "I'll get some blankets and pillows for you so you're comfortable on the couch."

"The... couch." I looked down at the far-too-small-for-my-large-frame piece of furniture and swallowed uncomfortably. A loud and clear message if there ever was one. She didn't want to share her bed with me.

She disappeared down a nearby hallway, then I heard a door open and close again. "You got lucky once. I'm not ready to be so... intimate with you. I have a lot to think about, and a lot has changed."

"For the better, I hope."

When she returned, she held a small pile of blankets and pillows. She was smiling, so I took that as a good sign. "I'm looking forward to getting to know you better. Right now, that's all I can promise. You wanted a chance."

"Yes." More than anything.

"This is it." She handed me the blankets. "Now, I was just eating dinner. Are you hungry?"

I nodded. My stomach still churned with nerves, but I would do anything for my one true mate. Every second we had to bond, I was going to take, even if it meant living in a foreign world. And sleeping on a tiny couch.

We ate, and Katerina told me more about her world. The small details about her life and more about the people she loved. Her students and how happy they made her.

Then we watched a television show she liked, and I sat through the whole thing despite not understanding the storyline.

She told me about the music she enjoyed listening to when she needed to relax. I took mental notes about everything.

Finally, she yawned. The clock on the wall read midnight.

"I should get some sleep," she said. "Can't believe we stayed up this late."

I could, and I didn't want the night to end.

"Sleep well," I forced myself to say even though watching her leave me was the last thing I wanted.

But she smiled and turned away and I watched her go. My dragon rumbled inside me but didn't fight hard against me. He knew we needed to take our time with her as well. She needed to be seduced, so we would just have to be patient.

I stood up, my body aching for my mate. *Fuck.* I ran my hands through my hair, a loud groan filling my throat. Get a grip and get ready for bed.

I arranged the pillows and the blankets, stripped out of my dusty clothes and climbed on to my makeshift bed, folding up my legs to try and fit. I wouldn't get much sleep on the tiny thing, but at least I could rest a little, knowing I was in my mate's house.

We might have been separated in body, but in spirit, I felt a whole lot closer.

Katerina

Lucian and I spent the whole weekend in my house, just talking and getting to know each other better. I studied his mannerisms and tried to decipher all the words he wasn't saying. He seemed like a genuine guy and I could sense he was actually telling the truth when he spoke.

But doubt crept in anyway, although that might have had something to do with the fact that my period was still late. Now it was late by five days—almost a full week—and I couldn't blame it on stress any longer.

"I'm going to the grocery store," I announced Sunday evening.

"We've already eaten," Lucian said, as though that was the only reason to go shopping.

"I'm out of coffee," I managed. It wasn't a lie, so I didn't feel guilty using that as an excuse. If my suspicions were right though, I wouldn't be drinking coffee for a while.

I went to the nearest store and got myself a pregnancy test. Completely distracted, I'd already paid for it when I realized I was about to go home with no coffee, so I doubled back and grabbed a bag of my favorite roasted beans.

Being away from Lucian felt... wrong. I missed him even for the few minutes I was in the store. Or rather, I missed the way I felt around him.

I thought about telling him what I was doing, I truly did. Having him with me as I bought the test then took it, would have stopped my body from shaking so much with stress.

But until I knew for sure what the result was, I didn't want to say anything. Why ruin the beginning of a possible new relationship with unnecessary drama?

When I got home, I put the test in the bathroom so I could take it after he fell asleep. But the joke was on me, and I fell asleep on the couch, my head on his lap, while we watched a movie. Eventually, I did make it back to my room, but I was too tired to worry about the test.

First thing in the morning, I couldn't put it off any longer. My alarm clock went off at five a.m., and I'd run out of excuses. Lucian was still sleeping on the couch, so I had the privacy I needed.

As my stomach flipped with anxiety, I summoned the courage to creep to the bathroom and find the box I'd stashed there. I took the test and did my makeup while waiting for the results. That was the only thing I could think of to distract myself so I didn't pace in front of the clock and accidentally wake Lucian. My hands shook the whole time, so it was a miracle I didn't end up looking like a clown.

Five minutes passed slowly. I checked the test. Positive.

My heart fell. "No," I whispered. "No, no, no."

I blinked back hot tears as I disposed of the evidence in the trash beneath used tissues and other random items. I didn't want Lucian to see the test before I could talk to him... and that wouldn't be happening until after I got home from work.

Hopefully that would give me enough time to figure out what to say—

and what I was going to do. No, I couldn't make a decision without discussing the situation with him. That wouldn't be fair. But I should at least think about it first.

He's going to be so pissed.

Thoughts of impending doom raced through my mind while I waited for my coffee to brew. A coffee I couldn't drink because of the caffeine but made out of habit all the same.

It sat in my thermal mug all day, mocking me.

For the sake of my students and my ability to teach that day, I pushed any worry about Lucian's reaction out of my brain. The thoughts kept trying to creep in, and I squashed them down until three o'clock.

As soon as my kiddos were on the bus, I closed the door to the classroom, sat down at my desk and cried. Full-on ugly sobbing.

I just got Lucian back and now he's going to leave again.

According to him, finding out I was his true mate had sent him spiraling out of control. A baby was going to push him over the edge. Talk about a life-altering change! We were going to be responsible for raising another human being.

Or were we?

Horror filled my chest, making the tears dry up. What if the baby came out a dragon? What if it came out with scales and magic? Was I even going to be able to give birth to it?

I'd seen the long talons and sharp teeth on Lucian when he was in dragon from. No way was I going to be able to push out a creature like that from my body without suffering some sort of damage. I probably wouldn't even survive!

Just the thought of giving birth to a normal baby terrified me. I'd heard it was the most painful experience a woman could go through. But a *dragon*?

And I'm going to get bigger. Even bigger than I already am.

There was no way I could avoid that. The baby would be growing inside of me, and I in turn, would get even fatter. I tried to imagine myself pregnant and didn't like what I saw in my imagination. Would people even realize I *was* pregnant? Or would they assume the worst about me?

I knew for a fact I wouldn't be one of those cute girls who looked like they'd shoved a basketball up her t-shirt. I'd look like a hippo.

If Lucian and I had been together for longer than a handful of hours, I might have felt less insecure. Even better—if the baby had been planned and not the result of a one-night stand. But circumstances weren't ideal, so my brain was on overdrive and my self-esteem was at a record low.

He was never going to stay with me, and he certainly wouldn't look at me with desire once I turned into a pumpkin.

"This can't be happening," I whispered.

I looked up at the clock and knew I had to get back home. Lucian was waiting and somehow, I had to find the words to tell him my news.

I drove home and rehearsed a number of approaches. Funny, cute, serious, matter of fact.

Hey, guess what? You knocked me up with one try. Pretty good, huh?

There were too many options, and I didn't know him well enough to guess which would work best.

He's a no-nonsense kind of guy, I think. So maybe I'll just state it point-blank.

When I walked into my house and saw him cooking dinner, I lost all my nerve. *I'm only a few weeks along. Maybe the test is a false positive.*

Yes, that made perfect sense.

Besides, what if something happens and I lose it?

That thought scared me just as much as having a baby did. I couldn't lose it. I didn't want to. But I wasn't far along, and a lot could change in a week. Look what had happened in just the last few hours.

And there he was, standing in my kitchen cooking dinner for me. His large form, performing such an ordinary domestic chore, gave me butterflies in the belly. Even the smile he shot in my direction as I walked in the door was perfection. Why destroy that the beginning of something that could be beautiful, when everything was still so new and fragile?

I'll wait a week or two. That'll give me more time to prepare, and us more time to know if what we have is real.

And more importantly, if it was going to last.

"You're home later than I thought," he said. "Though, that's for the better, because dinner might be a little delayed."

I set my purse down. "What brought this on?"

"What?" he asked.

"You cooking dinner," I said, gesturing to the stove. I leaned against the wall near the kitchen counter. "You're a guest, remember?"

He was so beautiful. Way too good for me.

"I thought the best way to get on your good side would be to make you food." He grinned.

I scowled at him, hating the inference. "Why? Because I'm fat?"

"What?" He frowned.

"The best way to get on my good side is food because I'm fat," I repeated, crossing my arms over my chest. "Fat girls love food, right? We don't like flowers or books or poems. Just lavish dinners and decadent chocolate."

He raised a brow. "Actually, the hope was to prove that I'm self-sufficient and reliable," he said coolly.

I rolled my eyes, wanting to contain my sudden annoyance but somehow unable to stop. "If you want to impress me, do the dishes when you're done and all my laundry. Then keep doing it for a week, then two, then a month, and for a whole year. Cooking one dinner doesn't prove anything to me."

"Right." He turned back to the pot on the stove and stirred vigorously. "But this dinner is a start. I thought."

It was. I couldn't argue with that, but somehow, I did anyway. What had gotten into me? "Sure, Lucian. Whatever you say."

"Why are you being so nasty?" he snapped.

I was. I couldn't deny it, and I didn't even know why. I shrugged. "I'm being realistic," I grumbled and marched off to go sit on my living room couch.

It was easy for him to say all of these things *now*. Life was still easy. We were in the honeymoon period of dating. The beginning, where everything felt magical and perfect. A place he was in, and I couldn't be, not when I had to plan ahead just in case.

And if I lost him for good, I didn't know how I would cope.

Katerina

Lucian turned down the pot on the stove and followed me to the couch. He sat next to me, his gaze never leaving my face. "Elaborate, please. I'm missing something. How is giving me sass and sarcasm being realistic?"

"It's self-preservation!" I exploded. "You can say until the cows come home that you're going to stick around and be a perfect partner for me. I'm not going to believe any of it until I see it. Sure, one dinner is a start. I get that, but you're going to ditch me. It's only a matter of time."

"Why do you doubt me?"

"Because every other guy I've been with has left!"

"I'm not them!" he seethed, his eyes flashing with anger.

I snorted. "Because you're my soulmate?"

"Yes!"

"Soulmate or not, you'll get tired of me eventually. Once you realize you can have a hotter girl..." I shook my head. "I'm great for conversation, but you know you deserve a girl who matches your looks."

He shook his head. "I'm looking at the most attractive woman I've ever laid eyes on."

"Stop! You're just—"

"No, I'm not." He leaned forward and took my hand in his. "Do I strike you as a man who just says things to placate another? No woman compares to you, Katerina. When you leave, all I can think about is when you'll be home again. Whatever physical flaws you think you have, I don't see. Even before we met, when I imagined my ideal mate, I saw *you*."

He cupped my face with his hand, the other settling on the curve of my waist. "The same figure. Your long hair. Perhaps not every vivid detail, but I craved you. When I finally saw you in the flesh, it was like my every fantasy came true."

Tears pooled in my eyes as I listened to him. Could he possibly be telling the truth? "But I'm... I'm... bigger than..."

"Why do you assume that's ugly?" he asked softly. "Who told you that lie?"

"Everyone," I croaked out. All my life. Everyone at school, growing up. Comparing me to my perfect, younger sisters.

Every boyfriend. The media. Magazines. Society.

He didn't say a word. He simply drew me into his arms on the sofa, and I broke down into sobs. The pain of past rejection, the pressure to live up to a standard I wasn't genetically designed for, the relief and love he felt for me... it all was too much to hold onto. I released it all hile being held in his arms and sobbing against his chest. When I finally stopped sobbing and my face was wet and hot, he lifted my face toward him.

"Better?" he asked.

"Yeah." I wiped at the tears, needing to blow my nose. "I'm sorry I was a bitch."

Now I really must look ugly. "I need a tissue. Give me a minute." I jumped up and grabbed for the Kleenex box, mopping my face.

When I finally felt like I'd gotten control of myself, I sat down beside him once more.

Then Lucian leaned in and kissed me. Soft at first, but as his lips touched mine, heat exploded between us. That same hunger and need that I felt the night of Sarah's wedding. It would be so easy to just fall into that same heat and pleasure. But I was scared.

"Tell me I can trust you," I whispered against his lips. "That you aren't going to break my heart."

"You can trust me," he said softly. "I'm not going to hurt you. My word is my bond, and ours is forever."

Swoon. I pulled him in for another kiss, pressing my chest against his, ready to have him right then and there. He did something that surprised me.

He picked me up. Correction. He lifted me up into his arms and I was being held in a classic damsel-on-a-romance-cover pose. Never before in my life had any guy ever attempted such a gesture of affection, let alone achieved it so easily.

I wrapped my arms around his neck and gazed lovingly into his dark eyes. My heart was already his, completely open and vulnerable. Lucian could do whatever he wanted to me and then some—for better or worse.

I was smitten, head over heels, and it was dangerous.

Lucian carried me to the bedroom, sat on my bed, and stroked a few strands of hair out of my face. "You're breathtaking. So beautiful. Would you stand so I can see all of you?"

"I... okay." I crawled off his lap and stood in front of him, awkward and shy.

He stood with me and circled around me, studying every part of me. Slowly, he undressed me, piece by piece. First, he slipped my blouse down my arms. Then he kissed my bare shoulders so tenderly that he sent a shiver of longing down my spine. Next, he helped me out of my pants, letting them drop to the floor. A hand ran along my bare legs, and I could barely hold in the moan.

Everything he did with me, and to me, was magical.

"I'm not sure which part of you is my favorite," he confessed, his voice husky and deep. "There are so many wonderful things about your body. Your soft skin, those legs for days..." He moved behind me and kissed my neck. "You taste delicious."

I giggled to break the tension around us. "Are you a cannibal now?"

"Ha." He undid the clasp of my bra and let that fall to the ground next.

I struggled not to cover myself with my arms. The light in the room was stark. He'd see every ripple of cellulite, my sagging boobs...

Lucian moved in front of me and took my breasts in his hands, plumping them up, then dropping his head to suckle on each of my nipples.

My weight forgotten, I threaded my fingers into his beautiful, thick hair and let out a moan of pleasure.

He glanced up at me. "Oh, I love that noise you make. And the look on your face... I want to see more."

"This isn't fair," I choked out as he slid my panties down my legs and continued to kiss along my skin. "You have way too many clothes on."

"I can fix that." He stripped quickly, revealing his muscled body to me. His eagerness was clear when I saw his large cock bounce up, red and swollen.

He wants me. And, God, I want him.

Lucian sat down on the bed and laid back. "I want to watch your pleasure. If that's all right, I mean. Your face is beautiful."

He wanted me on top of him? Seriously?

I swallowed hard, nervous yet excited. No one ever wanted to see me in that position, but the fact that he did, made me trust him even more. I slid my leg over his waist and straddled his ridged abdomen.

I didn't want to hurry, so I leaned forward and trailed kisses down his sculpted chest, rocking my hips so that I could feel his large cock beneath me.

I groaned when he shifted beneath me, found my entrance and entered me. I ached for him, and his length filled me so perfectly it was hard not to sob with relief.

"That feels sooo good."

Lucian grabbed my hips and guided me into a rocking motion. I put my hands on his chest and stared down at him, the intensity in his face making every moment better.

Together, we found our rhythm, and we were even more in sync than last time. Waves of pleasure rolled over me with every thrust of his body inside mine. I gave him exactly what he wanted, letting him see my pleasure. I was exposed and free. Insecurity fled and I relished in the sensation of the depth of his want—his love.

I closed my eyes and threw my head back, riding him faster and harder. I moaned, I gasped, and told him in every way how much I wanted him.

He let me take control, let me set the pace. I glided up and down his cock over and over again, building the pleasure inside my belly.

When he groaned and grabbed for my hips, I stared down at him. His face was set, his jaw clenched. He was close.

He began to thrust up into me, amplifying my pleasure. I gasped as he pushed me closer to orgasm.

"Oh... Ah..."

Lucian fucked me hard and fast, pushing me higher. The sensation was almost too much to bear, yet not anywhere near enough. I moved faster, needing more until we hit the peak together and climaxed. Lucian cried out and buried himself deep inside me, pulsing heat into my belly.

His orgasm pushed me into a rolling orgasm, making me scream and shudder.

I collapsed onto his chest, shivering in his arms. My orgasm continued to echo inside me, my pussy still pulsing around his cock. Lucian gently rolled us to the side, holding me close. I cuddled into his body for warmth now that the heat of the session began to dissipate.

He drew a blanket up and over us, then came back to lay his head against my chest. "Dinner will be cold now."

"That's what microwaves are for," I murmured, wrapping my arms around his shoulders and holding him to me.

"How about I go use it and bring dinner to you?" His eyes lit up, as though he was eager to serve.

I smiled at him, my post-orgasmic bliss stealing over me and making me drowsy. "Yes, please."

"I'll be right back."

I lay back in bed and closed my eyes, the whole night replaying inside my head. Once again, sex with Lucian felt like a dream.

I still couldn't believe that he'd picked me up and carried me to the bedroom. The attentive way he'd worshiped my body had been truly beautiful, and the fact that he wanted to bring me dinner in bed afterward was surreal. It all felt too good to be true.

But it *was* all real. My life wasn't just a fantasy playing out in my mind. Finally, I had the chance for a solid relationship that would go the distance.

My hand crept down and pressed against my still-flat stomach.

I also had a chance to have the family I'd always wished for. With my child, I'd have a deep connection. I wouldn't be distant like my parents were with me when I was younger. My child would be close with aunts, and siblings who may follow.

So much potential for happiness, and all of it within my grasp. At last, life was finally turning around.

CHAPTER
TEN

Lucian

I should have been living my happily ever after.

Katerina was mine at last, and she was willing to give me a chance to show her my love and commitment. From there, we should have been planning a wedding and making her home *our* home. We should have finally been at peace.

Unfortunately, that peace didn't last. We spent the first week engrossed in each other. While she left for work during the day, I tidied up the house and repaired any broken items in her home. Her dripping kitchen sink, and the toilet that ran incessantly unless the handle was jiggled. All while cooking and tending to her basic needs, so that our evenings could be spent in bed.

Making love to her was the highlight of my day. She was luscious and generous in bed. So fucking beautiful.

Over the two days she called the weekend, we went on a date in town, and I got to see more of her neighborhood. None of it felt like home, and the way the humans lived seemed strange to me.

I wasn't sure how they felt purpose in their lives or contentment, but I was willing to learn.

The following Monday morning, some of the glow began to fade.

"Are you sure you want to stay home alone all day?" Katerina asked while she was picking up her keys to leave for work.

I nodded, that tight feeling in my gut returning at the reminder of how out of place I was in this world. And how much I missed her when she was gone. "Where else can I go? I can't watch you work."

"No, I guess not," she mumbled. "That'd be a distraction. For me and the kids." She paused. "But you can meet them at the school social next Friday."

"I'd like that." I wanted to watch her with her students and get a taste of what she did at work.

"Great!" Her eyes lit up and her obvious excitement reduced my despondence at knowing she'd soon be gone for the day. "What are you going to do while I'm at work?" she asked.

"I'll find something around here to fix." I gave her a quick grin.

She kissed my cheek. "Thank you. I'll be back before you know it."

And then she was gone, and I was alone again. If I could find an actual purpose, then I might feel less bored and frustrated. Back in my home realm, I'd fly and patrol the lands on a regular basis to make sure it was safe from our enemies. Or I'd train. There, I felt useful and needed. Here in the human realm I was nothing.

I had to look on the bright side, though. I had Katerina. I'd figure something out. This world was new to me. I couldn't judge the place from living here for only one week. Settling in took time.

That's what Dymitri would tell me. Just give it time.

When her car disappeared from sight, the emptiness hit me like a solid blow to the gut. I looked about the house. How could I help her next?

My gaze landed on her front yard. The space had clearly been neglected for some time. The lawn was trimmed just enough to prove someone lived at the house. Her flowers looked awfully thirsty and were obviously struggling to survive.

Her yard in back was rather sad to behold in general. She had a few potted flowers, and the tiniest of patios. Maybe she'd enjoy her backyard more if there was a beautiful space in which to spend time. That was something I could help with!

I found a blank piece of paper and began to sketch out a plan. A better patio. No, I decided. She should have a deck in the back! With a place for a nice fire pit for bonfires in the evening. The thought of cuddling up to her in front of a fire brought a smile to my face. I could make a spot for flowers along the edges. She would like that, and then I'd make her a vegetable garden.

My heart lifted as I planned and sketched. When I finished the plans, I nodded in satisfaction. Now, I just had to build the thing. Katerina had tools in her garage. Surprisingly, a lot of them. All I needed was the wood. It seemed the human realm sold wood, cut and ready for use—quite different from my home, where we had to take an axe out into the woods and chop down what we needed.

Thanks to some cash Katerina had left for me, I was able to get my order delivered within a few hours. By the time she came home, I had the wood organized in piles, along with all the other supplies needed.

She didn't notice. Her backyard was a chaotic disaster, and she didn't once glance out the windows.

When I walked inside to greet her, she yawned loudly. "Ugh, I'm exhausted. Are you okay with just cuddling on the couch tonight? I don't care what we watch. I'm just so..." She yawned again.

"Whatever you need," I said, meaning every word. "I'll make dinner for us. Go ahead and relax. Your day must have been tough."

"Those kids have too much energy. I can't keep up sometimes," she said with a tiny smile, meandering over to the couch.

I frowned, disappointed at the fact she hadn't noticed the beginning stages of my latest project. However, this created a new opportunity. If she was always tired upon coming home, which she seemed to be, then I could reveal the new deck to her once it was finished. It'd be a great surprise!

So that's what I worked on every day to pass the time—the only way I felt I could be of use to her since she always seemed so run down and tired. All the while, I pondered how I could find my place in the human world.

When Friday rolled around, I was excited for the change of scenery and to see more of Katerina's world. She drove us to her school in her car —something I didn't need at home, obviously, with my in-built wings. School turned out to be a small, brick building, buzzing with activity as every student played outside on the playground while the parents and teachers chatted. Teachers at a table handed out ice creams.

As soon as we got out of the car, lots of young children ran up, shouting for Katerina.

"Miss Kat! Miss Kat!" one girl called out. Her gaze settled on me, and her eyes widened. "Is he your boyfriend!"

Katerina gazed up at me and laughed a little self-consciously. "Something like that, yeah."

Not quite the enthusiastic response I was hoping for, but it was better than her saying "no". The realization that she was finally attaching a level of commitment to our relationship was a good thing, though.

She *did* want me. Otherwise, I reminded myself, she wouldn't have taken me here to meet her students and co-workers. That gave me hope that she wanted the future I did too.

This is going to work. We are going to be okay.

"He's really tall," a boy said, coming over. "And big! I can't see! The sun is in my eyes."

I knelt down so I was closer to his height. "Is this better?"

The boy narrowed his eyes, studying me. "I guess you're okay."

I chuckled and took Katerina's hand as the boy ran off. Her fingers closed tightly around mine, as if she was grateful for the contact. She still wasn't saying much in relation to us, but small gestures like that were becoming more frequent.

We moved toward the playground, the kids talking so fast I could barely keep up. Katerina declined the offer of an ice cream when we passed the table.

"My stomach is still feeling off," she said, putting her hand to her belly. A problem she'd been having a lot more lately. Was she ill? Maybe going out was a bad idea.

"Are you okay?" I asked, squeezing her hand.

She nodded. "I'm great. Promise." She gave me a reassuring smile, and that was enough. For the moment.

I watched my mate in her element. She talked to the students like they were her friends, and she handled all of the parents with grace—including any who talked to her about concerns they had.

Her co-workers bombarded me with all kinds of questions. Where had we met? Where was I from? How long had we been together? I tried to keep all my answers simple, as Katerina seemed to value her privacy.

"My brother's wedding... A small town. You probably haven't heard of it... It's been a few weeks."

I hoped I was doing well, but still felt like a fish out of water. I wasn't used to following someone else's lead. Seeing her with her friends and her work family... it made me miss my own. I hadn't spoken to Dymitri since leaving home weeks ago. He was honeymooning though, so he was probably glad I wasn't there to interrupt.

I wanted to actually see him in person—taking to the skies together like we used to. The urge to let out my dragon and fly was becoming more urgent the longer I stayed here.

I assumed Dymitri was doing well. Someone would have arrived across the veil to tell me otherwise if he wasn't. And Damon... I had still been getting to know him when I left. Would our burgeoning relationship take a step backward because I wasn't home?

No, he'll understand. This is my true mate, after all.

I still missed him though, and the odd family bond we'd begun to build.

My brothers, my home, now felt like a place that only existed in my dreams. It was a feeling that left me anxious. A lot about Katerina's world did that. I was in a foreign land with only one ally.

I smiled my way through the event, being polite and keeping my grumpy dragon at bay while he screamed at me internally. For Katerina, I refused to falter. I was determined to never lose control of my shifter again.

We only stayed for an hour, but it felt an awful lot like five.

"Thank you for coming with me," she said as we climbed into the car. "But I can tell you weren't exactly comfortable there. If you hated it you don't have to come next time."

I shook my head. "I want to be with you. I'll get used to the crowds eventually. I've never been much of a people person."

"Not surprised by that at all." She laughed, turning on the engine and pulling out of the parking lot. "That brooding loner vibe you give off almost scared me away from talking to you at the wedding."

"It did?" I glanced over at her, surprised at the comment.

She squeezed the steering wheel a little tighter. "Almost, but I can't stay away from you. Even if my head tells me none of this makes sense... I feel..."

"The bond," I finished for her. "What you're feeling is our bond."

"It's definitely something," she admitted quietly, then louder she said, "I like it, though. What we have. It's different from anything I've ever experienced, and it's nice to have it all feel easy."

I nodded, showing I was listening, though I didn't necessarily feel the same way.

Being with Katerina felt safe—like home. But it was far from easy. I don't think she understood how much of my life was being changed or put on hold for her comfort. I didn't plan on telling her any time soon, though. The least I could do was try and adapt for her. She'd already done the same for me, letting me into her life. Lovers compromised for each other all the time...

Didn't they?

"When we get home, I want to show you what I've been doing all week," I said, feeling a flutter of excitement inside my chest.

"Besides cleaning my house and cooking?" she said, her eyes sparkling with light. "You know, I was starting to wonder how you didn't die of boredom. That night I said that, about doing all my cooking and stuff. I didn't mean you really had to. I was feeling pretty cranky and, well, I appreciate all you've been doing, but you don't have to."

"I want to," I said, glancing out the window as the houses flew by. And it was true. I did enjoy doing things to make Katerina's life easier if I could.

She cleared her throat. "I... err... there's something I want to talk to you about when we get home, too."

Her mouth snapped shut then, but her eyes were soft. What did she want to talk about? It didn't seem like anything to be concerned about. "Okay," I said, deciding I could be patient. "Me first, though. I really want to show you..." I broke off, nearly giving away the surprise.

"You've got me curious now," she said, and we shared a quick grin.

When we arrived, I put my hands over her eyes as soon as we were out of the car. "Trust me, I won't let you stumble."

She giggled and pressed her warm fingers over my hands. "I trust you."

I loved hearing those three words.

I guided her through the garage and to the back door. We entered the backyard, and I brought her to the edge of the new deck. "Now you can look." I removed my hands from her eyes and walked around her so I could see her reaction.

She squinted for a second, then gasped. "You... how... what?"

"This is what I made while you were at work this week."

"How did I not notice?" Her voice was full of wonder. She stepped up the small staircase and then sat on one of the built-in bench seats on the deck. "There's no way you did this all by yourself, surely?"

"Of course, I did." I sat next to her. "You didn't notice because you come home exhausted every night and you're early into bed, too."

"Do not."

I gave her a pointed look. "I've seen more brain activity from a zombie."

She gasped. "Zombies are real too?"

I snorted. "Not as far as I know. It was a joke, Kat."

A blush spread across her cheeks. "It's been a long week. And, yeah, I guess you're right. I have been extra tired, lately."

"I'm not judging you," I clarified. "Though I am worried."

She took a deep breath and let it out slowly, then whispered something almost under her breath. It was only my acute dragon hearing that managed to pick up what she'd said. "I'm afraid of losing you."

"Kat," I said, lifting a hand to stroke her cheek. She leaned into my caress and closed her eyes for a moment. "I'm not planning on going anywhere."

"I..." She took another breath in and out. "I'm good. It's just..."

"Been a long week. I know." I nodded and grabbed one of her hands with my own. "And now you have another place you can rest. Perhaps having some sunshine will help?"

"Maybe," she whispered. She bit her lip then shook her head. "Thank you, Lucian. For everything. Your patience. Everything."

I leaned in and kissed her sweetly on the lips. "I would do anything for you."

Even keep my dragon at bay.

I couldn't lose her.

For her, I'd find a way to make this strange world full of humans work.

"I don't know what I'd do without you," she whispered as she stared up at me with her big, beautiful eyes glistening with unshed tears.

Those words made the sacrifice feel worthwhile.

I wanted to tell her I loved her, to show her how deeply that love ran by taking her upstairs to bed and ravishing her until she screamed in ecstasy. Instead, I put my arm around her, settled her into my embrace, and we gazed across her fresh lawn. If the house felt like home for her, it could feel the same for me as well.

Home was a construct created by connections. My dragon family would understand.

CHAPTER
ELEVEN

Katerina

Every time I tried to tell Lucian I was pregnant, the words stuck in my throat. At first, it was simply fear of losing him that stifled my voice. What if telling him ruined everything? We'd reached the month-long milestone in our relationship with hardly any hiccups.

Then, as time went on, I was embarrassed that I'd said nothing, and it became even harder to broach the subject. How was I going to tell him? The right words just weren't coming to me. We got along so well. Everything felt so good. So... right.

I desperately wanted to tell him, I really did. But it had been so long now, I felt stuck. Three weeks passed quickly and I remained silent. I worked with my kids and Lucian worked on projects around the house. Every day he updated something. It wouldn't have surprised me if I came home one day, and he'd decided to gut the kitchen and start fresh.

I was just glad he had found something that he seemed to enjoy.

As the weeks passed, my morning sickness grew stronger, and my exhaustion became harder to ignore. I thought for sure Lucian would put two and two together, but he didn't.

He noticed I often wasn't feeling well, but he wasn't hugely familiar with my life or that of normal humans, so I guess he assumed that tiredness was a normal condition for me. After all, we hadn't spent much time together before he'd moved in. Not to say he ignored my health, quite the opposite. He asked me often if I felt okay, and if I was sick. Not once did he ask if I was pregnant, and I still hadn't told him.

"You need to eat," I whispered to myself as I stared down at the lunch I had brought to work with me. Once again the food was going to go uneaten.

I didn't know what to do, and wanted to ask my sisters for help. But Sarah was likely busy being a new wife, and Nadia hardly answered her phone. The reception in the other realm seemed to be terrible. Though I'd been able to get through once or twice, I could barely hear her voice, and vice versa. It became easier not to even try calling, in the end.

If they knew I was in such inner turmoil, they wouldn't ignore me, of that I was sure. Part of me didn't want to say anything anyway, because I knew they'd side with Lucian. It was so easy for them to tell me not to worry. They'd never known rejection like I had.

I gazed at my lunch, wishing I could will myself to eat. So far, I'd dropped three pounds. The internet said that losing weight was normal in the beginning of a pregnancy, so I tried not to worry about the baby too much. If a human baby sucked up a lot of energy from its mom, then I imagined a half-dragon baby might deplete even more.

"I have to tell him this weekend," I mumbled to myself and rubbed at my forehead with a hand. "I've put it off long enough."

I needed to stop being a coward. Come what may, Lucian had the right to know, and I didn't want to hide it from him any longer. I wanted him to know why I kept refusing wine with dinner, and why I wouldn't eat the sushi he'd bought. It was time, and I'd find a good way to break the news that hopefully put it in a positive light so he wouldn't run away screaming. Again.

"Tomorrow, I'm treating you for a change," I announced when I walked in the door that night after work. "So don't make any plans, okay?" That would buy me a night to think and plan.

If only he wasn't so distracting. With those lips... and the way he touched me... We made love practically every night. I didn't have a ton of energy, but I always managed to find time for that! Being one with him restored my soul in ways I'd never thought possible.

Lucian gazed at me, his head tilted slightly to the side. "Why?"

I coughed, startled. "What do you mean, why? Can't I do nice things for you too? You've been working so hard around here, and doing so much."

"Because I..." He swallowed. "All right. I won't argue."

"Good! I mean, you built me a freaking *deck*!"

"I was bored. You needed one." He shrugged like it was nothing.

It wasn't nothing, and it wasn't just the deck. He'd transformed my old, needing-some-TLC house, into a stunning place.

I shook my head. "Goof."

"That's a peculiar term of endearment," he said as he walked over and grabbed me. Then he kissed me deeply, and I melted into him. My nervousness grew and I made love to him that night like it might be the last time.

Being Friday, I didn't have to work for the next two days. That gave me plenty of time to plan, spill the beans, then deal with the fallout, whatever it might be. I slept restlessly, unsure of what the future would bring, but knowing it was time to step up and be an adult. I was going to become a mom! I needed to let Lucian know, and then we would deal with whatever happened next.

The next morning, I rose early and went straight to the store to get everything I needed for my big announcement. A light lunch for myself and something more substantial for him. If things went well, there were cupcakes. If things got awkward fast, I had fruit salad... and I'd save the cupcakes for myself later, if I could bring myself to eat them.

I set a blanket across the lovely new deck and some pillows on the blanket to soften the seating. It seemed such a small gesture in comparison to everything he'd done for me.

"Ready for lunch?" I asked, my stomach twisting with anxiety.

"Sure," he answered, sweeping his long hair back into a low ponytail and fastening it with one of my hair ties. "What's going on, Kat?"

Instead of answering, I took his hand in mine and walked him outside. We both got comfortable on the blanket, and I sat with my legs crossed and my hands in my lap. How was I going to even start?

He looked at me expectantly, so I just rushed into the conversation. "So... your instinct was right. I do have a hidden agenda."

Oh my God, that sounds terrible!

He frowned. "Should I be worried?"

"Maybe," I mumbled. "Hopefully not." I took a deep breath, and then just blurted out the news I'd been trying—and failing—to tell him for days. "Lucian, I'm pregnant."

Not the graceful, fun way I'd wanted to tell him, but nerves had gotten the better of me.

I braced myself for the worst, watching him carefully and barely able to breathe as I tried to gauge his reaction. He said nothing. He didn't even look at me. He just stared down at one of my pretty pillows, decorated with purple lace, and blinked a few times before reaching out a finger to trace the lacy pattern.

Had he heard me? Was he in shock? Horrified? Was he about to jump to his feet, shift into his dragon form, and fly off into the sky?

"Um, anyway," I said, when the silence continued. "I started suspecting right before you decided to knock on my door. That makes me think I'm about eight weeks along now, but I'm not sure. I haven't been to a doctor or anything yet. I, uh... think it happened the night we first..."

Finally, he spoke up. "The wedding."

"Yes." I took another shuddering breath, trying desperately to keep calm. My insides were churning, and my chest was tight. This was it. This was the part where he ran. "So, I'm sorry this happened. It's not like I wanted it to be this way. And I'm sorry I didn't say anything sooner, but I wanted to be sure. That's why I've felt so unwell lately, and exhausted."

More silence.

"If this is where you want to bow out, that's fine. I won't take it personally. I know having a kid is probably not high on your to-do list. I'll deal with this alone." I swallowed back my tears as my throat began to tighten. "Don't feel like you owe me anything, Lucian. You don't. You really don't."

"What are you talking about?" he asked, finally lifting his head and gazing at me. An enormous smile formed on his lips and his eyes shone. "This is *amazing!*"

"It... it is?" I blinked, unsure if I'd heard him right. I was so sure he'd be unhappy.

Was he serious?

"Yes! Of course, it is!" He reached over and tugged me into his arms. "We're going to be parents! We've bonded and mated and now there's going to be a little one as proof of our love."

I laughed awkwardly, swallowing hard against the clog in my throat. "It's proof of something."

That we'd jumped into bed the minute we met.

"I know I love you," Lucian said firmly, staring down at me.

I struggled to sit up properly, staying close, but not wanting to be in his arms anymore. I needed space between us, so I could study his expression.

"Please don't lie to me just because I'm pregnant," I whispered. "You barely know me. How can you love me? Because some witch told you I was your soulmate? Because an inner beast insists it's true?"

Nothing about his dragon soulmate tale made any sense to me. Not any logical sense, anyway.

Lucian's eyebrows lowered and he stared at me, hard.

"We've got our whole lives to discover everything about one another." He grabbed my hand and gave it a squeeze. "What I feel is real. I hope you feel it, too. That's what matters right now. Everything else will fall into place."

Deep in my bones, I agreed with him. It did feel real. And so damn right. But that treacherous voice in the back of my head wouldn't shut up. "Things are only going to get harder, you know that, right? Kids complicate life. I'm not going to be one of those graceful, sporty, awesome moms. I feel terrible, physically. I hate how I look and that's only going to get worse as I get bigger. I'm a hot mess, Lucian."

"Yes, you are indeed hot," he purred.

"Ha." I shoved at his chest, not sure whether to laugh or burst into tears.

"I'm being very serious," he said. "Why do you keep talking so poorly of yourself? I thought we'd discussed this already."

I looked away, unable to handle the weight of his gaze. "Because it'll be easier on me if we do this now rather than further down the road. The longer you wait, the higher my hopes get, and then when you leave... it'll destroy me."

And any child we had together.

"You're planning for a day that is never going to come." He stroked my cheek with his fingers. "You have to keep trusting me."

"What if I can't?"

My biggest fear of all. What if I was too damaged by the past to ever be the woman he needed?

"Take it day by day." He pulled my face toward his, so I was looking into his eyes again. "I'm not like any of those other men." One of his hands clenched into a fist. "Just thinking about how you've been taken advantage of... that is never going to happen again!"

The flash of anger in his eyes made my breath catch in my throat. He meant every word. And that anger had flared on my behalf. He cared. He really did care.

He took in a slow breath, and his muscles tensed. "No one will hurt you or our child. I promise."

"But what if—"

"No!" Lucian growled. "There is no what if. I'm not leaving you. I'm not leaving our baby. We are bound to each other for life. Not just because of the soulmate bond, but because of that child. I am not going to abandon you, or my future son or daughter."

My heart fell. The man before me was honorable, and I adored him for that. But I wouldn't take advantage of him because of that amazing trait.

I'd never be able to live with myself if he stayed out of a misplaced sense of duty.

"Don't stay in a relationship with me simply because of the baby, either," I whispered. "Let's not lie to ourselves like that."

Another growl and I actually saw a scale form on his forearm. "I am with you because I want *you*. I always will. One day you'll begin to trust me—trust *us*—and you'll see."

I gazed at the scales developing on his skin and shivered at the growl that came from his mouth and throat. "Please," I whispered. "If you can't keep control over yourself, I'm going to need you to leave. The dragon... I can accept that it's part of who you are, but it doesn't belong in this world. It's dangerous. For me, the baby, and for you."

He'd be locked up, or worse, if anyone from here saw him transform into a dragon.

"I'm not going anywhere without you!" His chest puffed up as he spoke, and he got more animated by the second. "Just let a puny human try to take me on! They won't get far!"

"Lucian!" I gasped. "*I'm* one of those puny humans!"

He gazed at me and the fear I was feeling on the inside must have been written all over my face, because the tension left his body.

"Yes, I mean everyone else. Like the men who've hurt you in the past."

"They're not here anymore," I said. "And I don't plan on ever talking to them again."

"Good." Lucian closed his eyes and the scales disappeared until there was only tanned flesh once again. He opened his eyes, and the man was fully back. "Does my dragon scare you?" he asked.

"It can," I said honestly. "Mostly when he tries to come out uninvited. Which seems to happen a lot, according to my sister. What if you get angry and..."

He shook his head. "My dragon would never try to harm you. Or the baby."

I knew *he* believed that, but dragons were so unfamiliar to me. How did I know for sure? How did he know, if he'd never had a mate before? "Regardless, you can't do that here. You can't change."

"Yes, I realize that would complicate things," he said.

We were both quiet for a long time.

Then his dark eyes lit up and he grinned at me. "We'll go back to my realm! We can live in the castle with my brothers and your sister. There I won't have to hide who I am. I can return to a normal life. You'll be safe, and we can raise our child together." He paused. "We can be a family. A real family."

Then in a whisper he added, "Everything I've ever wanted."

It was everything I'd ever wanted, too. Being with him, raising our child together in a home we built together... it sounded magical. Perfect. Perhaps too perfect.

I remembered the grandness of the castle. I'd been in awe and intimidated all at once. As beautiful as it was, I didn't feel drawn to stay there like my sisters clearly had. Nice to visit, but not a place to make a permanent home.

I shook my head. "I can't go back there. Your home... it's so cold. It's so far from everything I love here. My students, my father. I can't give them up. That castle didn't feel like home to me."

"I see," he said, nodding slowly and showing no emotion on his face.

Was it the same for him here? Did my home not feel like, well, *home* to him? How would we reconcile the fact that we were so different—and from completely different worlds?

"I don't want to keep you from your own kind," I said. "But you can't keep me from *mine*, either. I love this place, Lucian. Do you not think you could make it your home too? I hope you'll find a way to make this work, because I'm not leaving."

I hadn't planned to have any sort of ultimatum in this conversation, but there it was. I'd laid down the gauntlet, whether I'd wanted to, or not.

Neither one of us said anything for a long time after that. I worried that maybe I'd pissed him off and succeeded at pushing him away. After all, he was a dragon. Clearly, Lucian enjoyed being tough and in charge.

At long last, he cleared his throat. "Then obviously, the solution is that I stay. I learn self-control, keep my dragon in check, and I learn how to be human."

"Really?" I had to make sure I heard him right, that my ears weren't deceiving me.

He nodded. "Yes, really. It won't be easy, but the reward will be worth it."

Wow, he did love me like he claimed. "I thought for sure..."

"Katerina, you need to believe me. I'll do anything for you." He leaned over and kissed my lips softly. "For you and our child."

For the first time, I really did believe him. He was proving it.

Guilt stung my heart as the weight of what I'd just forced onto him hit home. I'd just asked him to deny his instincts for me. To hide half of his very being—his dragon. To give up his family and everything he was familiar with. To move to a foreign world where he knew no one and had nothing else but me.

It was so much to ask... too much, really.

And yet, Lucian loved me enough to do it.

I should have been elated, but instead I felt like a horrible person. I'd just demanded he do something that I myself had just declared I would never do for him.

"I'm so sorry," I whispered. "I—"

"What are you apologizing for?" he asked, frowning. "If you feel this is the best way for us to be together, I am going to trust that instinct."

His confidence in my decision helped and I moved forward to snuggle into his arms. But the weight of this conversation was going to haunt me.

I could already tell.

CHAPTER
TWELVE

Katerina

Time passed, and we lived together just like any other human couple. I went to work, and Lucian remodeled the bathroom to make it more efficient for me and the baby.

He continued to make my backyard gorgeous, installing a swing and building a playground. He drew up plans to fix my kitchen but hadn't gotten around to actually doing the work just yet. He seemed to enjoy construction; it was how he kept busy while I was out of the house, and when I was at home, he waited on me hand and foot.

I had mixed feelings about the latter. I loved how attentive he was to my needs and to those of our coming baby. Lucian was all in, in that regard. However, as the weeks passed, our interactions began to feel hollow. Like he was with me in body, but not in spirit. He listened to me talk but didn't say much in return.

I thought maybe he was just being broody, but then I noticed he'd had an entire shift in attitude, in general. He was very quiet. Somehow, Lucian didn't seem like the man I'd met the night of the wedding, and I wasn't quite sure what to do about it.

I was in week sixteen of my pregnancy and feeling a lot better. Once I'd gotten out of the first trimester, my appetite had returned, and life had gotten a little easier. However, now I was growing a bump, and becoming increasingly more uncomfortable. I had no idea how to tend to Lucian's emotional needs, or what the problem even was.

He wouldn't open up to me. How did I get him to do that?

Not that I was any better. I was going to my third doctor's appointment to check in on the baby, and I didn't tell Lucian that's why I was leaving for the day—only that I had errands to run for a few hours. He hadn't gone to any of my appointments, actually.

If I told him ahead of time, I knew he'd want to come with me. For the time being, I needed to go on my own. Part of me was still trying to wrap my head around growing a baby that was only half human and I needed to process what that might mean for the pregnancy itself, and for the birth.

I went to the clinic and sat in the lobby to wait. This appointment was the big one—the sonogram. I'd get to see our baby for the first time, and I was scared. What if the baby had wings or talons? The doctor would freak out. I would freak out. It'd be a mess.

A mess that I didn't want Lucian to witness. My falling apart would hurt him, I was sure.

Hearing the heartbeat for the first time hadn't been the picturesque moment I'd thought, either. I remember listening to the rapid whooshing and bursting into tears because I'd assumed that was abnormal—that I was listening to the sounds of an alien. It took the doctor twenty minutes to talk me down, and to tell me everything was in fact, just perfect.

Every visit I was told that, actually. The baby was practically perfect. That scared me more for some reason.

I didn't want to rob Lucian of these precious moments, but I was so tired of him seeing me crying, upset, sick, or anything potentially negative. No wonder he seemed so miserable all the time. He was stuck with *me.*

"Katerina Smythe," a nurse called into the lobby. I stood, and we began the process. She checked all my standard stats, then walked me back to the ultrasound room.

I lay on the exam chair and got comfortable. Warm goo was spread over my rounded belly, and a wand placed on top. To an outsider, I probably didn't look pregnant. I noticed the difference in my stomach's structure, though. I liked seeing the evidence.

My heart was pounding, and I felt like I was going to be sick. What was I going to see on the screen? Wings? Or something more human-like?

I focused on the screen and soon an image appeared. The baby looked... like a baby.

"There are the feet," the technician explained, pointing to the little white bones.

"And there's two of them?" I asked.

She laughed. "Yup! And two hands and two eyes and a nose. Your baby looks great! Let's take some measurements."

"Oh... okay." I adjusted a little and stared at the image on the screen. Sure enough, two eyes, a nose, a mouth. So human and normal. Was I wrong? Or had I dreamed that Lucian was a dragon?

No, he'd definitely turned into a dragon, and I'd been in my sound mind when I witnessed it.

The technician measured the baby's length. "Seems to be a little bigger than usual at this point. Are you sure the conception date is right?"

"Yeah," I said. "Positive." Before that night at the wedding, it had been almost six months since my last sexual encounter.

She made a note in my file, and I tried not to worry. "Did you want to know the sex?"

"For now, can we keep it a surprise?" I asked, though I was dying to know. That decision was definitely something I wanted to include Lucian on, though it was yet another thing he and I hadn't talked about. Did we want to know, or did we want to wait? Would there be a party to reveal the news to everyone? Who would even come? His family and my sisters were all in another realm, and my dad was too unwell to attend a gender reveal event.

The technician smiled. "I'll put it in an envelope for you, and when you're ready you can look. Or not."

"Thanks," I managed, though the weight of my guilt was growing by the minute.

I should have brought him today. He would have loved to see our baby.

"We're all done! I'll leave you to get cleaned up."

I nodded, grateful there wasn't much more to the appointment, because my mind was running a million miles a minute. The whole drive home, I tried to decipher my feelings from the facts. Sometimes, the two got jumbled together.

Fact: I was pregnant and starting to get excited about becoming a mother. The more time passed, the more connected I felt to the baby. I was coming to terms with the unexpected way the baby had come into existence.

Fact: Being with Lucian made me feel wonderful. He was a great man who deserved the world.

Fact: Lucian was a dragon shifter. He could change his form, and that was a trait my baby might have as well. Not might—did. Deep down in their genetic code, Lucian's dragon would live on in my child.

A baby—kids in general—I knew what to do. Dragons? Not so much. I wouldn't be able to teach him or her how to have control over their shifting, or flying, or about fated mates and the mystery behind how that worked. In fact, there was a lot about their heritage I was still clueless about.

Would Lucian be able to teach them safely in our current home? What if the neighbors saw? What if the baby breathed fire and the house burnt down? What if... there were a lot of those questions, and they all had a similar solution.

We had to go back to Lucian's realm. Our baby needed to be with its own kind. Not the answer I wanted to face, but I made peace with the hard truth on the ride home from the doctor's surgery.

I parked the car then walked into the house, rehearsing the coming conversation in my mind. Lucian would be disappointed I'd excluded him from so much, but hopefully he'd be relieved to know that we'd be moving back to his icy land and that large and not-so-comforting castle.

I shivered just thinking about it.

When I walked inside, Lucian was in the kitchen taking measurements. When his gaze fell on me, my heart sank. Despite the smile he wore on his lips, the light didn't reach his eyes.

And his face... it had sunken in. When had he gotten so thin? Even his broad shoulders looked like a shell of their former glory. How had I missed such a dramatic transformation? Lucian wasn't just miserable living here with me... he looked like he was *dying*. The longer he denied his dragon for me, the worse his condition became.

I put my hands over my face. "My God... Lucian... I'm so sorry."

"Hmm?" he asked. "For?"

"Everything," I whispered. "I don't know what to do."

He walked over and put his arms around me. "About what, beautiful?"

"About us."

His body stiffened. "What do you mean?"

"This isn't working!" I blurted out, which was far from the graceful speech I'd planned in the car. Lucian's obvious deterioration had snapped me into a terrible headspace. Seeing him in such a state shook me.

Lucian balked. "Again, what do you mean? I thought things were going well between us. We're not fighting. We're creating a home. Nothing has been bad!"

"Are you kidding me?" I shook my head, only just holding in my tears. "Lucian, I can see it all over your face. Your whole demeanor. Staying here is bad for you. You hate it here."

"No, I don't." He growled.

"Yes, you do!" I threw up my hands and turned away, because if I continued to study his thin face and frame, I'd break into ugly crying. "And I hate myself for doing this to you. You deserve so much better than staying here with me!"

He gasped. "Hardly. You are my true mate. You're the perfect one for me. Wherever you are, is the place I'm meant to be."

"I'm not the perfect one for you!" I snapped. "I'm *killing* you! You've lost weight. You don't look happy! You seem weak. This isn't right. None of this is okay! Stop lying to me to save my feelings and be *honest* with me for a change! How am I supposed to trust you otherwise?"

Lucian didn't respond right away. "Fine!" he said at last. "You want honesty? I'll give you honesty. You're right, I'm not happy. I'm miserable."

I cringed. Hearing the truth stung, but I also let out a breath I didn't know I'd been holding as relief washed over me. Truth. Finally. Now we were getting somewhere.

I spun back around to face him.

"I'm not happy because I feel like I'm worthless to you," he said. "Every day, you make it a point to tell me that you don't need me. That this is temporary until you determine if I meet your expectations. I work all day long trying to please you, and now it feels like you're throwing it back in my face."

"I'm not," I mumbled. "All I've asked is for a more realistic pacing. I don't want to run off and marry a guy I just met a week ago."

"It hasn't been a week. It's been—"

"Sixteen," I interjected. "Yes, I know." I patted my growing belly. "Believe me, I know."

He growled again. "Well, I didn't ask you to marry me!"

The way he said it made it sound as if he never intended to, either. "No, no you didn't."

"So I don't understand why you're so mad!"

"Because you just yelled at me for wanting something real with you." Tears fell down my cheeks. "That's all I've ever wanted. Something real. You play the part of a dutiful husband well. You take care of me physically, but you don't talk to me. You act more like you're my prisoner than anything else. And you're not."

I dared to look at him again and saw the deepest of glares. I shuddered.

"Where else am I supposed to go?" he asked. "I need to be with you and the baby to make sure you're both okay."

"No, you don't." I blinked away more tears. "We're doing just fine. The doctor said he or she is in prime health. And big." I still had the closed envelope that had the sex of the baby sealed away. "We can even find out what we're having, if you'd like to know."

I thought the news might soften him. I was wrong.

His chest puffed up. "You've seen our child? Why didn't you tell me? You're so quick to attack me for being silent, and you're keeping back just as much."

"You're right," I admitted. "Maybe this is a sign we're a bad match. We don't trust each other enough to open up and share."

Oh my God. How did this conversation turn so wrong, so quickly?

"You refuse to give me a chance." He shook his head. "Never have you said I'm your prisoner, but you treat me like one. You hint that I must remain locked away, out of sight of others, and I can't be myself. If I want to shift and let my inner dragon free, then I'm not welcome in your life. You said if I loved you, I would stay. If you loved me, you wouldn't have asked me to change who I am at my very core."

I hiccupped, sobbing. "Like I said, it's a sign. We're not good together. This was a mistake." My hand instinctively went to my stomach, and the reality hit me that I was about to be a single mother.

His eyes honed in on that gesture. "I see." He stormed out of the room, making his way to the back door.

I followed him, trying to think of anything that could possibly save what remained of our relationship. "Lucian, I'm so sorry."

I wanted to say that we'd be better in his realm. That I'd move there for him. But for some reason the words stuck in my throat and wouldn't spill forth.

"This is my fault," he ground out. "I was the one foolish enough to think the fated mate bond was real. That I could earn your love. I know now that's not how this works. You're the most incredible woman I've ever met. When you let me see your heart, it's gorgeous. I love you. I don't think you *want* me to love you, though. And that breaks me in two."

So much pain was in his dark eyes, it broke my heart to see it.

He stepped fully outside, then his body hunched forward and his skin melted into scales.

I stumbled back, both afraid and in awe of what was about to happen.

Soon, his whole body had transformed into a huge dragon. He turned his enormous head and stared at me for a few seconds, then, with a few graceful beats of his wings, he lifted into the sky. I watched him fly into the clouds and disappear from view.

I fell to my knees and broke down into sobs. The best thing to ever happen to me had just flown out of my life for good.

THIRTEEN

Lucian

"*This was a mistake.*" Katerina's words echoed in my head like a death knell as I flew away from the woman I loved.

She'd touched her stomach as she'd said it, and the message was loud and clear. Our baby wasn't wanted. *I* wasn't wanted. Everything we'd been building together these past few months was a lie. She didn't even think enough of me to invite me to that medical appointment that is one of the highlights of a pregnancy.

My anger was divided. Yes, I was mad at her for keeping so much from me. For not giving our relationship the chance it deserved. However, I also knew I could have done so much more to make her feel safe and comfortable. She didn't open up to me for a reason, and it was because I'd let her down and not opened up to her.

I'd stupidly believed that if I kept my thoughts and feelings to myself, she'd see me as patient and attentive—selfless—ready to step up and be an amazing father to our unborn child. Obviously, that wasn't the right approach, and I didn't understand what she wanted from me.

Why did I continue to get it all wrong?

You know why, I chided myself. *It's because you've never learned how to love. It's like the blind trying to lead the blind.*

That's why I'd failed so epically.

But I'd tried. I tried so damn hard. She didn't even give me an inch. Why did she still not believe me when I told her I loved her?

Leaving again was probably a mistake, but I had to get away. I had to breathe—to fly. I'd spent too much time in that house trying to make it a perfect home, and the result was destroying me. She was right about one thing—I was miserable, and I did feel trapped. I knew the only way I'd be able to think clearly would be to fly.

So, I left. And if I was honest, I wasn't sure if I'd be going back. Katerina had made it clear she didn't want me there. She was freeing me from my obligations to her and our child. Would she turn this around on me, or accept her part of the responsibility of failing as a couple?

Would she ever see that her fear of being loved—her absolute conviction that she was somehow unlovable—was breaking us before we even had a chance to be strong?

As I flew through the sky and toward the barrier between her realm and mine, I thought about my next action, which was critical. If I followed my anger, left and never returned, I'd be repeating the cycle started by my father. He abandoned Dymitri and me when we were young, and that created a hole in my heart I wouldn't wish on anyone.

But Katerina didn't want me, and continuing to stay and then fight with her would be disrespecting the wishes of my mate. Following my heart could be just as disastrous for us both. What if she hated me for being too pushy and aggressive? She could just as easily hate me for giving up.

I was damned either way.

On top of the rage, my heart ached in a way I had never experienced before. I'd just lost my mate—possibly forever. Katerina didn't love me.

She thought everything we'd done together was a waste. She'd kept me from being myself, quite deliberately. No wonder I felt so off in her world. I was depressed and hadn't even realized it.

Katerina saw my misery. That has to mean something...

She had the wisdom to see that we came from two different worlds that weren't compatible. *We* were not compatible, and that put me in a state of mourning. I'd been given the chance to bond with my mate, and we'd done our duty. It hadn't worked. Now it seemed that was all we'd get in our life together.

Those moments of bliss would forever remain in my memory. I'd remember what could have been, and always regret that I couldn't figure out how to make it work. As much as I wanted to blame my father for that, I knew it was *my* problem. Dymitri made his love and his marriage work. He'd learned how to push past his trauma and pain. Me? Not so much. It took a lot to ruin things with a soulmate. We were supposed to be perfect for one another.

But I'd managed to destroy any hope of happiness for both of us.

I crossed through to my realm, a shiver of cold passing over my skin. I was home.

I considered going straight to Damon's castle to speak with him about my situation. If he had advice or insight that could change my fate, I'd gladly take it.

However, there was the possibility that he'd call me an idiot, have no wisdom left to share, and tell me that I was a lost cause.

The ridicule could wait. I needed solitude and a place to properly vent my feelings so I didn't destroy the castle I'd spent so much time repairing. Besides, I felt more at home in the quietness of the woods than I did in the grandness of the castle. I wasn't the kind of man who needed luxury. I only stayed to be close to my brother and build my relationship with my family. We were stronger together.

Without them, I'm not sure I could hold myself together.

I turned in the direction of the rudimentary house I'd spent most of my life living in. Dark, ominous clouds hung over the forest. Lightning streaked the sky. I paused to assess, slowly flapping my tired wings. The weather seemed like some kind of sign from the divine, begging me to turn around and go back to Katerina. *"Make it work,"* the rumbles of thunder urged. A request I ignored.

There wasn't another settlement to land in nearby. I could cut through the storm to the house with minimal damage, or I could take the long way around and go to the castle after all. The thought of talking to either of my brothers before I felt ready was enough to make me scowl at that option. It was just a thunderstorm. Those were common. I'd flown through plenty of them before.

Forward was my choice, as I entered the thick, billowing clouds. The wind tossed me, and the rain stung as it battered my scales at full force. I welcomed the pain. It gave me plenty of distraction from the torture inside my heart. All I wanted to do was get back to the house and wallow in peace.

A sudden gust of wind gripped my wings, causing my whole body to tip and lose balance in the air current. The storm was stronger than I'd realized, but I was confident I could handle things.

Then the hail started to pelt my body. Small orbs of ice at first, that rapidly grew in size. They hit me so hard and so fast, they began to rip my skin. One tore through the softer flesh of my right wing and I screamed with surprise at the searing fire that came with the tear. Lightning flashed in front of me, and I had only a second to try and dodge it. Without the stability of two full wings, I lost control and tumbled backward through the sky with another surge of wind.

I rolled end over end through the clouds and toward the ground. The trees quickly came into view. If I didn't do something fast, I was going to crash land.

With a grunt and a growl, I managed to rightd myself again. My wing hurt so badly, the area was starting to go numb from the pain. More hail slammed into my body, the rain falling so hard that it might as well have been knives. This was much harder than it had ever been before. By neglecting my dragon for so long, being in that form felt foreign and weak. I didn't have the same instincts or the same strength that I'd had before I left my realm.

Lightning flashed, and this time I wasn't quick enough to evade. Flying into the storm had been a mistake, and it was one I would pay for dearly.

Electricity coursed through my system as a huge jolt of pain seared my whole body. The smell of burning flesh and smoke mixed in my nostrils. My vision blurred, and I spiraled toward the earth. I had just enough strength to flap my wings and push myself over the treetops and onto a nearby open field.

The top branches of one of the forest trees grazed my belly as I barely missed crashing into them. I landed hard on the ground, dirt and crops spraying everywhere as I rolled and eventually came to a stop.

I closed my eyes, feeling sick. My head... no, my entire body... throbbed with every beat of my heart. Spots of light lit my vision. I was so dizzy. Lightheaded, almost. Like I was floating.

Is this how it ends? Katerina, I'm so sorry. I shouldn't have left you and our child.

The lights disappeared, and the world went dark...

"We've got to get him to transform," someone said, the voice sounding distant. "It's the only way we can get him back to the castle."

"He's unconscious," another said with an annoyed tone. "How do you expect him to do that?"

Someone stroked my snout. "Wake up, Your Majesty. We need you to wake up!"

I groaned as my body coursed with pain.

"I told you he was alive!" the first person said. It was a man. "Your Majesty, we need you to turn back into a human. We can't carry you, in your dragon form."

Nothing he said made sense to me. I roared and tried to push him away, my dragon instincts taking over. The dragon wanted to flee, to lick his wounds alone. Every movement I made only increased the terrible agony. That was a good sign, I supposed. Before, I'd been feeling cold and numb. If I could feel pain and discomfort, then perhaps I'd live to see another day.

Live to try and make things right with Katerina.

Eventually, what they were saying began to make some sense. They wanted to move me, but as a dragon I was too large for them.

Turning back into a human, however, might be more of a challenge. But I had to try. I did my best to block out the pain and focus on my human shape. The familiar sensation of shifting fell over me, but it didn't last long. I reverted back to my dragon form almost immediately.

I was too weak to change.

"We could try and take him back to the castle on my cart," the second voice said, a woman. "They can help him more there than we can. And he might fit. Just." She touched my scales with a gentle hand. "Hold on, Your Majesty."

They manoeuvered a cart next to me, and somehow, with their guiding hands, I managed to lift up enough that they could roll me onto the vehicle. Though the anguish that ripped through my body at the movements was strong enough to make me pass out once more.

When I awoke, I was being transported in the cart. I barely fit, but it would suffice for travel. The storm continued to rumble overhead, though the worst of it had now passed.

I must have blacked out again because the next moment, a sharp jolt woke me. I was still in the cart. When my vision focused, I could see the gates of Damon's castle in front of us. My brothers were at my side, walking beside the cart.

"Thank God you were there to find him," Dymitri said.

"Lucian," Damon said. "Can you hear me? Do you understand where you are?"

I groaned in response, wanting them to know I did, but I couldn't shift back to tell them so.

"Here, this is for your help," Sarah said at the gate, offering the people who'd helped me something. I couldn't see.

"No, we don't need—"

"I insist," Sarah said, and that was the last I heard of her voice.

They brought me inside the castle grounds, and then multiple hands were on my scales and I was eventually inside the warmth of the palace itself. As soon as the huge front doors closed, something that felt like a soft cloud settled over my skin. Some kind of blanket? I was carried into one of the large dens and laid on a rug.

Dymitri rubbed my body with his hands, trying to warm me. "We need you to turn back into a human, brother."

"Then we can help you more," Damon said. He put another thick blanket over me. The extra heat helped to wake me up. Being cold always made me sleepy.

With the warmth, some of my strength returned. I tried once more to become human, and this time the transformation stuck. I shivered beneath the blankets, still wet and injured from my attempted journey through the storm.

"What are you doing here?" Dymitri asked. "Is everything okay?"

"Katerina…" Her name was the only word I could manage. My head hurt and my heart pounded fiercely despite its ache. Why was it so cold? I couldn't stop shivering.

Damon put a hand to my forehead. "He's burning up. We need to get him into bed."

I tried to stand on the rug beneath me, but my legs wouldn't hold my weight. My brothers each put an arm around my shoulders, holding me up between them.

"We've got you," Dymitri said. "You're going to be okay now."

"Kat…" I tried again.

"Is she in trouble? Is that why you rushed back here?" Dymitri asked.

I shook my head, wanting to tell him all about how she didn't want me anymore. Perhaps he could see it in my eyes, because his expression changed from worry to grief.

He sighed. "You need rest, then everything will be better."

I wanted to argue with him. Nothing would ever be okay again. Instead, I blacked out once more.

The next time I opened my eyes, I was in my own room, wrapped tightly in blankets, a moist cloth resting on my forehead.

"I'm not sure the fever is breaking," Sarah said, her voice just above a whisper.

Dymitri sighed. "I'm worried. He shouldn't be this sick. This isn't normal."

"The farmers said they saw him get struck by lightning. It's a miracle he's even alive!"

"His injuries mixed with the cold… it made him vulnerable. He might have pneumonia."

Sarah took in a slow breath. "We need to get Katerina here."

"We don't know why he returned home in the first place," Dymitri said. "What if there's a problem? She's not in danger, but something happened. I think it has to do with her. He keeps saying her name, even when he's not conscious."

"All the more reason to get her here *now*," Sarah insisted. "They need to be together. It's the only way he's going to recover."

I wanted to tell them both to leave Katerina alone. She'd been hurt enough because of me. But I was too tired, too cold. I couldn't fight them.

Dymitri let out a heavy breath. "I'll go get her. Tell Lucian to hang on."

"Be careful," Sarah said. I heard them kiss. A few seconds later, she moved her hand under the blankets to hold mine. "Hear that? Hang on., Lucian. Katerina is coming. Hold on for her."

Her and the baby.

Yes... I would do that.

I think I nodded. And then I drifted away once more.

CHAPTER

FOURTEEN

Katerina

I don't know how long I cried after Lucian left.

I didn't move from where I'd fallen to my knees. There was a vain hope running through my mind that maybe he'd return to me. And yet, I knew full well he wouldn't. Last time he left, it had been two weeks before he had the courage to come back. This time, he had no reason to return... beyond the baby, of course. But I'd made it pretty clear I didn't want him around, even though that was totally wrong. Of course, I wanted him. I loved him! Everything was a huge mess now, and it was all because of me.

Had I ever told him how I felt? No. I hadn't, and now maybe he would never know that someone loved him in return.

My fault, my brain kept taunting, over and over.

Why did I do this kind of thing to myself? Something good came my way, and I pushed it aside because I was too scared of being dumped later.

He was right. I had pushed away first. Why the hell would anyone stick around when they weren't wanted? The answer was, they wouldn't. Could I truly be upset with him for leaving? How could I possibly fix this?

My hands cradled my stomach. "I'm so sorry, little one. It's my fault you're not going to know who your dad is. It's my fault you're not going to have a solid home like I'd been hoping. It's all my fault."

I sat there on the deck until I felt completely hollow inside. How could I not feel empty? My true love had just left my life.

My true love.

I still didn't believe in the "fated mates" concept, but there was no denying that Lucian was my perfect other half. He might have flaws, but so what? I had plenty of my own.

The way he complimented my personality was unparalleled, and the way I missed him now that he was gone was devastating. This went beyond him being the father of my baby. Even without the child growing in my stomach, I'd miss Lucian like I'd miss breathing air. I wasn't sure how to live without him.

I'd get by if I had to. And I did have to. I was responsible for another life, now. There was more at stake than just my own happiness. But my life would never be complete.

I'd always feel hollow and like a piece of me had died if Lucian didn't come back to me.

I should have been calmer when speaking with him, had more patience and been clear about my intentions. When I'd left the doctor, the plan hadn't been to push him out of my life and go solo.

I wanted him to be happy, and it was obvious he wasn't happy with *me*.

We'd both come to the same conclusion. He didn't belong in my world, and denying his true self was making him a husk of the man I'd known.

Hot tears blurred my vision as I gulped in air. I'd let my insecurities get the better of me.

I'd been so blind. I had to speak to him, somehow. But how did I find him to apologize?

"I could call Sarah," I said, thinking aloud. "She's married to his brother."

If I could tell him I was sorry, then maybe we could at least find a way to move forward for the baby's sake. Some sort of connection with Lucian was better than nothing.

But the cell phone reception between realms was crap, barely there at all, and when I'd tried to contact Nadia a few weeks ago I'd gotten the merest hint of a word here or there, and then nothing.

Not enough to provide a heartfelt apology to Lucian, that was for sure. *Damn it.*

There was too much about that world I didn't understand. Why did I waste so much of my time with Lucian ignoring that part of him? I could have quizzed him about his world, and learned everything about it.

I would have been in a much better position now if I had.

I rubbed my stomach, feeling my strength return. I had a plan. "Don't be like me, kiddo. I should have asked him more questions and gotten to know him better. Magic is real. Dragons exist. You're one of them, and I never want you to feel like that is wrong."

I could at least do better with my child. I *would*. It'd be a small way I could atone for my sins against Lucian.

Finally I got to my feet, opening the back door and walking into the living room. There I swayed, exhausted. I was just about to lay down in bed so I could wallow some more, when I heard a male voice shouting my name from outside. "Katerina!"

"Lucian?" I called back, my heart in my throat.

It sounded enough like him. Maybe he was learning from his past too! Maybe he had no plans to stay away, after all. Maybe he was ready to talk and...

I ran to the front door and yanked it open. Not Lucian, but Dymitri. My sister's husband stood on the porch. He was shirtless, but blessedly wore a pair of jeans. God knew where he'd gotten them from, but I was grateful he wasn't naked.

He gazed about, frantic. "Katerina, thank God you're home!"

"What's wrong? Is Sarah okay?" The panic in his eyes said it all. Something bad had happened.

He shook his head. "It's Lucian. He…" He heaved a few heavy breaths. It was clear he'd flown a long way, and at speed.

I ran inside to get him a glass of water, my heart pounding. What had he meant about Lucian? "Come in!"

Once he stepped inside and closed the door, I handed him the drink. "Here. Now tell me. Lucian. He's okay, right?"

Dymitri gulped it down, shaking his head, and my stomach lurched. "Lucian is injured. No, sick. Well, actually, he's both."

"What do you mean he's injured *and* sick?" I demanded. I'd seen him an hour ago. Or was it more? I couldn't tell now how long I'd sat on the decking.

"He flew home, and some farmers found him. They said they saw him get struck by lightning in a storm, and he fell out of the sky."

My hand went to my chest. "Oh, God. Is he… is he…"

No. He couldn't die. Not now. Not after everything I'd said to him.

He fell out of the sky.

"He's alive? He has to be." My voice was a mere whisper.

"He is, for now. But for how long, I don't know," Dymitri said. "Our dragon forms are strong. We can withstand many things. Lucian doesn't seem to be at his full strength, though. His body seemed to recover from most of the injuries, but he has an awful fever. I think he's exerted too much of himself to heal and it's left him susceptible to illness."

I shook my head. He *had* to be okay. "Lucian is strong. He's the toughest guy I've ever met."

"Normally, I'd agree, but the man lying in his bed is…" He closed his eyes. "That's not the brother I'm familiar with."

"It's my fault." My voice cracked on the words.

"Hmm?"

I brushed hot tears away from my eyes. "It's my fault. He's been living his life here as a human. I've been making him ignore his dragon side. We got into a fight and… and…"

"That fills in a few gaps." Dymitri walked over and put his hands on my shoulders. "Dwelling on our mistakes won't fix our future. What matters is what you choose to do next."

I nodded, amazed at how gracious and kind he was being even though I'd basically admitted to killing his brother.

"I need you to come back to the castle with me," Dymitri said, his voice steady and calm. "If you return and show him how sorry you are, then it might give him the courage and the will to keep fighting."

That sounded too easy. Could it be? Would Lucian so easily forgive me? I'd only scraped the surface of our problems in my couple of sentences summarizing our issues. I'd done so much more than keep Lucian from turning into a dragon. I'd destroyed him. And his beautiful soul.

I didn't want to tell Dymitri about the baby. Not yet. My sister needed to know before him, and she needed to hear about it from my lips. Lucian would want to share the news with his brother, most likely. Who was I to rob him of that experience?

Not after I'd already taken so much from him already.

"Please, Katerina," Dymitri begged. "I'll take you back. Things can be made right again."

So much hope shone in his eyes. "Do you really think my presence will help him get better?"

"I think you're the only one who can save him." His voice was so quiet, so shaky. He was genuinely scared.

Lucian might die.

My heart thumped madly at the thought. Suddenly, I couldn't wait to get moving. "Let me pack some stuff. I'll be quick. But I'm going to need more than just the clothes on my back. If he's sick, this might be a long game."

Not to mention the fact that it was freaking freezing where he lived!

"Yes, good thinking." The worry on Dymitri's face shifted to relief. "I'll drink some more water while you pack and get myself hydrated for the journey back."

"Do whatever you need. My house is yours. We're family now, right?" I gave him a quavering smile.

He nodded, and after a moment, smiled back.

"I'll be ready in a flash." I hurried to my room and quickly packed a bag with winter-appropriate wear. It was always cold in Lucian's realm, and I hadn't been prepared for that last visit. Extra layers would be good.

I also packed my doctor-ordered vitamins and some other medical supplies. While Lucian's realm had witches and magic, I wasn't sure if there was a need for modern medicine. Silly, I suppose, but it made me feel useful and like I could make a difference.

That, right there, was part of the problem, I guess. Lucian was a dragon and from a world of magic, mystery, and things I'd only dreamed of. I was an ordinary woman from an ordinary world. I thought that by making him a part of my world—by making him more ordinary and ignoring the scaly elephant in the room—that we'd fit together better. That I could force it to make sense. But I couldn't.

The idea had only made things worse and now Lucian was paying the ultimate price.

I wasn't sure my presence really would make a difference. In fact, I was positive all I would do was take up space and get in the way. But I'd do my best, both to support him, and to earn that title of soulmate that he claimed belonged to me.

A title I'd never thought I'd hold in anyone's heart, and one I'd certainly never tried to live up to. Until now.

So much didn't make sense, but I'd made everything a mess. It was on me to clean it up and put things right. Even if we didn't end up together, I didn't want our child not knowing who his father was.

If Lucian died because of my selfishness, that was a weight I wouldn't be able to carry. How would I ever explain that to our son or daughter?

I hesitated and looked over at the envelope that contained the sex of the baby. Did I bring it along? Did I ruin the surprise? What if Lucian didn't make it? He could at least know what his future child was before he moved on. I hated the thought, but if life had taught me anything, it was to always prepare for the worst.

I packed the envelope into the bag, tucking it deep under my clothes for safekeeping, just in case.

We're not going to need to open it, though. Not unless you tell me you want to know.

A silent prayer, and I hoped whatever greater power existed heard it.

With my bag packed and the cloak I'd borrowed from the other realm wrapped around me, I went back to the kitchen to find Dymitri. He'd replenished with more water and whatever he could find in my refrigerator. Together, we cleaned up the small mess, and I locked up the house. Would I ever walk back through these doors? It might be a long time.

I hoped I'd return at some stage, and I hoped Lucian would be with me when I did. This place wouldn't feel like home without him.

"Let's go," I said.

I climbed onto Dymitri's back, closed my eyes, held on tight, and flew with him to the other realm.

Dymitri flew harder and faster than Damon had. Talk about a rush! As scary as it was, I also enjoyed the ride. I wondered what it would be like to fly on Lucian's back...

We landed near the snow-covered castle and Sarah was waiting for us in the foyer of the castle. She hugged me tightly.

"I'm so glad you came back," she whispered. "I think you're the only one who can help him."

I pulled back and nodded. "Take me to him."

Together we hurried up the stairs to his room. There, lying on the bed we'd once made love in, was Lucian. His eyes were squeezed shut, like he was looking away from something terrifying. Sweat beaded his face yet his entire body shivered under the heavy blankets wrapped over his body.

My heart thudded in my chest at the sight. I rushed over to him and placed a hand on his forehead. "He feels like fire."

And he did. He was boiling hot to the touch.

"It's bad," Sarah whispered. "I'm not sure what the actual temperature is, but I'm worried."

I pulled out the heat-sensing thermometer that I'd brought with me and ran it over his forehead, then gasped at the number. "One-oh-seven point four."

Any human would be almost dead with a temp like that.

"Do you think it's too late for him?" Sarah asked.

"I'm not sure what's normal for his kind," I said. "He's still here, and he's still fighting. That's a sign. We're not giving up." I gazed down at Lucian. "You hear that? We're not giving up!"

His body shivered. "Katerina... the forest... we..."

"Tell me all about it later," I said. "I can't wait to hear it when you're better."

"Father..." he grumbled.

I placed a hand on his chest, wanting to comfort him. His body seemed to ease at my touch. A step in the right direction. "Lucian, I'm here for you. Please rest now, and we can talk when you're better. You're not going to get well unless you rest."

His eyes remained closed, but they weren't so tightly pressed together.

The crinkles and creases in his face disappeared and his breathing became more even. Deep and slow.

Dymitri was right, my presence was making a difference.

I leant over him and pressed a gentle kiss to his hot forehead. "I'm not going anywhere," I whispered against his skin. "Promise. Hold on so you can meet…"

I sighed and glanced over at my sister, but she was folding linens in the corner of the room.

"Just hold on," I said instead.

For now, that would have to be good enough. I got comfortable by Lucian's side and settled into the chair beside the bed.

I was going to be here for the long haul.

FIFTEEN

Katerina

Over the next two days, I didn't leave Lucian's side unless absolutely necessary. I ate my meals by his bed, and I slept on an extra mattress in the room on the floor beside him. I was still pretty tired from being pregnant. Exhausted in body, but with not much else to do beyond being worried, I was also a little bored.

The general consensus for Lucian's illness was some kind of mystery virus that had gotten to him in his exhausted state. Everyone agreed he was lucky to be alive.

I dressed in loose clothing to hide the small bump growing in my belly. I'm not sure how obvious it was to outsiders, but to me, it felt like the whole world could see what was going on. No one said anything about it, though, so I knew it must all be in my head.

They didn't notice I wasn't quite eating as much as usual at breakfast or lunch. While most of my morning sickness was gone, my appetite had definitely been affected by the pregnancy.

I hadn't entered the glowing portion of pregnancy, nor that moment where I could eat whatever I wanted. Certain foods still turned me off— certain smells, too. Cooking meat especially, and dragons loved their roasted meat.

"Any ideas on how I can tell your brother to not make his food so rich in flavor?" I asked Lucian one afternoon. I often talked to him, even though he didn't answer, so he would know he wasn't alone.

I sighed. "Some of his cooking doesn't make the baby happy. I haven't told him about our kiddo yet. I thought you'd like that honor, so I need to find a way to tell him that I can't eat the rich food without insulting him. Because it's not bad food. It just... isn't sitting right with me. You know?"

I waited to see if maybe Lucian would answer this time. He didn't even stir, just continued to sleep soundly. At least he looked peaceful when he slept. When I'd first arrived, his face had often contorted into anguish. Now he fought his virus in peace and hopefully some measure of comfort.

We'd managed to drop the fever down to a lower one hundred point three. And there it had stayed. Lucian wouldn't open his eyes, though. I didn't know what to think, but it had only been two and a half days. My mother always said that sleep was the best weapon against sickness.

But I did worry. A lot.

"I guess I'll have to get to know him on my own and find a good way to ask him," I mumbled. "Though, I'm sure Sarah would have plenty of tips. I hate bothering her with anything."

"You shouldn't," Sarah said quietly from the doorway. She bit her lip and walked further into the room. "Sorry, I shouldn't have interrupted, let alone eavesdropped."

"How much did you hear?" I asked.

She walked over and put a hand on my shoulder. "Not a whole lot. Just that I might have tips on something?"

"Talking to your husband," I said. "I can't eat what he's been making."

"Yeah?" Sarah raised an eyebrow.

"Uh... yeah... it's a little too rich."

Hopefully Sarah would assume it was some kind of diet fad. I prepared myself for her speech on how I was beautiful and didn't need to worry about my weight or figure.

I always hated hearing it come from her because I didn't think she'd ever understand.

But it was a speech that never came.

"Because of the baby, right?" she asked instead.

I tilted my head to the side and my mouth dropped open. "You knew?"

"As soon as you came into the castle!" She squeezed my shoulder. "And I'm so happy for you!"

"How?" I asked, still floored.

"Your bump is not discreet," she said with a huge grin on her face. "And you're absolutely radiant!"

So, I was glowing... and no one was looking at me like I was just getting extra fat? They'd figured it out?

I closed my eyes and let out a breath, relief washing over me. "My pregnancy is another of the reasons we fought."

Sarah pulled another chair from its place against the wall and dragged it over to Lucian's bedside. "Tell me everything, Kat. Start from when he showed up on your doorstep, because I want to hear it all."

I nodded and readied myself to spill everything. "Okay, well... When he first arrived, I was surprised but excited. We'd had a... uh... really good night together at your wedding." I coughed, my cheeks growing warm with embarrassment. "Don't get me wrong, the dragon thing scared the crap out of me, but... we'd connected on so many levels. He lived with me for a few months, and I introduced him to my students. I showed him normal, boring, human life."

Sarah's eyebrows flicked up. "Did the two of you get along well?"

"Yes. He wanted to come back here with me, and I told him I wouldn't go." I sighed. "Because this world...it doesn't feel like home." I gestured at the castle. "Not quite my style. I'm not a fairytale princess."

Sarah opened her mouth, then closed it and sighed.

"I'm not," I repeated. "And it has nothing to do with how I look. The way I live doesn't mesh well with it either. Anyway, what I didn't realize was that in telling him I couldn't live in his realm, I forced him into my life which didn't suit him at all. That's what started the fight."

"He didn't like it?" she asked.

I shook my head. "He didn't complain or anything. It was me that told him I hated seeing him so miserable. I told him he should leave. I hadn't meant for it to come out the way it did, but we were both heated, and I was so tired. Not just physically, but tired of everything. He wasn't talking to me anymore. We weren't bonding. He looked miserable, and he was losing weight. I just knew I was the problem."

"Kat..." Sarah shook her head. "I highly doubt that was it."

"It was." I blinked away a few tears. "He fixed my house and did all the dutiful husband things without even having the title. Perfect on paper. His soul was missing, though. I saw the empty vessel I made him. Shouldn't I be making him feel complete? That's what a soulmate is supposed to do, right?"

"Were you hiding your true self from him too?" she asked.

Not the question I was expecting.

I had to think about that one for a moment. "Kind of. He said I was pushing him away, and I can't argue with that. I was. I'm scared of letting him get to know me properly. When I let the walls down, that's when guys leave."

"Lucian isn't like other guys, though. He's your fated mate," Sarah insisted.

"And that means nothing to me!" I snapped. "A magic bond that automatically makes us perfect for each other? Seriously? He loves me because of a mystical force? How is that real?" I thought she, of all people, would understand. "I want him to love me for me."

"He does." Sarah gazed over at Lucian's sleeping form. "If you asked him right now, he would say so himself. That he doesn't love you because of magic."

"How are you so sure?"

"Because the fated mate bond... it doesn't..." She pressed her lips together. "I'm trying to think of how to explain this. It's an attraction, right? Like the moment he first walks into the room, you feel complete, but you don't know why. How you just knew you had to talk to him. It's a force that puts the two of you together, sure. But it doesn't make the love happen. That's you."

I nodded, listening, wanting to believe. "Yeah, I did feel that way. Sort of. Maybe not so strong? Not at first. That came later when he was at the house. Like when he left after our fight. I felt it the worst then... the disconnect, I mean. Like part of my soul had just been severed."

"Right!" Sarah gave me a warm smile. "With the dragons, they feel these sensations at an amplified level. The fated mate bond pulls the two of you together because it knows that you are everything he'd ever want in a mate. Personality, sex appeal, all of it."

I scoffed. "Right, I'm so sexy."

"You are!"

"Have you seen him, though? He's gorgeous." I pinched the bridge of my nose. "In ways that I don't compare."

"Why do you assume that?" she asked, frowning. "Because I think the two of you look hot together. You get him to shine in ways I'd never seen. *You.* You bring that out of him! He didn't look anywhere near as good with Nadia whenever I saw them together. When Dymitri thought they were a thing, I didn't really see it."

"Nadia," I mumbled. "That makes things weird."

"Nothing happened, though," Sarah said.

I shook my head. "But he thought they were supposed to be together. Did he act all smitten with her like he did me? And then when he learned she wasn't the one, he turned it off?"

She laughed. "That's not how it went down. He knew the moment he saw her that she wasn't the one. It made him so upset he destroyed the castle. Didn't he tell you that story?"

"A version of it," I mumbled. "So, he didn't even... try? To make things work, I mean."

"Nope." Sarah shook her head. "He took care of her while she was sick." She motioned to Lucian in the bed. "Similar to this, actually. The moment she woke up and looked at him, he got all rough and grumpy. They were like oil and water."

Hearing it from Sarah made the doubt fade further. As much as I'd wanted to believe Lucian when he said it, I'd been lied to so much in the past. A few bad apples really did spoil the bunch.

But Lucian had never lied or led me astray.

I put my head in my hands. "What's wrong with me? Why can't I just trust him?"

"Why do you think you're not worthy of love?" Sarah countered. "And don't say it's because you're fat. Please. I hate hearing that kind of talk."

"Fat isn't a bad word," I grumbled. It was just… true.

"No, but saying you don't deserve love because of something so petty? That's negative thinking and unjust. Your appearance has nothing to do with your heart. So why?" She folded her arms in front of her chest.

I had no arguments. "Because no one has wanted to before, I guess."

"Lucian does."

"And I realize that now, but I've messed things up so badly."

"You can still fix it," Sarah insisted. "He's listening. Tell him what you need him to know."

I gazed over at him. "I need him to know that I do love him for him. Even the dragon side. It's a beautiful piece of his soul, even if he's rough and grumpy..,"

Sarah giggled. "Yes, he's definitely that. I promise he's a great guy, though." She paused. "Did I ever tell you about how he saved Nadia and me from kidnappers?"

"No!" I blinked. "You told me Dymitri rescued you from something bad, but… what? When were you kidnapped?"

"A few weeks before I married Dymitri." She looked down at the ground. "It's a long story. Dymitri and Lucian saw we were in trouble, and Lucian saved us, regardless. His heart is good. Pure. He does what is right and true. That's why I find it so funny you think him capable of lying. I don't think he's capable of it. He'll always be honest and pure like that. Even when you don't want him to be."

I soaked in her words. "You know, you're right. I don't know why I didn't see it before."

"You were scared."

"I was…" I sighed. "I am. I'm terrified. And pregnant."

"So I've seen."

"Does Dymitri know?" I asked.

She shook her head. "He's clueless. I didn't want to say anything before talking to you."

"Thanks. I thought Lucian might want to tell him."

"I think that'll be perfect."

Lucian groaned in the bed and his body stirred.

"It looks like this release of negativity has done some good things," Sarah said.

I put a hand to his forehead. "He feels much cooler."

"Stay with him." Sarah stood. "And I'll let Dymitri know to change up the menu."

"Thanks." I got up to hug her. "I love you."

"Love you too." She left me alone with Lucian.

I gazed over at him and grabbed his hand. "You need to wake up soon so you can spill the beans. I'm not sure how much longer Sarah is going to be able to keep it in now that she's got the news confirmed."

I kissed his knuckles. "More importantly, I need you. I want you. I always have. You've always been enough for me. Get better. We won't be able to be happy without you."

I lay my head down on his chest, then I lifted my legs onto the bed and lay down properly beside him. The rise and fall of his breathing lulled me into a slumber.

SIXTEEN

Lucian

I was plagued by the strangest of dreams. Katerina would walk over to me and slap me before telling me she was leaving me for a human. Then she said that the dragon in me scared her, and then I would change into my dragon and lose all control. I decimated the castle and the town, killing everyone I knew and loved before coming talon to talon with my father.

Then the dream would start over again. And again. And again. Constantly on repeat and showing me the parts of myself I despised the most. I couldn't escape. I was trapped in Hell.

Until one day, the dream changed. Katerina walked over to me like she always did. She raised her hand and I prepared myself for the slap. Only this time, she stroked my cheek.

"I need you," she said. "I want you. I always have. You've always been enough for me. Get better. We won't be able to be happy without you."

I pulled her in for a kiss, deep and passionate. Then the world faded to black, and I drifted off. When I did it this time, it felt more like flying. I was going home. I could feel it.

My eyes opened briefly. Katerina lay in my arms, sleeping soundly with her head resting on my chest. I tried to lift a hand to stroke her hair, but I was too weak to move.

Despite my frailness, I felt whole again, and safe.

I drifted off to sleep again, but for the first time I was not plagued by either nightmares or disturbing dreams. I simply slept, and when I opened my eyes next, Katerina wasn't in view. I stretched my arms and legs, and the movement felt refreshing—energizing! My muscles rejoiced, ready to do more than just lie in bed.

I yawned and let out a contented groan.

Katerina's face appeared out of nowhere. It took me a second to realize she had been in the room the whole time and had actually been lying on a mattress on the floor.

"You're awake!" She jumped up and hurried to my side. "You're okay!"

"Yes," I said. She grabbed my hands in her own and gave them a squeeze. Such a drastic change from the last time we'd seen each other. "I'm more than okay. I'm great."

"Yeah? You don't feel sick anymore?"

I frowned. "A bit tired, I suppose, but otherwise the same as always."

"It's like a miracle," she whispered. Louder she said, "We weren't sure if you were going to live or die. When I got here, your fever was so high, and you were delusional. Kept saying my name and something about your father and the woods. It didn't make sense to anyone."

"I was that far gone?" I asked. "The last thing I remember is being in a storm. I was hit by the elements. Wind, hail, lightning. I crashed." I frowned. "From there things start to get hazy."

She stroked my cheek with her fingers. "Yeah? Well what matters now is that you're better. We were able to get your fever down, and now you're awake. It's been about three days total."

"That long?"

"You were very ill."

"Apparently." I chuckled, glad to be alive.

"I was so worried," she said, her eyes filling with tears. "Dymitri came to my house and told me what happened. I had to be here. I needed you to wake up so I could... I could..."

I gazed at her, worried she was about to break up with me all over again. "You could?"

"Apologize." Tears fell down her cheeks. "I was wrong to push you away. It's not okay for me to dump the baggage of my past on your shoulders to carry. Just because others have hurt me doesn't mean you will too. I should have told you about the appointment to see the baby. You're his or her father! However much involvement you want, that's what you're going to have. That's how it always should be."

Her words touched my heart, but I wanted so much more. "I want to be a part of it all. Every check-up. Every diaper. The works."

I couldn't help but start grinning. Had I really just said I'd be happy to change diapers? What had come over me?

"There's more," she said. "I'm sorry I tried to get you to deny yourself. That I pushed you into a cell and put the chains around your neck. It was so unfair of me. Your dragon is just a much a part of you as the man. I had no right to ask you to deny your own soul. Please forgive me, Lucian."

I struggled to sit up and she hurried to plump the pillows behind me.

"I do forgive you," I said, finally sitting up. I grabbed her hand. "You talk about making me carry your baggage. I've done the same to you. It's why I keep leaving instead of staying to fight. I'm afraid of fighting. I'm afraid of losing control. I don't want to be like my father."

"I'd like to work on it with you. If you can help me open up, maybe I can help you calm down." She paused. "If you'll still have me. I'd understand if you don't want to, anymore. Not because of how I look or how I live, but just because I hurt you so badly. The fact you forgive me is huge already. Most people I know would leave forever."

I smirked. "It's a good thing I'm not most people. However, I do think we need to create some ground rules to prevent this from happening again."

"Yes. Like talking to each other more. Being honest when things aren't right."

"Naturally." I shifted so I could lean in and kiss her.

She smiled against my lips. "And I don't want to live here in the castle. I want our own place. I liked having a house. Smaller, sure, but simplicity is much more my style."

Was she saying that she'd stay here? In my world?

"A small house would be perfect," I purred. "Your wish is my command."

"I'm still not sure about this realm..."

"I know, my love." I kissed her again. "We can iron out all the details later. I mean, there's always the possibility of living part of the year here, and part of the year in your world, if we need to. But we have plenty of time to sort things out. Right now, I would much rather make up with you properly."

She blushed, and it was incredibly sexy. "Really? You're feeling that much better?"

We kissed again and a wave of lust rushed over me. I shifted more so she could join me on the bed, but then a sharp pain knifed through my abdomen. "Ah, it seems I'm still tender."

"I'm not going anywhere." She settled into my side and kissed me softly, before adding, "We have plenty of time, my love. We have our whole lives."

Katerina stayed true to her word. She didn't leave my side. She tended to my wounds and helped me recover my lost strength. Slowly but surely, the pain and trauma from my time in the storm healed.

Even though my body craved her during that week together, I enjoyed the time becoming one with her in a different way. We got to know each other on a deeper, more emotionally intimate level, as we both dropped our guard and let the other see the pieces we'd been hiding.

Katerina told me in more detail about the boyfriends who'd lied to her and left.

I, in turn, shared the full truth about what my father had done to my family. Talking healed the wounds of our souls in a way that I'd never thought possible.

"I didn't know that sharing my life with someone would be so freeing," I said to Dymitri as we walked slowly around town one day.

I'd rather have been with Katerina, but I needed my brother's assistance with a special errand.

Dymitri chuckled. "Well, tough guy, I hope this inspires you to let yourself soften around the edges more often."

"I'm ready," I said. "For all of it."

"Including being a father?" Dymitri raised an eyebrow.

"What part of 'for all of it' did you not understand?" I growled playfully.

He held up his hands, laughing some more. "You already have the protective side down. I'm eager to be an uncle and teach your son or daughter all kinds of mischief."

"Whatever you do, you'll get back ten-fold," I said. "Just wait until it's your turn."

"I hope it'll be soon," he said.

A shopkeeper returned with my purchase in a small bag. "It's perfect and polished."

"Thank you." I took the bag and peeked inside at the contents, still in disbelief as to what I had actually just purchased. "Now to return to Katerina."

We made our way back to the castle and found Katerina with Sarah and Nadia in the study. The three sisters sat at a table, hunched forward and talking quietly.

"My love, I don't suppose you'd like to accompany me someplace," I said, reaching a hand out to her and lifting her to her feet.

She smiled up at me. "I think I'd love that. I wanted to talk to you anyway about something important."

How convenient. "Let's go."

Slowly, she settled her hand more comfortably in my grip. I couldn't help reaching out to run my other hand over her burgeoning belly. Our baby was growing fast.

She waved goodbye to her sisters, and then we left the castle. I led her right to the edge of town and beyond, almost to the edge of my brother's kingdom. We strolled through the outlying streets, where it was quieter than the busy center of town where the castle was situated, and I made sure to give her ample time to absorb our peaceful surroundings.

"This is beautiful," she said, after a time. "Quiet and so cute!"

"I thought you'd enjoy it out here," I said. "Away from the busiest parts of the kingdom. We have one last place to visit."

I brought her to the end of the street we were in, where an iron gate stood blocking the rest of the path. I pulled a large key from my pocket and unlocked the gate. Then I led Katerina down the path. The town faded from view behind a small forest of trees.

"All day, I've been wanting to show you this," I said. We finally came up to an empty plot of land. "I haven't made any official decision yet because I wanted to make sure you liked this spot."

"For?" she asked, gazing around. "I'm not sure I understand."

"For a house."

Her eyes widened as she gazed up at me. "A house? You mean..."

"Yes. For us. I want to build a home here for us. I know how much you dislike the idea of living in the castle. This felt like the perfect place to make something of our own." My heart began to pound hard in my chest. I couldn't remember the last time I'd ever felt this nervous. "If you'd like to, that is?"

Katerina continued to gaze up at me. She was smiling, so that had to be a good sign. "You want to build a house from scratch?"

"Yes."

"All by yourself?"

"I might need a little help," I said with a smirk. "But you shouldn't doubt my skills after what I did to your home back in the other realm."

She laughed. "Good point."

"We can design it together," I continued. "Make plans and..." I swallowed. "I would love to do this as your husband."

"Yeah, I can see it now. We can..." She then stopped and her brow knit together. "Wait... what? Did you say..."

There was no taking it back now. "I want you to be my wife. Katerina, will you marry me?" I reached into my pocket and pulled out the simple yet elegant ring I'd purchased in town earlier with Dymitri.

I slowly got down on one knee in front of her. Her hands rose to her mouth and her eyes were like saucers as she stared at me.

"You're all I've ever dreamed of, and I would be the luckiest man alive to call you my wife. I'm already so fortunate that we're starting a family. Let's make this dream official."

She let out a shocked-sounding gasp, and then quickly followed with a chuckle. "I... Lucian... of course! Yes, yes, I'll marry you!"

She suddenly rushed forward and wrapped her arms around my shoulders before leaning down to kiss me. I got to my feet and kissed her back, not holding in any of my passion. I lifted her into my arms and carried her over to a blanket I'd already spread out over the grass when I visited here earlier. The goal had been to recreate the picnic she made for me the day she told me of her pregnancy.

Katerina picked up on it right away. "You remembered every detail." She gasped. "Even the color of the blanket."

"I remember everything you do," I admitted. I set her down carefully then joined her. "Especially something so kind."

Tears pooled in her eyes, and she kissed me. "Never leave me again, okay? Even if I say something stupid, I can't stand the thought of you not being in my life. It would devastate me."

"As you wish." I crushed my mouth to hers again, hungry and desperate to show her the depth of my love.

It was summer in my realm, and although it was still cool, this unusually warm day made my plans to seduce her very possible.

Words were not always easy for me, but actions? With those, I could get my message across. The dragon inside of me was burning for his mate, and I couldn't agree more. We'd waited long enough.

I put my hand up her skirt and pulled down her panties, pleased to feel her wetness against my fingers as I did so. Then I ripped open my pants. She helped release my cock from its confines and then climbed on top of me. There was no time for finesse. We had gone without for far too long.

I let out a quiet growl as I guided her down onto the fullness of my cock, impaling her fully. She let out a soft whimper of pleasure.

I cupped her full breasts through the material of her bra and enjoyed the feel of her warm body, her luscious curves, and her hot, wet channel tight around my flesh. Her fingers dug into my chest, and mine swept over her waist, her swollen belly and down to tease her clit as she rode me.

She moaned against my lips as she leaned down and kissed me. I cherished every touch. I pulled off her blouse and freed her breasts from her bra.

We loved one another until we were spent.

I panted, breathless and tried to keep her connected to me for as long as possible. She slowly, reluctantly, rolled off and lay down beside me.

"I've missed you," I said. "The taste of you. The feel of you. The little sounds you make when your desire ratchets up."

"Now I feel like we've officially made up," she said with a sigh. "Is that weird?"

"Not at all." I felt exactly the same way.

She kissed my nose and eventually stood to find and gather all her pieces of clothing that we'd scattered in our haste. She carefully dressed and adjusted her blouse to cover those luscious breasts, much to my disappointment. "Lucian," she said when she lay down beside me again. "I had something I wanted to talk to you about."

"Ah, yes, you did mention that earlier," I said as I rolled onto my side to face her.

"Yes, and you successfully distracted me from it! At least for a little while." She giggled, then her expression turned serious, and I couldn't help but worry. Katerina cleared her throat. "When I was at the doctor, they took a lot of pictures of the baby. They also were able to find out the sex."

My eyes lit up at the idea. "And?"

"I haven't actually looked," she said.

"Oh. What stopped you?" I asked. Surely, she would want to know if she was having a boy, or a girl?

"After you told me how hurt you were for not being involved, I decided it should be something we either do together, or not at all." My heart sped up. She wanted to wait and do this with me?

A huge grin spread across my face, and she cupped my cheek, smiling back at me for a moment, before she turned away and reached over for her purse. She pulled out an envelope. "What do you think? Should we find out? Or be surprised?"

I put my hand over hers and we held the envelope together. "This is a tough choice, Kat. It'd be like opening a birthday present early. On the other hand... I'm not known for my patience."

"So, we're going to look?" she asked, her eyes lighting up with pleasure.

It was obvious what her choice was, so I grinned at her again. "We are definitely going to look!"

"Okay. On three?"

"All right. One." I gazed into her eyes, seeing the love she was no longer trying to hide.

"Two." She smiled the brightest of smiles and my heart did a funny flip-flop.

"Three," I half-shouted, and together, weripped the envelope open.

EPILOGUE
TWELVE MONTHS LATER

Lucian

I sawed a piece of wood in half and added it to my pile in the backyard. Once again, I was working on building a deck for my beautiful wife. I was using the same design from her old house. She'd loved that one a lot, and I wanted to make our new home feel like one for her just as much as myself. So far, progress seemed to be going well.

In nine months, I'd been able to build the actual house. We'd made sure the blueprints included five bedrooms. One for us, at least three future children, and a guest room. There was also space on the land to create a guesthouse on the property, and that was next on my list once I finished landscaping the yard around the main house.

Katerina's dad wasn't well, and we had decided, after talking to Sarah and Nadia as well, that we should bring him here to live with us. He would have the guest house on our property for as long as he wanted it. And Katerina would have the pleasure of her father not too far away.

But first, I needed to finish this deck, and then I'd build the best of treehouse playgrounds for our active child. Katerina insisted that could wait until later. Babies couldn't climb trees, after all.

I suppose she was right, but I couldn't help it. I wanted whatever children we had to have everything. Spoiling Katerina and our beautiful son gave me the greatest of joys.

The sound of crying burst out of the windows from the top floor, my hearing picking up the moment my son was awake. I set down my tools and left the backyard for the nursery. I walked upstairs and quietly entered the room.

"Victor, you're awake just in time. Mommy will be home soon from work," I said.

He stood up on his little chubby legs, gripping the side of the crib I'd made him. One hand reached out to me. "Dadadada!"

"Yes, I'm here." I picked up my beautiful son and held him close.

I'd been so worried about becoming a father. I'd thought it wouldn't come naturally to me, and I'd struggle with learning how to love Victor properly. Taking care of his basic needs was never the concern. Just loving him, and learning how to love him in a way that didn't damage him. Like my father had done to me and Dymitri.

But from the moment he'd been born, it all fell into place. I held him for the first time and knew instantly that loving Victor would never be a problem. Much like loving Katerina had been as easy as breathing, the love for our son Victor came just as naturally.

After I'd proposed, and we'd told everyone here at the castle our exciting news, we flew back to Katerina's house in the human realm, and began our plans to settle down. Katerina wanted to finish the school year with her students, so we lived in her house until the summer. It was different this time, though, because things were good between my mate and me, and we had made the decision to return to live in my realm.

My dragon was sated by that news and remained quiet and content. At least, as quiet and content as it is possible for a dragon to be.

During that time, we got the place ready to sell and moved our things to the castle, all while planning a wedding.

The ceremony was simple yet elegant. We married on our property and honeymooned in the new house I built. Katerina spoke to Damon about teaching at the small school in town, for which he gave his grateful permission, and then she gave birth in the middle of summer.

Victor was now seven months old, and he'd just started standing with a little help. Watching him hit each milestone in development continued to blow my mind. I couldn't believe how smart he was, or how adorable. Watching him while Katerina worked at the school was not hard at all.

For the time being, my job was to keep working on the house, which I primarily did on the weekends and for a few hours after Katerina came home from work. Some small projects I did during Victor's nap time. When our house was finished, the plan was for me to expand my love of construction into a business.

There was so much to rebuild still in this kingdom—a legacy of my father's tyranny, but for the first time, I felt excited about the opportunities for building rather than angry at the previous destruction he'd caused.

We were close to my family, and also to hers. I flew her home to visit her father and her old school whenever she wanted, and of course, once our guesthouse was ready, he would come to live with us permanently. For now, he was happy with occasional visits. Sarah and Nadia loved to come over and babysit their nephew as well.

In our house in the forest, Katerina and I were finally able to be ourselves. In doing so, we saw how truly compatible we were with one another. She liked my quiet, strong, rough exterior, yet also appreciated my softer, hidden side. She didn't mind that I acted grumpy. My personality gave her a calm and safe place to hide when the world sometimes became too overwhelming.

In turn, I loved Katerina's boldness and newfound self-confidence. She didn't have any issues stating her opinions, and she wasn't afraid of putting me in my place when needed. There was a tender, nurturing side to her as well that left me never doubting if she loved me. Even when she was mad, I could still sense her love underlying it. A constant reassurance that everything would be all right.

For the first time in our lives, we both had balance. Katerina had her dream job and retained access to the world she loved. I had the freedom of letting my dragon fly and performing my duties for the realm. Life might not have been perfect, but we had gotten pretty damn close to it. Even if a situation rocked the boat in the future, I didn't worry about us capsizing in the storm. We'd sail through, stronger in the end. I could feel it in my soul.

The knob turned for the front door.

"Mamamama!" Victor squealed with delight.

"Yes! Mommy's home!" I made my way to greet her in the foyer. The moment she saw us, she shot me a huge smile and automatically reached for Victor.

"Hey, baby," she cooed and cuddled him close to her. He squealed and touched her face with his tiny hands. The way she smiled down at him with so much adoration and love... It was my favorite expression of hers.

I leaned in and kissed her lips. "How was school today?"

"Excellent. All the students are making me feel like a valued part of the community," she said. "Which is awesome and kind of a surprise since I'm pretty new here. They treat me like I've been around for a while."

"I knew you'd fit in perfectly."

A fact that relieved me, because I'd been nervous. Everything about my realm was new and mysterious to Katerina. She'd expressed so much hesitation when we first met. Since she had embraced my dragon, she also seemed to have fully embraced living in my world. I'd thought she might resent me, but I quickly learned Katerina was a woman of her word. If she said she was willing to go all in, she meant it.

And she went all in with me.

"I've been asked to help plan the next family event at the school," she said. "I can't wait to show you my classroom and introduce you to my students. A lot of them know of you but not much about you, so they ask me all sorts of questions."

I chuckled. "They'll be stunned when they see how normal and boring I am, compared to my brothers."

"It'll do great things for the kingdom, though." She smiled up at me, and I appreciated her thinking about that bigger-picture aspect of our life.

Regardless of whether or not I was a legitimate heir to the throne, my brother, Damon, had a lot of damage to undo. I'd be a willing part of that.

"What did you do today?" she asked.

"Worked outside," I said. "Victor did a lot of swinging while I got the planks ready for the new deck. It should be finished within a few days."

"A few days? Wow, you're a machine." She shook her head.

I winked. "Not only in the bedroom."

"Are you sure you're human?" she teased. "I mean, I know you're a dragon, but what about a robot? Are there mechanical dragons?"

"You know I'm all flesh," I growled playfully. "Or do I need to remind you later?"

She pretended to think. "Gosh, my memory is awfully foggy."

"Mama!" Victor interrupted.

"Oh, sorry. Are we traumatizing you with our love?" She bopped Victor's nose. "And do you help Daddy while he works outside?"

"He does by talking to me. I'm not sure what he was saying today, but he had a lot of opinions about it."

"Dada do," Victor said, lifting up his hands.

"Yes, Daddy does work hard," she said.

I gave her a weak smile. "He just woke up from his nap. I know, it's later than usual. I was so sucked into my work."

"Guess we'll have a later night," she said. "He's growing, so he's probably extra tired."

She brought him into the kitchen, and I loved how she made him a part of everything she did. Victor couldn't help by any means, but she talked him through her day and the process of whatever task she was completing. Whenever I wondered what I should do, I looked to Katerina as a guide.

From the moment I found out we were having a son, I knew it was an opportunity to break the cycle my father had continued. I had a choice: follow in his damaging footsteps or pave my own way and try to do it right. Doing my own thing wasn't as difficult as I thought with Katerina to help guide me and be by my side through everything. She was a teacher at heart, after all, and excellent at her job.

I was going to do far better as a father than I'd ever dreamed of, and Victor was going to grow up to be an amazing young man because of it. Together, Katerina and I would start a new legacy.

I watched my wife with my son and couldn't hold in the joy. I released a shout of laughter, and they looked over at me and both of them began to chuckle.

Our life was simple—beautiful. I couldn't ask for anything more. Love had won, and I had my heart's desire right here in front of me in the smiling faces of my loving wife and happy child.

~